ZOGARTH

THE
PRIMAL HUNTER
BOOK FIVE

aethonbooks.com

THE PRIMAL HUNTER 5
©2023 ZOGARTH

This book is protected under the copyright laws of the United States of America. No part of this publication may be reproduced, stored in a retrieval system, or transmitted, in any form or by any means, without the prior permission in writing of the publisher, nor be otherwise circulated in any form of binding or cover other than that in which it is published and without a similar condition including this condition being imposed on the subsequent purchaser. Any reproduction or unauthorized use of the material or artwork contained herein is prohibited without the express written permission of the authors.

Aethon Books supports the right to free expression and the value of copyright. The purpose of copyright is to encourage writers and artists to produce the creative works that enrich our culture.

The scanning, uploading, and distribution of this book without permission is a theft of the author's intellectual property. If you would like to use material from the book (other than for review purposes), please contact editor@aethonbooks.com. Thank you for your support of the author's rights.

Aethon Books
www.aethonbooks.com

Print and eBook formatting by Josh Hayes. Artwork provided by Antti Hakosaari.

Published by Aethon Books LLC.

Aethon Books is not responsible for websites (or their content) that are not owned by the publisher.

This book is a work of fiction. Names, characters, places, and incidents are the product of the author's imagination or are used fictitiously. Any resemblance to actual events, locales, or persons, living or dead is coincidental.

All rights reserved.

ALSO BY ZOGARTH

Also in series:

PREVIOUSLY ON THE PRIMAL HUNTER

J ake, reveling in his newfound power after his evolution to D-grade, did what any reasonable person would do: he went on a monkey genocide in the local forest. Poo-flinging monkeys, mind you, so his level-up spree was totally justified.

In the depths of monkey territory, he encounters a variant of these monkeys called a Prima, proving far more powerful than any beast he had previously encountered. After a tough fight with a monkey using time magic, he finally gets one over his opponent and slays it. After defeating the Prima, it dropped something called a Key Fragment of the Exalted Prima that will grant access to a place called the Seat of the Exalted Prima once he forms a full key. Totally not important in later books, I am sure.

After this, he also explored the area the monkeys once occupied. Within a temple guarded by this Prima, he discovered a time banana musa.

Okay, so, important sidenote here. It is a common misconception that bananas grow on trees, but in actuality, they grow on something within the musa genus. These are a form of plant that can sometimes grow as tall as trees but are not considered trees, despite something like a banana plant being able to grow over a dozen meters tall. A way to distinguish a musa from a tree is that their "stems" are not woody, making them herbaceous plants. The genus of musa was originally named by Carl Linnaeus in 1753, and... oh wait, this is a summary. Search up the rest yourself (after reading this book, of course). Anyway, yes, this was an essential part of the recap.

Back to the boring part, Jake decides to transport this time banana tree-that-is-not-a-tree back to Haven by lifting it. Quite a difficult and time-consuming task as he has to lift up the entire area surrounding it to make sure the transportation goes well, which does result in him nearly missing this tiny little thing called the World Congress.

An event that begins right after he gets back.

Miranda (the City Leader that Jake delegated pretty much all his responsibilities to), Jake, and two others head off to the World Congress as the system teleports them there.

In the World Congress, Jake reconvenes with friends and family he hasn't seen in far too long. He also finally meets the other influential people and factions of Earth. The Holy Church, led by Jacob from Jake's very own Tutorial. Jake's brother, Caleb, the leader of the Court of Shadows on Earth; Carmen from Valhal, a primarily human-focused mercenary faction, the Risen, with Casper as one of their leaders, another friend from the Tutorial. He also encounters another person with a Bloodline called Eron, who Jake honestly can't get a read on, and whom we have seen little of before this book, but he will be in this book and has a role to play, so I feel it pertinent to mention him. And, last but not least, the Sword Saint, leader of the Noboru Clan, a native faction of Earth and the second faction on Earth to obtain a Pylon of Civilization and create a city.

Politics ensues as Jake does all he can to avoid it while catching up with everyone he knows. Still, he cannot avoid it all.

Three votes take place during this World Congress. The first is a vote for World Leader, but seeing as this is the first time all the factions meet and quite a few of them don't exactly like each other, no one is elected for this. The second vote pertains to a system store that will help boost Earth by allowing them to buy different goods using Credits – the system-bound currency of the multiverse. This vote revolves around what this store will provide, and after Jake is forced to decide a tiebreaker with a coin toss (Politics 100 move right there), the store ends up selling Foodstuffs, Ores and Metals, and Herbs.

The third and final vote was to select a system event Earth would be able to experience. This vote ends up landing on an event called the Treasure Hunt... also known as the subject of book five of the Primal Hunter.

At the very end of the World Congress, Jake also speaks with someone who is acquainted with the beloved character William, and he finds out the dude apparently has PTSD after getting killed by Jake in the first book.

Speaking of William, we also had a nice POV of him returning to Earth and meeting up with a woman who used to work as his psychiatrist. William then proceeds to protect her and help some people claim a Pylon. Sadly, he has no presence in this book, something I am sure will disappoint the majority of you.

Back with Jake, he gets a new weapon from Arnold (the tech guy at the Fort close to Haven) and decides now is a good time to explore the dungeon revealed after he killed the D-grade mushroom below Haven. And what does he find in this dungeon?

Mushrooms. A whole lot of mushrooms. Also, some Deep-dweller creatures live in this place called the Undergrowth, and there is this troll with three kid trolls Jake becomes friendly with. At the very end, he encounters some facility created by the Altmar Empire, an elven faction some people may remember as the makers of his cauldron.

After a fight against a golem borderline immune to most of

Jake's attacks, he finally wins and ends up getting rewarded with an awesome ring giving a shitload of stats. The ring also functions as a tool for the Altmar Empire to identify talented individuals across the multiverse.

Shortly after getting back from the Dungeon, Jake meets up with a few people of note. One of them is once more Arnold, who he gives the Altmar Golem. A golem Jake totally didn't steal from the dungeon despite the projection of one of the dungeon creators begging him not to.

Jake also goes to a leatherworker who points out that a lot of her materials come from monkey bodies found dead in the forest nearby while questioning what kind of moron doesn't even bother storing the corpses. This is what is known as me, the author, recognizing that Jake not properly looting most of what he kills is pretty damn wasteful. Something he will continue to not do even after this moment, and just know that your suffering as you complain only brings me happiness.

Another person Jake meets is a man called Felix, a sculptor living in Haven who joined a faction known as the Primordial Church.

Now, what is the Primordial Church, you might ask? Well, I hope a lot of you won't ask, as I hope you still remember what happened in book four (it was only three months ago, man). Anyway, to recap, the members of the Primordial Church are peak-level fanatics who venerate the Primordials to a frankly unhealthy level. This means that once Felix finds out Jake is the Chosen of the Malefic Viper, he kinda goes wild, and the leader of the Primordial Church, the Eternal Servant, even momentarily possesses his body to fanboy a bit.

The sculptor naturally wants to make a sculpture of the Malefic Viper with input from Jake, but Jake doesn't really have any ideas but just makes some random mana constructs as he thinks... and the sculptor sees one of these and decides that must be the will of the Chosen. So definitely look forward to seeing the reveal of the sculpture in another five books or so (you may think this is a joke, and if you do, you would be wrong).

Jake then does some alchemy and stuff before a visitor by the name of Sultan arrives at Haven. A powerful man and a slimy merchant, he attempts to get in Jake's good graces but ends up pissing him off due to his flaunting of slaves, who were all former criminals. Eventually, this merchant still reaches an agreement with Haven and is allowed to stay, though only after Jake kills a few of his slaves, who he deems irredeemable. It is also made clear Sultan is on thin ice, and he is punished with one of the evilest things in the world - higher taxes. Frankly, Sultan survived only because he proved himself useful by selling Jake some highly valuable items, including a bow and an item he could use to upgrade his magnificent boots.

After meeting with Sultan, Jake heads back and continues doing his alchemy, focusing on elixirs while also eating magical time bananas for extra Agility.

Elsewhere, the hawk family that consists of Hawkie, Mystie, and Sylphie (10/10 names right there) is out fighting a bunch of eagles when Sylphie gets overeager and ends up attracting the attention of another Prima variant. The three hawks get in quite a precarious situation, but Jake is fast enough to get there and deliver a good smackdown on the eagle that dared attack his bird friends. Also nets him a second Prima Key Fragment.

Sylphie realizes she needs to get stronger after her near-death experience and quickly progresses. She eventually ends up meeting Stormild, a Primordial that the Malefic Viper convinced to look her way. Stormild, a chaotic living storm of lighting, wind, and fire, ends up Blessing Sylphie after a tough round of negotiation, giving her a special skill called a Union Oath. She uses this Oath on Jake, forming a special bond between them that will allow Sylphie to attend the Treasure Hunt event, something otherwise only intended for humanity. This bond does end up fragile and with a limited duration due to the Viper's interference in the middle of the ritual, but it still works for what they want to achieve.

Jake then proceeds to make his final preparations, including getting another upgraded sword from Arnold and stocking up on everything he could need. Across the world, humanity is gathered in their cities, and all the factions and elites prepare to enter the Treasure Hunt ahead of them.

With new equipment, poisons, potions galore, and a bird friend to enter with, Jake is as ready as the Treasure Hunt soon arrives - a system event that surely won't last an entire book, right?

... right?

Chapter 1

The Power of Haven

System Announcement:

The Treasure Hunt Special Event will commence in:
23:14:53

All qualified participants will be invited at the allotted time. Those within the territory of a Pylon will be able to enter together, while any not within a Pylon's territory will enter as individuals by default.

Neil, Christen, Eleanor, Silas, and Levi were all chatting in the room, waiting for the rest to arrive. It was right next to the newly expanded City Lord's office, where a large meeting hall had been made, primarily for this day. The five of them had all gotten the notification about the Treasure Hunt along with every other D-grade in the city. Likely across the globe.

"Gotta say, Miranda ain't a slouch either," Levi commented as they chatted about the other D-grades from Haven who would join the Treasure Hunt.

"You totally got a crush on her," Christen teased the man,

who had made similar comments many times before during their hunting trips.

"No, I'm simply acknowledging reality," Levi defended himself, faking offense. "By the way, you know who else is coming? Besides those randoms, that is."

The randoms, in this case, were something entirely unexpected.

Around a week before the Treasure Hunt began, D-grades had started appearing at the Fort and Haven. All of them had come for a few reasons. One of them was that they weren't sure if they could enter the Treasure Hunt without being within the area of a Pylon and had come to make sure. That reason had now been debunked, but another purpose was to hopefully enter with a stronger group and team up with others.

All the big cities wouldn't just enter with a dozen people. The party of five had spoken about how Sanctdomo, as an example, apparently had D-grades in the four digits associated with their city enter. Not all of them were members of the Holy Church, but a lot of them sure were. Independent parties who didn't want to join some powerful faction needed somewhere else to go, and it appeared that Haven became one such place. No doubt, along with a lot of other smaller settlements around the world.

So far, a bit over forty D-grades had come to Haven. That didn't sound like a lot, but it sure felt like it was, considering Haven didn't even have half that.

Haven only had their party: Lord Thayne, Miranda, Arnold, Sultan, and those two creepy women, along with one other guy who had joined a month or so ago. Phillip was one they had expected to enter too, but he wouldn't come. Christen had heard he was retiring, so that was a bit weird.

"Just those we discussed," Neil answered.

They kept chatting, only stopping when another person showed up.

"Ah, you guys and gals are already here," Miranda said as she entered. "Good, the rest should be here within the next half an hour, then we can get started."

Her words proved true when, not even a minute later, two men wearing medium armor and sheathed swords entered. Two minutes after that, a man and two women came, and five minutes after that, Sultan arrived. The room kept filling up, and close to the half-hour mark, Lillian entered, practically dragging Arnold, who had his head down and was reading on his tablet.

This would ordinarily not cause much of a fuss, except... Arnold was the highest-leveled person in the room, and practically none of them knew about him. He was the kind of guy who stayed hidden away in his workshop months at a time, so only people like Sultan—those who had gone to sell him stuff— knew the man properly.

Despite quite a few individuals with decent levels coming and Miranda herself having a respectable aura, however, the forty or so independent D-grades did notice an issue: Haven was weak. Their strongest party was decent, but there was another traveling party present equal to them in power. Miranda, Sultan, and Arnold were perhaps powerful in their own right, but ultimately they were outnumbered heavily.

Confusion and some discontent spread in the hall as people talked. Many had come to Haven because of rumors of the city's power and now found themselves incredibly disappointed. Five minutes passed without anyone showing up. Ten minutes. Fifteen.

They all just talked and discussed, their voices getting louder as many stopped bothering to hide their discontentment.

"Why is Lord Thayne not here yet?" Silas asked in a low voice to his party.

"I don't know... but looking at Miranda, I am pretty sure she has something planned," Neil answered in an equally low voice.

They could only trust she had predicted this would happen and made an adequate plan. None of them except Silas and Eleanor had met the owner of the city recently, and the last times they did, he'd just been shopping or interrogating Sultan. They knew he was strong... but was he strong enough to handle a hall of nearly forty D-grades who had come to believe Haven wasn't all it was made out to be?

———

Jake put the last batch of poison in bottles as he prepared to head back. He had gone a good distance away from the city to not contaminate anything as he crafted his uncommon-rarity Necrotic Poisons, and had now stocked up with a few dozen bottles at least. He didn't know if it was enough for the entire Treasure Hunt, as he had no idea how long it would be, but he had a feeling he could just craft some more in there if it came down to it.

Through this last push for more stats, Jake had gone on a full-on crafting spree to get out as many Perception elixirs as he could.

This meant Jake had consumed twenty-two uncommon-rarity Perception elixirs and a bunch more of the common-rarity ones during this time. In the end, through consumption of Perception-increasing elixirs, Jake had gained a total of 440 Perception over his crafting frenzy throughout this last month. Unfortunately, that was all he had time to make enough elixirs for. Yet, he had still wanted to get as strong as possible, so he decided to just cap himself out before the Treasure Hunt.

The rest, he had chosen to fill out with Agility. 40 uncommon-rarity Agility elixirs and 41 common-rarity elixirs had gone down his throat, and quite honestly, he was damn sick of the taste by now. He was now fully capped out at the 900 stats he could get from consumables. Additionally, he still had quite a few Vitality-based elixirs left, as well as plenty of Agility ones. He would have to hand those out.

Finally, he had gained a single more level in his profession, bringing him to 130. He was now officially at a stage where his profession was ahead of his class again. Something the Treasure Hunt would very likely change.

For the first time in a while, Jake opened up his full status and did a final check of everything before he headed back to Haven and that meeting.

Status
Name: Jake Thayne
Race: [Human (D) – lvl 129]
Class: [Avaricious Arcane Hunter – lvl 129]
Profession: [Heretic-Chosen Alchemist of the Malefic Viper – lvl 130]
Health Points (HP): 29573/29580
Mana Points (MP): 39888/40812
Stamina: 20021/24870

Stats
Strength: 2050
Agility: 3711
Endurance: 2487
Vitality: 2958
Toughness: 2124
Wisdom: 3265
Intelligence: 2781
Perception: 6708
Willpower: 2814
Free Points: 0

Titles: [Forerunner of the New World], [Bloodline Patriarch], [Holder of a Primordial's True Blessing], [Dungeoneer VI], [Dungeon Pioneer VI], [Legendary Prodigy], [Prodigious Slayer of the Mighty], [Kingslayer], [Nobility: Earl], [Progenitor of the 93rd Universe], [Prodigious Arcanist], [Perfect Evolution (D-grade)]

Class Skills: [Basic One-Handed Weapons (Inferior)], [Basic Twin-Fang Style (Uncommon)], [Basic Shadow Vault of Umbra (Uncommon)], [Hunter's Tracking (Uncommon)], [Expert Stealth (Uncommon)], [Archery of Vast Horizons (Rare)], [Limit Break (Rare)], [Enhanced Splitting Arrow (Rare)], [Arrow of the Ambitious Hunter (Epic)], [Arcane Powershot (Epic)], [Big Game Arcane Hunter (Epic)], [Arcane Hunter's Arrows (Epic)], [Descending Dark Arcane Fang (Epic)], [One Step Mile (Ancient)], [Mark of the Avaricious Arcane Hunter (Ancient)], [Moment of the Primal Hunter (Legendary)], [Gaze of the Apex Hunter (Legendary)]

Profession Skills: [Path of the Heretic-Chosen (Unique)], [Herbology (Common)], [Brew Potion (Common)], [Alchemist's Purification (Common)], [Alchemical Flame (Common)], [Craft Elixir (Uncommon)], [Toxicology (Uncommon)], [Cultivate Toxin (Uncommon)], [Concoct Poison (Uncommon)], [Malefic Viper's Poison (Epic)], [Scales of the Malefic Viper (Ancient)], [Blood of the Malefic Viper (Ancient)], [Sagacity of the Malefic Viper (Ancient)], [Wings of the Malefic Viper (Ancient)], [Fangs of the Malefic Viper (Ancient)], [Sense of the Malefic Viper (Ancient)], [Touch of the Malefic Viper (Ancient)], [Legacy Teachings of the Heretic-Chosen Alchemist (Legendary)], [Palate of the Malefic Viper (Legendary)], [Pride of the Malefic Viper (Legendary)]

Blessing: [True Blessing of the Malefic Viper (Blessing - True)]

Race Skills:[Endless Tongues of the Myriad Races (Unique)], [Legacy of Man (Unique)], [Identify (Com-

mon)], [Thoughtful Meditation (Uncommon)],
[Shroud of the Primordial (Divine)]

Bloodline:[Bloodline of the Primal Hunter (Bloodline
Ability - Unique)]

Jake went over it all with a smile. His stats had grown *a lot,*
and he felt far stronger than before. If he'd faced the Altmar
Census Golem now, the fight would have gone far differently.
Every part of him had improved, and his Agility and Perception
especially had experienced explosive growth.

Since the time he faced the golem, he had gotten nearly two
thousand more in stats from equipment, and about equally as
much from consumables, counting all the percentage bonuses.
All of this wasn't even counting the many levels.

Closing his status once more, Jake began his travel back to
Haven. For once, he wasn't actually late, even if it was later than
the planned time. This was all with directions from Miranda
about how to approach the situation. She had informed him of
the influx of D-grades and asked him one simple question:

Did he still believe he was the strongest human on Earth?

Jake had answered with "How the hell would I know?" but
made it clear he sure as hell would gladly fight anyone to find
out. That was good enough for her to assign him the role they
had decided he would play a long time ago.

He would enter as the overpowering owner of Haven,
squashing any doubt about the city's power. Jake could do that,
but there was one more participant in the plan. He had
mentioned her to Miranda, and her participation was also just
fine.

Because as Jake flew past a certain treetop, a green figure
zoomed up to him and began flying beside him. Jake smiled at
her when he saw her.

"Let's show them how awesome we are, eh?" Jake said with a
smile to the green hawk.

"Ree!" Sylphie happily screeched as she flew beside him, easily keeping up with his speed. She had returned as agreed, and as for his requirement for her to reach 110 in eleven days?

[Sylphian Eyas – lvl 117]

Yeah, she had smashed past it. The hawk had gone on a carnage during this time. Now in D-grade, she could truly show her full power. It barely had to be mentioned, but she was more powerful than both her parents by now. Jake wasn't even certain if he could have handled her right after reaching D-grade. He sure as hell would be unable to do jack shit if she decided to leave.

The two of them kept flying as he soon spotted the meeting hall. "Time for the grand entrance," Jake said with a smile, Sylphie mischievously screeching in agreement.

He had wanted to show off his Pride of the Malefic Viper when other people were involved, and what was a better opportunity than this?

———

Neveah wasn't as vocal as the rest of her party, but she too showed discontentment on her face. They had operated out of a smaller settlement for a while as a party of D-grades, but had had some disagreements with the local City Lord when he began demanding a portion of all crafting materials gained during hunts. This was, in their minds, ludicrous, and the breaking point had come when one of them acquired a spatial storage ring —only to be told they had to hand it over, as it was a tool to conceal goods.

Sure, the City Lord of Haven hadn't done anything similar, and the city had a great location with many great hunting spots so close, but that didn't mean it was great being there. There was a general lack of high-level craftsmen, and there were long waiting times on anything from those who were competent.

But hey, at least Haven was super powerful, right? So far, it seriously didn't appear to be. They had a pretty strong but super shady merchant who was probably the city's greatest asset with his valuable materials. The temple was also decent enough, but compared to the one in Sanctdomo, it was nothing. According to what the city folk said, the sculptor wasn't even there, but had been holed up for around a month now. It was ridiculous.

The City Lord also didn't appear overly strong. Sure, she was good enough, but not some dominating powerhouse. Neither was the one party that operated out of Haven. They were another case of "good but not great," and Neveah ranked their parties about equal. For reference, they'd been the fourth-best party in their old city, behind the three "sponsored" parties.

Finally, there was that nerdy guy with a tablet. His level was high—the highest in the room—but he gave off the aura of a pure craftsman. He could probably do a bit of combat, but he didn't strike her as a combatant at all.

So, in conclusion? Haven was a nice enough city to live in and seemed very secure and relaxed with the forest aesthetic, but calling it a powerful city was just wrong. She *had* heard that Sanctdomo—the closest other Pylon—hadn't come to claim Haven due to the owner of the city.

The thing was... Neveah couldn't see that making much sense. She and her party were aware of extremely powerful people. They had seen the premier party of Sanctdomo, which consisted of five absolute monsters, every single one of them likely able to take down their entire party. So she got how a single person could be strong...

But strong to cause the forty D-grades in the room to be careful, or even beat them all alone? Yeah, no, that wasn't something feasib—

"Huh?" she exclaimed as she suddenly got the chills.

Nobody else noticed it for that fraction of a second. Power

descended upon the entire hall as if an invisible pressure held them all down. Neveah felt like she was being watched by some powerful beast, and she drew her weapon without even thinking. She wasn't the only one, either, as nearly every single D-grade not associated with Haven did the same.

Why are they not doing anything? she asked herself, looking at the residents of the city. Her answer came immediately.

The door to the hall opened, and in walked a single figure. The air appeared to vibrate around them. They were shrouded in dark clothes, and a mask covered the face, leaving only two beastly yellow eyes peering out. She was unsure if the being was a human or not, and Identify...

[?]

Identify did nothing. She then noticed that perched on the figure's shoulder was a small hawk. It was green and looked a bit otherworldly to her eyes, and when she used Identify on the hawk...

[?]

She got the exact same response. When she Identified the hawk, it looked her way and did what she could only interpret as a scoff. Neveah didn't dare say anything, as her entire body was frozen. No one dared attack this newcomer. Everyone with even the faintest ability to judge the power of a person based on their presence was acutely aware:

This person could kill every single D-grade present in the room.

―――

Miranda stood up on the small podium. The entire hall was blanketed in a presence that sent a faint chill down even her back, and that was with her being used to him. She looked below and saw all the independents frozen, some of them even glancing around covertly for potential methods of escape. They were scared shitless.

Now, she knew that she had asked Jake to come in with a show of force and establish some dominance. She could own up to that.

But how the hell could she have predicted he was going to come in with a presence like that?

CHAPTER 2

TREASURE HUNT? LET'S FUCKING GO!

Man, people can get so tense sometimes, Jake thought as all the people looked his way. Most of them even had their weapons drawn! Even Neil and his party looked on the edge, and only Sultan and Arnold were rather unaffected by the entire situation. Well, Arnold did look up from his tablet, frown briefly, and just look back down.

Miranda threw him a glance he couldn't quite read, but he did get the faint feeling that he should maybe tone it down a little. He did so, and as if timed, Miranda spoke, "Lord Thayne, thank you for finding time to be here."

Jake just nodded her way as he stopped infusing his presence with mana. That took the pressure off of them, but all of those independents were still looking at him with fright. And honestly? He was okay with that. He scanned them all and found that not a single one of them was above 115. Not a single one of them was a threat. What did this also mean?

This meant the baby bird on his shoulder was likely the second-strongest person in the room—and she knew it.

———

Sylphie was happy, if a bit annoyed. She had worked *sooo* hard, and even when she was done working and wanted to go and spend time with Uncle, she couldn't, as he needed to play with his smelly pot. He had made her wait behind, and only now could they have fun together. Though she did think it was a bit boring being around so many weak humans. They weren't even proper humans, as none of them had shiny eyes like humans were supposed to. Or maybe they weren't supposed to? The lady human who looked to be in charge didn't have shiny eyes, and Uncle seemed to know her well.

The same was true for the guy who gave Uncle his new string-shooty-stick. Then again, he was a bad guy—who was sometimes a good guy because he had tasty treats. Sylphie still didn't like him, and Uncle didn't either, so that made her not liking him right.

As for all the other humans? She either didn't care or looked down on them as super weak. She felt like all of them were weaker than Mom and Dad and compared to Uncle. Sylphie was pretty sure they were some worse kind of human than Uncle for sure. Just as she was a super bird compared to all the stupid birds, Uncle was a super human compared to all the stupid humans? That made sense to Sylphie.

This was why she stood tall on Uncle's shoulder and threw judging glances at all the weak humans. They all looked back, scared of her and Uncle, which only made sense. They should be. Because super birds were better than stupid humans, and she would make sure they knew their place!

———

Well, at least Sylphie seems to be having fun, Jake thought as he sat, debating with himself if he could take a nap without being noticed. Sylphie had moved from his shoulder to the top of his head, throwing piercing gazes towards anyone who dared look their way.

Meanwhile, Miranda ignored his presence as he sat off to the side with his arms crossed. He would say he looked menacing, but the bird on his head kinda ruined that look. Or did it? From what he saw in his sphere, people still barely dared to look his way, and those who did clearly didn't look like they thought he was being funny.

Miranda spoke about the Treasure Hunt and did give out some good info. She offered general knowledge of other humans who would enter, not to mention general descriptors of those she was aware of that people should avoid. Overall, the purpose of this meeting seemed to be making sure everyone knew each other—at least, somewhat.

Valhal, the undead, the Holy Church, the Court of Shadows, and a bunch of other smaller factions were mentioned and described, as well as the powerful people associated with the factions. She also mentioned a few wildcards with little to no information on them. That included a lot of people Jake didn't really care about... except for two names.

The first one was Eron. Jake remembered him as the one other guy with a Bloodline at the World Congress and a man Jake had deemed "not worth fighting," as it felt meaningless. That didn't mean he was stronger than Jake, just that an eventual battle wouldn't lead to anything productive.

As for the second name?

William.

Jake wasn't even going to think about that guy. He had no desire to seek out the little psycho and would rather have someone else handle him. But again, if the guy did come to make trouble for Jake and his friends, he would happily end him for good the second time around.

The entire meeting continued for a little while longer until Miranda finished up and moved to the next important topic. Miranda looked Jake's way, and he nodded as he got up, all eyes moving to him.

He walked to the center of the room and waved his hand as a

wooden table appeared. Another few waves and potions upon potions were stacked on top of it. Mana, stamina, and health potions in the hundreds.

Jake enjoyed seeing all the independents' eyes go wide as they saw the display. There was something very satisfying about seeing others awed at your handiwork.

All of this was naturally a part of the plan Miranda had made. The good old carrot and the stick. Jake would come in, make it resoundingly clear he was the one in charge and suppress them with pure power, and then afterward show that he was far more than just a big stick. The purpose of the first part was to build fear and the other respect.

"Lord Thayne has prepared some potions for the Treasure Hunt; please take a maximum of five health potions and a mix of four stamina and mana potions," Miranda declared to the hall, surprising quite a few of them. "Not to worry, this is a gift sponsored by the city and Lord Thayne himself."

Jake just stood back, thinking about how a table full of colorful potions looked quite awesome. A sentiment shared by everyone else, especially one rather skinny guy who walked up and Identified one of the potions.

"This... this gives more than 8000 mana!?" the man exclaimed loudly.

Jake was about to defend himself, explaining that he hadn't practiced making potions much in recent times as a way to justify why they weren't top quality. Sadly, or perhaps luckily, a woman spoke up first.

"What!? Are you serious? How can it give that much!?" She ran over and picked one up.

This led to a bit of a scramble as most of the forty D-grades hurried over to the table. None dared to actually take any potions quite yet—until finally a person looked pensively over at Jake and, seeing him not react, put one in a small pouch.

This led to people picking out potions, everyone taking five health and mainly mana potions, from the looks of it. Everything seemed to be going well, but of course, there had to be an asshole. There always had to be an asshole.

The expected happened as a single person swiped his hand, and nearly forty potions disappeared. The man turned around before any of the other people could react, but he didn't even have time to take a step before his entire body froze up.

Jake sighed under his breath as he took a step forward and grasped the man by the neck before he could move again. He squeezed a bit as his fingers sank into flesh, and blood began running down into the man's collar.

"Really, this is what you're willing to die for? A few batches of potions?" Jake asked, disappointed. A level 103 human had risked his life for something so insignificant...

The entire room froze up upon seeing that all play out in less than a second. The man being held wasn't the first to answer; instead, it was Miranda.

"Please, I believe this is just a huge misunderstanding, is it not?" she said with a smile as she walked closer.

Jake knew she was addressing the man, likely not wanting the moron to just die there and then. He could understand why. It would be bad vibes and would ruin the nice carpet he was standing on.

"I... I..." the man tried to stutter out, but he was unable to.

Jake may have squeezed a bit too hard. Miranda threw him a glance, and he let the man fall to his knees, still shaking. Jake did consider giving him a little poke with Touch of the Malefic Viper but decided against it. Again, wouldn't wanna ruin the carpet.

Miranda walked up to them and pointed at the man as she sent out a small, green beam into his shoulder. "Now, please return what you took and stay around till we're done to discuss your conduct moving forward. Ah, and don't try to run; I have placed a little mark on you, okay?"

"Same," Jake said, his one word seemingly having more

impact than Miranda's very unveiled threat as the man shook at it.

Luckily, the rest of the meeting and distribution went through without any hiccups. Miranda made a few closing remarks and otherwise allowed people to figure stuff out themselves. They all seemed thankful, and a few even sent remarks Jake's way in gratitude. He didn't really see handing out a few potions as that big of a deal, but fair enough.

Afterward, people began leaving, and only those originally from Haven stayed behind—partly at the request of Miranda, partly at the request of Jake. The little thief was told to stay within Haven and be a nice boy until Miranda came by and dealt with him later. Jake would just let her handle that one.

Once everyone was gone, Jake handed Miranda a bunch of Vitality elixirs to hand out to those who wanted them. He also handed a few extra potions to those who were actually from the city to make sure they had enough. Jake planned on crafting a few more in the last few hours anyway.

He left with Sylphie not long after and headed back to his lodge. Now, Jake also had many elixirs of the Agility variety that he had not given out, even if they would no doubt be useful for people like Levi and Eleanor. As for why?

Because what else would Sylphie drink?

———

Casper sat on top of the castle wall, staring down at the courtyard where Priscilla was riling up all the D-grade Risen and humans alike. It was filled to the brim, and he reckoned there were around a thousand. Quite good, considering the undead faction wasn't the largest.

He grasped the locket at his chest and asked, "Are you ready, Lyra?"

"Naturally. Let's show them the strongest duo of Earth!" she answered in high spirits.

Casper made a rare smile as he looked into the horizon. "That we will."

———

Matteo played his piano as he tried to get in the right mental state before the Treasure Hunt. Nadia was working on making some specialized sniper bullets in the background, and a few other elite assassins were also present in the room as they made their final preparations or discussed the Hunt in whispering voices so as to not disturb the man playing.

The only notable absentee was their leader, Caleb Thayne, and for a good reason. His type of training wasn't one where others could be present. Matteo still remembered the last time he had come by. The chamber was hidden far beneath their main headquarters, behind wards and physical barriers alike.

It was a chamber set up for only the Judge to use. A magic circle of incredible power made the entire room one of soul-shattering pressure. Matteo had been knocked unconscious after only a minute in there. It was a room meant to amplify and direct the pressure of the dark heavens above. Nobody had lasted in there for more than a minute. Nobody except for Caleb.

He hadn't left for a week.

———

Carmen pulled out a bottle of water and poured it over her head to get some of the blood out of her hair. It normally didn't bother her that much, but it had begun sticking together a bit too much, getting annoying. As for the rest of her body? She could deal with that being blood-covered, and the Self-Repair enchantments would take care of that minor annoyance soon enough.

She hadn't bothered to return to her city in preparation for this Treasure Hunt. She didn't need to, as the message would allow her to join anyway. In her mind, there was no reason to enter together with them anyway. Her city was now already managed by Sven and his men, and she didn't have to do jack shit. So she just spent all her time fighting, as that was all she was good for.

When her leg stopped itching from being healed, she walked over to where the corpse of a huge lizard had been just moments ago. It had evaporated the moment it died, something she hadn't encountered before. In its place were two small things: a Beast-core and some weird small golden metal thing.

She picked the golden thing up and inspected it before just throwing it in her spatial storage.

What the fuck does the "Seat" in "Seat of the Exalted Prima" even mean anyway? she asked herself as she headed off to kill some more shit before Treasure Hunt time.

———

"The teams have been prepared and instructed according to your commands, Augur," the man said as he bowed.

"Good, you may leave," Jacob said, and the priest exited the room.

The parties for the Treasure Hunt had been pre-established according to what he and others believed would lead to the best results. He himself would move with Bertram and his party, using his abilities as an Augur to seek out treasures as fast as possible with as much accuracy as they could.

From all their deliberations, staying together as one big group would be inadvisable, which was why they focused on smaller teams and parties, ranging from single individuals with high personal abilities in stealth to a large group of around two hundred D-grades led by someone with a commander-like profession.

Everything was laid out for the Holy Church to come out on top, as they were without a doubt entering with the most people, and hopefully the most power. Jacob only saw two people on Earth able to truly challenge them, but he had hope regarding those two...

Jacob didn't need his Augur skills to know the Treasure Hunt would be a confrontation between Jake and the Sword Saint. Hopefully, one that would take the pressure off the Holy Church due to those two outliers distracting each other.

———

The old man opened his eyes as a blue sheen flashed for a moment. He watched the counter for the Treasure Hunt as it slowly ticked down.

Miyamoto smiled. "May this lead to a season of prosperity."

———

Jake sat with Sylphie and stared out onto the pond as the timer finally reached 0.

> **You have been invited to the Treasure Hunt. The Treasure Hunt will be an event focused on the acquisition of treasures through a variety of challenges. This is a combat and challenge-solving event, and death is an ever-present factor, so be warned. Exiting the Treasure Hunt early at the loss of obtained rewards will be an option. Do you wish to enter now?**
>
> **Time to decide: 9:59**

"You got it too?" Jake asked to make sure. The hawk gave him a nod, and he snickered. "Then let's fucking go!"

CHAPTER 3

TREASURE HUNT: A WORLD OF MIST

Mist rolled over the hills as the vast, open plains that were otherwise desolate suddenly saw movement. First, a figure appeared, a hawk still on his shoulder. Another person appeared a second later, and within two minutes, over fifty people stood there.

Jake saw Miranda had entered with both the slave woman and the thief. He wasn't sure what she had done, but both seemed to be under her charge for now. As far as he could tell, it wasn't any kind of slave contract or something like that, but there clearly was some kind of control involved. But, ultimately, it wasn't something he bothered dealing with.

The Treasure Hunt was far more important.

He noted they were currently within a transparent bubble of sorts, and would likely stay there until everyone had entered the Treasure Hunt. While the others were talking, Jake decided to spend this time more efficiently by testing some things. The first of which was his divine connection.

Jake felt inward, and while he could feel his connection with Villy, he couldn't pull on it. It was like the World Congress with the gods completely cut off. He was fully aware this was advantageous to him, and he was more than happy to have the system block it out. It meant far less bullshit would go on, and it would just be mortals fucking up other mortals.

Seven minutes or so later—when the original invitation time was over—a notification appeared as the bubble around them faded.

Welcome to the Treasure Hunt!

The Treasure Hunt takes place in the ruins of a fallen realm, one where civilization left behind many signs of its existence. Explore their world, challenge the many monsters that still roam these lands, and, most importantly, claim their treasures.

A mist hangs over these lands, hiding many secrets and forgotten places. Venture through it to discover the dangers and opportunities that lie within or stay in the safety of the plains. The choice is yours, but be warned of what the mist may hide.

Each Treasure Hunter has been given a Hunter Insignia that allows them to store treasures within. All spatial storages are restricted during the hunt. This insignia can be activated to transport the Hunter out of the Treasure Hunt prematurely at the cost of leaving all rewards behind.

The final reward will be calculated at the end of the Treasure Hunt. The Treasure Hunt will last a total of ten days. May fortune be with you!

Time remaining: 9 days, 23:59:59

Jake read it over and nodded to himself. He was currently standing on a grassy plain, except he noticed the grass had a neon blue color and was even giving off a very faint amount of light. The first thing he did was test the insignia versus his spatial storage. Jake tried to activate his spatial storage and easily took out his bow. He deposited it again without any issues.

Existing items I brought in are unaffected, he noted. Next, he picked up a small handful of grass from the ground and tried to put that in his spatial storage. It didn't work. Next, he tried to put it in the insignia storage, and that worked just fine.

All items from in here must be put in the insignia. Pretty simple, Jake thought with a nod. The insignia itself could be summoned anywhere on the body at any point and was just a box with some runes he couldn't recognize within. Some people had had it appear on their hands or arms, with the back of the hand seeming like the preferred position for most.

Jake also naturally listened in to the chatter all this time. It had been going on since the first participants entered, and he was looking forward to leaving, but he still took the time to hear if anyone had any interesting insights he didn't.

"The mist is dense," he heard someone with a bow say—an archer of some kind.

"I can't see shit," another one answered.

"I think we should stay in the plains for now..."

They were all currently standing in the plains, not very far from a barrier of mist. It was like a wall, but Jake could see it curving slightly, making it more circular in shape. If his guess was correct—he was certain it was—then the plains were the center of this entire Treasure Hunt, with a ring of mist around it. Jake looked to the side, and far off in the distance, he saw another group of people. Looking inwards, directly away from the barrier, he also saw people far off in the distance. Further, into the plains, he even saw a few buildings scattered about. The mist was still present in the plains, but it was far thinner and more just a light fog.

This place is fucking huge, he thought as he peered into the mist. He saw it moving a bit uphill away from the plains, and far off in the distance, he saw the outline of what looked like tall hills or mountains. Wait, wasn't a tall hill just a mountain? Or did it have something to do with how rocky they were? Hm...

"Everyone, let us split up here," Miranda said. "A larger group will be able to find far fewer treasures, and considering that our relative safety is guaranteed, there is no need to stay as a larger target, is there?"

Jake scoffed a bit internally. Of course, Miranda didn't want to bother with these independent D-grades either. Not that he thought they wanted to deal with her. He decided to be a bit nice for once and give them a warning.

"Be warned, there are unnatural movements within the mist; my guess is that creatures hide within," Jake said, having all the independents turn to him. Considering he still had a lot of goodwill from the potions and now the warning, he got a few thankful smiles and nods. They were the easiest brownie points of his life.

Five people took off individually just after he spoke without a word, still giving Jake a nod in thanks. They had likely just stayed behind to be polite to him and Miranda, and now saw both him and her speaking up as approval for them to leave.

Miranda looked over at Jake, and he looked back and smiled beneath his mask as he nodded. She would handle the rest, and now... now it was time for Jake to do what he was good at.

This was a Treasure Hunt, and he was a Hunter. A Treasure Hunter, even, as the system had called him and everyone else.

And Jake was very good at hunting.

———

Miranda observed as everyone left one by one or in smaller groups. Most went into the unknown mists after some discussions, while others left for the plains. Neil and his party had chosen to enter the mist, too, with Eleanor's abilities as a scout offering them some comfort.

The only people remaining were Sultan, the two slave women, the potion thief, and Arnold.

"I don't care what you do," Miranda said to the one slave woman and the thief, "just don't cause any trouble. Now, get out of here."

The two of them didn't have to be told twice, and they both took off towards the inside of the plains. Together. She didn't question that one, assuming they'd seen each other and decided to stay together for now. Miranda would bet a thousand Credits they were gonna fuck over each other the moment they found anything of value.

"What are your plans?" she asked Sultan, who was standing there patiently with his one remaining follower.

"I would ask you the same," he answered with a smile. "Should we perhaps go together? Strength in numbers, and I do believe we have powers that would mutually benefi—"

"No," Miranda said, shutting it down. "Thanks for the offer, but I am perfectly capable on my own."

The man shrugged. "In that case, we shall leave."

With those words, he and his slave entered the mist. He emitted an aura, and Miranda felt a slight prickle in her mind looking his way. No doubt it was some kind of soul magic, likely to scout the area after Jake's warning.

She turned to Arnold to ask him, but the man just stood there with his damn tablet out, pointed towards the ground. He also repeatedly looked at the insignia he had summoned on the back of his hand, and he even took a small needle to it, put the needle in a small slot in the tablet, and nodded in understanding just after. Miranda had some serious doubts regarding whether Arnold coming to the Treasure Hunt was a good idea, but he had chosen to attend. In the end, she just shook her head and asked anyway.

"What will you do, Arnold?"

He looked up at her briefly. "The objective of this Treasure Hunt, naturally."

Arnold was already looking down again as he paced back and forth; his tablet was still pointed down, and he sometimes did stuff on it.

Miranda shrugged as she also left. "Good luck, I guess."

With that, she also entered the mist to find her own fortune.

Now, if only she could see more than a hundred meters ahead of her... She summoned wisps of verdant light that flew out in all directions to at least give her some awareness of what was happening further ahead.

———

Arnold finished his scanning and located a suitable spot. He opened his jacket and took out a small pen, pressed a button, and saw it enlarge nearly a hundred times over. He placed it in the ground as it began drilling. Then, opening a small pouch on his belt, he took out a handful of small objects that he tossed into the air.

None of them fell to the ground, but instead took flight and began scouring the plains. Finally, Arnold took out what looked like a mix between a rifle and a cannon and pointed it upwards. He pressed the side of his glasses as they showed grid lines in the sky.

BOOM!

He fired, sending pain through his arm. Unpleasant but necessary work. Five more shots later, he felt like his entire arm was paralyzed. Thankfully, he was done with his part.

Arnold summoned dozens of mid-sized drones that he sent into the air, then into the mist. Once they were sent off, he saw that the drill was about done. It had managed to get nearly fifty meters down, which should be enough.

The drill was pulled back up with a command on the tablet, and he placed a final drone on the ground. Then he jumped down into the hole and let himself fall till he reached the bottom, where he sat down in the cramped space. Finally, he took out what looked like an umbrella that opened and pierced into the dirt, also making a platform beneath him to sit more comfortably.

A swipe on the tablet later, and the drone above began filling the hole up, the umbrella making sure he wasn't covered. Once it was done covering the hole, it would self-destruct to make it look like a fight had been going on, masking that a hole had been dug.

As a final thing, he took out an armchair from his spatial storage and sat back.

He looked down at the tablet as hundreds of small displays appeared from his many drones sent out. Then, a minute later, another message appeared.

Satellite uplink successfully established.

———

Countless factions and powerful individuals had entered the Treasure Hunt. Many had their own agendas, but the majority only hoped to find treasures to help themselves advance in this new world.

Anyone that had managed to reach D-grade was at least partly driven and competent. The majority of the larger factions quickly entered the mist, but a bit of reshuffling was necessary for some groups. An oft-forgotten ability was more essential than ever in this event:

Scouting.

The mist made seeing even a hundred meters ahead of you a major challenge for the common D-grade. An Archer or other class with scouting skills—especially the near-omnipresent Archer's Eye and its many upgrades—did help alleviate this issue somewhat.

A majority of these parties had made it as far as they did by being careful and organized. The Holy Church used light mages to create a path through the mist while carrying giant light-torches burning like the sun.

The undead summoned ghosts or apparitions to scout ahead for them when they didn't have a more regular scout class available. The Court of Shadows were naturally stealthy and carefully snuck through the mist, many of them spreading tendrils of darkness to warn them of any approaching threats.

People found solutions and were careful. Everyone tried different skills and tactics to safely explore the new environment they found themselves in. They knew things could turn deadly —not just by the hand of other humans, but also potentially the environment itself.

But... some parties and overconfident people did none of that. Some parties and individuals had gone with the tactic of trying to get as good a head start as possible. They were quick on their feet and identified that the better rewards would be deep in the mist, and the moment they got the chance, they rushed into it.

One such person was swiftly flying close to the ground, as he found flying any higher incredibly difficult due to the mist seemingly pressing him down. He was a level 104 caster, a competent fire mage who had never quite found a party he got along with, which was why he had entered this event alone.

He kept flying, sending out fireballs to light up the way. One of his blasts revealed something reflecting light ahead of him. Without any hesitation, he headed towards it. Yet, he wasn't a complete moron, so he stopped a distance away and surveyed the area as he landed.

Ahead of him was a metal staff driven into the ground. He Identified it and saw it was rare rarity... an item he could use for sure. The mage carefully approached, his eyes flickering back and forth as a mantle of flame covered his body in case he triggered any traps.

Nothing happened as he walked up to that staff. Then he

put his hand on it. Still nothing. He poured mana into it and bound it to himself, a huge grin on his face as he—

SWISH!

The air ripped from movement in the mist, but just as it appeared, it disappeared again. The mage's eyes opened wide. He didn't even think about triggering the insignia to escape... That function of his mind was already gone as he looked to the side only to see a gaping maw.

Half a minute later, all that was left was a dried-up corpse that soon turned to dust and became one with the mist, the creature that had killed him already gone.

Not a single trace of either's existence was left behind.

CHAPTER 4

TREASURE HUNT: NO FLYING TOO HIGH

J ake sprinted through the mist, Sylphie flying along with him. His Sphere of Perception was a bit over three hundred meters in radius as he scanned the area at the ground level, even scanning to see if anything was hidden beneath. With his eyes, he scouted the area ahead, seeing movement here and there within the mist. There were incredibly subtle shifts in the background, with patches of mist not moving as uniformly as the rest, or swaying in a too-predictable pattern.

Yet, he wasn't exactly aware of what lurked within. There were clearly some invisible creatures, and they were hiding from not only his eyes but his other senses too. None had entered his sphere, either, but seemed to keep a very healthy distance. He didn't doubt they were aware he had seen them.

Not simple beasts, he thought. On the contrary, they were careful and calculating. Smart... but not smart enough to avoid Jake's curiosity.

He threw Sylphie a glance, and she seemed to get it as he took a step forward. Jake teleported, took another, and teleported again. He repeated this seven more times until he was at the shimmering form that was hiding. It knew he had found it, and instead of trying to futilely run, it attacked.

Jake saw four long claws reflect a tinge of light out the corner of his eye as it swiped for him. No, they weren't claws; they were nails. Long—nearly seventy-centimeter-long nails—came for him, but Jake was ready. He blocked the blow as a barrier of mana appeared around one hand. With the other, he released a blast of arcane mana.

A high-pitched scream sounded out as his foe was blasted back, its invisibility now dispelled. He had naturally already seen its form in his sphere, but it was just something else when done with his eyes.

It was a thin figure with one large, black eye in the middle of its forehead and a giant, circular maw of teeth beneath. Its hands were disproportionally large and had what looked like useless thumbs and four extremely long nails. Its skin color was grayish blue, and it looked sickly and thin. Unfortunately, his Identify didn't exactly help him understand what it was.

[Young Ekilmare – lvl 118]

I would ask what the fuck an Ekilmare is, but this appears to be it. Huh, Jake thought. He was honestly more used to what were essentially just mutated Earth creatures. But this? This was something entirely else. Well, the Deepdwellers were also kind of weird, but they were mushroom-loving assholes, so that at least made sense.

At first glance, it actually reminded him a bit of the undead, but at the same time, he clearly felt a strong sense of vitality.

The creature stumbled to its feet, but this time it didn't attack. Instead, it slowly backed away and turned invisible again. This was totally okay for Jake, as he wasn't really that interested in them. He did find it interesting how this was only a Young Ekilmarre, making him wonder what the mature version looked like. But alas, he wasn't in the mood to bully some lower-leveled creature to find out.

Sadly for the Ekilmare... Jake's bird pal was totally fine with it.

Sylphie zoomed past him as she headed for the creature. A domain of green wind spread out around her, and Jake watched the mist freeze in place. Simultaneously, the creature's invisibility was dispelled, forcing it out into the open where it had to fight.

Jake saw it shimmer again, but this time it didn't turn invisible. Just as Sylphie got close, it swayed and teleported to the side. A fraction of a moment later, it teleported again, this time behind Sylphie, ready to cut up her small body.

Yeah...

A glowing wing met the claw as a blade of dense green wind cut forth, severing the arm of the Ekilmare.

That was dumb...

A sentiment the Ekilmare clearly agreed with, as it hastily retreated. Impressively enough, Jake saw its arm already regenerating. Alas, it was far too slow. The small hawk attacked again, and this time the Ekilmare didn't have a response in time.

In what would only be called a fly-by, Sylphie flew past in an insane dash, her wing extending like a lucent blade as she passed. Then she did half-loop in the air and flew back, landing gracefully on Jake's shoulder.

A few seconds later, a severed head landed on the soft grass.

He looked at it for a moment before the body also collapsed. The flesh wiggled for a bit, but soon it died for good. *Some kind of active regeneration skill... not like the Deepdwellers,* Jake concluded.

In the end, the Ekilmare was an ambush predator and not a tank. It was fast, had high attack power, and, of course, the ability to be invisible and even teleport. The invisibility was especially respectable. However, to Jake, it was far from enough. Even Sylphie could still detect them. As a hawk, she had high Perception by default, and she also had plenty of magic to detect foes.

Jake walked over to the corpse and saw that it hadn't

dropped anything of value—at least, nothing he could Identify. He did want to put it in his inventory anyway, as he had decided to just take everything, considering he had the special storage for this event. First, however, he would ask the one who had actually killed the thing.

"Sylphie, can you store it?" Jake asked.

Sylphie looked at him a bit and flew down. She poked the corpse with her talon, and the entire thing disappeared.

While it seemed like a great success, it instead made Jake frown. Because he just felt the corpse enter his own inventory. "Can you take it out again?"

She looked a bit confused for a moment, and after shuffling a bit back and forth, a corpse was dumped on the ground. This only made Jake frown even more. "Okay, Sylphie, I'll move back like a hundred meters. Then you try to put it in the inventory and take it out again, okay?"

He only added to her confusion, but she did as he said.

Jake used One Step Mile to get back and signaled for the bird to put it in the inventory. She did so without any issues, then took it out again.

Alright... shared inventory... I see no indication of a range limit... Isn't this just kind of overpowered? Jake frowned.

Making his way back to her, he said, "It appears we share an inventory... Do you know what that means?" Jake flashed an excited smile.

"Ree!" Sylphie screeched.

"Oh, yeah, good idea on that one," Jake acknowledged as he took a bunch of potions out of his usual inventory and put them in the Treasure Hunt one. "But, it also means we can split up and get twice the loot! Imagine how many tasty pellets you could get if you managed to collect some cool stuff?"

Sylphie's eyes went wide at the thought, and she screeched in agreement. It was lucky they could split up, as, quite frankly, they weren't exactly good at fighting together. Jake sucked at fighting with a partner, and Sylphie also had many flashy attacks and stuff like that.

As for the risks of splitting up? If Jake had learned one thing about Sylphie during their time together, it was how difficult she was to put down. In fact... he would say she had a higher chance of escaping than he did if they met a foe he couldn't handle. Her fully stepping into D-grade had not been a small upgrade. Far from it.

"Ree! Ree?" Sylphie screeched.

"Yeah, of course, just pull on that bond if you need any help; I will make sure to do the same," Jake answered with a big smile.

That was something else both had easily noticed after their contract. Both could vaguely feel the location of the other—mainly just the general direction, but also if the other was still in good condition. It was nice to have, as Jake believed he could only get a warning if Sylphie was in bad trouble without it.

"Then, bon voyage, and may your booty be plentiful," Jake said, snickering, only to get a confused head-turn from Sylphie. Rewording it, he said, "Good luck getting those shinies."

With those words, Sylphie nuzzled up to him, and he rubbed her head. Then, with a determined look, she took flight towards one of the hills in the distance, a green tailwind left in her wake.

Jake himself turned towards a more prominent mountain far off in the distance. Even the hill Sylphie had chosen was a far ways off, and this mountain was even further in... and damn, did he hope there would be more worthy opponents the deeper he went.

He took off, focusing on his sphere the entire way. He did spot a few minor things, like a rock his Sense of the Malefic Viper picked up on containing a lot of mana, a herb here and there, and stuff like that, but nothing truly worthwhile. Regardless, he took everything he found, as sending out a mana string or a quick sidestep on his path didn't slow him down much.

It shouldn't come as a surprise, but he noticed that the Ekilmare liked to cluster around these treasures, likely waiting for something to come by to try and claim them. Or were they just close because they themselves absorbed a bit of mana from the items? It was hard to say, and frankly, it didn't matter. The creatures ran whenever Jake got close, not a single one of them trying to ambush him, and naturally, he didn't bother chasing them either.

Throughout this time, he also made sure to completely ignore any other humans. Considering he was likely the one with the highest Perception in this entire Treasure Hunt, he easily spotted them all before they had a chance to spot him.

Surprisingly enough, he didn't notice anyone having a scuffle. Maybe they just hadn't spotted each other... or maybe there was some collective agreement that it simply wasn't time yet. Jake had no doubt in his mind that as more time passed, more humans would switch their goal from finding treasures to stealing from other humans.

In some ways, it was the tutorial all over again, except you would get *all* their treasures this time around. Even if the person were incompetent, over a week's worth of collecting would still add up to a lot. Certainly, more than one could feasibly collect in a short period.

Not that it was anything Jake particularly planned on doing. Though, of course, if someone wanted to rob him, it would only be fair to rob them back in kind, right?

His journey continued for nearly an hour as he ran at high speeds. He avoided using his One Step Mile to not miss anything with his sphere, and also to give those invisible stalkers time to get out of the way in time. Additionally, it gave him more time with his feet on the ground. And what did feet on the ground mean?

That's right—more time spent feeling his super comfy boots and their ability to feel earthbound herbs and natural treasures. This did expand his searching perimeter quite a lot, and Jake was essentially a one-man locust swarm, scouring anything of value in his journey.

He also checked the inventory and noticed many corpses appearing, progressively feeling more powerful as they grew in levels. *Sylphie seems to be having fun,* he thought with a smile as he pulled an uncommon-rarity sword from the ground and tossed it in the inventory.

Finally, he reached the base of a mountain. He looked up and saw that the fog got denser at higher altitudes. It even began changing color from white to black further up. Even with his insane Perception, he couldn't see more than a few kilometers up the cliffside.

All game logic told him the good shit should be up mountains like these. Jake had seen only two mountains and three hills from where he started, this being the smallest of the mountains. He honestly wasn't sure how tall it was, as he hadn't seen the top back then, and even as he stood before it, it was still a mystery to him.

Without further hesitation, he summoned his wings and began flying upwards along the cliffside. He had noticed a while ago that the mist seemed to push him down, making flying harder but not impossible. Sylphie also constantly rebuffed this effect with her winds to counteract it.

Jake kept flying upwards as the mist got denser and denser. Soon, he spotted something above. An angle that wasn't natural. It was a half-circle that should not appear on any regular mountain. As he got closer, he noticed what it was.

It was a balcony.

As it entered his sphere, he saw it truly was a balcony leading out of the mountain. He also saw that it had been carved into the mountain, making him frown a bit. Was this entire mountain actually some kind of construction? Or had it been carved out as a residence at one point?

This Treasure Hunt was meant to take place in a fallen world that still retained traces of civilization. This mountain appeared to be related to that, and was, beside those buildings down in the plains, the only sign this place had ever been anything more than a hunting ground for monsters.

Jake reached the balcony soon after and landed on it. It was substantial, nearly forty meters long and reaching out fifteen or so meters. He saw the entire edge was lined with what looked like plant boxes. Had they used this place to grow herbs and stuff for those within the mountain?

Looking up, he didn't see any other balconies. Why had they placed it this low down? Did it have something to do with the dark mist above? Jake decided to give a test. Instead of entering the mountain through the large gate on the balcony, he flapped his wings and flew upwards.

The first kilometer went fine, and he didn't spot any other signs of the mountain being inhabited beside his Sphere of Perception reaching inside, scouting it. He couldn't see much, as it appeared they had only built far inside the mountain.

Two kilometers up from the balcony, he noticed how it really began to darken.

Three kilometers up, he, for the first time, truly noticed a difference. His skin began prickling, and he covered himself in scales when he saw himself begin taking a bit of damage from the mist. Yet he decided to keep flying up.

The scales held back whatever damaged him as he sought to analyze it with Sense of the Malefic Viper. It was black, but he didn't sense any immediately familiar concepts in it. It wasn't dark mana or any kind of poison, as far as he could tell, and Palate didn't seem to have any effect either.

Five kilometers up, he began taking damage again. The pressure from flying also increased, and he felt like he was swimming through water. No, it was like his body was covered in glue. The damage also only kept increasing, and it was about that time he noticed something even worse... It was accumulating. It wasn't just some purely environmental effect... Something was invading his body, actively seeking to destroy him. Yet it also felt faintly familiar... like he had encountered something similar at some point. He stopped advancing and began slowly flying down towards the balcony again. Attempting to get any higher would just be needlessly reckless, and even he could only see a few dozen meters ahead of him with his eyes that high. Based on his sphere, he wasn't even close to the top.

When he landed back on the balcony, he took a knee and inspected himself. He dispelled his scales and saw thin, rune-like lines covering parts of his body. Upon further examination, he finally discovered what the energy reminded him of.

It was a fucking curse.

It was one of the worst kinds of magic. One that relied more on an odd, almost entirely metaphysical concept that Jake still wasn't entirely able to understand. One that relied more on emotions than raw power. One far harder to dispel than some average poison or nearly any kind of magic affinity.

Fuck me, he cursed as he entered meditation to dispel the foreign energy that had invaded his body. He made a mental note to himself, but also sent it towards Sylphie:

No flying too high.

CHAPTER 5

TREASURE HUNT: FIRE & ASH

"I fucking hate curses," Jake muttered out loud as he got up.

It had taken nearly an hour to fully eliminate the energies in his body, and he had only been up in those dark clouds for a minute or two. Shit, he had even lost over a thousand health during the process. When he imagined what was further up, he shuddered.

Seeing that traveling up the side of the mountain wasn't an option, he went for just traveling inside it. Before that, however, he took all the plant boxes on the balcony into the inventory. None of them gave off any special aura, but they were made out of some kind of metal, so he reckoned they could prove useful. Also... the storage given seemed borderline infinite, so why not just swipe anything you could?

Walking up the entrance of the mountain, he inspected the large black gate. He frowned a bit as he put his hand on it. He noticed how it almost seemed to reject him, and when he tried to pour in a bit of mana to inspect what it was made of, it was just repelled.

It wasn't that the door was enchanted either. Perhaps it was once upon a time, but not anymore. Instead, it appeared to be made out of some kind of metal that completely rejected all mana. Jake also saw further inside with his sphere, noting that another gate was only five meters inside the hallway leading into the mountain.

Considering that his danger sense was silent and he didn't detect any magic, he decided to head inside. Two handles were attached to the door, and he grasped one of them and pulled. The door was heavy as fuck, but he managed to get it open after a bit of struggling. He noticed some mechanism made it close by itself again, making it harder to open since it constantly wanted to stay shut.

Jake was pretty damn sure the door had been opened by some kind of enchantment when this place was actually used. That, or they actually kept it well-oiled. Anyway, he went inside and had the door close behind him nearly instantly.

Once inside, he noticed something—or rather, the absence of something. There was no mist inside, and what had entered with him was quickly dispersing. On a closer inspection... two gates... locking out stuff... Yeah, this was totally an airlock. Well, a mist-lock would be more accurate, as clearly it sought to keep out the mist.

Did those who used to live here fear the mist? Jake asked himself as he went through the second door, now truly entering the mountain. On the other side of the second door was just a long, boring hallway with several etchings along the walls and floor. No doubt old, inactive enchantments or something. He did test something, though.

BOOM!

The Pillar of Encumbrance was summoned, and he slammed it into the wall, feeling his arm hurt from the feedback. In retrospect, not the smartest decision. As for the wall? Well, he had taken a small nick out, so that was something. Needless to say, this confirmed the walls of this mountain were strong as fuck. It reminded him of the Challenge Dungeon and their indestructible walls. Man, he couldn't wait till Hank learned to make invincible houses.

He put the Pillar back in his inventory and began running forward, taking in the environment. After running nearly half a kilometer, he finally reached another door. All the enchantments or other tools to keep people out were long gone, it seemed, and now anyone who could open the door was free to enter.

Enter, and steal all their shit.

Well, at least he hoped they had a lot of stuff, because the entire place seemed quite bare so far. Getting through the third gate, he now truly reached the mountain and what was hiding within, and inside he found... more hallways. But! These hallways also had rooms attached to them—a massive improvement.

Sadly for him, what was inside the rooms was the opposite of interesting. All of them reminded him of those small, shitty cabins you got on a cheap cruise ship, with only a single small mat in each and none of them larger than the smallest of apartments.

The only objects inside were a few pieces of old furniture, most of them made of stone. He did see some signs of what had likely once been wooden furniture, but all of those had long since rotten away. Additionally, he did notice something else. Ash. Nearly all the rooms had ash, often on the mats that Jake assumed had once been used for meditation or maybe sleeping on.

An enlightened race for sure, Jake confirmed to himself.

Now, Jake did feel there were no real objects of value... but that didn't mean he didn't take anything. For example, if a stone looked slightly shiny, he swiped it. Something made of metal? In the inventory you go! Glass? Inventory!

So far, he hadn't spotted any signs of living creatures inside the mountain. Jake didn't rush through but carefully tried to get an understanding of the area. He counted thousands of residences. If the construction within the mountain had as many floors as he theorized, then a million people could have easily lived in there. Probably far more.

Walking down one of the long corridors, he passed a few stairways and what looked like a lift. A lift that had long ago become unable to operate, but he saw no other reason to have a long vertical hole going up and down the mountain.

After walking a bit further, he finally spotted something out of the ordinary. There was a large hall ahead of him. A communal area? It was towards the center of the entire mountain, and once he spotted it, he rushed out.

Entering the room, he came to realize it wasn't really a room at all. Instead, it was a huge, open space. Looking up, he could see pure darkness above... then the sky. The top of the mountain wasn't made of stone at all, but it looked like it had at least been partly hollowed out to make a huge skylight. The entire mountain was truly just a megastructure. More than fifteen kilometers tall, he now stood on one of the lower-middle floors of what he now rightly identified as an atrium.

This mountain... was a city. A large one. To explore it all properly would take a while, even with his sphere, as picking up all the information from it at once was more than a little challenging. So instead, he closed his eyes and focused on Sense of the Malefic Viper and the ground beneath his feet at the same time.

At first, he felt nothing. The entire mountain felt... hollow. Not a single ounce of life or trace of mana anywhere. No... there was some mana. The natural mana in the atmosphere was always there. Always seeping into the natural materials of the world. Yet, he noticed some areas had far less mana than others, which meant that something else had to consume it or keep it out.

Jake jumped out over the balcony and into the open space in the atrium. His wings spread out as he began flying upwards. The lower floors appeared to be where the common people had lived, while the higher floors were where this civilization's rich or powerful had resided.

That, or it was just where they kept the good stuff.

When he was nearly at the top, he took a turn and landed on one of the over a thousand balconies extending all the way up the structure. This specific floor was slightly different from the others, as within, he detected what felt almost like a vacuum of mana.

He soon found the reason: another black metal door. This one wasn't leading into a hallway, however.

Jake opened it with a good push and stepped inside. He found himself in a large room a few stories high with many tall bookshelves lining the walls.

It was a library with pretty much no books. All that remained was dust where the books had once been. Everywhere... except for one place. Directly ahead of him was a three-meter-tall bookshelf different from any of the others, in that it actually contained books.

Oh yeah, and a giant magic barrier sealing it in—no doubt the reason why this bookshelf still stood after this long.

It was also the thing that had sucked away all the surrounding mana. Jake walked closer to the barrier... at which point, something actually happened.

Because what was a good Treasure Hunt without a trap-filled room?

The door behind him sealed shut, the barrier in front of him intensified, and the entire floor lit up with an orange color. Jake didn't know what he had expected. Maybe some elaborate trap that fired out many weapons and different mixed concepts or something. But what did he get?

Fire.

A lot of fire.

Jake pushed a hand out to each side as he activated Limit Break at 10%, and a bubble of arcane energy began forming around him. At the same time, scales covered his body, and he even wrapped his already-summoned wings around his body.

The entire room began glowing orange, and soon the bookshelves caught fire. Next, the balconies and everything else not either within a barrier or made of stone began burning with intense heat. Jake was counted as within a barrier.

At least, for now he was. The room became hotter and hotter, and sweat began dripping down Jake's brow as he tried to hold it back. His scales protected him, but they were far from perfect, and for every moment that passed, it only got hotter in the room.

That was the exact moment Jake learned something new. If the heat got high enough, and the fire affinity was intense enough... even mana itself would burn. Everything would burn.

A dozen seconds later, the magic formation died down, and the fire stopped. The atmosphere ceased burning, and all that remained in the room was a single barrier covering the bookshelf. The barrier was the only thing that was not black ash, but one other place was slightly different: a sphere of ash, looking almost like an egg.

An egg that cracked a moment later as two crispy wings fell to the ground, an ash-covered Jake below.

"Tha—" Jake tried to say, but he ended up just making pained coughing sounds, as his internals had taken some damage from him stupidly breathing in.

That sure was something, he just thought instead as he shook his body like a wet dog, sending ash flying everywhere and revealing his mostly undamaged armor beneath. The only thing that had really taken a beating was the cloak, and even that was fast repairing, courtesy of the Self-Repair enchant.

Jake had to admit it was quite the trap. Perhaps someone with skills made to detect the trap would have discovered it earlier, but Jake really wasn't good at those magic formations. What he was good at was listening to his danger sense... and throughout it all, it hadn't really activated. In other words, the trap simply wasn't good enough to be a serious threat to him. Which made sense. Because if this room were a legitimate threat to him, it would kill nine out of ten parties from other factions.

It would still kill half for sure. Well, not really kill them, as they would have plenty of time to choose to leave the Treasure Hunt.

Either way, the trap was gone, and now he just needed to find a way to open the barrier and—

Jake heard a sound around him, like a gust of wind had picked up. He looked down and saw the ash-covered ground glow again, this time with an odd gray light. *Oh... the formation isn't done yet.*

All the ash in the room began swirling and gathering together in front of the door. Magic hummed to life as the formation transferred all its energy into the amalgamation of ash, which soon took the form of a semi-humanoid with two long arms. Jake immediately recognized it as an elemental and used Identify.

[Ash Guardian – lvl 141]

The elemental was nearly twenty meters tall, and faint embers were visible on its body as it moved to attack. It raised its large arm to smash it down towards Jake and—

BOOM!

An explosion sent ash flying everywhere as the arm was destroyed, and before the elemental could react, it was hit again.

BOOM! BOOM! BOOM! BOOM! BOOM!

Five explosions nearly scattered the entire elemental as Jake stood with his bow out, another explosive arcane arrow already at the ready. He naturally shot it and made the arrow split into five in mid-air, exploding the elemental again.

It attempted to reassemble itself, and parts of the ash moved towards him to stop his assault. A tornado of ash kicked up around him with red glowing embers mixed in between, but Jake easily dodged back and avoided being surrounded.

He kept bombarding it with arrows. The only thing he would admit was that it was durable. Everything else was just terrible. Maybe it could hurt him if it managed to completely surround and practically absorb him into its ash, but with how slow it was, that would never happen.

The inevitable result was that the elemental died within five minutes of being conjured.

You have slain [Ash Guardian – lvl 141] – Bonus experience earned for killing an enemy above your level

Jake saw the elemental slowly fall apart as the ash fell to the ground, showing no signs of moving again. He inspected it with his sphere and found himself disappointed at the lack of loot. Goddamn magical constructs. It didn't even have an orb like the cloud elementals, as it had been spawned by the formation.

With the death of the elemental, something finally happened at the barrier. Jake felt the mana in the entire room shift, and when even the door opened up, it seemed like all restrictions on the room had been lifted.

The barrier didn't disperse but instead coalesced into a figure of pure mana.

Jake frowned at it. It looked humanoid, but a lot thinner and taller. He couldn't see any details, as the figure was a dark blue color and more an outline than anything else. It didn't take a genius to know what this was, and Jake prepared himself for the exposition dump that was to come. Alas, it was okay, as any information about the Treasure Hunt area would be valuable. As for how he knew it was exposition time? What else would a damn library be for?

Almost on cue, the figure in front of him began talking.

"If you are hearing this message, it means you have broken through the defenses of the archives and that the last of us have

THE PRIMAL HUNTER 5

either fallen or entered slumber. I do not know which world you hail from or if you are even sapient, but I hope for the Records of this world to live on. It may be a lot to ask, but if you listen to the end, I shall reveal information related to the greatest treasure this world holds."

"Now that's just playing fucking dirty," Jake muttered out loud at the projection, which just continued without any pause.

CHAPTER 6

TREASURE HUNT: HISTORY LESSON

J ake searched his inventory and found a stone chair he had swiped before. He summoned it and sat back as he listened to the projection talk. This wasn't a case like in the Undergrowth dungeon and that Altmar elf. This was just a recording—nothing more, nothing less.

"This place is—or perhaps was—once called Yalsten. We were always a small, secluded world with few exits or entrances. For many years it was a paradise. A place of study and learning, free of war and conflict. A united people under the banner of the creator. We cultivated resources, trained fighters, and did as we were commanded. But, alas, this would not last.

"The creator was known as Yal, and the world was named after him. A mighty A-grade on the crux of advancement. Yet time was coming for him. He sought to advance but found himself unable. He sought power but faltered. Do not misunderstand; I do respect the creator for making this world... but I have long been disillusioned towards his person. He was just another greedy mage seeking to advance through any means possible. This world is ultimately nothing but a prison for his family to be kept safe forever. It was a place for his family to be kept safe..."

Jake looked up to the black, ash-covered ceiling as he

listened, hoping it would soon get to the good part. So, yeah, some space mage or something had made this world and put a bunch of people in here, including his family. He guessed the next part was about how shit had gone wrong.

*"While his life was long, he knew it was ending. So the creator sought ways to extend it. Natural Treasures consumed in droves, forsaken rituals of old... Everything in his power, he sought out. Everything appeared to be in vain... until **he** showed up."*

Jake frowned at that. The projection had perhaps not done it on purpose, but he felt the intent and will injected into that word—the pure hatred, powerful enough to survive even within an otherwise completely powerless projection.

*"**He** came bearing a gift that would turn out to cost more than Yal could ever afford. The creator accepted the gift as he underwent the Ritual of Blood and joined the vampiric race to extend his lifespan, and—"*

"Oh, damn, vampires," Jake muttered out loud. "So, this is vampire land? I hope it's the cool sort of vampires..."

"—throughout the years, he began offering this same gift to his family. Once his family converted, they spread it to their servants, who then spread it to their families, and within a few decades, nine out of ten had joined the vampiric race. The last ten percent were still on the fence or not deemed worthy. I must admit, my ancestors also joined them... and this entire change led to a period of prosperity.

"The creator reached S-grade not long after, and this world began creating C-grades like never before, all of whom left to join the wider world outside. Our kings grew to B- or even A-grade, and we became a powerful family under the banner of the vampiric race. All signs indicated that we would prosper more than ever before, and our future was bright. Until the Bloodless Night happened... and everything changed.

"Without the power of the True Ancestor, we were forced to feed... We were made to consume the lives of others to sustain ourselves. As a third-generation inheritor of the True Ancestor, the

creator was harder hit than anyone else and went insane. He died only a month after the Bloodless Night, hunted down by the Templars of the Blessed Sun. Our kings, fearing for the future, tried to hide our world away entirely, cutting off all connections to the multiverse."

It was quite a lot of information at once, and Jake frowned a bit at the many terms used. So... Bloodless Night, True Ancestor, Templars of the Blessed Sun... Jake had the feeling this recording expected him to know what all these were about. Naturally, he had no clue. But, man, True Ancestor and Bloodless Night? Totally vampire-related. The Templars? Jake remembered hearing those were often associated with the Holy Church, so had the vampires gotten hunted down by an army of paladins?

A bit cliché.

"However... this was not a suitable solution. We needed to feed to live, and if we locked ourselves away, we would not be able to get livestock. We tried to nurture some, but it was not feasible in any way. Our time of prosperous growth ended up being one of the primary causes of our downfall... Without proper livestock, the most powerful of us deteriorated and, in the end, had to leave this world behind to try and make it outside.

"Those that remained tried to find ways to survive without life energy. Alchemists kept us going for a while, but it was far from enough to sustain us. So we kept looking... and finally, someone came up with an idea."

"This is where he tells me about how they made some fucked-up experiment or ritual that ended up creating that mist which ruined the entire place for good," Jake spoke out loud.

"A ritual was theorized—"

"Fucking called it."

"—to change the nature of the mist that hung over our world."

"Shit."

"The mist was but a natural part of this world. It always had been. The mist held special magical properties, allowing certain Natural Treasures to grow, and was no doubt one of the reasons

why we could grow as we did. So, the one remaining Vampire King —a powerful A-grade—came up with the idea to transform the mist. Make it into one of life that could sustain us forever. The way of doing this? A grand ritual of more livestock than ever before."

"So the Vampire King left, and a century later, he returned. He came with several planets' worths of livestock. Most of them were humans, but it also included elves, scalekin, beastfolk, and most enlightened races. More than a trillion. All to be the fuel of the ritual."

"Okay, that's kinda fucked up," Jake said.

He knew—or at least hoped—that Villy was just joking with the whole planetary sacrificial ritual thing, and now he was hearing that was actually a legit thing. Seriously... a trillion was a fucking lot. That was more than a hundred times pre-system Earth's population. He did understand that planets could hold far more people now due to how massive they were, but it was still just too much.

"This Vampire King was a master of curse magic, so he thought it would be smart to create a special kind of curse to infuse all the livestock into the mist. He would not kill them... no, he would seal them. Make them constant batteries of life, turning their entire souls into fuel. I do not know the details... only that he succeeded. In fact, the ritual was a massive success, and for years everything seemed to be perfect once more. He was hailed as a hero.

"But the thing about curses is that they are very much alive. This particular curse evolved. Grew. It began to slowly develop, and so did those it affected. If you have been to the plains, you have seen the results of continued exposure... Monsters that dwell within the mist. Once proud members of the vampiric race, now reduced to nothing.

"We were forced to flee. Take refuge underground or hide within the towers to keep the mist out, live here, and try to survive on alchemical products and what little livestock we still had. The king was more affected by his own curse than anyone

else, and in an attempt to not be corrupted and fix everything, he tried a different ritual... one that ended up causing even more harm. Within the next decade, ninety-nine percent of this world was consumed by the black mist. Naturally, the king died too.

"Not a single being above C-grade managed to survive this period. Our most powerful kings, dukes, and marquesses died. Only the counts remained to lead us. They tried... I truly believe they did... but it never became the same. Thousands of years passed like this, us just hiding in towers, individuals sometimes venturing outside, but the creatures in the mist never disappeared. They were always waiting. Always hungering. Six hundred years before this message was recorded, the last gateway to the outside world closed, sealing us in completely.

"It was a slow death for us all. We deteriorated... but soon, we did see one spot of light. The mist began being cleansed. The curse weakening. All we needed was time... and so we waited. The counts entered Eternal Slumber, and the rest of us tried to make it. This recording being necessary should make it clear we failed."

Jake sat there, still listening to this massive history lesson. He did learn a few things. First, the mist was good for treasures and a natural part of this world. Second, the vampires had lived in these towers, and the creatures outside were mutated vampires. Third, the curse had been weakening. Fourth... there was something special about that center plain.

"Behind me is a recording of our history and some tomes with all the most valuable information we have learned through the ages. Be it regarding alchemy, smithing, construction, tailoring, or any other profession, it is there. I hope you will take this and spread the knowledge to allow Yalsten to live on, at least in some form.

"Additionally, there are many treasures hidden all over the plains and even within the hidden treasuries of these towers. Claim it all, for we have nothing to use it for anymore. All I ask is that you remember us."

The projection stopped talking and just stood there. Jake

stared at it intently for a while. *Don't you fucking dare scam me on the information about the greatest treasure...*

Just before he was about to waste his time tearing the recording a new one, it spoke again.

"Finally, I offered to provide the location of the greatest treasure in this world... and I will stay true to that promise. In the center of the Mistless Plains lies a hidden structure that contains this treasure. Power left by the True Ancestor Sanguine, brought here by the creator. One that can only be accessed when the keys of nine kings come together. These kings themselves have long died... but the Counts of Blood still lived at the time of this recording, and they now hold the keys. One of these counts resides within this tower. However, be warned... for the counts have entered Eternal Slumber, and if they still live and awaken, they will be hungry. If you can even reach their quarters, that is. I wish you luck."

With those words, the entire projection disappeared, leaving only Jake and the bookshelf behind in the room. Everything else was just piles of ash. Jake walked forward and looked over the bookshelf. He saw a shitload of books on so many topics. He counted about five hundred books total on the bookshelf... and there was no way in hell he was going to sit down and read anything here and now. Sure, maybe there would be some information within giving him information on where treasures could be located, but he would prefer to blindly just look for himself.

After putting the entire bookshelf inside the storage, he headed out again. He opened the huge gate and looked to see if the trap had managed to damage it in any way. It naturally hadn't, but he was more interested in whether the hinges were damaged. They were not.

The doors were attached through huge poles of metal on each side embedded in the stone. Jake very much wanted to steal them, but that wasn't possible without breaking down the stones. He had tried with the Pillar, and the stones were just too powerful. His arcane affinity also didn't help much. Jake had tried everything he could, and—

Oh...

Looking at all the ash, Jake remembered something. Something he probably should have remembered a bit earlier. What had Jake done the last time he came across contraptions he could not break?

Alchemical Flame.

Jake smiled as his eyes glimmered. It was time to steal the goddamn doors off their hinges.

––––––

Miyamoto walked through the mist-filled halls of the hill he had entered. A hill he came to learn was, in actuality, an underground bunker. One that had long been abandoned. Only the beasts that dwelled within the mist remained. Their claws were sharp and their attacks powerful... but compared to his blade, they all came up short.

Another figure flew in from the side as he walked past another doorway. It was only a faint shimmer in the air, but it failed to completely mask its presence. A single slice, and the beast was cut in two. Its bisected body splattered onto the wall.

This was but one of many. Beasts, not even the old man's own level, sought to challenge him. He would've found it insulting, had their general lack of intellect not been clear. At least the ones in the plains had learned to stay away. These beasts that had been sealed in were far more aggressive.

After walking through the halls for a long time, he finally saw a gate. One with a large, red magic circle inscribed upon it. He drew his blade and cut down the center where the slit of the gate was. The rune broke, and the door flew open.

Red mist poured out of the large chamber behind the gate. Inside, a coffin leaning against the far side of the wall slowly opened, revealing a figure within.

[Viscount of Blood – lvl 135]

The being's eye opened abruptly as an aura spread, and Miyamoto smiled. *Come.*

———

Jacob sat in meditation at the center of their hastily constructed basecamp in what he had come to learn was called the Mistless Plains. Little time had passed since they entered, yet they had already created large walls using earth magic and begun putting down preliminary enchantments.

He, as the Augur, was not meant to join any of the fighting. This was not his role. No, instead, he would be the one directing everything.

"Group 4 should move in the sixty-one-degree direction, and they will encounter a bunker," Jacob muttered. "Have them secure it and wait for Group 3 to arrive. Group 2 should move in the one hundred forty-six-degree direction, and they will encounter one of the mountains. There shall be an entrance along the base; I am not certain where. Once inside, scour it from the bottom to the top. I can see they will face challenges... it will not be as straightforward... The details are unclear. Oh, Group 8 should avoid their current trajectory and switch to the two hundred eighty-nine-degree direction."

Over a dozen mages and priests surrounded him, all with magic rituals and circles around them, allowing them each to communicate with a corresponding group. The only group Jacob personally directed was Bertram's, also known as Group 1.

"Bertram, once you're done in that bunker, head for the location of Group 2 and secure the tower. I fear we will have heavy competition."

Jacob had seen many futures and realities, but one thing was certain in all of them: for this initial part of the Treasure Hunt, those towers would be the gathering point.

CHAPTER 7

TREASURE HUNT: ARMOR OF MIST

One man's trash is another man's treasure. Many would say that in a Treasure Hunt with high-rarity items spread throughout a large area, one should not stay in a single place for a prolonged period to procure things that didn't even count as items. Most would argue that was a waste of time. But to Jake, the true treasure was not the huge metal gate; it was the sense of victory he got when the first door finally fell off the hinges and slammed into the ground, making the entire archive shake and lifting all the ash off the ground for a brief moment.

Totally worth it, Jake thought as he put the huge thing in his inventory. Swiftly he moved on to the next door and spent another half an hour slowly burning away at the hinge. Was this truly worth the metal of the door? Maybe. Jake really didn't know, as he was quite clueless when it came to metals. He had just decided he wanted the metal, so he got the metal.

All arguments for it not being worth it were swiftly removed, though, as the entire process forced Jake to take a different approach with a skill he often took for granted. Alchemical Flame was a core skill for all alchemists, and Jake just used it to control the heat of the cauldron usually. That usage hadn't really led to anything... but spending over an hour focusing on improving the flame as he got the doors off? That sure helped.

[Alchemical Flame (Common)] – The flame of an alchemist is one of the most critical aspects of the crafting process. The flame itself is affinity-less and not polluted by the impurities of burning a catalyst. The path to refining one's alchemical flame is a long and arduous one for all alchemists seeking the pinnacle. Allows the alchemist to create a small alchemical flame, emitting heat. Adds a minor increase to the effectiveness of Alchemical Flame based on Wisdom.

—>

[Alchemical Flame (Uncommon)] – The flame of an alchemist is one of the most critical aspects of the crafting process. The flame itself is affinity-less and not polluted by the impurities of burning a catalyst. You have just embarked on the path of refining your alchemical flame, and may your path towards the pinnacle be swift. Allows the alchemist to create a moderate alchemical flame, emitting heat. Adds a small increase to the effectiveness of Alchemical Flame based on Wisdom.

Jake got the notification halfway through getting the second door of the gate off. The change in the description was minimal, and honestly, he couldn't feel much of a difference aside from his flame growing slightly larger, heating up or cooling down a bit faster, and generally being all-around improved. Which was nice. Once again, stealing doors was totally worth it.

With the gate gone, he decided to head onwards. He still had a lot of the tower to explore, and according to the recording, there were hidden treasures. It made sense he couldn't just sense them outright, as, of course, hidden treasures were... well, hidden.

Walking out of the hallway leading to the library, he frowned as he heard sound echo up from the bottom of the atrium. Jake slowly walked over to the edge of the balcony with an overlook all the way to the base of the tower and towards the top.

He looked down and saw movement in the open space below. Jake saw several groups of humans running around, and even a few that flew or jumped up a few stories. They seemed hesitant to split up, though. He wondered why for a moment, but soon got his answer.

Out of one of the terraces flew a figure covered in dark armor. It seemed to emit black smoke from the gaps in the armor and swung a dark, two-handed blade as it chased after a mage who shot a fireball at it to try and blow it away.

[Reanimated Blackguard Golem – lvl 110]

Jake wondered why he hadn't encountered any of these himself. Then again... he had barely been around the tower. He had walked down two hallways total—one to get to the atrium and the other to enter the library, skipping everything in between.

Looking at this armor a bit closer, Jake felt that the black smoke coming out of its gaps was actually mist. The same mist he had encountered far above. This made him frown... How had the mist entered the tower? Were there breaches somewhere?

He kept looking down and watching how the humans below handled these golems, which they were doing quite well. A party of four took it on, and the mage who was being chased was swiftly saved as a warrior with a shield stepped in.

A Powershot from an archer hit the golem not long after, and when a rogue-like person struck it from behind, its end was clear. Yet, something still felt off. Jake frowned a bit as the golem was on its last legs, and just as the rogue struck it in the head from behind...

The golem exploded in a cloud of black mist.

A loud scream echoed up the entire tower as the rogue fell to the ground. A healer that was not from their party, as far as Jake could tell, came over as another two people joined the party of four. The healer began doing what a healer does, but Jake just shook his head.

Yeah, good luck.

The rogue had been hit point-blank with the cursed mist. Maybe they could fix it, but with the rogue's low innate durability, he doubted it. He was proven right less than a minute later as the rogue chose to activate his insignia and exit the Treasure Hunt.

When the rogue disappeared, a large, floating coin with the Hunter Insignia inscribed on it was summoned in his place, floating where he had been. The coin was about the size of a human head, and it didn't take a genius to figure out this was what contained the rogue's loot. Which made a lot of sense... Having everything a person had looted just appear in the air and not within a spatial storage would be silly—albeit extremely funny, as Jake could imagine a metal gate crushing some unsuspecting person if he ever left the Hunt.

Jake kept watching as the two groups got into an argument about the floating coin, and in the end, it ended up being a third party who came in from the side and stole it. Jake laughed a bit under his breath as he saw the thief use Shadow Vault of Umbra. It was nostalgic to see that old skill, and a little funny to him too. This was pretty much exactly what he had told Caleb the Court of Shadows should do during the Treasure Hunt.

Shaking his head, Jake decided to stop wasting any more time.

That humans would come into conflict during this Treasure Hunt was unavoidable, and he was actually a bit happy they didn't just try to kill each other outright. It had barely been a few hours since the entire Treasure Hunt started, so it would sure get bloody if people were already slaughtering now. Once again, though, he was sure that would come later.

Jake jumped out over the balcony and flew upwards. He felt a single gaze land on him from below, but that was it. He turned and saw a single archer look up towards him, but she swiftly averted her gaze when he returned her peeking.

He flew up all the way towards the top, where he had been told this count would be. If Jake could find any good challenge or good loot, it had to be in the vicinity of this boss-type enemy. He was still internally trying to figure out if all of this was "real" or more a scenario of sorts made by the system. Or perhaps a bit of a mixture of both. True history, but perhaps a made-up place?

Well, it was "real" in many ways, no matter what. But the tutorial, as an example, was partly system-constructed scenarios. Everything was just too neatly set up, much like this. Seriously. Collecting keys to access some big final boss, all of them conveniently sealed away in their respective boss rooms? All of it was just too artificial and game-like.

When he got all the way to the top, he noticed that the layout had changed a bit. The mountain narrowed the higher one got—as mountains tend to do—and Jake saw only four hallways total at the top, each of them a good stance from the very top too. Jake presumed all of them led into special rooms like the library.

Jake looked over towards one of the hallways and saw movement. While flying up, he had been wondering why no one had gone to the very top from the start. It turned out... some had. A group of five was far inside one of the hallways, battling three foes.

[Reanimated Blackguard Golem – lvl 132]

[Reanimated Blackguard Golem – lvl 133]

[Reanimated Blackguard Golem – lvl 132]

They were the same kind of golems as the one below, but at a higher level. One of the golems used a two-handed sword, another dual-wielded shortswords, and the last had a spear. All of them were quite competent with their weapons for being reanimated suits of armor.

Simarlily, the party was a coordinated group with two warriors, a healer, and two mages. The warriors each kept one golem busy, while the healer summoned magical barriers and hurled transparent chains of mana suppression at the last one. The mages were trying to swiftly finish off one of the golems, one using lightning and the other water magic. A nice combo, Jake reckoned.

They seemed to be doing quite well. As a general rule, he didn't intrude in ongoing fights, as he didn't really like when people did that to him. He still remembered the asshole birds up on the cloud island. Butting into their fights had been fine, as they did the same shit, and besides, he'd been with Hawkie then. It had been a bit of a dick move to force his own hunting policy on his feathered friend.

Just as Jake considered if he should go elsewhere and leave before the party noticed him, the situation changed. A wooden door at the far end suddenly slammed open as another figure stormed out. This one had a sword and shield, and its armor looked slightly different. He naturally Identified it.

[Reanimated Black Knight Golem – lvl 138]

With that use of Identify, Jake already knew the party was in deep shit, and while he generally wanted to avoid butting into the fights of others, saving their asses wasn't out of the question. So he summoned his bow, marked all the golems with Mark of the Avaricious Hunter, and took aim as he began charging.

At the party of five, the Knight entered the fray. The

warriors were all busy, but their competency showed once more. One of them used a skill to make his hammer smash one of the armored golems away from the group, allowing him to intercept the Knight.

He blocked with the handle of his hammer, and Jake saw him buckle under the pressure. The healer fired a spell towards him, and the warrior moved to get up and push the Knight back a step... At least, he looked like he did. Instead, the Knight simply stepped back as the warrior pushed to dodge the blow, then, with a dexterous blow, cut the warrior deep in his shoulder and smashed him in the chest with its shield.

The man was blasted back when the shield sent out a pulse of mana. By this point, the mages had picked up the pace and had just finished off one of the three Blackguards, freeing up the second warrior. Sadly, he had no way to intercept as the Knight went for the healer, who was still holding down a Blackguard by himself. Only the lightning mage could do anything, as the other was sealing in the explosion of mist in a bubble of water. And even if he wanted to help, the Blackguard that had been smashed away before was now charging towards him.

As the Knight raised its blade to cut the healer across the chest, it became clear this was a catastrophe to the party. But to Jake? To him, it was an opening.

He released the arrow, and an Arcane Powershot tore down the hall, leaving a wake of arcane mana. The Knight froze just as it noticed the blow and failed to do anything to minimize the damage. As a result, it was hit square in the chest, with the arrow piercing straight through and sending it flying back until it smashed into a wall.

The party stood frozen as Jake shot again. This arrow split in five and threaded between the five people and the two remaining Blackguards, heading straight towards the Knight. Five explosions of arcane mana filled the halls, the ensuing mana wisps barely missing the party.

Another arrow came just after, hitting one of the Blackguards in the side of the head and sending it smashing down the hall with an arrow embedded in the helmet. Arrow after arrow streaked down the hall, the party unmoving. The Blackguards had all been blasted away, and were now neatly grouped up at the end of the hall.

A good barrage of more explosive arrows later, Jake used One Step Mile and appeared amid the party. They looked frightened for a moment, but none made a move.

Jake looked down the hall as the dust cleared. The three golems were slowly getting up, their armor cracked and broken as pink-purple lines of pulsing arcane mana joined the black mist. He looked at the three of them and smiled beneath his mask.

Boom.

Three flashes of arcane mana lit up the hall for a split second as the Arcane Charges on the Marks activated. At the same moment the golems died, they all exploded with black mist, but Jake simply raised his hand and sent out a blast of arcane mana, blowing it away from him. With the distance between him and the golems, chances were the explosion wouldn't have done anything anyway.

You have slain [Reanimated Black Knight Golem – lvl 138] – Bonus experience earned for killing an enemy above your level

You have slain [Reanimated Blackguard Golem – lvl 133] – Bonus experience earned for killing an enemy above your level

You have slain [Reanimated Blackguard Golem – lvl 132] – Bonus experience earned for killing an enemy above your level

Jake quickly checked the notifications to confirm the kills

before closing them all and turning to the party. The last explosion the mage had handled was already fixed, as the bubble had been sent flying away and exploded harmlessly to release the mist. The healer—and leader of the party, as far as Jake could tell —was the first to speak.

"Thank you for the assistance, Lord Thayne," the man said with gratitude and a bow. "We surely would have lost party members without you. Once more, I thank you on behalf of myself and my party as well as the Noboru clan. Please, take this as a token of gratitude; we found it in the plains outside."

The man offered up a rare sword for level 105s that he'd summoned from his Hunter Insignia.

Jake looked down at it and shook his head. "Keep it. If you want to do something, deliver a message to the Sword Saint...

"I'm looking forward to the duel."

The party looked at him for a moment, bewildered, before the healer bowed again. "I shall be sure to relay your words. I am certain the Patriarch will happily test his mettle against you, Lord Thayne."

Jake nodded, and with that, he turned and walked over towards the three corpses of the golems. The five stared after him, their looks now far warier than before.

CHAPTER 8

TREASURE HUNT: THE GIRL & THE HAWK

Carmen sprinted through the mist-filled halls, smashing down any damn ghoul in the way. It reminded her a bit of the good old days of the tutorial, where she'd smashed zombies day in and day out. She snickered as she turned another corner. Before the waiting ghoul could react, she drop-kicked it square in the face, smashing its head between her heavy boots and the wall. She identified the undead-like thing with an oddly squishy head as she leaped back and landed on the ground.

[Vampiric Ghoul Thrall – lvl 114]

Even without its head, it kept swinging. She launched into a barrage of fists before she finally put it down for good, its body utterly pummelled apart within a few seconds. They were kind of durable, but her attacks were far from simple. Every single hit sent waves of destructive kinetic energy through her foes, destroying them from the inside.

Without slowing down, Carmen kept sprinting forward. She had entered this Treasure Hunt alone and would prefer for it to stay that way. She encountered a few more ghouls, but upon reaching a crossroad, she noticed something: corpses. Ones not made by her.

Curious, she stormed down the corridor, hoping to find this other person yet only finding more corpses than before. Finally, a few minutes later, she reached the exit of the hill... or what had been the entrance of the ghouls' killer. Cursing under her breath, she turned around and headed back inside after having gone the wrong way.

She stormed through the halls again, this time a bit angry, and she soon reached the same crossroad. Going the right way this attempt, she continued and passed through hall after hall with only dead ghouls. All of them had been cut up or ripped apart by some magic.

Carmen frowned a bit, as some of the wounds didn't look like they had been made by a human. She found deep holes in the skulls of the ghouls and jagged cuts that looked to be the work of a saw or something. Or maybe it was just some magic?

Not seeing it as important enough to think about further, she continued. A big part of her hoped it wasn't another human —or worse, a party of humans. *Should I just kill them if it is? No, they would teleport out, and it could cause trouble... Shit.*

Yet, she didn't want to just turn around and leave. With annoyance, she continued onwards and turned a few more corners. She noticed how she was going downwards, and the signs of battle got more and more obvious. Deep cuts covered the walls and dismembered ghouls littered the floor.

Finally, she heard a noise in the distance. A few hallways further, and she caught a glimpse of the action. A ghoul was blasted through the hall, smashing into the wall. Next, it was hit by a barrage of green crescent blades of energy that cut it into several pieces.

Carmen slowed her approach to get a better feel for what she was dealing with. That green magic wasn't a type she recognized. Another blast later, she felt the rush of wind blow through the halls. *Wind magic of some kind?* she asked herself. Nothing she had seen so far was a real threat, so she ultimately just rushed in to get a good look.

Turning the corner, she saw it. A small figure flew through the hallway ahead at incredible speeds, leaving a green wind in its wake. A small tornado revolved around it, inflicting shallow cuts on all the ghouls that got too close, and every time it waved a wing, a crescent green wave was sent out.

The three ghouls fighting it were quickly ripped apart. The last one had its entire midsection crushed by a single talon that began glowing green and enlarged as the beast grabbed it. Carmen Identified it as she was waiting, getting nothing valuable out of it.

[?]

Frowning, she wondered if this was some hidden boss. It was a beast. A bird of some kind. She wasn't all that sure about birds. Maybe it was a falcon, an eagle, or a hawk or something. Either way, it was nearly entirely green and damn strong, if not as strong as her. This was one of the few times Carmen wasn't sure what to do.

Not being able to Identify the beast was not normal—that was for sure—and she hadn't seen any boss or enemy during the tutorial or in a dungeon in the outside world she couldn't Identify. Well, not Identify in that she couldn't see anything. Sure, if it was a lot higher in level, not seeing the level was normal, but this clearly wasn't it.

The moment the bird finished off the last ghoul, it turned and looked over at Carmen. It stared at her for a while, then, without breaking eye contact, summoned a mana potion using a Hunter Insignia and drank it.

Ignoring how comical it looked to have the small bird gulp down a potion, Carmen was now more confused than ever. Was this a participant of the Treasure Hunt? Why was it a bird? Why was it green and a bit chubby-looking? Why did it have such big eyes?

Above anything else: Why the hell was the bird so damn cute?

"Hey, there, little fella," Carmen said with a smile, trying to look as approachable as possible as she began slowly walking towards the bird. She kept her hands behind her back to try and look as unintimidating as possible. Approachable and not intimidating... That should work, right?

The bird made a weird screech at her, making Carmen stop. Did it want her to back off? Well, alright... she would... after just one small head pat!

Carmen kept slowly walking forward, talking all the while. "Did you come here with anyone? Are you alone? You're sure a strong one, eh? I love your feathers, by the way. Those attacks were really powerful, weren't they? You're so pretty..."

As she talked, she saw the bird slowly calm down and just look her way, tilting its head back and forth in confusion. Step by step, she got closer, completely ignoring the many corpses she had to step over. The bird sat on top of a dead ghoul at around chest height.

Then, after only a few more careful steps, she came within reach. She slowly extended her hand to pet the cute bird on the head. It looked at her hand as she lowered it. The hand was mere centimeters from the bird's head when, suddenly, the bird dodged it by pulling its head back, still looking at her.

She refused to give up and tried again, and once more, the bird avoided her head pat. Carmen steeled her resolve and moved her hand a bit faster, but the bird was damn swift as it rotated its head to dodge her hand again and again.

Are bird necks even that flexible!? she screamed internally. No, this was not a battle she would lose. If the cute bird didn't want a pat... it could get a hug!

Carmen opened her arms and tried to hug the bird, but it jumped back, landing gracefully on the ground.

"Ree!" it screeched before turning around, strutting away from her as its tail swayed back and forth.

"Come on..." Carmen muttered as she ran after it.

The bird sped up as she ran and began making weird jumping movements before it reached a turn in the hall. She chased after it, and just as she turned the corner, she was face to face with a ghoul that had clearly been tossed her way with a blast of wind. The huge gust that hit her along with the ghoul was clear evidence of that.

The ghoul was still alive and began ripping at her, but Carmen easily pushed it away and kicked it into the wall. She didn't bother staying to kill it, instead chasing after the bird. Now it had done it. She would be damned if she didn't get at least get a tiny cuteness from the bird out of this entire thing!

Carmen looked on ahead and saw the bird jump down the hallway happily. She was certain it was having way too much fun with this. Carmen smirked as she chased the cheeky little bird. Yeah, she had to admit she found it amusing too.

The next fifteen or so minutes were spent with Carmen chasing the bird through the halls, an ever-increasing number of ghouls chasing them as the bird kept pushing them back towards her. Carmen really didn't wanna stop up to smash them, which would mean abandoning her chase.

Finally, they came to a dead-end in the form of a large metal gate with a red rune on it, forcing the bird to stop. Carmen also stopped and smiled triumphantly. Only for a bit, though, as she saw the bird look behind her. She turned around and saw more than forty ghouls chasing them.

"We'll settle this after the cleanup," Carmen said, preparing herself.

The bird jumped up beside her as it also prepared to fight. They exchanged a quick glance just before the horde crashed into them.

———

After Jake left the party from the Noboru clan, he headed further in the hall that he assumed the party was originally heading into. Sure, he was maybe stealing their path a bit, but honestly, they would have been fucked and forced to retreat without him, so he didn't feel that bad about it.

He encountered a few more Blackguards and a couple of Knights, but none were even close to his level of power. Jake was fully aware his current strength was far higher than necessary for this early in the Treasure Hunt, which was why he headed for the best stuff first. He wanted to find the Count of Blood before anyone had time to gather themselves and find it.

Jake wasn't stupid enough to think he was the only one who could kill them. He assumed someone like the Sword Saint and several of the stronger parties around would manage. Probably a few others too.

He did end up picking up some more treasures on the way, but most were bad. It was a bit surprising that the tower apparently held far less than the plains outside. Well, that, or they were just all bundled together in treasuries. Either way, count first, then he would look for hidden caches.

On a side note, Jake did get the weirdest message of sorts from Sylphie. Something about making a friend and needing to say hi or something. Jake was a bit worried she had gotten herself into something bad, but decided to be a supportive uncle. He took out a small pen and paper from his usual spatial storage, then wrote a short message that he tossed in the Hunter Insignia along with a few more potions. With that done, he soldiered on towards the boss.

Finally, he reached something new. Jake stood at a crossroad with paths leading to the left and right. At least, that was what the vampires wanted him to think, because the otherwise completely normal-looking wall directly ahead of him wasn't what it seemed. Instead of a solid wall, it was a magical barrier to block out physical stuff and confuse intruders.

But to Jake? Well, even without his sphere, he could see the faint shimmering on the wall. With his sphere? He looked straight through.

Without any hesitation, Jake took out his bow. Five barrages of explosive arrows were enough to dispel the barrier ahead. It went from looking like a sightly scratched wall to a big, gaping hole in the wall all at once, the marks left by the arcane explosions on the floor serving as the only sign that it wasn't a regular continuation of the hallway.

Jake looked through the hallway ahead with both his sphere and eyes, and the conclusion was unanimous: it was a trap room. Formations, physical traps, the whole shebang.

Anyway, to cut a long story short, Jake found himself at the other end of the trap room ten minutes later, not a scratch on his body. The entire hall behind him was now filled with black spikes glowing with poison, signs of explosions, broken stones, large blades pulsing with curse magic, and all the good old trap stuff.

With excitement, Jake turned a corner and finally laid his eyes on the end of the hallway. It was a black gate—a bit like the one he had stolen, but even bigger—with some very complicated script on it, as well as a rune that was glowing deep red.

Walking up to it, the entire rune changed as words appeared.

Present a Rune of Blood to unlock to be granted access to the Count's Chambers.

Well, fuck me, Jake thought. Why hadn't that shitty projection told him about needing a fucking quest item to get to the boss and get another quest item? It was a goddamn chain quest where Jake had skipped a step.

Jake grumbled to himself until he felt a slight mental nudge from Sylphie, making him break out in a massive smile.

———

Carmen leaned against the wall, breathing heavily. The bird was also sitting down and relaxing. She had to admit... the little feather ball was strong, even if she was a fair bit stronger. But even worse than that, she hadn't even gotten her hug or even head pat yet!

She took out a potion, ready to drink it, but the bird jumped over and made a screeching sound, interrupting her. Carmen looked down and saw the bird summon a health, stamina, and mana potion out of its insignia, as well as a small slip of paper.

Picking the stuff up, she noticed how the potions were far better than her current ones. She only took the stamina and health potion, leaving the mana one. "Just keep the mana potion; I don't need it," she said as she checked out the paper. On it was a written message with pretty bad handwriting. Not that she was much better. She read the note and frowned a bit.

"Hello, my name is Sylphie, and I'm a hawk. Please be nice to me; I am not dangerous and a part of this Treasure Hunt just like you, and if you hurt me, my uncle will get very mad."

"You have a strong and awesome uncle, huh?" she asked the bird she now knew was a hawk with a smile. Also, that part about "not dangerous" was just a goddamn lie.

"Ree!" Sylphie answered happily. This time she didn't dodge, and Carmen managed to land a light head pat with only a single finger. A major victory, in her head.

"That sounds nice," she said, a bit sad thinking about her own fucked-up family situation. "Anyway, we should—"

Another ghoul interrupted her when it came charging down the hallway towards them, likely having been attracted due to their fighting earlier. Sylphie seemed as annoyed as her, and together they attacked it. She punched it, and the hawk cut it up.

The ghoul was blasted through the hall, and once it got up, they attacked again. Their second strike ended up being from behind, and the poor ghoul was sent flying towards the large metal gate with a red rune on it. Contrary to expectations, the door neither of them could do anything to before gave way and opened to the ghoul, the rune shattering in the process.

Carmen frowned as she got a bad feeling—one confirmed right away as a red mist began creeping out of the room they had just opened. Walking closer to get a good look inside and hopefully avoid fighting in the tight corridors, she saw the cause of it all.

[Viscount of Blood – lvl 135]

"Hey, Sylphie... let's take this one together, eh?" Carmen said as she chugged the stamina potion the hawk had given her. She then smashed her now glowing fists together.

"Ree!" Sylphie agreed as she entered the room, a green aura already spreading from her body.

CHAPTER 9

TREASURE HUNT: VISCOUNT & COUNT

S ylphie had a lot of things she liked. She liked tasty things, her mom and dad, Uncle, biggest bird Stormild, shiny things, whooshing stuff, tasty things, whacking stuff. Oh, and tasty things. As for things she didn't like? Those were there too.

She didn't like all kinds of bad guys. Eagles were baddies, that was for sure. Anyone Uncle didn't like were bad also. Oh, and those bad monkey things that kept throwing around smelly stuff. Those were also super baddies for sure.

Now she had found something else to add to the list: smelly vampire things. No, two things. The vampire things that were kinda dead and smelly were annoying, and she didn't like them, but she was strong, so that was fine. But then the big vampire thing came. It looked totally like a human was not just annoying but also dangerous. She really didn't like that Vampire Vi-something thing.

The bad vampire's eyes were entirely red; its body looked a lot like Uncle's but was taller and super thin. It was super fast, too, and was glowing red as it tried to scratch Sylphie. But! While Sylphie had found something else she didn't like, she had also found a new friend. Maybe a friend? Sylphie wasn't sure;

she just knew the she-human was super good at hitting stuff, and when she got hit, she was totally fine. That was pretty awesome.

Sylphie flew through the large room with the bad guy vampire and avoided all the attacks. It used a long stick with a pointy end and kept yelling stuff Sylphie didn't understand. The she-woman did understand, somehow, and kept calling it corn or something. She kept saying corny, but Sylphie was certain the bad guy wasn't made of corn. It was also a bit weird she understood the weird gibberish of the vampire even though she couldn't understand Sylphie properly, which was why she'd had Uncle make squiggly things to tell her stuff. Humans liked to talk using squiggly things.

Oh! Back to the bad guy vampire. The she-human punched it super hard in the chest, making it fly back, but it quickly got up again and attacked with its glowing pointy stick. Sylphie was flying and avoided all the red wind slicers the bad guy sent after her while waiting for a good chance to strike with her super talons.

The fight wasn't one of those fast ones like with the dead vampire things. Instead, this vampire thing was faster and stronger. It used weird red glowing magic and the stick to avoid taking damage and hitting back, and whenever Sylphie managed to hit with a strong whoosh, the bad guy used cheating magic to heal.

Sylphie didn't like to admit it, but the bad guy vampire was maybe stronger than her. It probably wasn't stronger than the punchy lady, but Sylphie didn't think she could win against either. Both of them were just so super tough, and as she saw them fight, they kept using cheating magic to make their wounds disappear.

They could keep punching and stabbing each other for hours, she was sure. But that was without the awesome Sylphie there. Because while Sylphie didn't think she could beat either, she was sure she could cut them up real good, no problem.

When the vampire bad guy was distracted, Sylphie swooped

in from the side with a big blade of green wind. The vampire recoiled, also allowing the she-human to land a punch. Next, the punchy lady punched the vampire real good, and Sylphie super quickly swooped in and ripped off a big chunk of meat from the bad guy vampire with her super talons.

The entire fight was still super long, but the bad guy vampire couldn't keep up in the end. The cheating magic got worse, the pointy stick got slow, and the red magic the baddie made got so weak it couldn't even get through her Green Shield.

The she-human punched the vampire hard in the chest, sending it flying straight towards Sylphie, who flew over and, with her awesome glowing wing, made the head of the bad guy fly high up into the air. Without the body. This meant the bad guy was dead!

"Nice one, Sylphie," the punchy lady said, looking happy. "Name's Carmen, by the way. I totally forgot to introduce myself. We should keep this up; we make quite the team."

"Ree!" Sylphie said in recognition at the blood-covered she-woman. Compared to her, Sylphie looked as great as ever, and you couldn't even see she had been in a fight! She was a bit tired, though.

Suddenly, Sylphie heard a weird sound, and Carmen turned to look at it too. The sleepy-box the bad guy vampire had been hiding in began glowing red like the bad vampire, and it spat out a weird, round, floating metal thing with a shiny squiggle on it.

Also, just after, the wall to the side opened up and revealed a whole bunch of shiny things. Sylphie couldn't stop looking at the floating squiggly stone, though. It looked important. Oh, and Sylphie couldn't really use pointy sticks or cutty sticks or any of the other weird things humans used, because they didn't have awesome talons like her.

"Yo, if you take the Rune of Blood, I'll take the rest, okay?" Carmen, the punchy lady, asked. "We can just go for the next hill and split it the other way there. Does that sound good?"

Sylphie thought about it for a moment and decided she did

want the shiny disc. So she flew up and poked it with her wing, making it disappear.

A few moments later, she felt Uncle be happy! Oh! Oh! He praised Sylphie. Well, naturally, Sylphie knew the floaty shiny disc was the most important. She was good at finding good stuff like that!

————

Jake's annoyance at the chain quest was instantly dispelled as he felt the Hunter Insignia respond. Because it turned out this quest was one he had done in collaboration with Sylphie without either party knowing. He still wanted to punch the dude in the recording in the face for not telling about the trap room or any of all this shit, but sadly the guy was long dead.

He waved his hand and reread the words on the door.

Present a Rune of Blood to be granted access to the Count's Chambers.

The Rune of Blood appeared in his palm and instantly reacted with the gate. It floated up and inserted itself, causing red lines to cover the entire thing. He heard an odd noise as the large gate began slowly opening. It was nearly six meters tall, and seeing it slowly swing open was quite the sight.

Very fitting for a boss room.

Even more fitting was the dense red mist that slowly seeped out of the gate. Jake felt an aura spread from within, and he knew whatever dwelled in there had awakened. Jake walked forward through the gate and dense mist.

He looked through the chamber and saw the walls lined with beautiful paintings and a carpet covering the floor. What Jake could only assume was expensive furniture was also everywhere in the massive chamber. Contrary to everywhere else, this room was in perfect condition. There wasn't even a single trace of dust anywhere.

In the center of the chamber was a pedestal with a metal coffin on top. The coffin was made of a silver-like material and also looked expensive as hell. It was undoubtedly a treasure or item worth a lot, if not as a coffin, then for the raw materials alone.

Ever so slowly, the coffin opened. Jake stayed at the entrance to the chamber as he saw a figure rise out. He couldn't help but hold back a frown as he saw it. It was a... human? Or at least, it looked exactly like one. He had expected the Count to look more like the recorded projection. But this? This was just a black-haired, middle-aged man. He had to use Identify to confirm.

[Count of Blood – lvl 155]

Sure enough, it was the Count.

Just after he Identified the vampire, its eyes opened. They were red and beast-like. A bit similar to his own yellow ones, actually. Naturally, the vampire was also fully aware of Jake with his eyes open, and the Hunter had already prepared himself. He didn't want to attack right away, because these vampires weren't just stupid beasts, but humanoids like him.

"How long?" Jake heard a pained voice say. It sounded like someone with an incredibly sore throat.

"No idea, to be honest. A while," Jake honestly answered as he tried something else fun. "You're now part of a system event in the 93rd Universe, and you're pretty much just a quest monster."

"93rd Era!? How is that possible? It was barely the... the..." The vampire looked around, confused for a moment, before looking back up. "Who are you, and what are you doing here? Who is your master?"

Well, ain't that interesting—completely ignored the part

about it being a system event, Jake thought. It lent some more credence to his whole constructed scenario theory. Yet, the vampire was also clearly sapient.

"Well, I am a hunter; I came here to take a key off your hands, and my master is myself," he answered.

"A hunter!? A vampire hunter has entered my chambers!? That isn't pos—"

"No, no, just a regular hunter. I hunt pretty much everything; I don't discriminate. Actually, in this scenario, calling me a vampire hunter isn't entirely inaccurate? Though I guess that depends on you. The key, hand it over." Jake finished with a shrug.

The vampire looked at Jake for a moment, still standing atop his coffin. "How dare mere livestock demand anything of a noble!? I—"

"Hey, I'm an earl! Pretty sure earl is over count in the rankings. Or maybe they're equal? Not sure, to be honest." Jake again shrugged, thoroughly enjoying just fucking with the Count. He had a solid feeling the Count wouldn't give him any valuable info at all, and in the end, it would result in a fight. Better get the show on the road... after he had his fun.

"Are you mocking me?" the Count said, the intensity of his glowing eyes increasing.

"Not necessarily. Tell me, why didn't you guys and gals ever use the stuff left by that creator? You had the keys, right? Maybe with the stuff he got from that True Ancestor Sanguine, you could have made it out of here or traded it with a faction for protection or something. On a side note, who was Sanguine? I assume he is dead."

"YOU DARE SPEAK THE NAME OF THE TRUE ANCESTOR IN VAIN!?" the Count of Blood yelled. The entire room shook, and Jake sighed as he took out his bow. "TO BECOME MY FIRST MEAL UPON AWAKENING IS AN HONOR!"

Without any delay, the vampire waved his hand and

summoned a black sword in it. His clothes were replaced with a suit of chainmail armor, and a helmet covered the Count's head, except for an opening where the mouth was and two eyeholes.

Jake, in return, instantly summoned a few dozen stable arcane arrows in his hand and tossed them in the quiver on his back, along with the contents of a bottle of uncommon-rarity Necrotic Poison. One thing he had learned was that despite being vampires, they didn't really have anything to do with the undead. Quite the opposite, actually, as they seemed full of vitality.

He nocked an arrow, but he wasn't the one to make the first move.

The Count suddenly exploded into red mist, and a fraction of a second later appeared beside Jake with yet another poof of mist. Jake had to think fast. He quickly took a step forward, using One Step Mile just in time to avoid the sword slash.

Fast.

Jake turned on a dime as he fired the arrow after the vampire. The Count dodged the hastily fired arrow, then turned into mist again and pressed the attack. Seeing it coming this time, Jake had already jumped away, and this time had far more time to take aim.

While flying back, he shot it and froze the Count with Gaze of the Apex Hunter. Jake felt the strain from doing so and noted that the Count had quite the resistance. Still... he had faced worse, and the Count failed to move in time as he was hit in the chest by an arrow.

The vampire recoiled but swiftly ripped the arrow out and turned to mist again. Sadly for it... his poison was in his system, and even if he became incorporeal, he was still affected. But... Jake did notice one thing through his Sense of the Malefic Viper.

Innate resistance? he asked himself as he tried to create some more distance. He was lucky that the Count's chamber was freaking massive, easily over a hundred meters from one end to the other. Still, a bit confined, but manageable.

Anyway, the vampire had *something* that made his poison less effective. He felt the toxic energies quickly be broken down and eliminated, and what was in the Count's system didn't do the expected damage. It was like he had some kind of skill similar to Jake's Palate of the Malefic Viper.

"Fighting is meaningless. You are merely livestock—accept your fate," the Count said as he stopped up. His body began glowing redder than before, and he opened his hands wide as the blade disappeared.

"Grasping Claws of the Blood Feast."

The red aura around the vampire began shifting and changing, intensifying many times and growing almost tangible. The red light soon took the shape of four red arms ending in sharp, clawed hands. Jake saw all this happen, but that didn't mean he wasted his time.

Energy flared as he stood there with the string pulled back and arcane energy revolving around him.

When the four claws began flying towards him, he released the string to a mighty explosion of arcane energy. The four arms headed for him moved to defend, and while they managed to drain some of the shot's power, they failed to stop it.

All four arms lost their shape as they exploded, and the Arcane Powershot flew for the vampire. He didn't even dodge, but instead held out a hand to block it. The red aura around him moved to form a shield. The more Jake looked at the red aura, the more it looked like a red liquid.

A red liquid that couldn't stop his blow either. The Arcane Powershot obliterated the arm of the Count, sending him flying back into the wall at the far end of the hall. Jake followed up with a quickly fired Splitting Arrow of the five-arrow-explosions variant.

The Count sneered as the four arms rapidly reformed and,

together with the rest of the aura, managed to block the explosions.

"Fool, do you truly believe that mere livestock can stand against a count of the vampiric race!?" the vampire yelled as he flew towards Jake, the red aura around him growing even more intense.

I fucking hope those lines are due to system fuckery... Jake thought as he fired another barrage of explosive arrows, chipping away at the aura.

Well, at least he had taken an arm... or so he thought.

Jake watched flesh slowly form in real-time as a new arm grew out, giving him bad Deepdweller flashbacks. Except he soon noticed this was an active skill and not passive. At least, not all of it was passive. The aura became more focused around the growing arm.

Either way, the vampire was damn durable, and Jake knew he was in for the long haul.

A long haul... filled with horrible boss dialogue.

CHAPTER 10

TREASURE HUNT: ANNOYING BOSS FIGHT

The Count was truly a peculiar creature. He moved and acted like a fully intelligent and relatively competent fighter. It nearly fooled Jake into believing that he was fighting a smart enemy and not an absolute moron. However, the illusion was dispelled every time the Count opened his mouth.

"This is the part where you fall down and bleed to death!" the vampire yelled as he fired out a crimson wave of energy.

Jake dodged it easily, taking far more mental damage than physical from the exchange. The red glowing aura was still there, with the four clawed hands constantly trying to get hold of him. All in all, Jake would call the current attack pattern of the vampire more annoying than dangerous.

And yes, he would call the way the vampire attacked an attack pattern, as he could easily predict the next moves. He didn't even need his sphere or Bloodline.

Teleport. Jake stepped away, dodging the blade that appeared from the red mist as the Count of Blood teleported to attack him.

Claws. The four clawed hands chased after Jake's fleeing figure as he nocked and fired another barrage of explosive arcane arrows, burning away at the aura but failing to actually injure the vampire. It did stop the attack, though.

Ranged blade waves of energy. In response to being pushed back, the vampire sent out more crimson waves of blood that would for sure tear up the nice room. The fight had been going for a few minutes now, and Jake had switched his tactic a little bit by incorporating an important element: stealing shit.

Jake leaped back and touched two very comfortable-looking chairs, making them disappear into his inventory just before the sword waves came. To save all the furniture was impossible, but he would do his best to take what looked the nicest.

His next target was a bookshelf filled with old tomes as he summoned bolts of arcane mana to blow up the grasping claws. This bought him enough time to make a hastily charged Arcane Powershot. The aura around the vampire was resilient, but not resilient enough to block even his fastest-charged Arcane Power-shot using a stable arcane arrow.

Once more, the vampire was blasted back, an arrow embedded in his shoulder and seeping out poison. Said vampire ripped it out and chased after Jake. It was predictable to the level of boredom, but at least it bought Jake enough time to swoop up the bookshelf and even a nice dining table and accompanying chairs.

He didn't bother with the paintings, though. Too gaudy even for his taste, and all of them depicted the damn Count of Blood in different obnoxious poses anyway. Most of them were him leaning against the sword, trying to look cool. Some would perhaps argue he did... but Jake wasn't one of those people, though he was somewhat biased.

That was when the Count once more used his most powerful ability.

"I shall paint the carpet red with your blood!" the vampire boss yelled, making Jake cringe back.

"The carpet is already fucking red, you absolute moron!" Jake yelled back.

Balancing his desires to just kill the Count and actually loot stuff in the chamber before it all got destroyed by their fighting was a difficult challenge. Sadly, Pride of the Malefic Viper's defense against mental attacks didn't work against the bullshit spewed by the Count.

"Then I shall deepen it as I slit you open like the livestock you are!" the Count rebutted, making Jake groan.

Don't entertain his stupidity... Just clean out his room and finish him off... Don't let him get to you...

Before today, Jake had fought only one being that was higher in level than the Count. The Heartwarden in the Undergrowth Dungeon had been 162, seven levels above this vampire. If Jake were honest, he would say they were about even. Both were a bit strong... but not truly powerful for their level. The Altmar Census Golem had only been level 150, but had been far stronger despite its lower level compared to both the Heartwarden and this Count of Blood. Of course, one had to remember this was from Jake's perspective. Matchups mattered a lot too.

Considering how much stronger Jake was now than when he'd fought the Census Golem, his victory against the Count of Blood was pretty much assured. This was why he had the leeway to simply dodge attacks and take potshots while looting everything of value he could.

He had already tried to take the coffin, but that was clearly bound to the Count in some way, so that would have to wait. Besides that, there was only furniture and other knickknacks like chandeliers, candle holders, plates of different metals, a statue here and there, and even a few nice-looking blades that were more for show than combat.

Ten minutes later, Jake felt like he couldn't find anything more to perfectly legally acquire, as all the valuables that caught his eye were already nicely tucked away in the Hunter Insignia storage. With all that settled, it was time to actually finish the battle. The current standstill had only continued because, to be honest, Jake hadn't dealt any significant damage to the vampire. Instead, he'd been slowly emptying out his opponent's resources.

Jake dodged a final blow and cracked his neck. *Time to get serious.*

The carpet below him was ripped up as his body exploded with power upon activating Limit Break at 10%. Energy swirled around him even further when he infused his presence with mana. In a split second, the entire mood of the fight changed.

He stepped back with One Step Mile, appearing on a platform in mid-air. The vampire followed and appeared to his side, but Jake was ready with an extended palm.

BOOM!

His hand exploded with arcane mana as he sent a shockwave at the half-appeared vampire. Before even seeing if he had hit— he knew he would—Jake drew his bow and fired off a quick Arcane Powershot.

The vampire that was already flying backward was hit square in the chest and blasted back even more, with a large, gaping hole blasted through his midsection. When the Count hit the wall, five explosive arcane arrows also struck, exploding a large section of the chamber.

All throughout, Jake focused his presence on suppressing the Count and possibly making the vampire feel a sense of despair at the obvious difference in power. Instead, he got...

"Foolish human—to force me to go this far is an honor!" the Count of Blood said as he dodged an arrow by teleporting, appearing atop the silver coffin he had woken up from. "Now, behold! The true power of a superior being!"

Jake had never seen a more obvious transition to phase two of a boss fight.

The entire silver coffin began glowing as deep red as runes covered it. Like a current of blood, each of them spat out energy that entered the vampire, and the Count himself waved his hand to summon a bottle that looked a lot like a health potion.

His opponent gulped it down, and soon their entire body began changing. The Count grew nearly half a meter, all his hair fell out, and his clothes tore as two white, leathery wings sprang up on his back. His muscles also bulged and became far more pronounced. A more powerful aura than before spread throughout the room, and Jake also saw the extended aura retract back into the body of the Count.

The sword was now gone, and instead, both hands had grown in size to form large, beastly claws that Jake could see and feel excreting some kind of venom. The head looked to have almost been cut in two, as a slit went up between his eyes. A slit that Jake came to learn was its damn mouth when the entire front of the face split open to reveal several rows of teeth.

"To lay eyes upon the true form of a Balnar Vampire... You can now die with dignity!"

Sadly, even with a fucked-up mouth, the Count could still talk. It was now clear mental attacks would have no effect on the moronic vampire, so he would just have to finish him the old-fashioned way.

Jake fired another barrage of arrows, waiting to see what tricks the Count now had.

The Count saw the attack and swiftly dodged to the side with a flap of his wings before beginning to charge him. Jake swiftly adjusted and fired another arrow. The Count tried to dodge again, but Jake used Gaze as it penetrated his chest.

It failed to slow down the now roided-up vampire, which just continued his assault. He swung his claws while flying, sending out waves of red energy. Jake repeated his tactic of dodging around the room with One Step Mile to great success as he avoided the charge.

He turned and fired a Splitting Arrow with stable arrows. The vampire once more tried to dodge, and again found himself frozen as he got hit by all five. This caused him to crash down and tear up the carpet. The Count quickly got back up with an odd groaning noise, but he didn't charge this time.

"I tire of your running... **Chains of the Underworld!**"

For the first time in the battle, Jake was truly taken by surprise. Without even getting any chance to dodge, he suddenly felt himself being weighed down, as though heavy chains were attached to his body. There was nothing visible, but when Jake focused on the mana in the room, he could detect the incorporeal chains now trapping him.

"Escape is impossible!" the vampire yelled as he flew over.

Jake tried to use One Step Mile but found it impossible. He could still move, but slower than before. He began charging up a disruptive wave of arcane mana, but it was obvious it wouldn't be ready in time for the vampire's attack.

Fine.

Jake deposited his bow in his inventory and took out his two other weapons, quickly splurting some of his blood on them. The Nanoblade appeared in his left hand, and the Scimitar of Cursed Hunger in the right.

Have it your way.

If the Count wanted a good old melee squabble, Jake was down. Raising his blade, he clashed with the claws of the vampire and found himself slightly outmatched strength-wise. But when it came to speed...

The Nanoblade swept up and left a long, thin cut across the chest of the vampire, who barely even tried to defend himself. In turn, the vampire clawed at Jake's shoulder, but he moved in closer to dodge the blow. His disruptive mana wave was ready.

His entire body exploded with arcane mana, blowing back the Count of Blood and leaving light wounds on his chest. Jake pressed his advantage and moved in to leave a few more shallow cuts before being forced to block again, this time getting knocked back.

He landed on his feet and had to instantly block again when the vampire let out a loud, shrill shriek. For a fraction of a second, his entire body tensed up, and he failed to block the claw raking across his left shoulder. Blood flew through the air.

The shriek wasn't some mental attack, but pure sound. Not even reacting to his wound, Jake smirked and returned the damage in kind by cutting the vampire. The two of them continued exchanging blows, Jake landing ten for every wound he took.

Perhaps the Count believed his venom would do the work, but sadly for him, Jake barely noticed it. The toxins simply weren't potent enough to overcome the legendary-rarity Palate of the Malefic Viper. Meanwhile, Jake kept inflicting the Count with poison. Clearly, vampiric resistance didn't beat out viperic resistance. Bad puns aside, the vampire was slowly losing, and they both knew it.

In an act of desperation, the Count shrieked again, and his claw began glowing red as he tried to land a possibly lethal blow. Jake responded by freezing the large monster with Gaze simultaneously, completely ruining his opponent's momentum. Seeing his chance, Jake kicked the Count hard in the chest the moment he could move again, all the while releasing an arcane explosion to blast the Count away.

Both his blades disappeared the same moment he did this, and he drew his bow and fired another fast Arcane Powershot at the transformed vampire. The huge, bulky, winged monster didn't even need to be frozen this time, and was forced to block without Jake using Gaze.

Jake shot again, sending out a wave of explosive arcane arrows. He rapid-fired after the vampire as he was forced back, the chamber now more or less completely destroyed from their fighting due to explosions repeatedly blasting apart the environment.

His Mark of the Avaricious Hunter made him aware of where the Count was, and he had to admit, the charge had gotten big by now. Big enough for him to trigger it.

The entire chamber flashed as Jake drew his bow to

continue his attack. The vampire wasn't dead... but he sure wasn't feeling good either. Jake placed another Mark on his foe as he fired another arrow, aiming to finish off the damn thing already.

"I... **ENOUGH!**"

The voice echoed through the hall as a giant wave of red energy crashed towards Jake like a tsunami of blood. He put away his bow and held up a hand to summon a barrier of arcane energy to block it before—

With wide eyes, he stared at the Count of Blood zooming past him close to the wall. The vampire wasn't headed for Jake or even the coffin, but instead somewhere else entirely:

The exit.

That's right—the damn monster was running away.

———

Jason scoured the room, checking for anything hidden in what he and his party guessed had once been a meeting hall or something.

"Found anything?" he yelled over to his party member at the other side of the hall.

"Got a carving knife or something; it's uncommon rarity, so not bad," the warrior yelled back.

"I think that's all we're gonna find here. Let's regroup with the others," a third party member chimed in.

They were a party not affiliated with any large faction, thus joining as free agents. They had talked about joining a city or faction simply due to the conveniences it offered, but so far, they hadn't found a place to settle down.

Half an hour earlier, they'd met a group from Saya and the Noboru clan. They'd been heading out of the tower in a hurry but still found time to help Jason and his friends. Unfortunately, Jason's party lacked a healer, so it had been more than welcome when the other party's healer came and offered to top them all up. Maybe they should head to Saya after the Treasure Hunt? He liked that idea.

Jason and his two comrades left the hall and returned to the center, making sure to avoid the Blackguards. Those were nasty, and they had already lost a party member to one.

"Yo, any trouble?" their party leader, an ice mage, asked once they met up at the balcony, overlooking the huge atrium with the top and bottom both visible.

"Nah, this area seems pretty clean already; I think we should move on up a few floors," Jason answered with a shrug.

"Hmm, I guess you're right, we shou—"

SWOOSH!

Jason barely had time to react as a figure swooped down and crashed through the balcony. He swiftly turned his head and saw a hulking, winged figure kneeling down over his party leader. Jason steeled himself as he drew his sword, and the warrior to his side was already charging the creature. Being more reserved, he used Identify first instead.

The creature got up, and Jason saw his party leader... or what was left of him. A dried-up husk remained as the creature turned around, a large, open maw where a face should be. The warrior he was with swung his sword, but it embedded barely a centimeter into the thick chest muscles of the monster, who didn't even attempt to block. Its body was already covered in wounds for some reason, but Jason saw them all slowly begin healing.

With a single swipe, the warrior was smashed away by a huge claw. Jason's eyes widened as he turned to run. He had barely taken a step before he felt a shadow looming over him, and the final thing he saw was the result of his Identify as the maw of teeth closed around his head.

[Count of Blood - ???]

CHAPTER 11

TREASURE HUNT: COUNT DOWN
FOR THE COUNT

Fucking shitty bullshit boss, Jake thought as he chased after the damn vampire count. It had been barely a second ahead of him, but that second meant that when he reached the entrance to the trap room, the damn barrier was back, blocking his way. It had a slight red glow now, and there was no illusionary barrier trying to conceal it either... In other words, it was just there to slow him down.

Jake fired explosive arrows to blow it up, and while that process only took about ten seconds... ten seconds could be a lot. He rushed through the broken barrier and down the hall to the atrium. While he couldn't see the Count, he could still pinpoint the direction of his foe with Mark and feel the poison running through the vampire's body.

But... he could also feel the poison weakening significantly by the second. It was like the vampire was just chugging down healing potions or something, as his body kept getting infused with vital energy again and again.

Rushing even more than before, Jake soared down past the countless terraces towards his target, both blades at the ready. He just wanted to stop the Count from doing whatever he was doing to heal himself as fast as possible, and he didn't have a line of sight to shoot an arrow.

He saw what the Count was doing just a few moments later as the scene entered his sphere. Five dead, dried-up husks that Jake barely recognized as humans were on the floor, a sixth person was in the grasp of the Count and being rapidly drained, and a seventh person was lying on the floor with both legs crushed under the vampire's feet. Likely the next meal.

Luckily, that would never come to pass.

Jake crashed in from the side and swung his scimitar, which was now surrounded by a mix of arcane and dark mana. The guy the Count was holding was already dead, but the woman under his feet was still alive and even struggling to get free.

The Count tossed the nearly fully drained corpse away and moved to block Jake's blow. The blade extended and cut across the room, even cutting the flying corpse in two just before it struck the vampire. His opponent was blasted away with two nasty cuts on his palms from Descending Dark Arcane Fang, the wounds infected with the dark and arcane mana.

Jake quickly checked the woman with the crushed legs and tossed her a healing potion before he charged the vampire again. She looked confused but still managed to catch the potion by instinct. Jake was already gone before she managed to open her mouth and say anything.

To say that he was pissed was an understatement. While it was doubtful Jake could have stopped the Count from running away, he was still mad that other people had to get involved in their fight. He was equally mad at the Count for running away like that. Was it a good tactic by the vampire to go and consume the life energy of others to revitalize himself? Sure was.

It didn't make Jake any less mad, though.

He pushed Limit Break to 20%, and his aura intensified. His presence was infused with even more power as four arcane bolts condensed around him during his charge.

The vampire got up from being blasted away and yelled loudly, "Mere livestock dare interrupt my meal! I shall—"

"Just shut the fuck up," Jake answered as he pressed the attack.

The four arcane bolts were fired first, making the vampire dodge to the side. Jake responded by nudging them to follow the hulking monster using his presence-empowered mana control. At the same time, he reached melee range.

With the first swing, he broke his opponent's guard, and with the second, he left a deep cut. This was also the time the four bolts reached them, and the Count was struck in the side, leaving Jake another great opening to stab the vampire through the chest with the long Nanoblade.

"I SHALL NOT FALL!"

Jake was pushed back by another red wave of energy, but this time he didn't even bother using an arcane barrier, as he knew this attack wasn't meant to damage but only force him back. His scales were good enough.

The Count of Blood flew past him again, heading towards the woman on the floor that had just consumed a health potion.

Oh, no, you fucking don't.

Just as the vampire was about to grab hold of the woman, he himself was taken hold of as Jake used One Step Mile into the air and, with a flap of his wings, dragged the vampire out over the balcony and into the open space of the atrium.

Jake held one of the Count's wings with his right hand, and using the left, he cleaved down at the wing's base.

The Count shrieked as Jake cut off the entire wing and, with a spinning kick, sent the vampire flying downwards. He had also seen that the bottom of the tower was cleared of any activity, as people who had entered to explore had begun moving up the many floors... and he really wanted to keep the damn bloodsucker away from anyone else right now. Other people were just walking health potions for the vampire.

Jake took out his bow and fired off a quick Arcane Powershot. The vampire failed to stabilize himself properly and was hit by the arrow and sent crashing down into the ground. Jake began charging his Arcane Powershot right away, causing power to swirl around him.

Before this, the fight had happened in the confined space of the Count's chambers. No one had been aware that someone had already rushed to the top of one of the towers, somehow obtained a Rune of Blood and unlocked a boss in this short time, and begun fighting it. No one before now.

Only a few dozen seconds had passed since the Count entered the atrium—and even less since Jake had arrived—yet the balconies were fast being filled by humans. The fight had sent mana and shockwaves echoing through the tower, making anyone not deep within a room aware of the battle taking place.

Under usual circumstances, Jake wouldn't be a fan of so many people staring at him, and that was even truer now. All of them were just prey for the vampire. This meant Jake would have to finish off the boss before he got a chance to feed.

The Count below got up from the ground, a nasty wound on his chest. Jake stared down at it as his Arcane Powershot charged. His opponent had been hit by this specific attack of his many times and was prepared to dodge.

Prepared being the keyword here, as it still stood in the middle, getting ready to dodge. Jake needed to stop it, but Gaze wouldn't have enough duration... so he decided to take a card out of the Count's playbook.

His presence intensified as he prepared to land a mental attack. He opened his mouth and spoke in a taunting voice infused with his will. Even a bit of his heretic side joined in.

"That True Ancestor Sanguine was a coward and a weakling. Worse than livestock. Just. Like. You."

The words echoed through the entire atrium, and the Count froze. He looked at Jake for a moment, his red vampiric eyes wide as the slits on both suddenly narrowed and began glowing an even deeper red color. Jake had found his opening. His presence, infused by Pride of the Malefic Viper, struck right at the Count's mind, hitting him where it hurt.

In response, the Count didn't yell back. He didn't make a snide remark or cringy comment. He just shrieked as the mouth opened wide. A new wing instantly sprang out, fully regenerated, and he flew up towards Jake, now filled with pure rage.

So much rage that he didn't dodge when Jake released the arrow. Refusing to back down, the Count swung his claws and sent out an absolutely massive wave of blood energy. It was powerful for sure, likely the strongest blow the vampire had made this entire fight... but compared to a nearly fully charged Arcane Powershot?

The wave of blood was blown apart, and the onlookers from the balconies had to take cover from the explosion. The Count of Blood was struck by the stable arcane arrow just after. It blasted a huge hole through his chest and sent him smashing into the ground below, leaving a crater.

Still filled with rage, the vampire tried to get up again but was hit by five explosive arrows.

Jake stared down at the scrambling vampire as he drew the bow once more. This time, another kind of arrow emerged. A large one, looking almost like a spear and made of dense, arcane mana. It was the ability of his bow—and was about to scorch the damn vampire into dust.

"**I would take cover,**" Jake warned, infusing with voice with Willpower. He felt over a hundred eyes on him, and the warning was to them. He knew the destructive power of this blow, and luckily, there were no people on any of the lower floors.

Power swirled around him and the arrow as he released it, sending it flying straight down towards the vampire. The gemstones on his bow dimmed. The Count seemed to have finally come more to his senses and tried to avoid the massive, energy-filled arcane arrow.

He failed, thanks to Gaze of the Apex Hunter.

In a last-ditch effort, the vampire sent out a wave of blood-red energy that clashed with the arrow, and the entire tower became bathed in pink-purple light. Jake even focused his presence to attempt to concentrate the power of the arcane energy and prevent it from spreading out.

BOOM!

The ground shook, and Jake heard several yells as barriers and shields sprang up on the balconies with observers, all of whom moved to defend themselves.

Arcane energy scorched the entire bottom floor as the destruction wormed its away across the ground, leaving everything destroyed and pulsing with pink-purple cracks of arcane energy. Yet, despite the devastation done by the attack, Jake didn't let up his guard.

He threw a look at the closest party of humans to the bottom of the atrium and, in concert, the vampire. Jake began flying down—and just in time.

A figure flew out of the cloud of dust and debris, headed straight for the unsuspecting party. The Count was bleeding from everywhere, as his skin was cracked and broken. One of the wings had once more been ripped off, while the other one was filled with holes. Even one of the arms was gone, as the vampire had clearly tried to block. The only more or less intact part was the head.

Due to his preparedness, what the Count encountered in his path wasn't a party of living health potions, but a blade covered in arcane mana. The vampire moved to block the blow and ended up with a long gash on his one remaining arm.

The vampire was truly desperate now, and went for the only source of vitality nearby:

Jake.

The Count of Blood rushed him, ignoring Jake's two blades stabbing into his chest. A large, gaping maw opened up right in front of Jake's face as he ripped out only the Nanoblade and then did three things at once.

First, he triggered the Mark of the Avaricious Arcane Hunter, making the Count pulse with light from every opening in his body and dealing catastrophic damage to the vampire.

Secondly, he froze him with Gaze of the Apex Hunter, buying him enough time for the next part.

The third move was a horizontal swipe of the arcane-covered blade with both his hands. The head of one of the nine Counts of Blood was sent flying through the air, the mouth still wide open as the red glow in his eyes dimmed and finally disappeared.

You have slain [Count of Blood – lvl 155] – Bonus experience earned for killing an enemy above your level

* 'DING!' Class: [Avaricious Arcane Hunter] has reached level 130 - Stat points allocated, +10 Free Points*

* 'DING!' Race: [Human (D)] has reached level 130 - Stat points allocated, +15 Free Points*

The moment the light fully dimmed, the vampire's entire body turned to dust, leaving only a few items floating in the air. A blade—well, two, counting Jake's scimitar, which had been stabbed in the Count's body—a black key, and a large red gem.

Without any hesitation, Jake scooped them all up with the intent of checking them out later. Unfortunately, now wasn't a good time for several reasons. More than a hundred reasons, in fact.

People were staring at him from all around. Most of them with wide eyes, some with abject fear, and others with uncertainty over how they should react. One thing was certain, though... they all looked at him with some level of respect, even if more than a few seemed to hold some doubt. The party that the vampire had been headed for didn't look doubtful, though. They were on a balcony only a hundred meters from where Jake had finished off the vampire, looking at him with clear gratitude.

"What was that thing?" one of the people on another balcony yelled.

"Who are you? Are you a part of the Treasure Hunt?" another chimed in.

"What city are you from?" a third yelled from far above.

"That's Lord Thayne, the leader of Haven," someone answered.

Jake just closed his eyes briefly. He thought about if he should say something, considering he was the center of attention. A part of him felt like he should, and another made him believe it was expected of him to say or do *something*. The thing was... Jake didn't really want to, so he just said the simplest thing as he flew upwards, back towards the Count's chamber.

"Take care, people. Sorry for getting you all involved in my hunt."

———

Neveah stood shaking on one of the balconies overlooking the atrium. She was surrounded by her party members, all of them still alive and well. Looking to her side, she saw her party member just shake his head.

How fucking stupid had they been when they first came to Haven? They had heard rumors of Lord Thayne, but those were just rumors, after all. Then they'd met him during the meeting with the City Lord, and he had seemed absolutely terrifying... but afterward, they had talked.

Clearly, the man had used some kind of skill or something to make himself appear more intimidating. This made them unsure if he was truly that powerful or just incredibly good at fronting. Was he just all bark and no bite?

Well, today, they saw the bite, and it was absolutely terrifying. When Neveah had seen the Count of Blood for the first time, the only thought in her head had been to run. It was an absolute monster, and she'd seen it tear apart an entire party roughly equal to theirs in a matter of seconds. The only way to survive the wrath of such a being was to get lucky while running the fuck away.

And then... then an even bigger monster had entered the scene. The explosions of that odd energy, the sheer physical strength, and speed, the magic... Everything Lord Thayne did was just utterly overwhelming.

So... she asked not only herself, but the entire party the same question she kept asking herself. A question every person who had ever doubted the rumors was likely asking themselves right now.

"How fucking stupid were we when we said Haven was weak?"

Because why the hell would you need an army when you had a single individual that could rip one apart?

CHAPTER 12

TREASURE HUNT: THIEF!

J ake was in a hurry to get back to the Count's chamber, as he had a bad feeling in his gut. And no, it wasn't from just being the center of attention and feeling like that time when he was a kid and was in a school play, with all the parents staring at him. Instead, this kind of bad feeling was the kind he got when someone was about to steal his shit.

Okay, it was only was like that in retrospect. Because when Jake made it through the trap room and into the chamber, the silver coffin and altar were gone. He had only been gone for a few minutes to hunt down the Count down, and someone had taken that opportunity to rob him of his rightful loot?

Yeah, that didn't fly with him.

His senses spread in the room as Jake focused on both Sense of the Malefic Viper and Hunter's Tracking. There was no fucking way he was going to let the damn thief get away with it. Jake smelled the air and felt the mana, and soon picked up on something.

There were three traces of beings in the chamber. The most powerful was the Count's, then Jake's, and finally one far fainter. No doubt the thief. He tried to sense the mana type used, and it felt faintly familiar... It was... shadow mana?

Jake suddenly remembered someone. He had seen a member of the Court of Shadows steal that Hunter Insignia when someone was forced to teleport out less than an hour ago at the lowest level of the tower. His intuition told him he was right, which gave him an excellent starting point.

He knew assassins were good at hiding, but Jake had a secret weapon: an obscene amount of Perception.

Focusing on his Hunter's Tracking, Jake felt a faint trace leading out of the chamber. The thief had just run in, took the coffin and altar, and then run out again. Jake knelt down and saw a faint footprint that still had a bit of energy around it, then took a good whiff.

I'm coming for you.

He turned and followed the scent and the traces of mana still in the air. Every living thing left faint traces in their wake. Their presences passively soaked the environment, energy was burned and expunged as they moved, and, of course, all the good old physiological clues, such as smell, were also left behind.

Naturally, there were also ways to hide these trails. Any kind of stealth skill made one give off fewer traces and masked your presence. However, ultimately, this was done through magic, and through magic, one could still uncover these traces. This is to say, it came down to a contest between the tracker and the one being tracked. If the one being chased was more powerful and had better stealth capabilities than the one tracking them had tracking capabilities, they would escape.

Jake didn't really have exceptional tracking skills. He had his Sense of the Malefic Viper, but that wasn't really a tracking skill. His only real skill was Hunter's Tracking at uncommon rarity. He didn't have any experience with tracking things before the system either, so he couldn't really track anything without magic.

However, all of this didn't matter when one could just brute-force the entire thing with a Perception stat so much higher than reasonable at his level.

Jake ran through the trap room and stopped as he reached the crossroad. He knelt down and sensed his environment once more. *He went straight.*

For several reasons, he was also now confident his target was male. While he couldn't identify the figure he had seen steal the Insignia earlier as either male or female, he was sure it was a man now. Faint traces of a footprint were left on the floor, indicating a man due to their size, and the smell also told him it was more likely to be a male.

Rushing forward, he weaved through the halls, and the further he got from the chamber, the more obvious the traces got. It had only been a handful of minutes since Jake had killed the Count and the thief even became able to steal the coffin, so the person didn't have that long of a head start.

Jake eventually reached the atrium again. It quickly became apparent the thief had fled down to a lower floor and hidden, likely among the crowd. This meant it became a bit harder for Jake to track, as the traces became mixed with those of others, but by now, he was confident that he could recognize the thief's presence if he saw them.

He went three floors down by jumping off the balcony, where he then felt the trail continue down another two flights of stairs. The thief had clearly been in a hurry, and detecting the traces was easier than ever.

Storming down, he followed them until he heard people in the distance. Quite a lot of them. Through his sphere, he spotted a room through a few walls with around fifteen people in it. Some of them he recognized as observers of his battle earlier. In fact, he recognized all of them but three.

This crowd was gathered in front of a large magic circle on another gate, and through the gate, Jake spotted what looked like a display room. Or, as the recorded projection earlier had called it, a hidden treasury. Though calling it a hidden treasury was kind of wrong, considering the huge door with glowing runes on it and the magic circle.

He is in that room.

There was no doubt about it. Knowing the target was cornered, Jake casually walked into the large room with the metal gate in it as the people discussed.

"I think you need to focus more on the leftmost quadrant and open up the mana pathway to there."

"Hm, but won't that trigger that thing above it?"

"Will it? Hm, what if you..."

Jake listened in as he checked the gate and saw the message with floating magical letters in front of it.

Solve the magic puzzle to open up the treasury and obtain what lies within. But, be warned that failed attempts will have adverse effects.

Someone suddenly screamed out in pain as red runes appeared all over her body, burning with a familiar kind of magic: a curse.

The ones in the room looked at her but only shook their head. The only ones in distress were her party members, who tried to help her, but in the end, the woman triggered her Insignia and disappeared, leaving the large coin floating behind. Someone from her party took it with no one even attempting to steal it. Which was interesting....

Because the thief was standing right behind that party. A young man in a red robe, wielding a staff with a red gem embedded in the head that gave off faint traces of fire-affinity mana, stood there, staring at the gate, not seeming to mind the ruckus from the curse earlier. Everything about him screamed fire mage. Clearly he had changed his clothes and hidden among the crowd. Or maybe he was genuinely trying to solve the puzzle, just like everyone else, and was there for that, but that didn't change the fact that he had stolen from someone he shouldn't have.

Subtlety was often the name of the game, but not right now.

No one had noticed Jake yet, as he stood all the way at the back of the room, Expert Stealth active to avoid unnecessary attention while tracking down his target. But now that he had found him?

Jake stopped trying to be stealthy and did quite the opposite, infusing his presence with mana.

One had to remember... Jake still had Limit Break active at 20%. He hadn't deactivated the skill yet to avoid the period of weakness that would come afterwards. Considering the fact that the stat boost also helped him track his target faster, he preferred to just keep it active. Also... honestly... Jake was beginning to have enough resources to keep it active near-permanently as long as he wasn't in combat and using many skills. Shit, if he began lacking stamina, he still had the potion cooldown ready and could chug one.

All this meant that when Jake made himself known, everyone noticed and turned around in shock. Most of them had seen him before and instantly backed away. The ones who hadn't seen him before backed away even more than the others due to the fear of an unknown, powerful person.

Jake's eyes were trained on the thief as he used One Step Mile and appeared in the middle of the crowd. Before anyone could react, Jake grasped the guy by his robe and hoisted him up until his feet no longer touched the ground. He even made sure to wrap a few strings of arcane mana around the man, as Jake knew he was the slippery sort.

"You stole from me. Hand it back," Jake said, looking into the eyes of the thief.

The thief, appearing to have some balls, proclaimed his innocence. "Wha!? You have the wrong person! I've never stolen anything in my life!" The man addressed the next words not to Jake, but to the crowd. "He is trying to rob me! This is just an excuse! I haven't done a thing, I'm—"

"Five..." Jake said, staring into his eyes.

"I told you, I—"

"Four..."

Looking more desperate, the thief's eyes darted around, seemingly looking for some kind of assistance from the crowd. He got none.

Jake did notice, however, that a few from the crowd looked doubtful. It was understandable. No one had any proof, and it was just Jake's word against the thief's. The thing was... Jake didn't need proof. He didn't need a justification or a rightful cause, and deep down, they all knew it.

"Three..."

"This is simply ridiculous! Is this really what the world has turned to? Do we really allow such—"

"Two..."

Yeah, his attempt at riling up the crowd hadn't worked, though Jake did see some people begin to move away. No one went for their weapons. Being a D-grade of Earth this "early" after the integration meant you weren't a complete idiot without survival instincts.

"How can you just—"

"One..."

When Jake reached the end of his countdown, the thief seemed to realize the game was over. Only two things could happen from there. Jake would either kill him, or the thief would be forced to activate the Insignia and leave the Treasure Hunt. Both were bad options for him, and what did it matter if he had support from the public if he was dead or had lost all his gains?

So, he stopped fucking around. The thief's eyes changed as he looked at Jake.

"Is a few knickknacks really worth making an enemy of the Court of Shadows?" the thief asked, his voice no longer the same shrill, fearful one from before, but now confident and self-assured. "I was under the assumption we had a good working relationship."

"I don't remember ever giving any of you permission to steal from me," Jake answered, not taking any of that shit. He also noted the confusion among the crowd they had gathered.

"Oh, come on, is it even stealing? I just got there and took a few things you had missed. Besides, aren't we practically family? I fought both against and together with the Judge—your brother—and all of this is done under his instructions, so shouldn't we just leave it at this, Jake?" The man didn't seem scared in the slightest anymore.

The reason was clear... He was confident Jake wouldn't do anything to him. And Jake got that. The man was a subordinate of Caleb, Jake's brother, and the basic assumption that had spread was that Jake was practically a member, or at least a close ally. Miranda had briefed Jake on this before and made him aware of this assumption. Their friendly interactions during the World Congress had spread this, and the now widespread knowledge they were brothers had cemented it.

One could argue this assumption was partially correct. Jake didn't see the Court of Shadows as an enemy organization. Still, Jake didn't put that much weight on what organization people came from or belonged to. He wasn't blind to their existence and influence... but in the end, the individual was the one responsible for their actions, and Jake knew that Caleb was aware of Jake's point of view.

Because the thing was...

"That's funny. Caleb never stole from me, and I'm pretty sure our parents told us that was wrong. So as his big brother, let me teach his subordinate some basic fucking courtesy."

Before anyone could react, Jake tossed the thief across the room and into a wall. The man crashed into it and coughed up blood as he bounced off it. Jake hadn't thrown him that hard, as he knew the guy likely couldn't handle it.

Thinking this was a chance, the thief tried running, but Jake just took a single step and appeared in front of him. "I didn't say you could leave."

Seeing Jake appear, the thief used the good old Shadow Vault of Umbra to try and simply phase through him and away. Actually, Jake was pretty certain it was an upgraded version that allowed him to pass through humans. Anyway, his response?

Jake punched the guy in the face with an arcane mana-infused glove, knocking out a few teeth. Shadow Vault still had that big flaw of being unable to phase through magical barriers, and nothing was a more rigid barrier than Jake's arcane mana. Seeing all the blood fly from the man's mouth, Jake shook his head and thought about how fragile the thief was. He had to hold himself back so much to not break him, and it was quite frankly frustrating.

The guy tried to get up again, but Jake got in front of him, and this time the thief didn't try to run. "Are you really going to do this?" the man groaned as he held his jaw. Jake was pretty sure it was broken, so kudos to the guy for talking so clearly.

"I am. But sure, let's be nice for my brother's sake. Hand over everything you got, fuck off to somewhere where I never see you again, and I'll allow you to stick around for the rest of the Hunt."

"Or what? Are you gonna kill me? Damage me so much I'm forced to leave? Are you fucking serious, that you would cause such a big incident for a few items? This is practically a declaration of war. I looted an empty room, and now you come and claim everything is yours. What's next? You're gonna kill everyone here because they're witnesses? You're gonna claim that everything they have belongs to you too because you came to this tower first? Is this really how the almighty Progenitor and Lord of Haven acts?"

Jake didn't detect much genuine anger in his mouth. No, this guy was a snake, and not the cool, beer-drinking kind, but the lying and manipulative asshole kind.

Jake looked at him for a moment before he smiled. "Zero."

Before anyone could react, Jake slashed. Blood spurted as the thief was cut apart at his stomach, and his one hand—the one he was not holding his jaw with—also fell to the ground, cut off at the wrist.

The thief screamed, but Jake slowly raised his sword again above his head. The man looked up at him with wide eyes, for the first time showing genuine fear. The coward activated his Hunter Insignia and disappeared, leaving behind the large floating coin with the loot within.

"What an idiot," Jake muttered as he took the coin and put it in his inventory, quickly confirming he had indeed been the thief. Well, that, or he had found another suspiciously similar silver altar and coffin.

Jake turned to the observing crowd, all of them looking hesitant. It seemed like the thief's words had gotten to them, and they feared they were his target now. Jake shook his head as he walked over towards them.

"Relax—I'm done taking out the trash, so let's all move on, okay?" he said casually, following up with, "Anyway, what is this thing?"

He looked up at the magic puzzle-thing on the door, finding that far more interesting now that the thief business had been settled.

CHAPTER 13

TREASURE HUNT: JUDGING STUFF

J ake stared up at the puzzle door, no one answering his inquiry right away. He got why it could be a bit unsetting to chat with the guy who had nearly just killed someone, but in Jake's defense, the guy hadn't died. The lack of a notification confirmed that, and Jake was pretty sure people were healed when exiting.

"Uhm, it's a magic puzzle of sorts," some young man finally answered. He looked rather unassuming, and while Jake had seen him before as one of the observers, he wasn't exactly someone Jake had taken special notice of. Just another level 105 in the crowd.

"Hm, I see," Jake said, already inspecting the magic circle himself. Well, that was useless information, and exactly what the message written there also said. However, it appeared that no one had really made any progress with the entire thing, so Jake decided that he wasn't in a rush as he went over to the side of the chamber.

People looked towards him, but when they saw that he just summoned a comfortable chair and sat down, they turned back to the magic circle. A few glances were still thrown his way now and then, though. Once Jake was sitting comfortably, he deactivated his Limit Break and slumped down a bit. If push came to shove, he could reactivate it and suffer a worse backlash later if anyone tried to mess with him. It proved to be completely unnecessary, as it seemed to only make them relax more when Jake stopped giving off his aura.

Jake decided now was a good time to go through some of his gains before he could tackle the big puzzle-gate thingie.

The first items he went through were those he had looted from the Count of Blood, starting with the black sword.

[Count's Vampiric Blade (Rare)] – A blade wielded by a Count of Blood that has been soaked in the blood of countless enemies throughout the ages. Crafted using a special type of steel, the blade can absorb the lifeforce of Vitality-based lifeforms to repair itself. The Records left during this time have allowed the blade to evolve and transform even further, allowing it to steal a portion of the lifeforce of anyone injured. This blade was originally crafted in a set of nine using the unique environment of the hidden world and can absorb the weapons of other Counts of Blood to enhance itself. Note: This functionality is only available within the Treasure Hunt area and will disappear once the event concludes. Enchantments: Hemoabsorbant Self-Repair. Vampiric Blade.

Requirements: Lvl 125+ humanoid race.

Jake read it over a few times and reached one conclusion... It was pretty damn similar to his Scimitar of Cursed Hunger. Scarily so. Had Jake accidentally transmuted the cursed sword to make a vampire sword? Or were swords with vampiric abilities just not that rare? Thinking about it, it was a pretty basic effect to steal vital energy on each hit.

It was the kind of passive ability Jake didn't really notice while fighting. It was just there and nice to have, much like many of his other passive effects. Now, the sword was good, but Jake didn't really feel like using it. He liked the Nanoblade due to its longer length and insane sharpness, and he felt like the scimitar was still better as a vampiric sword. However, that wouldn't necessarily last forever.

The ability to upgrade the sword by absorbing the other weapons was super interesting and, once again, pretty game-like. It did mean that Jake would have to hunt down all nine Counts himself or possibly trade with someone to get all the weapons. Well... he would have to do those things anyway due to the other item he had gained: the infamous key.

> *[Key of Blood (Unique)] – One of nine keys held by the Counts of Blood within the Treasure Hunt area. When combined with the eight others, this key will grant you the potential to earn bonus rewards. Holding any of the keys, even if unused, will contribute greatly to your final reward.*

While the sword being able to absorb other weapons was "pretty game-like," having a set of nine keys one had to collect to open some secret place was super game-like. Or maybe movie-like? A plot about collecting MacGuffins was a prevalent trope, after all. Not that Jake was particularly complaining about it; he liked collecting stuff and unlocking bonus events.

Additionally, even if he failed to get all nine keys, he would still get bonus rewards. What this bonus reward entailed, Jake didn't know, as he felt like all the loot he'd gathered was enough rewards in itself.

Moving on, he got to the red crystal the Count had transformed into. It turned out to not be a crystal at all, but a heart.

> *[Starved Balnar Vampire Heart (Epic)] – The heart of a severely starved Balnar Vampire. This type of vampire is a rare variant with high physical Strength and incred-*

ible durability. The rarity has been downgraded due to the starved state of the vampire the heart has been claimed from. Has many alchemical uses.

Jake frowned as he read the description. Starved vampire? What? To him, the Count hadn't seemed in any way starved or weakened. Wouldn't the boss that loved exposition begin talking about how "even in my weakened state, I am still superior" or something like that?

In retrospect, though, it did seem to make sense. The vampire had been sleeping for a long-ass time, and while Jake wasn't a vampire expert, he could see how one that hadn't fed for many years could be weakened. Also... it was true the Count wasn't exactly a top-tier foe in Jake's mind. It was inferior to the Altmar Census Golem, but superior to something like the Monkey Prima. Now, this did make him consider how powerful a non-starved Balnar Vampire would be, especially with how the system recognized them as a rare variant.

Either way, figuring out what to do with it was for later. Chances were he would learn more about it as the Treasure Hunt progressed, and if he didn't, he could just research it once outside in the real world.

Now that he was done with the loot gained from the Count of Blood, he moved on to what had been in the Count's chamber. It was the items the thief had stolen, and upon checking them out... he suddenly understood the illogical actions of the thief a bit better.

The altar and the coffin were two separate items, both of ancient rarity.

[Yalsten Altar of the Damned (Ancient)] – An altar created by an extremely skilled crafter from the long-perished world of Yalsten, using a single, unbroken piece of an unknown metal. The metal of the altar itself makes it near-indestructible for any being below A-

grade. This altar has absorbed vast amounts of blood to empower it further, as countless sacrifices have been made upon it. It has been enchanted further to increase the effectiveness of all rituals made using it as a catalyst. Further increases the effect of all sacrificial rituals. Faint Records and echoes of old rituals remain imprinted upon the altar, making it passively infuse anyone lying upon it with the life energy of those once sacrificed upon it.

Requirements: N/A

Jake wasn't certain if he really had any uses for this altar, but he was damn certain Villy was going to make a joke about it if he knew about it. However, even if Jake didn't know what to use it for, its value was unquestionable, and it would surely count towards giving a good final reward.

Also, after the Treasure Hunt, there would be a big auction, and there was sure to be someone in attendance who could use it. Shit, couldn't Miranda use it? She was a witch who made rituals and stuff.

With the altar was also the accompanying coffin.

[Yalsten Coffin of Eternal Slumber (Ancient)] – A coffin created by an extremely skilled crafter from the long-perished world of Yalsten using an unknown metal that has been left untouched by the ages, slowly soaking in the Records of history and the concept of time. The metal of the coffin itself makes it near-indestructible for any being below A-grade. The runes on the coffin allow any who slumber within to be preserved longer, as time is distorted while inside the coffin. Once inside, enter a special type of meditation that will keep all resources fully replenished and allow you to enter deep sleep, making time pass unnoticed while lessening aging signif-

icantly. All effects are amplified for vampires, especially when used with Vampiric Slumber.

Requirements: N/A

This one was, in Jake's opinion, a fair bit more interesting. First of all, it was a coffin in a vampire tower, so it was already great thematically, and he also saw how well it worked with the altar. The altar would constantly infuse the vampire with vital energy as he or she slept in the coffin placed atop the altar.

The entire time magic part was also interesting, though not that relevant to Jake at all, as he didn't have any plans to enter some eternal slumber anytime soon. These two items were probably the worst ancient-rarity items Jake had ever obtained. At least for him. Oh, well. If he ever made a vampire friend, he had some cool stuff for them, and if not, he could always have someone melt all the stuff down and make something else. Because no, Jake was not going to sleep in the coffin. Ever. Fuck that.

Having fully inspected the two ancient-rarity items, Jake once more considered how the thief's actions made a lot more sense. He had likely banked on Jake not knowing the true value of the items, and had thus attempted to make Jake not think getting rid of the thief was worth the potential issues it could cause.

It was stupid to think the Court of Shadows would actually make an enemy out of Jake just because of one idiotic thief, but it did make sense he could think Jake would hesitate. The thief knew nothing about Jake. He had only seen Jake in this tower in person, and what had he done? He had fought a monster terrorizing others, helped many people, and even given out a healing potion to the woman with the stomped legs. This made Jake consider if the thief had somehow concluded that Jake was some kind of good guy with a hero complex who wouldn't just kill someone for a "petty crime."

Again, in some ways, this was a sound conclusion. Capital punishment for thievery wasn't exactly commonplace, so maybe the stupid thief had hoped for Jake just to file an official complaint and start a diplomatic conflict or something. The thing was, Jake wasn't big on politics, and hey, he had handled the problem just fine. What was the thief going to do? Go to Caleb and say, "Hey, so I tried to rob your big brother, the leader of another faction, and he got mad and made me leave the Treasure Hunt. Can we please declare war or something? A strongly worded letter, at least?"

Yeah, no.

Jake sat back in the chair he was in and relaxed. People had turned away from him again as he sat there and went through the items, slowly having the period of weakness disappear. Still not in peak condition, Jake looked up towards the magic-circle puzzle and began inspecting it more closely. *Seems interesting.*

———

"Four signals have disappeared within the last half an hour," the man said as he kept track of hundreds of floating wisps all around him.

He was standing within a cleared house in the central Mistless Plains, hidden by enchantments and a barrier.

"Could be better, could be worse," Caleb said, shrugging. "Any particularly noteworthy disappearances?"

"Hm, JN—the Shadow Thief who went towards one of the towers—disappeared less than fifteen minutes after he reported back about getting a big score," the Solicitor said as he kept control of his ritual. "Apparently, someone managed to fight quite the powerful monster and left the boss room unattended for him to loot."

Solicitor was a unique role in the Court of Shadows. They dealt with getting jobs, but also assigning them. More often than not, they took the role of handler for many assassins and kept track of their successes, failures, and potential deaths. While the Judge was the highest-ranking member in any individual Court, the Solicitors handled the day-to-day leadership.

"JN? That kleptomaniac?" Caleb said with a wondering tone. "He probably got found out and refused to hand over what he stole. I am a bit interested in who was able to catch him; he was quite the sneaky one, if I recall correctly..."

"I am not certain... Let me check if there have been any other reports," the Solicitor answered as he began going through the wisps. Each of them corresponded to a person, and each of them was linked to their respective member of the Court. They would send information through them, though only via simple messages.

Additionally, only the Solicitor could understand these messages. The number of people who could snoop in on such long-range communication wasn't small, after all, so it was all encrypted by the individual Solicitor who received it.

Caleb reentered meditation as he worked to steady the storm brewing within him. The reason why he wasn't out and about with all the others was simple... They needed protection at their main headquarters. Caleb was fully aware he wasn't an outstanding fighter in longer battles, but in short bursts, he was undoubtedly one of the strongest people on the planet. Quite fitting for an assassin, though Caleb didn't exactly view himself as one.

He had to admit, he found himself in a bit of an odd position. Caleb wasn't comfortable being some cold-hearted assassin killing people for money, yet he now found himself as the leader of an organization doing exactly that. So far, he hadn't needed to do many things that compromised his own moral compass, but he constantly found himself challenged. It was lucky that "killing" in the Treasure Hunt didn't necessarily mean actually killing someone. One just had to make them leave, and that was enough. Heck, killing people during the Hunt was extremely difficult, as unless killed instantly, one could exit with a simple mental command.

It was a bit lucky that as the Judge, he wasn't generally expected to be an assassin himself and go around killing people. And from the few conversations he'd had with both Umbra and a few higher-ranking individuals from the Court, it was actually preferable the Judge had some kind of moral compass and wasn't just a mindless killer. Mindless killing was neither profitable nor sustainable, and would only lead to the Court finding it more difficult to have a presence in the multiverse. The Court preferred to remain in coexistence with the existing establishments and be viewed as a necessary evil. The devil you know and all that.

In the end, this meant Caleb was actually more of a protector and guide to the Court. Someone who would decide what to do and make the important decisions based on his own judgment. So... yeah, a Judge. That was also why he was remaining behind right now. He was there in case the Solicitor needed to ask for feedback on anything and, of course, to serve as a protector.

There was also the fact that choosing to run around to loot things himself didn't make much sense yet, as the primary objective for all the Court members was to gather information for now and only obtain treasures when opportune. Ultimately, they weren't treasure hunters... They didn't need to obtain the treasures themselves.

They just had to take it from those who had before the event ended.

"Uhm, sir?" the Solicitor said, sounding more unsure than Caleb had ever heard him before.

"What's the issue?" Caleb asked.

"I got information from someone in the same tower as JN... Apparently a Count of Blood was slain there... JN looted the boss room, but was then tracked down by the killer of the Count and made to leave the Treasure Hunt..."

Caleb sighed as he facepalmed. *What a goddamn idiot.*

"Let me guess; it was Jake?"

"Yeah..."

"Whelp. Shit happens, I guess. Just write off the loss and put a note on JN's file."

"Yes, Judge!" the Solicitor said as he returned to work, relieved at Caleb's response.

Caleb just shook his head. Jake had always been a quite possessive person... To steal from him and expect to get away with it...

Yeah, he would have to have a nice, long talk with that moron JN after the Treasure Hunt.

CHAPTER 14

TREASURE HUNT: PUZZLE

This wasn't Jake's first time engaging with a magic puzzle, but it was his first time encountering this type. Before returning to Earth, the practice cauldron Villy had given him during his alchemy training session deployed similar methods to this gate's magic puzzle. However, the cauldron had been focused on alchemy, while this gate was more of a regular and more general mana puzzle.

Except... you couldn't really call it a regular puzzle. It was like those weird puzzle games with ropes and rings you could buy as a gift to a friend to piss them off because you knew they sucked at those kinds of things—which was totally not something Jake had ever done.

This brain puzzle did differentiate itself from even that by one huge thing: you couldn't test things. One could also compare it to having to do a puzzle, and while you could see all the puzzle pieces, you weren't allowed to misplace a single piece on the board. Doing that would result in being infected with a curse... In other words, every move had to be accurate from the beginning to the end.

Finally getting a proper understanding of the puzzle, Jake suddenly understood why so little progress had been made. It also had to be mentioned that this wasn't an individual puzzle, but visible to everyone. Therefore, any progress made on the puzzle benefitted everyone present. This had ultimately resulted in no one daring to try and make the next move in case it was a mistake, and they would be punished for it, possibly having to leave.

Now, Jake didn't actually think it would mark the end of the Treasure Hunt for him if he fucked up and got cursed here. He had seen that woman be cursed when he first entered, and while it was potent, it wasn't something he couldn't handle. He didn't want to do it, though, as curses were damn annoying and took so long to get rid of.

Jake furrowed his brows as he first observed the circle from a distance. *They have made a bit of progress*, he concluded. A few basic steps had been taken. About one-twentieth of the puzzle had already been solved by the crowd.

The first part did seem relatively simple. Like most puzzles of this kind, it got harder the further you got. At least partly. In some ways, it also got more manageable as you began to understand the logic behind the puzzle and how it all fit together to create a whole.

He had to admit... he liked that things like this puzzle door existed in the Treasure Hunt. He liked that it wasn't all about fighting, but also involved things like the trap room he had trivialized. It made it all feel less like just another murder fest. Well... it was still a murder fest. Which was good for Jake. Jake was good at murder, after all. But he felt like he was also usually pretty good at puzzles, so he wanted to solve this one.

It scratched that same itch alchemy did. Would Jake possibly be able to obtain more rewards if he decided to just leave and hunt down more foes or scour the rest of the tower for other hidden treasures? Probably... but now he wanted to solve this puzzle, so he would solve the puzzle.

With all that in mind, Jake got up from his chair and walked closer to get a better look at the whole puzzle in all its glory. He got a bit of attention, but most were either focused on the puzzle or had gotten used to his presence now. Or maybe they just realized gawking wouldn't lead to anything and ignored him consciously. Either way, Jake was left alone as he got closer and stared deeply at the gate.

What if you direct the mana through... No, false pathway. That way, then? Hm... No, another dead-end. Ah, but if you move it through—wait, no, that would trigger that thing.

Jake ended up closing his eyes and entering Thoughtful Meditation, the entire gate and magic circle still prominently displayed within his head, courtesy of the Sphere of Perception.

He began going through possibilities in his mind as he cradled his hands and made a miniature version of parts of the puzzle. The small construct broke apart time and time again, but it slowly expanded as well.

More and more people began entering the room, and more and more began doing their own small experiments. There were even groups forming. Many also left during this time, primarily those who were less magic-focused, likely believing their time was better spent searching the tower for treasures while leaving their party members behind. Hours passed by like this, and soon the large chamber had over a hundred people, nearly all of them mages or people with very mana-focused professions like Jake.

Jake was alone, but a few people did notice his construct and how his was larger and more elaborate than anyone else's. Yet, he wasn't happy, as he felt quite a few kinks in this method. He felt like he was missing a piece of the puzzle somewhere, as he had been stuck at the same point for nearly ten minutes.

"I got it!" an excited voice suddenly said, cutting through his meditation. "The top-left channel and the center-left channel are entangled based on their identical oscillation when probed."

Jake frowned and, without thinking, infused both simultaneously with equal amounts of mana. It was true; his construct didn't break apart.

He opened his eyes and found the speaker to be a young

woman who looked to be in her mid-twenties with two older men behind her. She had long, black hair and two dark eyes looking down at him as he sat in meditation. She didn't look at him in a condescending way, but rather a happy one from figuring out the magic puzzle thing.

Jake looked back through the holes in his mask as he tilted his head and answered, "Good catch."

Then he Identified all three newcomers. Jake assumed they had also tried to Identify him earlier, but he had kind of begun filtering out the sensation of being Identified, as people tried—and failed—to do so all the time. The two men with her were totally sizing him up, by the way.

[Human – lvl 113]

[Human – lvl 115]

[Human – lvl 116]

The woman was only 113, with the two men behind her higher level, but he didn't for a second doubt she was the strongest person in the group of three. Jake wondered why he hadn't heard of or met her before.

He stared deeply up at her as he also sized her up, neither speaking as she looked down at him. Her smile slowly faded as she broke out of her excitement. She instead took on a pensive look, seemingly deep in thought, as Jake also wondered who she was.

———

A few hours earlier, Reika had been exploring the small, hidden crypts spread across the plains, as she'd gotten a report from one of her two followers with a communication bracelet. They weren't truly guardians, even if they were a higher level, but more her supports. Needless to say, they were elites of the clan, but neither had gone for the Perfect Evolution. Instead, they had chosen to prioritize some immediate power for the clan over their own personal future growth. It was a decision she disagreed with but could see the necessity of.

"Miss Reika, a group of classers affiliated with the clan have made contact with Lord Thayne after he assisted them within a tower," the man said respectfully. "The tower should not be far from here."

"I see," she answered. She had told him to relay any information regarding Lord Thayne. Her great-grandfather was still set on having her be the leader of the diplomatic entourage heading for Haven, and she didn't wish to go against the Patriarch, even if she didn't agree.

If she was honest, she didn't like the person so respectfully called Lord Thayne by everyone, but she was also aware of it primarily being because she didn't understand him. The Noboru clan had looked into him and his background to see who he'd been before the system, and it was just a whole pile of... nothing. He was no one. A middle-tier office drone who'd worked in finance. Granted, his grades during university had been great, but he hadn't precisely attended a university she would put much stock in. He had also done a bit of archery, but she had at least three family members who were better than he had ever gotten.

Then there was his family. He had no heritage worth mentioning. No close family outside of his parents and brother. No long lineage or famous ancestors... Not even a single known noble anywhere in his family tree. There was *nothing* that made him special. Yet somehow, not only was the Lord of Haven an outstanding individual, but the little brother had become the Judge of the Court of Shadows. Somehow, two Lord Thaynes had emerged from nothing. His brother had been a damn teacher, and while that was a profession she held much respect for, it wasn't exactly one that lent itself to the position he was in now.

To Reika... none of that made sense. They had researched so many other capable individuals. Carmen of Valhal had been an extremely talented—if unstable and violent—boxer who had been hardened through incarceration. Eron was a savant-level surgeon with one of the best track records on the planet. The Augur of Sanctdomo came from a long line of successful businessmen and women, and had been a young prodigy and genius from birth. His bodyguard had served in the special forces before he retired to private security. Even the one known as William made sense in that he was a young, diagnosed psychopath who just happened to be talented in magic and got lucky with being blessed by a god.

This pattern repeated itself with all they investigated. All of them had been prominent figures, either infamous or famous. One simply could not hide the heaven-sent talent required to truly stand out in this new world. There *had to* be traces and evidence. Reika didn't believe in coincidences. So she surmised something did exist that made Lord Thayne special... Something that just hadn't been visible in the old world.

To make it even more confusing... this *special* thing also spread to others around him. Matteo of the Court of Shadows, formerly known simply as M, was a top-ranked assassin in the world.. and he had somehow been beaten by the school teacher Caleb Thayne. Even that Casper of the undead faction only seemed to be who he was due to his relation to Jake Thayne. He had been in a tutorial with both the Augur and William... making her sure he was the one common denominator of these odd occurrences. There was something about him, and she wanted to figure out what it was.

But... she wasn't going to upturn her life to do that. She had her own goals and objectives in this Treasure Hunt, and learning more about Lord Thayne was just one of them. Hence why she didn't interrupt their current task.

"We continue and finish off this crypt first," Reika
commanded as she drew her blade and continued down the hallway. "Have someone else return to the tower and see if he is still
there, and if not, have them explore it."

Hours later, they had wrapped things up and were headed
up from the crypt again as the man in charge of communication
gave an update.

"We have confirmation that Lord Thayne has slain a Count
of Blood within the tower and is now working on some kind of
magic puzzle to open—"

"Wait, he has slain one of the Counts?" Reika asked, stopping him.

Her great-grandfather had sent back information that a
Mark of Blood had to be used to gain access to the chamber of a
Count, and you needed one such Mark from a Viscount... How
the hell had the man managed to slay a Viscount and then a
Count within such a short period, only to now be relaxing and
solving a magic puzzle...?

Wait, a magic puzzle?

"Yes, he defeated it and—"

"Tell me more about this magic puzzle. Also, we're heading
there now," Reika interrupted.

Details about how he had slain the Count were just second-
hand information, and from what little she had heard of his
earlier exploits, it was just a mix of teleportation, bow and
arrows, magic, and dual-wielding blades. Explanations were a
waste of time, and she was certain she would have to see it herself
to comprehend his power.

"It appears to be a complex puzzle to open a hidden treasury," the man explained. "A collaborative project, it appears.
Current attempts seem to have..."

He continued explaining what they knew of the puzzle so
far, and even went back over some of the happenings regarding
Lord Thayne. Apparently, some absolute idiot of a thief had
tried to rob him or something. She didn't put much weight on

it, but instead focused on the information regarding the puzzle.

While she was a competent combatant with her sword, she viewed her true talents as alchemy and magic in general. She had chosen to pick up the blade due to prior experience before the system, but that didn't mean she only used that. Her great-grandfather had encouraged her to pursue her own unique path, and so she would.

Entering the tower was simple, as there were several entrances at the base of the mountain. Once inside, a member of the Noboru clan stood ready and led her to the puzzle room where she, for the first time, laid eyes upon the so-often-talked-about Lord Thayne.

She looked at him... and didn't get it. He just looked weird. He didn't give off any particular presence to her even though people had talked so much about it. Contrarily, he just looked tired as he sat in meditation with some glowing magic circle in his hands... *Huh?*

Reika looked up at the magic circle on the gate and compared it to the version in his hand... *How did he replicate so much of it? He hasn't been here for that long... What?*

Continuing to look at him for the next half an hour, she saw him make fast progress, but suddenly he stopped. She had inadvertently walked closer at this point to get a closer look at his mana construct. She compared it to the version on the wall and frowned. They were completely identical, and he had come so far, yet he was now stumped? What part was it? She could see that he repeatedly attempted to cause a change in a particular pathway. She activated a skill to better see the mana movement and another to analyze it. Getting lucky, she caught the issue and couldn't hold herself back.

"I got it! The top-left channel and the center-left channel are entangled based on their identical oscillation when probed!" Reika splurted out, a huge smile on her face as she figured it out. She only realized afterward she had done it as she inadvertently got the attention of the man—but not before he confirmed her theory to be true.

"Good catch," he answered, looking up at her. She met his eyes by instinct and peered into them.

Reika had been around elites for all of her life. Hardened military men, CEOs of some of the largest companies in the world, generals, and what many would argue was the best humanity had to offer. But compared to the eyes of the man in front of her...

He wasn't like any of them. All of them had an air of superiority—one of assumed influence, status, and confidence that seemed to invite respect. But Lord Thayne... he didn't invite respect. He didn't assume power or confidence. He demanded all of those. Not because he was a leader... but because he was powerful. It was a fact, not an assumption.

The only other person she had ever met that made her feel that way was the Patriarch, a man who gave off an aura that made one feel like he could slice you apart at a moment's notice yet could also explain to you the profound secrets of the world.

She didn't know how the man named Jake Thayne had suddenly appeared on Earth out of nowhere. She didn't understand how that could happen. But she wanted to find out. She always loved finding puzzles and understanding things she didn't understand... and something told her the man in front of her was possibly the most interesting and challenging puzzle she had ever encountered.

CHAPTER 15

TREASURE HUNT: COLLABORATIVE PROJECT

J ake stared up at the woman, who seemed to be deep in thought. Considering she had helped him, he started up the conversation.

"You have experience with these kinds of puzzles?" he asked her.

She seemed to exit her stupor, as she collected her thoughts and answered, "Yes, I have some experience from the tutorial, and through some practice objects I acquired."

"Practice objects?" Jake asked, his eyes lighting up. Had she managed to get something like the practice cauldron Villy had lent him? He still missed that cauldron every single day, but sadly he couldn't bring it back to Earth.

"From the tutorial store—I got an evolving puzzle box to keep practicing magic theory," she explained courteously, if still a bit tensely.

Why the fuck did I not think of that? he asked himself. He had so many damn points, and yet he had chosen to buy that damn Omnitool as the fifth item. Why hadn't he gotten a practice cauldron? Man, did Jake want a practice cauldron.

"Very neat," he said, nodding, thinking it would be too rude to ask to see it. "Name's Jake, by the way. Nice to meet you."

He got up from the ground, as talking to her while sitting down was a bit awkward. Jake was just about to extend his hand for a handshake, but luckily, before he had a chance to do so, she introduced herself with a bow, sparing him the embarrassment.

"Reika of the Noboru clan—it's a pleasure to meet you, Lord Thayne," she said, keeping up her courteous yet guarded attitude. The two men behind her also bowed but didn't offer up any names.

The silent types, eh?

"Pleasure is all mine," he said. "Real good catch on those entangled pathways; it wasn't something I had encountered before, so thanks. Did you come here to solve the puzzle door too?"

Jake had been aware of her presence but not really noted her. Sure, she had looked at his construct, but so had dozens of other people. However, in such a short time, she had managed to analyze his framework, understand the puzzle on the door, and find a solution. In conclusion? She was good at these kinds of things, hence why he asked if she had experience.

"In part, yes," she answered, not looking like she wanted to elaborate.

He just shrugged in response. "Either way, thanks for the help, and best of luck."

"If we both aim to solve this puzzle, would it not make more sense to collaborate and solve it together?" she quickly cut in.

"Hm," Jake said, a bit embarrassed to admit the thought hadn't even crossed his mind. But then again... Yeah, she was totally there to probe him or something. Well, he saw no reason not to give it a go. "I guess we could."

He wasn't really against it. On the contrary, it seemed like an interesting experience, and Reika seemed competent. He hadn't really worked with anyone else besides birds since... well, pretty much ever, and it seemed like a fun, novel experience. Also, Miranda would get super happy if Jake made friends with the Noboru clan, and the woman in front of him seemed to be quite the influential figure, considering her two followers.

"Great. Should we move elsewhere and do so in private?" she asked, her attitude still as tense and annoyingly courteous as before. She sounded like she was at work and interacting with a customer she had to talk to but would really prefer to avoid.

Jake nodded in agreement, as standing surrounded by people and talking with someone wasn't an optimal working environment. He moved to the side of the chamber and saw Reika tell her two followers to take off elsewhere. Jake wholeheartedly supported that decision—having two large men staring at him while talking to her wasn't exactly comfortable.

Once they had moved to the side, she waved her hand to form a magic circle that created a barrier around them. It was a basic isolation barrier, and Jake had seen Miranda and others use similar ones before. He should really learn how to make those. Anyway, being isolated and all, he decided to make his mask invisible, as it did seem a bit too impolite to keep his face covered. It should also be good practice for him, and besides, it would be easier to talk to her if she could see his face—if a bit risky, since she would be able to read his facial expressions.

"Just to know, what got you interested in these kinds of magic puzzles and general magic theory?" Jake asked his temporary partner. Once the barrier was fully active, he felt like it was okay to ask some more semi-personal questions, and besides, it would give him an idea of why and how she had her magic knowledge.

"Would it not be a better question to ask why I wouldn't be interested in magic theory? It's a fundamental power that opens numerous paths and possibilities. Is it not natural to want to solve the mysteries of this new world and discover the truth, especially when learning this truth can lead to tangible benefits?"

So, she likes magic theory but doesn't want to outright admit she finds it fun. Got it. It was an easy conclusion, given how she talked about it with such fervor, and her demeanor completely changed. It reminded him of Arnold in some ways, though Arnold was far weirder, and Jake found the dude hard to get a solid grasp on.

"True. You're a mage, I guess?" Jake asked Reika. He felt her aura, and she did give him the feeling of a spellcaster over a melee fighter. She gave off a magical presence more than a physical one.

"Once more, only partly. I primarily began learning about mana and its application through alchemy, and I then expanded upon that knowledge and applied it to other areas. Spellcasting is certainly an ability of mine, but I am uncertain if that makes me classified as a mage. To my knowledge, you also make liberal use of magic in combat scenarios, and does that make you a mage?"

Jake had chosen to bite onto something in the first part of what she had said. Alchemy. That did explain some things, as alchemy was a profession all about mana control and mana theory, but even more so... this was Jake's first time meeting and talking to another alchemist. Okay, maybe he had seen others, but he felt that the woman in front of him had achieved the Perfect Evolution title and was an alchemist to boot. To rephrase, she was the only talented alchemist he had met.

"Alchemy? Awesome. What kind? What do you specialize in? I myself mainly do poison, but I also got quite a knack for potions and a bit of off-brand transmutation here and there." He was quite excited to meet and talk to another alchemist. Especially one around his own level.

Sure, the Viper and Duskleaf were also alchemists, but they were so far ahead of him that they weren't even fun talking to about alchemy. Shit, he was certain he still sucked too much to fully comprehend how much better they were than him.

"I primarily create compounds and catalysts for magic rituals and other auxiliary items, but I have also dabbled in more classical alchemical works such as potions. Recently I have worked on making performance-enhancing consumables, also known as flasks. I take heavy inspiration from the chemistry of before the system, and I have also begun to apply some pharmaceutical methodologies recently." In a roundabout way, she was pretty much saying, *I mainly do catalyst-things, potions, and flasks.*

By now, Jake didn't need to be told what kind of person she was. He had met so damn many of her type before. She was the kind that had been practically living within the educational world for her entire life. This did make Jake think she was a bit younger than him. Physical appearances weren't always a good indicator of age anymore, so he couldn't exactly use that. As an example, Miranda and Reika looked about equally old, and Miranda was older than Jake by a few years. But her way of talking was just like so many of those driven people in university. He had to confirm, though.

"Let me guess—you were in Uni before the initiation?" he asked with a smirk.

Reika looked embarrassed for a fraction of a second, but quickly waved it off and grew somewhat defensive. "I was working on my dissertation when the system arrived. What of it?"

"Oh, nothing at all," Jake said, putting up his hands as he shook his head.

"What?"

"It's nothing. Everything's fine. Anyway, the puzzle?"

"No, what? Are you looking down on me just because I—"

"Hm, this next part seems a bit tricky. See those two pathways? Yeah, they're freaking moving." Jake kept smiling, appearing to focus entirely on the puzzle.

"Seriously?" she said, glaring at him.

"Yep, pretty weird to have moving mana pathways, eh? Two at the same time, even!"

By now, she had, of course, realized he was fucking with her, and Jake had committed to the tomfoolery. The reason was that he found her entire manner of speech and behavior oddly uptight, but also defensive. From the start, he'd had a feeling she had an odd interpretation of who he was. It wasn't Jake's first time experiencing something like this, and it was totally his fault such interpretations existed out there. He had acted like some kind of mysterious powerhouse who didn't consider others, mainly because that was honestly the easiest way to operate. Well, he didn't think his reputation was bad, as he hadn't done anything outrageous yet, but he couldn't say he was viewed positively either.

Having some status and position tossed his way when he just wanted to do his own thing and enjoy himself gave him a weird feeling. He was childish, and liked having fun and fucking with people. Especially those straight out of university or those still studying. They always acted so awkwardly—even by his standards—when they finally got out into the "real world," so to say. Reika gave him those same vibes. To break down the barriers that made her so uptight and annoying was something he would gladly do, mainly by going against her expectations and forcing her to reevaluate him. And it seemed to work.

At least partly, because she was pretty quick to shoot him down as she completely ignored his antics and just focused on the task at hand... not knowing this was partly Jake's plan. All along, he'd wanted to get through the small talk and unto the real task at hand, and for her to act a bit annoyed at him was far better than her acting fake. He also believed he would ultimately learn more about her through this puzzle-solving session than he would by talking to her with her guard up.

"It isn't that out of the ordinary and is triggered by the stabilized flux of mana from the previous step," she finally answered, getting the show on the road.

Jake expanded his construct of mana and made a particular section light up more. "Firstly, we will have to block this part not to break the equilibrium."

"Naturally, and then we need to open up that pathway," Reika said, pointing at a specific part of the puzzle, "or the pathway will be mana-starved and contract, leading to collapse."

"Hm, only that one? To keep the equilibrium intact, we need to also stabilize the other side of the section, or the entire thing will go out of balance and break apart." He wasn't really asking, but simply concluding.

"That's... true... Yeah, that's right," she answered while Jake smirked.

They continued to one-up and challenge each other. Reika truly did have a different mindset than his own, and their methodologies were entirely different. Jake was the type of person who relied way too much on his gut and would often make impulsive moves rather than planning the process from start to end. He preferred going in with a rough draft and then micro-adjusting and winging it, as he knew that more often than not, plans fuck up.

Reika was the type to have a solid method behind her actions and thoroughly plan the process from start to finish. A true academic that didn't simply try to understand an issue and solve it, but also to comprehend the underlying causes and theory behind why things worked as they did. Jake also liked figuring out how things worked, but he preferred to do so through testing and practical experience. Reika struck him as the type that would rather read all the research on the topic than half-arse an experiment. This was probably a good idea, in retrospect. Jake's approach had led to his cauldron blowing up in his face quite a few times. He doubted that had ever really happened to her, and being a chemist before the system, it did seem like good work ethic to not just mix chemicals and hope everything worked out.

If Jake fucked up something in his work before the system, it would just be a broken Excel sheet, or he would lose a bit of money in the short term for the company. Now, after the system, Jake was durable enough to avoid severe damage even if he fucked up during his concoctions due to Palate, Scales of the Malefic Viper, and, of course, his overall high stats.

Ultimately, this difference in basic mindset meant that Reika wasn't taking any risks and being slow and methodical, while Jake was fast and experimental. As they constantly challenged each other and played off each other, the puzzle construct got solved faster and faster.

Jake would get a clear view of the entire challenge very fast, and Reika would spot potential blind spots and flaws. She also eventually made her own floating magic circle that wasn't a copy of the puzzle, but instead an attempt to figure out the puzzle's internal logic. Like a predictive algorithm to spot where the most likely issues would be, she kept feeding it information with every step they passed, and towards the end, it came in handy by functioning as a great guiding tool.

Only two hours after entering their isolation barrier, they stood there, staring up at the puzzle in front of them. Every pathway was cleared. Every pocket filled with mana. To bring it back to the metaphor with a regular puzzle... all the pieces had now been placed, and the picture was complete.

They both just looked at it, both trying to spot any flaws. None of them saw any, and they turned to each other as Jake raised his hand in her direction.

"Up top!"

She looked at his open palm for a while before finally catching on and giving him an awkward high-five. Jake didn't mind it; he just smiled happily.

"Nice one all around. Should we flex on the populace?" Jake asked cheekily.

The puzzle outside had been visible to them this entire time, and the people present had made some progress during this time, but not much. There seemed to be an agreement that people were trying to solve the entire thing alone or in groups before opening the real thing. The reason? Because how the hell would they divide the loot if they had to split it between everyone?

That meant he and Reika were about to flex on the entire room and take all the loot for themselves while being showered in envy and resignation by everyone present. Now, Jake didn't really feel bad about it because puzzles like these were, in his opinion, a reward in themselves. It had only been a few hours of puzzle-solving, and Jake had already gotten a lot of nice ideas on how to improve some things—most of them courtesy of Reika.

Reika looked over at him, clearly elated at their success, and asked with a smile, "Are you ready to let down the barrier?"

Jake nodded as the mask appeared on his face again. A second later, the barrier fell away, and attention was instantly directed their way. The majority of the room was aware that he —the leader of Haven—and someone from the Noboru clan had gone in there, and he even saw a few looks of resignation when they noticed Reika in a good mood.

"Will you do the honors?" he asked her.

She looked a bit surprised at him, and her smile grew. "With pleasure."

Jake just watched on as she extended what looked like a beam of mana into the puzzle and the entire thing began moving. Section after section was unlocked, and the whole room was silent for the minute it took for her to do the entire puzzle. Not a single mistake was made, as she simply replicated the construct Jake had perfectly copied.

Finally, the last part was solved, and the entire gate lit up and began opening.

Sighs sounded out throughout the room, with a few muted "congratulations" and "good jobs" coming their way. Not a single person seemed to have any thoughts of stealing from them, as they'd all backed away from the gate, letting Jake and Reika be the first to enter.

For all this time, Jake had consciously held himself back from peeking inside to see what was behind the gate with his Sphere of Perception, but now he finally let loose and took it all in, and... well, there was a lot.

What was hidden behind the gate wasn't a treasury.

It was an armory.

CHAPTER 16

TREASURE HUNT: PURE ONES

J ake wasn't the only one staring at what lay beyond the
gate. Reika seemed somewhat surprised too, and the
many others who had attempted the puzzle also seemed
highly interested in figuring out the big prize for
solving it.

Yet, he doubted many of them noticed the uniqueness of the
room. Jake felt an odd aura in the room, different from anything
he had encountered prior, yet also slightly familiar. He sensed
curses within. Not just one, but many. Yet even these curses felt
different. They somehow felt less insidious, like they didn't carry
any hatred towards him. Usually, curses seemed to just want to
destroy anyone and everything, lashing out at whoever came into
contact with it... but not these ones.

He walked inside with Reika, none of the observers daring
to follow.

"It's an armory of some kind... but these items..." Reika
frowned and inspected a common-rarity sword that looked to be
made of silver.

Jake also threw it a look, and the conclusion was obvious.
"These are anti-vampire weapons."

He identified a random one placed on a rack.

[Sword of the Pure Ones (Common)] – A shortsword made of an unknown metal created by the Pure Ones— enlightened inhabitants of the Yalsten world who had not turned to vampires and were hunted down and made into food as the hunger of the vampires grew. The enchantment placed on the sword is specifically made to hunt down vampires and will deal extra damage. All attacks against vampiric foes will deal extra damage to their vital energy.

Requirements: Lvl 100+ in any humanoid race.

"Quite the lore," Jake noted after he read over the item.

Reika looked his way and asked, "Just to make sure there is no disparity in information, what have you learned of this world so far? To my knowledge, it was inhabited by some humanoid race that eventually chose to become vampires, some catastrophe happened, and their civilization devolved and fractured, especially after the dimension became isolated."

Jake proceeded to give the information he had gained from the projection and also came to learn that the other factions had found a lot of similar things. Small crystals with recordings on them located in the plains, written messages or even projections in the abandoned houses in the Mistless Plains, and, of course, also information from other towers. However, Jake also came to learn that the information didn't precisely match up everywhere.

The projection had told Jake some people either hadn't chosen to turn or hadn't been judged worthy of being vampires... but the existence of this room and some information Reika had learned made him believe it wasn't quite that simple. No, there'd been an entirely different faction in this world who opposed the vampires, known as the Pure Ones. People who'd refused to become vampires and opposed the establishment.

How they hadn't just been slaughtered by the kings or something like that, he wasn't sure. Maybe they'd been deemed a necessary evil? Good fighting practice? Or perhaps they'd coexisted until shit hit the fan and the vampires began hunting down anything they could.

Or maybe, just maybe, this entire world was just fake as fuck, and set up as a scenario by the system for the Treasure Hunt, and everything was just background lore to make it all more interesting. Either way, it didn't matter. What mattered was that they had just found an entire armory of anti-vampire weapons.

"There are hundreds of weapons here," Reika noted as she checked the weapon-lined walls.

The armory was cross-shaped, with a long hallway at the start and a path to each side. Weapons lined the walls, including swords, spears, knives, crossbows and bolts, scimitars, glaive-like weapons, and overall just a lot of stabby things. Interestingly enough, no blunt weapons, making Jake think blunt damage probably wasn't very good against vampires. He would have to try hitting one with the Pillar next time.

"That there is," Jake agreed before adding on, "But let's get to the good stuff."

He could see that she also wanted to check out the central room, where a large cube of opaque glass gave off an aura, making it obvious valuables were within. The glass had a magical opening where it seemed to almost be made of water. In fact, the entire cube seemed more like a mix between a magical barrier and a physical one.

"I'll head inside first," Jake said as they stood in front of it. He decided to be the first to enter in case it was a trap. He was confident he could escape due to his danger sense if things went south—and if not, he could probably just tank the damage.

Upon entering, he finally discovered where all that curse energy came from... It had been leaking from that cube. Jake saw a total of five items within. Four weapons, all surrounding a central pedestal with a floating... wooden... stake.

Is the system actually fucking with us?

Jake motioned for Reika to enter after him, and when she did, she also saw the wooden stake and stopped up.

"Isn't that a wooden stake?" she asked pensively.

"Sure is," he answered in a deadpan tone.

"Made by vampire hunters."

"Yep."

"I... Why... Is the system messing with us or what?" she asked in exasperation, mimicking Jake's own thoughts.

"It appears to be completely serious," Jake answered with a smirk as he identified the stake.

[Stake of the Pure Ones (Unique)] – A cursed wooden stake created by the Pure Ones—enlightened inhabitants of the Yalsten world who had not turned to vampires and were hunted down and made into food as the hunger of the vampires grew. The stake gives off an aura that hides the wielder from a Count of Blood, and it will deal substantial damage if driven into any vampire. The curse will inhibit the regeneration of the impaled vampire. Only works on Counts and below. Holding this item will contribute significantly to your final reward.

Requirement: N/A

It was indeed a real item with very real effects. In addition... it was a damn quest item, one hundred percent. The item also made something else clear... Jake had really done this entire Treasure Hunt in the wrong order. The intended plan was likely to first collect information, get to know of the vampires and the Pure Ones, discover this armory and get a Mark of Blood, and then go for the Count.

Jake had identified the stake as similar to the quest items during the tutorial he had used to fight the King of the Forest, though those had been far stronger. In retrospect, it was actually quite insane. That shadow bead and the tusk both held curses and energies more powerful than even this stake...

"This wooden stake appears to be the primary reward of this puzzle, and considering you were the primary contributor to solving it, I believe you should take it," Reika said.

"Oh?" Jake exclaimed, a bit surprised. He was sure she would have wanted it. There was just one thing. "Nah, I don't want it."

"Excuse me? What? Why not" she asked with a perplexed expression.

"Why would I? The purpose of it is clearly to weaken a Count of Blood to fight them more easily. Why would I ever do that?" Jake just shrugged.

"I..." She looked at him for a moment before pausing and nodding. "Thank you. I believe it only fair, then, that you take the rest of the weapons here."

"Sure thing," Jake agreed. They could figure out what to do with the rest of the armory later, but clearly, this room was where the good shit was at.

Jake looked at one of the four weapons—a spear—and Identified it.

[Spear of the Pure Ones (Rare)] – A long metal spear with a wooden spearhead created by the Pure Ones—enlightened inhabitants of the Yalsten world who had not turned to vampires and were hunted down and made into food as the hunger of the vampires grew. The enchantment placed on the spear will deal extra damage to vampiric vitality by injecting them with a unique type of venom specifically concocted to kill vampires. Enchantments: Venom of the Pure Ones.

Requirements: Lvl 110+ in any humanoid race.

Yep, it was a potent vampire-hunting weapon that even had venom that worked especially well against vampires. The other three weapons were a sword, a halberd, and a dagger. All of them rare rarity, and all of them with the same venom enchantment.

Jake tossed them all in his inventory as Reika put the stake in hers. As they moved out of the room, Jake took out the dagger again and casually stabbed it into his shoulder, not even stopping his walk.

"What the hell!?" Reika yelled as Jake made sure not to drip any blood on the floor.

Jake shrugged. "What? Just getting a taste of this venom."

Part of it was to fuck with her, but the main reason was to actually get a feel for the toxin and analyze it with Palate of the Malefic Viper. He didn't plan on replicating it, but just having experienced it would allow him to maybe use some of the concepts of the venom with Touch of the Malefic Viper.

"... How does that even work?" Reika asked, her voice a mix of resignation and genuine curiosity.

"I have a skill that allows me to learn about anything alchemy-related I consume and absorb. That includes poison that has afflicted me. Very handy to have, but it does have its downsides... such as being forced to eat copious amounts of mushrooms." That brought back some bad memories.

"Is that seriously a skill?"

"Yep, a great one. Anyway, let's move down the next corridor."

Jake led her towards one of the wings of the armory. Reika followed him in silence, seemingly deep in thought. She looked internally conflicted between staying cordial and being incredibly curious.

Entering the left wing of the armory, they found a smithy and a bookshelf filled with books. Jake swiftly pulled one of the books off the shelf and checked it out. He saw it contained recipes and blueprints for making anti-vampire weapons.

Reika also went over, pulled a book off the shelf, and quickly scanned through a few pages.

"This stuff seems great for the Treasure Hunt itself, but I'm unsure about its usefulness outside," Jake commented on the books, not very interested in them himself. "Unless the Noboru clan has some vampire problem I don't know about?"

His puzzle partner just threw him a glance. "This Treasure Hunt is my first time encountering one."

"Damn, and here I was hoping Earth secretly had hidden vampires trying to meld in with humanity," he joked as he skimmed a few more of the books. They were truly all about smithing, and there weren't even any mentions of the venom.

"Pretty sure we would have found any Earth vampires already, as they would surely be glinting under sunlight."

Jake stopped up as he looked at Reika, and she looked back at him, clearly a bit embarrassed. *Did she just make a joke?*

He smiled as he nodded and went along. "Yeah, but I doubt they would even be an issue, as they would all be too busy stalking teenage girls and spending all their time creepily watching them sleep."

"Or battling werewolves who have the magical abilities to somehow preserve their pants when exiting their transformations," Reika doubled down with a smile.

"System fuckery for sure," Jake said, nodding and faking seriousness. During this time, both had been skimming over all the books in the smithy, and eventually, they had to return to actually doing work. "Anyway, do you have any interest in the things within this smithy? There doesn't seem to be any materials to use, but considering there are still nearly one and a half weeks left in the Treasure Hunt, I could see some smiths who would have time to make something useful."

"I do believe the Noboru clan would have interest in this smithy, yes," she responded, also back in professional mode. "Are you certain Haven doesn't want to acquire it?"

"No idea, really, but we barely entered with any people, so as long as you guys are fine with letting in one or two people from Haven, it should be fine. It would be a bit of a dick move to just claim the entire smithy for the potential that someone may want to come here."

"Thanks," she said with a smile. "Let's check out the other wing?"

"Sure."

They quickly went over to the other wing, and on the way, he saw that people were still gathered outside the gate. None had dared to take a step inside. It was a bit weird, and he couldn't help but pose a question to Reika as they walked.

"Does your clan want all of those common-rarity weapons? I just considered if we should maybe just hand them to the people who tried to open the gate."

Jake himself didn't need them, and he didn't really think they would contribute much to any kind of final reward. He would rather just hand them over to the people who had spent a good while trying to solve the puzzle to make sure they at least got something out of it. Also, he was pretty certain most of them could use them to fight the vampires. From what he had seen, while many had okay gear, all of the weapons in this armory were D-grade anti-vampire weapons. So they were bound to be useful.

"Hm, while the clan could use them, I believe that handing out the common-rarity ones and keeping the uncommon-rarity and above weapons shouldn't lead to any issues," Reika agreed after thinking for a second.

"Great, let's tell them when we're done. Let's check out the alchemy lab ahead first."

Yeah, he had taken a sneak-peek with his sphere—earning a surprised look from Reika—but she didn't say anything. They quickly got to the right wing of the armory and opened the door, leading into an alchemy lab, just as Jake had said.

It quickly became clear this was where the venom used on the weapons had been made, and here too was a bookshelf on alchemical anti-vampire creations. Jake and Reika split the books, Jake taking all of those related to poison—which was the majority—and Reika taking those related to creating anti-

vampire materials and catalysts, such as some way of transmuting wood to make it better against vampires. It was a fair
split, in Jake's opinion.

Reika told Jake that everything else was his, as she had been
given the smithy, and Jake gladly stole everything in the entire
lab. All the tables, a few common and uncommon-rarity caul-
drons that still worked, a slew of other tools, and even the bookshelf the books had been on. While he was looting, Reika went
and took all the uncommon-rarity weapons from outside, also
splitting those fifty-fifty with him. When Jake was done in the
alchemy lab, the room was bare, and Reika looked at him
weirdly.

"Do you really need *all* of it?"

"Would it not be better to ask, how can I know I won't need
all of it? Why would one not claim all one can in the event it
becomes useful down the line?" Jake countered, making a throw-
back to their first interaction. She was just jealous that most of
the things in the smithy couldn't be easily moved but were built
into the room.

She looked at him, a bit embarrassed as her ears turned red,
but swiftly changed the subject. "We're done here, right? Let's
get out of here and tell those waiting outside they can take the
weapons they want."

Jake resisted the urge to shake his head and just nodded in
approval instead. He had to admit, all of this was a nice intermission between vampire hunting. Because he would go hunting
soon again... and the stake earlier had also revealed one other
thing that Reika didn't seem to have taken notice of.

The stake said it worked on Counts of Blood and below.

That meant there had to be vampires higher in the food
chain than the Counts still present in the Treasure Hunt.

CHAPTER 17

TREASURE HUNT: BLOOD

J ake considered what his next step would be as Reika was hard at work.

After dividing all the loot and telling the people outside they could enter, Reika called her followers to keep watch over the smithy, with several blacksmiths also included in this group. They only took a few minutes to arrive, and Jake saw they looked a bit more haggard than before, carrying the remnants of curse energy on their bodies. It was easy to see they had been fighting those cursed armor golems.

The two followers stood guard at the smithy as they waited for members of the Noboru clan to arrive. A few had already been in the gallery of observers before, and now, more were coming from a basecamp in the central plains.

Reika and Jake walked out of the armory, and the room with the puzzle was now close to empty.

"Something has been on my mind for a while," Reika suddenly said. "Why would one hide an armory in the middle of enemy territory like this? It doesn't make any logical sense, much less to ensure it with some magical puzzle and not a key or something like that."

"I actually think it makes a lot of sense," Jake said. "Especially to make it a magic puzzle. That meant one had to have some level of power and experience to open it, and you couldn't just take a random unturned human and have that person open it with just a bit of mana."

"What stops a vampire from just solving the puzzle?" she asked him, genuinely confused.

"Vampires don't have mana. At least, not the same kind as you and I or really anything else I have met do. Instead, they seem to have some kind of unique energy that serves many of the same functions but is fundamentally different. I think this energy may have also been the cause of their downfall."

He had fought the Count and noticed this difference in energy pretty much right away. He just called their energy "blood energy" in his head because it was red and looked like blood, and knowing the system's naming sense, he was probably right on the money.

"They don't? That... I didn't even consider that." Reika looked to be deep in thought as she considered the implications of that.

As Reika stood there, Jake noticed one of her followers come out of the armory towards them. It was the communications guy, as far as Jake could tell.

"Mr. Thayne, I bring a message from the Patriarch," the man said, confirming he was the communications guy. Reika also perked up at the mention of the head of the Noboru clan, and Jake raised an eyebrow—hidden under his mask, of course.

"Do tell," he answered.

"The Patriarch relays the message that you should have your meeting in the center of the Mistless Plains at the hidden tower once all keys are gathered, and he would like to propose a bet. There are nine keys... so the one to bring five will get priority in exploring the hidden tower. He also expresses his hopes that you and his great-granddaughter are getting along and that you treat her kindly."

Jake bit onto that first part. "Oh, so he's out there hunting

Counts too, huh? Better tell him to hurry up. Also... I don't mean to be an ass, but let's not assume it's only he and I who are capable of matching those vampires. Especially not after what we just found."

The man smiled almost triumphantly as he added, "He knows you are one key ahead and that others are also capable of defeating these Counts... but he still stands by his words to bring five. Because if you don't, he will."

I'll take that as a challenge, Jake thought. The Noboru clan had made it clear they were willing to challenge any other faction who managed to obtain a key, which meant Jake would either have to do the same... or just get those five keys by himself.

"Well, then, tell him the game is on," Jake said, smiling as he turned to Reika. "Oh, and do remember to make use of the wooden stake. Maybe give it to him. Perhaps he will need it to help him make up the difference."

Reika had been looking a bit embarrassed since the conversation began, no doubt due to the whole thing about treating her well. Jake got it. It was always awkward when a grandparent said something like that in front of others, making him smile a bit internally. Jake had also had a good relationship with his grandparents before they passed, and it was only good that Reika seemed to have a positive one with her great-grandfather.

She looked up at him before she steeled her look. "Don't think he will be the only one from the clan hunting down Counts."

Jake looked at her and smiled. "Good luck to you. But be warned they aren't that easily taken down, and I would advise you against trying to beat one with numbers, as weaker humans are little more than walking health potions to a vampire, as far as I can tell. Of course, you also have the stake, so, yeah, happy hunting!"

"Thanks, and you too," Reika replied, giving Jake a bow. That they would naturally split up after the puzzle was done and the loot distributed had been a tacit understanding. Besides, they didn't really have any reason to stay grouped up.

Jake did add on one more line as he left with a wave over his shoulder while walking. "Cya around, Reika. It's been fun."

"You too... Jake. Take care and stay safe," she half-yelled as Jake smiled under his mask.

Well, he didn't know about that last part. Jake wasn't known as the type to take care of himself, nor to stay safe. He was more the type that would head straight for danger. Sadly, he could not go to the next tower right away; he had to find a Mark of Blood first. He did throw a mental message towards Sylphie, and she sent back something about having fun, but that the next floating Mark thing wasn't Sylphie's but her friend's. So he would have to get one himself.

Jake knew there were likely other treasures still in the tower; in fact, he was certain there were. He hadn't called the structure a mega-structure for no reason, after all. Even just sprinting down the stairs, he felt mana in the distance and a response from his boots that there were treasures. However, he also felt the mana of other people, and he didn't have any inclinations of coming in and stealing any loot. He was confident that what had been in the chamber of the Count and the puzzle room was the best there was.

It didn't take him long to get out of the tower, and when he reached the bottom, he saw many other entrances. So, yeah, no need to enter from some balcony.

People made way for him as he exited out into the plains, and Jake had to hold back the impulse to steal the gates. It would be a bit too much for even him to spend half an hour slowly burning off a gate with people passing by and looking weirdly at him all the meanwhile. No... he would have to play it smarter and find isolated gates to steal.

Because he was one hundred percent still going to steal some gates.

The Viscount of Blood stumbled as she landed another slash of her long claws on the human in front of her.

Her claws cut through the man and sent blood splashing everywhere as his entire body was ripped apart. The severed arm hit the wall, and his guts spilled all over the floor.

The man's body was fully healed the next moment, and he stood in the same position as before the Viscount had attacked as if nothing had ever happened—the only sign being the newly made splatter of blood and some more guts on the floor. He stood in the exact same place he had been standing from the moment she awakened. Where he had been standing for the last five hours, just staring at her.

Exhaustion was apparent in the movements of the vampire. Her attacks and steps were sluggish and slow, the red glow in her eyes dimming. Meanwhile, the man only moved to comb back his hair and continue staring at her, never allowing her to leave his sight.

When his head was severed, the eyes of the severed head stayed on her body. Even when the entire head was squashed, it returned a moment later to observe her.

The vampire tried to drink his blood but found itself poisoned by the vitality she consumed, dealing even more damage. It was not the first time she had tried, but she was desperate. Finally, the vampire just slumped back and sat on the ground, heaving. The tomb was completely locked, with just the man and the Viscount inside.

Once the vampire was done fighting... unable to go on... the man made a sad smile and nodded towards her.

"Thank you." He went forward and lovingly placed his hand on the top of her head as he comfortingly spoke, "Your sacrifice will not be in vain."

The vampire looked up at him, her eyes dimming as her life came to an end, not a single wound on her body. She turned to ash and left behind the Mark of Blood while a side room with treasures opened up.

At the same time, the door to the tomb opened, and a dozen or so people stood right outside it. They all looked at the man, complicated emotions in their eyes, yet none said anything. They just looked on as he slowly went over and claimed all the loot before walking out of the tomb, all of them making way.

Once outside, a man and a woman were ready to receive him. "How did it go?" the woman asked with genuine concern.

The man, still dirty from the happenings before this, sighed. "The sparks are corrupted... broken... yet whole. I know more now, but still not enough. Come, let us continue as we seek out one of these Counts."

Back at the tomb, one of the people who had been waiting took a look inside and stared wide-eyed. It was pure carnage inside. Guts everywhere, severed limbs by the hundreds, and a horrific smell. Everything was just red—even the walls and ceiling. Yet the worst was the floor.

The floor looked like that of a flooded cellar. The liquid on the floor wasn't water, but blood—thousands upon thousands of liters of it.

All of it human.

———

Jake ran through the dense mist, heading towards a hill far away from the tower. He was headed towards one he was certain no one had been to before due to the long distance and how it was slightly hidden behind two other hills and several actual towers. Not mountain towers, but buildings made to look like buildings. He decided to check those out first and sprinted along the plains, scanning them with his sphere all the while. He noticed everything had already been cleaned up, and considered who it could be until he saw faint movement ahead.

Something small was flying through the air silently, barely

visible in the mist, as it was camouflaged and nearly invisible, a lot like the vampire's invisibility. But, as he saw it, he also spotted a common-rarity staff of sorts embedded in the ground, seemingly just left there when someone went "fuck it" and stuck it into the ground before leaving.

Jake went closer to get a better look and saw this small, flying thing descend towards the staff. The moment it flew down and made contact with the staff, several metal wires were sent out, wrapping themselves around the weapon before pulling it from the ground.

The second the staff stopped touching the ground, it just disappeared.

Now he was really curious about the thing's identity. He used One Step Mile to get over there quickly, and in a snap, he stood before the flying thing—which he now recognized.

"Arnold?" he asked the drone in front of him as it promptly dispelled its camouflage. It was nearly entirely circular, about the size of a basketball in diameter, with one large, completely silent rotor at the bottom.

"What?" Jake heard from the drone, the voice completely unrecognizable. In fact, there was nothing about the drone to even indicate someone controlled it.

"How the hell did you put the staff inside the storage?" he asked. Probably not the question most would have asked, but it was what Jake was wondering the most.

"It's done through touch, and I touched it," Arnold answered through the drone.

"Okay... and how does the mist affect the drones, by the way?"

"The mist is based on a curse. Curses target living entities. Drones and robots don't count as living, so curses don't work—at least, not this variant."

Jake got the hint that the dude really didn't want to chat, but just get on with it. "Cool stuff. See you around."

With that, the drone became invisible again and flew away

without another word spoken. Jake was pretty darn confident Arnold had found a loophole or something. He wasn't entirely sure how he had managed to loot stuff through the drones... but then again, he and Sylphie shared an inventory due to the peculiar way the Hunter Insignia worked.

It was good to see that people from Haven were doing well, though. He was sure the others were managing too. They were all competent in their own rights, and even if they got in trouble, he was certain they could get out using the Insignia.

Jake continued on his journey toward the towers. When he got close, he saw they were made of a mix of wood and stone, with each of them having a metal gate. Sadly, it wasn't the awesome super metal like at the mountain towers, but just some boring metal.

He opened the gate and got inside. The entire tower was only about fifty meters tall, and while that was a lot by old-world standards, it was just a small building in this new world. It was pretty wide, though, and inside, Jake found that this one had clearly been a living space of some kind.

The primary clue for this was the bones. Yes, bones. Which meant this place had not been inhabited by vampires, but more regular enlightened species. Jake saw several kinds of bones— some he clearly recognized as humans, but many were also slightly different. Some bones were different in shape, while some of the skeletons were just too small.

Small, but still robust. *Dwarves?*

Another kind of skeleton was thinner than humans, and their shape reminded him a bit of the projection he had seen during the Undergrowth dungeon. So, elves. He also saw some that were bigger and some even smaller, and some that were just weird, including those with tails.

Jake quickly went through the entire tower and found only a few minor items and a few pieces of furniture. He also noticed that while the tower's first floor was a living space, the ones above were certainly not. They were cells.

"I guess I just found out where they kept the livestock..." Jake muttered as he left the tower again.

He didn't even bother checking any of the other towers, instead heading straight for the hill ahead. Considering none had entered any of the towers, he was certain he was the first to be there.

Time to speedrun this vampire hunt!

CHAPTER 18

TREASURE HUNT: BROKEN TOWER

The Viscount tried to close his mouth, but was unable to as it encountered material far too tough for his razor-sharp teeth to get through. To make matters worse for the vampire, he was repeatedly stabbed in the chest with an envenomed anti-vampire weapon while he struggled against the merciless human finishing him off.

Jake only lifted his foot, which he had stomped inside the vampire's mouth, when he got the notification, also quickly checking that the vampire hadn't even managed to make a single mark on the boots. To be honest, he felt genuinely bad about this kill. Nevertheless, he had gone in and stuck with his desire to test out the anti-vampire weapon... and he had done so.

The hills were actually grave hills filled entirely with ghouls. The doors to keep them closed weren't able to keep out the mist entirely, making the halls filled with it. He had stormed through and easily located the tomb of the Viscount. There, he'd found one of the great metal gates with a magic circle to stop him from getting in. Well, he'd broken that one with some arcane energy, and the moment he'd done so, the vampire had awakened... revealing what looked like a damn kid.

Mind you, it hadn't been a kid, but what Jake guessed was a

dwarf. Still, Jake had felt bad about the entire ordeal. The vampire dwarf could at least have had a beard to make it all less awkward as Jake borderline curb-stomped the much smaller enemy.

Am I racist? Jake asked himself as he looted the Mark of Blood, went over to a newly opened side-room, and also swiped that empty. *Is it considered racist to feel bad about fighting certain races?*

He began burning off the gate with Alchemical Flame as the thoughts kept coming. *I remember it being a common trope that men refuse to fight women, which is often called sexist. Now, that would be incredibly dumb with the system making physical differences not matter... and size doesn't really matter too... but... why the fuck did the dwarf have to look like a kid?*

Seriously, it had felt like a mental attack struck him every time he hit the dwarven vampire. To make it worse, even the voice had sounded childish. If it had at least been overly manly, he could have looked past it, but come on... Shit, he still held doubt that it hadn't been a kid, considering the trope about vampire children never growing up.

No, Jake, your murder of little people was fully justified.

Jake committed himself to hunt down enemies without any prejudice and bigotry. He would be an equal opportunity hunter.

After finishing burning off the door, he did a final check of the room. Surprisingly enough, the wooden coffin the vampire had been in wasn't an item at all. But upon closer inspection... he had a feeling it had been. Maybe it had run out of energy or stopped working, or maybe it was just a cheap one-time thing, with the Counts having the good coffins.

Leaving the tomb, he swiftly moved on and stormed towards the next tower. The issue was that there were more than nine of the large mega-structure mountains, but only nine Counts, as far as he could tell. Or maybe there were more than nine, and they only had a chance to drop a key? Wait—perhaps just the first nine dropped one?

Either way, he would have to find a mountain that wasn't already being attacked by another powerful faction. He didn't really feel like getting into some big fight with the Holy Church or that Valhal place or anything like that. Not quite yet, at least.

So, he headed towards a mountain tower even further away from the Mistless Plains. The plains were the center of this Treasure Hunt, and the further you got away from there, the fewer people. He went deeper into the dense mist than he had been before, and deeper than he had seen anyone go.

While he ran, he inspected the weapon in his hand. It was the sword from the Pure Ones' armory, and it was now pristine and clean once more, as the vampire blood on it had evaporated. He had absorbed a bit of the venom on it earlier and gotten a basic understanding, but he now understood it even better after the live test.

As the name said, it was anti-vampire venom that had the primary function of stopping healing. It was actually a bit like his hemotoxin, except this venom only worked on vampires. And it truly did only work on vampires.

Jake hadn't taken any damage from the venom he had afflicted himself with—at least, not from the venom directly. Of course, it had still taken a small number of health points to dispel the inherently antagonistic energy, but he would compare it to the time he used poison arrows on the cloud elementals. Sure, the poison did technically do a bit of damage simply due to it being foreign energy, but the anti-vampire properties of the venom didn't actually do anything to a human like him.

If he compared it to his own uncommon-rarity Necrotic Poison, Jake's was far superior when it came to dealing damage, even to the vampires. The venom from the weapons was better at stopping them from healing themselves, though. Judging by the Viscount, it also seemed to make it harder for the vampires to use their magic, at least somewhat.

Determining what was better was difficult, but only if taken in isolation. Because using the venom meant Jake had to use the Pure Ones' weapons. And among those weapons was no bow or arrows, and while the melee weapons were fine, he preferred the Nanoblade and the scimitar. Also, no, he couldn't use his regular poison with the fancy anti-vampire weapons. Toxins just didn't play well together like that.

With the way the venom worked, he also had to compound it by dealing constant damage. Which meant less time spent shooting with his bow. Also, while he now had a lot of recipe books to make a poison to counter the vampires, it really wouldn't be worth his time to sit down and do alchemy here and now.

Exiting his thoughts, Jake entered another mountain building. This one was much like the other one, but once he got inside, he did notice some differences. More accurately, one major damn difference: the mist hadn't been kept out.

It filled the halls, and as Jake sprinted through them, he made a mental note to steal the gate on his way out.

The further inside Jake got, the more apparent the difference between this mountain and the other one became. While the other mountain had been a mess, he wouldn't exactly have called it a ruin. The walls had been whole, all the stone furniture had still been there, and overall it hadn't looked like a tornado had torn through—unlike this one.

Walls had been broken somehow, the rooms were unrecognizable, and the entire thing looked absolutely ruined. Jake frowned at first but soon felt something from beneath his feet. A faint pulse that he instantly recognized as the response his boots had to a natural treasure.

It came from far above. Jake chose to head towards where he expected the atrium to be to get a faster way up than looking for a stairway that wasn't completely broken. He had seen a total of two former elevators, but both of those were blocked, making them unfeasible too.

However, just as he crossed a corner, four signs of movement entered his sphere. Judging by their reactions, it was obvious they were aware of his position too.

How? Jake wondered as he recognized their forms. The four of them turned a corner not long after, entering his line of sight.

[Reanimated Blackguard Golem – lvl 113]

[Reanimated Blackguard Golem – lvl 111]

[Reanimated Blackguard Golem – lvl 109]

[Reanimated Blackguard Golem – lvl 111]

Jake stared at them as they charged him with abandon, then just sighed, raised his hand, and fired out a blast of arcane energy, stopping them in their tracks. He then took out his bow and fired down the hallway. While it was around ten meters in width and six meters in height, making it a large-as-hell hallway by Earth standards, it was still considered a narrow space by D-grade standards. Much more so when one got bombarded by exploding arrows.

It took him only a few minutes to finish them off and promptly continue on his journey. Yet he had barely managed to get down a single hall before another group of those Blackguards appeared. Only three this time.

A few more explosions later, and they were dead. If living armor could even die. Well, the system said Jake had "slain" them, so he counted it as killing. Too bad they didn't give any experience, but then again, they were weak as hell. Their only really dangerous attack was their self-destruction upon death, but Jake used this awesome technique called *not being close* to avoid that.

Jake moved down another corridor with even more golems coming. This repeated over and over again, Jake leaving a trail of carnage behind him until he finally made it to the atrium. When he got there, he saw that the destruction wasn't limited to the entry area.

What looked like a grand indoor space in the other tower now looked like an absolute ruin. Several of the balconies were broken, pretty much every railing torn apart. To make it worse, Jake saw golems. Not just a few, either.

Standing in that open space, Jake felt the attention of hundreds of beings upon him. *Well, that's something, ain't it?*

Now, the usual and reasonable response to being seen by hundreds of foes between level 105 to 140 would be to run or maybe try and find a better position to fight them from. What Jake did wasn't reasonable at all. He stayed in place and welcomed them. If he wanted to explore the tower... he would have to clean it out first. That much was certain.

Like a horde of rampaging zombies, they stormed him. By now, it was clear... this tower would not hold secrets like the last one. That didn't mean it would hold no secrets, just not the same ones, and he also severely doubted a Count still resided within. When he looked up the atrium, he saw the dark mist hang above, including around the floors where he would expect a Count to be.

I'll go check in a while, Jake thought as he cracked his neck at the hundreds of approaching golems.

To describe what transpired next as a fight would be facetious. It was simply the desperate struggle of an unfeeling army of golems trying to slay one person. Jake felt them all close in, and with his bow in hand, he moved.

Arrows flew and exploded, arcane bolts blasted everything away, blades appeared and cut and tore apart his foes. Through it all, he moved in between them, teleporting away whenever necessary. Jake was bombarded with attacks himself, including some golems with bows, but none even got close to hitting him.

A hundred golems died within the first half an hour, Jake barely with sweat on his brows.

Two hundred and fifty died within an hour as he began to get the hang of it.

Five hundred were dead after two hours, with Jake getting a bit sweaty and taking a few minor wounds.

Seven hundred golems and two and a half hours after the battle began, they stopped coming. The mist turned silent once more, and the only thing that moved was a single human sitting and breathing heavily in the middle of the atrium, the ground around him blackened from his bow's Scorched Plains attack. He had seen the result versus the Count and had repeated it again, this time to kill nearly forty grouped-up golems at once to finish the fight.

As he closed his eyes and entered meditation to relax, he went through the notifications, but only the ones that gave experience. The rest, he just filtered out.

You have slain [Reanimated Blackguard Golem – lvl 134] – Bonus experience earned for killing an enemy above your level

....

You have slain [Reanimated Blackguard Golem – lvl 132] – Bonus experience earned for killing an enemy above your level

Besides the Blackguards, there had also been five Knights sprinkled in for good measure towards the end, as they had descended from the upper floors.

You have slain [Reanimated Black Knight Golem – lvl 136] – Bonus experience earned for killing an enemy above your level

...

You have slain [Reanimated Black Knight Golem – lvl 140] – Bonus experience earned for killing an enemy above your level

It sounded like a lot... seven hundred or so golems... but only twenty-three had actually granted him any experience, including all five Knights. In fact, he had a feeling those five gave more experience than the eighteen Blackguards put together.

To his surprise, when he was done with spring cleaning, he had actually gotten a level.

* 'DING!' Class: [Avaricious Arcane Hunter] has reached level 131 - Stat points allocated, +10 Free Points*

It shouldn't be a surprise to get a level after so much killing... but his class drawbacks weren't there for nothing. He knew that any other class would have gotten a lot more experience overall. At least, he'd thought so, but now he wasn't entirely sure.

Jake knew his level-up couldn't simply be due to those twenty-three golems. Unless he'd been damn close to a level after the Count, he didn't see it happening. So... maybe it was due to the presence of all the other golems? Due to the added difficulty? Jake knew experience gain wasn't just black and white, where an enemy at X level gave Y experience when killed. It depended on an endless amount of variables that even Villy wasn't sure about.

Jake was also acutely aware that skills like Mark of the Avaricious Hunter and hidden buffs to experience gain from higher-leveled enemies muddied the water. This was why he ultimately decided trying to figure out some grand formula was a waste of time. Him knowing wouldn't change his level-up speed, and he already knew the most optimal way to level up was to fight foes many levels above himself.

During the fight, Jake had been smart enough to drink potions to limit his downtime once done, so he would soon be ready to go again. More than resources, he needed to relax his mind after the fight. He sat in meditation for a good fifteen minutes while thinking over all of those experience-related things and going through notifications. He was still relatively low on mana, around forty percent, but he would manage. Also, it was mana potion time in twenty minutes.

And while the bow wouldn't empower his arrows while it recharged itself, he was okay with that and would manage without.

He continued up the tower, and was soon forced to do something he'd hoped he could avoid. He stopped flying just before he reached the black mist, then covered his body in dark green scales. Using his hands, he formed a barrier of arcane mana around him as he entered the mist.

The layout of the topmost floor was identical to the one with the Count on it, besides a few minor changes.

Jake got to a large gate that wasn't there in the last tower, right at the entrance to the web of halls that would eventually lead to the Count's chambers. And behind the gate, he saw the movement of black living armors wandering aimlessly. He sighed internally. *Well, these ones are at least all Knights.*

He went closer to the gate, and it instantly responded to his arcane barrier's touch by beginning to open. As it opened, the entire gate cracked and slowly fell apart into hundreds of fractured chunks of metal. Thick, black mist gave off a strong sense of danger, forcing Jake to quickly retreat.

As he did so, the golems behind the door reacted too. Nearly fifty empty helmets turned his way. Even more of them were deeper within. Jake did the only rational thing he could: he turned around and began running back through the halls to get a better fighting position. In other words, somewhere that wasn't surrounded by cursed black mist, such as the atrium down below. Mind you, Jake hadn't actually planned to pull them right away... but what's done was done, and now he would have to fight.

He needed to clear these Knights out anyway—not just for

experience, but because he was certain of one thing... the natural treasure was located where the Count's chamber would usually be. By now, he was also beginning to believe his original assessment of there not being a Count's chamber was wrong.

Jake just seriously doubted he would find any Count within... which made him think what else could now dwell within.

CHAPTER 19

TREASURE HUNT: ROOT OF RESENTMENT

The difference between Knights and Blackguards was slight, and primarily registered in the level difference. They even looked the same, with the Knights being slightly slicker and a bit faster and more agile, but that also came with the Knights being slightly less tanky.

Now, slightly less tanky didn't mean they weren't tanky. In fact, due to their levels, they were tankier than nearly all Blackguards. The only good thing about them was that they were what Jake would classify as trash mobs. Filler enemies that, individually, would rarely be a challenge to anyone of equal level, and who didn't really possess any interesting skills or dangerous abilities. The only thing the Knights could do was to blow up when they died, just like the Blackguards.

However, what they did have were numbers and durability. Enough numbers and durability to make Jake pretty much run out of mana after he had killed thirty of them. Luckily, he had a mana potion at the ready and consumed one to keep fighting with close to optimal power.

Even during the previous fight, he'd used Limit Break at 10% throughout, and now he pushed it to 20% to finish it off as quickly as possible. He could afford to lose the stamina, as his mana expenditure was far larger.

In the end, while the Knights were stronger, Jake was far stronger than even that. One had to remember that these Knights were enemies that could be taken down by the regular parties of humanity, by groups often more than twenty levels below them.

His only struggle was with his resources, but he could kind of keep up by using potions and switching to a more low-maintenance fighting style. He stopped using Splitting Arrow and One Step Mile whenever possible. He limited his use of magic attacks and returned to an older style, swiftly switching weapons between melee and ranged. The only active skill he used was his arcane arrows.

Yet to his dismay, they kept coming. The gate that had fallen apart when he touched it had housed an army of those Knights. He had believed there was perhaps a hundred total, with an average level around 135. After killing that number and seeing how more came, he had to reevaluate and realize he had severely lowballed it.

They just kept fucking coming. Jake's low-maintenance style could keep him going for a while. Still, he did have to make some sacrifices in the form of willingly taking less dangerous hits to avoid wasting stamina or mana on teleporting or making a barrier.

But another, perhaps even larger issue was just how tiring it was. More so mentally than physically. He had to constantly dodge and filter information from his sphere. Constantly consider when to attack and find openings. Even a second of inattentiveness would result in him taking severe damage.

Jake kept retreating inside the mountain, going down hallways as he fired arrows after those who chased him or cut them with his blades. Sadly, their self-destruction did nothing to harm their comrades but only cursed Jake whenever he was hit. And he did get hit by the remnants of some explosions, as it simply became unavoidable.

The entire ordeal began taking far longer than it should, due to him constantly having to flee and wait for the moment he could chug down another mana potion to get another period of serious damage output. His brain ended up going on half-autopilot as he dodged sword swing after sword swing, narrowly avoided black waves of dark mist sent his way by spear thrusts, and ducked under arrows surrounded by black mist.

He cut a golem and kicked another as he finally used a mana potion. He also used the oft-forgotten enchantment on his pants —Life Burst—flooding him with both vital energy and mana at the same time to give him a second wind.

Jake pressed the attack by firing off explosive arrows, cutting down golems, and tearing them apart one by one. The curse in his body did accumulate, but the scales still on his body took the brunt of it, even if it was yet another source of mana expenditure.

This continued as he killed Knight after Knight. Jake was little more than a machine churning through golems. Hundreds of hallways had been left scarred. The atrium had been passed a dozen times as he circled the building, with clear signs of their battle. Then, finally, he kicked away a golem; it exploded a moment later as he drew his bow and prepared an arrow. Yet he stopped up, a flash of confusion passing his otherwise tired, blank eyes.

There was no movement in the hallway.

Jake just stood there with an arrow nocked for five or so seconds. Realization finally struck him, and he lowered his bow and dispelled the arcane arrow. He exited his battle haze and only had the energy to summon the same comfy lounge chair he had used in the puzzle room.

He fell back in it and breathed loudly, not caring about the blood he dirtied it with or the bow that fell on the floor beside him. Jake closed his eyes and slowly slipped into meditation, which quickly became him just taking a nap.

Hours later, he reawakened, his body still sore from the incredible overuse of Limit Break and from having his pools so strained during the fight. "Fuck those tin can fucks," Jake muttered. They weren't even fun to fight; it was just goddamn tedious.

Looking at the timer, Jake saw the Treasure Hunt had now officially entered the second day—and by quite a few hours, even. He had spent far longer killing those damn Knights and Blackguards than expected, just because he felt a natural treasure somewhere above.

Sadly, he couldn't just go up right away, as he was still low on resources and felt sore. So he chugged a stamina potion and entered meditation again, going through all the notifications.

You have slain [Reanimated Black Knight Golem – lvl 131]

...

You have slain [Reanimated Black Knight Golem – lvl 142] – Bonus experience earned for killing an enemy above your level

* 'DING!' Class: [Avaricious Arcane Hunter] has reached level 132 - Stat points allocated, +10 Free Points *

* 'DING!' Race: [Human (D)] has reached level 131 - Stat points allocated, +15 Free Points *

* 'DING!' Class: [Avaricious Arcane Hunter] has reached level 133 - Stat points allocated, +10 Free Points *

*** 'DING!' Class: [Avaricious Arcane Hunter] has reached
level 134 - Stat points allocated, +10 Free Points ***

*** 'DING!' Race: [Human (D)] has reached level 132 - Stat
points allocated, +15 Free Points ***

Jake had killed... a lot. Three hundred and eleven Knights in
total, two hundred and ninety-two of which gave him any experience points. That had resulted in three whole levels... which
meant that in the day since Jake entered this Treasure Hunt, he
had already gotten five total class levels. He had to admit that he
hadn't thought it would lead to this much experience when he
entered the Treasure Hunt. However... it wasn't all great.

While the levels were good, there was one negative aspect...
he had just spent nearly a full day without getting a single piece
of loot. The damn reanimated armors blew themselves up upon
death, and whatever metal was left behind was rusted and shattered like the metal gate that had broken apart. They also only
fell into smaller pieces that tried to curse him when he touched
them. In addition, Jake had killed so many, but none of them
had dropped an orb or a fragment or a shard or anything like
that.

At least he still had more than eight and a half days left to get
something, as he could well and truly say that his idea of
speedrunning the Counts had been utterly ruined.

Hours passed as Jake healed up and consumed potions
whenever he could. He was a bit surprised not a single person
had come to the tower during all this time... but maybe it was
because it looked abandoned and held constant mist within? Or
they'd chosen to focus on towers closer to the Mistless Plains
and their basecamps? According to Reika, all the large factions
had made temporary camps on the plains, so it made sense if
they wanted to stay close.

When he felt up to snuff, he picked up his bow with a string
of mana, got up off the comfortable lounge chair, and put it

back in his inventory, hoping he hadn't lowered its value too much by getting it bloody. He had also discovered that the reason it was so tiring to recover was that damn curse again. He was really getting fed up with these curses.

So, of course, his next course of action was to dive straight into the cursed mist again, scales and arcane barriers at the ready. He had slaughtered a damn army of Knights, so he sure as hell wanted to see what they were hiding.

He flew up and began walking through the now empty halls, trying to keep the curse at bay, heading straight for where his boots told him the natural treasure was. Neither Sense of the Malefic Viper nor any of his other senses gave him information about the treasure; it was only his boots. He reckoned the curse was why his Sense didn't work. As for why the boots worked? Because they were awesome, that's why.

Jake finally made it to the final corner-turn, and by now, he could only see a dozen meters ahead of him even with his insane Perception. He reckoned most more normal D-grades would barely be able to see their outstretched hands.

With the Sphere of Perception, he could naturally see far further, and soon the gate into what he presumed was the Count's chambers appeared. To his utter surprise, the gate was there, good as new, with the same magic circle encountered last time that required the Mark of Blood to open.

The chamber is still intact? What?

He was genuinely confused. Everything else was broken and completely eroded by the curse, yet the gate leading into the chamber didn't look any different. The magic circle seemed utterly unaffected by the curse, and as it protected the gate, no signs were left on that either.

Jake pushed onward through the cursed energy, walking up to the gate. Behind it, he saw destruction, yet it was all a bit vague. It was like how he hadn't been able to see in the dark-affinity Forgotten Sewers before he got used to the dark affinity. In other words, it wasn't that he couldn't see anything; it was that there was too much to see. The fact that it was only like that behind this gate meant one thing... the curse was magnitudes more powerful on the other side. Far more than even what it had been when he tried to fly up along the side of the mountain.

At the same time, his danger sense didn't respond. It was an odd dichotomy... His logic told him what was behind the gate was more dangerous than anything he had ever met in this Treasure Hunt, yet his instincts told him there was no enemy. He looked up and saw the same words on the gate as the last tower, and Jake promptly summoned the Mark of Blood. It resonated with the gate, dispelling the magic circle and opening it.

A flood of pure darkness washed out of the chamber, yet Jake stood in his place as the mist, oddly enough, just skirted around him. It only went a few dozen meters down the hallway behind him, mingling with the existing black mist, before it stopped spreading. By now, it was apparent this mist wasn't natural, but controlled.

Within his sphere, he saw something. A shape appeared, looking oddly human, yet not entirely. It was made up entirely of the cursed mist, and the moment it appeared, an aura spread that was even more powerful than the Count.

Jake narrowed his eyes, and simply by using Identify on the black mist before him, he got a response.

[Yalsten Shade of Eternal Resentment – lvl 160]

"Hello, there," Jake greeted into the darkness.

It squirmed and changed, evermoving, and suddenly the voice of a man sounded out. "How do you carry the Mark of Blood yet remain unturned? Who do you serve?"

Before Jake could answer, another voice came... followed by a goddamn choir.

"It's a human."

"How did he come here?"

"He is with the vampires, is he not?"

"A traitor to the Pure Ones."

"Perhaps he is with the Pure Ones?"

"I wanna go home..."

"Silence, child."

"Are you with the Pure Ones?"

"Who do you serve?"

"Who are you?"

"What are you?"

"Identify yourself."

Jake stood there, bombarded by the voices. Many of them echoed and were hard to discern, talking over each other and interrupting in the middle. These were only what could be construed as sentences too... for in total, hundreds, if not thousands spoke. Thank Villy for high Perception once again.

"I'm a hunter, squarely not on the side of the vampires, and I'm here to hunt down the Counts and kill all the vampires in this place," Jake said, leaving out the part about stealing all their stuff or the Pure Ones being all dead. "I have already killed one Count of Blood, and as for who I work for? Well, I would self-identify as more freelance than working for anyone."

A moment of silence followed before the voices came back with a vengeance.

"Enemy of the vampires?"

"A paladin? A holy warrior?"

"Slayer of the unclean."

"Kill them all?"

"Ally?"

"He has a free lance?"

"He said hunter... A vampire hunter?"

"But does he lie?"

"A liar?

"Lies?"

"He may work for the Counts."

"He said he killed one."

"He lied."

"Traitor."

"We demand proof."

"Evidence."

"Show us proof."

"Proof."

"Proof."

"Proof."

Rather than using words, Jake responded by summoning the key and the heart of the Count. He held them both high before speaking towards the intangible form before him.

"I told you, I'm a hunter here to slay all the vampires. Will you get in my way, or what's the deal?"

The last words were spoken after he unleashed his mana-infused presence. He hadn't been speaking only for the fun of it, but to try and understand what kind of creature he stood before, and he soon found what it was. Behind the pitch-black form of mist was an item that connected to it. Right where the altar had been in the last chamber. It was also this item that gave off the response of a natural treasure.

Once more, the Shade was silent for a few seconds, just taking in his presence. Jake had infused it with his desire to kill the vampires. A genuine emotion that he believed the personalities dwelling within the Shade understood.

"Truth."

"He has slain one."

"But can he slay them all?"

"Counts, he can."

"But what of...?"

"No..."

"Impossible."

"But what if we help?"

"Help."

"We help."

"If you swear to slay them."

"Slay them all."

"Slaughter them."

"Kill them."

"Kill."

"Kill."

"Kill."

"Kill."

"Yeah, I'll kill the vampires; that's the damn point, I promise," Jake said. He was beginning to get a damn headache from the many voices echoing throughout the hall simultaneously, and the constant infusion of will trying to afflict him. While the curse didn't try to harm him, it did try to make him into a bloodthirsty vampire slayer.

Just as he was considering if this entire ordeal was worth it or if he should risk a fight, the Shade once more responded.

The dark mist in the area began swirling and gathering towards the natural treasure like a black hole. Jake was entirely unaffected, and only a second later, he noticed how he could already see a bit farther ahead as the density of mist decreased.

Jake observed the natural treasure for the first time as it gathered energy. It truly had been the chamber of a Count, and he saw the coffin and altar just like in the previous tower. Or what was left of them.

The altar had been cracked into many pieces, and the coffin shattered as a root descended straight down from the ceiling and penetrated the coffin and broken altar. Within the coffin lay only ash, and Jake saw that the entire descending root was rotten and hollow aside from the sharp tip and the meter or so up its length.

He used Identify on the root, and at the same time, he felt the presence of the Shade disperse as the intensity of the curse in the room returned to normal. Except the curse energies didn't hurt him... for no black mist got within five meters of the black root.

[Root of Yalsten's Eternal Resentment (Unique)] – A wooden root from an unknown tree that has absorbed

the curse energies of the black mist that has hung over Yalsten for innumerable years. The deep and eternal resentment towards the vampires that permeates the curse has now been absorbed and concentrated. Will cause disastrous damage and curse any vampire it comes into contact with; however, it can only be used once. While in possession of this root, the cursed mist will not see you as an enemy. Be warned that while the curse will not seek to damage you, it will still influence you. This effect grows as it absorbs the curse energy of any cursed vessels related to the curse in Yalsten.

Jake stared at the description as he walked up to it, and with an easy pull, he got it out of the coffin. The rest of the root that extended towards the ceiling also turned to dust the moment he claimed the item.

He saw that the mist still didn't get close to him; he now had a five-meter area around him completely cleared of black mist.

I'm sure this will come in handy.

CHAPTER 20

TREASURE HUNT - COUNT HUNTING

J ake walked through the hall as the black mist parted around him. He found that even with the Root in his inventory, the mist still parted for him. The Root was an interesting item that he was certain had some specific, intended use already.

Also, the wood the Root was made of was a bit recognizable. He had a strong suspicion that whatever tree this Root came from was the tree that had been used to make the Pure Ones' anti-vampire weapons and, of course, the Stake. However, the Root was clearly far superior to the Stake. In fact, Jake had a strong suspicion that if he stabbed a Count with it, it would be a near-instant kill.

The mere fact that it was even useful outside of being a stabby tool was awesome, and he saw several possibilities to explore areas filled with black mist. But for now, he planned on just keeping it hidden away in his inventory... At least, that was the plan.

Just as he reached the atrium again, he felt something from his Hunter Insignia. The Root wanted out, and Jake obliged by summoning it in his hands. The moment it emerged, it functioned as a black hole of curse energy once more... but not towards the atmospheric mist.

No, it was from some of the nearly one thousand golems he had slain. A large number of them below sent energy up towards the Root, which absorbed every bit of it, and Jake felt the curse amplify as it subtly influenced him. It wanted him to slaughter vampires, and made him feel anger and hate towards them... or at least, it tried to. The thing was, Jake had been walking around with a cursed blade for months and had gotten accustomed to its constant influence—plus, he had to deal with what was essentially an emotional minefield caused by his Bloodline, too. So, yeah, while the curse on the Root was powerful, it failed to really do anything. Also, one shouldn't discount the now legendary-rarity Pride of the Malefic Viper, which facilitated his resistance and amplified his will to resist the curse.

It only took a few seconds before all the curse energy had been collected, and when Jake jumped out over the railing, he got in range of even more dead golems and felt yet another rush of cursed energy. He kept holding the Root throughout the halls, letting it absorb more and more curse energy.

He decided to give the tower a quick rundown for any hidden treasures. Considering the Count's intact gate, maybe there were other hidden places too?

Well, after half an hour, he did finally spot another closed gate, and once he got close, he saw that behind it were another five Knights. They were gathered around a chest, making it damn obvious they were guarding some kind of treasure or something.

I guess I can kill a few more.

He went up to the gate and broke it with a quick kick. All the gates in this place were just shitty. Jake had expected the five Knights to react when the gate was suddenly destroyed, and they did... just not as expected.

They all turned towards him for a second before returning to standing around the chest, ignoring him completely.

"Huh?" he said out loud as he walked closer. Jake went straight up to one of the golems and poked it with his finger, not getting any reaction. He then looked down at the Root and got an idea.

He lifted it up and hit the golem gently on the helmet with the blunt end of the Root.

You have slain [Reanimated Black Knight Golem – lvl 135] – Bonus experience earned for killing an enemy above your level

The black mist that inhabited the golem was instantly absorbed into the Root as the armor fell to the ground and crumbled into scrap metal. Jake's eyes lit up as he went over to the next golem.

"Bonk."

You have slain [Reanimated Black Knight Golem – lvl 135] – Bonus experience earned for killing an enemy above your level

With childlike glee, he bonked the next three too. Seeing the enemy that had given him that much grief getting one-shotted with the Root and falling apart was so damn satisfying. Also, he was fully aware that while he got notifications for the kills, it wasn't like he actually got any worthwhile experience. It was like that rat swarm in the Forgotten Sewers he had killed with the control staff. Sure, it had *said* they gave experience, but it had been negligible due to the way he killed them.

Once they were all turned to scrap, he opened the chest and saw a pillow with a collection of small orbs on it.

[Bead of Curse Resistance (Common)] – A bead that, once crushed, will grant the user temporary resistance to all kinds of curses by coating the user in a veil of

mana. One-time use. The veil of mana's rate of
wearing down is dependent on the power of the curse it
blocks.

Correction—he saw a pillow with a collection of small *beads*
on it. He counted about thirty of them, and he was amazed at
how useless they would be to him after obtaining the Root. This
was the puzzle room all over again, in the sense that it was clearly
intended to be found before he headed for the Count's chamber.
That way, he could have used the beads to defend himself while
exploring the upper floors.

Needless to say, Jake had no need for them now with the far
more effective Root. Hence, he moved on.

Because *now* it was time to speedrun some Counts.

————

While Jake had been busy fighting an army of cursed golems, the
different factions had stayed closer to the center of the Treasure
Hunt area, also known as the Mistless Plains. Additionally, they
had chosen to focus on the Counts first above anything else, and
it soon became obvious that the faction named the Pure Ones
had hidden armories or weapon stashes in nearly all the towers.
All of them hiding a Stake specifically created to severely weaken
a Count.

News spread that the Sword Saint had slain a Count after
around a full day of the Hunt. Whether a Stake had been used or
not was unknown. Either way, that would be the second person
to kill one after the Lord of Haven. As for the Holy Church?
They were aiming to get the third at this moment.

"Noor, Joshua, how long till the barrier is ready?" Bertram
asked as they stood outside the room to enter the Count's
chambers.

The caster and healer of the party were hard at work collabo-
rating to lay down a barrier, hoping to seal the Count of Blood

to avoid it running down the tower or, worse yet, fleeing outside the chamber.

The first kill on a Count had made it clear that one couldn't let the vampire run free and consume people, hence why they decided to seal it in. Jacob had also warned them that it could become a very tough fight if the vampire ran rampant.

Lucian and Maria, the swordsman and archer of their party, were just hanging back, both also making subtle preparations. Maria was preparing her bow by temporarily making it stronger and boosting its enchantments, courtesy of her profession. Lucian was sitting with a small pen, engraving small runes upon one of the swords related to the Pure Ones, each rune pulsing with magic.

They were going all-out in this fight.

"It will be done within the next minute," Noor answered him as she finished up the final parts.

"Good. Lucian will sneak in first and use the Stake on the Count. The moment he does so, he will retreat to the rest of us, and we'll deploy the tactics discussed and used against the Viscount. Any questions?"

Seeing only nods, Bertram motioned for Lucian to get ready. The swordsman donned a robe enchanted with stealth-improving properties and went up to the gate. The moment Noor gave the sign that the barrier was ready, he presented the Mark of Blood, and the gate opened.

Lucian slipped inside, sensing no movement as he held the Stake in his hand. The vampire didn't react until the moment the Stake penetrated its chest, making it scream loudly in pain as black veins spread from the wound.

"YOU DARE USE THIS HERETICAL TOOL TO HARM ME!? MERE LIVESTOCK DESERVE ONLY DEATH FOR SUCH TRANSGRESSIONS!"

The Count screamed, but all of them had been prepared and steeled their mental defenses. Luckily, they all had skills to resist the constant mental attack from the Count, which slowly corroded the will of his foes through what, granted, did sound like horrendous speeches.

Bertram stormed the Count first, and his team followed up. They had planned for this using the last half a day or so, and that preparation showed itself. They continually suppressed the Count, Joshua searing it with powerful light magic and Maria bombarding it with fire arrows that left flames that refused to burn out.

The fight ended up still taking nearly half an hour, with the Count of Blood struggling throughout, but it was far from powerless. It used whips of blood to try and cut them up and summoned snake-like creatures from bloody spots it left on the ground. These attacks had not been predicted, and the Count seemed far less melee-focused than they had come to believe. Ultimately, while this did add some difficulty, the party of five still proved superior.

Bertram cleaved down with a mighty swing of the blade and finished off the already-haggard vampire. From Lucian building up poison with envenomed attacks to the two powerful ranged fighters, they had significant damage output. Bertram constantly smashing the Count down and keeping him controlled had also been a major contributor to what made them victorious. Noor had been supporting them throughout it, of course, and she especially proved her worth when she used a healing spell to regenerate Joshua's arm when he got it whipped off.

As the vampire turned to ash, Bertram claimed the key as well as all the other loot. The entire group was tired, and Noor was already sitting down from being out of mana along with Joshua. Maria was in the best condition, as she had managed to avoid all hits and stayed as far away as possible throughout the fight.

Bertram looked at his party. "Great job, everyone... This was a tough one. We can all be proud."

Three of them smiled, but Maria shook her head as she looked at the ashes of the vampire. "And the Sword Saint and

Lord Thayne each killed one alone... No one reported seeing signs Lord Thayne had even used a Stake; in fact, they found one in that tower later... Do we even know the Sword Saint used one? Is this really anything to be proud of?"

I get it, Bertram thought but didn't say. *But do not compare yourself to monsters, for it will lead to nothing good.*

"Stop being a downer," Lucian scoffed. "No one says we couldn't have beaten it without the Stake either. We don't even know how effective it is, and maybe he used something else to weaken it. Also, clearly they were not identical monsters, so comparing them one to one is just moronic."

"Do you seriously believe that?" Maria shot back.

"Unless you present proof that shows otherwise, why wouldn't I? We don't know which is true. Maybe that other Count was just weak in comparison." Lucan shrugged. "Point is, nobody knows, so why be a downer and assume we're weak compared to that Thayne guy?"

"You—"

"Because we *are* weak in comparison," Bertram said with a sigh, getting everyone to turn their attention to him. "That is simply a fact. But he is also alone. His support system is weak compared to ours. He may have the biggest stick, but we have thousands of sticks. So don't be discouraged... We don't need to be the most powerful people on Earth. The Holy Church just needs to be the most influential faction. And the best way to make the Church stronger is to do as we are doing right now and progress. Got it?"

He got a few glances, but they all eventually nodded. After that, Bertram just closed his eyes and entered meditation. One thing he had left unsaid, though...

While the Holy Church certainly was powerful on Earth... Bertram didn't need to voice his doubts that their numbers would ultimately be useless before true monsters in human skin.

———

An unlikely party traveled through the tower. Two women and a small, green ball of fluffy feathers tore through the halls with incredible speed, tearing apart anything in their way. It was mainly done by the woman at the front as she slammed her fists into the cursed black golems.

Behind her was another woman with green magic revolving around her. She summoned bolts of what looked like shimmering green fire and pelted the enemies, but it was only when the golems died that she truly showed her worth.

A golem neared death as it exploded into black mist, but the woman simply waved her hand, and the golem suddenly sank into the ground. A moment later, a few scraps of metal remerged where the golem had just been, emanating black mist that made it clear it had just exploded.

Another golem tried to attack them from the side, but the feather ball flew up to it and cut a deep gash into the black metal before sending it flying back with a green gust of wind.

This unlikely party consisted of Carmen and Sylphie, now joined by another friend.

"I feel like I'm getting carried on the backs of you guys," Miranda said, miffed, at the woman and bird both displaying power above her own in these direct fights.

"You're doing great; those explosions are shitty to deal with," Carmen comforted her.

"Ree!" Sylphie added. Neither woman understood the bird, but they still gave her a nod as if they did.

"Well, I'm trying," Miranda said, smiling in return to Carmen.

Miranda had coincidentally run into one of Arnold's drones, and when she asked it for information, he'd told her the location of Sylphie and Carmen inside one of the many grave hills. Miranda had believed there was a chance Jake was also there, or at least nearby, but had found only the two comrades she now explored the Hunt with.

Carmen had especially been welcoming. As for Sylphie?

Miranda had luckily made it a habit to always carry some of those pellets the bird liked. Yes, it was one hundred percent a bribe to make the small hawk like her, but what can you do?

Funnily enough, Carmen hadn't asked Miranda about the bird other than if she knew it. Miranda had just responded that it came from Haven, and they had left it at that. Honestly, she appreciated it, as she wasn't comfortable divulging it had entered with Jake. Not without his permission, at least.

"Do you think we can take down a Count?" Carmen asked.

"Ree!" Sylphie chimed in. Both of them understood that clearly; she believed they could.

"We need a Stake—that's for sure," Miranda answered. "Perhaps a few more allies too. I heard a group tried to take on that Count the Holy Church was after and ended up being slaughtered within minutes. It even wasted a Mark of Blood, as the gate slammed shut after their deaths."

"You sure we can't do it just us three?" Carmen asked again.

"A hard maybe..." Miranda reiterated. "But I would argue it would be better to get some more powerful people involved."

Miranda was naturally trying to get Carmen to do something. And...

Carmen sighed as she gave up. "Fine, I'll call Sven and the others."

The Mistress of Haven just smiled in return. "With them, it should be more than manageable."

CHAPTER 21

TREASURE HUNT: ACTUAL SPEEDRUNNING (MOSTLY)

T his time, Jake actually did as he'd intended when he called it a speedrun. An hour after leaving the tower, he was already within another, a new Mark of Blood in hand. Well, in his Hunter Insignia. Whatever.

He stormed up the tower, noticing many others already within it. There didn't seem to be a singular faction that dominated, but just many smaller forces and parties, which was perfect. This was one of the towers still not consumed by mist, and it would contain a Count, from the looks of it.

When he made it to the upper floors, he saw a great number of people grouped up before the gate. There were around thirty in total, and Jake saw that their levels ranged from 109 to 116. There were two people Jake couldn't Identify without squinting a bit and penetrating whatever they used to hide their levels. Needless to say, their puny skills were nothing before the might of the mega-Perception build.

Jake's appearance wasn't exactly unknown at this point, and everyone turned to him when he appeared.

Being a recognizable figure, a few people backed away, while others seemed to take up semi-defensive positions. It was a bit useless, as neither of those would help anything if Jake had come to rob people. Luckily for them, he hadn't, but that didn't mean he was just going to leave them be.

"I'm here for the Count. Leave."

To his surprise, more than half of the people there just looked at him for a brief moment before leaving without any arguing. A good amount of people did stay, though. The ones at higher levels. Fourteen people remained; all of them were above 112.

"Lord Thayne, do you have a Stake?" a man from the group of fourteen asked him. "If not, we can offer one and work together on taking down this Count. You can have the key; we just wish to split the rest of the loot."

"No, thanks. Just leave," Jake said as he walked closer to the gate.

"Would it not be better if—"

"No. Leave."

The man looked at Jake with an open mouth, clearly not entirely sure what to say. A party of five among the fourteen people behind him exchanged looks before they left. Half of the remaining eight beside the leader seemed to take this as their cue to bail, leaving only four behind him—probably his party members.

Jake threw him one final glance before he summoned the Mark of Blood and the gate began to open. The man saw him do this, his eyes wide as he yelled for his party to run. While retreating, Jake heard him mutter something about Jake being an "unreasonable asshole."

He wasn't really going to disagree on that one. But it only made sense. It was foolish to expect a hunter to be nice when you came between him and his prey.

As the door opened, Jake spun a web of arcane strings that he attached to each side of the gate, keeping it at the ready for when the time was right. It was ready just in time for the gate to fully open, at which point a relatively small form appeared from the silver coffin with long, tendril-like hairs extending from all over his body.

"Who are you? How dare mere livestock awaken this Count? I—"

BOOM!

"You'll die," Jake answered as Limit Break activated at 20%, his presence blanketing the entire chamber. With blades and arrows poisoned, he went forth, holding nothing back.

What followed was a lot of explosions alongside a vampire with oddly stretchable limbs and the ability to grow out hair that tried to grasp Jake and consume his blood. That feature turned out well for Jake when the Count got a good slurp of his poisoned blood. In not that long, the Count was already on its last legs.

The Count tried to run, but Jake was ready. He activated his arcane strings, and the gate slammed shut in the face of the fleeing vampire. The hairy bloodsucker screamed and fired off magic to try and tear off the strings and keep Jake away, but that wasn't going to happen.

Jake caught up to the vampire, gripped his head from behind, and slammed his face into the gate as he began channeling Touch of the Malefic Viper. The Count tried to pierce his hands with his long hair, but Jake had already infused his gloves with arcane magic, making them incredibly tough.

The Count struggled, but Jake kept smashing his head into the hard metal gate over and over again. Blood splashed everywhere, and the head of the vampire became more and more squishy from the Touch. The long hair repeatedly tried to penetrate his body, but Jake either shrugged it off or avoided being hit in any vital places.

Ultimately, the Count of Blood was too weak, and with a final smash, the entire head popped like a watermelon fired from a cannon into a brick wall.

***You have slain [Count of Blood – lvl 155] – Bonus
experience earned for killing an enemy above your level***

* *'DING!' Class: [Avaricious Arcane Hunter] has reached
level 135 - Stat points allocated, +10 Free Points* *

Second Count down.

Jake looted the key that dropped as well as the heart. Instead
of a sword, this Count dropped a dagger. The dagger and key
were both items he already knew about, as the knife was the
same as the sword in pretty much all ways.

The only interesting drop was the heart—another beautiful
red gem.

> *[Starved Hilsic Vampire Heart (Epic)] – The heart of a
> severely starved Hilsic Vampire. This type of vampire is a
> rare variant with high Agility and controllable hair that
> is more durable than most metals. The rarity has been
> downgraded due to the starved state of the vampire the
> heart has been claimed from. Has many alchemical uses.*

"Hilsic Vampire, huh," Jake muttered, the name meaning
absolutely nothing to him.

He was impressed with how many different vampires there
were, though. It was pretty neat. He did wonder why the
Viscounts didn't drop any hearts, though. Was it because they
weren't rare enough variants? Or just system fuckery? Either
way, Jake now had two epic-rarity hearts.

Next up, he looted the altar and coffin, finding them both
identical to the ones prior. He had no idea what he would use
two damn altars and coffins for, but now he had them.

With everything done, he began another important job...
stealing the gates. Now, that wasn't very speedrun of him, but
the gates were awesome.

Jake spent the next twenty minutes burning off the first door, then only eighteen for the second one. He was getting better; that was for sure. It did look a bit funny with the gate completely gone, faint marks as if something had torn it off from where it had been attached to the walls.

Gate in his inventory, he chugged a mana potion and headed onwards to get another Mark of Blood and kill another Count. He summoned his wings and leaped up as he took flight, feeling like going by air this time around. He repeated the battle in his head as he flew, also sending a few mental messages back and forth with Sylphie.

———

"He's just some stuck-up, arrogant piece of shit who thinks he's better than everyone else," the man complained loudly to the dozen or so people gathered around him.

"Why are we even staying here when the dude is probably already dead?" another one chimed in, sounding equally mad and annoyed.

"Yeah, is the seal still not reactivated?" the first guy said, turning to someone in the group with a small, compass-like item.

"No, it's still down, so he is probably still alive somehow," the one with the compass answered with a shrug. "I guess the vampire is taking its time getting a good meal."

"I hope that fucker dies and doesn't leave like a coward."

"A damn narcissist is what he is," the first dude muttered as he paced back and forth. "If he had just teamed up with us, the Count would be dead already. It's been over a fucking hour, for fuck's sake."

"Maybe he will have weakened it, and we can capitalize?" the second guy came in again.

"Perhaps. He did kill one before, but let's not risk things more than—"

At that moment, a figure flew by, coming from the direction of the Count's chambers. They saw the black wings and, for a moment, thought it was the vampire, but soon realized it wasn't... It was Lord Thayne.

He flew by them without even acknowledging their existence. More important was that they didn't see any hints of heavy injury in his movements.

The twelve people who had stayed behind looked at each other in disbelief before taking off towards the Count's chamber. When they got there, they were absolutely dumbstruck. The entire chamber was completely ruined, and there was blood everywhere... but more so than that...

"How... how did he destroy the gate?"

It was a question they all asked themselves as they saw its absence. They had all encountered that black metal and knew exactly how tough it was. None of them could even leave a noticeable mark on it. And yet Lord Haven had blown it off during his fight.

"He... is he human?"

"I... I think I'm gonna leave."

"Do... do any of you think he heard us? What if he holds a grudge?"

"What a monster..."

While their responses differed, one thing was certain... none of them dared shit-talk him ever again. In fact, they would prefer to never even meet him or get his attention.

Ever.

———

Someone else that would agree that Jake was a monster was his next foe. Three hours after he killed his second Count of Blood, Jake was at it again. The entire chamber was covered in toxic mist—not the cursed kind, but the highly toxic variant from Wings of the Malefic Viper.

Five figures attacked Jake, each of them holding a black rapier. Jake ignored four of them and slammed his Scimitar of Cursed Hunger infused with arcane mana into the fifth one, sending the vampiric woman stumbling back. Yes, it was a woman, and double-yes, it was still called a Count of Blood.

Jake suddenly saw the entire hall in front of him shift and change. The walls collapsed in upon themselves, as if space was a piece of paper being crumbled, him caught within. He ignored it again, took out his bow, and fired a quick shot into empty space.

He hit the Count of Blood. She shrieked at having yet another poisoned arrow sticking out of her chest.

Next up, Jake felt like a hundred voices invaded his mind, and his vision shifted as everything became entirely red. But, once more, he didn't really react; he just kept shooting arrows at the vampire, which he could still see within his Sphere of Perception without any issues.

You see, Jake had found out that this next Count of Blood used some interesting magic. One part was mind magic. It reminded him a bit of the Minotaur Mindchief, but was clearly a different variant. The essence was the same, though, as it aimed to make him fail to block blows properly. These blows would be delivered with a rapier, with the damn vampire always going for his heart.

The second type of magic it used was illusion magic. It was quite the combo to not only mess with your opponent's head, but also actually change how things looked in the real world. A real double-whammy, that one, and Jake could see many others having issues with this Count. It was the trickiest one so far by a mile.

Except it had met Jake. It was one of those situations that wasn't really fair, and proof that matchups mattered a lot. If two people were equal in power, but one person countered the other, it wouldn't really be a fight. Sure, the Count still had her usual magic, and she seemed quite adept at that too. Still, when her two strongest tools were utterly nullified by fighting someone with insane Perception and a legendary-rarity ocular skill to see through nearly all her illusion... it just made it feel unfair.

The mind magic also did little against his Pride of the Malefic Viper, and considering how Jake was completely confident and barely breaking a sweat, he sure as hell didn't despair.

Oh, and finally... none of those things would have mattered anyway, as his Bloodline made both the illusion magic and the mind magic used to amplify the illusion magic completely useless. She could make the world look as fancy as she wanted, and Jake's sphere and instincts still wouldn't give a shit.

So... yeah. It ended up being anticlimactic, with Jake slowly killing her and taking his sweet time in robbing the entire chamber of furniture. He even took the gaudy pictures this time, all of which featured the vampire he was currently fighting. Him taking them had nothing to do with them depicting the scantily clad, goth-looking vampire lady in various risqué poses. Not at all.

A bit over an hour after he entered the chamber, he killed his third Count of Blood.

You have slain [Count of Blood – lvl 155] – Bonus experience earned for killing an enemy above your level

He didn't get a level for this one, and Jake wasn't sure whether that was because the fight had been easier than the previous ones or something else.

Making his way over to the corpse of the Count—she was at the far end of the chamber, as Jake had finished her with a Powershot—Jake passed the coffin and altar, putting both in his inventory. Which meant he had three of each now. He continued over to the ashes of the vampire to loot the three items she had dropped.

Jake first picked up his second heart of the day, Identifying it as he did so.

[Starved Nalkar Vampire Heart (Epic)] – The heart of a severely starved Nalkar Vampire. This type of vampire is a rare variant with extremely high innate abilities in illusion and mind magic, and often possesses a larger reserve of blood energy than most other vampires. The rarity has been downgraded due to the starved state of the vampire the heart has been claimed from. Has many alchemical uses.

First of all, Jake felt vindicated. This heart confirmed vampires had a resource called blood energy, which he assumed was their form of mana. Or maybe their form of fused mana and stamina? Health and mana? All three? All of these and more were things he could likely learn if he read some of the books he had swiped. Anyway, the heart was as he expected.

Besides the heart, he also naturally got the key. The weapon this Count of Blood dropped was the rapier, and he picked it up and tossed it in the Hunter Insignia with the two other Count weapons... which was when he felt something.

A resonance came from within the Insignia, and as he had bound the three Count weapons, he instantly understood...

They wanted to fuse.

CHAPTER 22

TREASURE HUNT: BLADES & BROTHERS

J ake was aware that the vampire weapons could fuse, but he had kind of assumed that would happen when he got all nine, not just three of them. He wasn't going to complain, though. He summoned all three of them on a wooden table he had also just tossed out.

Instinctively, he felt the three weapons' desire to devour one another. He just had to permit them... so he did. Jake had to choose a weapon to absorb the others, and he chose the blade over the dagger or rapier, as he was more used to using swords.

The three weapons acted almost magnetic, attracting each other and clashing when he gave permission. The moment they touched, their black metal became liquid, and within a few seconds, all of them had turned into a weird glob of what looked like black mercury. It did kind of keep the shape of a sword throughout this process, but it didn't exactly look stable.

He observed the entire process closely, feeling them slowly become one. Throughout, it became clear that they'd been made for this. Their Records fused, and the metal itself gladly mixed and consolidated, though the size of the weapon didn't increase.

Around a minute after it began, the blade returned to its original shape. It did not look any different at all—just a simple, black metal sword—but its aura had been amplified significantly, and Identify also confirmed the changes.

> *[Count's Vampiric Transforming Blade (Epic)] – A weapon created by fusing three weapons wielded by Counts of Blood, all of which have been soaked in the blood of countless enemies throughout the ages. Crafted using a special type of steel, the blade can absorb the lifeforce of Vitality-based lifeforms to repair itself. The combined Records of the three weapons have allowed the blade to evolve and transform even further, allowing it to steal a portion of the lifeforce of anyone injured as well as change form between a sword, a dagger, and a rapier. This blade was originally crafted in a set of nine using the unique environment of the hidden world, and can absorb the weapons of other Counts of Blood to enhance itself. Three have now been fused, and six remain. Note: This functionality is only available within the Treasure Hunt area and will disappear once the event concludes. Enchantments: Hemoabsorbant Self-Repair. Vampiric Weapon. Transformation.*

> *Requirements: Lvl 130+ in any humanoid race.*

The level requirement had gone up by five, and the rarity had increased to epic. Those were the most obvious changes. Besides that, the only real change was the ability to transform.

Jake picked it up, and with an easy mental command, the entire weapon changed into the shape of a black metal dagger. The entire process took less than a second, but that still made him frown, as it meant it wasn't something he could do in live combat. He had mastered the art of fast weapon switching using his inventory already, and it was far faster just to do that. It could also only transform into the set shapes of a dagger, a sword, or a rapier—in other words, weapons he had used to fuse it.

This led to the ultimate question... Would he switch using this blade over any of his other weapons? Jake honestly wasn't sure yet.

The Scimitar of Cursed Hunger was in a weird place, in that Jake couldn't determine exactly how powerful it was. It looked to be made of black steel or iron, and the metal itself didn't strike him as anything significant. What was significant was the curse on it. The weapon grew with every fight he was in, as it absorbed excess vital energy, so even if it was Soulbound and didn't have a level requirement—if it did have one—he guessed it would be around 115 or 120 by now.

He also had to admit he had a bit of an emotional attachment to it, as it was the first weapon he'd created using Touch of the Malefic Viper that was actually worth a damn. It would also be a waste not to keep improving it. The power curses could hold was also evident to him, especially after exploring this Treasure Hunt.

Curses were essentially just emotions, Willpower, magic, and possibly other stuff mixed oddly together to create something he didn't fully understand. No two curses were the same, and there didn't seem to be many rules or standards to how curses functioned either.

He wasn't going to replace his scimitar, as he saw too much potential in it, which left his Nanoblade. The Nanoblade had a lower level requirement and even a lower rarity than this vampiric blade. All the statistics would make one believe it was weaker, but... it just suited him too well.

It was a no-nonsense weapon. Discounting its unbelievable sharpness and durability, all it did was make his arcane energy better when Jake coated the blade in it. Perhaps the vampiric blade would be better, but there was also something to be said about familiarity, and Jake had to admit that he just liked using the Nanoblade. Meanwhile, the vampire weapon didn't sit well in his hand when he held it, and he just didn't click with it. Was it more powerful? Perhaps. Would he use it? No.

Not yet, at least. If Jake got his hand on more vampire weapons and upgraded it again, his chosen weapon could very well change.

With everything done in the chamber, Jake left. Now, one may wonder how he found another tower so readily available without anyone getting in his way or messing up the fight. The reason for this was the same as why he hadn't stolen the gate.

Walking out, he smiled, dispelled his mask, and gave the person waiting for him a wave. "Count is officially down for the count."

"That was bad, and you should feel bad," the person standing outside answered.

It was a man clad in a black robe. A thin metal pole with an orb at the end floated behind him. He looked a lot like Jake, but that was to be expected, considering it was his brother.

"Oh wow, are you *judging me* for my humor?" Jake shot back, grinning at Caleb.

"You are getting awfully close to a declaration of war here."

"You won't even take me to court first?"

Caleb looked at Jake before cracking a grin himself. "I apologize for my impoliteness, oh glorious Champion of the Malefic Viper, Progenitor of Earth, and the true chosen one and hero of our age. Please show mercy upon this lowly mortal."

"This one forgives thy transgressions," Jake joked back, refusing to see himself beaten by his little brother. Well, he did make some concessions. No way he was going to burn off the gate with Caleb staring at him over the shoulder while judging him for taking it.

Caleb chuckled and turned a bit more serious. "Any issues with the Count of Blood?"

"Nah, it was a great matchup for me," Jake answered, giving Caleb some quick details about the Count and how he had beaten her. There was no one else present, and Caleb was at the gate just in case the vampire made it out. While he had admitted to Jake he didn't think he could kill a Count, he was confident about holding one back long enough for Jake to reengage the vampire.

"That does sound like a tough enemy for any regular group," Caleb noted. "We would have needed a Stake for sure."

The reason the Court of Shadows hadn't killed the Count was that they didn't have a Stake. They were still in the process of getting it, but they had gotten very unlucky with the kind of method they had to use to open the gate it was hidden behind. It required them to correctly craft several special metal keys to open the puzzle, and while their crafters had worked hard at it, it still took time. Of course, they were still going to open it, but now Caleb could just keep the Stake.

"Yep, I could see those illusions causing some issues," Jake agreed before swiftly changing the topic. "How is everyone? Do you have any problems or need any help?"

Jake hadn't asked before, but just rushed for the Count—also by request of his brother to get the boss done—but now that it was a silent moment, he had to ask.

"They're doing well, and I got things handled. Just focus on what you need to do. Your presence alone is a shield." Caleb gave a comforting smile. "We named him Adam. Just like Maja had been talking about."

"Mom was also a big fan of that name; she must be ecstatic." Jake smiled, remembering a simpler time. A time so simple it appeared gray and dull in his mind... It was cruel to think. But he couldn't lie. He had to admit he had just been bored before the system. Even when he spent time with his family, there had been a cloud of boredom hanging over him.

"She is," Caleb answered, throwing Jake out of his thoughts. His brother's smile slowly faded, and he grew more serious. "Jake, after the Treasure Hunt, you're coming to visit. I'm not asking. Got it?"

Jake sighed. "Got it."

Caleb returned to his usual smile. "Good. Here, take this Mark before heading out. You may be lucky and snatch another

Count before all of them are slain. From all the info we have gathered, this is the sixth key to be claimed. The Noboru clan has two, Holy Church one, you three, and last I heard, the last three are under heavy contention."

"I'll keep that in mind, and thanks," Jake answered as he received the Mark of Blood.

"No problem, isn't that what family is for? Helping each other hunt down vampires in some separate dimension?"

"Naturally," Jake said with a teasing smile. "I am surprised you guys don't have a key; you seem to enjoy stealing stuff related to the Counts."

"Yeah... that moron will be heavily reprimanded when we get back. But, seriously, he once stole a damn uncommon-rarity dagger and refused to give it back until his dad told him to. I am not even joking." Caleb shook his head in utter disbelief.

"Sounds like a grade-A member of the Court," Jake kept teasing.

"That's the issue... he is," Caleb said with a large sigh. "The guy is damn talented at stealing stuff, and even more capable at making tools to steal things."

"Tough being a boss. You should just delegate everything and only do stuff when you feel like it." Jake shrugged.

"It is what it is. Anyway, I think you should get going if you want to get another Count before others do," Caleb said, adding on a final warning. "Be careful of the Sword Saint; he isn't simple at all. The man named Eron also isn't to be taken lightly, though he seems to have little interest in the keys. I heard he fought a Count before it went on a rampage throughout a tower, consuming everyone it came across, and the Sword Saint ended up putting it down. And somehow, Eron still walked out of that tower unscathed."

"I know. I already have a bet with the Sword Saint on who gets five keys first," he said, nodding. "I'll be off. Take care, and see you in the Mistless Plains for the big reveal!"

With those words, Jake turned around to make his way

towards the next Count of Blood, hoping he would make it in time.

———

Reika stood with her two followers, the Mark of Blood ready and the path cleared. She still had the Stake from the Pure Ones ready, too, in her Hunter Insignia. She had sent the message to her great-grandfather already, and her follower had used a skill allowing the Patriarch to pinpoint their location. Navigating the mist could still prove difficult, so it helped tremendously.

She waited with anticipation as she slowly got updates about the happenings of the Treasure Hunt. Reika sat down with her alchemy cauldron, practicing making stamina potions. She listened attentively as she heard the news that Lord Thayne, Jake, had killed another Count of Blood and had last been seen entering a tower that had been claimed primarily by members of the Court of Shadows.

His level of power was something she had difficulty understanding. It was hard for her to see him as the powerful person he was. It wasn't like her great-grandfather, where she understood his power. Her time with Jake had not helped her truly comprehend him, either, besides the fact that he was driven. Driven to a ridiculous degree. He also seemed to always just enjoy himself... It was very odd to see someone smile and not frown when they encountered a complex problem.

As she sat there in thought, she heard a sound. Soft footsteps echoed through the halls, and Reika instantly recognized the familiar way of walking.

She stopped her crafting and got up, just in time to see the Patriarch around a corner. His steps were immaculate, and every one of them slid oddly across the ground, making him travel far faster than his casual stroll would indicate.

"Patriarch!" she greeted with a bow as he came to a stop

before them. "I have prepared the Stake and Mark of Blood as promised!"

Reika summoned the two items and held them out, one in each hand.

Her great-grandfather looked at her and chuckled. "Good work as always, Reika. I thank you for the Mark of Blood, but do keep hold of the Stake."

She looked up at him, a bit confused, her followers doing the same. "Do you already possess one?"

"No," he answered, shaking his head. "It would simply be wasteful to use an item that provides extra rewards unnecessarily, don't you agree?"

The implication was clear.

He didn't need it.

———

Miranda, Carmen, and Sylphie were prepared as the reinforcements arrived.

A party of five walked through the hall towards them, making Miranda frown. At the front was Sven, the man that had primarily represented the faction of Valhal during the World Congress, and with him were four others. She recognized one of them as another participant of the World Congress, and she was certain of one thing... that party was powerful.

Carmen went up to them to meet them, and Miranda noted how they were all oddly respectful. It had to be noted that while Miranda had been in a group with Carmen and Sylphie for the last day and a half or so, they hadn't exactly met any strong foes. In fact, it was Miranda who insisted they needed assistance with the Count. She had heard the Counts were powerful, and she didn't want to unnecessarily risk it.

Once Carmen was done talking to them, Sven turned his attention to Miranda. "I must admit, I was surprised when I heard the Rune Maiden was with the City Lord of Haven and a peculiar hawk. Is it yours?"

Before Miranda could react, Sylphie answered for herself with her usual loud, "Ree!"

Sven looked a bit taken aback as Miranda answered, unfazed, "No, she is a member of this group like Carmen and me. I can't reveal more; just know she is powerful and an ally. Also, I see nothing weird about us women spending some quality time together."

Miranda said the last part teasingly, getting a smirk from Carmen and another screech from Sylphie. She did think about the odd title Sven referred to Carmen by, though. Rune Maiden. Perhaps it was her class? Profession? Miranda *had* seen Carmen deploy some rune magic, but not much. Once again, their fights had been relatively easy so far.

"I see. Well, then, are we ready?" Sven asked.

"Should we not strategize first?" Miranda implored. Sven should have brought a Stake to use, so he should sneak in first and stab the vampire before it awakened.

"Is that truly necessary?" Sven asked, directing this question at Carmen.

"Maybe, maybe not. Let's see for ourselves." Carmen just smiled as she, without further ado, summoned the Mark of Blood and opened the gate before anyone else could react.

"Wait, don't we need to go in with the Stake first to make sure the Count doesn't awa—"

"I HAVE AWAKENED! WAIT! LIVESTOCK DARE INVADE MY CHAMBER!"

Carmen looked at the rising form of the vampire, then briefly back at them, before quietly muttering, "I forgot?"

CHAPTER 23

TREASURE HUNT: PUNCHING BACK

Miranda felt a moment of distress as the vampire rose, spreading its aura out the gate and into the hallway. Sylphie didn't seem to be that on edge, but the same couldn't be said about the people behind Sven. Sven himself didn't display anything, but just drew his weapon and yelled for his party to get ready.

She also took this yell as her wake-up call and waved her hand, summoning magic circles around her. She doubted she could do much direct damage to the Count of Blood, as the Viscounts already outmatched her, but she would do her best nevertheless.

Carmen threw a glance towards Sylphie, and without further ado, the two made their move. Sven followed, wielding a large, two-handed sword, with his four party members also doing their own thing. One summoned runic lines that appeared on the armor of Sven and Carmen; another began summoning root spears; the third charged with Sven, wielding a sword and shield; while the last one was the most impressive, at least visually. He roared as his body slowly began morphing, and before long, a large, armored bear had joined the battle.

The Count of Blood was a large male who summoned armor

of bone upon seeing the charging humans, a black spear also appearing in his hands. Red energy exploded out of his body. Miranda had to defend herself by doing what she thought was most valuable: creating a barrier between her and the two casters in Sven's party. Not one that could hold back the vampire for long, just long enough for them to react.

Magic filled the air, and the two sides clashed, a powerful vampire on one side and a group of humans on the other. Oh, and a green bird that fast proved to be one of the most dangerous things in the room.

Sven could only chip off parts of the bone armor with his swings, making it crack and sometimes knock pieces off, but Sylphie? Sylphie did a fly-by and cut up the vampire's back, sending blood flying as the armor failed to block her glowing green wing. How the hell the bird had such potent attack power, Miranda truly didn't understand.

The bear proved to be impressive-looking but unable to do much. All it did was try and preoccupy the vampire by holding onto parts of it, sometimes landing mostly ineffective blows with its large paws. On the other hand, the bear-man did prove to be very durable, but the vampire handled that by simply not attacking it.

Besides Sylphie, Carmen was the one who found the most success. Her glowing fists cracked the bone armor with every hit, and with her far higher rate of attack, she was by far the main danger of their entire group. Fortunately, the vampire seemed to lack attacking power besides the spear—which he did wield skillfully—but even so, the human side took quite a few injuries.

Miranda worked on her barrier while the wood mage fired off wooden spears, and after seeing they did nothing, she switched to summoning roots, trying to restrain the vampire and limit its movements. The rune caster was some kind of healer and used his magic to temporarily make Carmen or Sven stronger while also creating runes that summoned shields.

Overall, their group was balanced, and it became a battle of attrition. The vampire kept yelling horrible dialogue about how it would drink their blood and feast on their flesh, but from what Miranda had learned, that was just par for the course.

She was beginning to feel confident, even if the vampire healed any wounds they inflicted, and the wounds accumulated on primarily the bear, Sven, and the woman with a sword and shield. On a side note, Sven had attempted to use the Stake, but found that it failed to penetrate the bone armor and only made the vampire even madder. After that happened, she feared for a moment they would have to flee and hopefully find Jake to help them, but that didn't seem neccesar—

"ENOUGH!"

The Count of Blood screamed as his entire body exploded in white light, sending all the melee fighters back and interrupting the spellcasting of everyone, including Miranda. Then the vampire raised its spear and stabbed it into the ground.

"Forest of Bones."

Miranda barely had time to react before the ground erupted with thousands of spear-like bones shooting up from below. The barrier she had made also protected downwards, but only barely. She dodged back but still ended up being speared through the thigh and an arm, making her yelp in pain and lose her concentration.

Those who had been close to the Count and were blasted back now faced angled spears of bone aimed at their backs. Sven turned in mid-air, blocking with the flat side of his large blade but still taking a few minor stabs to his chest.

Carmen didn't even bother with it all. She was speared from behind, but the bones barely penetrated a few centimeters, allowing her to quickly shoot back towards the vampire as her wounds visibly healed. The one who handled it the worst was the woman with a shield. She had already been wounded by a spear earlier, and now failed to dodge the spear that impaled her through the chest.

Miranda turned and saw that the runic healer had also been

stabbed by a spear and was trying to get to healing again. The wood mage had handled it well by shooting his own vines up from the ground, shooting him into the air.

The bear was the one that took the most spears due to its size, and the man had now reverted back to his human form, retreating towards the back wall as blood dripped from dozens of wounds on his body.

This isn't good, Miranda thought, gritting her teeth. The only one unaffected by the attack had been Sylphie, courtesy of her small form and being airborne.

Would she have to call Jake? Could Sylphie do it?

Carmen clashed with the vampire again, but the vampire appeared stronger than before. The armor of bone began changing into a smaller version, and the spear moves became faster and even more deadly.

While Miranda seriously considered if they should retreat, Carmen jumped back and quickly glanced around the room. Sven had also gotten up and looked Carmen's way. He only looked at her for a moment before he nodded.

"Retreat!"

The bear-man didn't have to be told twice. He began running out of the chamber while the wood mage summoned roots to extract the damaged shield-wielding woman.

But... two "people" didn't retreat. One of them was Sylphie, and the other one Carmen.

Miranda was practically pushed by Sven to leave and exit the chamber, leaving the bird and woman behind. She frowned but didn't resist, as she knew she truly couldn't do much. Carmen kept clashing with the vampire while Sylphie hung back.

"What are we going to do?" Miranda asked once outside.

She could still see inside the room due to a mark she had left on her magic circle, and all she saw was Carmen still fighting the Count on her own.

Sven was working on closing the gate and securing it using his sword as he turned and looked oddly at her. "I don't follow?"

"Shouldn't we do something? The Count proved stronger than expected, and—"

"Ah, Ms. Wells, you worry needlessly," Sven chuckled, the rest of his party also shaking their heads. "I am most certain Carmen is more than happy about the state of that room. The only one I am worried about would be the bird, but it seems to be able to handle itself."

———

Inside the room, Carmen stared at the Count of Blood. Sylphie looked at her, and she threw the hawk a glance. She seemed to understand, and gave a small *ree* as Carmen smiled and got to work. The Count was weakened and about to be out of resources, so it was time to finish the fight. As Carmen prepared, Sylphie flew towards the Count and began flying around it to kick up a whirlwind, keeping the Count locked in place.

Carmen knelt down and placed both her fists on the ground as she spoke.

"Sacred Battlefield."

A pulse went through the ground as an odd aura overtook the entire chamber.

"Regalia of the Fallen."

A golden set of phantasmal, almost ghostly armor covered her body in a veil of energy.

"Runes of the Valkyrie."

Runes appeared all over her arms. She felt an influx of power in them, and their resilience significantly increased.

"Exaltation of Valhal."

Behind her, an illusory hall full of feasting warriors appeared, all seeming to lift their mugs in her glory. Carmen felt like she suddenly got a huge boost to her stamina, and the energy moving through her body sped up.

"Blessed Echo."

A see-through woman wielding a large axe floated above for a fraction of a second, then slowly descended into her body, buffing up all her physical attributes.

"Ruinous Drive."

All her internal energy burned as her body became significantly more powerful. Her skin started flaking, and blood dripped out of cracks on her skin. For but a moment, she was at her strongest. All of the skills came together and boosted her at once, pushing her incredibly durable body and healing ability to their absolute limits.

With all those skills active at once, she couldn't fight for long... which was why she would finish it quickly.

She drew back her fist as energy began revolving around it. The Count looked out of the green whirlwind caused by Sylphie, crossing its arms in front of its chest just in time.

"Fist of Ragnarok."

In a flash, Carmen appeared before the Count of Blood and punched.

Her fist literally exploded when she struck the vampire. Two bone-covered arms flew into the air as her fist penetrated through the chest of the vampire, blasting it towards the back wall of the chamber.

Carmen knelt down on the ground with only a stump left where her arm had been. Yet, she was only grinning. Sure, the vampire was still alive, but...

A green flash appeared as the vampire, which was already embedded in the wall, had its head separated from its neck by a small figure flying by. A notification confirmed the kill, and Carmen just laughed as Sylphie claimed the items dropped.

That was when Carmen remembered something else she had forgotten... She had promised that Sylphie would get the loot from the next boss besides the Mark of Blood... Considering this one didn't even drop a Mark of Blood...

Carmen began laughing even more, already imagining Sven's reaction.

Jacob had made many decisions he now doubted were wise, and the one he had made that day was one of them. With Jake having obtained three keys for Haven and the City Lord working with Valhal to get another... they needed to ensure the last one. And right now, or at least very soon, Jake would be headed their way.

They needed to delay him. The issue was... who or what could delay the Progenitor of Earth? The likely most powerful person on the planet? Jacob had thought about this for a long time in case things went south... so he had made contact with someone else who was a wild card of their newly initiated universe. His only purpose was to delay Jake, and as far as Jacob was aware, it wasn't like his friend would come to harm, since he seriously doubted anything would come out of their fight.

At least, Jacob didn't believe so... but had to admit that out of the many people on Earth he had difficulty comprehending, Eron was perhaps the biggest mystery to him.

There were many unknowns in this choice, but he had to take some risks. While he did consider Jake a close friend, he still valued his responsibility to the Church over personal relations. He simply had too much responsibility on his shoulders to make decisions based on emotions alone.

This was also why he had made an alliance not with Haven, but the Noboru clan. Perhaps the clan had realized that with the Court of Shadows firmly on the side of Haven and Valhal working with their City Lord, they also needed allies.

The Holy Church reciprocated. Jacob saw a lot of value in nurturing the relationship between the Church and the clan. It was work, not personal business. With the Church already having one and now getting another, and the Noboru clan close to claiming their third... it would mean the clan and the Church having five.

Of course, all of that depended on Eron's ability to delay

Jake long enough for Bertram and the others to finish off the Count of Blood.

There was one other thing that irked him, though. It had been two full days of the Treasure Hunt by now, and outside of the first hour or so of the Treasure Hunt, he had heard nothing of the undead faction at all. Considering the antagonistic relationship between the Holy Church and the undead, this was a major cause for concern...

Jacob sighed as he once more entered meditation, trying to discover what would happen the moment all nine keys came together. One thing was for certain, though.

He had talked to many individuals from the Holy Church and done a lot of research before entering the Treasure Hunt. General investigation into system events and the general tendencies and stages they went through. Based on all that research, Jacob was confident of one thing:

This entire Treasure Hunt was being completed far faster than was usual.

———

Jake used One Step Mile through the plains as he approached the tower in the distance. There were three unkilled Counts, and Jake was going for the closest tower to the one he had just done. He had been told that the Holy Church had already claimed one, and considering how a fourth key had appeared in his inventory halfway to this next tower, he wasn't going to play nice. He just needed one more, and he would do all he could to get it.

He made it inside and sprinted through the halls, frowning a bit as he encountered no one on any of the lower floors. His frown only grew the further up he got until he finally detected a presence.

A single man stood within a large hallway with a metal gate at the end. Jake instantly saw that the gate wasn't there naturally, but placed. It had been almost welded to the walls, and with his sphere, he saw enough to realize it would require a bit of burning with Alchemical Flame to get it free. Or a lot of Arcane Powershots.

But... that wasn't the most important concern right now. It was the man who stood in front of the gate.

The man smiled as he saw Jake. "We meet again, Mr. Thayne. I must admit, it is good that we met again so soon. It always gladdens me to see sparks grow and rekindle."

It was that madman Eron.

CHAPTER 24

TREASURE HUNT: INVINCIBLE

Jake studied the man's combed-back, slick hair and casual demeanor. He wore a simple white robe that reminded Jake of the coat doctors would wear, though it was clearly magical and enchanted. However, he wasn't there to judge fashion, but to kill a vampire.

"Move."

Eron looked back at Jake and shook his head. "I apologize; I'm unable to do that."

"You're gonna stop me?"

"Delay. I was contracted to delay your arrival in the Count's chamber by one and a half hours," Eron explained forthcomingly. "Ah, only around an hour now. In case you wonder, yes, it was the Augur and the Holy Church who contracted me. I shall be honest; I would prefer for this not to devolve into needless violence, so would it be too much to ask for us to simply sit down for a cup of coffee and wait? Or do you prefer tea?"

Dumbfounded, Jake looked at the man. With a light smile on his face, he summoned a small coffee table and a pair of chairs. The issue was... Jake needed to go down this hallway. Like with the other Count chambers, the way there was linear. There was one way in and one way out.

Within his Sphere of Perception, he saw the other side of the metal door. A group of fifteen people stood close to the gate on the other side, channeling mana into it. With them and Eron in front of him, the situation had suddenly gotten a lot more annoying.

Well played, Jacob.

Jake had to admit this wasn't expected. Eron was one of the few unknowns of the planet that he couldn't really understand. He was the one other person on Earth with a Bloodline, as far as Jake was aware, instantly making him a person of interest.

Sadly for Eron, Jake had no interest in being delayed.

"Yeah, no. Fuck off, or I'm gonna make you."

Eron looked up at Jake. "Rude, but I guess your anger is understandable. Fine. I am looking forward to seeing your attempt at making me leave, as, if violence becomes a necessity, let it at least have a purpose. I have heard much of you and your capabilities, so please show me your methods."

Jake narrowed his eyes. He had already used Identify on the man, but the result had been disappointing.

[?]

No matter what he did, Jake couldn't pierce it. It wasn't that bad, as Jake still got a feel for the madman's Strength... but all that told him was the same as during the World Congress. A feeling that fighting him would be a waste of time.

In the end, Jake sighed and took a step. He appeared straight in front of Eron, who was still making his coffee. Drawing his blade, Jake placed it at the neck of Eron, who stood unfazed.

"Nothing?"

Eron twirled the spoon in the cup of hot coffee. "My reaction would warrant a belief that decapitation would do me any harm. I would prefer to do without, though, as it would ruin my drink."

Frowning, Jake put his blade away and just ignored Eron as

he went over to the gate. He had already inspected it with his sphere, and it was far from as well secured as all the others. While those had taken him twenty minutes to remove, he could easily do this one in five.

Just as he began burning the hastily assembled hinges, Eron waved his hand. An odd flame appeared and formed into a bolt. Jake stopped what he was doing and looked back to see a pure-white, flaming bolt being fired his way.

He decided to block it primarily out of curiosity. The moment the flame hit his hand, it just sank into Jake's body, and instantly he felt a warm flow going through his body... before it began burning. Jake had to grit his teeth from the pain. It was only for a moment, at which point his own internal energies dispelled the foreign energy, but Jake saw and felt he had taken damage directly to his health points.

What the fuck was that? Jake asked himself as he backed away. He genuinely had no idea what the fuck that magic was, but he knew it was dangerous in large quantities.

"Once more, I am to delay you. So, please, can just we just relax for the next hour or so? Or at least have it be you attacking me?" Eron took a sip of his coffee.

"No to the first one."

This time, Jake didn't hold back. Eron struck him first, and he would respond in kind. Then, brandishing his Nanoblade, Jake attacked. He expected the other party to dodge, but the man just stood there as Jake effortlessly bisected him at the stomach.

"I expected more originality," Eron said. A split second later, his severed lower body simply disappeared in an explosion of red mist, and Eron landed on his newly healed legs.

Now Jake really frowned... for he had seen the entire progress. This wasn't nullification of damage. Eron had just taken some significant damage; Jake was sure of it. His Mark confirmed as much too. Yet the man seemed unaffected... He had just healed it instantly, without Jake even detecting any magic being used.

Natural extreme regeneration?

"What are you?" Jake asked, Eron having not even let go of his cup.

"A human, just like you. I do not mean to sound cliché, but we are not so different, you and I. We both seek the pinnacle of what is possible—to explore behind all the doors this new multiverse has opened up! We have just chosen to open different doors. While you aim for destruction and death, I seek preservation and life. Ah, but do not see this as me admonishing you. Both are necessary, even if I may personally dislike your path."

Jake didn't know if he enjoyed monologuing because the dude had time on his side, or if he really was such a talker.

"Then let me see if I can destroy you," Jake said as he attacked again. He infused his blade with arcane energy and stabbed Eron, who just kept talking.

"Evolution is an interesting concept, is it not? To develop towards your own version of perfection... yet some things will forever be in common. I am not talking of the vain, outward features, but what is beneath the skin. The viscera—oh, excuse me, internal organs—will slowly disappear in the ranking of importance. The spleen, liver, large parts of the intestines. All of these are judged unimportant as we humans stop needing them."

Jake had already cut him into many pieces, including half of his head and the brain. Yet the man kept talking as if unaffected.

"However, it is not these I find the most interesting. It is those that remain... or, more accurately, why they remain. Tell me, Mr. Thayne, why do you need lungs when you do not need to breathe? Why do you retain a stomach when you do not need to eat? Is it not fascinating how the reason why we keep those is not for their original purpose?"

"How you seem to not need any organs at all sure is fascinating," Jake said as he repeatedly turned Eron's insides to mush with Touch of the Malefic Viper, only to see his poison constantly be nullified by a flood of vital energy—but not before corroding his entire chest away, everything within included.

"The lungs do not remain to inhale air, but mana. We breathe to regenerate ourselves; it's why meditation is so closely interlinked with breathing techniques. We keep our stomachs not to get nutrients, but simply for pleasure. In fact, many things remain only for pleasure. Human vanity. Now, some things remaining make sense. The sexual organs will forever serve the purpose of reproduction, as we are biological creatures, but why retain the anus when it is no longer used for the excretion of waste? I surmise it's only retained for se—"

"Dude, what the fuck, too much information," Jake blurted out as he smashed Eron into the ground again, making half of his body explode, including the head. His entire body regenerated within a moment, and the man kept speaking.

"Very well. Let me just skip the details, then, and get to the point. Besides those vanity organs or features, do you know what the last organs to disappear are in all biological creatures of the system? What has been deemed essential, and that we, even in our pursuit of perfection, can never get rid of?" His question was not rhetorical this time.

"I dunno, the dick?" Jake shot back, honestly starting to get annoyed. Touch did nothing, his arcane magic did nothing, and even Gaze of the Apex Hunter only managed to freeze the guy for a bit. With his arcane energy, he stacked his Arcane Charge to the largest one possible... and yet it did nothing.

"Well, yes, that does remain... but besides that, what remains is the heart and the brain, despite their presence being less and less relevant. I do believe that I myself am a great example of this. In fact, no organs are vital to continue existing."

Jake decided to switch up his tactic, wrapping Eron in strings of arcane mana. His thought process was that if he couldn't kill Eron, he would just displace him and toss him somewhere far away. That would give Jake enough time to burn the gate off.

Yet just when Jake was done wrapping up Eron, his danger sense reacted for the first time. Jake jumped back from the man just in time. Eron's entire body burned with energy, and the madman exploded in a red explosion of pure vital energy and mist—a bit reminiscent of the Deepdwellers, but far smaller and more localized.

Another difference was that the Deepdwellers did not instantly appear again before the mist had even subsided.

"Case in point, I believe," Eron said as he quickly summoned back the robe to cover himself. "You see, we as living beings no longer exist solely dependent on our bodies. As long as our sparks remain alit, we remain alive. This spark does not exist within our bodies... No, it exists beyond that."

Jake looked at him before asking, "Are you unkillable or what?" He had just seen him literally return his body from nothing. Not even a drop of blood had remained, yet he'd regenerated.

Eron looked at Jake. "No. No, I don't believe anything in this multiverse is truly unkillable. For every spark there is, a force that can blow it out must also exist. At least, I believe such a balance is necessary. I do not doubt for a second that any god could whisk me out of existence if they so pleased."

The two men stood for a while as Jake considered what the fuck to do, while Eron wouldn't stop talking.

"To return to the earlier topic... the brain and heart remain. The brain controls the body and speeds up reactions. It no longer houses who you are, but is more like a complicated muscle that serves to amplify your bodily functions. Once more, I can see this making sense as anchoring physicality, and physical prowess outside of the metaphysical is sensical. But... this brings us to the heart.

"Why do we need the heart, and why is the heart the center of our beings? You hold a Bloodline, so I am certain you know that the heart is linked to the core of your soul. It's the point of contact between metaphysical existence and our tangible forms. When I heal, my heart is the first to appear." He promptly ripped out his own heart as a demonstration. He then exploded the rest of his body, and his entire person reformed around the heart.

"The heart still pumps blood and now even creates the blood itself. This naturally begs the question of why blood is even necessary. I believe this refers back to grounding the tangible. To transfer energy through a physical medium is simply far more effective than not. To have blood deliver vital energy to the body only makes sense, does it not?"

While Jake did find the guy's words more interesting than he dared to admit, he still knew his objective. The issue was that he wasn't certain how to actually do anything... because he was fairly certain that his theory was correct.

"You have limitless or at least near-limitless health points, don't you?"

It was the only thing Jake could see making sense. Eron had learned to control his vital energy like Jake controlled his mana, and could use it actively to instantly regenerate his body. Of course, the expenditure of vital energy—health points—to do this had to be ridiculous... but what if you had a near-limitless supply?

"That is correct, if a bit oversimplified. I will not share how I have achieved this, however."

"I see... What was the bright white flame before?" Jake asked, now acting far more willing to talk.

Eron's smile deepened. "As I am certain you can guess, my ability to stay alive in most situations is great. However, this does have some drawbacks, including certain limitations to my options in combat. I needed a tool to defend myself. My thought process behind it was to take a part of my own spark and use it to displace a portion of my foes, effectively eliminating a portion of their health pool. This magic is by the system, called an arcane affinity."

That one sure got Jake's attention. An arcane affinity? Sure, Jake was aware that arcane affinities varied person by person and were unique to the creator... but to see that Eron had made one too? And one so substantially different than his own? While Jake's was all about stability, destruction, and the dichotomy of those two, Eron's seemed entirely Vitality-based.

"You're awfully open about your abilities," Jake remarked. Unfortunately, he didn't have time to ponder more on the man's abilities, as it would soon be time.

"Naturally. I hope for you to find the chink in my armor and pierce through it. To expose my weaknesses and exploit them. My pinnacle is one of infallibility. So once more, please. The soul attack earlier was interesting, but I have recently learned counter-methods to that kind of attack. Your mana attacks are effective, but ultimately they are just regular attacks."

"Yeah... I'm really not sure how to kill you... but can I try something anyway?" Jake asked.

"Please, go ahead," Eron said, almost elated at Jake's willingness.

Jake drew his Scimitar of Cursed Hunger and stabbed it into Eron's body, right through his heart. Eron just looked down at it with obvious disappointment before his eyebrows raised, and he commented, "A Vitality-absorbing curse? I have been battling vampires with similar abilities for days. Do you really think this will be enough?"

Jake looked at him. "Nah... but it will delay you."

A cube of arcane barriers appeared around Eron at that moment, just as Jake used Gaze of the Apex Hunter to freeze the man. Jake didn't let his eyes leave his opponent as gates he had stolen so far appeared on all four sides of the man, trapping him between the ceiling and floor. Jake pressed down on Eron from above with the arcane barrier, intending to make him completely immobile.

The arcana mana barrier closed in and pressed the gates together. Jake finally lost sight of Eron, resulting in his constant channeling of Gaze stopping. His eyes dripped with blood. Eron would still be frozen for a bit longer, and Jake pressed the barriers together even more as Eron got squished, the blade still in his heart. Jake made a final push as his entire construct stabilized.

"Let's hope this works," Jake muttered as he rushed towards the gate. He kept a part of his consciousness on the barrier to keep it active and began channeling his flame.

Inside his makeshift prison, he saw Eron struggle. The man exploded into a mist of blood but only regenerated in the same spot, the blade still stuck in his heart. He felt the energy from the scimitar increase through his connection to it; the blade consumed vital energy from Eron constantly, the absorption only increasing further the more it consumed. Jake felt Eron fight back as the white flames spread and began seeping through the imperfect gaps between the gates and into his arcane barrier... but Jake's stable arcane affinity won out in that duel, and it became clear Eron wouldn't be out any time soon. His barrier was being corroded, but slowly.

Behind the gate that Jake was attempting to open, he saw several people channeling mana into it to stop him... but they didn't stop his burning of the gate; they only made a barrier behind it. Jake sadly couldn't see what was happening further down the hallway towards the Count's chamber, but he hoped he would make it in time.

CHAPTER 25

TREASURE HUNT: UNREASONABLE PEOPLE

J ake burned through the sides of the gate to get it free from the wall, simultaneously keeping Eron trapped. However, it ended up taking him nearly ten minutes to get the door off, as he had to split his focus, and he felt Eron attack his arcane barrier with more and more power.

Once Jake got the gate off, he grasped hold of it and pulled. The moment it stopped touching anything, he put it in his inventory and saw the barrier behind where the door had been. The people there, surprisingly enough, didn't look alarmed, but just kept channeling their mana.

Jake walked up to the magic barrier and placed his hand on it. Touch of the Malefic Viper pulsed out from his palm and began corroding the entire barrier. It had only been there to make sure the gate stayed in place, making it far from durable.

With a final punch, the entire barrier shattered like glass, and Jake made it through. The moment he did so, all the casters and healers formerly channeling their power into the barrier just disappeared, leaving Hunter Insignias in their places.

They just fucking left like that?

He frowned while quickly claiming all of them... and saw that every single Insignia was empty. The fuckers had handed off all their loot to someone else already, and this entire thing had been planned. Jake rushed forward, having now wholly cut his connection to the arcane barrier behind him.

Passing through the halls, he soon looked down the hallway to the Count's chamber. The gate was open, and in front of it, he saw only a single person he didn't recognize sitting on the ground, waiting. Jake realized, there and then, that he hadn't made it. Eron and the gate had together delayed him by over half an hour, which had proven long enough for the Church to kill the Count and leave with the key.

Jake slowly approached the chamber and the man sitting there. It was just a random level 101 human who didn't look special in any way, shape, or form. It was just a D-grade from the Church who had barely qualified to enter the Hunt. Or, as the Church had clearly viewed it, a disposable messenger.

"Lord Thayne," the man said as he stood up and bowed.

"Where is the Count and the key?" Jake asked, already knowing the answer.

"I apologize. The Count of Blood was slain a quarter of an hour ago, and the key claimed. The Augur expresses that he finds this entire situation unfortunate, but he made the choice he believed was the most advantageous for the Holy Church. Therefore, he hopes that these treasures can serve as an apology." The man summoned a number of items.

Jake narrowed his eyes as he saw the altar and coffin appear. The same ancient-rarity ones he had already claimed four of each. This was all the loot the Count's chamber usually held. However, that wasn't all.

There was also a black metal claw and a metal pike, as well as two red gems. The hearts and weapons of two Counts of Blood.

"Due to other obligations, we cannot provide the keys, but the Augur and Church as a whole truly hope this can be viewed as recompense," the man kept explaining. "The Noboru clan has already made prior claims on the keys, and how could we as a Church be trustworthy if we didn't fulfill our obligations?"

Trying to play both sides... Classic Jacob.

He really wasn't sure how to feel about this entire thing. On the one hand, Jacob was an asshole for getting in his way, and on the other hand, Jake was an asshole for trying to kill the Count under the Holy Church's nose. Giving him some kind of compensation for claiming a kill—one that most would right-fully point out was theirs to begin with—was a bit weird.

Jake swiped all the loot the guy had thrown on the ground, and the moment he did so, he saw the guy light up a rune on his hand. "The Holy Church hopes this does not create bad blood between Haven and the Holy Church, or between the Progenitor and the Augur. Sometimes you lose, and this is simply the nature of the competition."

"Oh, for sure," Jake agreed.

It was also the nature of competition to openly rob people and kill them during this Treasure Hunt, so was that fine too? Jake had a strong suspicion that the last part wasn't something Jacob had instructed the guy to say. Because Jacob wouldn't have said something that dumb, that could be interpreted in so many ways.

Without further ado, the guy activated his own Insignia and disappeared, leaving an empty one just like everyone else from the Church. Jake walked further towards the Count's chamber, and right in front of the gate, he found remnants of a magic circle. As he stood in the middle of it, he vividly felt the traces of space-affinity mana in the air, as it became apparent that those who had killed the Count of Blood had left through teleporta-tion straight after.

It was another smart move, as Jake would have absolutely gotten the key from them if they hadn't.

Jake really wasn't sure how to handle this entire situation. He just shook his head and reminded himself, *Keep things simple, and take the complications as they come.*

Seeing as there was nothing left to claim in the chamber, Jake turned around and headed back towards the Mistless Plains, unsure of how he would confront the Holy Church. He sent a mental message to Sylphie letting her know, and received a response that she was headed there too.

As was the majority of the significant forces of the Treasure Hunt, Jake reckoned.

"Ms. Wells, I believe we should at least discuss the distribution of loot properly," Sven tried as Miranda and Sylphie traveled towards the Mistless Plains with the people from Valhal.

"Dude, just cut it out; I already told you this is what Sylphie and I agreed," Carmen butted in, staring daggers at Sven. "Are you saying I'm a fucking liar or what? Oh, or are you arguing that it wasn't the two of us who did the majority of the work?"

Miranda quite honestly found the entire situation utterly bizarre. Carmen was fully aware Sylphie was related to Haven, but she still chose to support the small hawk over the faction one would expect she should. It made Miranda believe that perhaps the relationship between Carmen and the nominal leader of Valhal on their planet wasn't the best.

Carmen's position in Valhal was one Miranda wasn't certain of. Clearly, Sven recognized her as of higher rank than him, and Miranda wasn't sure if that was solely due to Carmen being more powerful. Miranda knew that Valhal placed much importance on combat prowess, so it was a possibility... but none of that explained why Carmen sided with Sylphie and Haven over her own faction.

Of course, even if Carmen supported Sven... Miranda couldn't really do anything about the hawk. Something she had tried to explain several times, but Sven seemed to doubt her words.

"As I told you, I am not able to command Sylphie," Miranda asserted once more. She wasn't sure if she could divulge the actual relationship between Sylphie and Jake, but she was pretty damn confident both Carmen and Sven had figured it out. Primarily by the process of elimination.

A few members of Valhal had beasts they had brought into the Treasure Hunt. Only two people, but it still set a precedent. They knew a human had to have some kind of bond with the beast to bring it into the Treasure Hunt... and who else but the Lord of Haven could bring in a small, green bird that was one of the most powerful individuals in the entire Hunt?

"Please understand why I find it hard to believe that the City Lord of Haven doesn't even have the authority to give simple orders to the pet of—"

"Not a pet," Miranda and Carmen said at the same time, exchanging a smile.

As for Sylphie? She was just silently floating through the air alongside them as if perched on an invisible branch. Miranda had noted how she tended to refuse to sit on anyone except Jake. That part was kind of cute.

"Companion, then," Sven corrected, as Miranda was sure he thought of both herself and Carmen as unreasonable women.

Miranda had to admit that she had approached Carmen partly with purely political intentions, but from their first encounter, she had liked the woman, and Carmen was starting to become someone she would consider a friend. In some ways, she reminded Miranda of Jake. They were both highly individualistic, powerful people who were more than a little unreasonable and unpredictable most of the time.

Is it weird I'm beginning to find those likable traits?

It probably was, but it was probably also fine for things to be a bit weird sometimes.

So she continued to talk to Carmen as they made their way back, ignoring Sven for the most part, with only Sylphie joining in sometimes with screeches.

Overall? She was having a good time.

———

The group of hundreds walked through the black mist.

The curse, which everyone else who had dared venture into the mist was forced to wrestle with, appeared calm and even gave away to the large group. Shades of Resentment and other creatures of magic born from the powers of the curse swirled and flew around the group in excitement, welcoming them.

At the front of this group were three people. Two Risen and a wraith, with a man walking slightly ahead of everyone else as he showed the way.

It was naturally Casper, Lyra, and Priscilla, leading the D-grades of the Risen in the Treasure Hunt. They were a group that had not hunted Viscounts or Counts, nor solved puzzles, nor sought after loot, but had instead headed where no one else could. Beyond the wall of mist, away from any mountains. They had ventured into a land that had been covered in darkness for countless years.

Casper listened to the Shades as the powers of the curse bore into his body but did no harm. Instead, it encouraged him. Cheered him on. The curse wished for them to reach their goal.

"The final Count has fallen. It's only a matter of time now before they activate the device," Casper said to Priscilla and Lyra, relaying the Shades' words.

"We still have a head start," Priscilla answered. "Once the Vaults unlock, we will be in position."

Out of everyone in the entire Treasure Hunt, the Risen were the ones that had entered with the most information. It was a pure stroke of luck, or perhaps what some would call fate. For when they'd entered, and Casper felt the curse on that very first day, he knew.

When he'd practiced during the tutorial and been taught about magic and curses, one of his topics of research had been the one that had afflicted Yalsten. It was an example of a curse that hung over an entirely separate world in its own subdimension, and had been studied for years before the world was sealed off.

There was also one other interesting snippet of information. The ritual performed on the mist to attempt to help the vampiric race had not been thought up by the King, as many believed. It was one he had acquired. What the vampire king had not known was that the creator was undead.

For even if some of the world's history had been altered and parts of the world changed, one fact still remained...

The state of Yalsten had ultimately been engineered by the Risen. This was their world, and to them, the curse was no obstacle. They also knew about the next phase the Hunt would enter, based on what the Shades had told them... They just had to be ready for the moment the people in the Mistless Plains initiated it.

To Casper, it was never a question of if, but when that phase would activate. But he had to admit... it had gone faster than expected.

———

Jake walked back the way he came and saw the cube of white fire. His arcane barriers were being corroded at an ever-increasing speed. Finally, after a few seconds, the entire box exploded in white flames, the arcane barrier collapsed, and the gates fell to the ground, making the entire hallway quake.

Having his priorities straight, Jake hurried up over to get the four gates back in his inventory before Eron could claim them. His arcane barrier had made it so Eron couldn't put them in his Insignia, but Jake feared that the guy could now that the barrier was broken.

He also saw that his scimitar had been blasted away and was now lying on the ground. He went over to pick it up but hesitated for a moment. It was practically humming with power, as it had absorbed unprecedented amounts of vital energy... more than it had in all the time he had owned it. Usually, the absorbed vital energy would first heal Jake and then empower the blade afterward. When in combat, he always took a bit of damage from minor things... but not today.

Today, it had been stuck in a guy with seemingly infinite health, with no other purpose for the energy than to empower the curse.

Knowing it was a bit risky, Jake steeled himself and put his hands on the Scimitar of Cursed Hunger. When his hand made contact with the handle, he felt a pulse of emotion invade his mind. The endless hunger and avarice of the blade flooded his mind, and Jake just made a toothy smile. *Sated, eh?*

He knew the blade was now stronger than ever before.

Where the makeshift prison had been a moment prior, Eron walked out, looking to be in near-pristine condition. But only near-pristine. He actually looked a bit tired.

"An unexpected approach," Eron said as he eyed the Scimitar of Cursed Hunger. "The curse on that blade is not simple, and most certainly not of earthly origins. I would tell you to watch out, but I think it fits you very well... It also brings comfort to know that should you die, the curse dies with you."

Jake held onto the blade as he looked at Eron. "I didn't make it in time, so I guess you're happy?"

"I simply fulfilled my duty, even if you made a valiant attempt to make me fail."

"So you wouldn't mind me stabbing this blade back into you to empower my weapon more?" Jake asked Eron.

"Truthfully? No. But, sadly, the blade seems satisfied for now, as it stopped absorbing Vitality a minute or so ago."

Jake inspected his weapon again and indeed found that while it hungered, it was also full. So it would need some time to digest all the vital energy before it would be worth it to go stab the unkillable healer in front of him.

"Bummer."

"Quite so. With this, it appears all nine keys are assembled. My hypothesis is that you are now headed back towards the Mistless Plains, correct?"

"Yep," Jake agreed as he put the weapon away.

Eron smiled at his response. "Mind if we travel there together? I believe we have much to learn from each other. The type of mana you used is part of your arcane affinity, is it not? A curiosity, don't you think? That both of us possess Bloodlines and that both of us have managed to create our own affinities? While that is only two data points, it still does not feel like a coincidence."

Jake looked at Eron for a moment before he shrugged. "You know what? Sure. Let's take our time and have a nice, long chat as we go there."

While he couldn't get payback on anyone for his loss right away... he could delay the entire event involving the nine keys by being incredibly petty and not hurrying back to the Mistless Plains.

Also... he genuinely did believe he could learn some interesting things from Eron. As for getting revenge or something like that against Eron? Jake honestly didn't care that much. He would just take learning a bit about controlling vital energy as payback.

———

Not even three days after the Treasure Hunt began, the forces of Earth had gathered all nine keys and were ready to unlock the second stage of the Treasure Hunt.

While the Noboru Clan was the faction to acquire five keys first, determining a winner was not easy, if even possible. Because while they had obtained five of the keys, Jake had obtained more of the loot from the Counts. All of this also disregarded the many individual actors of the event who'd stumbled across lucky opportunities and treasures.

The Treasure Hunt continued... as determining an overall winner was far too early with more than a week to go.

CHAPTER 26

TREASURE HUNT: EXCHANGE

Jake hated to admit it... but Eron was a genius. And no, not the hyperbole version of a genius, but an actual genius. Even before the system, he had been a damn monster in human skin. Jake even had suspicions he'd been doing things that could be considered magical before mana and magic were even a thing.

He was awfully open about his Bloodline too, not hiding many details. He explained how he saw sparks, and how he believed these sparks were the representation of life and existence itself. He told Jake about how he had forged his path entirely around these sparks... entirely around his Bloodline.

In some ways, it wasn't that different from Jake. The main difference was that while Jake had grown up and lived in the old world suppressing his Bloodline, Eron has explored and embraced his. This was also why Jake reckoned the guy had a far higher understanding of his Bloodline than Jake did. Or maybe they were just vastly different Bloodlines?

Another interesting point of discussion was arcane affinities. Eron's affinity was interesting, if a bit odd. Jake was pretty damn sure his own was better. Eron's was far more limited, and the man confessed he hadn't acquired his arcane affinity before he was already D-grade. Another point for Jake.

There was one thing that still bothered him, though. An ultimate question of sorts.

"So, if it gets down to it... could I kill you based on what you've seen?" Jake asked Eron. He thought, hey, the guy had been truthful so far, so no harm in asking.

Eron looked at Jake a while before nodding. "Yes. As I said, I am not invincible—at least, not quite yet. If we'd continued our battle, I do believe I would eventually have been withered down. To regenerate my body takes mental energy and concentration. Differently from yours or most other's vital energies, mine does not simply reform my body passively... it requires active input."

"So if you get knocked out and then your body is destroyed, you die for good?" Jake asked.

"Astute observation. This was the first weakness I worked to alleviate, so no, not quite. I do have fail-safes in place for most scenarios I have come up with, but not all work as well as others, and some I cannot test out, as doing so means risking true death."

Jake nodded, a few plans already forming in his head. Eron easily took damage, so what if he made a poison specifically engineered to make it harder to regenerate? He already had experience with poison working not only on the body, but in the metaphysical plane of existence. Some type of hemotoxin, perhaps, considering that poison already made healing harder.

"So... what's the drawback?" Jake finally asked.

Such power had to come with significant drawbacks. Jake did not believe a D-grade could achieve immortality or near-invincibility without it having severe consequences. He was already aware that Eron's physical abilities were pretty damn bad, and his offensive prowess with his magic was also bottom-tier. The only reason he held some fear towards the magic was due to his lack of understanding of it. But if they were to fight? Jake would just summon an arcane barrier around his body to block the white flame, as it sucked against mana-based shields.

"Hm... that, I believe, would be unwise to disclose. But I guess I can share the simplest one. I have no mana or stamina, and any task requiring either forces me to manually convert my health points. This includes a constant conversion of health to stamina for me to simply be walking and talking right now."

This made Jake stare at him for a bit. "That just sounds fucking exhausting," he noted, shaking his head.

He was aware that the transformation of energy from one type to another was possible. He did this in part when making potions. But it was not one-to-one, and if he tried to make his health into stamina, as an example, it would take concentration and time, and he would spend way more health than he would get stamina. In other words? It was practically never worth it.

Yet apparently, that was how Eron now lived. *What the fuck?*

"Oh, hey, what do your Endurance and Wisdom stats even do now?" Jake asked curiously.

"Add to health instead of their respective resources," Eron answered.

"Let me guess, you also put all Free Points in Vitality?"

"A significant amount, yes, but I also invest in Willpower. As I said, abilities that take away my autonomy in any way—or any attacks that hamper my mental faculties—could prove potentially deadly. In fact, the soul attack you used earlier was a great example. While incapacitated, I was unable to heal myself even if I wanted to, allowing you to trap me."

Jake nodded. "Got it; I'll have a special vat of toxins ready to trap you next time."

Eron just smiled, and Jake began asking him more about the control of vital energy. The man gladly explained his insights, with Jake listening and learning. He even did some basic testing as the two of them casually strolled down the tower and into the plains.

The man had a level of insight into vital energy that was

quite frankly insane, only matched by his willingness to teach Jake. Of course, Jake also taught him in kind. He talked about how mana shaping and manipulation worked, and how Eron could possibly try and better stabilize some of his magic or possibly even control his arcane affinity more. His white flames were crude, and Jake believed that their corrosive properties could be significantly improved.

There was truthfully no bad blood between them. Jake learned that the reason Eron helped the Holy Church was because they offered him a certain treasure, as well as the ability to study those who had died and become Holy Spirits.

Holy Spirits were apparently the result of someone with a blessing or even just a baptism dying. While regular folk would just die when they were killed, the Holy Church somehow saved people in their ranks. At least partly. Their souls would be extracted and taken to an artifact in the closest Holy City, and from there, be sent to the Holy Land, the realm of the Holy Mother.

Jake had to admit it all sounded kinda shady, but Eron explained his own Patron god had assured him it truly did work like that. This was probably why the Holy Church was the most prominent religious organization in the multiverse. Who didn't like the thought of a life after death?

Well, Jake. Jake didn't like the thought of that.

Eron admitted he would also just prefer to avoid death altogether, but how a soul could exist without becoming undead was still of interest to him. Jake also tried to get Eron to spill the name of his Patron god, but got no answer. Just a long tirade about how the god had the most beautiful spark he had ever seen, besides Eron's own.

On that note, Jake also learned that Eron was well and truly a narcissist who believed himself superior to everyone else around him. Well, nearly everyone else, as he didn't seem that obnoxious when he talked with Jake, even if there was a hint of superiority. Eron liked to be the one teaching Jake, and was standoffish when Jake gave him tips in return, even if he did ultimately acknowledge them. Perhaps because Jake was the only other person with a Bloodline and at least publicly recognized as possibly the most powerful person on Earth.

Jake was totally fine with being on the receiving end, as he learned more about vital energy and even how to control it than ever before. Eron even enthusiastically placed a hand on Jake's shoulder and showed him how he could direct his vital energy to heal a wound faster. Of course, to be like Eron and just pop in and out of existence wasn't possible for Jake... but to learn to regrow an arm within a minute or two if he used a healing potion? It should be possible.

He even got some ideas about his own arcane affinity and vital energy, but nothing worth testing quite yet. It also became more and more evident that Eron truly didn't have any bad intentions towards Jake or Haven or pretty much anyone. Instead, he seemed apathetic and openly stated that he believed killing others was such a waste. He believed all life should be preserved if possible, including not snuffing out sparks.

Finally, as they walked through the plains and Jake saw that they were closing in on the Mistless Plains—Eron didn't, as his Perception sucked—the healer asked Jake a favor, clearly a bit uncomfortable doing so.

"Would it be possible for me to see your mask for a moment?"

Jake stopped up and looked suspiciously at Eron. "Why?"

"I believe you know why," Eron said, giving Jake a knowing smile. "The spark is faint, but most certainly there. It burns in a way and glows in fashions I have never seen before. I merely wish to observe and inspect it. Nothing more, nothing less."

"What once was inside this mask has died—notification, experience, even a title and everything confirming that," Jake rebutted. He did know there was something about the King slumbering, but he didn't truly believe it was the King of the Forest.

Perhaps it would be a vision of the King or some fragment of it, but the Unique Lifeform itself? Villy had told him that one doesn't simply circumvent true death. It wasn't like Jacob and his skill to avoid it... The King had truly died, just like William. William had only returned to life due to some special and incredibly valuable item. Jake didn't think the King of the Forest could do the same.

"You are only making me more curious when you say that... and you killed this being at least before the World Congress, yet the spark grows only brighter," Eron said, his eyes practically shining.

Jake looked over Eron once more, seeing his unabashed curiosity. "Got anything to trade? Also, you can only look at it with me right here, and not for that long."

He didn't fear Eron stealing it. The item was Soulbound, so Jake could always feel its location, and no one else could bind it. So letting Eron see it wouldn't even be a risk, as Jake knew the guy couldn't put the mask in his inventory or anything like that. But that didn't mean he wasn't going to get something in return. Sure, they were friendly, but this entire interaction was ultimately an exchange of knowledge.

Eron looked even more reluctant as he sighed. Finally, he took out a small notebook. It didn't look to be larger than a few dozen pages, but the man held tightly onto it. "This notebook contains some insights I have into the metaphysical existence of the living. It may seem inadequate in your eyes, but these are things I've discovered through the sparks of existence. Do with it as you wish... but do be aware this knowledge may not be useful to you, as it deals with concepts I have only theorized and not proven. But... do keep it safe."

This was the most serious Eron had been since they met, as he looked Jake dead in the eye. Jake was confused for a moment, then took the notebook and began reading through it. He saw odd diagrams and runes, as well as drawings with lines that messed with his head, due to seeming straight yet curved. Everything on the pages seemed to move as he looked at it. *What the hell is this?*

Yet a part of him understood soon after... Eron was a researcher. Did he fear that what he had learned and discovered would disappear if he died, and had thus chosen to pass it onto someone he believed could keep it safe? Was that maybe why he wanted to become unkillable in the first place? Was Jake just theorizing based on little to no information and deciding this entirely on gut feeling?

Probably yes to all these, and definitely yes to the last one.

Having been shown sincerity, Jake relented by taking off his mask for the first time in he-didn't-know-how-long. He usually just made it invisible, and as he could eat and drink potions through it, there was no reason to ever take it off.

It did feel a little weird to have it off as he held it out to Eron, the man staring intently down at the mask. "You got a few minutes, okay?" Jake asked, not really asking.

"Of course," the healer said as he took hold of the mask and looked at it curiously. He examined it all around and even took out a tool and tried to pierce it, all to no avail. Finally, Jake saw the guy enter the final stage. He poured his weird energy into the mask and peered deeply down into it. Jake felt like he saw two faint sparks in the man's eyes, and then...

Then Jake lost connection to the mask.

His mana fell by 25%.

He reached out towards Eron to grasp it back, as the man stood in a daze... and then everything returned to normal. The connection was back, the mana enchantment restored. Jake hurriedly Identified the mask and saw the description was exactly the same. The only trace of it ever happening was that he truly had lost the mana, as the increases to his maximum had temporarily disappeared.

Eron still stood there in a daze for a moment before he handed the mask back to Jake, his hand shaking slightly.

Jake glared at him suspiciously as he took the mask from the man's shaking hand. "What did you just do?"

"Nothing..." Eron answered. "I couldn't scour any information... I apologize."

Looking down at the unchanged mask again, Jake seriously couldn't find anything different, and his danger sense was utterly silent when he went to put it on. Once he did so... still nothing.

"I... I believe we should separate from there. It would not be good if the Holy Church believes we are in collusion after I allied with them temporarily... I shall take my leave," Eron muttered as he turned around, not even giving Jake time to respond or keep asking him what had happened.

Jake could only stare after the man, confused. Then, after Eron had gone into a building in the distance, Jake took off his mask again and looked at it inquisitively. "What happened back there?"

It was not quite certain if he was asking himself or the mask.

———

Eron walked inside a small, secluded building. He appeared relatively normal except for his one shaking hand, not showing anything outwardly.

But once inside and away from any prying eyes, he fell to his knees and started quivering. He balled his fists as blood began dripping down from his fingernails digging into his skin, and he took long, heaving breaths as he stared at the floor, trying to make himself stop uncontrollably shaking.

His eyes were bloodshot from the image replaying in his mind. He felt a genuine fear he had not felt since the tutorial. The horror he had seen was not one he wished to ever lay eyes upon again. Yet, at the same time, he felt an equal level of excitement and relief from the encounter. Relief that he was alive.

For he had just gazed upon death and escaped.

CHAPTER 27

TREASURE HUNT: PHASE TWO

J ake had, in usual Jake-fashion, returned late to the center of the Mistless Plains. As there was no mist in the Mistless Plains—hence the name—it was easy to see everything, far and wide. He saw several basecamps scattered about, some of them even having tall walls and magical barriers.

Finding Miranda and company would have been difficult if he didn't have a living GPS locator in the form of Sylphie. Jake made his way over, feeling many gazes upon him as he did so. Scouts from the myriad factions kept an eye on his casual stroll, none of them approaching him or making him aware they had even seen him.

Oh, but someone did come to meet him.

A fluffy green ball of feathers soared through the plains right towards him with incredible speed, kicking up a cloud of dust in her wake. Jake opened his eyes as the small hawk barrelled into his chest, and he hugged the cute little bugger.

"You got faster!" Jake commented as he cuddled the bird nuzzling up to him. He kept walking towards the place where Sylphie had come from, and his pace picked up a bit.

"Ree!" she heartfully agreed, proud of herself.

She kept making screeching sounds and green apparitions of

wind, manifesting and narrating her adventures around them as
they got back to Miranda and the others. Jake didn't even know
she knew how to make those wind constructs, and honestly
thought they were kinda cool and very artistic-looking. Primarily
due to their fluid forms, which made them look very abstract.
What he did piece together was that she had hunted down
vampires and cursed armors like everyone else.

He did get confused about the part with a giant bear-looking
creature that Sylphie, for some reason, depicted as resembling a
cartoon bear that kept getting whacked around by a vampire.

She was still putting on her little show when Jake spotted
Miranda in the distance, surrounded by quite a few people. He
recognized them as ones associated with Valhal right away,
including that Sven fellow and the woman Carmen, whom
Sylphie had been hanging with. He was a bit surprised not to see
Sultan or Neil and his party, though. Whether they had left the
Treasure Hunt or were still out there was hard to know. But,
then again... did they need to return to the middle? They had
their own stuff to do, and the event about to take place wasn't
anything they could affect.

"Lord Thayne," Miranda said with a respectful bow when he
made his way to them, putting on her courteous persona in
front of the onlookers. The aforementioned onlookers kept a
watchful gaze, with Carmen staring at him with an odd look.

Jake nodded to Miranda in response. "Good job as always,"
he said, not quite knowing what she'd done that was a good job.
She had been part of getting a key, so she had done something
good. Also... he was just happy she was still around, so he had
someone to handle the talking.

Although... Nah, it was still too early to begin beating
disagreeable people up and taking their stuff.

Dispelling his thoughts, Jake turned to Carmen. "Thanks for
taking care of Sylphie."

He had noticed that Carmen didn't look weirdly at Jake
alone, but also Sylphie. The bird had now climbed from his

chest and shoulder to stand atop his head, establishing her dominance.

"So, the hawk is your pet?" Sven asked him as he saw the bird standing on top of Jake's head. It was more a statement of fact than a question, as the man had made assumptions Jake quite frankly found insulting.

His response was to look at the people behind Sven as he asked, "So, are those humans your pets?"

The entire mood instantly became weird, but Jake didn't care. The guy had insinuated something Jake wasn't cool with, so he'd pettily shot back in kind.

That the guy didn't understand newer cultural nuances of post-system sapience and autonomy wasn't Jake's problem. In fact, from what Villy had told him... a human having humans as pets was more normal than a human having beasts in the multiverse.

Everything was still for a moment until Carmen began laughing loudly. "That was a damn good one! Sometimes it bloody feels like it, them doing everything he says like loyal little puppies!" She kept laughing for a few more seconds, with Miranda smiling a bit uncomfortably as she stood beside the laughing woman. Carmen followed up with a question after she stopped laughing and looked at Jake. "Anyway, what is your relationship with Sylphie?"

Jake returned her gaze and answered, "Eh... she is the kid of some friends? So, kind of my niece? Not sure exactly how you would classify it, but does it really matter?"

He kept rubbing the soft feathers of the bird that sat on top of him, her happily just sitting there like his hair was her nest.

Carmen looked at him and shrugged. "I guess it doesn't."

The entire atmosphere improved somewhat, and Miranda took the chance to redirect the conversation. "How did it go? Did you get the items you wanted?"

Jake shook his head. "Nah, the Holy Church got two and the

Noboru clan three, as far as I can tell. So, yeah, it sucks; I only got three myself, with Sylphie getting one."

"Ree!" Sylphie agreed, proudly puffing herself up.

"What happened?" Miranda asked. "I was told by Arnold he estimated you would make it in time."

"Eron got in my way, as well as some defensive measure to seal off the Count's chamber. On a side note, Eron is pretty much unkillable, so, yeah, that's a thing." Jake was fine with the people from Valhal also hearing him. Heck, he half-expected them to know already, considering they were a major faction. And if they didn't know, the only thing he did was spare them wasting their time.

"He's a healer, right? Can't you just wear him down?" Carmen butted in.

"You would think so, but I'm pretty sure I could blow him up a few hundred times without him minding," Jake said, shrugging in response. "Either way, if you meet him, I would just recommend walking away. The dude is slow and can't really do any worthwhile damage, so just ignore him."

"He sounds lopsided as fuck... Did you try separating his heart and head from the rest of the body?" Carmen asked in a wondering tone.

"He totally is lopsided, and when I tried to wrap him up, he just blew up his entire body and reformed, so I reckon he could do that if you try to separate his body parts."

"Anyway!" Miranda came back in, clearly trying to stop the conversation from derailing more than necessary. "As you have the keys, should we head for the center? It has already been scouted out, and the nine alters for the keys found. The other factions are there too."

Jake agreed, and Miranda began explaining about the placement of the altars designed for the keys. She made a construct of mana, showing the Mistless Plains and how they were spread in a circle around the center of the Plains. It all matched what the projection had told him so far, and it did look like they would open up some kind of hidden tower.

The Noboru Clan, the Holy Church, the Court of Shadows, more people from Valhal, and many other factions were present to see what would happen when the nine keys were brought together. Notably absent was the undead faction, but Jake didn't consider it further. He seriously doubted they could have been wiped out, so they were probably just up to their own shit with their own weird undead agenda.

Jake and the others soon met up with a group of people that had clearly been waiting for them, making Jake feel pretty good about himself for wasting their time just a little bit. It was the pettiest of revenge, but short of going on a murder spree, it was all he was gonna get.

At the front of the group stood the Sword Saint and Reika. At their side were Jacob and Bertram, as well as a few parties of decently powerful people. He saw his brother and his folk gathered a good distance away; Jake threw him a nod before he went up to the group with Miranda, Carmen, and the others. A big crew from Valhal had also joined them at some point.

"I must admit... this competition did not transpire as I had hoped," the Sword Saint said, opening the conversation. "In the end, perhaps it was foolish for only two individuals to make a bet with so many uncertain factors." The old man still smiled at Jake. "Nevertheless, despite the flaws, It appears I won. I possess five keys, and to my knowledge, you have four."

Jake looked at the old man and his way-too-cheeky smile. *Patience, Jake, we got like three-quarters of the Treasure Hunt left... You'll have your duel.*

"Seems so. I guess you were better at splurging and hiring help," Jake answered.

"Indeed, yet it proved barely enough to win out over the power of nepotism," the Sword Saint counterattacked.

The two of them stared at each other until Reika broke it up. "Patriarch, should we not focus on the matter at hand?"

"Mm, we should," the Sword Saint acknowledged. "We both agreed on the terms that I shall be the first to explore whatever opens up, correct?"

Jake just looked at him and reluctantly nodded, throwing Jacob and Bertram a look—with perhaps a bit of Gaze of the Apex Hunter mixed in.

"Well, then, should we begin?" the old man asked. "Each altar requires a key, and from what some of the good folk at the Holy Church discovered, we need to input all keys at roughly the same time."

He then motioned to Jacob. Jacob tossed over four small stone medallions of some kind, which the Saint then handed to Jake.

"We have nine of those medallions, and when one of them breaks, all nine do," he explained as Jake inspected the medallions, finding just a small magic circle on each. Simple stuff, really.

"Sure," Jake agreed, tossing a medallion to Miranda and another to Carmen beside her. The last two, he kept for himself for now.

"Half an hour should be enough for all to be in position to insert the keys, I hope?" Jacob suddenly butted in.

"I don't know, Jacob. Are you sure I won't get delayed?" Jake asked as he looked his way.

Jacob winced and gave an apologetic smile, while Bertram just shook his head and palmed his face. The other people behind him looked downright hostile at Jake, clearly not happy that he had dared take a jab at their glorious Augur.

"Half an hour it is. Simply insert your key when the medallion breaks," the Sword Saint said, un-derailing the conversation. He made a circle with his finger, showing nine dots and a general outline of the Mistless Plains. "We shall take these five while you handle the other four. Are we in agreement?"

Jake once more just nodded and turned back to the other people. He nonchalantly handed Miranda and Carmen a key each and let the two of them pick out two altars. For the last two keys, he went over and gave his brother one along with a medallion. He and Sylphie would handle the last one.

No, he didn't trust Sylphie with doing it. Sure, she probably could, but then again, she was not even half a year old. It was a lot of responsibility for someone so young.

The entire process was easily handled, as everyone wanted to get the next phase started. They all got in position, and Jake saw that each altar looked to be made of the same black metal as the doors. He spent his entire half an hour trying to figure out if he could steal it, but found the task impossible.

Once the half an hour was up, he felt the medallion crumble, and without further ado, he inserted the key in the very obvious slot on the altar. For a brief second, nothing happened—then, suddenly, he felt it.

Red light exploded out from both sides of the altar, creating a wall of pure energy towards the two adjacent altars. All of the altars around the Mistless Plains fired off these walls of energy at once. When a circle was formed, the interior of the circle began slowly filling with red runes.

It was a giant magic circle... one far more powerful than any he had ever seen before. Well, besides the one in the vision from the Path of the Heretic-Chosen skill.

The entire magic circle kept powering up, and Jake spotted quite a few panicked faces around the circle, as they were unsure of what was happening. Jake was relaxed due to his silent danger sense... Also, he didn't believe the system would be so dickish as to make this into some suicide ritual. The charge-up of power continued for a few more seconds until, finally, it culminated.

It felt like the entire Treasure Hunt world shook as the ground opened up and a mighty structure began ascending. What came was a spire that looked to be made entirely of some pure-white crystalline material. It sent shockwaves through the land as it finally made its way into the world after countless years of being hidden away.

Energy washed across the plains, and the spire pulsed with power, growing taller and taller. It didn't simply get elevated from the ground, either... it truly grew. So much power had been packed into it that Jake quite frankly found it insane.

Finally, the tower made it all the way up to where the dark mist began. The moment it touched, the true purpose of this creation became clear.

Like soap touching dirty water, the cursed mist parted and exploded out to both sides, the sky seeming to be torn open. The sound of thousands upon thousands of screams echoed through the entire world as the spire attacked not only the black mist, but the curse itself.

From the beginning, this spire had not been built as a treasure tower or residence... It had been created for the day when the curse had weakened enough—and the spire had accumulated enough power—to strike back at the curse and try to reclaim their world.

Looking at the sky far above, he saw the darkness of the mist throughout the sky begin to turn white, the darkness and the power of the curse slowly fading away. At the same time, the entire crystalline spire began growing darker. Jake realized it wasn't dispelling the curse... it was absorbing it. Containing it.

What also became clear... was that this tower could not be entered. Thus, the Sword Saint's price for winning their bet meant nothing.

"Lucky one!" Jake cheered. He high-fived Sylphie, who sat atop his head, just as the system notification signaling the second phase of the Treasure Hunt appeared.

CHAPTER 28

TREASURE HUNT: VAULTS

J ake and everyone else in the Treasure Hunt all got the notification at the same time.

While the curse slowly claimed their world, the inhabitants of Yalsten did all they could to fight back. As a final gambit, they created a device to seal the curse forever and banish it from their homeland. Yet the curse was too powerful and the device too weak... so they waited, empowering the device as the curse slowly weakened.

During this time, when Yalsten deteriorated and the nobility began weakening, they sought ways to preserve their heritage and wealth for future generations. To do this, Vaults were set up with the most priceless of items, hidden away within the cursed mist till the day Yalsten was ready to rise again.

That day never came... and now the Treasure Hunters from another universe have come to seek them out. Nine Counts have been slain, the keys assembled, and the spire

summoned. As the curse is made to retreat and the mist
washed away, the Vaults have been reactivated once more.

However, the keys to these Vaults have long been lost
and forgotten. To acquire the treasures in the Vaults, the
Treasure Hunters must overcome their defenses, and
whilst these defenses have weakened with time, they are
not to be underestimated.

Be warned... that legends long forgotten may be released
as the Vaults begin to open.

May your continued Hunt be fruitful.

*What is a good system message without ending with a
warning and then telling you to do the exact thing it just warned
you about?* Jake joked with himself.

He was somewhat surprised at the system just spelling things
out like that, but perhaps that was a part of the rewards for
clearing the first phase? Or maybe it was to get everyone up to
speed, as it assumed most of the influential forces who had
hunted down Counts knew this already.

Which, from what he had gathered, they did. Most had
found out through old recordings or messages or such left
behind. Jake was pretty sure he had lucked out with the projection, even if the information he had received was flawed. It had
said there would be a treasure left by that True Ancestor in the
center of the Mistless Plains, and Jake had a hard time seeing that
be the big crystal spire. Primarily because the True Ancestor
should have left the treasure there long ago, while the spire was
made to fight a curse that came to be later on.

Jake also wasn't sure if that crystal tower could be called the
"greatest treasure" either, so he felt pretty damn lied to.

Well, technically, the projection hadn't lied... for in the eyes
of the vampires, this tower probably was the greatest treasure to
be found in this world. It was their final hope of fighting against

the curse—a way to seal it in and then possibly take the entire spire and toss it away somewhere.

Of course, that would still leave all the usual vampire problems, but at least they would have cleaned up one issue.

But... there was still one thing bothering Jake. Why was this entire plain devoid of mist while it existed everywhere else? The spire didn't remove the mist itself; it only absorbed the curse in it. Perhaps the altars had absorbed the mist? Or was it something else?

While he saw many others around the plains begin to group up again, Jake headed straight towards the spire to get a better look at it. The red runes still dominated the inside of the circle, with the energy walls still present, but Jake didn't feel any danger from the energy. It was just there for the spire and not harmful to him.

He made his way towards the spire and, with his sphere, saw complicated devices that appeared to be made of the same black beneath the ground. All of it was organized in a highly complex matter, giving the magic circle both a magical and physical form.

Jake noted that the complexity only increased the closer he got to the crystalline spire. Sadly, he had to stop when he got within a hundred meters of it, as the power of the curse began invading his body, proving that while it was contained, it wasn't fully suppressed.

This would have stopped him if not for his special little Root of Eternal Resentment. He summoned it, and instantly the curse let him pass. He moved closer to encompass more of the spire, but more importantly, what was below the spire.

A coffin.

The bottom part of the spire encased a coffin that was even more intricate than any of the other ancient-rarity coffins. Within it was a figure. The moment he saw it, a shiver went up his spine. *Strong.* Below the coffin itself was not an altar, but what looked like a giant safe of some kind... a giant safe that was pure darkness when he tried to look inside it. *Like a system lock-box,* Jake noted.

He was pretty damn certain he'd just spotted the final boss of the Treasure Hunt, as well as that special reward.

Jake was uncertain if he should share this knowledge, but decided to do it with his closest allies. Primarily to tell them to move their basecamps out of the Mistless Plains, as he had a feeling whatever was sleeping below the pillar wouldn't be in a good mood when it awakened. At least, not if any of the other creatures he had awakened during this Treasure Hunt were good references.

Now, when he said, "tell others to move their basecamps," he naturally meant his allies. So, Caleb, the folk from Valhal, and, of course, Miranda, in case she wanted to warn anyone.

He was confident the Noboru Clan and Holy Church could handle things themselves and didn't need a heads-up, right? And if they didn't prepare, and some powerful creature went on a rampage and began tearing things up... those in the camps would need to be fast on those Hunter Insignias. If they weren't? Well, that was just too bad, and not Jake's problem.

Oh, who am I kidding...

Jacob probably already knew with his weird-ass prediction skills, and the moment the factions saw everyone evacuate the Mistless Plains, they were sure to follow.

Jake shook his head as he made his way over to where Miranda was supposed to be. He sprinted to meet up with her and Carmen, but was surprised to see that Caleb had also come and was currently conversing with the two women. Sven and his "pets" weren't anywhere to be seen.

"... it was really funny, and you just had to be there. Jake's face was priceless, and he was so embarrassed."

He heard his brother's voice as he got closer, then only began rushing even more, as the little traitor was clearly sharing stuff he shouldn't. Miranda was smiling, and Carmen laughed loudly at whatever he had said.

"Anyone wanna clue me in?" Jake said when he appeared before them.

"Oh, no, it had nothing to do with you," Caleb confidently stated with a smile, the two women not even trying to hide their smirks.

"I heard my damn name."

"Must have misheard. It happens."

"I wanna bet I have more Perception than all three of you combined," Jake argued.

"And yet you managed to mishear... Truly a wonder of the multiverse," his brother said as he stared questioningly at the sky, acting all philosophical.

Jake nodded as he smiled and turned to the two women. "Caleb faked having diarrhea for eight hours straight because he was too scared to ask out his now wife and hid away in the bathroom."

Caleb just stared at Jake for a moment. "It wasn't eight whole hours, and it wasn't like I hid away all the time..."

"No, you just ran back there every time she tried asking you something," Jake kept piling on.

"I was like sixteen, and—"

"She ended up asking him out because he was too much of a chicken."

"Now, let's just move o—"

"He then booked them a table at a family restaurant but accidentally chose the wrong day."

"I believe we have something more important to do!?" Caleb yelled, waving his hands dismissively, then muttered under his breath, "Besides... it was fine... They had plenty of free ones..."

"What?" Jake asked his dear brother. "I didn't say anything; you must have misheard me. See, that's what happens when you don't invest properly in Perception."

"With these Vaults opening up, I assume you will go and explore them?" Miranda finally came in, saving poor Caleb.

Jake finally showed mercy and nodded in agreement. "For

sure. Also, tell everyone to evacuate the Mistless Plains. I believe we have a final boss on our hands, sleeping right below the large crystal spire. No doubt it will be released at some point, and ancient entities that have been sleeping for a long time tend to be grumpy when woken up."

Caleb returned to a more serious mood, too, and nodded. "We already planned on de-centralizing all control personnel to not risk a direct attack on us. The members of the Court of Shadows will spread even more out from here... Do be warned that when three days remain of the Hunt, we will switch from simple thievery and obtaining loot ourselves to acquiring treasures more forcefully."

"Should we be worried?" Miranda asked, a bit in doubt.

"I hope not; they should be aware of the members of Haven," Caleb answered, turning to Carmen. "I cannot say the same about the members of Valhal. While those unassociated with larger factions will be prioritized as targets, those from Valhal will undoubtedly also be hit. The orders are to avoid lethal force if possible and just make people leave... but accidents do happen."

"Oh, that's fine," Carmen said dismissively. "I don't really give a shit."

"I... alright?" Caleb answered, perplexed, before just shaking his head. "I'll have to head back now. See you guys and gals around."

Carmen and Miranda gave him a nod in acknowledgment, with Jake giving him a big wave as he headed off to soar into the sky. Sylphie mimicked his waving movements, looking cute as hell. Jake felt the intensely jealous gaze of Carmen, and it was easy to understand why.

Everyone wanted a cute feather ball like Sylphie, but only his head was a satisfactory home for one.

He chose to ignore her jealousy and instead simply said, "I wanna go and find these Vaults, and possibly do near-suicidal and reckless things to clear some of them quickly... Would you two be fine taking care of Sylphie meanwhile? You can always contact me through her if any problems come up, and I can feel her location at all times."

While he liked spending time with Sylphie, the reality was that she simply wasn't powerful enough to travel with him, and his entire style functioned better alone than with others. Miranda and Carmen also both seemed to have taken a liking to Sylphie—especially Carmen—and the woman from Valhal also felt pretty strong, so the little hawk should be safe.

Not that Jake had seen anything he believed could slay her in the Treasure Hunt quite yet, besides maybe that Shade of Eternal Resentment, but his belief it could was primarily based on him not knowing what it was capable of. In truth, he wasn't aware of what Sylphie could do either, but he did know she was incredibly difficult to put down.

"Of course!" Carmen answered before Miranda could answer.

She even tilted her head a bit towards Jake and Sylphie, expectantly. Sylphie looked at her and then down at Jake. Jake just shrugged, letting the bird do what she wanted.

Sylphie decided to meet Carmen halfway. She jumped down onto Jake's shoulder, rubbed her head against his cheek in good-bye, and then flew over and landed on Carmen's shoulder. While the hawk had not graced Carmen's head with her presence, Sylphie had still granted her the privilege of having the mighty Sylphian Eyas stand on her shoulder.

Truly an honor.

Jake smiled as he waved them goodbye, once more reminding them to take care of the little hawk. Mentally, he also sent Sylphie a message telling her to take care of Miranda and warn him if anything bad was happening. Once he got a mental approval from her as well as a semi-angry screech in his mind, admonishing him for how he dared believe there was anything she couldn't handle, he left.

———

Casper stood with the other undead as the energy washed over them. The darkness and curse energy within the mist drew back, the mist around them returned to pristine white once more. Casper held out his hands to feel the energy and sighed.

"They activated the device," he concluded.

The curse had been pushed back in all directions, and had more or less expanded the scope of the entire Treasure Hunt by opening up areas otherwise dominated by the curse, allowing only those of the undead race to enter. Yet now, with the disappearance of the curse, it was open to everyone.

They continued their travel for a bit longer until, finally, the pulse of energy reached the edge of the Treasure Hunt world.

At that moment, not far in front of them, a red pillar of light fired up towards the sky like a massive flare. Not long after, a similar red pillar arose in the distance to the side, followed by a third and then a fourth.

"The Vaults have been revealed," Priscilla said with surprise before quickly recomposing herself. "Remember, our primary goals are the Seed and the Core. The Core should be in the Vault we are headed for, but be warned that finding the Seed may take longer. Not even the Shades were sure of its location."

She spoke primarily to the Risen, who had been scouting the immediate area until the system message appeared, getting them all up to speed and on the same page. "Additionally... do not enter any Vault without proper preparations, and hand over all acquired loot before doing so in case you are forced to teleport out, or the worst happens."

They all nodded and continued towards the red pillar of light, where they suddenly reached a cliff... if it could truly be called that.

Casper stared down into the abyss as he stood at the edge, knowing where he was. He had reached the edge of the world... At least, he was close to it. For before him was the Vault they had been looking for. It was on an island floating in the middle of nowhere, the dark abyss below.

Yalsten was not a planet in the multiverse, but a separate dimension. One that had begun slowly eroding and falling apart many, many years ago. It remained stable enough to not break entirely, as an equilibrium had been reached... but the edges were still damaged.

Casper looked back at the others, then towards the Vault in the distance. "I'll handle this one alone. Go for the next Vault before other participants arrive."

They had already looted everything that had been within the mist on the way to where they were now. It had been done partly hoping that it would make people believe the area was desolate of treasures... but they hadn't known the red pillars would appear, marking all the Vaults. While there were many of them, people were bound to come sooner or later, so they would have to move fast to press their advantage.

"Remember to hand over what you acquired so far first," Priscilla reminded him. "I promise you will get it all handed back when you return successfully."

He turned to her. "No."

"We have a protocol and a process you are not excluded fro—"

"I said no," Casper said again. "If I fail, we all fail. So just do your job while I do mine."

Dark energy began revolving around him as he jumped off the edge and began flying towards the floating island in the distance. The turbulent space mana in the area tried to distort and rip his body apart, but the moment it got close, it was rebuffed... the curse of Yalsten still echoing out of Casper's body, blessing him and granting him power.

CHAPTER 29

TREASURE HUNT: OUT OF PLACE

C asper flew towards the island with the Vault, the curse energy revolving around him as he soared through the unstable space. The cause of the disturbance in the natural balance of space was naturally the world having been partly broken by the curse, but also due to the battles that had taken place within.

Many high-level beings, including A-grades and possibly even S-grades, had fought within the world known as Yalsten, and such battles rarely left the area unbroken. Yet space also had a natural inclination to always stabilize itself. It wanted to be as solid and as stable as possible while returning to its original form. This was why space could so often be shattered—or its worlds borderline torn apart—only to nearly always find a way to stabilize once more. Of course, if large parts had been broken for good... those parts remained broken, and space simply had to find an equilibrium to avoid a chain reaction.

In these unstable places where space had been shattered, the physical realm constantly shifted and turned, overlapping in places to keep this equilibrium. They were patterns of failed attempts at repairing themselves, which meant that any outside entity entering often resulted in space simply trying to shift and stabilize around them. Diving head-first into unstable space would be a quick way to be torn into several pieces.

However, Casper didn't fear this. The curse that empowered him helped shroud and protect him, but even without it, he was confident. While his class revolved around curses, his profession did not. He was a Dungeon Engineer, and one of the basic elements of dungeons was space magic. His understanding was still simple and very specialized, focusing on dungeons and not general combat or even making things like spatial items... but what little insight he had was more than enough to survive the unstable space in the Treasure Hunt. In fact, his knowledge was especially suited for this kind of thing.

Now, had this world been undergoing actual collapse, or had he found himself in a full-on space storm, he would've been utterly fucked, but luckily it wasn't that bad. Though Casper doubted it had much to do with luck and more to do with design. All of these system events were designed, after all.

They were set up to challenge those who participated—not that different from most dungeons, albeit far more tailored to the participants. It was interesting, as the system even made its own dungeons, and in some respects, one could view this entire Treasure Hunt as a collaborative dungeon of sorts specifically made for Earth. The comparison was actually quite apt, as this was even a completely separate space, and none would likely ever enter Yalsten again. At least, not this version of it.

Just focus on your task, Casper reminded himself as he made it through the unstable space and got close to the island.

Once he got close enough, he noticed that a bubble of stable space had formed around the island. In fact, it was the reason this island was even whole and not broken into tiny fragments like everything else around it. This was no doubt due to the Vault, which had been formerly hidden on what had likely once just been part of the plains.

This was evident from the blue grass and the familiar-looking environment. The only real difference was a single structure smack in the middle of the island, emitting a giant, red pillar of light. Casper ignored everything else as he made his way towards the structure.

When he got close, he saw it looked just like an old house with unassuming features. It was camouflaged well, or at least it had been. The issue now was that the building was whole with no broken parts, and even looked recently cleaned, giving away the high tier of the materials used and the enchantments placed on it.

Casper walked up to it and placed his hand on the door handle. *Enchantments.* He knew something was off the moment he sensed them, but frankly, there was nothing he could do about it. He sighed and opened it without any problems, then stepped inside to see a perfectly regular-looking room—at least, by post-system standards. It was an entrance area to greet guests, and once more, it all looked way too clean. The door automatically closed behind him, startling him a bit. He upped his guard.

Slowly making his way forward, he said, "Lyra, do you detect anything dangerous yet?"

"No... it feels almost too safe. I can't even detect the outside," she answered, her voice echoing in his head.

This made Casper frown, then turn around and open the door he had just entered through. When he did so, he saw a living room where the outside of the island had been before.

"Great... a damn maze," he sighed as he got to work.

The worst part? He was pretty sure he hadn't even found the actual Vault yet; this was just the automatic defenses to trap people, probably until someone could come and investigate. But, naturally, no one would come to investigate, so all this meant was that Casper would have to find a way out himself.

Closing his eyes, he took out a small compass-looking item and tapped it, sending out a pulse of space-mana that mapped the building—or at least, attempted to. It projected a structure to him, and when he saw it, he sighed again. All he'd gotten was a jumbled mess, showing the same rooms repeating tens of times over.

"I think we'll be here a while," he said to Lyra, in all honesty not finding the situation that bad. At least he could now be alone with her with no other annoyance around.

———

Someone else heading towards a Vault was naturally Jake. He used One Step Mile through the plains, not taking any detours or finding any distractions. Not that many, anyway. He passed several people and parties on the way, and he even noticed a few of them changing course when they saw he was headed towards the same Vault they were.

The Vaults themselves were damn far away. Past all the towers and buildings, all the way to where the black mist had dominated in the distance before. Jake did wonder if he could have scouted it using the Root of Eternal Resentment before this second phase began, and while he probably could, he didn't really regret his decision not to.

Even with Jake's speed, it still took him over one and a half hours to make it to the Vault. He only had a handful of brief stops on the way to take some loot that was too good to pass up on. A part of him just couldn't run by a rare-rarity herb or a super shiny piece of metal giving off dense mana.

Jake didn't encounter many enemies on the way, but there were some. They were the vampires from before—those weak ones that had previously avoided him—but now at a far higher level. He even encountered a few variants that were more powerful.

Not that any of them were a threat.

The most usual kind he found, deeper in, looked a lot like

the usual Ekilmares he had seen before—with the long fingers, willow form, and sharp claws—but instead of their pure white and sickly-looking body, these were an almost impossibly dark shade of black.

[Young Nocturne Ekilmare – lvl 132]

When he fought one, he found out it was because it *was* an impossibly dark color. They used magic to make themselves appear even darker than usual, and even had some dark-affinity magic and illusion magic tossed in there. Overall? A lot stronger than the typical ambush predators.

They did have one little problem, though... Their stealth abilities were shit. With the mist turned white again, they stuck out like sore thumbs. Luckily for them, they were far stronger, so they couldn't only ambush things.

Jake killed only a single one of them in a two-minute bout, mainly to get a look at what it could do before executing it.

He did find it interesting how these had clearly been living within the black cursed mist. It seemed to run contrary to the notion of the curse being anti-vampire and wanting them all dead. Actually, thinking about it, with vampires having to feed... had these vampires just evolved and mutated to feed off the mist? It was fascinating how both cursed and non-cursed variants appeared. Maybe they were both cursed?

Anyway, it was interesting but not at all something he should spend his time trying to find out—especially with just over a week of the Treasure Hunt left and many Vaults to loot.

The red pillar of light soared towards the sky right in front of him, soon entering his line of sight. He passed over a small hill and into a valley... and... it was honestly hilarious.

Within the valley, he saw several broken trees that were little more than stumps. They had clearly been eroded by a combination of the curse and a lack of proper mana to feed them. Yet, smack in the middle of it all stood a perfectly normal-looking tree—at least, by this world's standards—utterly unaffected by anything. It was so out of place Jake couldn't help but chuckle under his breath.

He was confident that back in the day, this place had been a forest of some kind. In fact, the only stumps remaining were those closest to the totally-a-real-tree, as whatever had protected it likely had extended slightly to those around it. He couldn't detect anything suspicious about the tree with any of his senses; it really did just look and feel like a regular tree.

A long time ago, when this place was a forest, he didn't doubt it had been pretty much impossible to find. A single, unassuming tree in the middle of a forest wasn't exactly what many would assume was a hidden treasure vault. Jake made his way into the valley and towards the tree, and once he got closer and it entered his Sphere of Perception, it all began making more sense.

It wasn't a tree at all—shocker, that one—but merely a thin covering of bark-like material and fake leaves. Below the bark was a metal structure shaped like a tree with advanced runes carved into it, with the top of the crown concealing a sphere of metal.

Walking up to it, Jake decided to just poke it to see what would happen. He extended his finger and lightly touched the tree, expecting something to happen.

A few seconds later... nothing.

Jake tried casually punching it, still doing nothing. Then he tried infusing some mana, but found that the bark-like coating shielded the structure beneath. Which, funnily enough, was what bark on actual trees did after the system had arrived.

He did find that at places in the bark, a little mana seeped in through small holes if he tried to direct his mana into them, with each hole corresponding to a hidden rune. Jake did a quick run around the tree and found hundreds of these tiny openings.

Okay... totally some sort of password system.

It was also notable how this worked with mana and not that weird blood energy. Had it been made by some other enlightened race? Probably. The core of the whole tree structure was also obviously the metal sphere on top, and when Jake peeked into it, he saw how complicated it was.

Is the sphere the Vault?

It was large enough to contain some valuables, but if it had the name "Vault," he assumed it was more likely a spatial storage of some kind. No doubt he would have to input the correct password on the tree to make the sphere unlock and grant him access to the loot. It was the logical solution, and he was sure the creator had spent a long time making an elaborate puzzle.

Anyway, Jake decided to set it on fire.

He pressed his hand on it and let his Alchemical Flame slowly erode the bark. Now, could Jake have tried to solve it? He sure could've, but that honestly just seemed like a lot of work. Was it possible this would end up breaking the tree, thus barring him from any treasures? It was possible... but he doubted it. It would be a horrible way to design the device, as there was a big chance someone would try to break it. Also, if he did break it, then all he would lose was an hour or so of travel time. Way better than spending what could be days trying to figure out the password, as he could just head for another Vault.

It didn't take him more than a few minutes to remove a small patch of the fake layer of bark, and the moment he breached the outer shell, the tree got mad. Really mad.

The entire structure lit up with runes that began humming with power, destroying all of the fake bark at once and revealing a metal tree with the sphere cradled where the crown had been. At the same time, the entire valley Jake was in began glowing, and he came to learn that those burned-out-looking tree trunks did serve a purpose.

A wave of mana was sent out, followed by a dozen beams of light descending from the metal branches of the trees into all of the broken black trunks. The entire process took only a few seconds, and soon Jake heard creaking sounds from all around him.

The trunks all began growing with insane speed as branches resembling arms spewed out. Some of them had only two branches, while others summoned over ten. He felt the curse energy emanating from all of the growing creatures, and he had a strong feeling this entire defense system was kind of scuffed from the long exposure to the curse and the passage of time.

Nevertheless, the creatures weren't entirely broken.

Around him, eleven figures were rising. Feet of roots erupted from the ground as the creatures dislodged themselves. Finally, a twelfth figure erupted from below by crawling out of the earth. It was larger and more brutal-looking than any of the other creatures, and Jake Identified a few of them, including the biggest one.

[Cursed Vault Guardian Treant – lvl 140]

[Cursed Vault Guardian Treant Lord – lvl 150]

[Cursed Vault Guardian Treant – lvl 140]

"Treants, huh," Jake muttered.

This was his first time fighting those, but it was quite the common enemy, as far as he knew. They were also objectively superior creatures compared to the accursed fungi. Yes, even if these treants were literally cursed, Jake still believed that the natural existence of a mushroom was more cursed by default. Because fuck mushrooms.

The treants began closing in on him from all sides, the largest of them in the back. They were all semi-large, around five meters tall, with the Treant Lord standing at eight meters. Their bodies were all sorts of messed up too. Long, squishy, tentacle-like vines protruded from the Lord's body, flailing around. The other treants had far too many arms, and some even had more than seven leg-like appendages. They had really been fucked up by the curse, but they were still relatively dangerous—for the usual Treasure Hunt participant, that is.

As for Jake? Jake was just happy he had skipped the overly long and unnecessary puzzle-solving sequence and found the more straightforward solution. Taking out his bow, he cracked his neck and got to work.

It was time to do some deforestation.

CHAPTER 30

TREASURE HUNT: ARROGANT YOUNG MASTER

Treants, oh, treants. It was a creature type that was present across video games, fiction, and general fantasy. No doubt, humans from ages past had seen trees and wondered, "What if that massive fucking tree could walk around and smash stuff?" and just let their imagination take things from there.

Yet when Jake finally got to meet them, he got some scuffed, broken versions that were far closer to elementals than actual trees. He felt cheated and betrayed that they even kept the treant tag. They couldn't even do proper tree magic! No spearing roots, no long vines extending from them, no razor leaves fired after him. Just a bunch of rotting trees that blew up with a single arrow and reassembled themselves using their curse energies.

Jake did what he could as he worked to make the world right. He tore the trees apart one by one, starting with the Lord. It was the biggest of the bunch, and the only one Jake hoped would at least give him a bit of entertainment.

Well, the first thing he did was take out the Root of Eternal Resentment, hoping he could just bonk them to death and be done with it. Sadly, it didn't work. Jake assumed it was because these weren't truly part of the Yalsten curse... just generally fucked up by curse energy. If the Yalsten curse directed them, wouldn't they hold more hate for the vampires sitting around the edges of the valley trying to take advantage of the fight than Jake?

No, even if cursed, they were still directed by the fake-metal-tree-that-wasn't-even-a-metal-treant tree. That damn tree was a big disappointment too. Sure, Jake had gotten cheated out of fighting real treants, but a mech treant could still be cool, right? But *nooo*, he just had to fight these shitty, rotting things. They even smelled.

Still... not as bad as mushrooms.

As for the fight itself, it was just the usual stuff. The wannabe treants used simple attacks, mainly just trying to smash Jake with a touch of curse magic mixed in here and there. The Treant Lord used its weird tentacles to try and grasp Jake and infuse him with its curse, which was also the reason he targeted it first. Those damn vines were a bit too mushroomy for his liking. Cursed *and* mushroomy, even.

What he had to hand to the treants was their durability. He kept blowing them apart time and time again, yet they kept regrowing the broken wood. In the end, Jake blanketed the entire valley in toxic mist and, with his blood-soaked arrows, poisoned the fake treants one after another, whittling them down. While his poison didn't do much... it did take its toll.

Needless to say, destructive arcane energy also did plenty of damage.

For nearly an hour, the valley was a hellscape of broken and rotting pieces of wood flying everywhere, pink-purple explosions, and a constant, poisonous mist blanketing everything. Occasionally the entire valley would light up for a brief moment as a Mark of the Avaricious Hunter was activated, making it quite the show from an outside perspective.

Sadly, all the vampiric observers had taken off in fright, not wanting to get involved at all. Probably a good decision on their part.

In the end, Jake stood in the middle of the valley, destruction all around him as he cleaned his cloak—which now looked to be covered in mold. Cursed mold. Good thing he'd gotten it upgraded. Altmar technology sure was something. To his surprise, he had even gotten a level from the entire endeavor.

You have slain [Cursed Vault Guardian Treant Lord – lvl 150] – Bonus experience earned for killing an enemy above your level

You have slain [Cursed Vault Guardian Treant – lvl 140] – Bonus experience earned for killing an enemy above your level

...

You have slain [Cursed Vault Guardian Treant – lvl 140] – Bonus experience earned for killing an enemy above your level

* 'DING!' Class: [Avaricious Arcane Hunter] has reached level 136 - Stat points allocated, +10 Free Points*

* 'DING!' Race: [Human (D)] has reached level 133 - Stat points allocated, +15 Free Points*

In retrospect, it probably shouldn't surprise him. He hadn't gotten a level after he killed the last Count of Blood, and he had gotten more experience since then. Granted, the fights hadn't been the hardest, but Jake hoped he would encounter something worthwhile later on... If not, then at least that final boss should be worth something.

If he had to place these cursed fake treants on any kind of power hierarchy, he would say they were about the level of the Warlords or Fungalmancers—AKA, creatures Jake had been able to kill relatively easily dozens of levels and hundreds of elixirs ago. On the other hand, he had a feeling these enemies weren't truly designed to kill anything, but just stall people more than anything. They were overly defensive, after all.

With all the fake treants dead, Jake summoned the Root of Eternal Resentment again, and this time it reacted. It began absorbing some of the energy from all the dead enemies, but only a bit of it. Once it was done absorbing the energy, he put it back in his Insignia and also stored all of the wood that remained of the fake treants. It looked like shit, but who knows? Maybe it was worth something to someone.

He walked up to the metal tree and placed his hand on it again. This time, he got an entirely different response. It felt almost like an invitation... Without further ado, he accepted it and disappeared, teleported into the hidden space of the metal sphere.

As for how he knew he was in the metal sphere? Because he could vaguely feel the outside of the tree through his Sphere of Perception. He now found himself in a perfectly spherical room. He stood on a platform surrounded by a barrier in front of him, with the space behind him filled with furniture and other amenities, like it was a living area. The entire sphere was only about ten meters in diameter, so not exactly a huge space.

Behind the barrier, Jake saw plenty of stuff that he assumed were treasures. The issue was... he had no idea how to get through the barrier. He placed his palm on it and felt like it was utterly impenetrable with usual means... Maybe he could wear it down with enough time if he used—

Before he could finish his thought, a figure suddenly appeared off to the side of the metal sphere. It was a woman in an odd uniform, and Jake instantly recognized that it was some kind of projection and not a real person.

Jake looked at her and saw the red eyes indicative of a vampire. Her pale white skin also made him think the same, and she had an odd symbol on her forehead, reminding Jake of a third eye. Identify didn't return anything, as it wasn't actually a person, but he still had the feeling that whoever left the projection hadn't been weak. Quite the contrary.

"Who are you? How dare a mere D-grade enter this place?" she said, her voice filled with venom. She made it sound like Jake had just killed her entire family.

"I'm here to claim whatever is stored in this Vault, so would you kindly lower the barrier and allow me to take it all? Yalsten has long fallen, and there will come no one else to claim it." Jake said this while looking straight into her eyes. If she was going to be an ass about it, so would he.

Weirdly enough, she took offense to his response.

The entire room became flooded with an aura Jake could only recognize as above D-grade. C-grade? Possibly even B-grade? Either way, it wasn't one with any true intent, just the aura and nothing more. While Jake knew that would often be enough of an intimidation tactic against most other D-grades, Jake just kept staring at her, unfazed.

"Well?" he asked.

She looked a bit perplexed, which surprised Jake. A part of him had assumed this projection wouldn't show any real intelligence, but just be like the Counts or something. There were predetermined responses and such... but the look of utter confusion on her face seemed very genuine. So... closer to the Altmar one?

"Who are you?" she repeated.

Jake had taken this time to properly inspect the room, as well as what was behind the barrier. While he couldn't see through it with his eyes or other magical senses, his Sphere of Perception sure could, and behind it, he saw a few interesting things. One of the items was more interesting than any others, as it had a certain motif engraved on it that he recognized... and based on its prominent position...

He decided to take a gamble.

Jake stared at her, faking anger and relaying his own aura. "A better question is who you think you are to ask me that. Has Yalsten really fallen that far?"

As his aura washed over the room, he happily mixed in a dash of an aura that was normally concealed by Shroud of the Primordial—the one marking him as the Chosen of the Malefic Viper.

For what Jake had seen in the Vault was a medallion with the motif belonging to the Order of the Malefic Viper. Prominently displayed on a pedestal in the middle of the room for all to see.

His actions were a pure gamble... and they paid off.

The projection of the woman paled—something he was impressed that a vampire, much less the projection of one, could even do. Jake allowed her to bathe in his aura and gradually recognize his presence, gladly playing the arrogant young master to get some benefits.

After a few seconds, she seemed to come to her senses. She practically prostrated herself on the floor. "This member of the Nalkar line greets the Malefic's Chosen; I apologize for my disrespect and not recognizing you!"

She stared at Jake with amazement in her eyes, which made Jake feel both uncomfortable and amazed at the overdone response. However, he had to keep up his persona and toss around his clout. "I don't really care either way, and didn't I tell you to open up the damn Vault already?" Jake asked, literally staring down at her.

"This... I am under strict order to only open it if a member of the Nalkar line arrives, or someone holding the key..." Her domineering attitude was utterly gone, replaced by meekness.

"I wasn't asking," he said before shaking his head in fake disappointment. "And here I thought the Nalkars were smart... but it appears even your intelligence is merely an illusion. How disappointing."

Considering how she had named herself a part of the Nalkar line, Jake naturally remembered that he had a heart from a Nalkar vampire. The Nalkar vampires were talented in illusion and mind magic, and were more casters than warriors, unlike most vampires Jake had encountered. As for the insults? Well, he was a young master, was he not?

"I..." she said as she pulled herself together and got up, still keeping her head lowered. "I shall naturally unlock it. Apologies for the continued disrespect. I was simply too caught up in old customs and procedures. I hope this has not led to any bad blood between the Nalkar line and the Order."

With that, the vampire made some motions, and different runes around the room began glowing, unlocking the barrier. That was when Jake realized this was actually just another puzzle. One he had bypassed by fooling the projection into helping. But then again, perhaps that was also just another option. One he could totally see someone like Jacob exploiting.

The barrier slowly faded as more and more runes were activated, and Jake decided to be a bit nicer. "I shall make sure to mention it to the Malefic One that the Nalkars aren't all that bad."

"My eternal thanks," she said with a bow. "It gladdens me that those who fled from Yalsten made it safely to the Order... It may be overreaching, but how is the clan doing?"

Jake hadn't expected that one. He stopped up, looking as if he was thinking. He was actually just waiting for the barrier to fully disappear, as he didn't want to say something dumb that could make the projection change her mind.

If he said he had no idea, it would be suspicious, considering he clearly knew of the Nalkar vampires... or would it? He didn't know how common they were. If they happened to only originate from Yalsten, it would be suspicious as hell if he was super knowledgeable. On the other hand, if he lied and said they were doing well, it would be a bit out of his fake arrogant-master character, wouldn't it? Mainly the part about him even bothering knowing if they were doing well.

Man, did he wish he could just ping Villy and ask him if his

Order happened to have a bunch of vampires in it, and if any of those were of the Nalkar variant.

Luckily, the barrier went all the way down without any issues, and Jake stepped inside past where the barrier had been before, ready to One Step Mile out if the projection became hostile.

Then he answered, "Are you questioning if the Malefic Order doesn't take care of its own? That I even bother knowing of the Nalkar vampires should be answer enough about how they're doing, shouldn't it?"

It wasn't a perfect answer, but it seemed to be good enough, as the projection was visibly relieved. Jake totally understood that... This projection had been left in this Vault a long time ago, only to be activated at some unknown future time. If Jake's theory was correct, these projections were more or less just clones, which meant they had their own thoughts, even if they were only temporary existences. To give the projection some relief wasn't too much to do... and he decided to actually check in with Villy after the Hunt to ask about them.

"Naturally," she finally answered, a smile on her lips.

Considering the projection seemed satisfied, Jake began inspecting the loot. He initially wanted to start with the medallion related to the Order of the Malefic Viper, but decided against it. He was the Chosen of the Malefic Viper; why would he care about some small token? Thus, he went for the other stuff first. Also, there was something to be said about saving the best for last.

The first item he went for was the one giving off a rather impressive magical aura. There were three items in total giving off strong auras, which he did find a bit weird, considering this was meant to be a Vault made by powerful beings far above D-grade. No doubt, the system had curated what was handed out.

He went over to the item, and even if it was the one giving off the weakest aura... it was quite the impressive item nevertheless.

[Wand of the Mindbreaker (Epic)] – A wand created from an unknown type of wood with the ability to project a portion of the abilities of a Mindbreaker. The wand has been soaked in the blood of a dead, high-tier D-grade Mindbreaker variant, and been infused with the core of one, granting it some of the Mindbreaker's abilities. Allows the user to cast the spell Mindbreak, sending out a wave of pure mental force to damage the outer layers of the soul for anyone nearby. Enhances all mind magic cast using this wand. Enchantments: Empowered Mind Magic. Grants the skill: [Mindbreak (Epic)]

Requirements: Lvl 120+ in any humanoid race.

It was a wooden wand that honestly didn't look that special besides its carvings and the slightly reddish-brown color that appeared uneven in places. Jake considered experimenting with it, but decided to pick up his pace to avoid spooking the projection. Looking impressed with a measly epic-rarity wand wasn't something an arrogant young master would do, now, was it?

So he nonchalantly tossed it in his Insignia and moved on, trying to fake utter indifference like swiping epic-rarity loot was just another day in the office for the arrogant young master of the Malefic Viper.

CHAPTER 31

TREASURE HUNT: TEST OF CHARACTER

W ith the wand in his inventory, he moved on to some of the other stuff. The next item of interest was a white crown sitting on top of a pillow. The crown had a relatively simple design and was made out of some kind of white metal, reminding him a bit of white gold. In the center of the crown was a small, red gem that looked to almost be glowing. It also gave off an impressive aura, reminding him a bit of the Nalkar vampires, and it became clear why upon identifying it.

[Nalkar Crown of the Dominant Mind (Ancient)] – A crown created by a powerful crafter from the Nalkar vampire line. The crown is made of an unknown metal and is extremely durable. A processed heart of a powerful Nalkar Vampire is embedded in it, soaking it with magical powers. The Nalkar Heart enhances all mind, illusion, and phantasmal-based magic. Passively grants resistance to all mind-affecting magic while worn. Enchantments: +200 Willpower, +150 Wisdom, +100 Intelligence. Dominant Mind of the Nalkar.

Requirements: Lvl 130+ in any humanoid race.

Well, damn, Jake thought as he looked at the stats. That was some impressive stuff. The pure stats it gave were quite insane, and with the added benefits of making mind magic better? A pure win. Especially considering the wand he obtained earlier. Jake reckoned a mage using mind magic could go far with those two together. Even if one wasn't a mind mage, he reckoned most mages could make good use of them. The pure stats and mental resistance granted by the crown were likely considered enough by most people.

He also wasn't going to ask about the ethicality of using the heart of one's brethren to make a crown. Because, honestly, that was less weird than people getting their loved ones cremated before the system and turning their ashes into jewelry. He wasn't judging; he just found it weird, and it was probably a cultural thing.

As for the question of whether Jake would use it... he would find that out later. He had a feeling he couldn't, due to the mask on his face getting in the way, and he really didn't want to try and put it on his head there and then, potentially looking like an idiot with the projection watching.

Thus, he just put it in his inventory, not showing any visible signs he was impressed.

Jake finally went over to the token with the Order of the Malefic Viper symbol on it and picked it up, the projection looking on nervously behind him. Once he did so, he used Identify on it... and was honestly taken aback.

[High-tier Alchemy Token of the Malefic Order (Legendary)] – A token created by the Order of the Malefic Viper. This token represents a deal made with the Nalkar vampire line to grant a set number of the Nalkar clan vampires membership to the Order, and includes a set number of benefits. This token has never been turned in, and doing so may lead to certain

rewards. Gives off an aura that encourages growth in toxic alchemical products.

First of all, legendary rarity for a token that would grant access to the Order of the Malefic Viper? Was this just Villy and his Order flexing by having such a high-rarity item do that? Or was there actually something special about it? Was that aura really enough to warrant the rarity?

He was also surprised such an item was present in this Treasure Hunt. Was it like the Altmar things in the dungeon? A method to recruit people? But from what Jake had gathered from Villy, the Order wasn't really that big on recruiting, and had quite high standards usually.

Maybe the Nalkar vampires were just that great? Considering the starved heart of one was epic rarity, he assumed the regular version was ancient rarity. With their natural magic abilities and the stats granted by the crown likely corresponding to what their race gave... he could see how they were well-dispositioned to doing alchemy.

It would be pretty funny if they had a big presence in the Order, he joked to himself. He kept walking around the room, trying to look as disinterested as possible as he emptied it out.

"Sir... I may be speaking out of turn... but for what purpose do you acquire the furniture?" the projection asked with a very nervous tone.

"Are you saying this furniture is of poor quality? I just don't believe anything, even with low value, should be wasted. That is the true path to strength—always strive for more and take anything you can. I am a man of avarice; this is simply my path." He stole a sofa while delivering his sage advice.

The projection slowly nodded as Jake left the Vault's interior an empty husk, taking everything and anything he came across.

The rest of the loot after the token wasn't much to write home about. Jake was more sure than ever that the system had kind of curated things and chosen what should remain. This

Vault had supposedly been left behind by beings several grades above Jake, so for it to only house D-grade equipment and items a D-grade could feasibly use wouldn't make much sense.

During his looting spree, the projection just looked on, appearing to reflect deeply on his words. A bit useless, considering she was a projection who could never leave the Vault. Jake found this entire practice of leaving projections behind odd, albeit useful. He just couldn't imagine how a projection with sentience must feel... knowing it would cease to be in not that long, existing only with a single purpose. Or maybe they were programmed somehow? Either way, Jake felt a bit sorry for them.

Once he was all done in the room, he turned to the projection and nodded. "While there was nothing of use to me, I still found some items of value I can give to my subordinates. I shall remember the courtesy of the Nalkar line and be sure to pass it on."

"If... if I may ask a single more question," the projection said, then asked inquisitively, "Is... is the True Ancestor truly dead?"

Jake looked at her, suppressing any reaction. He should have known this one was coming, shouldn't he? The True Ancestor, Sanguine, was without a doubt a powerful god. As a Chosen of a Primordial, it probably made sense he would know.

If he said, "yeah, he dead," it could possibly have some bad effects, but so could lying and saying the guy was still alive. Heck, if it was even a guy. Was Jake even sure of it being a man? Sanguine wasn't really a name Jake could place gender on. Wait —maybe the Ancestor was some genderless monstrosity?

Jake tried to look calm as he considered his answer, and eventually settled on a noncommittal one. "What do you believe?" he asked her. Considering he didn't know, he preferred to try and stay mysterious. Any answer could backfire, though at this point, he had a feeling he could answer anything he wanted without any negative consequences.

"If the True Ancestor remains alive... why would he have

abandoned us like this? Why would he allow us to suffer, and see his children be hunted and slaughtered for no reason? Why would he permit so many lines to be extinguished?" She had more bite to her now, her frustration evident.

Oh, a great way to bait some more info out, Jake thought.

For this one, Jake actually had an answer. Perhaps not the right one, but the one he was sure Villy would give... and in many ways, the same one Jake would.

"Why not? Why would the True Ancestor care if the weak are culled? Would it not only give space for the truly powerful to rise? For the lines that remained to become more powerful than ever? Perhaps it was a cleansing. A test. All you need to know is that the Nalkar line remains... and if the True Ancestor died or not, does it really matter? If the Nalkar line was so weak as to require the help of Sanguine to remain viable, it was never worthy of existing to begin with." Jake allowed his aura to bellow out of his body to reinforce his words.

It was harsh, but in Jake's opinion, the truth. If a race existed only by relying on some powerful god, was that truly a race that should exist? Clearly, the vampires hadn't all ceased to be after the True Ancestor disappeared or died or whatever. Being caught up in some old geezers vanishing was just a waste of time. Jake knew the gods had probably created some races throughout the ages... but those races remained even after the god died. If a race would disappear with the death of a god, that race would just suck, in his opinion.

The vampire woman just stood looking at him for a while, her face a bit offended and angry, but she didn't say anything. Jake saw this and decided to double down.

"Don't misunderstand; I am complimenting the Nalkar line. You have reached a stage where you don't need the True Ancestor to be powerful. You don't need the Order of the Malefic Viper. You can stand on your own feet and show the multiverse the Nalkars are not to be trifled with. That is true power and worthy of respect."

Jake had no idea if this would work... but the look on the projection's face quickly changed as she went deep in thought. Jake himself was considering if now wasn't the time he should get out of the damn Vault, considering he was done looting it, and for every sentence he spoke, he got closer and closer to saying something he really shouldn't.

Yet before he could say anything... the room shook. Everything around him seemed to shift and move.

He looked over at the projection, and she smiled and bowed to him. "Thank you... truly. It gladdens me to know the Nalkar line remains powerful and under the umbrella of the Order of the Malefic Viper... With your words, I believe I can rest. None will come here, and none will need to know of our fate... Please take care of the Nalkars in the future."

When she was done saying this, the entire projection turned to wisps of energy and flew into a formerly hidden compartment Jake hadn't even noticed with his sphere. He had simply thought it was part of the magical construction of the metal sphere and some power source... and in some ways, it was. It had been the source of the projection.

The compartment opened, and within, he saw a familiar red gem that still gave off an aura similar to the projection. It was a vampire heart—the projection's heart. Jake hadn't expected it to turn out like this... but when he used Identify on the heart, he was totally fine with how things ended up.

[Nalkar Vampire Heart (Legendary)] – The heart of a powerful, C-grade Nalkar Vampire. This type of vampire is a rare variant with extremely high innate abilities in illusion and mind magic, and often possesses a larger reserve of blood energy than most other vampires. The rarity is higher due to the high innate talent of the Nalkar Vampire that left behind this heart. Has many alchemical uses.

From this, Jake also learned the vampire he had been talking with had been C-grade. A part of him felt proud he had just managed to fool a C-grade, but another part of him felt a bit shitty about his deceptive tactics, especially considering how the projection had made itself cease to exist by giving him the heart. Not that he believed being stuck in this sphere was much of a life... but still.

Jake didn't even have time to consider how he should get out before he felt the pull of space on him. He quickly stored the heart in his Insignia before he was pulled away from the space. He was tossed outside of the metal sphere and landed on the ground where he had killed the fake treants.

The metal tree in front of him began rusting before he had even landed, and within less than five seconds, it had turned into silver dust and fallen to the ground.

He walked up to the dust and found it gave off no mana. He tried burning a patch of it with Alchemical Flame, discovering it wasn't even resilient either. It was just useless dust. Shaking his head, he stood up and turned to walk towards another red pillar of light in the distance.

Jake promised himself that if the Nalkar vampires truly did exist out there and within the Order, he would do them a solid in the future. They had just given him some awesome loot, and he was likely the first to clear a Vault... so that was the least he could do.

———

"Patriarch... was it truly wise to antagonize the Lord of Haven like that?" Reika asked her great-grandfather somewhat nervously.

This was just after they had opened the spire and caused the curse to be absorbed by the large, crystalline structure. Reika was worried that this could hurt the relations between the two factions and potentially even make them enemies.

Her great-grandfather just looked at her, smiled, and shook his head. "My dear... if he chose to make us into mortal enemies over this, is he truly someone we want to ally with? If his ego is so fragile, and his emotions so immature, he would lash out from losing such a minor competition, then he was never worthy of admiration or respect."

Reika looked a bit at the Patriarch, taking the words in. She admonished herself for thinking about the situation so simply... Her great-grandfather hadn't only made the competition to get some potential benefits; it was also a way to scout out Jake's character. And she had to agree. If he chose to make either them or the Holy Church outright enemies over a competition with loosely defined rules, where it could be argued neither side truly honored the spirit of the aforementioned competition... then he truly wasn't someone worth working with. If even such a minor slight turned into conflict, then working with him would be hell.

She already knew he wouldn't act out, based on her brief encounter with him. Sure, he was competitive to the extreme, but he wouldn't begin killing people for minor things. At least, she didn't think so. Their time had been brief, but during that, he had never gotten angry even when she one-upped him, or he was wrong.

"Besides," the Patriarch said, continuing, "Wasn't I the loser here? I now owe the Holy Church, and my price for victory was to be the first to enter a crystal spire that cannot be entered."

Her great-grandfather laughed and shook his head, clearly not caring that much. She looked up at him and couldn't help but wonder who would truly win in a duel between him and Jake. From a purely analytical standpoint, Jake was stronger. But, for some reason, she just couldn't see the Sword Saint losing either.

"Now, let us not miss out on more rewards than necessary," he said, looking out into the horizon before turning to her with his usual relaxed smile. "I shall head south; you take the north-eastern area. Remember to report in... Oh, but before you go, remember to evacuate all of those under your command from the Mistless Plains."

Reika nodded, not even questioning why. She had already seen the Holy Church packing up and retreating out of the plains. It looked like they were relocating to one of the cleared-out towers, and Reika decided to do the same.

The Sword Saint nodded to her and, with a final wave, spoke, "Happy hunting."

CHAPTER 32

TREASURE HUNT: RUBIK'S CUBE

T he second phase of the Treasure Hunt started out as a mad dash for the closest Vaults. The Risen had a head start and had already located and mapped out the location of several before the phase began, looting everything in and around these Vaults.

Other factions simply rushed for them. For most, it would be a half-a-day journey or more to the closest Vault, including much combat and challenges along the way, making it potentially take even longer. One had to remember that someone like Jake had a powerful movement skill, while a party often had at least one member—often the healers or the heavy warrior—who had difficulty traveling fast.

Due to the danger, as one moved further away from the central Mistless Plains, it wasn't viable for most people to go solo either. Only the more powerful individuals could do this, as the average rogue, caster, or archer from a party would find themselves in hard-fought battles against several Ekilmare variants.

All of this ultimately resulted in only the most powerful parties or individuals making it to the Vaults first, and while this would, in the eyes of many, look like an advantage... in many cases, it wasn't.

———

Jake made his way through the mist towards another Vault. The journey took him more than half an hour due to the distance, even with the constant use of One Step Mile. This one was about as close to the center of the Treasure Hunt as the one with the Nalkar vampire, just in another cardinal direction.

He had spent a good while killing fake treants and talking with the projection and looting. He knew it was unrealistic to be the first to reach this Vault, too, but still hoped for it. Yet as he got closer, it became clear he wasn't the first.

Flashes of light lit up in the distance, only visible through the mist due to his high Perception. No doubt a fight was going on, and Jake considered if he should interfere or try and head elsewhere further in, hopefully being the first to reach that one.

Ultimately, he decided to say *fuck it* and just head to his current target. With around a week left of the Hunt, it was fine to begin robbing a bit if people wanted to compete. If it was a puzzle or something, he could just beat people fair and square, and if it was solely a fight to unlock the Vault... well, he would deal with that situation too.

Making his way over another hill, he saw that this Vault was also in a small valley. The plains had many valleys, and the further one moved from the Mistless Plains, the more verticality got added to the terrain, with hills, valleys, and even the occasional small mountain beginning to pop up—real mountains this time, not the live-in mountains.

He had a good vantage point at the top of the hill leading into the valley and saw the situation below.

A mishmash group of people was fighting an even larger group of vampires of the Ekilmare variant. It was the usual Nocturne version, except for one larger than any of the others. It didn't have the same sharp claws, either, but something far closer to human hands. Its head was also disproportionally too large, and it had a huge belly.

Jake used Identify on them to get an idea.

[Young Nocturne Ekilmare – lvl 133]

[Young Nocturne Ekilmare – lvl 135]

[Juvenile Nocturne Ekilmare Matriarch – lvl 142]

He then turned his attention to the humans. There were eight vampires in total, while the human side had four. One of them used shadow magic and dodged around while firing bullets from a magical gun. Another was a mage alternating between fire and ice magic, the third was a rogue with two swords, and the final person was a mage surrounded by massive stone armor.

From what he could see, these four weren't party members, but individual fighters. They clearly weren't used to working as a team but did so nevertheless. Jake used Identify on them all, seeing they were fairly similar in level.

[Human – lvl 121]

[Human – lvl 118]

[Human – lvl 119]

[Human – lvl 124]

The rock mage was the highest-leveled one, followed by the guy with a magic gun. Observing from the hilltop, Jake saw that he didn't need to get involved—at least, not right away. While the fight wasn't easy for the group of four, they did seem to be winning. The Matriarch was more like a support variant than a true fighter, as far as he could tell, and Jake saw the guy that he determined was from the Court of Shadows slowly wear it down with his shadow gun quite nicely.

Instead, he turned his attention to the thing giving off the massive pillar of red light and marking a Vault's location. The thing in question was... nothing. The pillar just fired up from the blue grass on the plains, making Jake theorize the thing was underground.

Jake was in a bit of a conundrum. Should he walk into the valley to investigate? That would undoubtedly shift some attention to him and interrupt the fight, considering they were sometimes battling even within the red pillar. He hated interfering with fights without any reason and robbing others of a good challenge... but he also hated wasting his own time by sitting around.

He tried looking from a distance, narrowing his eyes to inspect the area with the pillar. He felt the mana given off by the area was different—probably also explaining why the vampires were there. Monsters just loved areas like this with special mana or a higher mana density. It allowed them to passively level and stay powerful while also making their resources regenerate faster. Well, Jake and other humans also got the benefit of faster mana regeneration.

As he was thinking all this, something great happened. The lowest-leveled of the bunch—the ice-and-fire mage—was suddenly jumped by four of the vampires at once in a coordinated attack. The Matriarch even empowered them all with some magic, making their claws glow-in-the-dark color.

Excuse!

Jake happily saw his chance to interfere when he saw the poor guy about to be ripped to shreds. If this had been an actual party and not just four random people, this situation would have never happened, but none of the others present had really considered defending their most vulnerable member.

The mage summoned walls of ice around himself, then used flame magic to launch himself into the air. The Matriarch opened her large, circular mouth and fired off a black beam that made the wall explode and throw him off course, allowing a vampire to grasp his foot and drag him down.

Just as he was about to be torn limb from limb, Jake arrived. Or, well, his arrows did.

All four vampires froze at once, and a fraction of a second later, four arrows pierced a vampire each and sent the blood-suckers tumbling back. It was a hastily fired Splitting Arrow with stable arcane arrows, and it wasn't enough to truly down the vampires... but it was enough to buy Jake time.

Jake manipulated a string of mana and wrapped it around the mage's ankle. Then he pulled with his mind just as the vampires stabilized themselves and tried to jump the caster again, only to see him be dragged across the ground away from them.

He fired off another round of arrows, this time more focused on killing and not only delaying. He rapid-fired, each of his arrows now covered in his own blood. The vampires barely had time to react before they were pierced straight through, leaving festering holes.

The Matriarch shrieked and turned her attention to Jake, then opened her mouth and fired off another beam. Jake simply looked over at her and took a single step, avoiding the beam at the very last moment, before he loosed another arrow—this one towards the Matriarch.

A good thing about the Matriarch was her isolated position... making her a perfect target for explosive arcane arrows. The arrow split at the very last moment, and she was hit by five massive explosions, blasting her backward and tumbling across the plains.

He refocused on the regular vampires again and saw that, after the initial confusion, the rogue, gun-guy, and earth mage had all resumed their own assault. With Jake preoccupying half the vampires, they swiftly made progress.

The earth mage had grasped one in his massive hands and had begun smashing it down into the ground, reinforcing said ground and making it slightly spiky all the while. The assassin with guns was blasting a single vampire repeatedly with black bullets that exploded on impact. Finally, the rogue with the two swords was fighting two vampires, adeptly cutting them up while expertly dodging.

With the ice-and-fire mage out of danger, he also got back on his feet, threw Jake a grateful glance, and returned to the battle. He helped the rogue with swords by summoning a giant, flaming ice spear, penetrating a vampire through its back.

It took them only a few minutes to finish off all the vampires, Jake likely doing most of the work despite joining so late. He wasn't entirely certain, though, as the group had worn down the vampires quite a bit and, based on the corpses on the ground, already killed three before he got there.

Once everything had calmed down, Jake finally entered the valley. The four people looked at him, with only the earth mage and the rogue looking a bit apprehensive.

"Thanks for the help, mate; I would've been fucked without ya," the elemental mage said as he laughed.

Jake finally looked him over properly and saw he was a middle-aged man with a full beard. He was solidly built, and if he'd been smaller, Jake would have assumed him to be a dwarf.

"No problem," Jake said, his attention already more focused on the Vault than anything else.

Clearly, the earth mage noticed this. "It's hidden approximately fifty meters below us."

Jake nodded, having already walked closer to see it in his Sphere of Perception. It was a magical cube, reminding Jake a bit of a Rubik's cube... and giving him a feeling about what they were in for.

"Can you get it up?" he asked, looking over at the earth mage.

The man looked back at Jake, not the scared type. He was still in his armor of stone, making him a five-meter-tall golem-looking dude. Jake could still see him within, and Jake looked straight at the chest where the man was hidden.

"How do I know you won't just take all the treasure from the Vault, leaving us all with nothing?" the earth mage asked with an accusing tone.

Jake looked at him and smiled beneath his mask. "First of all, from what I have learned, these Vaults aren't just something you instantly open and empty out. My guess is this one is a puzzle of some sort, and without solving the puzzle, there is no way to get the loot."

He said this first part while being nice and diplomatic, explaining some of the mechanics of this second phase of the Treasure Hunt. He wasn't as nice with the second thing. His aura bellowed out, infused with his presence as he looked at the earth mage.

"Secondly, you don't know if I will just take the Vault, but what the fuck makes you think you can do anything about it? If I really wanted everything, I would have put an arrow through your head before you even knew I was here, *really* taking everything from you. Would you prefer that?"

Jake felt like the guy was a moron. He had just helped them, so if he'd really wanted to do them harm, wouldn't he just have killed them too? Or was he so blind he thought Jake couldn't? Because then he would truly be a moron.

It ended up not being the earth mage, but the bearded man that said something in response first. "Aye, if he wanted to fuck ya up, ya would be fucked already. Also, stop hidin' in ya little shell of a stone. It ain't gon' help for shit. I know ya low on mana, so stop actin' like a dumb cunt already."

"The man has a point; let's just play nice, alright?" the shadow assassin chimed in.

Jake figured that if anyone were going to turn on anyone else in this group, it would be the guy who was an actual assassin.

The stone mage grunted and dispelled his stone armor, allowing himself to fall to the ground. He was a young man in a brown robe, and he looked suspiciously at everyone present.

Does the dude have trust issues or something? Jake asked himself, not really caring all that much.

What he did care about was having the mage help bring it up to the surface. While Jake could do it alone, it would be a long and time-consuming task, while he had a feeling an earth mage could handle it much more easily.

"Fine... but swear that you're not letting us all leave empty-handed," the guy agreed, not even having to be asked as he felt the gazes of everyone present on him.

"I'm not gonna promise you shit," Jake said, dismissing him instantly. "But I'm not gonna rob you if you manage to open the Vault first; I can promise you that. But if I end up doing it all alone, then you can take the scraps I leave you or fuck off."

The earth mage grunted again, then just shook his head and muttered something under his breath.

"Still betta than those religious freaks," the ice-and-fire mage said loudly, shrugging. The shadow assassin and the woman with two swords also stayed behind, giving their tacit approval.

Jake saw the earth mage plant both his hands on the ground and begin channeling mana into it. Then the earth began shaking as it churned and moved. The soil was being displaced, and a small hill began forming on the side of the valley in response to the earth mage's magic.

At the same time, Jake saw the cube slowly lifting up towards the ground, pushed by the soil underneath. Jake saw in his sphere that it had been anchored before, but those anchors were now broken—likely by the system, or perhaps just the erosion of time.

Not long after, the cube got within a few meters of the surface, and once it did, it seemed to take on a life of its own. It suddenly shot out of the ground, sending up an eruption of soil and stone. A pulse of mana went through the valley, washing over them as the cube was revealed.

Yep, that's a Rubik's cube, Jake confirmed to himself.

The entire cube was more than five meters on each side, and

wasn't the usual sort with bright colors and three-by-three dimensions. It was the sort made by people who were honestly too much into Rubik's cubes. It was a fifteen-by-fifteen cube.

Jake stared at it and noted the magic sigils on the cube, making it obvious this was a puzzle.

"Yeah, fuck this," the bearded caster said as he just turned around and walked away. "Thanks, mate, but no way in fuckin' hell am I doing that."

CHAPTER 33

TREASURE HUNT: VALUABLE ASSET

Four people stood staring at the massive cube. The bearded man had truly just taken off, not bothering to stay and try to solve it. The earth mage, the rogue, the gunman, and Jake were the only ones left, and from the looks of it, the gunman and rogue were also close to leaving. Jake wasn't sure if the earth mage actually had a clue about the puzzle or if he was just staying out of pride.

The puzzle itself was very much a Rubik's cube, but not the kind with colors or easy symbols. There weren't only six types of symbols, but instead hundreds, and from Jake's initial assessment, he believed that before one could figure out how to solve the Rubik's cube part of the puzzle, one had to first determine what each of the six sides should look like.

Compared to the puzzle he had solved with Reika, this one was far harder.

"Could we just try all the combinations and solve it like that?" the guy from the Court of Shadows asked.

"Sounds like a great way to waste the rest of the Treasure Hunt," the rogue woman said, speaking for the first time.

Jake nodded. While he had never been that much into Rubik's Cubes, he had watched online videos on them while bored. A simple three-by-three cube already had possible combinations in the quintillions. He doubted he would manage to brute-force a fifteen-by-fifteen cube even if he spent the remainder of his entire D-grade lifespan.

He considered if even trying to solve it was worth it. It would no doubt take a while, and he could clear more Vaults if he found some he could open just by killing stuff. Well... he could try, if moving the rube around incorrectly would trigger some combat mechanism like the tree.

"I'm going to try and manipulate the cube. It may cause enemies to appear, so be on guard." Jake then extended a string of mana. The cube happily responded as Jake moved one of the rows, making it turn, and—

"—oody waste of—wait, what the fuck?"

Just as Jake manipulated the cube, the bearded man suddenly appeared. Jake looked at him, confused, and he looked back at them with a similarly confused expression.

"Did you drag me back, or what the actual fuck just happened?" the bearded man asked.

"We just moved the cube," the shadow assassin explained.

"Oh."

Jake ignored their conversation as he sensed the area. Faint traces of space-affinity mana surrounded the spot where the bearded man had appeared, and when Jake really focused on himself, he noticed something. A small mark, not dissimilar to his own Mark of the Avaricious Hunter, was on his body—or, more accurately, his soul.

"Someone try to leave the valley," Jake said, needing a guinea pig.

"Here we go again," the bearded man said, not even asking twice as he took flight and began flying away.

Meanwhile, Jake turned the cube repeatedly. The moment the ice-and-fire mage was a few hundred meters away, he got teleported back where he had originally been, still firing flames out of his feet.

"Okay, fuck this," he complained. "Ya messin' with me, or we actually stuck?"

"Seems like it," the shadow assassin said, looking quite worried.

The others did too, with the ice-and-fire mage and the rogue looking especially bothered. The earth mage didn't visibly display any signs of being annoyed or put off, though Jake theorized that had more to do with honor than his actual feelings.

Jake sighed internally. That pulse earlier had likely been the source of the mark, and when Jake inspected it more closely, he had no idea how to remove it. He did feel like it would disappear within a day or so, though. He guessed the lower duration was the tradeoff for it being hard to remove... or maybe it was just far above his level.

So, solve the puzzle or be stuck here for a day doing nothing... I guess this is the system's way of not just letting people run between the most straightforward challenges.

"What's the game plan?" the rogue woman asked, looking up at the cube. "I don't know anything about these magic things."

"I know a bit," the shadow assassin chimed in, seeming truthful.

"I fucking hate shit like this," the ice-and-fire mage said, making it obvious he was quite knowledgeable on the subject.

"I am quite well versed in magic circles," the earth mage said, making it clear he wasn't very good at it.

They all looked at Jake. He just shrugged. "I don't really know much."

It was the truth. Jake really didn't have any solid grasp on these kinds of magic circles or runes or anything like that. He was just a fast learner and generally good at magic, which he leveraged when it came to solving puzzles. During the puzzle in the tower, Reika had been the one with the knowledge of magical runes, not him.

"So, we're basically fucked," the shadow assassin sighed.

"The mark keeping us trapped will be gone in around a day,"

Jake informed the others. "Also, the teleportation only triggers when the cube is moved."

Jake only stated these things as he stood there, observing the cube. He hadn't realized the way his words could be interpreted before he saw three of them back away from him slightly. The three—all except the elemental mage—looked warily at him.

"What?" he asked, throwing them a glance that only made them back off more.

"They think ya gonna kill us all to make sure no one moves the damn cube," the elemental mage answered.

"Oh," Jake said with a nod. "I guess that works, but it also seems risky. Someone else could just come around and move the cube and teleport me back. Imagine if that happened during a fight..."

"Sounds like a get-outta-jail-free card," the ice-and-fire mage answered with a laugh.

"Yeah, no thanks... Let's just solve this crap," Jake said, turning to the three wary people. "The best way to not tempt me into believing going full murderhobo is the best option would be to actually prove yourselves useful and help solve the damn puzzle."

"Way ahead of those morons," the elemental mage snickered as he took out a small notebook and began writing stuff down.

The tentative onlookers, seeming to realize Jake's idea was their best choice, all got to work.

But not before Jake tried firing an arrow at the cube.

That didn't work either.

———

Relying on the natives had always been a good tactic when it came to finding and exploiting the resources of the local land. It was why settlers and explorers always tried to subjugate or ally with the local forces upon landing on foreign ground.

They knew the lay of the land. They were familiar with

where all the valuables were hidden. However, often these natives were not friendly. Sometimes diplomacy simply wasn't working, or, more often than not, it wasn't considered worth it to ally with them. With superior power, forced servitude was simply the easiest and most efficient solution.

Sultan was more than aware of this when he appeared in the Treasure Hunt. He had done what few could and forcefully employed the local wildlife. The Ekilmares were, in his eyes, not foes to hunt down, but beasts to use. They knew of the land and where the valuables were, just like a native of a conquered land.

He only had a single slave by his side going into the Hunt. It was the pathfinder named Summer, whose primary skill was her ability to mark and see through the eyes of others. This ability proved extremely useful during this Treasure Hunt, especially in concert with the temporarily dominated vampires.

Sultan had a hard time deciding if keeping the woman around or not was the smart choice. He was aware of her stalker tendencies, and he was surprised that when Ms. Wells had given her the choice of being under the confinement of Haven or staying with Sultan, she had chosen to stay.

That is, until he'd realized that those stalker tendencies had been turned to him. She was the kind of lunatic that fixated on a single target, and her type seemed to be the man who had every-thing... and apparently, Sultan fit that description. He would have thought someone like Mr. Thayne was more her type, but perhaps even she had a tinge of sanity in her mind, making her not pursue him.

Sultan naturally didn't have any positive feelings towards her, but that seemed to only attract her more. This is why he found the entire situation unsettling. It had all become more complicated, and as he was no longer allowed to torture her—a rule he had followed—she had only become more servile and obsessed. Ultimately, however, he decided just to make use of her. She was, in his mind, an indentured servant, working with him until anything else was demanded of him or circumstances changed. He did not fear betrayal, either, as she was bound by the rules in her contract... and Sultan also had certain skills he hadn't fully disclosed to Haven related to mind magic that gave him assurance. Not because he didn't trust them—he trusted them as much as he would trust anyone that wasn't himself.

Haven had been good to him so far. They had some talented craftsmen and women, and he had made ample use of the System Store. However, it was more what simply being related to Haven granted him. It was like a protective shield hanging over him. Once people knew where he was from, they didn't dare to strike at him out of fear of retaliation. Retaliation he doubted Lord Thayne would dish out even if people went for Sultan, but the fear of the possibility proved enough most of the time.

Not that he feared getting into a bout. He could handle himself.

Sultan had always been alone, and as such, had always needed to handle his own matters. He had learned the value of money from an early age and had resolved to never be poor. Not again. Wealth in the old world had been synonymous with power. Money could buy you the local police; it could make you immune to borderline any scrutiny. At least, where he had been from.

His father had been wealthy, so the day he took advantage of Sultan's mother, no one dared complain, not even she. His mother had been a servant, but was in all but title a slave. She'd had no possibility of fleeing and no passport to travel, and had been worked to the bone with only a single bed and a bit of food as payment.

So when the man who would become Sultan's father had taken a liking to her and started taking advantage, no one stood up or said anything. When she got pregnant, the man simply tossed her out onto the streets, not a penny to her name.

Sultan had grown up poor. Not the "no birthday presents" poor, but the "barely surviving" poor. His mother had done what she could to survive and raise her son, but he still had to do many things to survive. Out of all the people he had ever known, his own mother was still the person he respected the most. That was also why he would never take advantage of a slave in the same way his mother had been taken advantage of.

That didn't mean he would ever claim to be a good person. Quite the opposite. He had learned to find pleasure in inflicting pain upon those he believed deserved it. He still remembered the day he'd looked his father in the eyes as he took everything from him. The day he destroyed his own "family" and left the formerly prestigious man in shambles, a poor beggar on the street. His wife divorced him, his children shunned him, and all his former business partners cut him off, acting as if he was dead. It had been pure euphoria.

It was only beaten out by the day he'd seen his own father working as a servant. Sultan had believed the old man would have killed himself, but no, the old bastard had been too much of a coward to do that. Could Sultan have ended his father's life? Yes, easily... but the day he saw the pure misery in his eyes, he knew a life of servitude was a worse punishment than death. He had come to believe that for those in power, being dragged from their high towers into the streets to struggle in the lowest rung of society was the best punishment. Ah, but that didn't mean there hadn't been celebrations when he heard his father had died of a heart attack from overworking himself.

Sultan was also fully aware many would view him as a hypocrite who was just as bad as those he despised, and he wasn't going to argue against it. He didn't need to be a good person—just competent enough to make sure none could drag him from his own tower. His way of doing this? Not being the one sitting at the top.

Lord Thayne was at the top of the tower, and Sultan was perfectly fine with that. He had his own rules and his own creeds, just like Sultan himself, and as long as the merchant managed to identify those and play within the Chosen's rules, he should be fine. In the end, it was all about benefits and Perception. So as long as Sultan stayed a benefit to Haven and not a liability, he would have a tower to weather all storms.

"Master, the vampires have located the closest Vault and begun fighting the guardians there," Summer said.

"Then let us move," he answered.

Sultan controlled his ship—because of course he'd brought his ship to the Treasure Hunt; anything else would be silly—and set course for where Summer directed. He leaned back as they sailed through the air at high speeds, rivaling most individuals with powerful movement-related skills. His vessel was not cheap, after all.

It didn't take them long to reach their destination, where he found the Ekilmares fighting. Those controlled by him were clearly losing, but that was only to be expected. An unfortunate downside with domination was that the dominated targets often weren't as powerful. It wasn't due to a reduction in stats or anything like that, but simply the fact that any being not moving according to its own will wouldn't be as strong.

Sultan had many theories as to why, but none seemed quite right. Ultimately, it could simply be system-imposed rules, but alas, it was just something he would have to deal with.

He took a deep breath and prepared himself for combat. Waving his hand, a musket appeared in it, gilded symbols of gold adorning the beautifully crafted weapon. The ship shifted and turned its side to the combat in the valley below, cannons appearing at starboard.

While his vessel was a great tool for transport, that didn't mean it couldn't be used for combat. Quite the opposite.

Summer also summoned her own bow, not even having to be told to. Sultan trusted her to simply do her job.

He raised his own weapon and muttered, "Fire."

A barrage of magical explosions overtook the valley with no regard for the Ekilmares he had dominated earlier. This was one of the advantages of using them—friendly fire wasn't a thing.

The vampires quickly noticed they were being assaulted and

began running towards the floating ship. Sultan simply smiled and shot one of the vampires in the front. It stumbled back from the impact and, instead of continuing to run for the ship, attacked another of the vampires beside it.

At the back of the vampires was one called a Matriarch, and it was by far the most dangerous foe present. It opened its maw and fired off a beam of energy, forcing Sultan to activate the shields on the ship while navigating it to move. Unfortunately, the ship was impacted, and the shield managed to block the blow successfully, but it still left some cracks in the barrier.

Sultan shot for the Matriarch, and she didn't even dodge as she was hit by one of his bullets. He tried to use his mental domination but felt a rebound, as if something had hit him in the head. *Too much resistance.*

The more intelligent and higher in level a creature was, the harder it was to dominate. This was why sapients like humans were impossible to directly control, no matter their level. One could still control their movements, but not their mind. From the response the Matriarch gave him, it was either too strong or too smart to have its mind and body controlled. Luckily for him, he had other ways.

He took out one of the many items he had acquired from the Hunt: a rare-rarity, anti-vampire sword left behind by the Pure Ones. He held no doubt it was an item many others would greatly value. Sultan valued it too... but he valued victory more.

With his hands on it, he channeled a certain skill from his profession. The sword began to warp and distort, then suddenly imploded into a small metal ball, the item destroyed forever. He took the metal ball, put it into his musket, and took aim once more.

It was an expensive shot, and not one he planned on wasting. The skill could also not be used repeatedly, truly only giving him one chance. He directed the vampires he still had dominated to head for the Matriarch as he controlled the ship to bring it closer. Meanwhile, all the usual Ekilmares were still being bombarded by the ship and Summer, who continually used Powershots and other magical arrows.

Turning the ship, he made the front face the Matriarch. A compartment opened up to reveal a large cannon. Energy began swirling as he aimed his musket. The ship fired first, making the Matriarch dodge the blow while being hounded by its own brethren. Her movements were predictable, giving Sultan the perfect opportunity.

BOOM!

The musket released a blast of mana and propelled the pellet forward. The Matriarch's instincts clearly made it aware of the danger this attack represented, but it failed to dodge due to being mid-air.

What had once been a rare-rarity sword, now reduced to a single bullet, penetrated the body of the Matriarch and drew screams of pain. Silver veins spread from where it had been hit as the attack did its job. The skill allowed him to reduce an item of rare-rarity or below to a single bullet, amplifying the power of its enchantment significantly and delivering a good portion of the power found in the item's Records at once.

The Matriarch stumbled and screamed at the significant damage, but more importantly, the vampire became utterly unable to heal from the wounds inflicted by its brethren. Cuts and bruises soon covered its body, and Sultan kept shooting with Summer as he also repositioned the ship to keep up the assault, the cannon at the front being single-use.

It still ended up taking them a good while to finish the job, as the vampires were incredibly durable. The Matriarch died from accumulated wounds, and Sultan claimed the Vault.

Above all else, Sultan was a merchant. Yet, in this new world, a merchant had to be able to defend himself. He knew he could never reach the same level of power through his own efforts as others. He wasn't as naturally talented at combat or magic, so he simply did the second-best thing: he bought all the power he could. His profession and class both amplified his abilities to do so.

He always carried many weapons to turn into bullets in his inventory, some of them rarer than others. Rarity, however, wasn't always everything. For he had found that a certain set of weapons Haven had given him access to were incredibly potent. Ones he saved as trump cards.

It was the toxic scrap metal Lord Thayne had created and discarded in large quantities a while ago while practicing trans-mutation—now reformed into weapons. Unfortunately, these weapons were all impractical and impossible to use as actual weapons due to their fragility, but for Sultan?

Sultan only needed them to last for a single shot.

So one could say that Sultan didn't only leverage the Lord of Haven's strength socially, but also in many ways literally—something his Patron god had continually expressed was a path he should keep walking. Because even the strongest would require a support system, and Sultan planned to become part of that system and stay an invaluable asset.

CHAPTER 34

TREASURE HUNT: ANOTHER COLLABORATIVE PROJECT

The valley was nearly unrecognizable compared to its state less than a day ago. Several ice cubes were spread throughout, a few models of stone were carved, and the environment was totally changed, with many symbols arranged into potential magic circles carved into the ground.

"Ya can't fucking do that; it fucks over the fourth side," the ice-and-fire mage commented.

"Not if we turn it in this way—then the circle will be restored again," the shadow assassin countered as he manipulated the large cube.

"Aight, but that doesn't fix the problem with the first side still being a damn mess."

"True... but the edges look right."

Jake listened to their conversation while making symbols appear around himself, manifested through his arcane mana. He arranged and rearranged them repeatedly, trying to get the magic circle to look right. They had already "solved" five of the six sides of the cube, and Jake was working on the last one.

When Jake said "they," he meant primarily Jake, the elemental mage, and the guy from the Court of Shadows. It turned out the gun guy was also a talented gunsmith and knew quite a bit about enchantments and runes due to that. Magic guns were just fancy magic wands, after all.

The elemental mage was just naturally talented, as far as Jake could tell. He already made magic circles sometimes during combat and said he was actually a builder who didn't like building stuff. Instead, he was solely focused on reinforcing objects and making them more durable. He even had skills similar to Transmute or perhaps Cultivate Toxin, in that they hardened objects and could slightly change properties.

As for Jake? Well, Jake wouldn't have said he knew a lot about runes and the like a day or so ago, but by now, he had become quite knowledgeable. The reason for this was simple: he had cheated.

Alright, it wasn't really cheating, though Jake still thought it kind of was. What he used wasn't truly his own knowledge, after all, but that of the Malefic Viper.

It wasn't something Jake thought a lot about. In fact, it was something he often forgot about. But he couldn't forget that he was still carrying around a drop of blood from Villy somewhere in his body. In actuality, it was more like it resided within his soul, and more than a drop of blood, it was a fragment of Records. It was a fragment of pure knowledge that his ancient-rarity version of Sagacity of the Malefic Viper was partly designed to explore, as reflected by the description:

[Sagacity of the Malefic Viper (Ancient)] – To hold just a fragment of the wisdom of a Primordial is more than most ever achieve. Much less to be personally taught that knowledge directly by the god himself. Allows the alchemist to peek into a fragment of the Malefic Viper's Records to seek his knowledge. Grants the Alchemist of the Malefic Viper far better understanding of mana and of most affinities. Allows the alchemist to make creations he does not have the associated crafting skill for. (Does not receive stat effectiveness bonuses without associated

skill). Passively provides 1 Wisdom per level in Alchemist
of the Malefic Viper. May your search for knowledge be
as inexhaustible as the Malefic One.

In fact, Jake believed having the drop of blood was likely a primary contributor to him getting the Sagacity skill to begin with.

Jake had used the fragment actively a few times in the past, but it was rare. He did it while practicing transmutation, and sometimes, while crafting, it passively gave him some insights—courtesy of the Sagacity skill—but to truly delve into it wasn't easy or simple.

After the first hour or so trapped within the puzzle area, Jake had entered deep meditation to truly explore some of the knowledge within the drop of blood. Of course, Jake was fully aware it was only a fragment of knowledge, but even that fragment proved invaluable to him. Even the tiniest of fractions of the Viper's knowledge was worth more than everyone in the valley combined, after all.

Magic runes and such appeared to have some basic rules or at least tendencies Jake began recognizing. While different sets of runes could vary significantly, they had to possess internal logic and consistency. Runes weren't as simple as something like letters in an alphabet, but were something Jake wasn't quite certain how to define. It was like one could faintly predict their elements and how other runes would look based on previous runes, so maybe runes were more like sentences?

Jake's surface understanding deepened as time passed, and he started making some logic of the madness on the cube. He began to see how the different runes "fit" together and how magic circles could be formed. With the help of the ice-and-fire mage as well as the shadow assassin, he slowly ironed out some novice misunderstandings and quickly began surpassing the both of them in certain areas.

The runic language on the cube was actually rather simplistic. It was clearly one made to be learned fast, and Jake was ninety-nine percent sure it had been altered or created by the system for the Treasure Hunt, because it would honestly suck as a legitimate defense. Sure, for the five D-grades, it was difficult, but even for more regular D-grades with some magic knowledge, it was still something that could be done within a few days. A C-grade, even one bad at magic, could probably have opened the cube in a few hours tops.

Also, after nearly a full day, they were still only five people. After some hours, this had become odd to them, and Jake had decided to try and discover why. He found out they were isolated by a space barrier of some sort. The mark left on them by the cube didn't only teleport them back; it also allowed them access to the hidden space the cube now occupied. Others who went towards the cube would likely find themselves unknowingly passing the valley due to the distorted space around it.

This meant it was truly only the five of them able to do anything. Throughout it all, the earth mage and rogue with two swords had tried, but neither had proven very useful.

The earth mage seemed to rely solely on skills, and was more like a warrior than a mage. His manipulation skills and armor of stone appeared to be the bulk of his abilities, and he hadn't done much to learn magic outside of skills. His profession wasn't useful either. At least, Jake didn't think it was. The dude didn't share what his profession was and overall seemed very defensive and annoyed by being trapped. His "I don't care" attitude fell apart within an hour, though, and he just became an ass whose only good trait was not getting in the way. In the end, he ended up mainly just doing his own thing, using some odd device.

As for the rogue... well, Jake believed it made perfect sense she didn't know much about magic runes. She was a pure melee fighter, and Jake doubted she even had more than a skill or two that actually used mana. Her profession was blacksmithing, too —more specifically, swordsmithing. While that did include some amount of magic, the skills did all the work for her, and she had focused on improving the handiwork and not the nitty-gritty details of enchantments.

They had still helped a bit. The earth mage had resigned himself to making models of stone for the first hour before he became a downer, while the rogue worked on arranging different test circles and just doing whatever she could here and there. While the earth mage seemed almost offended at having to do more menial tasks, the rogue seemed more embarrassed by not being able to help more. She also kept helping throughout, just doing what she could.

Anyway, back to Jake and his peeking into the drop of blood he had stolen from his best buddy snake god.

Usually, it took him more than ten minutes to really immerse himself, and that was while using Thoughtful Meditation. This led to Jake usually spending a few hours sitting in meditation while everyone else worked around him. For anyone else, this would mean they were cut off from the world, but not Jake.

His Sphere of Perception still allowed him to see the Rubik's cube. However, he did cut out everyone else and what they were doing, focusing solely on the cube. During the first half a day, the ice-and-fire mage and shadow assassin were the primary contributors, with Jake a close third, but as time progressed, Jake overtook them both.

He began comprehending the circles and possible combinations. He could usually start with a small quadrant on the cube and make those fit together, and then expand from there. Whenever Jake solved these parts, he would open his eyes to share his realizations and make new models for the elemental mage and assassin to work out.

This was how they solved five of the sides of the cube within twenty-three hours. But for Jake, more important than solving the cube was how much he learned about magic theory and magic symbols and circles.

Jake had never been the best at learning pure theory. He was the type of guy that needed to apply his knowledge practically to truly get it. That was why he didn't get much out of simply reading a book on alchemy without also testing out what the book said. It wasn't that he failed to understand the theory; it just didn't "click" for him.

A cube puzzle such as this was a perfect opportunity for Jake to learn theory and immediately try to apply it in the real world. He could see how they potentially fit together and turn the cube and experiment all he wanted while even getting feedback and discussing with others. Jake also got the feeling from the two others that they'd also progressed nicely in an extremely short amount of time.

To be honest, Jake wouldn't put it past the system to make a puzzle like this especially suitable as a training tool. While the system seemed unfeeling most of the time, Jake did view it as somewhat benevolent.

Time kept moving, and when the twenty-fourth hour passed, Jake felt the mark placed upon his soul disappear.

"The mark keeping us here is gone," Jake shared with the others.

The elemental mage and shadow assassin both nodded in acknowledgment, neither showing any intentions of leaving before the task was done. The earth mage also didn't do anything in particular except take out one of the devices he had been playing with occasionally. The rogue woman closed her eyes, and Jake guessed she tried to look inward to confirm the mark was gone.

After a bit, she opened her eyes. "I'll just be heading out, then... I haven't contributed much anyway," she said with some resignation. The woman had tried to help, and Jake would honestly be fine getting her something. Well, she *had* gotten something, as she now had some knowledge, but honestly, she lacked the foundation to properly understand much.

"Wait, why not stay?" the earth mage said, stopping her as she was about to head out. "I'm certain there is enough loot for everyone. It would be a shame to miss out on something due to a bit of impatience. You'll soon be done opening the cube, won't you?"

"Aye," the elemental mage confirmed, throwing Jake a confused look. Jake returned it. It wasn't about the puzzle, but the earth mage.

Why the hell did he think they were going to give *him* anything? He had just been a beacon of negativity from start to finish. In fact, Jake was surprised he hadn't taken off, as he seemed more than annoyed being stuck there.

"I'm fine sharing, I guess. It depends on Lord Thayne," the shadow assassin said, also looking at Jake.

"Let's just open it first," Jake said, dismissing them. It wasn't even certain solving the cube would lead to instant loot.

The rogue chose to stay after a bit more assurance from the earth mage that she would surely get something. It was all very odd, but Jake and the other three refocused on the puzzle.

It still ended up taking one and a half hours more before they were done. Jake had performed another round of delving into the drop of blood, then put the last piece of the puzzle together. He summoned a construct of arcane energy showing the solved cube. They double-checked it, and once everything seemed right, they began spinning.

The cube turned tens of times a second, soon speeding up to hundreds. This part was easy enough. They had done so much to figure out the possible magic circles and how to put them together that the actual solving of the Rubik's cube was little more than a formality.

As the turned parts of the cube clicked into place, one after another, all five of them stood with anticipation. When the final turn was done and the Rubik's cube solved, they all just stood there for a second. Nothing happened.

"Ya gotta be fucking kiddi—"

Suddenly a loud click sounded out, and the metal cube began shining. Then it released a bright light, and once the brightness subsided, the entire cube was gone, leaving instead three floating items with seven more items lying on the ground.

Jake didn't even need to use Identify to know the three floating items were the most valuable. Two of them gave off impressive auras, with the final item giving off none. The one not giving off anything was the central item: a cube identical to the one they had just solved, except shrunk down the size of a regular Rubik's cube. He identified it right away.

[Safebox of Perennial Sustainability (Legendary)] – A cube containing a spatial storage within, specially made to store items of high value safely. The cube can be manipulated and sealed with a password. Due to the construction of the cube, it is near-indestructible by anyone below S-grade, and if the item is destroyed, a space storm will be released. The time of all items will be frozen within, and mana leakage will be severely allevi- ated. Mana leakage is nullified entirely for lower-value goods. The difficulty of the password is determined by the user.

He smiled and quickly also checked the two other items. One of them was a staff, and the other a metal mask.

[Staff of Elemental Confluence (Ancient)] – A wooden staff with a mounted gem at its head. The gem is a merged product of the orbs of powerful earth, air, fire, and water elementals, condensed into a single gem that amplifies all elemental magic. The wood is likewise a merging of different elemental-affinity woods and is enchanted to be durable and further amplify the user's mental abilities and casting capabilities. The gem passively absorbs fire, water, earth, and air-affinity mana, and this stored mana can either be used as a supplementary mana reserve or released all at once as a

quad-elemental blast. Enchantments: Elemental Conflu-
ence. Quad-
  element Blast.

Requirements: Lvl 125+ in any humanoid race.

[Mask of Shifting Faces (Epic)] – A mask created to
change the wearer's appearance. Allows the user to store a
set number of humanoid appearances that can be freely
changed. This is an illusionary technique and not actual
morphing. Changing appearance will also hide the user's
mana signature and aura. This effect can also be applied
without changing appearance. The mask itself is incred-
ibly durable. Enchantments: Appearance Change. Pres-
ence Masking.

Requirements: Lvl 115+ in any humanoid race.

The seven items on the ground had two rare rarities among them, and the rest were uncommon rarity. Before Jake had time to consider the items deeply, the elemental mage raised his fists to the air. "Fuck yeah!"

The shadow assassin also smiled. "Nice one."

Jake himself couldn't help but flash a smile behind his mask. It felt good, and he wouldn't have been able to do it that fast without the two of them. "Fuck yeah, indeed. Good job, guys."

The three of them stared at the items for a bit, all smiling. Next would be the distribution of loot, and Jake found it interesting how the best items were—

He stopped his train of thought. Jake felt something. Presences approaching... Not just from one direction, either. A realization then struck him. He and the four others had been stuck inside a valley all this time, isolated in a bubble of space, meaning Jake couldn't see the area around him. With the ever-present mist also hanging over the area, obscuring presences, and him being so focused on the task, he hadn't noticed them before now. The approaching people had also kept a good distance too.

Jake turned his head and saw that a single figure had appeared on the top of the hill leading into the valley, followed by many more not long after. Mana washed over the entire valley, forming a semi-transparent dome. A barrier to lock them inside.

In his sphere, Jake saw the earth mage snicker... which was when Jake realized why he had chosen to stay. Why he hadn't wanted the rogue to leave. Because she would have seen them. It would be hard not to, considering Jake detected over a hundred people.

While everyone else had been trying to solve the puzzle, the fucking earth mage had had his own plans:

Setting up a trap.

CHAPTER 35

TREASURE HUNT: THE IMPORTANCE OF WORD CHOICE

While Jake was the first to notice what was happening, though everyone naturally became aware when a huge magic barrier surrounded them. People suddenly appeared on all sides.

"What the fuck?" the elemental mage asked as he readied himself.

Jake's first course of action was not to answer, but to take a step towards where the cube had been and quickly swipe all the loot. This did earn him a few glances, but he was happy to see there was nothing accusatory in them from the rogue, the assassin, or the elemental mage. However, the earth mage did glare daggers, as the man had already begun backing away.

The shadow assassin, who had also realized the earth mage was in on it, turned to him. "Are you for real? What the fuck is wrong with you?"

"Oh, please. Stop acting all surprised; you're a fucking assassin and a thief," the earth mage replied in a snarky tone. "This is a Treasure Hunt, and I'm just playing by the rules."

Jake didn't bother with the earth mage, as he had turned his attention to someone else. It was a man who stood at the top of the hill, surrounded by others. Jake was pretty sure he recognized him and a few of those around him. *Those are...*

That was when Jake recognized them from the World Congress. These were city leaders and people related to cities that weren't involved with any specific factions. The independent forces. He remembered Miranda talking about them making internal alliances, and that seemed to be true... He did wonder why they had chosen to attack him, though. Jake looked at the man at the helm and Identified him.

[Human – lvl 130]

He was the strongest person Jake had seen in quite a while. Nearly Jake's own level. Then again, he was a city leader, and those tended to level quickly. Looking at those standing with the man, Jake saw that nearly all those closest had levels above 120.

"Lord Thayne," he heard the man yell from atop the cliff, "I had hoped not to meet again under such strenuous circumstances, but here we are."

Jake looked up at him. "I think you accidentally activated a barrier or something."

"No, no, this is quite the purposeful act," he answered with a smile.

The elemental mage, rogue, and assassin all scurried closer to Jake as it became clear what this was. Jake looked around himself a bit more and counted one hundred and seventeen people—one hundred and eighteen, counting the earth mage. All of them were naturally D-grade. Most were between 100 and 110, but a lot were also above 110.

"Are you sure you want this? I'll give you a chance to wisen up," Jake said. This really seemed like an entire *thing*, and Jake felt like this could all turn real complicated quickly. There were many city leaders there, and he could already begin to predict the issues this would create for Miranda.

At the top of the hill, the man shook his head and began

rambling. "Do you know how screwed up the current status quo of Earth is? A large religious organization is the largest faction. A goddamn assassination cult is among the most influential forces. We even have non-human monsters sitting in the high seats. This planet is slowly being claimed by outside forces. Gods and their factions from outside *our* universe are claiming *our planet*. I—no, we—will not stand for this."

The man paced back and forth, while Jake just listened to him rant.

"The choice is either to be subservient to some higher power or get screwed over. Yet, that is something some of us won't do. We refuse to give up our world and deliver it on a silver platter to exploitative foreigners. We are here because we refuse to be ignored. We will reclaim our planet, and we will make things right. Purge the undead and return to secularism."

Jake scratched his head, not exactly sure what the guy was getting at. Wasn't this guy as extreme as everyone else?

"What has anything of this got to do with me?"

"Hah!" the man laughed. "It has *everything* to do with you. You, a chosen puppet of some god. The so-called strongest person on Earth. Do you know the reason we're not listened to? Because people think we're weak. That we can't stand up for ourselves. That's why we have come here. To show we can. And what better demonstration than taking down the first city owner of the planet and the most prominent slave of the gods?"

"Not to mention the bounty from it," the earth mage said with a huge grin, the greed in his eyes evident. "I heard he killed three Counts of Blood, and he sure as hell got a lot more besides that."

"I believe what my comrade is trying to say is, just surrender with dignity," the leader said, smiling.

One hundred and eighteen people stood surrounding four people. A barrier was sealing them all in. One side had come prepared and the other taken by surprise. All of this had been done to make Jake into an example. For the independent faction to prove that while they may have been weak individually, together they were strong.

While they were certainly aware they likely couldn't kill Jake, they were confident in forcing him to leave the Treasure Hunt. A few of them were even using magic to record the scene to have proof of what had happened. The independents would prove, once and for all, that they were not to be ignored.

Jake was fully aware that a lot of what he relied upon was reputation over actual feats of strength. He was powerful because people said he was powerful. He was a Progenitor, but most didn't know what that entailed. He had killed Counts of Blood, but the other six had been slain by several different factions. None of the people present had seen him actually fight. While they had heard of his public slaying of the first Count of Blood, that was, in the end, still hearsay. Also, even if he genuinely was more powerful than all of them individually, they'd come prepared with numbers.

Perhaps they also relied on him being mentally exhausted from solving the cube, which he partly was. He was also isolated, and the three people he had to assist him would not be able to do much. All in all, the approach of the independent forces had been calculated and well-thought through.

While their tactic wasn't entirely asinine, they had made several mistakes. The first one was to seal off the entire space, giving not only Jake and the three others issues escaping, but themselves too. The second mistake was to not attack, but instead stop up and monologue. Perhaps even giving them a chance to trigger some powerful, large-scale attack that Jake couldn't have dodged to wound him from the get-go.

The final and perhaps most egregious mistake was what the man said. Not the information he gave, but his choice of words. For while Jake could handle a lot of insults, there were some things he couldn't take. Some words and insinuations triggered him and made him have very extreme responses.

Jake really didn't like being called a puppet.

THE PRIMAL HUNTER 5

Much less a slave.

The man atop the hill was preparing to open his mouth again, but didn't get the chance to.

A presence overtook the entire valley. Jake jumped, black wings and scales covering his entire body as he took on an inhuman and monstrous form in the eyes of his foes. Power swirled around him from Limit Break activating at 20% instantly. His mana-infused presence blanketed everyone present, pressing down on them with not only sheer, almost physical pressure, but also the full brunt of his primal rage.

Jake flew up and looked down at all the people present as they were mentally torn down. Weakened. Fragile. *Slaves* to their own fear. *Puppets* to whatever moron had convinced them to participate in this ambush.

Pathetic.

No longer bothering to hold back, his eyes glowed yellow with a visible sheen. Killing humans was something Jake tended to avoid. It was messy and led to complicated situations. It was something he only did if he felt forced to—or he really wanted to.

This was a case of the latter.

Gaze of the Apex Hunter landed on every single one of the ambushers. The fear of a predator so far superior to themselves flooded their entire beings and souls, making them shake with fear. Most were frozen, cold sweat soaking their backs.

But for some... for some, everything simply cracked.

More than forty people fell to the ground like puppets with their strings cut. Their eyes glazed over, not a hint of life in their body. In an instant, the force of nearly ten dozen was cut down by a third, the weaker of the group dying.

Jake stared down, red now mixed into the yellow of his eyes as two small drops of blood ran down his cheeks. It didn't stop him from summoning his bow. He aimed, and just before people were able to move again, an Arcane Powershot soared down.

It hit the man to the left of the group's leader, penetrating straight through his skull. The man didn't die instantly, but he became unable to act. Unable to teleport himself out of the Treasure Hunt. Jake followed up with another barrage, the people below now able to move.

Everyone except the guy with a pierced head retreated, none of them even trying to help their downed comrade. Five arrows fell upon the man, exploding on impact. Jake had just set the scene for the "battle" that was about to take place.

"GET IN POSITIONS! ACTIVATE THE—"

The man in charge stopped yelling, forced to take out a staff and summon a shield around himself as Jake fired an arrow at him. The shield cracked but didn't break, sending the man reeling back nevertheless.

A healer.

Jake quickly recognized the man's class. A rarity among the truly powerful, as more often than not, healers were more in a supportive role. Their personalities often leaned towards the dependent types and not the independents. Of course, there were exceptions. People who simply reveled in the sense of power that came from wielding the life of others in their hands... or fanatical individuals who had an unhealthy relationship with the concept of the preservation of life. Eron came to mind there.

This man was the former. He raised his staff and sent out a wave of light, pushing back the effect of Jake's presence. While that did stop them from continued exposure, it didn't dispel what they had already experienced. Pure dread was already ingrained in many of those present. Dread that would hamper their abilities to put up a proper fight and react adequately.

Down in the valley below, it wasn't silent either. Instead of hiding away or taking cover, the only three people not affected by Jake's initial salvo moved. The rogue, assassin, and elemental mage had been excluded from everything, as they weren't the target of Jake's ire, while the earth mage standing close by had been. With him distracted, the shadow assassin was the first to move.

Before the earth mage could properly awaken from his stupor and unfreeze from Gaze, he was shot several times in the chest and smashed into the ground by a sledgehammer of ice before his one arm was cut off by a sword. The other blade of the rogue tried to decapitate him, but a passive defensive skill activated and began automatically assembling the armor of stone.

Within five seconds of the ambushers making their intentions clear and Jake making his move, the mood was set. The formerly confident group, believing that outnumbering the group twenty-five to one would make it easy, came to a stark realization.

Teamwork was important, and in many situations, numbers did matter. The Holy Church was proof of this working. They were known for conducting grand rituals with hundreds, if not thousands of people. Through the power of the collective, they could take down foes they otherwise couldn't... but the crux of it was that they were a collective.

They worked as one unified being. The individual was discarded for the sake of the whole. Meanwhile, the people attacking Jake were just a group of individuals with a few parties. They had all come to intimidate, believing they were far superior. Sure, Jake was strong, but was he stronger than a hundred people? Would he risk fighting them?

Even if he did choose to fight, could he truly kill them when they had so many people around them to assist? To put it simply... they had clearly come without fully realizing this would be a fight to the death. They honestly believed it was all just intimidation, and that the "weaker" side would back down without actually fighting.

Jake fully shattered that illusion in his opening attack. Of course, this shouldn't mean the fight was over already, but in many ways, it was. He had only wiped out a tenth or so of the enemy fighting power with Pride and Gaze, meaning that if the other side truly fought, they could likely put up quite the struggle.

But all of that was dependent on their intention to actually fight. Jake had also killed an enemy leader, showing that even the more powerful among them could die. That they could be rendered unable to exit using the Insignia and save themselves. It had become life and death.

Many of them hadn't signed up for that. They began retreating, only to be faced with their own barrier.

"Rally! Don't panic!" the leader of the enemy faction yelled.

"Activate the shields!"

"Defensive positions!"

"Bombard him!"

Others of those more willing to fight also joined in. Jake was still flying in the air and firing arrows down, only to see more and more of them be blocked. Jake realized what he had to do and began spreading poison mist with his wings, but not to attack his foes. The mist around him quickly turned black from dark-affinity mana, obscuring himself completely.

He then opened his palm and began summoning his Arrow of the Ambitious Hunter, all while dodging in the air. When he first got the skill, it had taken him quite a while to summon an arrow, but that summoning depended on many things. Summoning speed was based on how powerful Jake was, his ability to control energy, and his understanding of the skill itself, but more so than anything, his familiarity with the target.

Ever since getting the skill, Jake had never summoned an Arrow of the Ambitious Hunter to kill a human. Yet when he did, it quickly became obvious... of any target he had ever chosen, humans were the most obvious. Of any foe, what could Jake be more familiar with than one of his own race? He was fully aware of his own weaknesses, and comprehending his own body was a necessity. He understood the way energy moved within him. He knew borderline everything.

So when he summoned an arrow to kill one of his kin, the skill responded promptly. At high speed, a simple-looking arrow grew out of his hand. It was just wooden with a metal tip. Of all the arrows Jake had summoned with the skill, this was perhaps the simplest-looking one. But Jake knew that was just perfect.

From start to finish, summoning the arrow took five seconds. This had barely been enough time for the ambushers to collect themselves and organize a bit. Most of them—primarily those dragged along just to push up the numbers—had all just retreated, hoping the more powerful people could handle it.

Jake would make it loud and clear they couldn't.

While being bombarded with a few attacks, Jake nocked the arrow and took aim at the healer below. The man was rallying his troops while maintaining a barrier in front of himself. It was not a barrier Jake could break with regular arrows... but he could no doubt break it.

He pulled back the string and began charging Arcane Powershot. At the same time, he focused on his surroundings, which were still affected by his infused presence. With the ease of controlling mana within that area significantly increased, he did something he hadn't been able to before.

As he charged his shot, arcane bolts began condensing in the air. A dozen bolts of highly destructive arcane mana came into being in the air, some of them tens of meters from Jake, serving two functions. First of all, they became targets of range spells, and secondly, they were naturally tools to attack with.

Jake began bombarding the perimeter with arcane bolts, doing little damage but creating panic aplenty. All of these bolts were hastily constructed except three. These three bolts floated around Jake, all of them meticulously constructed.

His plan was simple... kill the leader in a single shot, and make it absolutely clear that if one chose to attack Jake and make him an enemy, no matter how much they tried to plan or how many people they gathered, the only thing they would get out of it was death.

Oh, and also...

To never call him a fucking slave.

CHAPTER 36

TREASURE HUNT: NOT EXTORTION

The dark ball of mist hung above the valley with mana swirling around it in a spiral. Bolts of arcane mana were condensed by the dozen every single second, falling on the many people around the valley as they tried to attack the person hidden by the mist.

Jake, who stood within, had his aim set. Arcane Powershot had been charged to the maximum, and the three bolts hanging above him were ready. He released these three powerful bolts down towards the healer and leader of the ambush.

The healer swiftly reacted once he saw the bolts exit the mist and poured more mana into his barrier. The people around him also helped as the three bolts arrived. A massive explosion was kicked up, sending soil and dust flying everywhere, but it didn't do much damage to the barrier itself. Not that the blow was meant to... It was just a smokescreen.

It was simply there to make the healer feel a slight moment of relief before the true blow arrived.

BOOM!

For this second attack... the healer didn't react in time.

The entire ball of black mist exploded, the mist scattered by the sheer release of power from the Arcane Powershot. Arcane energy burned in the wake of the arrow as it tore through the air. Before anyone below could react, it reached the barrier of the healer. The man only managed to open his eyes in fright as his defenses shattered like broken glass and the arrow pierced straight through his chest. Usually, Arrow of the Ambitious Hunter couldn't pierce magic barriers... except Jake had come far in his understanding, especially of humans. He viewed mana as simply an extension of the body, so why the hell couldn't his arrow pierce a barrier constructed from it? The skill had clearly agreed with his conclusion.

Once the arrow hit, there was no grand explosion, just the man smashing into the ground. Yet, at that very last moment, something activated. His body began glowing. Jake recognized it as some kind of life-saving skill. Perhaps one to nullify some damage or ensure he couldn't die to one attack... Jake didn't know, but what he did know was that the healer wasn't ready for the follow-up.

Because before he even saw the arrow land, he began firing the next one. This one wasn't simple either. The two orbs of power on his bow channeled all their energy into the arrow condensed on the string. Jake was preparing to make the area into a Scorched Plain.

He fired the second arrow only two seconds after the first, not leaving the healer any time to prepare. Seeing their leader suddenly go down had already created even more panic and doubt, meaning no one reacted adequately.

Jake released the arrow and, at the same time, used One Step Mile. While Arrow of the Ambitious Hunter was his most powerful attack by a fair margin and archery was his best tool in combat, his greatest damage per second didn't come from ranged attack.

It naturally came from Touch of the Malefic Viper.

The large arrow infused with all the energy from his bow

landed just before Jake did. The Scorched Plains effect activated as it exploded, sending a wave of destructive arcane energy burning through the area; all the blue grass it encountered turned to nothing.

Jake landed amidst this explosion, the arcane energy washing over him. He took it unbothered, as his scales blocked what little damage it could usually do to him. Out of everyone in existence, Jake was the one with the most natural resistance to his own affinity, meaning he could tank it pretty damn well. Far better than the other humans.

His target within the inferno of arcane energy was the healer. The man was still alive, but that would soon change. The guy was still thrown off and semi-conscious as Jake jumped him. The other party failed to respond before Jake smashed his face into the ground, and his hand began glowing green. Jake pressed down with all his might as power swirled around him, the arcane energy still dominating the environment.

Jake squeezed his hand tighter and tighter, pressing down until, eventually, Touch of the Malefic Viper had weakened the skull enough. With a final push, he completely squashed the head of the formerly oh-so-confident leader of the independent factions.

The already-damaged man didn't survive.

You have slain [Human - lvl 130 / Auspicious Mind Mender – lvl 108 / Pioneering City Lord of Earth – lvl 152]

Jake stood up but didn't continue his attack. After killing the man, he felt far more relaxed than before, and his rage began to subside. He closed his eyes for a brief moment, focusing on getting his emotions under control. Jake was fully aware that this had been another case of his emotions—specifically anger—going wild, no doubt due to his Bloodline. Jake just *really* didn't like being called a slave. Luckily, the guy was dead, and Jake could now relax, as he didn't feel the need to murder anyone anymore. Instead, he simply assessed the situation.

Everyone in the area had been hit by the Scorched Plains, and the moment the destructive force that was his affinity began destroying someone, they reacted with fright, activating their Hunter Insignia to escape. In fact, while Jake's attack did do significant damage, he reckoned nearly everyone should be able to survive—and many even block it—as the Scorched Plains attack was more about widespread destruction than killing individual foes. However, based on everything else Jake had shown so far, those that were hit chose to react with caution, preferring to forfeit rewards over death.

It was a wise choice, and one Jake would now implore them all to take. As the effect from the Scorched Plains attack subsided, everyone saw where Jake was standing and the corpse beneath him. Once Jake felt their gazes upon him, he knew this entire "fight" was truly over.

Flashes of light appeared all around the valley as Jake looked at the four people he had been solving the puzzle with. His attack earlier had hit not only his enemies, but also those within the valley. In fact, the arcane energy had hit anything and everything within the barrier, with even the barrier itself having taken significant damage.

The elemental mage, rogue, and shadow assassin had all managed to somewhat handle the blow. The arcane energy had still left some wounds, but as they weren't attacked by anything else, they had managed to put up some defensive measures. The same couldn't be said about the earth mage, who'd had his armor of stone eroded halfway through and was now trying to reconstruct it and escape.

Jake stared at the fleeing man, having none of that. He raised his bow and fired a quickly charged Arcane Powershot. The arrow landed true, making the armor of stone explode and sending the man tumbling through the air with a large hole in his chest. The earth mage was already heavily injured, but hadn't yet chosen to leave for some reason.

The elemental mage moved to attack and finish off the earth mage, but the man defended himself at the very last moment by yelling, "We will remember this!"

With those words, he activated his Insignia and disappeared.

Even more flashes appeared all around as people chose to flee. They no doubt feared they would be the next target of an arrow and have their head pierced or something similar, making them unable to flee. Jake noticed that some people did stay behind, all huddled together in a defensive position. He saw around thirty people, including several of the more powerful humans who had been around the healer. None of them had taken any significant damage, as they had managed to actually display some level of teamwork.

Jake looked over at them as one of the people at the front spoke, "Lord Thayne, please, I believe this is all a misunderstanding."

Tilting his head, Jake stared at the man and asked, "In what way am I misunderstanding you trying to trap and kill me within a barrier?"

"Sir, it was not done with the intent to kill, merely to give us grounds for negotiation. We—"

"I don't give a shit," Jake shot back. "If you want to negotiate or talk, come up to me like a normal fucking human being. If you want to negotiate from a position of strength, at least make sure you can actually back it up. Oh, and last of all, don't fucking insult someone you want to negotiate with. I'm no expert, but that doesn't seem very smart."

The man looked at Jake, troubled. He didn't look particularly bothered by the death of the healer, but more by the prospect of being forced to leave the Treasure Hunt with more than half of the time to go without any loot.

"What do we have to do to get out of here alive or without having to leave the Hunt?" the man finally asked sensibly. He seemed far less moronic than the healer, cutting to the crux of it without trying to justify himself.

"That's a really good question," Jake answered with a nod before turning to the three people inside the valley. The elemental mage had already swiped up the loot from the earth mage and now stood with the assassin and rogue. "What do you guys think?"

Jake hadn't been the only one under ambush. These people had been implicated, too, and Jake had to admit he felt a bit bad about it. He hated getting others involved in his own matters without any reason, and this ambush had been made with him as the target.

Would the earth mage have maybe done something similar even without Jake's presence just to steal all the loot? Probably, but Jake couldn't know for sure. In fact, he had a feeling the guy would have tried to rob it all by himself to not share with anyone, being the greedy moron he was.

"They could start out by apologizing for being such cunts," the elemental mage yelled. "Who the fuck brings a fucking army to rob one guy? And to then, worse yet, fail so miserably? That's just shameful, man."

Jake smirked beneath his mask as the elemental mage gave him a thumbs-up. "Great fucking display, by the way, but ya could have not hit us with that damn explosion, ya know? Bloody hurt. Also, why is it that weird-ass color?"

"Hey, it is what it is," Jake said. "I didn't choose the color. Also, I just trusted you guys and gals to know how to block a massive explosion. I'm sorry if my assumption of competence was incorrect." He and the elemental mage had thrown more than one dig at each other during their puzzle-solving, and Jake was happy the guy hadn't changed. People usually started acting weird after seeing Jake fight and kill people. Odd how that works.

The guy with the group of thirty or so didn't dare interrupt, and from what Jake could detect, the man seemed happy to let the two of them talk, lightening the mood. Jake didn't doubt the guy would prefer less killing to be going on. He was lucky that Jake didn't plan on killing anyone, but there was no way he was getting off easy.

"I sincerely do apologize," the man said. "I do not mean to misdirect blame, but most of us who came here didn't do so expressly with intent to cause harm, but simply to back up an ally. It was ill-advised and a mistake, and I take full responsibility for that. I just want to make it clear that the words of Jakob weren't spoken for all of us, but were his personal views only." It wasn't certain if he was fully telling the truth or just trying to get out alive. However, Jake chose to bite into one part he probably shouldn't, as it really wasn't that important.

"Wait, the guy was called Jakob?"

"Yes," the man answered, a bit uncomfortably.

"Huh. With a C or a K?"

"It was with a K, I believe." The guy now just looked confused.

Jake nodded, feeling even more justified in the kill. Even if one was with a K, having two Jacobs would just be confusing for everyone involved.

"Hey, how about that compensation?" the elemental mage suddenly chimed in.

The stand-in leader of the group of independents looked somewhat bewildered for a fraction of a moment, then realized what the man meant and nodded. "Naturally, we will compensate you all for this unfortunate situation." He turned specifically to Jake. "We sincerely hope this will not cause a rift between Haven and the independent factions."

Jake stared at him, not revealing his actual thoughts. *I have no fucking idea where any of you are from...*

Sure, he knew they were related to cities, but he didn't know the city names or their locations or anything. So if these people just didn't come to the World Congress or some other event, he would never recognize them. Well, he could understand that if these people had a lot of their time and power invested in being political leaders, them not being able to participate due to fear of Jake would be a bad thing.

With all that in mind, he gave the guy a chance. He did have to give the guy and everyone else some credit, as when he counted all the floating Insignias around the valley, not a single one was missing. That was very lucky for them, because if even a single one was gone, Jake would have made them all leave. He still could, but he had a feeling that pissing off every single one of the independent forces present for a bit of loot wouldn't be worth it.

Those who had attacked him today were probably just part of some fringe group. Haven, being a small city in itself, would do best with positive relations with pretty much every faction. At least, Miranda had repeatedly claimed this. She insisted that staying what was effectively a neutral force was their biggest strength, and Jake really didn't want to shatter all her plans.

"Fine. What are you offering?" Jake finally said, seeing the guy visibly sigh with relief—a bit too telegraphed, honestly. The guy clearly wanted Jake to see him be all humble and nice... and to be fair, Jake was totally fine with that.

The guy ended up giving Jake and the three people with him some good stuff. Jake even noticed some of them weren't from the Treasure Hunt, but things from the outside. Primarily, he gave Jake herbs he wanted, and the ones behind the other leader even handed stuff over. Jake discovered that there were a whopping four additional city leaders in the group of thirty or so. Upon discovering that, they also coughed up some extra stuff.

Throughout the negotiations that were totally not just extortion, Jake did feel a few glances of hatred and resentment, but he paid them no mind. He had undoubtedly killed comrades of some of those present, and a dash of hate for that was only to be expected. If they didn't act on it, he wouldn't fault them.

In the end, the entire ambush situation ended with Jake looting more than seventy dropped Hunter Insignias filled with loot, all of which he collected while the elemental mage and the others did their own totally-not-extortion. Most of those Jake had killed or made to leave had very little, except the healer and the guy beside the healer. Both of those had some good stuff, and he even had a theory they had hoarded the stuff of others.

After the survivors among the ambushers handed over loot to Jake, the shadow assassin, the elemental mage, and the rogue, Jake allowed them to leave. Only the elemental mage didn't look very uncomfortable during it all. By the time they were done, the barrier was about to dissipate on its own.

"Jakob thought it would be smart to make a barrier that would last for a set amount of time," the enemy leader said, reminding Jake of how much confusion he had saved the world from with the whole Jakob-Jacob thing. "That would mean no one would be occupied with maintaining it, and he said that even if things took a bad turn, we could just stay defensive and escape when it went down... Yeah, that turned out well."

The guy finished it all off with a bow as he prepared to lead people away. "Thank you for allowing us amnesty... and I hope we can work together again in the future. My name is Ja—"

"I don't care," Jake said, cutting him off. "Talk to Miranda about all that stuff, not me. Now, fuck off. We got loot to distribute."

With those words, Jake turned back to the three people he had solved the puzzle with, ignoring the city leaders behind him. They still had the actual loot from the Rubik's cube to distribute.

CHAPTER 37

TREASURE HUNT: SPATIAL STORAGE & PARTING

"I want the staff."

The elemental mage said this the moment the kind people who'd given them stuff were gone.

"Didn't you already swipe the loot from that asshole earlier?" the shadow assassin said with an accusatory tone, adding on, "Also, could I perhaps see that mask one more time?"

"The guy didn't have much, man, just a big fucking rock collection. Shiny rocks, sure, but ya ain't gonna take an old man's rocks, are ya? Unless ya really want it?"

The last part was spoken towards Jake. He just shrugged. "Keep it. But... can you even use the staff?"

Jake summoned it from his inventory to check on his own.

[Staff of Elemental Confluence (Ancient)] – A wooden staff with a mounted gem at its head. The gem is a merged product of the orbs of powerful earth, air, fire, and water elementals, condensed into a single gem that amplifies all elemental magic. The wood is likewise a merging of different elemental-affinity woods and is enchanted to be durable and further amplify the user's mental abilities and casting capabilities. The gem

passively absorbs fire, water, earth, and air-affinity mana, and this stored mana can either be used as a supplementary mana reserve or released all at once as a quad-elemental blast. Enchantments: Elemental Confluence. Quad-element Blast.

Requirements: Lvl 125+ in any humanoid race.

Jake didn't have any need for it himself. Could he find a use for it? Probably. As far he knew, every single human was bound to have at least one of the four elemental affinities, if not several of them. However, Jake had his arcane magic, and that was good enough.

He then compared the staff's level requirement to the elemental mage who was standing there and admiring it.

[Human – lvl 118]

"Dude, he's right; you can't even use it," the shadow assassin very accurately pointed out.

"So? I will be able to soon," the elemental mage shot back. "Why do you want it? You know what—you can have it, but only if I can shove it up your arse."

"Fuck off. I'm just saying." The assassin shrugged dismissively.

"Ya lucky I'm not as petty. I fully support giving this bastard the mask to cover up his ugly mug."

"Oh, yeah, real mature," the rogue fired back. "At least I can actually put it on. What do you plan on using the staff for? A walking stick?"

Jake had also summoned the mask and checked that again too.

[Mask of Shifting Faces (Epic)] – A mask created to change the wearer's appearance. Allows the user to store a

set number of humanoid appearances that can be freely changed. This is an illusionary technique and not actual morphing. Changing appearance will also hide the user's mana signature and aura. This effect can also be applied without changing appearance. The mask itself is incredibly durable. Enchantments: Appearance Change. Presence Masking.

Requirements: Lvl 115+ in any humanoid race

Both the staff and mask were interesting, and the mask especially played with some interesting concepts to allow someone to change the appearance and even hide or change their presence. Not that Jake wanted it. His mask was already infinitely better, even if it did probably have a Unique Lifeform slumbering within that may or may not cause issues in the future.

Jake just stood back, ignoring the two rather childish men, as he checked out the stuff. He exchanged a glance with the rogue woman, who just sighed. The two immature mature men kept arguing for a while before she finally cut in.

"As I mentioned before, I didn't contribute much, so I'm leaving now."

That got the attention of the two bickering men.

"Now ya making me feel bad, lass," the elemental mage said, scratching his beard in embarrassment.

Jake decided to finally make his own position known. "I am fine with giving the staff and mask to you two, and I assume you are fine with me keeping the cube?"

He got nods from both of them.

"Great," Jake said as he took out an item.

It was a ring he had previously held in his normal storage on his neck. Newly acquired from the healer guy and not something from the Treasure Hunt. One had to remember that while he got the stuff from the Insignia from all those who fled, he got everything from those who died.

Well, besides what he broke. Jake's arcane affinity liked to destroy stuff, so a lot of defensive gear was broken, and of course, all Soulbound items were lost. But he had still gained a lot, the ring included.

"Since I get the cube, take this," Jake said as he tossed the woman the ring.

[Protective Spatial Ring (Rare)] – A ring created from a very durable metal by a very talented crafter from the newly initiated 93rd Universe. The ring has been affixed with a gem with powerful space-affinity mana that has been transformed into a spatial storage. All items within the storage are frozen in time. Latent space-affinity energy not consumed by the storage can be activated to create a temporary barrier of space-affinity mana around the wearer. Enchantments: Spatial Storage. Protective Barrier.

Requirements: Lvl 110+ in any humanoid race.

Jake had noticed that the woman carried her blades at her hips and didn't appear to have any storage. She probably had a skill for her smithing-related stuff, but not for everyday use. Jake was also fully aware that spatial storage items were quite hard to get for those unaffiliated with larger cities or factions.

Making a storage item wasn't actually that difficult. Jake had heard that even Neil could do it, despite not being very talented at creating equipment. The system was very happy offering skills specifically made to create those storages, giving them out left and right. Heck, Jake had a feeling that if he really tried, he could receive a skill to create spatial storage items the next time he chose a profession skill.

However, like elixirs, it required one to at least be D-grade to make them. Additionally, the required materials and ingredients weren't that easily acquired, and even with the System Store, the demand simply outweighed the supply by magnitudes. Who wouldn't want spatial storage, after all? Shit was just so damn convenient.

With how factions worked, they naturally prioritized themselves first. As an example, the first spatial storage Neil had crafted was given to Miranda because she was the City Lord, so for the healer guy to also have a spatial storage only made sense. Naturally, Jake didn't need it, hence why he handed it off to the rogue so she would at least get something.

"I can't take this," she said after looking it over and realizing it wasn't even from the Treasure Hunt.

"Too bad, because it's yours now," Jake said, waving her off.

"If ya don't want it, I can take it?" the elemental mage happily offered.

It was entirely possible he didn't have a storage either. Jake had seen the man summon a staff out of thin air, but that might have been from a skill and not a storage. As for the shadow assassin, Jake had seen him summon a chair at one point, so he had one for sure—which, again, only made sense. He was from the Court of Shadows, and as far as Jake could tell, not an insignificant member either.

"Fine," the woman relented, clearly wanting it from the beginning.

Seriously, who wouldn't like a spatial storage? She bound the item and put her two swords in it, happily seeing it work. After that, they distributed the staff and mask to the elemental mage and shadow assassin, respectively. As for the seven rare items, they also distributed those evenly. Jake, the shadow assassin, and the elemental mage got two each, with the last one going to the rogue. She didn't even try to argue that one.

Jake himself claimed the Rubik's cube, also known as the space-magic box. He identified it again as the three others admired their own newly acquired items.

[Safebox of Perennial Sustainability (Legendary)] – A cube containing a spatial storage within, specially made to store items of high value safely. The cube can be manipulated and sealed with a password. Due to the construction of the cube, it is near-indestructible by anyone below S-grade, and if the item is destroyed, a space storm will be released. The time of all items will be frozen within, and mana leakage will be severely allevi-ated. Mana leakage is nullified entirely for lower-value goods. The difficulty of the password is determined by the user.

He had to admit he wasn't entirely sure what to personally use it for. It was a spatial storage no doubt better than anything else he had and was nearly indestructible. The thing was, Jake's necklace already did all he wanted… but that didn't mean the cube would be useless, because items like this did have value.

Now, one may ask, why not just use normal spatial equip-ment like the ring or his necklace over the cube? The reason for that was actually simple: all of those were bound to the user. Things always got a bit dicey when it came to sharing stuff with spatial tools. Personal spatial storages were incredibly hard to switch around, and often the only way to get it off someone would be to kill them as Jake had done with the healer. Unbinding them wasn't like usual magic tools, but it often took a long time—way too long for it to be convenient.

Yet, there were many situations where one might want a shared spatial storage that didn't rely on a single person acting as a bank. The person acting as the bank had to be powerful and able to keep things safe and easily accessible at all times if someone needed anything. To put it simply, it was highly impractical. One could say that the way Haven did things currently, with Lillian acting as the bank most of the time, was highly unsecure. It put both her and anything she carried at risk.

That is where something like the cube came in. The cube

wasn't a piece of equipment, but an unbound item. It was one opened simply through a puzzle of some sort and not through owning the item. This meant several people could unlock it and use it at the same time. However, Jake had a feeling the actual password one could set would be borderline impossible to solve for most anyone. Because when Jake twisted the cube in his hand, he saw that it had changed slightly.

While it was still fifteen by fifteen, he felt that he could change it. Not just through some subtle manipulation, either. For when he poured a bit of mana in, a screen appeared before him:

Welcome to the default menu of the Safebox.

Options available:
1. Choose a compartment to access.
2. Choose cube composition.
3: Choose password layout.
4. Claim Administrator role (once an Administrator is set, only the Administrator can assign others with the role. If the Administrator dies, a new one can be assigned after (please set time)).

Jake stared at the options for a bit. It wasn't a system message, but one directly given by the item. It was also a message only he could see, based on no one else reacting. So, without further ado, he claimed the Administrator role.

After that, Jake studied it further before tossing it into the Hunter Insignia. He knew he could play around with the box a lot, but now wasn't the time or place. Also, he kind of wanted Miranda and Lillian present. Based on how the cube worked, it likely wouldn't be Jake using it much in the future. It seemed like this item could serve as Haven's vault of sorts after the Hunt.

He also saw that the others had put away their items. The

rogue now stood without her swords out, keeping everything in her new ring. The elemental mage had put away the staff somewhere, with the shadow assassin now wearing his mask. Jake looked at the guy and saw he now looked exactly like the elemental mage at first glance.

"Oh, no, which of you is which!?" Jake exclaimed with fake confusion. He looked at the shadow assassin and squinted his eyes until he saw the flaws in the illusion, courtesy of his high Perception. Well, he also had his sphere and instincts telling him the guy was faking it, so he really wasn't gonna fool Jake.

"Ya daft cunts will neva figure it out!" the assassin yelled, trying to sound like the elemental mage.

The elemental mage responded by flinging a fireball after the guy.

"Who's the daft cunt now, eh? Come in, little shadow boy. Use your fire magic!"

Jake chuckled beneath his mask as the assassin dropped the illusion and laughed himself. "Anyway, it works quite well, eh?"

"As long as you shut up, I guess it does," the rogue answered.

The three of them stayed to talk a bit more before the time finally came to part. They had spent over a full day together, just chatting and solving puzzles. If there was anything those escape rooms back before the system had demonstrated well, it was that these puzzle-solving events were great bonding experiences.

"What do you guys plan on doing now?" Jake asked them.

"Heading back to the Court," the shadow assassin answered first. "I got a message the moment we solved the puzzle about a new rendezvous point, so I'm going there to check up on things and report in."

"I'll just keep exploring as before," the rogue answered with a shrug.

"Aye, me too," the elemental mage said. "We should team up, lass; two is better than one and all that. Also, it's way fucking easier to cast spells when things aren't chasing or hitting me."

"Sure," she agreed without hesitation.

"I'll head out too," Jake finally said. "More Vaults to open, puzzles to solve, and things to kill. You know the deal."

"Before ya go, I been wondering... That city of yours still looking for fresh meat?" the elemental mage asked. "Ya know, recruiting? I usually just drift around, ya know? Figured I could stop by."

"Not sure recruiting is the best word, but sure, just stop by. Just ask for me if you ever make it."

"Nice," the mage said, smiling. "Name's Roman, by the way."

That was when Jake noticed an oddity... Throughout it all, they had never exchanged names. Jake had never volunteered his, as sharing names just wasn't that usual. The shadow assassin guy hadn't either, likely out of habit, and besides that, it just never came up. They had just been too busy.

"I'm Jake," he responded.

He felt close enough with these people to share his name, and he couldn't really see any harm in it. In fact, he had a feeling the shadow assassin likely already knew or could easily find out from Caleb or the Court of Shadows.

"We don't really use names much in the Court, so everyone just calls me KL," the shadow assassin shared.

"Felicia," the rogue woman put in before also asking, "Would it be fine if I also came by Haven?"

"Sure," Jake once more answered. "I'm not really in charge of stuff like that, but just ask for me when you come by, and things should be all fine and dandy."

She nodded with a smile, and the four of them stood there for a bit.

"Take care, people," Jake finally said in farewell.

"Don't die!" the elemental mage chuckled to them as he headed off with the rogue.

The shadow assassin stayed behind and looked at Jake. "Want me to give any message to the Judge or something?"

He was clearly aware Caleb was his brother—again, not a

secret—so Jake just answered, "Nah, I'll see him soon anyway. See you around." He waved to the people in the distance and the assassin both. He got a big wave from Roman, and a more muted one from Felicia as the assassin KL nodded in acknowledgment.

With that, Jake turned around as he headed onwards to open more Vaults and get some more of that good shit—better known as loot.

CHAPTER 38

TREASURE HUNT: VAULT RUN = LOOT 5.0

Time passed by with the Treasure Hunt in full swing. Everyone chased for Vaults all over the place, many finding more than they bargained for as they got trapped or were faced with foes far above what they could handle.

Jake was naturally one of these people. Not the trapped and in over his head part, but the chasing Vaults part. He went from Vault to Vault and did as any reasonable person would do: looted everything.

On his way, he encountered plenty of people who tried to argue with him or put up resistance, but none willing to actually fight. Jake himself tried to be accommodating and diplomatic, but seeing a party struggle with a single level 130 vampire just made him so darn impatient. If they were that weak, how the hell did they expect to actually claim a Vault?

Word of his encounter with the independent factions hadn't really spread in the first day since he split up with Roman and the others, but on the second and especially third day, he began to realize many were more apprehensive. Some just bolted if they noticed him.

Finding out exactly which faction people belonged to was

difficult. It wasn't like everyone had matching uniforms, and many had only joined a faction partly, functioning more as temporary members. The Holy Church and the Noboru clan in particular had many of these, simply due to their sizes and influence.

However, Jake did become relatively sure that the majority of humanity still wasn't associated with any of the larger and well-known factions. It was just that the large factions were always at the forefront, dominating events and the political arena, pushing the smaller ones to the side. Also, while they may not dominate in numbers, the larger factions dominated in strength.

The people who had ambushed Jake were an excellent example of this. The healer had been level 130, but the vast majority of those levels had come from him being a City Lord. His class had been low, and Jake even suspected the guy hadn't gone for a Perfect Evolution either.

Yet, he had been a significant leader of the independent factions. A bit disappointing, really. Sure, he had no doubt been one of the more powerful people on Earth, maybe even in the top one percent among D-grades, but compared to the top elites of Valhal, the Noboru Clan, or the Holy Church, he wasn't worth much. In level, maybe, but not strength.

In fact, Jake was fully aware his own level wasn't that high. The same was true for many others of the top elites or even just those slightly below the top elite. Jake reckoned Neil and all of those in his party could be five to ten levels higher if they had just ignored the Perfect Evolution, if not even more. If Jake chose to neglect his profession and just grind class levels, he would also gain far more levels faster.

The problem with that was how much it would fuck one up further down the line. Villy had told Jake that while leveling fast was all fine and dandy, it wasn't something one should actively pursue. The path to godhood wasn't a sprint, after all. Better to take it slow and steady and do everything well than just rush along. Rushing would mean missing out on many potential titles and Records. Heck, if Jake had just rushed to D-grade, he likely wouldn't have gained his arcane affinity and the Arcane Prodigy title.

Jake was thrown out of his thoughts as he exited meditation, sitting in the midst of what could only be described as the scene of a slaughter. Piles of dead vampires littered the valley. All of them had been on the weaker side. However, once they were all dead, he'd tried to open the actual Vault—which was concealed within a very out-of-place pond—and ended up summoning a damn golem.

So then he'd had to kill that one too. It wasn't all bad, though, as Jake finally got a level.

You have slain [Jadewater Guardian Elemental of Yalsten – Lvl 145] – Bonus experience earned for killing an enemy above your level

* 'DING!' Class: [Avaricious Arcane Hunter] has reached level 138 - Stat points allocated, +10 Free Points *

* 'DING!' Race: [Human (D)] has reached level 134 - Stat points allocated, +15 Free Points *

It had been four days since he split up with the group from the Rubik's cube puzzle, and Jake had to admit they hadn't been as eventful as he had hoped. A lot of time had been spent just running between Vaults, as the space between them only widened. He even tried running towards a certain Vault for hours only to see the red pillar suddenly disappear.

This meant that Jake had only managed to clear four other Vaults besides the one he was at right now. That was only about a single Vault a day. At least he had gained two levels in his class from killing guardians and getting through defensive measures during this time.

Jake got up from his mediation and headed towards the pond again. It had started glowing after the Guardian Elemental's death, the elemental itself having been a water elemental. The fight with it hadn't been that interesting, consisting of Jake blowing it up with arcane arrows for a few minutes before discovering he could merely shower it in toxic blood and kill it that way.

He stepped onto the lake and felt himself be teleported into another space. Not his first time either. Of the four last Vaults, three had teleported him away, while one had been like the Rubik's cube and instead sealed off the space around itself. Only one of the Vaults had been focused on combat, too, with the others just being more magic puzzles.

By now, Jake was convinced this Treasure Hunt had some agenda to teach everyone magic theory. Not that he was complaining—he had learned a lot, but he did prefer simply killing stuff. The one Vault requiring him to actually kill stuff had been the best, though, netting him a level in his class and being the fastest besides the first one where he scammed that Nalkar vampire lady.

As for what he had gotten out of these few days? Well, quite a lot. Each Vault appeared to have a legendary-rarity item, but Jake also noticed a pattern with these items. A pattern that became clearer over time. The first Vault had been a puzzle and had transported him into what seemed like a smithy. He'd had to get some machine working there. He'd fucked it up a few times too many and ended up fighting an army of war golems. That probably only sped up the entire challenge, as Jake had killed them and been rewarded with something called a Forgestone.

[Forgestone of Eternal Embers (Legendary)] – A Forgestone infused with incredible quantities of fire-affinity mana. The concept of embers burns strongly within this stone, never allowing the flame to truly die out. Unknown alchemical uses.

Jake had no idea how to use it, but he reckoned a blacksmith or someone like that would really appreciate the stone. Besides that one, he didn't even get any ancient-rarity stuff, just some rare-rarity things and a single epic-rarity spear he wouldn't use.

Anyway, after that, Jake had done a Vault where he was transported to an empty space with hundreds of stars and planets all around him. He'd had to somehow map out the correct path of all the celestial objects, and only then did he complete the puzzle—high Perception really came in handy for that one. His reward for that? A damn weird item.

> [Orrery of the Godless One (Legendary)] – An orrery made by a man who refused to acknowledge any gods during his life, only viewing the celestial concept as worthy of being recognized as divine. This orrery will passively map out all nearby celestial objects and give insight into their basic properties. This effect is entirely passive and cannot be altered by outside means, and may take a significant amount of time. This effect bypasses all attempts to hide or mask these celestial objects done by anything below divine-level skills.

This one was even odder than anything prior. Jake wasn't even going to waste his time thinking about its uses, and just moved on.

The next Vault had been the one that didn't transport him to another land. Instead, the entire area around him had changed and warped into an odd illusion of how Yalsten had likely once been. There, he'd had to talk to illusory vampires of ages past to figure out the true path into the Vault and—

Anyway, he cheesed it with his Sphere of Perception after figuring out the goal. It still ended up taking a while, as he had to figure out what the fuck to do first. In the illusion, he met several people who talked about some weird stuff until he finally figured out he just had to find a special tree. Locating the tree was probably meant to be difficult, but the moment he heard of it, it also appeared in the real world outside the illusion.

On to the loot.

[Paint Brush of Ephemeral Power (Legendary)] – A brush made from the wood of an ancient tree with a powerful time affinity. The concept of time has been further amplified by using the hair of a C-grade Temporal Fox variant. All paintings or illustrations made by this brush will hold significantly higher effects; however, they will also cease to be within a short amount of time. Allows the user to release a blast of Ephemeral Power, having unpredictable effects based on the last five creations made using this brush. This effect cannot cause direct harm to others.

Requirements: Lvl 140+ in any humanoid race.

This one was a lot simpler than anything else. Once he found the tree in the real world and placed his hand upon it, it transformed from a tree into a small wooden brush along with an ancient rarity bo staff. He put them away and moved on, having little use for either.

In the fourth and final Vault, before the one he had just entered, he'd been faced with another kind of magic puzzle. It was one he didn't do alone. Instead, he ended up working with a bunch of random people—nearly a hundred or so. It was all about crafting and creating weapons to fulfill some quota, and there Jake noticed the system only really cared about the rarity and level requirements of weapons.

So, Jake kinda cheesed that too by transmuting nearly all the crafted weapons with his arcane affinity, making them useless, quasi-Soulbound items, before feeding them to the mechanism to unlock the Vault. It had sped up the process significantly, and in the end, Jake was given—totally voluntarily, not at all because people were a bit scared of him—the best reward.

By far the best reward for him personally, too.

[Supreme Carbonic Focusing Catalyst (Legendary)] – This item is made of a rare type of carbon and is known to be able to bond and mix with most other materials in existence, making it incredibly potent as a catalyst in most crafting endeavors. This Carbonic Focusing Catalyst is of extremely high quality and has absorbed affinity-less mana to allow itself to grow for countless years, making it reach legendary rarity. Has a wide variety of uses in alchemical creations and will increase the power of most crafts where this item is used as a catalyst.

The sort of things half his alchemist skills talked about when they mentioned how a catalyst could enhance the final product. The Catalyst itself was just a small, perfectly black, marble-like ball that was incredibly durable. Yet as he held it, Jake was acutely aware it would easily melt to Alchemical Flame. He wasn't sure what he would use it for, but this was the one he wanted to keep the most out of everything.

These were all the legendary-rarity items he'd found so far. He had shared some loot at other places if others had helped, and also at one point because he felt sorry for others. There had been a party trapped in the illusory space with the tree since the first day the Vaults opened, and Jake gave them some rare-rarity stuff, as he kind of came in and swept up all the loot.

As for what else he would use all these legendary items for? Well, he would have to ask Miranda, but if Haven had no use, one had to remember a tiny little detail... This Treasure Hunt wouldn't be the end of this event. It would be followed shortly by an auction. An auction to sell off all the useless stuff and extra items everyone had gained during this Hunt. Jake was certain there would be many ancient-rarity items acquired by every faction, and Jake was more than looking forward to it.

In regard to the legendary-rarity items, it also quickly became obvious they all had a certain theme. Not a single one of them was a weapon or even a tool that could be directly used. The brush kind of could, but that was for a profession and even stated the effect couldn't cause direct harm to others.

These were not items to cause more war or destruction, but to infuse Earth with rare and valuable Natural Treasures along with created ones from this ancient civilization. They existed to push the Earthlings further and speed up their progress on the path of creation.

Well, okay, there was some good shit too when it came to equipment made to be worn.

Of all the equipment he found, most weren't worthwhile objects. Except, for some fucking reason, he found three rings. The first one was a rare-rarity ring from the first of the three Vaults. He had happily taken it on, as it increased his mental stats.

Then, in the next Vault, he'd gotten another rare-rarity ring, this one increasing his Agility and Perception. Jake was over the fucking moon at it. It was so much better than the shitty Ring of Brilliance he had gotten from Abby's body way back when, with its measly +50 Intelligence, +50 Wisdom, +35 Willpower enchantment.

Yet in that exact same Vault, he also got one more ring that he only noticed a minute after being so happy at the first one. He hadn't known what to expect, but when he had used Identify on it, he wasn't disappointed. Far from it.

[Ring of the Starseer (Ancient)] – A ring once worn by a powerful Starseer. The Starseer sought to comprehend the celestial concept and intimately understand the stars, and this ring was made to do exactly that. Allows the wearer to use the Starseer ability inherent in the ring.

The Starseer ability significantly reduces visual distortion caused by the space and celestial affinities. This effect can also be activated to temporarily grant the wearer the ability to peer at a faraway, pre-known celestial object. Enchantments: +400 Perception, +200 Wisdom. Starseer.

   Requirements: Lvl 130+ in any humanoid race.

Needless to say, he tossed it on and became happy as a clam. At least he was happy.

Back in the present, Jake had just entered the water to explore his fifth Vault. The pond he entered through had been at the very edge of the world, where he saw space break apart just in front of it. Jake even had to get through some spatial distortion to get there; he'd partly chosen this Vault to test out the Starseer ability.

However, the moment he appeared inside the Vault, Jake's eyes opened wide. He felt himself floating.

Fuck me, he thought.

It was a fucking water level.

CHAPTER 39

TREASURE HUNT: SUBMERGED

S omewhere, a long time ago, a group of game developers sat in a room together. They knew they needed more content in their game to expand the playtime, but they had no idea what to add. Technology was limited, and there were only so many mechanics to add when all the controllable characters could do was to move up, down, and to the sides.

Then suddenly, one of them got an idea. "What if we make our character able to fly?"

But no, that was quickly shot down. The movements would be too fast, and it would be too hard to control. Once more, they were stumped until someone else spoke up.

"What if instead of flying, we make it swimming..."

And thus, one of the worst ideas ever was conceived.

At least, that was how Jake imagined the absolute moron who'd thought up water levels. No one liked water levels. They always sucked. Jake believed this was inherently down to how water affected movement and limited how one could usually control the game.

Water had to slow down movement, and while it allowed lateral movement, this was often slow and frustrating and incredibly "floaty" due to it being in the water. It also meant enemies could attack from more directions, and overall just caused a lot of issues. However, perhaps the biggest obstacle was how one often lost their usual means of combat.

Suppose you killed stuff by jumping on it. Well, becoming unable to jump made that difficult. If you shot a gun, chances were it wouldn't work underwater. Swinging a melee weapon was also often limited. In conclusion? You didn't only have severely inhibited movement underwater; you also couldn't fight properly.

Now, how does this relate back to Jake? Quite obviously so, actually. Because Jake currently found himself submerged in water, having no idea what the fuck he was supposed to do. He was just floating there, in the middle of nothing. Yet, for the first time, he also experienced something he hadn't in a long time...

Blindness.

Jake couldn't see anything in his surroundings. It wasn't limited to his eyes either. His Sphere of Perception was being overloaded with information, mostly due to the powerful mana inherent in the water. It filled the sphere, making it seem almost solid to his senses.

To his eyes, it was also utter darkness, which was new to him. Usually, he could see even without any light. Entirely sealed-off caves weren't any issues due to his high Perception, but he truly was blinded under this water.

For a brief moment, he panicked and began moving around, trying to find something to hold onto. However, he quickly found there was nothing and no one. He was utterly alone, trapped in nothingness.

Constant pressure was upon him from the water too. It didn't deal any damage to him, but he felt it. Also, while he didn't have to breathe, being unable to do so was incredibly uncomfortable for him. Jake had never had any issues with water and could swim with no problems... but this wasn't okay with him.

Calm down, he told himself as he tried to stop moving

sporadically. His instincts told him to get out of the water and find solid ground. He felt exposed. Jake closed his eyes as he entered meditation and attempted to do what he had done in the Forgotten Sewers dungeon with all the dark mana—acclimate himself to the environment, filtering out the mana in the water.

Yet shortly after he closed his eyes, he was thrown out of meditation by his danger sense activating. His eyes shot open, and he moved to try and defend. The blade appeared in his hand but moved incredibly slowly through the water in his attempt to raise it and block the incoming blow.

He failed.

A warm feeling and a sting of pain filled one arm as something hit him. He had been cut, he knew, but he didn't know by what or whom. Jake felt more and more unsettled as he felt something come by him again, not attacking this time.

The water made him feel like he was moving in slow motion. Taking out his bow was also utterly out of the question, as how the hell was he supposed to shoot an arrow while submerged? It would be a waste of time.

By now, he also noticed something else with his wound. It kept stinging, and soon he detected some foreign energy invade his body. It was venom. Jake frowned as he thought of what to do, then summoned his wings to try and use them to move around.

He could feel something still moving around in his sphere. He couldn't properly see it, only notice the mana's subtle displacement whenever something fast moved by him. Jake once more tried to filter out what he assumed was water-affinity mana, but the moment he closed his eyes, his danger sense activated again.

Jake once more tried to block, and this time he was partly successful. He released a blast of mana from his body, hitting the creature attacking him just as it came close. It was repelled for a brief moment, then began circling him again. Believing he had found a temporary coping mechanism, Jake felt momentary relief. Then he had the sense of danger again, this time from two directions at once.

There is more than one.

Gritting his teeth, Jake released his presence and infused it with mana to try and get a better understanding of the situation. When he did so, he suddenly became able to see a bit more of his surroundings due to the mana displacement. However, he also felt a severe drain on his resources. The water pressed down on not only him, but everywhere his presence dominated, wearing it down and forcing Jake to choose between deactivating it or risk running out of mana within less than half an hour.

Jake felt forced to choose the former, but not before one final push. He channeled more mana into Pride of the Malefic Viper and also summoned a net of arcane mana. When the next creature came to attack him, Jake was ready.

The creature zoomed towards him, and at the final moment, Jake manipulated the net of mana to be positioned in front of him. At the same time, he angled his body, allowing his foe to penetrate his stomach with its attack. He felt like he was pierced with a sword. The net of mana wrapped around his foe as he tried to grab hold of it with his hands.

He felt something slippery squirm, but he managed to keep hold of it with the net. The wound on his stomach got worse as it moved back and forth. Jake raised his blade and stabbed it through the creature to make it stop, but found that it only made things worse.

Finally, he managed to wrestle it into a position where he could place his hands on it without slipping. He began channeling Touch of the Malefic Viper as the creature struggled. Yet he just kept going, the wound in his stomach growing and more, and more venom being injected into him.

With a final push using Touch, he felt the creature stop struggling. A notification appeared.

You have slain [Deepgorge Terror – lvl 127]

Jake stared at the notification for a while. Only level 127. A being several levels below himself had caused him quite a bad wound and left him reeling from its simple attacks. It wasn't even some powerful variant. Heck, it just felt like a creature that was some weird mix between a swordfish and an eel. He knew he needed some way to fight back, and quick, before—

His danger sense activated, and he was forced to block a blow with his arcane barrier. The creature was repelled, but soon after, it activated again. Focusing on his surroundings, he saw signs of movement. Not just one or two either.

That was when Jake realized that he was truly in deep shit.

———

How exactly they had come to be in their current situation was a bit hard to understand. It had all begun when they ended up at the same Vault, which proved to have certain competitive elements. The Vault had opened up a large maze all around itself as the geography changed, and everyone had been teleported and split up.

Miranda had found herself alone, separated from Sylphie and Carmen. The three of them had stayed together and done well, even clearing a few Vaults together. She had heard that Jake had an incident, though the details were still unclear. All she knew was that it involved killing many people, and many of the smaller independent forces were now afraid of anything related to Haven.

She would handle that later. What mattered now was the situation in front of her.

Standing in a hallway, she faced a man she had only ever seen once before but heard of many times. His slick, combed-back black hair and casual demeanor gave him an off-putting presence as he stood there, staring at her.

"Eron," she said.

"Miranda, I believe?" the man asked rhetorically.

In a situation that mirrored the one where Jake had met him, she was now faced with a conflict she would prefer to avoid. Under normal circumstances, they would have no reason to fight; however, this Vault fostered battles.

When they were teleported, each had gotten a small mark that others could claim. These marks allowed the challenger to open certain passageways, granting them more access to deeper areas of the maze and eventually the Vault itself.

This Vault was perhaps the largest of the bunch with the most rewards, and, from her estimates, in excess of a thousand now found themselves inside it. Miranda had already used a device given by Arnold to send out a distress signal, so she could only hope someone would come... because she wasn't certain how to handle the supposedly immortal healer.

"An unfortunate situation, and the peculiarity of the circumstances are not lost on me," Eron spoke. "I hope we, too, can have a friendly bout like I did with Mr. Thayne."

"I don't suppose we can't just go our separate ways?" Miranda asked, having a feeling her time in the Treasure Hunt was about to be over. Sadly, one couldn't simply hand over the mark from the Vault. It was only dropped by leaving the entire Hunt or dying.

She should know. She had already made a handful of people leave, which was also the reason she knew Eron wouldn't simply let her go. He also had quite a few marks, too, but less than her.

"Sadly, I don't believe that is a course of action worthy of consideration."

With those words, he exploded in white flames and began manipulating his magic.

Miranda also used her own skills as she began retreating, having been warned by Jake of the odd affinity Eron possessed. While considering what to do, a voice suddenly entered her mind and made her eyes open wide.

———

She was chased through the halls, firing magic after Eron as he pursued her. Miranda turned a corner, with Eron turning it soon after. He found that the woman had erected a wall of stone to block his way. He burned through it within a minute, and on the other side found Miranda surrounded by a barrier. She had reached a dead-end.

"I can at least waste your time," the woman said as Eron walked forth.

He waved his hand, and white flames blanketed the barrier of mana. Miranda kept up the shield as he slowly burned it down, waiting for her to run out of resources. Because he knew she would run out before him.

Seconds turned to minutes, and soon a quarter of an hour had passed. No one else had arrived during this time besides a woman who saw Eron and then swiftly ran the other way. That put his mind at ease, as she would serve as a distraction if anyone else came down the same way. As they were at a dead-end, no one should come.

"I must admit, I expected more," Eron said. The woman had been defensive through it all—besides the first few minutes, where she'd at least attempted to stop him. "One would think the City Lord of Haven had more tricks up her sleeve."

"Trying my best here," she answered as sweat pooled beneath her.

Eron looked on, knowing she would soon reach her limit. "A valiant attempt, indeed, if the purpose is only to waste my time," he muttered.

A minute or so passed.

"I do hope you are aware this is in no way personal," Eron told the woman. He saw blood come out of her mouth and her one leg wobble as she knelt down. "Just leave now, Ms. Wells."

"Why would I?" he suddenly heard a female voice say. His

eyes opened wide as he looked to the side and saw the City Lord of Haven standing on a magic circle more than ten meters away from him. Completely unscathed.

"How is—" Eron began, but his vision shifted.

The room expanded, revealing the absence of the barrier of stone he had made a hole through, and a long hallway opened up in front of him where a dead-end had been. Beneath his feet was a magic circle that had not been there before. He whipped his head to see what he had been burning, only to find a figure standing beside what looked like a metal mannequin with white flames on it.

The figure was one Eron recognized.

"The pleasure is all yours," Sultan said with a smile, staring mockingly at Eron.

Eron knew himself and his powers very well. He feared very little and knew few things could truly harm him. However, that didn't mean there weren't people on Earth he would avoid at all costs. People with magic and methods he wasn't sure how to handle or who countered him.

Sultan was one of these people.

The man took out a black notebook, whose pages began turning. Eron couldn't move. He tried to, but the command simply didn't register. Instead of moving, he chose to blow up his own body to escape.

BOOM!

White flames blanketed the hall, and he saw Sultan and Miranda both get pushed back. Able to move again, Eron swiftly retreated back where he had come from. He ran through the halls, and the two people chased him. He sent back a wave of white flames, making them both stop their pursuit. His escape continued for a minute or so until he turned several corners and felt like no one was chasing him anymore.

Eron sighed with relief as he resigned himself to—

"Verdant Feast Of the Lagoon's Insatiable Depths."

He hadn't moved. He hadn't self-destructed. The realization struck him as a hand reached up from the magic circle below him. The entire floor turned into murky green water, and countless greedy hands pulled him under. He tried to explode again, but still found himself frozen.

The last thing he saw before being pulled under was the smile of Sultan, who stood there with his black book.

———

Miranda collapsed with fatigue as the man disappeared, devoured by the ritual. She looked at Sultan, for the first time feeling a bit of fear towards the man. He had spoken in her mind and told her what to do, even being aware of her Feast ritual.

"Well, that's that handled," Sultan said as he closed his book.

"Will he die?" Miranda asked.

"Doubtful. However, the Feast is self-perpetuating, correct? So let him be the fuel of his own prison till the Hunt ends." Sultan shook his head.

Miranda gave the man a look again, slowly nodding her head. A small pool of green water remained on the ground where Eron had once been, no other signs of him present.

"It should keep him trapped till the end of the Hunt."

Miranda once more nodded. Eron could probably find a way to break free eventually if he was truly invincible, but it shouldn't be possible in such a short amount of time.

Sultan himself stood there nonchalantly, motioning as if to ask whether they should continue their journey. The slave woman also soon came up to them, having served to put Eron's mind at ease before.

Miranda couldn't wrap her mind around how Sultan looked completely unbothered by how they had just put someone out of commission that even Jake had told her to avoid at all costs.

At that moment, Miranda had to admit... she was happy he was on their side.

CHAPTER 40

TREASURE HUNT: THE DEPTH OF WATER

J ake had a headache. Not the kind of figurative headache, but the literal kind. It felt like he was constantly being smashed in the head with a sledgehammer while wearing a motorcycle helmet. At the same time, his body hurt, as he had countless bleeding holes all over.

In his surroundings, corpses of dead fish floated, polluting the area around him. Jake had killed eight of them so far, all of them rotten through by his Touch of the Malefic Viper. While the fish had also taken some damage simply by being in the water around him, that hadn't been the primary killer. The blood he was constantly leaking—infused with Blood of the Malefic Viper —was the source of this pollutant, and it had ultimately resulted in the fish leaving him alone for the most part, yet still circling him.

He had also tried to release his poison mist but found it useless. The water simply consumed and suppressed it instantly. The only reason his blood worked was due to the tangibility of the toxicity being bound to the blood. Touch of the Malefic Viper also didn't do shit if he just used it on the water. He tried doing some stupid stuff like absorbing the mana with his new space cube, but spatial items always had the issue of needing to deposit an object. Turns out an ocean's worth of water didn't count as an object.

However, what ultimately saved his ass hadn't been all of his poison or his arcane affinity or any of his usual go-tos. No, it had been the Expert Stealth skill coupled with his cloak. He had wrapped it all around him and focused on Expert Stealth to try and meld into the environment. It hadn't worked at first, as he still had to kill the fish already aware of him, but once those had died, it seemed to work—kind of.

The fish circling him didn't do so because they were aware of him, but because of the blood of their brethren. They knew this was a "special spot," but not why. Jake, wrapped in his cloak, once more focused on comprehending his surroundings, which was the cause of the headache.

Jake knew the affinity surrounding him was solely the water affinity. His Sense of the Malefic Viper told him that, and Jake also knew he had that affinity himself based on his talks with Villy. Not because he had been tested, but because, according to Villy, every human who started at G-grade had it. Something about water being the basis of life in their newly integrated universe, making everyone have it by default.

With that in mind, he knew he just had to explore the affinity and learn of it to become able to filter it out with his Sphere of Perception. It should be easy... but it wasn't. For it wasn't only the water affinity dominating his surroundings.

There was also a concept Jake wasn't certain about. All he knew was that it mixed incredibly well with the water and was the primary cause of the pressure upon him. It was clearly related to water in some ways...

Was it gravity? Just weight? Jake wasn't sure. He had no idea how far down he was and if it was just sheer water pressure. Wait —was water pressure a concept in itself? His head was filled with many questions, making it only hurt more.

Time slowly passed as Jake tried to filter out the excess information in his sphere. The first thing he did was focus on limiting its scope from the usual few hundred meters down to only a few dozen. Usually, he didn't really "look" at his sphere when it was just that large; it more functioned as a passive detection system, only alerting him to movement. It worked especially well with his danger sense to alert him of potential dangers.

However, as had been shown before—like just after his evolution to D-grade—it could also be a bit of a double-edged sword at times. Jake didn't have the passive assistance of the system to help him not overload his brain, and thus had to solely rely on himself. He was lucky that his Bloodline was semi-self-regulating, in that he would instinctively try to avoid things that would cause severe harm to him.

His Bloodline wasn't omnipotent, however, and ultimately relied on Jake himself. Which was why he sometimes needed to step up with his more conscious mind, like in his current situation.

Ever so slowly, his sphere shrank. He analyzed and took in the mana around him with Sense of the Malefic Viper. He kept trying to identify the concept but couldn't exactly put a name on it... Still, he did get a good feeling for what it did.

The concept wasn't as simple as just being water pressure. Water pressure would solely be a physical force, while this was not. It didn't only pressurize the physical water around him, but also the mana density and even Jake mentally. It simply compressed and pushed on everything. In some ways, it did remind him of what the Lighttail Monkeys did.

Yet it wasn't entirely the same, as this clearly wasn't some magical attack, but simply how the environment worked. Also, the fish were clearly unaffected by it based on their agile move-ments. If they were under the same pressure as Jake, they sure as hell wouldn't waste their energy swimming around as they currently were.

Which naturally begged the question—why weren't they affected? Was it some passive skill? Perhaps they were affected but were just used to it, and this was their norm? Crazy-insane physical stats making them god amongst fish outside of water? Either way, before Jake could figure it out, he would have to actually be able to see what the hell was going on.

Jake focused his mind and entered meditation, slowly exploring the area around him. He began filtering out certain kinds of information and found that it helped to focus on one of the fish. The fish appeared to just be made of water in his sphere, yet it was also an autonomous creature separate from its living environment.

With it as a catalyst, Jake began separating the fish from what was around it. He tried to discern the details of the creature, filtering out the atmospheric mana that dominated the water he found himself trapped in.

One small detail at a time, he began seeing the fish. It was long and eel-like as he expected, but contrary to eels, it had visible scales covering its entire body. Jake didn't detect any gills, but it did have four large fins on the side of its body. The head was the most peculiar of all.

It had a mouth full of razor-sharp teeth and a long, sword-like nose. The sword's edges were jagged, and Jake felt toxins embedded in each of the jagged edges, making the entire nose look a bit like a poisoned saw.

As the fish became more and more defined, its surroundings also began standing out more. It became murkier, the darkness fading as Jake focused on filtering all the "sameness" away. He naturally also focused on Sense of the Malefic Viper to correctly identify the water-affinity mana as he also became more familiar with that.

Ever so slowly, he began to see. The immediate surroundings of the fish were the first to come clear, and it left a trail of clearness as it swam. It spread and spread, and soon the area thirty meters around him became visible to his Sphere of Perception.

One problem down... Next up, how the hell do *I move properly?*

As mentioned, Jake knew how to swim already. He had even

done some light training for fun in his pond, and while water did inhibit movements, the depths he currently found himself in took that concept to the extreme. He felt like he was a human from before the system stuck in water, and—

Wait, is that it?

All this time, he hadn't thought of the most obvious reason why the water was harder to move in... It was simply because it was water. No, not normal water, but magic water.

Water was harder to move in due to friction and the higher density. You had to always displace some amount of water whenever you moved, the same as with air. Of course, water made this harder. Soil and sand were even harder, as you technically could move in loose soil; it was just a damn struggle—something anyone who had ever been buried in sand at the beach could attest to.

After the system, this displacement in both water and sand had become far easier. Jake was far stronger than before, making it incredibly easy to move some water with a light motion. Yet what would happen if this density were amplified? If this denseness and friction were heightened to a supernatural level by making it a concept?

That was what Jake was currently experiencing. It wasn't that it was some other concept mixing with water... It was merely a concept naturally born of much water affinity being together.

The reason had been so simple all along. Jake was stuck in magic water, not normal water.

He had a strong feeling his insight was right, and it also allowed him to see his surroundings more clearly. The mana was so damn dense because magic water didn't only compress physical space but also the magical space. It also explained the mental pressure. In fact, he had a feeling that perhaps his soul was getting pressured.

Jake was happy at his realization. There was just one issue: what the fuck to do with it?

Sure, Jake now knew he truly was just stuck in super-magic water, and that was why it was so dense, but that didn't magically make him able to move about in it. Furthermore, considering how much harder it was to properly analyze the affinity, he was also damn certain his water affinity was pretty crap compared to his dark affinity.

But... there had to be a solution. For this, Jake once more turned to the fish. These creatures were utterly unaffected by this denseness. In fact, the water seemed to give way wherever they swam. His first thought was that their bodies were coated in some kind of barrier displacing the water, but he couldn't detect anything.

Next up, he wondered if they were immune due to system fuckery and them being fish. However, that didn't seem to stick either, as clearly, they were doing *something*. He felt magic from them. A constant hum of mana. It was passive, but there, a bit like when his own Limit Break was active...

Whatever method these fish used wasn't external, but internal.

Which made Jake consider if he was able to copy it... because as he currently was, he couldn't fight for shit. The fish also kept circling him, so he couldn't move without them noticing him... Actually, he had a feeling his cover wouldn't last much longer. The blood was thinning around him, slowly spreading out and floating away. This meant him hiding under his cloak would soon begin standing out more.

Jake's hiding place already stood out, but as the blood and corpses stopped functioning as cover, he was certain the fish would discover him. While his cloak and Expert Stealth were nice, he was ultimately still free-floating in the middle of the water.

Gotta hurry.

He needed to at least find a way to make himself semi-able to fight back. Those eight he had killed so far had come with him losing over half his health pool and forcing him to drink a health potion, and currently, he detected over ten in his immediate surroundings. Jake was not looking forward to dealing with all of them at once.

Now, how the hell do you manage to be unaffected? Jake asked the fish. He didn't get any answer.

No, he knew he needed to scan them somehow. He needed to be able to see their interiors... and the only way he knew how to get a better look was through Sense of the Malefic Viper. More specifically, by using it on a poisoned foe. At least, that was what he needed to develop his own method. For now, he just needed to find a way to survive and put up a fight.

Jake was, in his current state, at less than ten percent solely due to his environment. Swinging a sword was slow as fuck, his bow was out of the question, any magic he summoned consumed far more resources than reasonable, and even his poison was significantly weakened, as he couldn't summon his mist.

There was only one thing that had improved. Now Jake could see—at least, somewhat. As he became able to perceive his surroundings through his sphere, he also slowly became able to see with his eyes. Everything was still murky, but now he could at least make visual contact with his foes, which meant Gaze of the Apex Hunter was back on the menu.

Just as he was about to formulate a plan, the situation changed. A fish seemed to spot Jake hidden behind his cloak. It abruptly shot towards him, nose-first.

Not so easily this time!

Jake narrowly dodged by swimming to the side, grasping the fish under his arm as it squirmed. It did cut up his side and his arm a bit, but he managed to hold it. He infused Touch of the Malefic Viper into it while trying to carefully see the inside of the fish's body.

Emphasis on *tried*, as just when he began, another fish came. Jake was forced to let go of the first one and push it away. The second one charged Jake, but he froze it with Gaze right at the last moment. It stopped swimming yet still floated straight towards him. Jake had, at this time, managed to get both his scimitar and Nanoblade out.

He stabbed the frozen fish with the scimitar, purposefully soaking the Nanoblade in the blood from some of his wounds to poison it. The Scimitar of Cursed Hunger didn't look or feel any different than before his encounter with Eron, except he felt its hunger even more than before. Clearly, both the curse and the weapon had become more powerful in concert.

A third fish dove for him, and Jake turned his head to also freeze that as he skewered it on the Nanoblade. With a fish on each blade, he was at an impasse when yet another one came towards him. Thinking fast, Jake raised his foot as it came barreling into him. It hit him on the boot, completely failing to do any damage to Jake's awesome footwear. His foot did hurt like hell, but not as much as the fish that had its nose bent from the impact.

Jake struggled as he was pulled in different directions from the fish squirming on his swords. They struggled, trying to swim away and get themselves lose. He saw how every fin movement displaced a humongous amount of highly condensed water, making it difficult to keep hold of his weapons.

He failed to react as yet another fucking fish came from behind, and as he couldn't turn his head, he failed to even use Gaze. He angled himself to avoid a bad hit, but still had the damn fish pierce him through his stomach.

With a bit of reluctance, he let go of one of his blades—still binding a string of arcane mana around it—and infused his gloves with arcane mana, then grasped the nose that came out of his stomach. He began infusing it with Touch of the Malefic Viper to poison that one, too. It quickly decided stabbing Jake was a bad time and backed away in what Jake saw as an almost impossible motion. It seemed to practically swim backwards as the sword nose exited him, leaving yet another nasty wound.

Jake yoinked back his sword with the string, the fish getting off the blade. The one on his scimitar had also managed to dislodge itself and had now retreated. None of the fish attacked him right away, as they were nursing their wounds or being apprehensive with their attack. Some of the fish were poisoned, and the one he had grasped first was on death's door, but there were still many more.

Overall? Jake was having a very shitty time.

CHAPTER 41

TREASURE HUNT: BE LIKE WATER

This is bad, Jake thought as the school of fish around him grew. He quickly chugged down another healing potion as he considered his approach. However, one thing was certain: he couldn't abandon his focus on how to better move.

The poisoned fish around him became his stepping stone to understanding this. He felt the toxins circulating through their bodies, gradually battling to remain. It was a struggle between the vitality of the fish in question and the poisons Jake had infused, and he saw this battle clearly.

Yet, he also noticed something else. Not in the clash of vital energy and poison, but more what was around it. Everything just felt so odd inside the bodies of the fish. The toxins constantly moved about, and he also detected large amounts of water-affinity mana inside them at all times.

It was a constant stream... but the amount of mana they had to consume at all times to circulate that amount of energy was just utterly insane. Again, one could compare to Jake's Limit Break, where he naturally expended more stamina by circulating more stamina. In the same way, these fish constantly circulated large amounts of water-affinity mana.

One would think this was tiring, but they all did it in the same way. If it was Jake doing the same thing, circulating mana inside or around him, he would be out of resources within an hour. Yet these damn fish didn't give a fuck, pumping mana through themselves like it was nothing.

He felt like none of this helped him. On the contrary, it only made him more uncertain of exactly how they managed to cope.

Firstly, how did they even deal with the sheer load of mana running through them? Or was the water affinity just suited for it? Water was naturally able to flow and seemed like a gentle force. From what Jake knew, water-affinity mana liked to be together and condensed. It also liked to conform to whatever shape it was in, being a liquid and all.

Was this why the fish could handle it? The water allowed them to handle it? Was it perhaps because it was in constant motion? So many questions, so little time. The fish grew bolder and bolder, drawing closer with every swim-by.

He wasn't sure what to do as he prepared himself. Right in front of him passed a smidge of red that seemed completely out of place. The blood of the fish wasn't red, but transparent and water-like. Which meant it was human blood from his own wounds.

Jake watched his own blood effortlessly flow through the water, unaffected by the pressure or the concepts Jake had observed before. It seemed to almost meld into and become one with the water. In fact, when he observed it with his sphere, it appeared nearly the same as the water around him. His Sense of the Malefic Viper also told him that the blood had simply integrated the water. Allowed itself to be integrated. It was mixed with the water, yet it still remained separate, with the poison within it. Integrated but not assimilated.

That was when Jake remembered a certain quote that honestly didn't fit that well in his current scenario:

Be like water.

Because that is exactly what the fish did... They became one with the water around them. They, like his blood, integrated themselves without being assimilated. With this realization, another one also came... He asked himself why he fought his environment so much.

The mana didn't hold any intent. It simply was. The only reason it damaged Jake was due to the sheer density and that concept, and while he wasn't sure that could be eliminated entirely, he should be able to alleviate it, right?

Jake opened his mouth and took a deep breath, letting the water enter his lungs and body. He felt like choking but resisted. Instead, he also focused on absorbing as much mana from his environment as he could. His mana pool couldn't contain all of this excess mana, which began damaging him... so he released it again.

He did discover that drinking the water was a grade-A idiot move, as he only needed the mana—but in his moment of desperation, he wasn't thinking very clearly. All he knew at that moment was that he had to not fight the water or find a way to cope with it; he had to allow himself to acclimate by taking it in. This was only possible because it was neutral mana and not something summoned by anyone. If this Vault had been made with water that held inherently antagonistic properties, Jake wasn't certain how anyone could survive.

After around thirty seconds, Jake began seeing some results. His entire body was affected by the water affinity, and he actually felt his own weight increase. However, what he also felt was familiarity. His surroundings became clearer, and he began feeling like he could move. His headache also lessened a lot.

Jake wasn't out of the woods yet, though. Because while he had found a way to adapt, this method wasn't instant. He had to absorb the mana into his body and release it again to do this process, but if he did it too fast, he damaged himself and risked losing control. Too slow, and what was about to happen would be the result.

Three fish came at Jake. He instantly responded by brandishing his two blades. He managed to swing far faster than before, taking one opponent by surprise. A long, nasty cut was left across its side. The second one found itself suddenly confronted with the edge of a blade that skewered it through the mouth as Jake angled it to avoid being hit himself. The final fish was frozen just before it hit him and collided with an arcane barrier.

Because one other thing had come from his realization. It had led to him recognizing that it was insane not to use his arcane magic, too, using the environment and not fighting it. Before, Jake had tried to use his own mana far too much to summon his magic. This was a necessity in the outside world, where the atmospheric mana was never this dense.

But here? Here, Jake just had to not fight the neutral mana. Instead, he had to create a spark of arcane energy and then transform the surrounding energy with that as the base. Because Jake had learned that water very much wanted to conform once directed. Did this mean he could turn this entire shithole of water into arcane energy? Sadly not, as Jake couldn't cast magic that far away from him, and he still had to direct this transformation.

What he could do was easily summon plenty of low-mana-cost mana bolts and barriers.

However, their explosions and speed proved to be lacking when he fired one into the crowd of fish. More than an explosion of arcane energy, it was an implosion. The moment the bolt lost its form, it was just compressed and consumed by the water, not doing anything to the fish.

Thus he switched to going full-on stable arcane bolts, pretty much just creating small crystal spikes and larger crystal spears of pure arcane mana to pierce his foes. He focused on this while also trying to absorb more and more water mana... which led to another wonderful discovery.

In this place, he had near-limitless mana. In fact, the fish were expending copious amounts of mana every single moment;

they just didn't give a shit because they regenerated even more. Not that it helped these to have near-limitless mana, for they were utterly doomed now that Jake had a way of fighting back.

With every moment, he grew faster and stronger. His magic sped up, too, and soon all that surrounded him was the blood and bodies of fifteen newly killed fish.

Jake cheered internally as the enemies stopped coming, naturally continuing to absorb the water mana and adapting. He checked his notification, which instantly put a damper on it all.

You have slain [Deepgorge Terror – lvl 119]

...

You have slain [Deepgorge Terror – lvl 128]

To feel proud about slaying these fish was honestly a bit... sad. Yeah, sad had to be the right word. These fish were weak—as in, among the weakest any D-grade of their level could be. They had no skills or abilities. All they could do was swim into people and try to poison them with their nose swords. No magic or anything had ever been displayed by them. They weren't even durable or overly fast...

They were just fucking fish. Barely magical fish.

Of all the D-grades he had killed, he didn't doubt these were the weakest on paper. Yet, he had to admit that this had been the most danger he had been in since fighting the Altmar Census Golem, a level 150 foe created by an ancient faction to test talents. And he had gotten significantly stronger since then in every way.

Matchups aren't a fucking Joke, he told himself, shaking his head.

Jake chose to remain where he was, slowly healing himself and getting used to the water for the time being. The entire acclimation thing was fast in the beginning, but he soon noticed it slow down significantly. Finally, after an hour or so, with him having also consumed another health potion, he noticed nothing more was happening, to his disappointment.

While he could now move far more easily, he still felt like a pre-system human in water. But, then again, could he expect anything more? In the end, he wasn't an aquatic animal, but a human. Shaking his head, he closed his eyes and reentered meditation, not reemerging until all of his resource pools were full.

On a side note, Jake was forced to continue the mana circulation from the environment. The moment he stopped, he felt the pressure on him begin to accumulate, making him restart the process. This meant that there was a constant mental element to keeping himself functional while underwater.

It took him another three hours and two potions before he was back in top condition. He also had to wait out the Limit Break weakness, as he had naturally used that during the fight.

Opening his eyes once more, Jake believed it was ripe time to actually begin exploring the shitty Vault he found himself in. He had moved little more than ten meters from where the teleportation had originally taken him, and he seriously doubted all there was to this Vault was a bunch of fish.

Maybe he could have stayed put to try and think up more methods for fighting in water, but he had to remember he was already on a timer. He would hate to miss out on anything important happening outside just because of his own tardiness.

Jake began swimming upwards first, but after less than a minute, he saw a ceiling. On the subject of his sphere, he had chosen to keep it at thirty meters. Anything more, and the headache from information overload would resume. While he now understood the mana and could see through it, he still had to filter it.

The ceiling he encountered appeared to be made of rock, yet he noticed it was just a small layer when Jake got closer. Behind the rock was metal, affirming that he truly was just stuck inside some artificial space. Was this a giant cube of water or a sphere or something? A labyrinth?

Either way, he followed the ceiling until it began sloping downward. He then followed the wall until he reached the bottom of wherever he was. When he reached the bottom, Jake got a brilliant idea. He waved his hand, and a much-helpful metal staff appeared.

[Pillar of Encumbrance (Rare)] – A metal rod made of a type of metal with the natural ability to change weight based on the intensity of the mana infused within. Incredibly durable.

Requirements: N/A

He wrapped it in arcane strings and infused some mana into it. At the same time, he infused his feet with mana to anchor himself to the bottom... and voila! Jake suddenly felt like he was standing on solid ground. The seabed—if you could even call it that—was made of stone too, and he doubted this method would work on sand, so he had to do it while he could.

There was something inherently entertaining about walking at the bottom of a pool of water. It became even more entertaining when you didn't have to breathe. So, finding some amount of fun in this Villy-forsaken place, Jake continued his journey exploring the bottom of the Vault—or at least, what he assumed was the bottom.

For he soon came to learn it wasn't. After exploring the edges of the area, finding nothing, he walked to the center and found a circular hole with a peculiar magic barrier covering it. He frowned when he saw it was a path downwards into a new section, and his new theory was that he found himself in some kind of giant metal cylinder.

Jake leaned closer to the barrier and tried touching it. To his surprise, his hand just phased through without any problems.

Well, *without any problems* weren't entirely accurate, as his hand began feeling weird as hell on the other side. It almost felt like it wasn't really his own hand, or that it was wrapped tightly in a glove or something like that.

He quickly noticed why. The other side of the barrier wasn't the same kind of water as where he was now. There was another density to it—one far lower. Either way, he would have to dive through, as he saw no other exit to where he currently was. Clearly, this was the way forward.

Phasing through the barrier, he found himself in a new room. This one was actually a room and not a cavern of any kind. The walls were made of metal, and he saw several instruments and magical devices scattered about. All of them looked broken and corroded, but he had a feeling this place had once been used for research of some kind. He scouted the room out a bit, finding nothing of particular value. Everything was attached to the walls or the floor, and while the devices looked complicated, they were all ruined.

That is, until he spotted something. A faint light. He moved closer, removed some debris, and saw a still-glowing panel of some sort. Jake looked at it and saw a big red button with huge letters over it: ACTIVATE COMPRESSION.

Jake pressed it. It was big and red—he had to.

Also, it did exactly as he expected it to. A loud noise occurred, and dormant magic circles activated all around the room. The mana density—and thus, pressure—in the room began heightening at a steady pace, and Jake began adapting once more. It quickly became clear that this next area would be even more pressurized than the last.

He severely hoped this would be the last part of this water level, but alas, water levels also had one more important trait:

They were often too fucking time-consuming and dragged on far longer than they had any right to.

CHAPTER 42

TREASURE HUNT: BOSS ROOM, PLEASE?

C asper solved the puzzle and shattered the spatial bindings holding the final fragment as Lyra flew up and grabbed it. She returned it to him, and he inspected it to make sure everything was in order.

> *[World Fragment of Yalsten (Unique)] – One of five World Fragments of Yalsten, the cornerstones of the miniature world. As Yalsten began falling apart, the World Core was split into five and scattered in the cardinal directions of the world to stabilize it. What has broken cannot be restored, but the fragments can be combined into a Quasi-Core once more. Be warned that creating a new core from the fragments will permanently destroy the world known as Yalsten. Cores will automatically reform if close to each other.*

When coming to this place, the undead faction had held two primary goals. This was the first of them. A World Core was something even gods sometimes desired, as it allowed one to create a true world. Not a full universe, but a world that existed within the endless Void between the universes.

These worlds could vary vastly in size, from no larger than a single room to millions of galaxies. Compared to a real universe, this was still only a mere fraction, but these worlds were far easier to control, customize, and defend compared to managing a section within a universe. However, they also had many drawbacks, such as their fragility and the fact that the world would become effectively inaccessible if all access points were cut off. This was what had happened to Yalsten.

What Casper and the undead would get wasn't a true World Core. That ship had already sailed, and what they would instead get was a World Quasi-Core. This core would not allow them to establish a stable world, but it could serve other means. Of all the treasures in the Treasure Hunt, this core was possibly the most valuable.

To assemble it, Casper began heading towards the center of the Treasure Hunt—the crystal spire. The final fragment was stored there, and now was the time to make their final preparations for the battle against the guardian.

But for now, Casper needed to keep his distance from the spire. At least a kilometer or so. If he went too close, he would trigger the merging of the fragments, and then the world known as Yalsten would begin its destruction. The unstable space at the edges failed to spread only due to the fragments Casper had taken, so once combined, nothing would hold the world back from slowly collapsing in upon itself.

Waiting was done not only for the undead, but also for the other factions. After all, there were many other valuables to collect. Casper had also naturally seen the opening quest about the Vaults and knew that soon the final stage would begin whether he triggered it or not. In the meantime, the undead would make their preparations while searching for the other thing they wanted.

The second item the undead faction really wanted was the Seed of Eternal Resentment, the fulcrum of the ritual that had placed the curse upon Yalsten. Needless to say, an item with the ability to store and facilitate a curse able to destroy an entire world wasn't to be looked down upon. It would no doubt be weakened if removed from Yalsten, but it was still worth it.

However, with this, they reached an impasse. They discovered that the Seed had already sprouted long ago. Wood had been created from offshoots of the Tree of Eternal Resentment, then turned into weapons and tools of the Pure Ones faction.

The main tree itself would have had to be thousands of kilometers tall, towering over the world. Yet now, no such tree was to be found, and the undead scrambled to locate any remnants of it. There had to be at least some leaves, bark, or just any wood left... or perhaps just a single root.

———

"Blub blub blub," Jake complained as he peered down the hole leading into yet another damn cavern, his words roughly translating to, "You gotta be fucking kidding me."

Of all the Vaults, he had now officially spent the most time in this one. In the first cavern, he had killed fish before proceeding down to the second. Inside there, he had killed slightly stronger fish. In the third cavern he'd also killed fish, but there he'd met different kinds—including a second variant added with the ability to spew water bullets or something.

Fourth cavern? Two same kinds of fish, but—get this—also traps trying to hurt him. Fifth? More fish, more traps, more everything. Sixth, seventh, eighth? Same fucking shit, over and over again. Some were more focused on foes, some more focused on traps, and all of them equally a waste of fucking time.

Jake had gotten a grand total of *nine* kills that actually gave experience throughout the entire shitshow that was the water vault. It was just cavern after cavern with those airlock-type things in between to increase the pressure. Jake adapted every time, and he honestly barely noticed the difference between each level.

Perhaps it would screw over someone with less physical stats, but Jake handled it easily. The only real consequence was him having to limit his sphere by a little every time. In this ninth room, he had shrunk it down to only fifteen meters, which still served him fine. His eyesight had gotten rather good, so he managed.

Entering his ninth Vault, he checked it out with his sphere to see what this place had to offer. It appeared to be more of the same, seeing as he was instantly assaulted by a school of fish. Jake sighed internally as crystalline bolts of arcane mana began condensing around him.

Some of the crystalline shards, Jake still embedded with a bit of destruction, making them explode. The explosion wasn't meant to damage anything but simply sent smaller splinters of crystal-like arcane mana flying. Arcane frag grenades, if you will.

At the same time, he drew his weapons, preparing for his foes to arrive. Jake still hadn't found any feasible way to use his bow and arrow underwater, so for now, this was what he had to do. Just before the first fish reached him, his danger sense faintly warned him. He dodged a harpoon fired out of the wall.

Jake dove forward, staying mobile to avoid the traps. He cut and weaved, swimming primarily by condensing and hardening the water under his feet. Sometimes he appeared to be dragged downwards, courtesy of the Pillar on his back, which he sometimes used to increase his weight.

For a lot of the rooms, he had simply reached the bottom and killed everything from there, feeling almost as if he were fighting flying foes. However, that hadn't worked for the last two sections, as the bottom was now a forest of large, vent-like openings spitting out extremely hot water whenever he got near.

His eyes tired as the fish were slowly culled. Sometimes he even made use of a trap, slapping a fish into an incoming spear or perhaps impaling one and sending it flying down to the bottom to become a steamed fish.

Jake could easily handle the Terrors with large noses, but he did take some damage from the second variant—the Spitters. They fired bullets of pressured water after him, each of them able to leave small, circular wounds. One or two were fine, but it was just tiresome when a dozen assaulted him at once.

Ultimately, he spent nearly an hour cleaning up yet another fucking samey session. He found yet another airlock at the bottom and entered it. He instantly went to the floor of the small chamber and sat down to meditate, his body looking like Swiss cheese from all the bullet holes. While meditating, he naturally went through all his lovely notifications.

You have slain [Deepgorge Terror – lvl 131]

...

You have slain [Deepgorge Terror – lvl 141]– Bonus experience earned for killing an enemy above your level

And the only other type of foe—because who needs proper enemy diversity in a fucking water level?

You have slain [Deepgorge Spitter – lvl 133]

...

You have slain [Deepgorge Spitter – lvl 143]– Bonus experience earned for killing an enemy above your level

Once more, a lot of the same shit with far too many foes he didn't even get experience from. The Deepgorge Terror fish were, as previously mentioned, bottom-tier D-grades, and the Spitters were barely a level above that. If these were translated to land-dwelling animals, Jake would be able to slaughter them even more easily than the Deepdwellers back in the Undergrowth dungeon.

As he thought this, he reached the end of his notifications and saw one more that made his eyes open wide.

* 'DING!' Class: [Avaricious Arcane Hunter] has reached level 139 - Stat points allocated, +10 Free Points *

This shit actually gave me a level?

Doing the math, it seriously shouldn't have. While Jake had certainly killed a lot, these were weak D-grades and barely any levels above himself. *Could it be it's because of the environment?*

Jake did know that a part of how much experience one got was determined by the difficulty of the fights, and he did have to admit that fighting these fish wasn't easy. He had to apply new methods, and not a single room had left him with more than half of his health remaining.

Shaking his head, Jake simply focused on his meditation, not bothering to think too much about it. Instead, he focused solely on recuperation so he could swiftly move on to the next area. The next one would be the tenth cavern, and he dearly hoped that would be the last one. A part of him had hoped it was only nine, but ten also seemed "fitting," if that was the right word.

A few hours passed before Jake got up, ready to continue. There was now only a bit over a day of the entire Treasure Hunt left, and he seriously couldn't dally and play around in these shitty water levels anymore.

The next cavern turned out to not be a cavern at all. Jake looked around and saw what looked like a flooded underwater chamber with large metal pillars everywhere. He was also fairly certain this place was larger than any section prior. This change could only mean one thing:

It was a boss room.

And what did a boss room also indicate? That's right—the end of the challenge.

Jake made a toothy smile, prepared to face whatever monstrosity was hiding within. Yet, just as he was beginning to get himself riled up, he spotted a figure out the corner of his eye. It was a long, snake-like creature that was more than five meters long. He turned towards it and Identified it.

[Fulgarian Eel – lvl 140]

The slithering beast also saw Jake at the same moment. It darted towards him with its mouth open, even faster than the Terrors from the other chambers. He reacted by drawing his blades and winding up his arcane magic.

With a slash, he met the charging beast. It angled itself to bite into his sword, catching it between its razor-sharp teeth. Jake thought it moronic to do so until the very next moment. His danger sense reacted, and he quickly let go of the Nanoblade he had used to attack.

A thunderclap was heard as the area lit up with blue light from his blade. Electricity, and not a small amount either. Luckily, he had let go at the very last moment, avoiding being zapped. He was still hurt by the electricity, but not as much as he would expect, being in water and all.

His body was temporarily paralyzed, but it did little to stop his arcane magic. Crystalline bolts hammered into the side of the eel, leaving nasty punctures along its side. It made an odd screeching sound in anger and pain, but all that did was make Jake continue his assault.

Covering his body in Scales of the Malefic Viper, Jake dove in, scimitar at the ready. He retrieved his Nanoblade and attacked the eel with both of them, leaving a few nasty cuts. The eel turned around in the water, sending out a pulse of electricity after Jake, but this time his scales were up. The paralysis was negated, and the beast didn't bite down on a tasty Jake, but instead a blade stabbing into its open mouth.

Frowning, Jake wondered if this could truly be the boss. It was stronger than the fish, sure, but it wasn't exactly boss-level or anything. Dislodging his blade, he attacked yet again. At the same time, another current of electric energy was emitted—this time at higher power, actually managing to penetrate his scales. Clearly, this was not done with the intent to paralyze, but damage.

Jake felt the current run through his body, burning him a bit internally but far from enough to stop him. He retreated for a brief moment, poisoning both his blades with his own blood before he attacked again, leaving a few more cuts. The beast was heavily damaged by now, and Jake was confident he would finish it shortly.

Sadly for him, it had friends.

He became aware of several presences approaching—not from his sphere, but his Sense of the Malefic Viper. Mana of the electric variant approached him from three sides, and he quickly oriented himself toward the joining foes.

[Fulgarian Eel – lvl 139]

[Fulgarian Eel – lvl 141]

[Fulgarian Eel – lvl 142]

Four at once... Still better than the other sections, Jake told himself as he activated the Pillar on his back to sink downwards, avoiding being surrounded.

Three of the eels chased him, one of them lagging behind due to its injuries. Jake faced them all as they clashed. He opened his eyes wide and froze them with Gaze, proceeding forward with his blades. Arcane power swirled around his blade as he cut the first one deeply. The second one got stabbed through, with the third getting four arcane crystal bolts puncturing its side.

If this fight had happened in the very first section, Jake considered, he would've been utterly screwed. But now, nine caverns later? By now, he was confident fighting underwater, and while he was still far weaker than on land, handling a bunch of eels wouldn't be an issue.

Lightning rolled through the water, and poison and blood spilled everywhere, but the winner was clear from the beginning. Jake cut and poisoned the eels till they all stopped struggling, barely taking any damage from it. He did have to block a few blows, which resulted in him taking a bite on the arm, but it wasn't anything he couldn't easily ignore.

He noticed that the eels couldn't discharge electricity all the time. They had to slowly build it up, and from what Jake saw, they did this by absorbing the water mana in the area and transforming it into lightning or electricity-affinity mana.

This meant he knew he could attack an eel with no reservations just after it released a blast or tried to fry him, giving him ample openings.

Jake shook his head and dispelled his blades again, disappointed. Was this shitty place really going to continue? He couldn't see those four eels being the final challenge of—

CLICK!

The loud noise echoed through the water, and a moment later, Jake heard what sounded like a generator starting. The metal pillars all around the room began glowing as electricity wormed up their sides, and Jake's eyes opened wide when he saw something move far beneath him. It looked like part of the room itself was moving...

He squinted, then saw the faint reflection of deep blue skin that faintly crackled with lightning. He promptly used Identify.

[Giant Fulgarian Eel Lord – lvl 158]

Thank fucking Villy, it really was a boss room.

CHAPTER 43

TREASURE HUNT: A SCALY INTERMISSION

J ake readied himself as the creature swam beneath him. He knew it was aware of him, since he felt its attention upon him. The eels before had been about five meters long, but this one... this one was on another level. More than an eel, it was a giant sea snake. He estimated it to be in excess of a hundred meters, with a large, bulky form over six or seven meters in diameter.

However, this didn't mean it was slow. It slithered around the pillars lining the large room, seeming to enjoy the jolts of electricity that ran through them. On the other hand, Jake really didn't, as he was forced to keep his distance from all the pillars or risk getting zapped.

The large Eel Lord didn't seem to be in a rush to attack him. It appeared to have only awakened when whatever powered the room also turned on. It happily absorbed the electricity and empowered itself. Deciding not to waste his opportunity, Jake held out his hand.

Mana condensed as an arrow began appearing from his palm. More than an arrow, it looked like a harpoon, with jagged etches and a large broadhead. It was naturally Arrow of the

Ambitious Hunter. While he didn't know much of these light-ning eels, the Terror and Spitters were close cousins, and ulti-mately, they were flesh-and-blood creatures.

Jake kept an eye on the eel as its massive form made its way around the chamber, keeping an eye on him too. It was appre-hensive, far more so than any of its brethren. This indicated at least some level of intelligence, as it had no doubt noticed the four dead eel around his more-or-less uninjured form.

It wasn't that smart, though, as it allowed Jake to fully summon the arrow. Now his only issue was how to deliver it. He had no confidence firing an arrow with all the pillars lining the room to function as cover, not to mention the tiny little detail that he was still underwater.

Underwater archery didn't have a good historical track record, in that it didn't have any track record. Because under-water archery wasn't a thing. Because underwater archer would be stupid. Jake didn't plan on inventing it in mortal combat.

So, he wrapped the Arrow of the Ambitious Hunter on his back with arcane strings and took out his blades. He coated both of them in uncommon-rarity Necrotic Poison and added a small layer of stable arcane mana on each blade to encapsulate the toxins and not have the water dilute and weaken the killing power. Also, he had a very advanced attack tactic called "stabbing both swords into the eel to their hilts" planned.

Next up, he began condensing what looked like cubes of highly stable arcane mana. Whenever he made one, he sent it flying out into the large chamber, simply floating where it was. He did this tens of times, making hundreds of these cubes. The mana expenditure was insane, but he had the natural environ-ment to keep him topped up. As for the purpose of these cubes? That would become clear later.

Being fully prepared, Jake narrowed his eyes as mana began condensing around him. Crystalline bolts assembled by the dozen. The eel noticed what he was doing and knew it could no longer continue what it was doing. It moved around a few more pillars, rapidly making its way towards Jake.

Far more rapidly than Jake had expected.

Shit, he thought as he released the bolts of arcane mana towards his foe. Despite its massive form, the eel managed to dodge most, while the rest only left surface wounds. Four tendrils of pure lightning condensed around its head when it got close and moved to grasp him.

When he got a closer look, he noticed they were a mix of highly condensed water and electricity. The Eel Lord used them almost like hands. Jake dodged backward and, in his moment of temporary panic, fired off a blast of arcane mana, sending himself flying back and getting a bit too close to a pillar. The hair on his head stood as faint amounts of lightning entered him.

The eel dove forward, lunging as it tried to bite down on his significantly smaller frame. Jake was more prepared this time, and had already made a path of escape. He condensed some water below his feet and stepped down. One Step Mile activated, and Jake found himself standing on a cube of stable arcane mana more than two hundred meters away.

He had come to learn that One Step Mile really didn't give a shit about what kind of environmental mana it had to make him travel through. Sure, the water was far denser, but in the end, it was still neutral and not antagonistic mana, making his One Step Mile work as well underwater as on land.

However, there was the issue of having something to step on. Condensing water far away from him was incredibly difficult, as Jake usually used his Sphere of Perception for this, but with the Sphere limited, he required pre-prepared stepping platforms. That is where the cubes came in.

Why cubes? Well, because they had more sides, and while Jake had tried discs, they often weren't oriented properly. Cubes were far better at that, as they tended to spin randomly around from the currents and whatever movement in the water his fighting instigated. The cubes of stable arcane mana also lasted longer, since they had more real estate to pump mana into. So, yeah, that's why he used cubes.

Jake teleported again just after landing, getting on the other side of the eel to confuse it. It sent out a large wave of electricity, but Jake was ready, and he simply tanked it with his scales. The large form of the beast allowed him to take yet another step and appear on top of it. Electricity ran up his body, but it failed to paralyze him as he slammed both his swords down into the Eel Lord's body.

It made a loud squeal of pain, sending a soundwave through the water that made Jake's ears bleed. Yet Jake didn't let up. He dragged both the blades across the body of the beast, leaving two incredibly deep cuts. Not to mention the poison that now flowed within.

Sadly, he couldn't continue his assault. The eel shook its body and amplified the voltage. Jake was forced to jump off, and just in time. An almost shockwave-like jolt of blue power ran through the eel. The massive creature fled from him and slithered around several pillars, absorbing even more electricity as its wounds also began healing.

Jake responded by summoning even more bolts of arcane mana. However, he didn't simply do that, but also coated them in his own blood before he sent them flying through the water. The eel avoided most of them, but a few did find purchase.

Annoyingly, he found that the electricity of the pillars helped speed up the elimination of poison in its body as well as heal it. Ultimately, he still chose to fight it at range and wait for it to get close. His arcane bolts petered it as it tried to hide behind the pillars. Jake still did more damage than it healed, making him unsure what the hell it was doing—until he noticed its skin slowly turning blue and crackling.

It was storing electricity not only in its body, but its skin and small scales hidden beneath the skin. Each of the scales served as small batteries. Jake felt his own poison slowly draining into these scales, the poison wearing down. The entire thing reminded him of how the Malefic Viper's scales had—

His eyes opened wide as he stopped what he was doing. Without thinking, he poked a certain skill, impulsively activating it without any hesitation.

Do you wish to experience the Legacy of the Malefic Viper? Uses remaining: 2

———

The nine council members surrounded the dragon that was the Malefic Viper, having activated their trap and sealed the beast within a grand barrier. They were confident and saw no reason why they shouldn't be able to slay it.

Their magics activated, raining down upon the dragon's scales. Yet the moment they did, something wondrous happened. The scales seemed to almost come alive, consuming the magic and storing it within themselves, nullifying or at least delaying much of the damage the Malefic Viper would have taken.

Everyone present was taken back, except for two other consciousnesses present. Naturally, the Malefic Viper had expected it. This was all part of the plan to make them all fear him, which would amplify the effectiveness of the presence he would release soon after.

The second person who wasn't surprised was Jake. Back during the first time, he had noticed this peculiar phenomenon, and now that he'd experienced it himself, he truly understood. However, comparing it to the eel was simply shameless.

This was on an entirely different level. Jake saw the scales consume the mana with absolute avarice, and he felt that it didn't stop there—far from it. The mana stored in the scales was being broken down by an odd mix of Touch of the Malefic Viper and Palate of the Malefic Viper. The two skills seemed to fuse, existing within each scale as they passively did their work. The purpose of this was clear... to transform and then absorb the mana. Claim it as his own, with absolute gluttony and greed—a concept Jake understood very well, and perhaps a part of the reason why he comprehended this skill so easily.

He felt it, he understood it, and, as he focused his mind, he applied it. The vision around him began breaking down soon after, being the shortest Jake had ever experienced and even repeating the same scenario. Jake understood why... for he had wished to experience this again. He had wished to finish his comprehension, and the system had acknowledged his desire and granted it.

As for why it ended so soon... because Jake was done, and he didn't need to see any more. He had seen this end before, and he had his own battle to attend to. The notifications appeared before his eyes as he was transported back again.

[Scales of the Malefic Viper (Ancient)] – The Malefic Viper's scales are the first, and often the only required, line of defense. Allows the Prodigious Alchemist of the Malefic Viper to turn parts of his skin into scales, vastly increasing the effect of Toughness and adding a certain damage threshold. All damage below the threshold is nullified. The scales are exceptionally resistant to magic, allowing the alchemist to handle toxic substances better. Passively provides 1 Toughness per level in any profession related to the Malefic Viper. May you continue down your path, o chosen of the Malefic One.

—>

[Scales of the Malefic Viper (Legendary)] – The Malefic Viper's scales are the first, and often the only required, line of defense. Throughout the ages, as the Malefic Viper became a dragon, he too was granted the power

inherent in the well-known dragon scales, making him a bane of all magic. Allows the Alchemist of the Malefic Viper to turn parts of his skin into scales, vastly increasing the effect of Toughness and adding a certain damage threshold. All damage below the threshold is nullified. The scales are legendarily resistant to magic and will store excess mana from any magical attacks that would have otherwise damaged you. If the damage taken by the scales is too high, this mana will be dealt as direct damage after a certain amount of time. Otherwise, this mana will be slowly refined and absorbed or dispersed into your surroundings. Passively provides 3 Toughness per level in Heretic-Chosen Alchemist of the Malefic Viper. May your scales be as perennial as the Malefic One, and may the sight of your scales let all know their resistance is futile.

* 'DING!' Profession: [Heretic-Chosen Alchemist of the Malefic Viper] has reached level 131 - Stat points allocated, +10 Free Points *

* 'DING!' Race: [Human (D)] has reached level 135 - Stat points allocated, +15 Free Points *

———

The eel was clearly flummoxed when Jake returned. He had only been gone for a few seconds, but it was enough to throw it off momentarily. His trip away had been brief, but Jake was still experiencing the euphoria of the skill upgrade, and he had no patience or willingness to delay experimenting.

Scales had been the first of the "of the Malefic Viper" skills that granted him stats. The skill had been the beginning of it all. It had served him well and been his primary defense for such a long time... and now he would see what the improved version was truly capable of. Scales covered his body, looking no different than before visually, but the assumption that no changes had happened couldn't be further from the truth.

Each scale was a small magical treasure in itself, holding concepts and power Jake couldn't fully understand. Yet the knowledge of the skill made him aware this was because the scales he summoned were true dragon scales, or at least a very close imitation of them. He was certain an actual dragon would have far more powerful ones, as the Viper's were still on another level, but that didn't mean his scales weren't already ridiculous.

The Eel Lord collected itself, its body now shimmering with electric light. Jake noticed the Arrow of the Ambitious Hunter was still on his back, and he couldn't help but smile. He began condensing mana under his feet as the massive beast charged towards him, its gaping maw open and ready to rip him apart.

Jake stood still when the eel released a massive shockwave of blue light. If it had hit him only a dozen seconds ago in real time, he would have been paralyzed and found himself in quite the pickle... but now? Now the electricity simply rolled over his body, small sparks absorbed by the scales here and there.

This didn't deter the beast. It sought to consume him; that much was clear.

He chose to oblige, but on his own terms.

Jake leaped forward, arcane energy exploding behind him as he was propelled like a torpedo towards the open, razor-sharp-teeth-filled mouth of the eel. Naturally, the beast noticed his near-suicidal attack and prepared to chomp down with a strike that no doubt could pierce even his shiny new scales. Unfortunately, they still carried the same relative fragility to physical damage as before, even if that had also improved.

Not that it was an issue in this particular instance, for the moment before the Eel Lord managed to close its jaws around him, its entire body froze, affected by Gaze of the Apex Hunter for the first time. It failed to move as a figure barrelled straight into its open mouth and summoned a bow.

Arrow of the Ambitious Hunter still had to be shot from one, after all.

And while archery was utter shit underwater, it was still useable if you only had to make a magical arrow move a short distance forward and puncture a beast.

The arrow was released just as the beast was able to move. He shot it upwards towards where he assumed the brain of the Eel Lord would be, but didn't wait to find out.

A blade appeared in each hand, and he headed not out of the mouth, but further in. Simultaneously, the eel's internal defense system activated. Everything around him contracted, and electricity unlike anything ever before dominated the environment, far more powerful within the beast than outside.

The energy rolled over Jake, and his eyes lit up from the electricity. The scales blocked nearly everything, but some damage did still manage to seep through. He reckoned most things would die from being crushed by the contracting muscles of the eel and the massive amount of electricity... but Jake wasn't most.

With his two blades, he cut up the eel from the inside, storming through the inside of its body down the length of the beast. It squealed and resisted. It tried to crush him, it tried to fry him—it did all it could as it thrashed around, but failed to truly do anything. Jake made things even worse by cutting up his own arms and spraying his blood inside the body of the eel.

One step at a time, he carved his way through its body, leaving only rotting, necrotic flesh and blood in his wake. At the same time, his scales were pulsing, absorbing more and more mana. If he had done this before the upgrade, things wouldn't have ended well, but now?

Now all the beast could do was slowly realize it had swallowed more than it could chew.

You have slain [Giant Fulgarian Eel Lord – lvl 158]- Bonus experience earned for killing an enemy above your level

'DING!' Class: [Avaricious Arcane Hunter] has reached level 140 - Stat points allocated, +10 Free Points

In the end, the water level didn't turn out to be that bad. Jake just had to leave with Path of the Heretic-Chosen and do something else to truly enjoy it.

CHAPTER 44

TREASURE HUNT: SERENITY & CONFLICT

Throughout the multiverse, different species and races were famed for different things. Humans were famed for their diversity and their ability to become nearly everything. You could meet humans as strong and tough as the most powerful beasts, or mages with magic and skills that employed concepts in line with the most powerful elementals or spirits.

A cat-like monster would often be agile and fast. A fish would excel underwater and have skills well suited for underwater combat. Among all these species, some were more famous than others. Not only for their relative strength, but for simply being a powerful race.

Unique Lifeforms, beings that were not truly a race in themselves, stood at the pinnacle of this. Any Unique Lifeform was an existence that all knew were powerful solely by hearing what they were, but this was far from limited to only them. Some races fell under other archetypes but were nevertheless extremely powerful due to the subcategory their race fell into.

The most famous of these were what humans before the system had often referred to as mythical beasts. A phoenix, no matter what, would be a powerful beast by courtesy of being a phoenix. The krakens, champions of the sea, chimeras, beings that could adapt to nearly any foe and had oh so many abilities. Yet, one creature was more known than any of these: dragons.

There did not exist a creature with the word dragon in its name that was weak. Dragons naturally also had subcategories, but all of them were powerful. There were lesser types of dragon-like monsters, also known as wyverns, land drakes, or such things, but these were not True Dragons.

The word dragon also came with certain expectations. Assumed abilities that one would be correct about, for all dragons had at least two skills.

Dragon's Breath was a destructive weapon heightened to a concept in itself. The form these breaths took could vary widely. A blue frost dragon would, as expected, spew something ice-related, while the classical red dragons would no doubt release fire. Yet all of these breaths had one thing in common: their unimaginable power.

Jake had read in a book that the weakest Dragon's Breath ever recorded was of legendary rarity, which meant most were above even that. He had seen the Viper release his breath and seen the power therein. This would be enough for most to fear dragons, but their other trait made them absolute nightmares to deal with if you attempted to slay one.

Dragon Scales. Known as the bane of all magic, these scales would make any mage grit their teeth in anger. More often than not, it would be useless to try and cast magic on a similarly leveled dragon unless you yourself were also a supreme genius.

Naturally, the nature of these scales also varied. Many simply provided ridiculous defense and magic nullification, and the scales always resisted magic more effectively based on the dragon's own affinity. That is to say, using frost magic against a blue dragon was double stupid.

What Jake acquired weren't true dragon scales. He wasn't a dragon, so it would be very weird if he did. However, if he had picked the Malefic Dragonkin race back then, there actually was a chance he could have gotten them by now.

Instead, what he had were imitations of dragon scales. They served much the same function but weren't simply a passive ability he had at all times. Jake had a feeling he could take his scales in that direction if he wanted, one day making them a permanent fixture, but he really didn't want to, as he would rather upgrade them in other ways.

Also, Jake's version of the scales did have one small drawback.

"Holy fucking shit, it hurts," Jake said, his words naturally just coming out as water bubble due to him floating there, the massive frame of the dead Eel Lord beneath him.

The scales on his body were all supercharged with energy, slowly being refined, but a lot of that energy couldn't be. So what did this energy do?

It directly damaged his own health pool, which was essentially a minor soul attack. It fucking hurt, to put it mildly. His decision to simply tank all the power the eel had at once hadn't been the smartest, and had honestly been risky as hell, but, hey, he'd gotten the job done.

He also discovered that he couldn't dispel his scales if they were charged with any magic. Jake even tried to cut off some scales, but saw that it didn't do shit. New ones automatically regrew, the old charge within. So, yeah, he couldn't hack the system that way.

Soldiering through the pain, Jake instead focused his attention on the corpse of the eel. He felt something within it, and with his blades, quickly dug out what looked like an oddly shaped heart.

[Giant Fulgarian Eel Lord Heart (Rare)] – The heart of a Giant Fulgarian Eel Lord. This heart has potent light-ning-affinity energy within and will passively generate electricity if infused with mana. Many alchemical uses.

It was nearly the size of Jake's entire body, and when Jake infused some mana into it, it beat like the eel was still alive. Very freaky. He tossed it in his inventory and moved on, still wanting to exit the Vault sooner rather than later. Oh, and to get the loot.

Diving down, Jake encountered yet another opening, this one larger than any of the others. Coming out of it, he saw countless cables. The cables went to the pillars spread across the room, each of them fastened to the bottom.

Could I have broken the cables to make the eel unable to absorb electricity? Jake asked himself. He quickly tested it by firing a crystalline arcane bolt into a cable and saw the bolt easily pierce it. *Guess I could. Huh.*

Moving on.

He entered the next area and, to his surprise, found that when he went through the barrier, he did not find water on the other side. Instead, he found air. As he had just hurried through, his entire body suddenly found itself falling to the floor, and to say it felt weird would be an understatement.

Momentarily, he felt like his entire body was weightless. Then it suddenly felt like it weighed a ton. He fell straight down onto the floor, bracing himself. At the same time, he actively pumped mana out, not only due to his scales but also just from his constant cycle of water mana to adapt. It felt weird as hell to suddenly leave the depths and enter a normal atmosphere so suddenly.

Jake lay on the ground for a while as he collected himself. He had quite a few things to focus on, including expanding his sphere a bit to get a look at the room he was now in, all the meanwhile dealing with the scales and adapting to not being under the crushing weight of that odd water-affinity-concept-thing.

This new room was quite small compared to any of the others, but was far cleaner and well maintained. Instruments lined the wall, there was a single bookshelf with books that looked unaffected by the moisture, and overall there was a lot of

stuff that looked to be worth swiping. Two things in particular
stood out. One was an altar with a large tome and an orb right
next to it, while the other was a large bowl of water placed on a
pedestal. He noticed that some of the water from above had
dripped down as he fell and landed in the bowl of water—clearly
by design.

He lifted himself off the floor, then walked closer to the
bowl and looked within. There, he saw a stone no larger than a
child's fist at the bottom of the newly fallen water. Jake focused
on the stone and used Identify.

*[Dewstone of Serenity (Legendary)] – A small stone
created by the combined effort of a group of water
nymphs to help heal a close friend. This stone was eventually acquired by a powerful vampire and brought to
Yalsten, where it has been ever since. Will passively
transform surrounding water by infusing the power of
serenity into it. Effect lessens, and the transformation
process becomes slower the larger the pool of water. Has
many alchemical uses.*

Well, this is interesting, Jake thought as he looked at the
stone. It looked simple and nondescript, and had it not
given off the aura it did, he would've easily mistaken it for
some random stone found anywhere. It did look like it had
been polished by water quite a bit, as though it had come
from a beach or a lake or something, but other than that,
nothing.

He also felt it influence the water around it, but as the water
had just dropped there, it had yet to be fully affected. Thus, he
decided to not touch the bowl quite yet, and instead moved to
the altar with the large tome and the orb.

The tome looked faintly familiar to him, and it didn't take
him long before he made the connection. He had seen two of
these before—once when he got his profession for the first time,

and the other after he killed the Great White Stag. Identify confirmed it truly was such an item.

[Akashic Tome of the Fulgarian Depthcaller (Unique)] – Allows the user to acquire the class Fulgarian Depthcaller if compatible.

Requirements: Lvl 99-199 in any class. Compatible user.

It was exactly what he expected. From all the research Jake had done, Akashic Tomes were quite rare but not impossible to create. However, they did still take significant investment, meaning all of them were considered very valuable. Of course, it all ultimately depended on how good the given class was.

The other item on the altar was an orb that clearly came with the tome.

[Storage Orb of the Fulgarian Depthcaller (Ancient)] – A storage orb containing items to assist a Fulgarian Depthcaller, including equipment and guidance. This orb is near-indestructible by anyone below A-grade, and any item within will be destroyed if the orb is.

Requirements: Fulgarian Depthcaller.

This one was a bit surprising. Would one just be handed the class's full set of equipment and supportive items or something? That seemed excessive. Jake himself didn't have any use for it, but it would probably fetch a pretty penny in the big auction after the Hunt. Surely there would be a bonus for having a set, right? Package deal and all that.

Now, he still had to figure out how good the class was, and he had a feeling the bookshelf would help him answer that. Jake waltzed up to it, his scales disappearing one by one. By now, most of his scales had vanished as the mana within was neutralized, and he was beginning to feel normal after being so suddenly de-compressed.

The bookshelf held around thirty books, all of them seemingly related to the class, the Vault, and generally just stuff about water magic and such. Jake didn't want to check them all out now, but he did find one book aptly named Fulgarian Depthcaller.

Jake opened it and quickly skimmed a few pages to get some basic knowledge of the class. He came to learn that the class had once belonged to an A-class Vampire King of Yalsten, and this entire Vault had been created with the intent of preserving his own legacy.

The book included quite the detailed description of the class, as well as a damn history lesson about how the king got his class after training for many years underwater. There, he had battled and trained with eels, learning from their powers and slowly beginning to mimic them. Before that, he had already been a lightning mage, and through his evolution, he had merged water and electricity.

Exact details on the class were limited, but the mere fact that an A-grade had found it worthy of creating an Akashic Tome for future generations should say something. Jake put all of the books and the bookshelf in the Hunter Insignia. Some of them he would keep for himself, while others he would use to heighten the price during the auction.

Taking another look around the room, Jake once more noted how everything seemed to be in far better condition than anywhere else. A bit like a Count's chamber. Considering that... wouldn't it be a shame to just leave it behind? Surely it would.

In all his generosity, Jake began ripping everything off the walls, burning the instruments from their fastenings, and storing anything his inventory would allow. Computer-looking devices, shiny pieces of metal, and even some wall platings were ripped loose and thrown in there.

It took him a good half an hour to tear the room apart and

take everything that looked to be even vaguely of value. He even ripped down a lot of the wiring leading up to the chamber above. He did remember copper cables selling quite well before the system, so magical high-conductivity wires had to sell well, too, right?

With everything done and looted, he turned his attention towards the one item still left in the room. One he had left for last on purpose.

He returned to the bowl of water and, this time, noticed a difference. The water in it had changed and now gave off quite a bit of mana, making him naturally use Identify on it.

[Serene Water (Rare)] – This water calms the mind of anyone who consumes it, allowing them to more easily focus while suppressing the effects of most mental afflictions. Continued consumption will help heal minor soul injuries. Has many alchemical uses.

Jake smiled. He was reasonably confident he had just found something very useful for the future. Lifting up the bowl, he took a small sip of the water, feeling a cool stream go through his body. He felt his mind soothe a bit, the mental stress of the adaptation process lessening. It was some good shit. He quickly scooped up the entire bowl, including the water and Dewstone within.

Now, with all of that done, Jake sat down on his ass and entered meditation to fully recuperate. There, he turned his attention to the next subject on his to-do list:

Avaricious Arcane Hunter class skills available

———

As Jake spent far too long inside the damn water-level Vault, the Treasure Hunt outside progressed as before for the most part.

However, something had changed. Before, working together and progressing towards mutual goals had been the norm, with human-on-human conflict being rare, often only happening in cases of preexisting antagonism.

Now, things had changed. When around three days remained, the Court of Shadows changed their MO. Their goal changed from seeking out Vaults themselves to claiming the loot from what had already been opened.

Them doing this led to a cascade effect, changing the dynamic when people met. No longer would it simply be apprehensive greetings. Instead, chances were it would lead to a straight-up battle. No one trusted each other, and many believed this had been a part of the Court's plan from the start.

It allowed them to swoop into the battles of others and claim all the treasures, being the premier masters of stealth and deceit within the Hunt. Another thing that certainly didn't help were rumors that some members of the Court could change their appearance and even aura, appearing to be someone else. A recording of this soon surfaced, showing a man suddenly transformed into an assassin with two guns donning a black metal mask and ambushing the people who'd thought he was a member of their own faction.

Some factions were hit harder than others by this. The Holy Church had already bunkered down and centralized their loot in their base within a tower, making it impossible to claim much of what they had. Members would just send everything of value there with heavily protected escorts, meaning the members of the Church rarely carried anything of value on their person. The undead were still rarely seen and moved in large groups. This meant that primarily the Noboru Clan, Valhal, and all the independent factions were hit repeatedly, forcing them to change their tactics and group up more.

One of the only factions generally left alone—at least, to begin with—was Haven. Rumors of Jake's slaughter when ambushed had spread far and wide, and the Court naturally left the members of Haven alone. They seemed to be the only ones viewed as untouchable until something else happened.

The tower in which the Court of Shadows had set up their base of operations was attacked. Not by an army, but a single man. Their barriers were broken, the defenders forced to leave or face death, and all the supportive staff escaped through their Insignias. In the end, only those not in the tower and a few elite members managed to escape—including a heavily injured Judge. More than two hundred members of the Court either died or had to leave the Hunt within less than an hour.

After that... no one dared to go after the Noboru Clan, either, lest they face the wrath of the Sword Saint.

CHAPTER 45

TREASURE HUNT: ARROW TIME

A bolt of black lightning struck from a clear sky. It impacted the ground, leaving a crater smoking with dark mana. As the dust settled, a single figure could be seen kneeling within the crater, holding his shoulder as blood dripped down on the ground beneath him.

Caleb slowly got up, breathing heavily, exhausted from using the skill. It had drained a good ninety-five percent of his mana pool, making him not worth much at the current time. He took out a mana potion to at least be functional as he reflected on mistakes made.

It turned out that being a shadowy organization had quite a number of challenges, especially if they had a lot of enemies due to the nature of their trade. It made everyone an enemy and forced you to look out for more threats than you possibly could.

The Court of Shadows had faced quite the challenges trying to mobilize themselves and secure their position. Not with getting the loot—that part had gone relatively easily—but keeping ahold of it. Most assassins operated alone or in very small teams of a maximum of three, so facing a large group was difficult. Hit and run was the name of the game.

Stealth was their only true weapon to hold onto the loot

they obtained. Against the usual enemy of independent factions, lone individuals, and small parties, that was all fine and dandy, but they began having issues when all their couriers or smaller groups got hit repeatedly. They then tried to centralize the loot with the stronger people in the Court, but then the couriers just got ambushed during transport.

Their ambushers? The Holy Church.

To hide from someone with the ability to divine the future and peer into fate became a challenge they honestly should have predicted. The Holy Church discovered that there was a lot to be gained by stealing from the thieves, and they could even claim the moral high ground while doing so, making it a purely win-win situation for the religious fanatics.

This forced the Court to pool the loot more on people who were either strong enough to defend it or good enough at hiding. The Augur seemed to know who was worth hitting at all times, and the Court of Shadows took more and more precautions. In the end, they began having a large central group, with the majority of loot being carried by Caleb. He and others could veil them all constantly to keep them hidden, and they escaped the Church and went on with their business without any major issues for a few days.

Keeping an eye on other notable figures was something they also did. Eron had disappeared, so that made them worry a bit. The people of Valhal seemed to just take the losses from the occasional assassin, seeing it as a sign of weakness and a teaching moment for those hit. The undead were rarely targeted, as they moved in big groups, and they had shown no signs of significant movements against other factions. The people from Haven? They were naturally left alone, and besides, they had been stuck in the massive, maze-like Vault for a long time. A few from the Court had also been trapped in there, too, as well as over a thousand others.

As for the Noboru Clan? Their notable members were either trapped in the big maze or moved around in one large group these days. The Sword Saint was spotted often with the group, so the Court followed it to keep an eye on him. The man himself disappeared occasionally, but he never strayed too far from the central base of his faction.

Until he did.

Out of nowhere, he was suddenly *there*, right in front of their temporary base—one hidden behind endless barriers that had primarily focused on obscuring divination and hiding them. The Sword Saint had cut through them all, and the Court had reacted too slow.

He was just a single man, and in all their arrogance, they had believed he wouldn't be able to break them himself. They'd had a few hundred people there. Barriers. Traps. Caleb himself, as well as Matteo, Nadia, and a few more of the most powerful assassins. Even Caleb had believed the man was arrogant for truly believing he could defeat them all alone.

How wrong they had been. Caleb had faced the Sword Saint with all the others... The result?

Well, him having to flee, fourteen dead, and one hundred and ninety-one forced to leave the Hunt—including Nadia and Matteo, who had both tried to hold him off. Those who'd died were the weakest, mainly people who had been arrogant and tried to face him head-on.

The only consolation was Caleb having carried over eighty percent of the Court of Shadows' total loot, as he was the one with the highest level of confidence in retreating due to his near-immunity to divination and his many methods of escape. But, even then, it had gotten far more dangerous than he was comfortable with.

All of this made Caleb wonder. He had known Jake was monstrously strong before, and him having even trounced all of those independent factions had once more confirmed his strength, yet now Caleb couldn't help but worry...

Because the Sword Saint was also an absolute monster.

Ah, skill selection. Always a good time to get a better feel for one's progress and see what the system had conjured up. From fucked-up skills telling one to become a sadistic slaver to telling someone they should really consider getting a proper arcane barrier skill. Or, as it most often ended up doing, just giving Jake ideas on how to improve his existing freeform version of magic.

Thus, as always, Jake went into it with high expectations, looking for a skill doing things he himself could not, or at least something so darn complicated or weird he wouldn't have figured out how to do it himself anytime soon. Or, you know, just something that sounded cool.

The first skill was neither of these things.

[Hunter's Natural Adaptation (Uncommon)] – A hunter must always adapt to the environment in which they hunt. Allows the Hunter to acclimate to new environments more easily and grants resistance against neutral mana you do not possess an affinity to. This effect is amplified by Toughness.

This skill was just the system going, "Oh, hey there, I saw you just experienced something new! Here, let me give you a skill retroactively after you already figured out how to deal with it. Sure would have been nice to have earlier, eh?"

It made him wonder how many people had died a level or two before being offered skill that would allow them to avoid that death. Sure, he got how the system couldn't just give skills and predict the future, but...

Anyway, he didn't want it. It was uncommon rarity, too, which was just icky. Moving on.

[Explosive Arcane Orb (Rare)] – By your will, explosive arcana shall come into being. Allows the Hunter to

*summon an explosive orb of arcane mana at a target loca-
tion within their range of Perception. The arcane orb will
be highly unstable and will automatically explode mere
moments after being conjured. Adds a bonus to the effectiveness of Intelligence when using Explosive Arcane Orb.*

It appeared Jake's explosive arcane orb-like things had finally
become different enough from arcane bolts to warrant their own
skill, so that was nice. Proof he was going in the right direction
with that one, which naturally made him happy.

Arcane Orbs, rather than bolts, were more just manifested
bombs at specific locations and weren't really designed to be
fired, just summoned and then made to explode where he
summoned them. A bit of a by-product of his Pride of the
Malefic Viper upgrade and his infused presence, making mana
control more straightforward in his surrounding area. There was
just something about summoning bombs in mid-air that was
funny.

Didn't make him not skip it, though. Next!

*[Arcane Shotgun (Rare)] – Your arcane mana can take
many forms, so why not mimic a weapon of old? Allows
the Hunter to fire off shards of highly stable arcane
mana, functioning as a shotgun. These shards will pierce
and deal significant damage at close range while
becoming less effective at long distances. Adds a bonus to
the effectiveness of Intelligence when using Arcane
Shotgun.*

Jake wanted to pick this one just from the name alone, but
his logical mind managed to hold him back. It did give him an
idea to have Arnold design one just to look cool. Either way, the
skill had clearly come from the crystalline bolts he kept making
against the fish, and he *had* kind of mimicked how shotguns
worked when he fired arcane mana shard with a good spread.

You needed good spread when you fired many small projectiles, after all. Also, it helped with him not having to be that accurate.

Another funny one, but not one Jake would ever pick. So far, this skill selection had been a case of "See what you have done in the past in the form of uncommon and rare skills," which wasn't very interesting. At least the next one was epic rarity and a bit different.

[Conjure Arcane Armaments (Epic)] – A weapon or piece of equipment is always within grasp when you can simply conjure them yourselves. Allows the Hunter to summon armaments of stable arcane mana. The shape of the weapons or equipment is determined by the summoner. Armaments can be given to others. The duration and durability of all equipment summoned is based on mana expended. Adds a bonus to the effectiveness of Wisdom when using Conjure Arcane Armaments.

This was the one... if Jake wanted to become an arms dealer. If he read it right, he could create weapons others could temporarily use with his arcane mana. It was an upgraded version of the Spectral Weaponry he had seen oh so long ago. Back then, he had skipped it, as he'd believed it was something he could do himself with freeform magic, and he still believed that to this day.

The only possible thing that could make him pick the skill was how it explicitly stated others could use what he created. Not because he wanted to have others use it, but because it could possibly give him some inspiration when it came to using Touch of the Malefic Viper and transmuting items. If he could make transmuted stuff useable by others, that would be great, and would no doubt also allow him to heighten his own skill significantly... maybe even get that to legendary rarity too.

But why would he do that when he could just pick up a legendary skill here and now by choosing the fifth option?

[Steady Aim of the Apex Hunter (Legendary)] – When the string is taut and the arrow ready, the hunter's focus reaches new realms. To aim and shoot the perfect shot is what any hunter aims for, and as one who stands at the apex, you refuse for even time to hamper your accuracy. Allows the Hunter to significantly heighten his focus when the bowstring is fully pulled, tapping into the concept of time to slow down his Perception of it while simultaneously boosting all effects of Perception significantly. Your eyes receive this boost to Perception at twice the effect of all your other senses. All effects scale with Perception.

Jake had to admit... the name was incredibly boring to the level of nearly being criminal. It was pretty much just a "steady aim" skill with some fancy title added on and a flavorful description. Also—let's be fair—the name was bad, and Jake didn't understand why the skill hadn't just called it by its rightful name: Arrow Time. The bowman version of bullet time.

Alright, in all seriousness, the skill description and simplicity of the skill really did speak for itself. It was a skill made for better aiming taken to an absolutely extreme level and made into a legendary skill. Perhaps it was one of those times where Jake was meant to be offered some version of Steady Aim, and the system then analyzed Jake or something and decided he had reached some threshold to get the legendary version.

As for how that would have happened... well, the skill did feel awfully similar to his Moment of the Primal Hunter. Likely there was even a bit of Gaze of the Apex Hunter mixed in there, considering the similarity in name between the two skills and the extra bonus to his eyes. Perhaps it was just an amalgamation of a few different skills, Jake's practice with aiming, and his ability to quickly aim and make decisions.

Honestly, he had no way of ever knowing. He just knew he had the skill offered and that he would be an utter moron for not picking it up. Which is to say he naturally picked it.

The moment he did so, he felt... nothing. Yeah, he just picked the skill and stood there expecting something to happen. Not to be misunderstood, he was only anticipating some instinctive knowledge, not some grand understanding of the concept of time. Just something.

Yet nothing. Jake frowned, checked his status, and saw the skill there. Shrugging, he decided to just take the most straightforward approach and test it out. With his bow in hand, he casually summoned an arrow and nocked it. He raised his bow as he drew the string, and then... then the world slowed.

Jake's eyes began glowing with even more power than before. He felt the droplets of water dripping from above slow down significantly... in that, to the naked eye, they had entirely stopped. One had to remember that under normal circumstances when Jake focused on aiming, it already felt like time slowed down simply due to his high Perception. Same as when he was fighting, It was something everyone experienced simply due to the growth of stats. If not, how else would anyone be able to react to an arrow flying faster than any sniper bullet or a sword swung several times the speed of sound?

But this? This was different. This was like the difference between when Jake perceived his surroundings while still in E-grade and now. With this new skill, he had ample time to think, react, aim, and locate the optimal target. He even felt that many aspects of his shots would be improved... for didn't his passive Archery of Vast Horizons make his arrows stronger based on Perception? And make his stable arcane arrows deal more damage?

He attempted to move, as the entire world seemed to have stopped moving, and found that it wasn't only the world, but him too. It wasn't like Moment of the Primal Hunter, where he could move unaffected with everything else slowed down. This time around, he was also affected just as much as everything else. In other words, it was only Jake's mind and Perception of time, not time itself.

Shifting his aim a bit could still be done slighter faster, and micro-movements were naturally more precise when he had more time to adjust. However, it quickly became apparent he didn't have infinite time to just stand there with the string fully pulled. He began feeling a faint headache slowly come on, at which point he finally released the arrow.

It slammed into the wall, failing to truly leave any mark due to the indestructible nature of the underwater Vault, but he still felt that the arrow had been more potent than usual. Jake instantly drew his bow again, and the moment he had the string taut, time slowed once more. This time, the headache came quite a bit faster. He shot and pulled the string a third time. The headache came super fast now.

Some separate limited resource meter for Arrow Time? Jake wondered. He had been standing there for a damn long time with the string fully pulled with the first arrow. At least a dozen seconds in real time with everything slowed down, just observing his surroundings and himself. He would have to avoid doing that in the future.

Jake sat down to meditate a bit more, getting up every hour to consume a potion and do a light amount of practice with his new skill. He instantly discovered a few very interesting things he couldn't wait to test out in live combat.

Overall? The skill felt awesome, and he had a feeling it had great future potential. Now he only needed a good fight to truly test it out.

Luckily, he had a feeling he would soon get one.

With around twenty hours of the Treasure Hunt remaining, Jake left the water Vault through a teleportation circle in the center of the room, ready for the final stage of the Treasure Hunt.

CHAPTER 46

TREASURE HUNT: THE FINAL STAGE

Miranda walked together with quite the group of people through the giant maze. It was a Vault far larger than any other, and they soon found out why... because it wasn't only one. It was several Vaults hidden within one Vault in some complex pattern, and one had to solve all of them to open the final one in the middle.

Coupled with that, it was a massive maze with dead-ends, traps, monsters, and—worst of all—other participants. Fights happened all the time, forcing people to group up whenever possible, and small factions had ended up forming.

As for who Miranda found herself with... well, it was a nice mix of new and old. Sultan had stuck with her after the whole Eron business—something she wasn't sure how to feel about. They had later been joined by Sylphie and Carmen, who had managed to find each other. Then, suddenly, a drone from Arnold had passed by, which was how they got to their current size, as he apparently had over a hundred in the damn Vault scouting things out.

Neil and his entire party, people from Valhal, a few members of the Court of Shadows, random individuals who Arnold had "employed" prior, and even people led by a woman named Reika from the Noboru Clan ended up joining them. It was a mighty political mess, only made worse when Priscilla and a large group of undead also turned up.

Miranda, Priscilla, Carmen, and Reika became the leaders of this small band of misfits—although some would argue Sylphie was the true leader—as they explored the Vault and solved challenges one by one. The difficulty increased further in, and as more and more powerful foes and dangerous traps appeared, their collaboration became quite the boon.

The four women and bird handled everything far more easily than expected, and Miranda had to admit things went a lot more smoothly than anticipated. She had expected it to be a political nightmare, but it actually turned out quite pleasantly. She was already friendly with Carmen, Sylphie accepted her, Priscilla was very accommodating and open to any positive relations, and Reika was also surprisingly friendly for someone associated with a faction Miranda felt wasn't exactly an ally.

Solving the final Vault itself was done through their teamwork, and more than the final rewards which they shared, Miranda felt like the foundation of trust built among their factions was the true gain. Not that she was complaining about the legendary-rarity Magic Circle Foundation she got—a large disc of odd stone specifically made to carve magic circles on and amplify them significantly.

Upon exiting the Vault, Priscilla turned to them. "I believe it pertinent to warn you all that the final phase of the Treasure Hunt will begin shortly... Heading towards the central plains would be the wisest to do."

Reika nodded. "I also just got word when we got out of the Vault that the Holy Church has been preparing there for a while for what is to come. The rest of the clan too."

Miranda listened, a bit jealous of the women's information network, while also wondering how the hell Arnold had managed to communicate and help guide them through the

Vault while still hiding outside. Because it appeared like everyone else had been cut off.

Nevertheless, she nodded. They all split up yet stayed fairly close to each other as they all began heading back towards the Mistless Plains. Even Miranda, who was not a fighter or in possession of particularly honed instincts when it came to this kind of thing, knew a big battle was on the horizon.

———

Jacob opened his eyes and shook his head at the uselessness of his divination of the upcoming fight. The system wasn't the one making things difficult; it was the presence of so many extraordinary people. All he knew was when and where it would begin. Thus, the Holy Church made preparations. In fact, they had done so for days already.

A mighty magic circle was being prepared to face the final opponent of this Hunt.

"Think we will even need it?" Bertram asked as he stood beside him.

"I truly don't know... This fight just has too many unknowns. Better safe than sorry, right?"

"Hm," the large man said, nodding.

Jacob looked at his old bodyguard and friend. The man was powerful, one of the strongest people of Earth, and the party he was in was likely the strongest on Earth... yet Jacob was fully aware the five of them couldn't truly stand tall before the best Earth had to offer. They were all geniuses, but people like Jake and the Sword Saint were more than that.

———

"Great-grandfather," Reika reported in as she met up with the Patriarch.

The man stood staring into the horizon. Reika followed his

gaze and saw the figure she recognized as the Judge from the Court of Shadows. He looked back their way, his gaze icy, but he didn't look like he was planning to pick a fight. It would be foolish of him to, for the Patriarch had already shown mercy when he taught them a lesson.

"Has your time been fruitful?" he asked with a friendly smile.

Reika couldn't help but sense how he looked so weak standing there with his thin frame, long sparse white hair, sunken eyes, and wrinkled face. Yet his eyes remained strong, making her admonish herself for even thinking such things.

"It has," she said, returning his smile. "How about you, Patriarch? Is all well?"

He shook his head as he answered, "We always have more to strive for, and there is always more to do."

Reika hid her frown at the melancholy in her great-grandfather's eyes. She didn't understand why and looked questioningly at him. He returned her gaze and gave a comforting smile.

"It's nothing. Just the ramblings of an old man who has to realize perhaps his time in the sun will soon be over. This world is for your generation, Reika. Ah, but don't worry, dear... I shall remain long enough to play my role and have the clan experience this springtime season at least a little longer."

She only got more confused, but she didn't say anything... until she noticed him moving his arm a bit, revealing a few black spots that still emanated faint amounts of shadow mana. *He was hurt.* He had not trounced the Court of Shadows for free... and the wounds still lingered. She couldn't help but worry, but he just placed a comforting hand on her head.

"I told you not to worry. I still have a role to play, and I shall not bow out before it has been played to completion. The wound is merely a reminder of my own incompetence and the constant need to strive for improvement."

———

Jake broke out of the Vault, mentally spitting at the shithole that was the water level. He was a bit sad he hadn't learned the subspecies of vampires responsible for the Vault. That would have given him some easy targets in the future to carry out justice on. Fuckers probably liked mushrooms too.

He had barely gotten out of the Vault when he noticed someone... or rather, *something*, looking at him. He looked up and saw something float far above. It looked to be made of metal of some kind, and before he could properly investigate it, the thing flashed a small light in an odd pattern.

The issue was, Jake had no idea what it was trying to tell him. He was pretty sure that was one of Arnold's satellite-like things, wasn't it? Staring way longer than he should, he finally noticed something else looking at him. A small drone flew towards him at pretty high speeds, and this one he knew for sure belonged to Arnold.

"Hey, there!" Jake yelled to it as it got close.

The drone stopped in front of him, and Arnold's voice sounded out. "The satellite should have already informed you that the City Lord and others have organized a rendezvous in the central plains."

"It did?" Jake answered, staring up at it again, noticing it had stopped blinking.

"Through Morse code."

"I don't know Morse code?"

"Apologies for my assumption of competence," Arnold acknowledged in the most insulting way Jake could imagine phrasing it, yet he felt not the slightest hint of intent to insult in his voice.

"Anyway, where do we meet exactly?" Jake asked. "Also, how has the Treasure Hunt treated you?"

"I have had adequate success in this event. To get to the central plains, simply head that way"—the drone fired off a small beam of light towards the distance—"and spotting someone should be natural. However, be warned that there may be others in the path."

"Got it. Thanks, mate," Jake answered as he turned and took off, waving to the drone.

It was difficult to explain how damn good it felt to run across the open plains and over the small hills after just being stuck in water or that small final room for so long. He felt faster than before, but knew it was only marginal and due to his stat growth.

Jake ran without using One Step Mile to enjoy the wind on his face. He passed a few groups of people and soon made it to the top of a hill, giving him a good look at the Mistless Plains. Looking in the direction where he felt Sylphie, he could faintly spot Miranda and Carmen with her. Sylphie sent back a mental greeting asking if she should come, but Jake declined and said he would come to her.

Just as he was about to head off, someone approached him. A man was flying through the air surrounded by odd energy, and when Jake got a closer look, he recognized it was his old colleague-turned-undead.

Casper landed in front of Jake, touching down elegantly before not-so-elegantly yelling: "So *you* have it!"

"Oh, hi, Casper. Nice to meet you too," Jake said a bit snarkily. "Also, I have what?"

"A byproduct of the Seed of Eternal Resentment. You know what I mean, right? It can take many forms, including a small, pebble-like seed, perhaps a large spore or a weapon forged of it or something."

"Something like a Root also works?" Jake asked as he turned his wrist and made the Root of Eternal Resentment appear.

[Root of Yalsten's Eternal Resentment (Unique)] – A wooden root from an unknown tree that has absorbed the curse energies of the black mist that has hung over Yalsten

for innumerable years. The deep and eternal resentment
towards the vampires that permeates the curse has now been
absorbed and concentrated. Will cause disastrous damage
and curse any vampire it comes into contact with; however,
it can only be used once. While in possession of this root, the
cursed mist will not see you as an enemy. Be warned that
while the curse will not seek to damage you, it will still
influence you. This effect grows as it absorbs the curse
energy of any cursed vessels related to the curse in Yalsten.

Casper stared at the black root in Jake's hand before he slowly nodded, having clearly used Identify on it himself. "That's the one. How much do you want for it?"

"Before I answer that, tell me first what you will use it for," Jake countered. He did know Casper was into curses and stuff, so maybe he wanted to make a weapon out of it or something? Jake didn't really wanna give it up, as he had a strong feeling he could still find a use for it.

"I will use it to absorb the curse energy in the large spire and then against the final boss of the Treasure Hunt to weaken it," Casper answered. "At least, that is the official story I was supposed to give you. In actuality, we will use it on the spire to still absorb the curse, act like it has no other uses, and beat the final boss without it by using people like you and the Sword Saint. We will then bring the Root back to Earth, where we will use it as a power source in a ritual together with the World Quasi-Core we will get from this final stage. All to construct a special dungeon especially suited for us undead and inherently antagonistic to anything and anyone else."

"Oh," Jake said, taking it all in. "Sounds fancy. Do you absolutely need the Root?"

"Absolutely? No, but it would be very useful for us."

"You know what—let me think about it, okay? If I don't find a use for it, I doubt there will be much interest at the auction. Also, thanks for the tip. I didn't even think about bonking the big spire."

Casper just smiled and shook his head. "I guess it's about time to get the show started. Once the two of us move closer to the spire, the final phase of the Treasure Hunt will begin. You good with that?"

Jake quickly took a glance around, noticing a slew of familiar faces. He saw Jacob far off in the distance with Bertram beside him. The moment Jake looked at him, Jacob looked back. Jake felt the guy was using a skill to see that far, but didn't consider it more, as he saw Jacob just give him a nod. Clearly, the Holy Church was ready. He then tossed a glance the way of the Noboru Clan, seeing the Sword Saint and Reika both stand ready, also fully aware of what was about to happen. In fact, Jake felt like he was the last to know. That did suck a bit.

"Let's go," Jake said as he summoned his wings.

Casper followed him as they flew to the spire. Once they got within a certain distance... something shifted. Like the sound of a massive mirror being broken, the sky above shattered, and Jake's eyes darted around as he felt the entire world change.

Casper was enveloped in light. An item appeared in his hand before swiftly disappearing into his Insignia, and at the same time, the system responded.

Quest Received: Cursed Monarch

The world of Yalsten has reached the end of its lifespan as the last anchors keeping it together have been removed. A foregone conclusion, as suppressing the curse would inadvertently lead to this fate anyway. Space will crumble as the world slowly turns to nothingness.

Yet, in this final moment, an ancient figure has awakened: the husk of the once glorious King of Blood who cursed the

World of Yalsten, resurrected by his own creation, morphed and twisted by eons of pain and torture, his Records and existence morphed into something unrecognizable.

In his greed, this Cursed Monarch chose to be buried with not only his entire clan, but a mighty treasure. One their world had been tasked with keeping safe by the True Ancestor—a treasure still untouched by the curse. The Cursed Monarch must be returned to the soil along with the soldiers he raised alongside himself to claim this treasure.

Objective: Defeat Cursed Monarch and his soldiers.
     Final Rewards will be calculated after the Treasure Hunt concludes.

Warning: Due to the destruction of the world, the Treasure Hunt will end in: 11:59:59

Jake skimmed it as he made his way to the massive spire. He bonked the Root into the crystal spire without any hesitation, making it shatter just like the sky above. It turned to crystalline dust the moment the Root touched it, and Jake felt the curse in the Root of Eternal Resentment amplify to extreme levels as it absorbed far more than anything prior. The intent and emotions of the curse invaded his mind while this happened, assaulting every inch of his being. Gritting his teeth, he channeled his Pride and suppressed the desire to slay the vampire he knew dwelled beneath and was about to awaken, getting himself fully under control. No fucking way he was going to let a stupid, ancient curse able to destroy an entire world ruin a good fight.

He tossed the Root back in the Hunter Insignia as he flew over to Miranda and the others, the crystal spire slowly turning to nothing behind him. He had barely landed and given them a friendly nod before another message appeared before him and everyone else.

> **System Announcement: The Cursed Monarch will awaken soon. For the next fifteen minutes, anyone can choose to exit the Treasure Hunt while retaining all currently obtained treasures and without any penalties besides the inability to participate in the final stage. During this time, no items can be withdrawn from or deposited into the Hunter Insignia or any other spatial storages or items.**

Countdown: 14:58

Jake read over the messages, and before he even had time to open his mouth, the plains were filled with flashes of light as people began leaving the Treasure Hunt. He even saw quite a lot in the distance, making it clear that this wasn't even a question for many. A way to escape without having to fight some final boss and potentially even risk more human-on-human conflict? Jake could kind of understand it.

Not that he himself had any plans of leaving.

The same couldn't be said for those around him.

"I believe it would be wise of me to take my leave," Miranda said. "I have gotten enough... and quite frankly, I'm not confident in my ability to fight on a stage like this."

She looked like she was afraid Jake would disapprove, but he just nodded at her. "Understandable. This is more my kind of thing, so I'll happily be the representative of Haven."

"Ree!" Sylphie screeched at his side.

"With Sylphie, of course," he quickly added on with a smile. Miranda nodded and disappeared.

Arnold also said his goodbyes without any explanation, and the drone he kept with Miranda just poofed out of existence. The rest of the people from Haven chose to stay behind. Neil only gave Jake a brief greeting, the man and those with him fully aware they were not there to fight the Monarch himself but the soldiers the message mentioned. No, those who would fight the Monarch were the best Earth had to offer.

Jake peered all around the plains and saw everyone who would face the Cursed Monarch.

The Sword Saint, Casper, Priscilla, Carmen, Sylphie, Reika, Caleb, as well as the most powerful parties of Earth with Bertram and Sven in them. Others also remained behind. In fact, many chose to face the final stage and help assist them, including a large group from the Holy Church and another large one consisting of undead.

Jake exchanged glances with the Sword Saint, who stood beside Reika. The man gave him a knowing smile. Jake nodded with understanding as he also prepared himself to face the final boss.

With that, the fifteen minutes expired... and the Cursed Monarch awakened.

CHAPTER 47

TREASURE HUNT: STARTING SHOTS

At the edges of Yalsten, destruction was unfolding. The equilibrium of space that had been formed for so long was now broken, and the world began collapsing in upon itself. Earth and soil were turned to nothingness as everything began shrinking, any matter being cut up endlessly.

It progressed fast, and a few people who had not been close to the Mistless Plains found themselves with no choice but to leave the Treasure Hunt or run from the world's destruction. But it was only a few, for the vast majority had already gathered, ready to face the Cursed Monarch.

———

Inside a maze of metal, a magic circle suddenly stopped functioning. The caster had disappeared, and all connections cut. A few seconds passed until, suddenly, a hand emerged from the ground that appeared to turn liquid.

The man dragged himself out and stood up, covered in green water.

Eron frowned as he saw the quest but didn't decide to leave. Instead, he walked casually out of the Vault, making a mental note to avoid Haven for the time being, or at least until he came up with a valid countermeasure. Issues for later, because he saw no reason to miss out on contributions against this final enemy calling himself a Cursed Monarch.

"So, you guys have any tactics in mind?" Jake asked the people around him.

"Stay the fuck back," Christen said, getting nods from Neil and the rest of her party.

"Good call—one I think I will follow," Jake said while looking around, finding a spot in the distance. He felt energy gather as the Cursed Monarch slowly came to life. All the mist from Yalsten was gathering at the coffin that was now visible due to the spire being broken.

Jake took flight and headed off, getting a few odd glances on the way, but nothing that bothered him.

He was an archer after all, right? Hence, he was looking for a good vantage point.

A pulse went through the entire Treasure Hunt. Then, a few seconds later, a second one. It soon began rhythmically beating like a heart as an ancient being that had slumbered for an untold number of years awakened.

Yalsten was now nearly entirely devoid of mist, except for a few dozen meters right around the coffin and the sky far above. Then, as if appearing from nothing, figures suddenly stepped out of the mist. Hundreds of beings resembling the Reanimated Armors were the first to become visible, all of them pulsing with power.

[Cursed Soldier – lvl 135]

The mist around the coffin slowly dispersed, revealing a single cloaked figure. A black crown adorned his head, a cloak dark as night behind him, and he had piercing eyes that were entirely red beside the deep red irises. He was over two and a half meters tall, but his form was willow and thin, his eyes sunken, his appearance decrepit. Around him stood five heavily armored beings, one with a sword, another a spear, a third a bow, a fourth a staff, and the fifth with two floating orbs revolving around it.

It was clearly a party setup, the five of them all called Royal Guards.

[Cursed Royal Guard– lvl 160]

The final one was naturally the cloaked figure. A being that absolutely pulsed power as he stood there. The vampire looked up towards the sky before releasing his aura, truly making himself known as the Cursed Monarch.

[Cursed Monarch – lvl ???]

Most everyone present was intimidated by the absolute power of the Cursed Monarch, yet they also breathed out a sigh of relief because, while the boss was powerful...

He was still D-grade.

Jake observed it all happen from far away. The boss and those around him didn't move to attack right away, but seemed to need to collect themselves after just awakening. Or was it that none of them were truly intelligent anymore?

The primary evidence for this being the case was the Cursed Monarch not yelling out something like, "I HAVE RETURNED TO FEAST ON YOUR BLOOD" or another likewise cringy way of announcing himself.

What argued against it was him looking towards the sky. It was a needless action unless he detected something up there, and Jake didn't think that was the case. If that was true... was it simply that the Cursed Monarch didn't view any of them as a threat?

No, that couldn't be it either... for at least he and a handful of others sure as fuck were.

Jake held out his hand and began his own true preparations now that he saw them. A part of him hoped to just get an easy opening shot, but it appeared that wasn't going to happen. The first to make a move wasn't Jake or the Sword Saint or even the Holy Church, but a single person.

Casper flew up and opened his arms wide as he regarded the army of vampires, the Curse of Yalsten burning within him. The Cursed Monarch looked up at him with blank eyes before the undead pointed down at the resurrected king.

"Resonance."

Then... both of them froze. Jake had not been informed much of what was going to happen, courtesy of him being stuck in a goddamn water level, but it very fast became clear these people had planned more than just coming together and attacking.

Whatever Casper had done had frozen the entire group of cursed vampires. Behind him, Jake saw two giant pillars of power ascend towards the sky, one of them a mix of white and black, exuding a ghastly color and powerful affinity of death, while the other was a pillar of holy light.

It was quite the deadly combo when mixed, Jake came to learn, as two huge blasts released by rituals with hundreds behind them descended on the group of frozen vampires. Or... at least, they looked immovable, for at the very last moment, Jake saw the Monarch release a faint pulse before the explosion engulfed the army.

An explosion more powerful than anything Jake had ever caused ravaged the Mistless Plains as the powers of death and holy light mixed, not much different than Jake's Corrupted Mooncore back in the day against the King of the Forest. It worked in the same vein, with two very much opposing concepts mixing to create something more powerful than the sum of their parts.

Jake heard cheers from below but knew it was premature. At the very next moment, the Monarch moved. The remnants of the explosion were parted by a screen of red light that cut across the plains and directly into the camp of the Holy Church. Barriers activated but shattered like wet paper before the attack, instantly killing a dozen or so members of the Church.

Another wave was released towards the undead, but they were prepared and managed to avoid losing anyone. A third then came, aimed towards the campsite of the Noboru Clan. This one wasn't dodged.

An old man stepped in front of the group from the clan, which hadn't made any barrier in preparation. He waved his blade, causing a blade of water to appear and shoot towards the deep red slice of pure blood power. It didn't crash with it or enter a contest of strength. Instead, it subtly hit the side of the wave and almost seemed to be absorbed into it as it guided it in its path, making it curve slightly.

It completely missed the old man and the camp, none of them even looking worried as they charged up some kind of magical ritual themselves. It felt and looked far weaker than whatever the undead and Church had made—and even weaker than the second magic ritual the Church was cooking up, hidden away behind a hill.

As the dust settled around the Cursed Monarch, his undamaged form was revealed along with the Royal Guards and the closest soldiers. Jake did a quick headcount and noticed over a hundred Cursed Soldiers were gone, and the Royal Guards had clearly expended some resources too.

They had lost many Cursed Soldiers right off the bat, and hopefully... one Royal Guard.

For while Jake had been an onlooker so far, that didn't mean he hadn't been preparing. The Cursed Monarch had turned his attention to the one person who had blocked his blow. Five

Royal Guards stood around him, three of which were of the fighter variety, while two were casters.

Jake aimed for the one with the staff, as it gave him healer vibes. The show earlier had given him ample time to prepare an Arrow of the Ambitious Hunter—formed using his knowledge of vampires and the cursed golems as the basis—and charge a full-power Arcane Powershot.

It was tight on time to get everything ready, but he managed to without pulling out any new tricks. The enemy hadn't noticed him before he released his attack, with too many other people and sources of potential danger around the plains.

BOOM!

Jake had shot from the balcony of a building nearly fifty kilometers away from the Mistless Plains. It tore through Yalsten, the unstable space breaking and cracking in its wake from the destructive arcane power. Reality rebuilt itself nearly instantly as the arrow passed by, but even so, it proved that both that space was unstable... and that Jake's shot was damn powerful. More powerful than any he had released before.

Steady Shot boosted his Perception, which boosted his archery, which boosted everything related to archery. It made the arrow fly fast and hit harder—hard enough for the Royal Guard to not notice before it was too late.

Or, it did notice... but Jake was already ready, and he drew the string of his bow. When it was taut, he felt the world slow down, and at that moment, he used Gaze of the Apex Hunter on not only the healer but all five Royal Guards.

At the same time, arcane mana swirled around him far faster than ever before—at least, from an outside point of view. To Jake, it was business as usual. He manipulated the energy to charge up Arcane Powershot, but with his perception of time slowed down, it meant his actual manipulation was faster in reality.

Physical movements were limited by this slowdown, making Jake unable to move his limbs as he wanted, but mana was something entirely different. The speed at which mana moved and how fast Jake could manipulate it was primarily limited by three things: One, Jake's own skill at manipulating it; two, his ability to impose his control—reliant on the Willpower stat—and finally, Jake's own durability, both mentally and physically. There were a few other minor details and contributing factors, and time sure did affect him still, but compared to before, his Arcane Powershot was charged approximately three times faster. With practice, Jake reckoned he could improve it even more.

Ultimately, this meant that Jake already had another two Arcane Powershots in mid-air just before the arrow hit his target, all of them charged for only a single second, but all still packing potent power.

The frozen Royal Guard that was his target still managed to muster some response. An entirely white barrier appeared around the Guard as well as the vampire's comrades. It was hastily constructed and, needless to say, not enough.

Like glass, it shattered. The Guard was hit by Arrow of the Ambitious Hunter, sending it tumbling back from the impact. Its comrades stood frozen as the Monarch turned and looked Jake's way. The Monarch began moving, but Jake smiled.

You stop too.

Gaze of the Apex Hunter activated. Jake felt himself pierce the soul of the Monarch—a soul even more powerful than all of the Royal Guards put together. Yet the Cursed Monarch still froze, unable to resist the skill powered by his increased Perception. The big boss vampire still managed to break free in only half a second, but it was enough for a second Arcane Powershot to hit the healer Guard.

The first arrow had merely sunk into the body of the healer, its effects serving to not only damage it but severely hamper the natural regeneration of vampires. The second arrow hit the healer in the chest, blasting a palm-sized hole through it. The vampire was sent flying even further away—right in the direction of two people in particular.

Black lightning struck from above as a powerful magic circle activated with intense curse energy at the healer's landing spot. Caleb and Casper both struck together, and the healer was blasted even further. His brother had landed with his staff and smashed the healer into the ground, and spinning his staff in the air, he smashed the vampire in the side, sending it flying even further away from the Monarch and the four other Royal Guards.

The other vampires tried to come and help, but only Caleb was there. He dodged back as another attack from the Monarch arrived, his entire body turning into black lightning. However, the power difference was too high. Caleb took a nasty cut on his shoulder just before he transformed and retreated.

Ranged attacks began raining down on the healer as Jake fired towards the Monarch and Royal Guards, but found his arrows blocked by the Monarch, who had also blocked his third Arcane Powershot originally aimed for the healer. Even then, bullets, bolts of all elements, spears, beams of light, and over a hundred attacks descended on the already heavily damaged healer as the Royal Guard still managed to form a barrier.

The armor of the Royal Guard was broken now, clearly revealing female features and a completely blank face—one that didn't show any emotions or even that she was so hurt. Her one arm was dangling, the wounds not healing as they should due to Jake's arrow and poison combined with the black lightning and curse. One had to remember she and everyone else were also still affected by whatever magic Casper had activated at the start.

Jake knew he didn't need to do anything more to the healer himself, so he just focused on distracting the Monarch a bit longer. The boss-level vampire stood there, and Jake let his own aura flare up to attract attention. The Monarch didn't strike him as truly intelligent, based on how he reacted, and it proved to be correct, as the vampire clearly focused a lot more on powerful

THE PRIMAL HUNTER 5

foes than making the smart choice of trying to save the healer vampire.

As for how Jake knew he didn't need to do anything more? Because a second later, the barrier around her was shattered when a woman smashed it apart with her fist. Carmen moved forward and punched the vampire in the stomach, sending it flying upwards. A green dart of pure death came from behind the pugilist and, in a fly-by as fast as Caleb's lightning, severed the head of the vampire.

Back in the center of the plains around the Monarch and Royal Guards, the Cursed Soldiers had begun finally waking up and looking about to notice the enemies in the distance. They began running amok, each of them as powerful as some of the strongest Ekilmares around. They would surely be powerful foes... except they were severely outnumbered and outmatched. The best Earth had to offer, barring a few people, were present in these plains.

From the start of the fight, Jake had a feeling that this stage was inherently unfair. The vampire Monarch was incredibly powerful, the strongest foe Jake had ever seen. Each of the Royal Guards was as strong as a Count of Blood too.

All of this is to say that it was truly unfair... for the vampires.

CHAPTER 48

TREASURE HUNT: QUITE THE MIX

About twenty kilometers from the center of the plains, six figures suddenly appeared—five humans and one vampire. The vampire instantly turned towards the humans and charged without any hesitation.

Neil blocked the Cursed Soldier with a barrier, giving Christen time to engage it in melee. Levi was already flanking the vampire as Silas cast buffs on Eleanor, who was charging up a Powershot. Neil had managed to teleport them all to the circle he had prepared in the distance, isolating them with the Soldier just as planned.

The Soldier and Christen crashed, but she easily held on as he redirected the sword swing with her buckler. This particular Soldier had a sword and a shield, and while it was quite powerful, it wasn't very talented at using its weapons.

Levi came in from the side, his sword aflame. He cut the Soldier across the back, making it growl and turn to hit him. Christen took the opportunity to try and stab the vampire with her rapier, but found her blow blocked by the shield.

Neil moved his magic to create spatial pressure on the Soldier, trying to suppress it and allow his comrades to land blows. Eleanor was finally ready just as Neil's own magic also finished, and with a combined attack, the Powershot empowered by Silas was released in a wake of silver light.

The vampire was blasted back, allowing Levi to strike again with a crosscut that sent out a small whirlwind of fire and wind. The rest of them also kept up the pressure, dominating the Soldier from start to end. They killed it within a few minutes, and once it was done, Neil disappeared.

Ten seconds later, he reappeared and nodded towards Eleanor, who stood ready with a charged arrow. He activated his spell, and space warped as a Soldier was teleported. The Powershot hit it before it could get its bearings—at which point the group attacked it, using many of the same tactics as with the last one.

Neil and his party had naturally chosen to stay and fight, yet they had no delusions about their presence truly having a large impact. They had seen the monsters that would handle the most dangerous foes and knew it was not their place to stand beside them... at least, not yet.

Because while they knew they weren't extraordinary, they were still hopeful. Neil was a space mage, a very good class that took a lot of natural talent to comprehend. The rest of his party weren't slouches, either, and all five had managed to get the Perfect Evolution. After they all reached D-grade, things had truly taken off. They'd grown more in levels than before, their teamwork also improving.

They had constructed a strong foundation and were now building upon it further to improve their strength. Their time in the Treasure Hunt had been very fruitful, with plenty of treasures obtained and levels gained. It also helped tremendously that they had avoided all human conflict due to their affiliation with Haven—at least, after Lord Thayne had had that confrontation with the independent factions. Before that, there'd been some rather passive-aggressive people.

Neil had even spent quite a while with that guy Casper inside a Vault. Neil had detected one that was heavily based on space magic, so he had sought that out while the rest of his party hunted and leveled up against those Reanimated Armors in an abandoned tower.

He had to admit, the undead had some interesting and very different insights into space, but that also meant Neil had actually managed to help a lot. It felt good and affirmed that Neil wasn't as untalented and useless as he had begun feeling while only spending time in Haven.

There'd been a strong feeling of inadequacy when he and his party had to compare themselves to Lord Thayne for the longest time. Neil had then seen the World Congress, where he felt like one of the weakest people present. Besides Lord Thayne, there was Arnold—an insane scientist of sorts who Neil wasn't sure about, but he seemed smart—and, of course, Miranda. Then Sultan had come, another man more talented than any of them. Miranda wasn't a combatant and had always been clear about that. Oh, but it had helped when some unaffiliated D-grades began showing up, and Neil began to realize that none of them seemed even close to as good as he and the party were.

But... they still had a long way to go. Neil teleported another Soldier away from the center and to their ambush spot as he took a good look at the battle between the true elites. A stage where they did not belong yet, but one he yearned to stand on.

For now, all they could do was help with the small fry. The same as thousands of other people who knew directly engaging the foes in the center of the Mistless Plains would be utter suicide.

———

One Royal Guard down, Jake snickered as he stared at the battlefield in the distance. The Soldiers were running towards the many humans lining the perimeter of the plains, many already fighting. There were foes in all directions, meaning most groups of Soldiers weren't more than five or six, with many even being alone. Parties of humans had engaged them, some employing interesting tactics, such as Neil and those guys and gals teleporting Soldiers away and fighting them there.

Jake himself didn't bother with the Soldiers. They were a good source of fighting experience for those on the weaker side. Instead, he would focus on the Royal Guards and Monarch. The death of the Royal Guard healer at the hands of him, Casper, Caleb, Carmen, and Sylphie had now truly woken up all of the more powerful vampires.

The eyes of the four remaining Royal Guards lit up as a bit of clarity returned to the Monarch's gaze. Coupled with the "resonance" stuff Casper had done beginning to fully wear off, it was time for the true battle to begin.

As expected, the four Royal Guards moved as a party to take up a defensive perimeter around the Monarch. The big boss regarded his surroundings, looking like he now fully understood the situation.

"I see."

For the first time, he spoke, his voice reverberating throughout the plains. Jake felt the power it held... perhaps vestiges of a being that had once been A-grade. He looked into the horizon, Jake following his gaze. With the mist gone, for the most part, Jake could see the sky in the far distance shattering as space broke apart, and so could the Monarch.

"Yalsten has fallen, its inhabitants gone."

He turned his attention towards the people attacking him, throwing a glance at Jake and the Sword Saint in particular.

"Is this my final role? Is this meant to serve as punishment? Tell me... how many eras have passed?"

All of the Soldiers still ran and fought people, but the center of the Mistless Plains was devoid of fighting. Everyone had stopped when the Monarch began talking, with the Royal Guards also doing nothing. The Monarch did not seem to carry any hatred towards those who had come to slay him, nor even toward those who had killed one of his comrades. Or maybe subordinates was a more accurate term?

"We have just entered the 93rd Era. Not even a year has passed since then," a voice echoed out as a figure in all white stepped forth from the Holy Church camp, flanked by Bertram and his four party members. It was Jacob, who Jake had honestly thought would have left the Hunt.

The Cursed Monarch looked towards Jacob as he stood there. Jake tried to Identify him on instinct but hit a barrier.

[Human – lvl ?]

Jake frowned, but he knew his Identify didn't fail because Jacob was too high in level; the dude had just gotten a skill to resist it. Sadly, Jake didn't have time to try and peer around it before the Monarch spoke again.

"You give off the stench of the Holy, yet I feel no trace of lies in your words... Truly, so long has passed. Tell me, slave of the Holy Tyrant, have you come to finish the job at the behest of your masters? Or have I simply become the subject of the system's limitless mercy?"

Jake saw Jacob frown in the distance, his façade falling for a moment under the pressure of the Monarch's aura.

"Ah... my words strike true. A second chance, given as my world crumbles. Another life. Escape, gifted with only a single requirement..."

Power suddenly enveloped the entire Mistless Plains as the Cursed Monarch released his aura, and his body began burning with power.

"...I merely have to claim my own future... by taking all of yours."

He raised his hands and released two beams, one towards Jacob and the other, interestingly enough, headed straight for Jake. Jake watched it as he fully drew back the string on his already-nocked arrow, allowing his perception of time to slow down.

A fraction of a second before the beam hit him, Jake released the string and sent the stable Arcane Arrow barreling down. It hit the beam and parted it, causing two red screens of light to fly by Jake on either side. He snickered beneath his mask.

It's on.

As for Jacob, he did perhaps the most interesting thing. He just stood here and had a hole blasted through his body, sending him flying back with worried gazes upon him. Yet he had barely landed before he stood back up, the wound on his chest already healing—not from some healing spell, but solely due to his insane Vitality.

His old boss had clearly gotten some pointers from Eron, and Jake also knew the lopsided stats of Augurs gave them a shit-load of Vitality.

As for the people around Jacob, they took the chance to charge towards the Royal Guards and Monarch. The same was true for Sven and those from Valhal, Priscilla and an undead party, two groups from the Noboru Clan, and a few other talented or overconfident people.

One of the groups from the Noboru clan had Reika in it, and Jake watched her summon four swords above her head and charge forth. All of the swords burned with intense blue flames, giving off a rather dangerous aura.

Yet the Monarch cared not for any of these parties. He suddenly turned to mist, appearing several kilometers in the air, then looked down. Jake met his gaze and saw him also observe a few others, primarily the individuals Jake also knew were powerful.

Jake drew his bow and fired an uncharged arrow, which the Monarch easily swatted away, but just after, a bolt of black lightning came from below, followed by two kinds of crescent waves —one green and one blue.

If it had been the Monarch before his "awakening," he

would have just taken them... but as he was now, he had intelligence, so he merely dodged by turning to mist again, appearing a bit to the side with a smile.

More attacks arrived soon after. Space began warping around him as a group of space mages from the Holy Church below tried to restrict his movements. The Monarch scoffed and merely pointed down at them, making five people explode in mists of blood and disrupting their ritual.

He turned in the air toward a figure flying towards him at high speeds, holding out his hand as he blocked the glowing fist of Carmen. He furrowed his brows at being pushed back slightly, and quickly had to react again as a metal staff descended with dark lightning crackling around it.

Jake's arrow then arrived from the side, forcing the Monarch to dodge back, only to find himself confronted by an old man who looked even older and more derelict than the vampire that had been dead for countless years.

The Sword Saint slashed down, and for the first time, Jake saw the Monarch open his eyes wide. He exploded with a wave of blood, sending everyone flying back away from him— including Sylphie, who was preparing to strike from behind.

Another teleport later, and the Monarch found himself free of enemies.

"Not bad for a bunch of low and barely mid-tier D-grades... or have I truly become that weak? No, that isn't it. Tell me, what factions would send you all to such a perilous land? I already see those of the Holy Tyrant and the undead, even a warrior of Valhal, and an assassin of the Court, but as for you two—"

The Monarch motioned towards Jake and the Sword Saint in particular. **"You two, I cannot quite place. Free agents? Hired help? I must admit, this entire entourage is quite the mix."**

Jake stared from afar, not able to answer due to the vast distance. Or maybe the Monarch would still hear him? Eh, it didn't really matter, as Jake didn't feel like answering. He was totally fine with being a far-off sniper.

Who did answer was the Sword Saint. "I serve only my clan," the old man said, staying alert.

"Hm, I guess it does me little good to know; I am certain many new factions have emerged. What of you, Hunter?"

Jake stared back again, still not sure what to answer... but he decided to anyway. The Monarch knew of most already, and he saw no reason to hide himself. Besides, the Monarch would probably figure it out himself. If he had once been A-grade or at least contained many of the memories of an A-grade, it only made sense he would be familiar with an ancient faction like the Malefic Order. Also... everyone else knew.

He released the aura otherwise suppressed by Shroud of the Primordial. The power of his Bloodline, mixed with the signature, marked him as the Chosen of the Malefic Viper as he let it wash out of him.

The Monarch stopped and stared deep into Jake's eyes, the deep red gaze of the Monarch meeting that of the hunter. No one moved for a while, as the Monarch just looked confused more than anything else.

"Why?"

Having noticed the confusion, Jake frowned. He saw Casper looking a bit weird, and Jacob too. It looked like they expected him to know something. *Did I miss something?*

"What has happened throughout these eras for the Malefic Order to decide to hunt us down? Why would the Malefic One make such a decision..."

CHAPTER 49

TREASURE HUNT: PROPOSITION

Jake stared, confused, as he had a feeling he had *really* missed something. Also, why did Casper look so weirdly at him? He got Jacob, but even Casper knew? Shit, even Carmen threw him a confused gaze. At least the Sword Saint wasn't in the loop either...

He tried to focus his voice, infusing it with some will and projecting it into the distance towards the Monarch. **"Being real honest here, I have no idea what you're talking about; I'm just here to get treasures. Do feel free to clue me in."**

This only got him more confused stares from everyone, including the Monarch. Jake, on the other hand, was just happy his voice projection had worked so well.

Casper, in the distance, just began laughing and shaking his head. Jacob face-palmed, and Carmen nodded like his answer made sense.

"Hah.... ha. I must confess, this is quite the situation. Who would think the system would throw me into such a bizarre situation? Tell me, does the Chosen come here at the behest of Malefic One or of his own volition?"

"Nope, I'm here all on my own," Jake answered truthfully, just wanting to get back to the fighting.

"I see... It does sadden me that our race is so insignificant that not even his Chosen would know of us... but more than eighty eras have passed, have they not? Perhaps it is to be expected." The Monarch said looked truly disappointed.

Jake was beginning to feel a bit bad for the poor guy. It must suck to be resurrected and find out that your entire race has potentially been wiped out without any way of finding out. There probably was, but Jake just didn't know—and even if he did, would it help to tell him?

Also, more than eighty eras... and with what Jake knew, it had to be nearly ninety, as to his knowledge the Viper had been "gone" for more than eighty. He didn't know the exact timeline yet, and he had never asked Villy, as he didn't want to dig up old wounds by asking about stuff like that.

"I wouldn't say that," Jake answered. "I'm just not the most informed when it comes to matters like that. Besides, does it matter? I reckon if you win here today, you can leave, and if you lose, well, you'll be dead, so that's that."

He really wanted to finish off the conversation, as it was tiring to project his voice like this. The fighting below with the army of Soldiers and even the four remaining Royal Guards was ongoing, so in that sense, talking was to their advantage. Humanity and the undead were clearly beating the army of cursed vampires handily, and Jake would be lying if he said he didn't find the Monarch's indifference slightly surprising, if not downright worrying.

"You may have a point, Viper's Chosen," the Monarch acknowledged. "And as you said, the system has given me a new path. I merely need to defeat all of you, making you leave before Yalsten collapses to escape. Meanwhile, I assume you lot have to exterminate me."

The Monarch didn't need any answer to get his theory confirmed, as the silence of those present was good enough.

"Chosen, I have a proposition," the vampire Monarch

said as he looked towards Jake. **"Assist me in slaying the slaves of the Holy Tyrant and the filthy undead as well as those who side with them, and I shall allow you to finish me off afterward or do anything else you wish with me. My only other request is that if you choose to slay me, you will promise to assist in the survival of the vampiric race in the multiverse, or at least not be their enemy."**

Jake stared at the vampire as he waved his hand and did something. He was surprised at the proposition, and even more so at the quest that suddenly appeared before his eyes:

Quest Received: Friend of the Monarch

As you stand before the Monarch, he has given you a choice. Side with the Monarch to defeat everyone else by either making them leave the Treasure Hunt or slaying them. The endless gratitude of the Monarch will be yours.

Slaying the Monarch or choosing to fight him will nullify this quest. Accepting it will nullify the quest: [Cursed Monarch].

Objective: Defeat all other Treasure Hunters present. (4.2%)

Rewards: Final rewards will be calculated after the Treasure Hunt concludes.

Warning: Due to the destruction of the world, the Treasure Hunt will end in: 11:28:52

The atmosphere of the Treasure Hunt seemed to change, and he felt the gazes of all present and not occupied with fighting. Even Casper looked his way, worried, with Jacob looking especially troubled. The only ones who looked unbothered with it all were Caleb and Sylphie. Sylphie just seemed confused, as she had also gotten the quest, but she either couldn't or didn't do anything, allowing Jake to decide.

Now, for the large pros and cons list, first of al—

"No, thanks," Jake said. "Can we just get to fighting already and stop chatting? Oh, but I have nothing against vampires; I just don't really wanna make any promises."

Seriously, why would he accept such a bad proposition? Also, he could only begin to imagine how pissed Miranda would be if he decided to make pretty much all other humans on the planet his enemy. It wasn't like he would actually kill them and make troubles go away even if he had a momentary lapse of judgment and joined the vampire. They would just leave, and he would return to Earth with everyone hating him. On top of that, he would miss the best part:

The fight with the Monarch himself.

Jake visibly saw the relief of the anxious onlookers, Caleb just shaking his head with a wry smile.

The Cursed Monarch didn't look surprised or even mad. Instead, he just nodded in acknowledgment. "Very well... I must admit, to fight the Chosen of a Primordial just after my return... the system has given me quite the path."

A bit of a miscalculation there, mate, Jake thought. *I'm not the only one you have to be careful of.*

Almost as if his words were prophetic, a figure flew up towards the Monarch. Carmen appeared and punched with her glowing fists, sending a wave of force out. The Monarch blocked easily but was once more attacked from behind when black lightning struck, and before he could even register that, a bird attacked from above.

The first blow was blocked by a palm, the lightning dismissed as he simply tanked it, with the bird's attack narrowly dodged by him turning to the side. With a palm strike, he leaned forward and sent Carmen flying away with a hole in her chest and a trail of blood in her wake.

An orb of blood appeared in his one hand, and he sent it flying towards Jake. It began morphing in mid-air as a clone of the Monarch appeared, flying at high speeds in Jake's direction. Jake scoffed and fired a barrage of arrows towards it. The clone was fast, but just as it tried to pass through the projectiles from the Splitting Arrow, they all blew up, taking the clone with them.

It was the first time Jake had used an explosive attack, and it worked quite well, as the clone clearly wasn't made to be durable. It was just a distraction that allowed the Monarch to continue his attack towards Carmen, who he apparently viewed as the one he wanted to take down first.

He pointed down and fired a red beam towards her still-falling form. No one could get there fast enough to help block it, but luckily they didn't need to. Carmen somehow punched the red beam, making it explode and sending her smashing into the ground even faster. Her fist was mangled, but she was already self-healing at a visible rate.

The Monarch plainly wanted to try and finish her off, but had to block another blow as the Sword Saint appeared. His blade fell, and the Monarch coated his hand in a red aura while blocking. Just as the sword made contact with it, however, it seemed to almost pass through, and the Monarch was truly wounded for the first time.

A small cut appeared on his one leg, making his eyes open wide. He attacked the Sword Saint by summoning twenty orbs of blood around himself and bombarding the old man, but the swordsman didn't let up. The sword fell two more times, making two large cuts on his arms before the Sword Saint was forced to retreat from the orbs. The old man appeared to shimmer as he fought, making even Jake frown in confusion.

Seeming almost offended, the Monarch began glowing red. He moved like he wanted to tear the old man to threads, but for the umpteenth time during the fight, he was forced to face something else. An arrow came in from far away, making him dodge back and away from the Saint, clearly not wanting to block the Arcane Powershot directly.

Jake himself was currently flying closer to the battlefield. Hitting reliably from such a distance was hard, and he wanted to at least get within a few kilometers, where his arrows would arrive within a second with every shot. Currently, Jake had to calculate every blow far too much, and the last Arcane Powershot was fired on the way. Oh, yeah, that was another thing—he had to use Arcane Powershots to make the arrows faster, and that simply wasn't sustainable.

He fired a few arrows a second as he flew forward, aiming at the Monarch and throwing off his momentum. Jake deliberately avoided using Gaze, as he wanted to save it for a more opportune time and not tire himself out.

The Monarch fought the Sword Saint more, and with the support of Jake, the old man avoided taking any injuries. Caleb and Sylphie were incredibly fast strikers, coming in and landing glancing blows from time to time too. Carmen also joined their assault not long after, completely healed from her previous injuries.

Below, Reika, the party with Bertram in it, the ones from Valhal, Priscilla and the undead, and several others were fighting with a huge advantage against the Royal Guards, who were a member down. Each of the Royal Guards was about as strong as a Count of Blood and, like the Counts of Blood, could also be weakened by stakes. It didn't take long for the human side down there to figure that out. Each of the Guards was stabbed through, every faction having more than enough stakes left over.

Jake saw that the Monarch's confident grin began turning into a frown. A few more minutes had passed, and Jake was now only a few kilometers away and had stopped to bombard the Monarch from there. After all, as an archer with so many melee fighters to support him, why get close?

Casper did something similar to Jake, preparing some magic off to the side. Several wraiths flew around him, and Jake faintly felt the Root of Eternal Resentment react within his Hunter Insignia, making him aware those wraiths were like that Shade of Eternal Resentment he had seen back then. Ghosts of sorts, born from the curse... and from the looks of it, Casper was preparing an attack using them.

The battle continued both above and below. The Monarch was faster and stronger than anyone else present, but he was pressured by so many strong people around him. Anytime he was close to landing a blow, he was forced to block or dodge—something that seemed to miff him quite a bit.

However, this also meant that the Cursed Monarch had only taken minor wounds so far. The few wounds he did suffer healed nearly instantly, too, and Jake began to realize something as the fighting went on. *Time isn't on our side.*

For some reason, the Cursed Monarch, at least, believed so. Was it because of the world breaking down? Would that result in default victory for him? Or was it something else? Jake did notice how the Monarch never really committed in any attacks. If he had to trade blows, he would rather avoid it altogether.

Or perhaps the Cursed Monarch just had confidence in being able to outlast their resources and win through that... which actually wasn't out of the question.

Jake himself would be fine due to his high and diverse stats, alchemy, and even the mask increasing mana regeneration. Casper also looked like he would be fine, as he mainly borrowed power from other sources, but the Sword Saint, Carmen, Caleb, and Sylphie? Jake could see all of them running out if this kept on. Especially Caleb and Sylphie, who now burned their resources to land swift and deadly blows. This was all fine and dandy if you only had to land a few and win a battle through a burst of power, but in a drawn-out struggle, it could spell disaster.

He sent a message towards Sylphie asking her about her

resources and got a bad response... She was spending way too much. She herself didn't see any issues, but Jake clearly felt how unbothered the Monarch was.

Was the talking also part of his plans to drag things out? Jake had no idea, but he knew he would have to change up the game, so he did what he always did when people wanted to play the long game against him: he proved that was a really bad idea against a poison alchemist, much less the Chosen of the Malefic Viper.

Jake drew his bow and got even closer than before. He drew back the string, and just as time began slowing, he spat some poison on the tip of the arrow. One had to remember that his most effective version of Blood of the Malefic Viper came from the poison excreted by his canines using Fang of the Malefic Viper—a skill he really didn't think about much.

Taking aim, he fired at the Monarch. As always, the vampire tried to dodge, but for a brief second, his body tensed as Jake used Gaze, allowing the stable arcane arrow to hit the vampire in the left arm. Jake followed up with another arrow, also with spit on it. At the same time, he had summoned two bottles of uncommon-rarity Necrotic Poison and poured it in his quiver.

He shot again and then swiftly moved his hand to just above his quiver. He began summoning stable arcane arrow after stable arcane arrow, allowing them to drop down into the quiver and soak in the poison. In less than a second, he summoned thirty arrows into his quiver, and with that done, he chugged a mana potion. Unfortunately, all the Arcane Powershots earlier, as well as the Arrow of the Ambitious Hunter, had drained his mana quite a lot, and if this was going to be a long one, he would prefer to get ahead of it.

On the good side, the Monarch had been hit by two arrows, and Jake would now begin to build up damage. Now the only problem was if the rest of them could keep the Monarch busy and outlast him long enough for it all to accumulate. If not, Jake would have to take matters more into his own hands.

The problem was how they could possibly outlast the Monarch. One would have to be—

Suddenly, light washed over the Sword Saint and Carmen, who were engaged in melee, making the old man heal at a visible rate and speeding up Carmen's regeneration. The Monarch opened his eyes wide and saw the newcomer. In a flash of mist, he disappeared. Clearly, he knew a healer would complicate the situation... There was just one problem for the poor guy.

The Monarch's fist penetrated through the chest of the white-robed man, and with a palm-strike, his head exploded. Wanting to make sure—or perhaps just not seeing a notification —the Monarch blew up the rest of the healer's body, leaving nothing behind.

That is, until a second later, when a new body appeared right in front of the Monarch, making him stare down in confusion.

"My, my, quite the rude welcome," Eron said with a smile as white flames began burning on the madman's body.

CHAPTER 50

TREASURE HUNT - TARGET
PRIORITIZATION

J ake watched Eron stand before the Cursed Monarch,
unbothered as flames wormed across his body.

The Monarch took a step back and asked, "**What are
you?**"

"A rude welcome followed by a rude question," Eron said,
visibly upset while looking at the Monarch. "I have had not the
best time these last few days, so please excuse my own rudeness...
but I have never seen a more disgusting spark than what glows
within you.

"Broken and flickering like the wind can snuff it out at any
moment, you burn out your very essence and need to consume
the sparks of others to keep yourself alive... Disgusting beyond
belief. Truly your existence itself is cursed, Monarch or not."

The white flames exploded out of Eron. The Cursed
Monarch was pushed back, or rather, chose to fly back. He
didn't take much damage from the flames but was still left
disturbed. As Jake already knew, the flames were more eerie than
dangerous. A bit of exposure did nothing but some damage to
health, but with enough time, Jake could see it becoming lethal.

Jake also learned for the first time that Eron could actually
heal people. He wasn't just an immortal wall, but a wellspring of

health. One that would make this battle even more one-sided, as they now also clearly had the advantage in durability and had the resources to outlast the boss.

It was clear to see that the Cursed Monarch hadn't learned this yet. Perhaps he didn't believe Eron was truly unkillable, or perhaps he just couldn't comprehend it even being possible. Without any hesitation, the Monarch attacked the healer that had just called him disgusting. He opened his palm towards the healer and sent out a red wave of energy.

Flying out, it touched Eron's body and made it erode, yet the man just kept standing there and staring at the vampire. A second after the wave passed through, obliterating his body, he was back. This made the Monarch frown even more.

Jake totally got the frustration. He had been faced with it himself. And he was sure the Monarch could figure something out with just a bit of time, but that time wasn't something anyone else present planned on giving him.

An arrow was nocked and released, a sword brought down, and a fist smashed forward. Black lightning fell from above, and Sylphie attacked with blades of wind, having been told to relax it with her powerful dive attacks.

Once more, the Monarch was on the back foot.

For a while, he tried to keep up the same tactic as before, but the arrival of Eron made that plan unfeasible. Jake noticed Eron didn't use any shields or buffs or anything like that; he only healed people. In many ways, his white flames were a kind of reverse healing, too, making it clear the guy really was the purest form a healer could take, with a bit of immortality sprinkled in for good measure.

When it became apparent this passive approach wouldn't work, the Monarch switched gears. He took a step back after blocking a sword swing and turned to mist.

Jake felt a sense of danger as he stepped down on the platform of mana he was standing on. He appeared on another one a hundred meters away just in time to dodge a red claw trying to penetrate his chest. The Monarch had clearly chosen to switch his focus from the melee fighters to taking down or incapacitating Jake first. Jake felt that the claw the Monarch used wasn't like any attack used prior. Instead, it gave off a very familiar and much-hated feeling; it was a curse.

One had to remember, this Cursed Monarch was born from the remnants of what had once been an A-grade King of Blood specialized in curse magic. So for him to retain some knowledge and abilities to curse people was only to be expected.

Turning around, Jake fired a potshot that missed when the Monarch turned to mist again. Jake, in turn, dismissed his bow and summoned his scimitar and Nanoblade. Just in time, too, as he blocked a claw coming from behind.

He was still sent tumbling back, being outmatched in strength, but was otherwise unhurt. The Monarch had hit his Nanoblade, and Jake quickly saw the result when black veins began spreading on the sword. *Not good*.

Jake was forced to block again as the Monarch didn't let up. The others tried to get to him, but the Monarch purposefully made Jake retreat away from them through repeated attacks. Each time the Nanoblade was hit, he felt it become more and more damaged, but the scimitar took the blows without any problems. In fact, it felt almost like the blade enjoyed the power of the cursed claws.

"Once more, this is not personal," the vampire boss said without letting up for a second.

Jake found it funny the guy was still worried about him getting mad from this entire situation, but even more funny that the Monarch seemed so sure of this victory.

"Neither is this," Jake answered as he counterattacked.

The Monarch had a sliver of hesitance within him to attack Jake. A faint opening. That weakness was blown right open as the infused presence of Pride of the Malefic Viper spread around him, attacking the vampire's psyche.

For a brief moment, the Monarch hesitated. It was barely

there, but that was enough. For the first time, Jake activated Limit Break at 10% and dove in. He dismissed the Nanoblade while stabbing the scimitar into the arm of the Monarch, making him unable to attack. Meanwhile, Jake placed his palm on the chest of the vampire, channeling Touch of the Malefic Viper.

The Monarch reacted fast with a swing of the other arm, but Jake didn't stop. The claw was just in front of Jake's face when a sword narrowly passed by behind Jake's shoulder, stabbing the Monarch's hand and pinning it to the vampire's body.

With a groan, the Monarch freed the hand Jake was trying to block with his scimitar, but Carmen came in from the side, twisted the arm, and held it in an armlock. At the same time, Caleb attacked from behind by placing the tip of his staff on the body of the Monarch.

Jake kept channeling Touch of the Malefic Viper throughout it all, and he saw the chest of the vampire begin corroding and rotting away as black veins spread from the wound. The Monarch released a red wave of energy, but to the surprise of both him and the humans attacking him, it didn't go as expected. Well, it surprised everyone besides Caleb.

The red wave didn't release in all directions, but instead shrank instantly as black lightning ate at it, with Caleb's staff consuming it. Jake's brother was blasted back, but he had managed to buy them a second or so more before the Monarch could make another move.

At that moment, a loud shriek sounded out from behind them. Casper had come over, hundreds of Shades flying around him. Jake saw the eyes of the Monarch open wide as the many spirits flew towards him, worming past Jake and the others to enter his body.

Casper directed the many spirits like a maestro, guiding them into the body of the boss vampire. The Monarch, in turn, groaned with a pained expression. The five strongest people on

Earth were currently holding him down, with Sylphie and Eron also incoming to keep up the assault.

Yet Jake didn't feel confident. He met the eyes of the vampire, who looked back with a sinister smile. **"Impressive."**

The vampire simultaneously tore his hand through the blade of the Sword Saint and kicked away the old man, the freed hand aimed at Jake's head. The arm Carmen held was twisted free as he willingly broke it, and his entire body began burning in a deep crimson flame while the ghosts shrieked—this time in pain and not delight from getting a chance at revenge.

Jake watched the incoming hand, narrowly moving his own hand to the side and answering, "Likewise."

Twisting his body around, Jake got to the back of the vampire, only taking a small claw attack in return. The Monarch was distracted by the descending blade of the Sword Saint and a few wooden stakes fired off by Casper, allowing Jake to summon his Nanoblade again and stab it through the back of the Monarch.

Carmen punched him in the side, too, with Sylphie flying over and cutting his one arm deeply. The Sword Saint managed to land a few more nasty wounds, with Caleb now having regrouped with Casper. They worked together to make ranged attacks of wooden stakes and needle-thin bolts of lightning that seemed to pierce the Monarch's body like a poison.

The crimson flames barely hurt Jake, clearly being focused on incorporeal beings and the vampire's insides. With the shades still weakening the vampire, they all went all-out to deal as much damage as possible without revealing any of their most powerful cards, Jake going HAM with his blades and plenty of poison.

Within a minute, the group had managed to leave hundreds of wounds, a few of which would be lethal to a human, yet the Monarch took it all. The shrieks of the shades slowly died down until, suddenly, they fell silent—a moment that served as a shift of momentum too.

The Sword Saint brought down his blade, but the clawed

hand of the vampire flew with incredible speed to catch not the blade, but the arm of the old man. The Sword Saint's eyes opened with surprise, but he still reacted swiftly by practically tossing his sword to the other hand and cutting down in a fluid movement.

With a snicker, the Monarch just let go of his arm. He dodged the blade, opened his palm, and fired off a blast of red energy, sending the unprepared Sword Saint flying back. Then, with both hands free, he pointed a finger above his own shoulder, aimed straight at Jake.

Jake's danger sense exploded. He let go and jumped back just before a beam cut through the air, making space crack in its wake. The rest of the humans and the one undead were also pushed back. At the same time, several globes of blood were summoned and began sprouting tentacles of blood that whipped at them.

The vampire tossed a glance at everyone, then chose his target. Out of everyone present, Jake had been the one to cause the most damage, and from his Sense of the Malefic Viper, he felt the poison burn through the Monarch's body, but that did not mean he was necessarily the most dangerous.

Because he also felt how the Monarch had a harder time healing himself. The cause of that was clear. Another energy mixed with Jake's poison—not amplifying it, per se, but making anything harmful to the Monarch more effective and harder to heal: curses.

Which is to say, the Monarch had recognized Casper as his first target to take down. Permanently.

Casper—to his credit—had predicted this too, and the moment the mist coalesced to his side, the area exploded in black curse energy as a pre-prepared trap triggered. For the most part, the Monarch ignored it, his claw ripping through the energy and towards Casper. The undead dodged back, but two red beams were released, one of them penetrating his chest and the other his stomach.

Everyone else tried to come to his assistance, and Jake glanced towards Eron and noticed something. The man didn't even attempt to heal Casper, but just frowned... Jake soon realized the guy wasn't just being an ass. He couldn't heal undead.

Shit.

If Casper was forced to leave the Hunt, it would make things difficult, as the Monarch was still quite healthy, and Jake also feared the current effects of the curse would disperse.

Clearly, the Monarch was aware of all this and moved to finish off the man. The clawed hand descended towards Casper, cutting up his chest with a long, deep wound, and the other hand penetrated his chest, his heart skewered and grasped in the hand of the Monarch.

Jake's eyes opened wide, afraid Casper was at the risk of dying, but saw that his friend just grinned. His undead friend pulled the Monarch closer and stabbed him in the stomach with a wooden stake, and the next moment the Monarch fled back in fright—just in time, as the locket on Casper's neck released a ghastly light and gave off a powerful aura as something flew out.

A figure collided with the Monarch, sending him flying back in a bright explosion of energy, the vampire forced to block with a barrier.

"You aren't simple either, huh? A servant of the Blight-father?" the Monarch said as he saw the ghost that now stood in front of Casper protectively.

Jake also Identified her.

[Blightwraith – lvl 146]

Jake didn't recognize her, but knew from what he had heard that she was called Lyra and had also been in their tutorial. He wasn't aware of everything that had happened, but knew Casper had made a deal that ultimately resulted in her being resurrected as a ghost that resided in the locket. What he hadn't known was how powerful this ghost was.

She was stronger than most anyone present, and from the energy she gave off, Jake had a feeling she and Casper working together was the primary cause of his strength.

"Not quite," Casper answered as he took out an odd potion Jake didn't recognize and chugged it down, his body healing at a visible rate afterward.

The Monarch looked towards the sky, muttering, **"This is harder than I thought... You are a bunch of monsters, aren't you? Or has the average level of the enlightened races heightened so much? No... doubtful..."**

Shaking his head, the Monarch just got back to the action, red energy burning around him as he charged Casper again. Lyra blocked him, screaming and releasing a shockwave of blight energy. The Monarch turned to mist and avoided it, appearing right beside Casper, who reacted quickly once more and blasted himself to the side—in the direction of Jake and the others.

Carmen managed to get in front of him just in time to block an attack from the vampire. She managed to stay still as they clashed, using some skill to negate the impact, much to the annoyance of the vampire. Two red globes of blood still floating some distance away suddenly flew towards her and exploded against her back, but a second later, her wounds began healing, courtesy of her own magic and Eron's.

Seemingly having realized that Eron was too annoying, the Monarch finally decided to deal with him. He turned to mist and appeared right behind the man, who released a burst of white flames out his back. The Monarch ignored it by turning to mist again and appearing right in front of Eron.

The Monarch stared into Eron's eyes and spoke, **"Sleep."**

He then turned to mist again to avoid a barrage of arrows from Jake, while Eron fell to the ground, unconscious.

The dude really needed to work on mental defenses.

CHAPTER 51

TREASURE HUNT: WILL OF THE TRUE ANCESTOR

Reika manipulated her weapons as she battled the Royal Guard in front of her, the male vampire using an odd mix of blood and water magic against her. The other Royal Guards also assisted him but were otherwise busy as they got swamped by everyone else present.

The people from Valhal were absolutely pummeling one of them, another one being dominated by the party from the Holy Church, and the fourth primarily fighting the undead woman Priscilla and her followers. Behind them, many others assisted or simply killed the many Soldiers also coming in and disturbing their battle.

Durability-wise, the vampires were all high-tier, but they simply didn't get any opportunities to properly show their offensive might. Especially not after each of them was stabbed by one of the cursed Stakes originally intended for the Counts.

So while the battle still took a while, it was an utterly one-sided affair. Reika had wanted to join the fighting in the air with the Monarch very much but knew it was beyond her. She had caught glimpses of the fight and knew she wouldn't last long, possibly only being a burden.

Among humans on Earth, she had always thought she was at

the pinnacle, but she had to admit that her combat prowess was lacking behind that of others. Reika had perhaps focused too much time on her profession and not enough on actually improving her combat skills. This didn't mean she was weak, though.

Four swords flew through the air, burning with blue fire as they cut at the barrier of the vampire before her. A Soldier approached from behind, and she directed two of the swords to stop it. They flew towards the vampire, and while one was blocked by an old rusty shield, the other stabbed the Soldier in the arm. The flames instantly began spreading, but instead of heat, they left signs of frostbite.

Reika had formed a cold flame that she used primarily for alchemy, as she found that most of her crafting worked best in low temperatures. She wasn't an alchemist like Jake or others with a more classical approach. Instead, hers was more modern, at least by human standards, where she used a cold environment to preserve the effects of the medicine more effectively while combining it through a hardening process.

This flame had also proved very useful when it came to fighting foes. The flames spread on the Soldier as Reika used her hands to manipulate the swords, and at the same time, she drew a simple magic circle using her feet and pure mana manipulation.

Her attack on the Soldier didn't impede it, as it kept charging her. Reika finished the magic circle just in time and flew to the side, the Soldier stepping where she had just been. The circle activated and spat out chains of frost, stopping the vampire.

Without further ado, she took out a small, crystalline bottle and tossed it at the Soldier. It exploded with a cloud of odd silver dust, and a moment later, she tossed another bottle that exploded in blue light. All of the silver dust was activated and expanded as it froze, forming thousands of localized ice explosions. The soldier, caught in the middle, was completely frozen both inside and out.

With that done, Reika gladly turned her attention towards the Royal Guard again. The vampire had tried to do something, but was hit by a blast from the side by the odd ship of the merchant from Haven, making it fail its spellcasting. This gave her ample opportunity to direct all four blades when she spotted one of the Royal Guards being finished off by the fire-using archer named Maria from the Holy Church's party.

By now, it was only a question of time before the Royal Guards would all be wiped out.

The many Soldiers weren't faring any better, as they were so heavily outnumbered.

———

Jake fired another arrow, hitting the Monarch on his thigh when he didn't turn to mist fast enough—courtesy of the Sword Saint trying to cut his head off and Carmen attempting to rupture whatever organs could possibly remain within the Cursed Monarch.

Lyra had reentered the locket with Casper. Based on him only really attacking after that, he proved Jake's theory that the two of them were using some combo attacks by channeling both their energies.

Caleb and Sylphie kept up their work as strikers, occasionally hitting with powerful glancing blows when the Monarch was unprepared and often at the same time. Finally, the Sword Saint and Carmen kept the Monarch engaged in melee, with Jake shooting his bow from only a few hundred meters away.

Eron was uselessly unconscious on the ground below, still under the effect of the Monarch's spell. The vampire had tried to use a spell on the Sword Saint at one point also, but it appeared to have little to no effect. Carmen was affected, but the pain she caused herself with her magic seemed to snap her out of it instantly, rendering her effectively immune. Below, the Royal Guards and soldiers fell one by one.

Reflecting on the entire battle—while still shooting arrows —Jake had a feeling this couldn't be it. The Monarch was around 190, as far as Jake could tell, which meant he was nearly C-grade, but so far, the battle hadn't been that hard at all.

He did think that the Monarch wasn't at the pinnacle for someone his level—quite the opposite, actually. He was clearly severely weakened, and the Cursed part of his name was not a positive moniker. It was something that restricted him, same as how the Counts had been starved.

There was also the fact that the Monarch still had a far too casual approach of just dragging out time. He had landed some wounds on them, but primarily Carmen, who self-healed. While he had gone for Casper earlier, and even Jake and Caleb had taken some blows, it was nothing serious. It was like the Monarch was waiting for something and still hiding a part of his power... Not that Jake was particularly worried.

They were all holding back.

Every fighter present had more to show and was just waiting for it to be required. Blowing your load too early was an excellent way to turn a good situation bad, after all.

But, more convincing than any of his own postulations and belief that the Monarch had more to show were the actions of Jacob. The Augur was still preparing some ritual with hundreds of people below, hidden behind a barrier meant to obscure them —a useless attempt before the power of the full-Perception build.

Alright, entirely useless it wasn't, as the Monarch hadn't noticed yet. Perhaps just specially designed to be hidden from vampires? Either way, the ritual proved that Jacob was preparing for something that was to come, clearly having at least some sense that there was more to the Monarch.

Which made perfect sense... What boss fight was good with only one phase?

The fighting kept up for a few more minutes, the Earth side more dominant everywhere. After the first of the four remaining Royal Guards fell, the others quickly followed as they were swarmed and overwhelmed. The Soldiers were slaughtered wholesale, many of them having ten or even twenty people gang up on them. Rituals from the undead side and the Holy Church activated to blow them up continuously, and the Noboru clan even joined in with some long-range barrages that had pinpoint precision. Not to mention all of the parties like Neil's, who were killing the vampires with almost machine-like efficiency.

Jake kept up the assault of the Monarch, feeling his poison accumulate. The large dose he'd injected with Touch was especially still doing harm. He also discovered that the stake Casper had stabbed the Monarch with earlier was a modified version of the ones used on the Counts, this one able to be used on the Monarch, even though it appeared to be way less effective. As to how he had learned this? Well, because Casper had more of them. Jake had seen him summon another, giving him a better look.

In a final clash, the Sword Saint managed to land a deep cut on the Monarch just as Jake hit the vampire in his hand, ignoring the attempted block. Carmen, Sylphie, and Caleb also all hit at once, with the final attack made by Casper being dodged as the Monarch turned to mist.

He appeared far above them, floating and looking down. Jake stared up and saw the vampire standing there, his clothes shredded in nearly all places, his body filled with wounds and marks as black veins spread across it. Yet he smiled.

"I must admit... this is not going as I had imagined. This body is truly not what it once was... if it ever was. I am beginning to question if I am truly a King of Blood or merely a specter formed of his memories. Perhaps a bit of both? I am not certain it matters, but one cannot help but question." The Monarch looked down at them again, then up towards the sky.

Jake considered shooting an arrow, but he wanted to see
what the Monarch would do next if he was perfectly honest.
Also, it would not hit for sure, and none of the others seemed to
want to attack right away, either, preferring to take the breather
instead. Jake knew it could be mentally taxing to constantly fight
and be on your toes, so he got it. Partly.

"Back when Yalsten was founded, the True Ancestor
handed a treasure to the founder. A treasure meant to
preserve the Legacy of the True Ancestor, hidden here
away from sight. Perhaps this treasure was the cause of the
fall of Yalsten to begin with... Did you know that I caused
the isolation of our world on purpose?

"The Church, undead, and many others were closing
in, and on my way back after I collected sacrifices for the
grand ritual, I was discovered. I was forced to sever all
spatial channels leading to the outside world to stop them
from getting in and safeguard the treasure. Naturally, this
could not be shared with the inhabitants. I just had to say
that the curse damaged the channels and eventually broke
them. I was even made to kill all those who wanted to leave
and make those who stayed behind believe their relatives
safely got away."

The Monarch spoke while floating in the air, his wounds
dripping blood.

"This was not a proud moment, but one of necessity. I
believed we could restore the connection... do something.
But no, the curse ritual was tampered with or failed.
Everything began breaking down, and I was forced to seal
myself while working on a device to try and restrain my
own curse."

He sighed, shaking his head.

"An utter display of failure. All of it. Now, I am a mere
husk of what I once was... but one thing remained with
me. For I had kept one promise: to safeguard the treasure
left by the True Ancestor. I was unable to do anything

with it myself; all vampires were, due to the Law of Ancestry... but the rule is gone, it seems. I had hoped to avoid using this, as even I am uncertain of its effects, but would the system have left it with me if it led to catastrophe?"

On the ground below, the coffin that the Cursed Monarch had been lying in suddenly exploded as a hidden compartment was opened. A small, glowing red item soared up and stopped right in front of the Monarch. He looked at it with excitement and reverence.

"Behold."

He spread out his hands, revealing the red item to be a necklace. A necklace that held a small glass bauble with some red liquid stored within it.

"The Blood of Sanguine."

Jake Identified the necklace as fast as he could, and his eyes opened wide.

[Sanguine's Blood Legacy (Divine)]

He failed to see any more information than that; perhaps his Identify was not good enough, or the item was too far above him. Yet, he could not understand how a divine-rarity item could be present in the Treasure Hunt of D-grades, and he didn't have time to find out.

The Monarch looked at the necklace as it responded. Not aloud to him or anyone else, but simply by imposing its own will upon the world around it. The sky became red when it released a subtle red wave of energy that pulsed across the entire Treasure Hunt, nearly unnoticeable.

It passed through Jake and everyone else without any effect... but the same could not be said for those of the vampiric race. The first to be hit was the Monarch, who simply let the energy wash over him, and as it did, he began changing.

His husked form healed instantly. His wrinkled skin tightened up, deep red hair grew on his head, and a black beard appeared at impossible speeds. Muscles grew and wriggled as his entire body went from a deathly-looking, dried-up husk to a man who looked to be at his prime. At the same time, all traces of the curse of Yalsten left his body.

On the plains below, the wave hit all of the corpses of the vampires. Hundreds of Soldiers had been slain, and all of the Royal Guards. Their bodies released black smoke as the curse disappeared. Furthermore, when the wave hit them, their bodies melted into red puddles and joined the blood they had already spilled in the battle before. All of this blood began gathering to form humanoid, vampire-looking shapes of blood.

Jake looked down and saw dozens of these blood creatures form all over the plains. He quickly worked to Identify them.

[Vampiric Blood Elemental – lvl 143]

[Vampiric Blood Elemental – lvl 151]

[Vampiric Blood Elemental – lvl 164]

Their levels varied widely, and so did their strength. Jake glanced at the people below, many of them exhausted and now faced with powerful enemies once more. The most powerful elemental was level 169 and had been formed around where the Royal Guards had been slain. He already saw the people from the Holy Church preparing to face it, looking almost as if this was expected. Perhaps because Jacob had seen this coming. In the end, hundreds of those elementals were formed.

Finally, Jake turned his gaze to the Cursed Monarch... and noticed, upon using Identify, that he couldn't use that name anymore.

[Monarch of Blood - 170]

The newly born Monarch of Blood stood with his eyes

closed as Jake wondered what exactly had happened. The level of the Monarch had dropped by more than twenty levels... yet when he gauged the vampire in front of him... he was stronger. Not just by a little.

"I see... all is planned indeed," the Monarch said while opening his deep red eyes, magic circles glowing within as he looked at them. **"The True Ancestor was truly crafty."**

The necklace that had released the pulse continued upwards. The red sky intensified, and the mist all over Yalsten was completely and utterly evaporated. Then, the necklace above transformed itself, releasing a flash of red light before revealing a blood-red celestial object hanging above. Jake was uncertain if it was a moon or a sun.

At the same time, the Monarch of Blood released his aura. The unstable space of Yalsten appeared to shake and quiver at his display.

Jake felt the power and could only smile. He exchanged a glance with the Sword Saint and saw the old man return a nod. Outwardly, he displayed worry... but Jake saw the man's excitement.

The Monarch also smiled as he spread his arms wide and yelled, **"Come. Let the Will of the True Ancestor be done!"**

CHAPTER 52

TREASURE HUNT: A LEVELED LOOK AT POWER

L evels truly worked in peculiar ways, and the correlation between levels and actual combat prowess was often muddy and difficult to pin down. For example, a low-tier genius D-grade could sometimes beat even pinnacle D-grades who focused primarily on crafting if they also happened to counter their skillset well, and if the individual they fought was just overall weak for their level.

Jake was a great example of this, having a class focused on fighting more powerful foes and a profession offering him many benefits in combat too. For him to fight an enemy tens of levels above himself was just to be expected. He was the Chosen of the Malefic Viper, after all, and a Progenitor. He had titles making his stats far exceed what one of this level usually would have, a class and profession offering even more stats further amplified by this, powerful skills, and so on.

This did mean that level itself was truly a poor indicator of actual power, yet it was the best people often had if someone didn't outright release their aura and kept their presence and whatnot suppressed. Of course, anyone could still feel the grade someone was, but it was uncertain if the Monarch had any idea as to Jake's actual level, considering he couldn't be Identified.

Now, Identify not being a good way to gauge anyone's strength didn't mean there was no way to do it. In fact, almost anyone with any talent in fighting could get a rough estimate for how powerful someone was merely by looking at them.

Jake's Bloodline didn't create new instincts; it merely enhanced those that were there before to wholly ridiculous levels. As many beasts had shown, some basic danger sense was present, some spatial awareness was to be expected, and even intuition was just a natural occurrence everywhere.

Intuition and danger sense working in tandem was what allowed one to estimate how powerful someone was by simply looking at them. Jake had both these boosted to levels beyond perhaps any other being in the multiverse, meaning his instinctual gauge of how powerful someone was proved far more effective than merely using Identify. Of course, it was not entirely perfect. Something like the damn blue mushroom down in the biodome was a good example of this, as while Jake had felt it was strong, he couldn't properly understand it either.

Now, all of this is to say that Jake noticed some people looking relieved after they saw the now-named Monarch of Blood had dropped more than twenty levels. Perhaps they believed he had given up some of his own power to spawn the elementals and the huge, blood-like celestial object hanging above. But, unfortunately, this was an entirely incorrect assumption.

Because while they breathed out in relief, those in the air all prepared themselves. The Sword Saint got into a defensive position, Carmen used some magic to fully heal herself right away, and Sylphie, Casper, and Caleb all backed off even further away, knowing the situation had changed.

The Monarch spread his hands and launched the final act. **"Come. Let the will of the True Ancestor be done!"**

Jake had no time to think about what the whole "crafty True Ancestor" thing was about before he was attacked. He wasn't the only one either. The Monarch had raised his hand and fired off a beam in each of their directions.

The Sword Saint pointed his blade up, causing water to revolve around it. The beam struck the tip of the sword and was redirected away, hitting a Vampiric Blood Elemental below. Carmen crossed her arms and blocked, her bracers activating some enchantment to facilitate this. Caleb dodged to the side along with Sylphie while Casper summoned a black wooden shield, successfully blocking the blow.

Jake simply stepped to the side, his danger sense having given him ample warning, and released an arrow in return. Not towards the Monarch, but someone else. He had noticed that the many spawning elementals below actively ignored a certain unconscious man, making Jake guess something.

If Eron was so useless that he could be knocked unconscious and die for real to a single arrow, he wouldn't be worth shit anyway, so Jake decided to take a gamble and shoot him with one. The arrow fell and exploded when it hit the man below, blowing up his body entirely.

He didn't have time to observe the result, given the mist condensing behind him. Jake took a step forward, appearing on a platform ahead of him just as the air ripped where he had just been standing. In his former place was the Monarch, who wielded a clearly summoned sword made of blood-red crystal.

The Monarch didn't seem to be in a mood to talk much more. He attacked Jake again, this time simply flying towards him. In response, Jake decided to get a bit more serious himself. Mana began condensing around him, and soon crystalline orbs of highly explosive arcane energy appeared.

He drew his scimitar and Nanoblade to block. Jake clashed with the vampire, finding himself outmatched in skill, speed, and power. But not diversity and defensive abilities. Dodging the sword several times, he didn't manage to retaliate, but he *did* finish his arcane bombs.

Jake wanted to pack more power into them but found

himself forced to block more and more from the left side. That was when he noticed the Nanoblade, which had already taken a beating, begin to struggle. He saw a faint smirk on the face of the vampire when, suddenly, a red aura washed over Jake, restricting his movements slightly.

Fighting back with his own Pride of the Malefic Viper to wrest control of the domain back, he was still not fast enough. The crystalline sword of the Monarch grew to resemble a two-handed heavy sword and, with a mighty swing empowered further by the vampire's energy, barrelled for his left side, trying to bisect him at the stomach.

He was forced to block with the Nanoblade despite knowing it was a bad idea. He heard the crack as the heavy sword hit the far more narrow and fragile-looking Nanoblade, and Jake could only grit his teeth as he was blasted away—with just half of the body of the Nanoblade in hand.

Oh, and a dozen or so arcane bombs.

A second shockwave rocked the terrain as an explosion blew up where Jake had just been, sending him flying even further away. He didn't have time to mourn the loss of his weapon. Instead, he drew his bow again and fired into the remnant arcane energy left by the bombs. He ignored the wounds left by the blade and his bruised arm and side, not having time to deal with it right away.

The arrow split into five as it got close, and soon after, another explosion sounded out. However, Jake knew that this one had done nothing. He still vividly felt the Mark of the Avaricious Arcane Hunter he had left on the vampire, and with this attack, the charge did not increase.

Two crescent blades—one of water and one of wind—cut through the terrain towards the Monarch, parted the arcane energy, and impacted the barrier the boss had made around himself. Two large cuts were left on it, one leaving a barely noticeable trace, while the other caused faint cracks. The Sword Saint was naturally superior to Sylphie when it came to fighting prowess, but the bird was no slouch either.

With a swift hand-motion, the Monarch made the barrier explode. Shards of glass-like blood crystals flew everywhere, even hitting the people below who were now in a bitter battle with the blood elementals. A few of the weaker ranged fighters found themselves taking deadly injuries, while others were caught off-guard.

Gotta get him away from here, Jake reckoned.

There was also a risk the Monarch could absorb the blood of those below like the Counts could, making them all living health potions. He didn't want to risk that happening, as he could see what kind of shitty situation that could lead to.

Jake fired another barrage of arrows, but his shots were swiftly dodged by the Monarch, who chased him again. By now, it was clear he was the primary target. Perhaps the Monarch believed Jake was dangerous if left alone, or maybe the boss just wanted to fight him because he seemed the strongest. Either way, Jake invited it.

Retreating as he blocked, the Monarch gave chase and repeatedly swung the crystalline blade. To make it more difficult, the weapon changed shape to a heavier version sporadically, seemingly everchanging. Yet when he focused on being purely defensive, Jake could handle it.

His danger sense and ability to survive were what had allowed Jake to get where he was today. The first truly strong foe he had fought was the Alpha Badger back in the first tutorial dungeon, and against that beast, he had been so outmatched when it came to physical stats it wasn't even funny... but he had still won and survived.

Because while Jake was good at archery and magic and all that, his survival instinct were his greatest weapon.

The Monarch cut and changed the weapon, summoned magical attacks one after another, yet Jake was always one step ahead—sometimes literally with One Step Mile. The game of cat and mouse was one where the mouse clearly had the upper hand, as every move of the cat was predicted and countered near-perfectly.

Jake saw and felt the frustration of the Monarch but paid it no mind. He was in the zone, focused only on his sphere and danger sense. Every faint movement of blood energy, every twitch of a muscle, every instance of slight tension in the vampire's body lay bare before him as the two of them got further and further away from the Mistless Plains.

He felt Sylphie chase after him, followed by the others, with the Sword Saint dragging along Eron. She kept him updated so Jake could focus on the Monarch and not divert his gaze for even a moment. Finally, the Monarch made a too wide swing, and Jake pounced like a starved beast. His own scimitar flew up and left a cut on the Monarch's arm.

Instantly, the Monarch refocused and tightened up his technique. His magic burned bright to summon blood clones all around him, each summoning their own crystalline weapons of blood energy.

Jake swiftly used One Step Mile to get away, leaving a Mark of the Avaricious Arcane Hunter on each of them to keep track. There were five clones in total, and three of them headed towards the approaching humans—and Casper—while the other two joined the Monarch in his assault.

Arcane bolts condensed around Jake as he took this slight reprieve to counterattack, sending all of them towards one of the clones while preparing himself. The clone dodged two of the arcane bolts but was hit by two as they blew up, sending it tumbling back slightly, meaning only two figures appeared before Jake a moment later to strike him.

The Monarch teleported to his back while the clone attacked from the front. Jake chose to charge ahead towards the blood clone and engage that, avoiding the blow of the Monarch by a slight margin as he clashed with the far weaker clone.

Yet even the clone was able to block Jake and fight him

rather well, giving the Monarch ample time to get close again and attack. Narrowing his eyes, Jake went back on the defensive for a while, simultaneously secreting poison mist from the wings on his back. He knew this would have little to no effect on the Monarch, but the blood clone was another story.

He also noticed that his arcane mana burned strongly within the clone. As a magical construct, it was far more susceptible to his arcane mana, he reckoned. The poison also seeped into the clone quite happily, and while it didn't affect its movements, it did put it on a timer.

Dodging back even further, he let the chase continue, eventually detecting the destruction in the distance. Not towards the plains, but far away from it. The cataclysmic power of the world breaking apart as space collapsed could be felt from over a thousand kilometers away, and it was clear that it was coming closer by the second.

Far enough now, Jake decided, not wanting to get any closer to the spatial collapse. Even at this distance, his danger sense made him acutely aware that he didn't want to enter the edges of Yalsten and experience that kind of destruction firsthand.

This meant Jake changed up his tactic and began fleeing downwards instead of flying through the air. Over time, Jake had gotten quite good at aerial combat, primarily through practice against birds on the cloud island, but he still felt more comfortable on the ground. Sure, it could be argued that dodging in a fully three-dimensional space was easier than when you only had to the sides and upwards, but he still preferred the ground.

Flying down, the Monarch gave chase. Jake dodged orbs of blood and beams during his descent. The clones were lagging slightly behind, not releasing any ranged attacks, making Jake believe they could only fight in melee. Or maybe ranged attacks were just a waste of their limited energy pools.

Honestly, Jake had to admit that he was surprised at the lack of diversity in the vampire's skills. He had many types of blood magic, but most of it could be boiled down to orbs, beams, clones, and melee fighting. Alright, he also put Eron to sleep and done some mental magic, but nothing Jake had noticed so far really put him on edge.

It was inarguable that the Monarch was still powerful, but there was no way he'd retained the skills he had as an A-grade. Far from it.

After his transformation, he had gotten stronger, but not overly much. It was more the reset that had caused that had the biggest impact, as it healed his wounds, and as far as Jake could see, the guy now had more resources than before and used them more liberally.

But... ultimately, the question was... could Jake win? Because while this was indeed the strongest foe he had ever faced, that didn't mean it was the most dangerous foe. Jake was also more powerful now than ever.

Could he beat the Monarch alone? Uncertain, but maybe? It would take a while, though.

Could he beat the Monarch with the help of nearly all the strongest people on Earth?

Well... yeah.

Unless the Monarch had more interesting things to show, that is.

CHAPTER 53

TREASURE HUNT: ONE DOWN

*S*trong.

Carmen saw the old man from the Noboru clan obliterate the blood clone within a few dozen seconds, his blade moving incredibly fast and seeming like it could cut anything. She really didn't want to block that sword directly—that was for sure.

Yet the other person Sven had warned her about was even worse. She had just finished off the last of the blood clones with help from Sylphie, the Judge, and the undead called Casper taking care of the third one. This still meant they had only destroyed three clones, while that Chosen guy had singlehandedly taken not just two clones, but the far more powerful true body of the Monarch.

She was worried as he had quite the firepower, but as an archer, his melee prowess would likely be severely lacking. Archers were ranged fighters, and while their Agility and Perception both tended to be high, their durability often wasn't up there.

But when she watched him land in the distance, she didn't see what she'd expected. Two clones attacked him with the Monarch, blood magic flying everywhere, yet he kept dodging and weaving better than any fighter she had ever seen before. It was uncanny to the level of being straight-up ridiculous.

If there was the slightest gap, he was in it the moment it formed; the tiniest opening to escape a pincer attack was chosen, and it didn't matter what angle the attack came from. He was aware of it and reacted, clearly possessing some skill to give him vision all around him.

Is he specialized in avoidance? she wondered as he somehow ducked and jumped at the same time, avoiding two strikes and blasting a mana attack out of his hand. The force sent him flying back slightly to dodge a red beam from the Monarch.

Carmen wasn't delusional. She knew she was strong but not the strongest. Yet, she still felt like there was a gap wider than expected. Sure, she could see herself putting up a good fight, and with all of her boosting skills, she could deal great damage... but could she even hit him?

Moreover, his constant focus was just too ridiculous. One would think that there was a chance to get distracted, or that a wayward thought could sneak in and toss you off for a brief moment, yet such a thing had yet to happen. She herself had many times taken a hit because of a moment of inattentiveness, but that didn't look to be a concept the Chosen even had to deal with.

He was just a monster.

The Sword Saint drifted through the air, using a skill to move faster, and struck at the Monarch from behind. A clone moved to block his blow, and the old man reacted by simply empowering his blow further. His blade seemed to be surrounded by water for a fraction of a moment while falling. It warped around the weapon the clone wanted to block with and cut off its arm, and before it could reform its body, the Sword Saint used another skill. His blade flashed, and the clone was cut into six parts.

Another damn monster, Carmen thought, just shaking her head. Yet, she didn't want to see herself too beaten as she also used a movement skill. Golden wings of light condensed behind her, speeding her up and sending her charging straight at the Monarch.

Energy whirled around her as she struck forward, releasing blasts of pure kinetic force. The vampire naturally noticed her and summoned a circular barrier to block her blows. At the same time, the Chosen guy also moved to attack—with his blow clearly being prioritized and viewed as the most dangerous.

She didn't blame him. Poison was nasty.

Shattering the barrier in a few blows, she got in closer. The Monarch was now forced to address her. And address her he did.

He moved his hand to summon a magic circle beneath him, and before she could react, one appeared beneath her too. Carmen tried to get out of it, but before she knew it, her vision turned entirely black for a moment. Then she found herself in new surroundings.

Carmen instantly recognized that they had been teleported back in the direction of the Mistless Plains. More than a thousand kilometers, passed in a moment. That the Monarch also knew some kind of space magic was something she nor anyone else had expected, and Carmen cursed herself for not having any proper resistance against such attacks.

This was one of her weaknesses... She couldn't do jack-shit against most magical effects due to the way her class and profession worked. Not having any mana did have some downsides.

The Monarch looked her way and flashed a creepy smile. *He wants to make me leave before the rest get here?*

He didn't talk or taunt her. He simply attacked, more or less proving her theory. Mist suddenly appeared behind her, and she was too slow to react to the cut he delivered across her back. The Monarch she had just been looking at dissolved into nothingness. *Mental magic?*

She twisted around to block and found herself faced with three identical Monarchs. All of them gave off power, and when they attacked, she had to block all of them. That was when she noticed they were all "real," to some extent. More clones.

The clones were usually just red... but these weren't, and without spending a long time, she couldn't tell the difference.

It would take the others several minutes to arrive at a minimum, and it didn't look like the Monarch wanted to give her that long. All of the clones began burning with energy as they charged her. Carmen blocked what she could, but it was a losing battle. She was pushed back and took several severe wounds that would be lethal to a pre-system human.

Fuck.

Originally, the fight had seemed to extend into more of a marathon than a sprint... but she couldn't afford to keep a steady pace as things were.

Carmen smashed her fists together and released a shockwave while, at the same time, jumping back. When she landed, she pressed both her fists to the ground and spoke,

"Sacred Battlefield."

A faint pulse went through the terrain, establishing the battlefield, and she felt herself grow stronger. But this was far from enough... so she went all out.

"Regalia of the Fallen."
"Runes of the Valkyrie."
"Exaltation of Valhal."
"Blessed Echo."
"Ruinous Drive."

Golden armor covered her body, and she began burning from the inside. Runes covered her skin, blessing her with power far above what she could usually handle. Skills from both her profession and class working in tandem, making her far more powerful for a short amount of time. The entire summoning process for all the skills didn't even take a second, and by the time the Monarch reached her, the clash was far more even.

On her battlefield, the masking of the clones faltered, and she saw the real Monarch. Her fist clashed with the blade of the

Monarch, and this time she didn't lose out. An explosion rocked the area as the two separated, but Carmen charged again to press the assault.

Usually, it would seem smarter to be defensive, but when Carmen was in this state, she had to fight. Her entire body burned with stamina, and her health depleted by the second. Her only way to remain stable was to both release the energy and lifesteal through dealing damage to her foe.

Carmen attacked the Monarch, who met her blow for blow. She gritted her teeth as her hits were blocked every time, but at least she managed to release her pent-up stamina. She pushed more and got in closer while trading hits. Her fist connected with the flesh of the vampire, and she felt her energy intrude and pulse through his body. In turn, she herself got some health back.

"Truly a warrior of Valhal... Impressive," the Monarch said as he jumped back and pointed towards her to release beams of blood energy.

Her golden armor blocked the blows, and she stormed forth again. The clones attacked her still, but they had trouble breaking through her armor and outmatching her self-healing, meaning she could keep it up for now.

But not for long.

The Monarch was clearly aware of her powers, yet he kept fighting her in melee. For now, she actually had the upper hand, but she felt herself slowly running out of fumes. She had to do something, and quickly. The others were coming. She just had to hold on.

Carmen pulled out as much power as she could and charged for the umpteenth time. Her fist glowed with energy as she smashed it forward. The Monarch smiled and turned to mist at that very moment, but Carmen had expected it.

"Honor's Call."

Instead of teleporting away, the Monarch appeared right in front of her, compelled by some unknown concept Carmen didn't understand herself. It appeared that the Monarch did, but understanding and being able to counter something wasn't the same.

"Fist of Ragnarok."

Space imploded as her fist struck the blocking blade of the Monarch. The crystal sword shattered into thousands of pieces, the energy from her fist penetrating the stomach of the vampire and releasing a massive internal shockwave. Her physical fist failed to penetrate, however.

Right as she finished her blow, her entire arm up to the shoulder exploded in a mix of golden energy and blood. Golden veins spread from her shoulder and down her body. The Monarch was blasted back several kilometers and into a hill that now found itself with a newly made cave.

Carmen quickly used her other hand to take out a special potion she'd had one of the alchemists of Valhal prepare. It contained a golden liquid that made the energy ravaging her insides subside. She would be able to regenerate her arm again in only a—

"You know, this reminds me of a fight I once had."

She hadn't seen him. The Monarch suddenly stood right behind her, the wound still on his body and her energy still pulsing through him. Yet he smiled.

Carmen tried to get away, but her skills were weakening. She only managed to get a few meters away before the Monarch attacked, not giving her any time. Raising her remaining arm, she tried to block, but the vampire didn't let up. Claws tore into her flesh, the wounds not healing as they should.

"I would recommend leaving this system event," the Monarch said as he blasted her with blood energy.

She summoned whatever energy she could muster to block it, but all that did was create another opening. The claw of the vampire flew forward and closed around her neck, forcing Carmen to focus all her energy on strengthening it.

Dark energy spread in her body, and she felt her limbs

become limp. She knew it was a curse and that she had no way to fight it. Carmen cursed both the curse and herself as she resigned herself and activated the Hunter's Insig—

And then she was free. The claw on her neck suddenly let go, and she opened her eyes to see the Monarch gone from where he had been. Now he was flying into the distance—an arrow stuck in the side of his head.

A millisecond later, she saw a figure pass by, surrounded by a mix of green energy she recognized as Sylphie's mixing with pure burned stamina. A crude and wholly inefficient method of boosting the body... but clearly enough. The archer had only appeared before her in a brief flash before he stepped down again and appeared right in front of the vampire, which he proceeded to kick in the head, embedding the arrow further.

She had to admit... that was very satisfying.

———

Jake had to admit that he was kind of miffed. He had baited the vampire so far away, wanting to fight him. Yet the fucker had just teleported himself and Carmen away like an absolute asshole, leaving him and everyone else hanging. A serious dick move, in his opinion.

His Mark of the Avaricious Hunter at least told him where they had gone, and he noticed it was quite the distance. To make it worse, four wayward globes of blood from earlier suddenly transformed into blood clones to get in their way. Jake knew he couldn't stay behind and exchanged a look with the Sword Saint, who nodded.

He also sent the message to Sylphie. While Sylphie was faster than him in a sprint, it was simply too far to Carmen, and he let her know this. She seemed worried, so she did what she could. She used some magic and flapped her wings, and Jake felt a green aura envelop him as the wind around him seemed to give away and even support him. It was like his old bow enchant, except way more potent.

"I'm off!" Jake yelled as he sprinted, only a few seconds having passed since she was teleported away.

Jake used One Step Mile faster than ever before, pushing Limit Break to 20%. He flashed across the rather flat ground of Yalsten, and he even felt how it was easier to travel here than anywhere else. Space was more fragile and bent more than before.

The wind carried him forward, too, making it all easier and faster. The terrain passed him by in flashes, and within only a handful of minutes, he was close. It didn't take much longer before he felt like he was close enough. He took a step that sent him slightly airborne and drew his bow. While still in the air, he nocked a stable arcane arrow and, as time slowed down, charged the Arcane Powershot, his vision amplified just enough to see the head of the Monarch far in the distance.

An explosion ravaged the area around him, but he had barely released the string before he took another step—the just-fired arrow passing over his head as he landed. He kept running and squinted at the Monarch far in the distance. He was holding Carmen by the neck, and Jake reacted.

Gaze of the Apex Hunter activated, and the Monarch froze. The boss vampire was frozen just long enough for his arrow to pierce the side of the vampire's head and blast them away. With another five steps, he appeared right beside Carmen, who was falling limp to the ground. Two steps more placed him right in front of the Monarch, which he proceeded to kick in the head, making the arrow pierce through and out the other side— straight through the brain.

No way he thought it would be lethal... but it had to hurt like hell, didn't it? Besides, poison on the brain was never fun.

Jake wasn't done yet either. He drew his blood-poison- soaked scimitar and cut at the Monarch a few times.

To his credit, the Monarch reacted fast. He used one hand to blast at Jake and the other to pull out the arrow in a pained groan. Jake dodged the blast by using another One Step Mile, appearing right behind the vampire and trying to cut his head off. His scimitar was sadly blocked when he failed to sever the spine, as it had been magically reinforced.

Finally, the Monarch managed to get him off. He grasped the blade and used it to make Jake choose between losing the weapon or being thrown off. He chose the latter. Jake flew in the direction of Carmen and used one Step Mile as he went over to her, as he didn't want to give the vampire any chance to finish her off.

He looked at her form as she kneeled and breathed heavily, her entire body weak. She tried to stand back up, but her legs wobbled and she fell to the ground, her eyes barely open as she tried to stay conscious.

"I believe that is one opponent down," the Monarch said as Carmen lay unmoving due to the curse, now truly forcing Jake to relocate her to relative safety.

CHAPTER 54

TREASURE HUNT: PATHS

J ake stood defensively in front of Carmen as the Monarch looked at him. The others would be arriving, but it would still take a bit. Carmen had closed her eyes, and Jake felt like her energy had become calmer, making him think she had passed out.

"**You have no need for concern,**" the Monarch said casually. "**I possess no desire to slay her— or you, for that matter; I merely need to win and make you leave.**"

"Yeah... don't fault me for not trusting you," Jake answered, totally fine with talking for now. "Also... you said earlier you sealed off the entrances to this realm. Does that mean no vampires escaped Yalsten?"

The Monarch gladly answered, for some reason not in a rush either. Maybe he genuinely wanted Jake to know the answer. Or maybe, just maybe, it was the gaping hole in his stomach with wriggling flesh trying to heal. "**Some did make it out beforehand. Quite a lot, actually. Yalsten also was only one of many places where we vampires lived—just one more sealed off than most others, hence a great refuge and easier to defend from outsiders.**"

"To be honest, I would find it odd if an entire race just died off like that. I have a feeling the system or at least interested parties wouldn't want that."

"I would agree under normal circumstances... but the vampiric race is not a naturally occurring one. It is difficult to say, to begin with, if the system cares for the survival of any race, and as for allies and interested parties... the Malefic Order was one of them." The vampire shook his head.

"Yeah... again, the Order could be filled with vampires, and I wouldn't know. I've never been there or met any members of the Order, for that matter. At least, not any normal members."

"...How has the Chosen of the Malefic Viper never been in the Order or met anyone from it?"

"Eh, it's complicated, but as the universe is newly integrated and all that, I haven't had a chance to go anywhere and have only met him a few times. We do speak quite often, though." Jake didn't really care that much about giving information out.

Jake wasn't leaving the Hunt, so either he would kill the Monarch or the Monarch would kill him. Either scenario would end in whatever he said not mattering. Also... he didn't really care.

"You speak directly with the Malefic One?" the vampire asked after trying to figure out who "him" was, growing more and more confused.

"On a regular basis, yeah. The last time we met in person, it was to do some alchemy and chill together with him and Duskleaf. We had a good time. The time before that, we had beers and talked about life and all that." Jake sensed he was dealing mental damage with every sentence.

The Monarch just kept staring at him, Jake staring back. Carmen was apparently still conscious as she lay there, as her pained face had changed to one very visibly saying, "What the fuck?"

Yeah, he had actually assumed she had passed out. Turned out she hadn't. *Well, then... Nah, it should be fine.*

It wasn't like him and the Viper being buddies was a secret anyway, and he didn't see it causing any problems. Even if it did, he would deal with those problems whenever they arose. There was no reason to make things more difficult than they were. He would just keep things simple and take the complications as they came. Same as always.

Luckily, he didn't have to keep narrating about himself as reinforcements arrived.

Black lightning stuck down beside him to reveal Caleb's arrival, electricity running across his body. The Monarch regarded him as Caleb asked Jake, "What happened?"

"Curse."

Jake didn't need to explain anything more, judging by Caleb's glance. Jake nodded in response, and they moved simultaneously. The brothers went in opposite directions, with Caleb picking up Carmen and Jake engaging the vampire. Not fighting was what Jake would have preferred... but they had both felt it.

While the Monarch may have spoken truthfully about his lack of interest in killing Carmen, he sure as hell did want to kill Caleb. His killing intent, at least, flared as he looked at the younger of the two brothers.

"Just a shot in the dark, but let me guess... the Court of the Shadows were on the anti-vampire side?" Jake asked as he appeared in front of the vampire. He only had his scimitar after the destruction of the Nanoblade, so that would have to do for now.

The Monarch responded by blocking his weapon and pausing, holding Jake in a standstill. **The Holy Tyrant and her slaves, together with the undead, were our true enemies, but the Court of Shadows sure happily took payment from both to speed up the genocide.**

Jake was pushed back when the Monarch got free and tried to turn into mist again, but Jake quickly used Gaze to freeze the vampire for a brief moment. He engaged again, noticing that the Monarch took it relatively slow at the moment. Maybe because of that entire gaping-hole situation in his stomach.

Yeah, that was probably it. Carmen's ultimate attack had left quite the injury, and Jake had to admit it was powerful. Likely as strong as a fully charged Arcane Powershot with an Arrow of the Ambitious Hunter, if not stronger. Which made sense, considering it was a skill that had clearly left her severely drained afterward, while for Jake, it was just a bit of mana and stamina gone.

The wound left by Jake firing an arrow through the guy's head had already healed like it was never there. Probably still did some good damage, but the vampiric race's durability and natural regeneration skills were honestly quite insane.

"It has been a long time—not sure it makes sense to judge the current factions for crimes of the past," Jake argued, mainly just trying to waste time. He had left a Mark on Caleb and Carmen both to keep track of them.

The Monarch held out his hand and released blasts of blood magic, Jake dancing in between them while the boss answered, **"Perhaps, but just as the Will of the True Ancestor echoes true so many eras later, so does the will of Umbra, the Holy Tyrant, or the Blightfather. While the mortals may have changed, and perhaps even the Pantheons underwent a transformation... those ancient gods are still in command. Their power is unshakeable because their will is unchanging in principle. Their paths are set in stone, so to not blame someone for choices made in accordance with their path only shows your inexperience."**

Jake frowned, dodged the final beam, and stopped up. "People do change, no matter how ancient. The gods you know of are now more than tens of times older or something like that. That should be plenty of time for at least minor character developments."

"Hah, truly words of naivety. It surprises me you know so little of how the world works. They became gods *because* they followed their paths. They remain the most

powerful *because* they keep following their path. Their path is the deepest creed they follow, their very fundamental principle of life. Their meaning. If their dedication to their path was so weak that something such as time could change it, they would have never become gods or stayed powerful to begin with."

"Even if a basic principle does not change, so can many other things. There is nuance to everything," Jake countered, more just to argue than anything else. He was out of his depth, and he knew it. He had never understood that paths thing entirely... He was just argumentative.

"The Malefic Viper is a god that believes in freedom through power, that the pursuit of progression and improvement is the only true path of the multiverse. He is uncaring towards most, sees little value in nearly all mortal life, and views those who he deems unworthy as less than insects, not even worth acknowledging their existence. He will stop at nothing to achieve his goals, and while he may show kindness towards those he has shown interest in, that kindness only extends to them and not anyone else he does not view as valuable.

"I would bet that even as his Chosen, the Malefic Viper has no interest or sympathy towards your family, friends, or anyone else. To him, they are insects that will become dust in the blink of an eye, forgotten by both of you. You say he is a friend... If that is so, the only reason is that he genuinely believes you will become a god, hence worthy of being seen as someone of value. Anyone that does not at least strive with all of their heart to attain immortality is but a blip on the canvas of time. Beings that only exist to be forgotten. That is the Patron you serve. You said a long time has passed... but you also know that every one of my words was as true then as they are now."

Jake stood there, taking it all in... and he couldn't really outright dispute anything. He didn't know if what the vampire said was true or not, especially the second half... but the first half sure was spot-on. The Malefic Viper did seem to care little about mortal life, he viewed killing as natural, and he did treat Jake as equal to him in some ways, though Jake wasn't delusional enough to think that wasn't in large part due to his Bloodline and potential.

But this did make Jake think... what exactly was his path? What was something so fundamental to him it wouldn't change? For the Viper, it was apparently all about getting stronger all the time or something like that, and while Jake was on board for that, that wasn't really something he would call his path. In fact, just thinking about his path felt like a waste of time. Because while he did like having some conversation once a while... well...

Caleb was far enough now.

And another person had just arrived.

The old man's hair whistled in the wind as he seemed to almost skate across the landscape. His stance was strong, and some faint energy from the slain clones still remained on his sword. Jake felt Sylphie was also not that far behind... but the Sword Saint was faster.

What was even more surprising was that, clearly, the old man had heard their talk. Either his Perception was stronger than expected, or... Well, actually, the Monarch did kind of project his voice all over. The Sword Saint addressed the vampire's words as he stopped right beside Jake.

"I cannot argue with your view of a path, but to make meaning so static shows a rigid mind. Freedom has many forms, and while I do not know this Viper myself—far less what impact of having walked a path for time immemorial can have—I do know a bit of having walked through life with a single path from start to end. While the fundamental drive and motivation may not change... the person walking it can. His perspective may shift... and his dream be realized through achieving other goals than originally intended." The old man finished with a smile.

Jake looked at the old man and vampire, who stared at each other. One was a vampire with age at least in the thousands, and the other an old human who, even if he was the oldest on Earth, couldn't be more than a hundred and some change.

Yet the Sword Saint gave off the aura of a wise old man far more than the Monarch. *Guess his looks as an old man ain't all for show,* Jake joked with himself.

"The goal is always immortality and godhood. It is power. That is the root of all progress. Protecting your clan or the survival of your race, trying to better the world or bring it to ruin, attempting to become known as a saint or a calamity... In the end, it all returns to power. Without power, nothing can be achieved. All else is merely a justification. Power is the ultimate goal, always. At least, it is for gods or those who reach the truly high grades, for if you do not pursue power for power's sake... what happens when you achieve your goal? When you do save your clan and ensure its safety? What if it dies out due to something you failed to stop? Does that mean you perish with them? Or do you wish to protect your race forever? An impossible path is a way to ruin just as much as a too unambitious one is. No, in the end, the only true path is the pure pursuit of power for power's sake. In your mind, you may view this as false... but my words will only ring true to you when you fail your breakthrough and hit the wall that is your limit."

"Perhaps a path you do not view as worthy is merely one not properly explored," the old man said with a grandfatherly smile. "Power comes in many forms... Do you merely quantify it as levels? Skill rarities? Is there no power in the growth of a group? In the prosperity in your family? In what you build and the legacy that is made to further empower the new generation after you? Perhaps this may not be the path to godhood for the individual... but it may make you a god in spirit when your child, grandchild, or many generations later achieve it, and you will be the one whose shoulder they stood on to reach it.

"I myself have walked this path... for to me, death was merely a fact. In the end, we all die in body, but our souls can attain immortality through history. To become a name that would never be forgotten as long as humanity existed... was the closest to immortality a human could ever come. Some achieved this through good or bad, but all had an impact on the world. They were not remembered for their own power, but for what they built, what they shared, or what they destroyed. Some were monsters, some heroes... but in the end, is godhood not the same? A god has many faces, for, ultimately, they are people. A god that has not left an impact on the world to be remembered by is far less worthy of being viewed as immortalized than a mortal man who will be eternally remembered."

The Monarch looked at the Sword Saint, and Jake just listened. Through it, he kind of understood the old man's philosophy... or perhaps, his path. At least somewhat.

"Words of someone who will forever stay a pathetic mortal."

"Spoken by he who died as one."

The Monarch's smile instantly faded, and Jake just smiled under his breath. That was a damn good burn. One the Monarch *really* didn't appreciate.

"I think it is time to stop wasting any more time."

With those words, the wound left by Carmen healed nearly instantly. The vampire had clearly focused on getting himself fixed up during the conversation. Sylphie, Casper, and even Eron had also arrived during this time. Caleb was still a good ways away, closer to the Mistless Plains and seeking a safe place for Carmen.

The Monarch spread his arms, and the dark red celestial object hanging above began glowing more than before. The light descended towards the many towers spread throughout Yalsten, pulling something toward them. Soon enough, he felt a large blob of blood begin condensing far up in the sky, making Jake guess the Monarch had another trick up his sleeve.

Jake cracked his neck as the old man wryly smiled, chuckling and readying his sword.

While the Sword Saint may have won in the battle of words, it is now time to begin the battle of killing, Jake thought, instantly regretting what his own mind made up.

Alright... that was bad, and I should feel bad... I suck at this...

For some reason, Jake was fairly certain being a wise old master filled with sage words wasn't ever going to be part of his path.

CHAPTER 55

TREASURE HUNT: COUNTERMEASURES

Sven and Jacob stood side by side as healers from both camps surrounded Carmen, who now lay unconscious to preserve her resources and heal faster. She had chosen to pass out, and Jacob had to admit that her perseverance was admirable.

"So?" Sven asked as he stared at the two healers who inspected her.

"The curse is embedded in her veins and throughout her body, both physically and spiritually. It isn't harming her, but..."

"She won't be able to join any more fighting?" Jacob asked pointedly.

"Right," the healer responded with a nod. The other one also concurred, adding, "Trying to heal it as an outsider might do more harm than good, and it looks like it will disappear in its own time within half a day or so."

Jacob sighed. The Monarch of Blood had been a master of curses before his death, so for him to have such means was only to be expected. These kinds of curses were of an incredibly high level, and Earth simply didn't have anyone who could deal with them yet. Moreover, Carmen was an ideal target; she'd used all her temporary boosting skills and was in a weakened state. All

THE PRIMAL HUNTER 5

the curse effectively did was extend that weakened state while amplifying it slightly.

"Do you think they will win?" Sven asked Jacob, a worried look on his face.

Jacob understood... Carmen was the most powerful person from their faction on the planet, and top five overall on Earth. She was powerful, but so were others.

Besides... he knew both he and the undead had more cards up their sleeves.

"I do. Especially if they bring the Monarch back here," Jacob answered, the magic circle they had hidden now finally ready to be fully activated. He had mentioned the circle to Caleb, and Jake's brother had promised to pass it on or lead the Monarch back himself.

Looking out over the Mistless Plains, it was just a slaughter of Vampiric Blood Elementals. A near-endless struggle that seemed to just keep going, the creatures reanimating again and again due to the Blood Moon hanging above. Luckily, they also got weaker every time.

Sven looked out over the area with him and muttered, "If anyone can, it's those two monsters."

Jacob had to agree with that one.

———

The Sword Saint swept his blade across the ground and cut upwards, making the Monarch block. An arrow flew right past the old man and hit the Monarch in the stomach, injecting poison and doing plenty of damage.

Blood magic condensed around the vampire, but the old man responded as curtains of water surrounded him. Each of them reflected the images of the blood orbs, and before they had a chance to attack him, the old man cut all of the reflected images, also making the real orbs disperse.

He smiled and lunged forward, but the Monarch was ready.

His weapon suddenly transformed, and the Sword Saint was forced to retreat as a long spear suddenly stabbed towards him. The Monarch waved his other hand to summon a blood-red crystal shield, then took up a more defensive position.

Jake, who stood behind the two fighting old geezers, took aim once more and fired. The vampire blocked with the shield, also keeping the Sword Saint at bay with the spear.

He shifted things up... Jake thought. He wasn't the most talented when it came to fighting, but he did know that spears tended to be good against swords due to the longer range, especially if one could make sure the other person never got close. If the Sword Saint managed to enter his range, he would have an advantage, but the Monarch didn't let him do that.

Well, normally he wouldn't, but that was where Jake came in.

Jake took a step and appeared off to the side. Two more put him at a ninety-degree angle. He began running as he fired arrows, circling the Monarch, who was dealing with the Sword Saint. The cocky vampire wanted to block his arrows with a shield? Well, that seemed hard to do from behind.

Something the Monarch clearly also noticed when he was hit with an arrow in the shoulder that held the spear. Another arrow came for the back of his head, but the Monarch summoned a helmet of crystal. It was heavily nicked when hit and still rattled him from the impact.

At the same time, the Sword Saint managed to close in and force the Monarch even more on the defensive. The spear transformed again into a sword as he blocked, but Jake also attacked him at the same time, making him take a few injuries here and there.

It seemed to be going well until, suddenly, the Monarch grinned. The Sword Saint cut down, and Jake fired an arrow, and both were surprised when they hit. The Monarch was struck in the back of the head with the arrow, the helmet pierced, and the sword nearly bisected the vampire from the shoulder to the groin.

Yet, just at that moment, Jake's danger sense reacted. "GET BA—"

BOOM!

A shockwave rocked the terrain. The explosion sent the Sword Saint flying back and made Jake summon a barrier of arcane energy in front of him as he was also pushed away. However, the Sword Saint was hit the hardest, and the old man barely managed to stabilize himself before he landed, several wounds now covering his body—all of them pulsing with some odd energy.

Now it was pertinent to mention why Eron, Sylphie, and Casper weren't helping. Well, they were busy. Three new blood clones were now fighting them, but another figure had also suddenly appeared from above. A monstrosity of blood and magic, wriggling and ever-shifting flesh marred its form. It was an absolute monster.

[Blood Abomination – lvl 160]

It was what had been resurrected by the Sanguine's Blood Legacy item from the nine dead Counts of Blood, and the thing that had dropped down from above earlier. It was another unexpected newcomer to mess up their plans, and one the Monarch had clearly been waiting on during their whole speech and path discussion.

Speaking of the Monarch of Blood...

When the Monarch had exploded earlier, he had simply switched places with and detonated a blood clone. He now stood right in front of Casper, who had been dealing with three clones.

Casper reacted fast but was still taken by surprise when the blade dug into his body. He gritted his teeth as the curse energy revolved around him, but the Monarch just smiled, holding out his hand and sending out a faint pulse that dispelled whatever Casper was trying to do.

Just before the Monarch managed to land another hit, his body froze and an arrow arrived. While the Monarch's disappearance was a surprise for sure, it hadn't fooled his Mark, which allowed Jake to adapt instantly.

However, this entire interruption had let the clones run wild. The only positive thing was the obvious lack of intelligence in the Blood Abomination, allowing Eron to handle it alone for now. Perhaps the Monarch had some control over it, but clearly, he couldn't spare the mental focus to do so even if it was possible... until he could, as suddenly the Abomination charged for Jake.

With Carmen out of the picture and Caleb still returning, they were rather short-staffed. Sylphie was helping Eron keep the damn Abomination busy. To call the entire situation frustrating was an understatement, as the Monarch plainly didn't want to just fight Jake... He wanted to kill a select few people, Casper and Caleb among them.

Jake supported Casper as much as he could, but soon the blood clones who'd been fighting his undead pal came for him along with the Abomination, which Sylphie and Eron luckily held back for now. All of the clones were just getting in the way of his arrows after the first one, giving the hulking monstrosity time to arrive. *This seriously isn't good.*

The Monarch had wanted to isolate Casper... and he was doing a pretty good job at it. Repeated blasts sent the undead flying further and further away, while Jake could only try and kill the blood clones as fast as possible.

Luckily, he was soon joined by the Sword Saint, who was back on his feet and engaged the clones. He threw Jake a glance, and with a nod, the Saint engaged the Abomination while Jake fought the clones before he took off to follow the Monarch and

Casper. All he could do for now was hope Casper could hold on until he arrived.

———

Casper concurred... this situation wasn't good. His curse magic was repeatedly dispelled, the Monarch having hidden that ability. He repeatedly summoned his pre-prepared wooden shields, but seeing them breaking one by one made it clear he couldn't hold on for long.

Ultimately, Casper was not a fighter but a trapper. He created pre-prepared tools and traps to battle his foes and take them down, but to do that, it required research. Casper had used these ten days primarily to do the Vaults and spent all time in between preparing for this exact fight.

Several modified Stakes, weapons created from the research of the Pure Ones, traps, devices, shields made specifically to battle the blood energy of vampires... all of it ultimately faltered before superior power. Without Lyra lending him her power, he would have been downed already.

"We need to use it," Lyra stated in his head. Casper groaned as he blocked, sending him flying even further away from everyone.

"If we—" Casper tried to argue, but he was interrupted both by Lyra and a beam of blood that penetrated his chest and sent him tumbling even further back. A follow-up beam nearly severed his arm as he registered Lyra's voice.

"NOW!"

Casper was blasted back once again, and only had time to react because Jake fired an arrow at the Monarch from far off in the distance, forcing the vampire to redirect his attention momentarily. Focusing his energy, Casper activated a seal, and his locket began glowing.

"Blightform."

His flesh melted to reveal white bones beneath, and at the same time, Lyra came out of the locket, her body superimposed upon his. Power surged through Casper as he felt himself transform. This was their ultimate weapon, and their most potent temporary boosting skill.

Soon, all of the flesh on his body was gone, and Casper had transformed into a lich-like creature with ghastly eyes and the blight energy revolving around him, his entire body glowing. When the Monarch looked his way, Casper held out his hand and released a beam of pure blight energy.

The Monarch turned to mist to avoid it, and Casper prepared another attack with the intent to—

"**Ah, blight,**" the vampire suddenly said with a huge smile as he appeared off to the side. "**A potent affinity that is difficult to grasp, even for me... much less you... One used to kill countless vampires.**"

The Monarch made four clones all around him, and they spread out in a circle. Casper tried to release another blast to get them away, but he found an odd barrier covering each of them.

"**Is it not only to be expected that we made countermeasures?**"

All of the clones exploded at once, creating a giant, magical sphere all around him. Casper's eyes opened wide. He tried to release an attack but found his blight magic completely ineffective. Soon after, his vision began blurring as the magic circle truly powered up. Before long, he was entirely blinded.

"*Casper... what's happening? I can't see anything...*"

Casper was truly panicking now. He still felt his body, but nothing else. Blightform made him rely entirely on magical senses, as he'd lost all the usual biological ones, but now it didn't work. Instead, he felt the burning blight on his body suddenly dim as he weakened.

He needed to escape. He tried moving to the side, but he didn't know if it worked. He couldn't feel anything. There was no way of knowing if he had moved or just stayed where he was. There was no way to know anything besides his own dimming strength as the blight energy began burning out.

Blightform was supposed to be their ultimate attack. A skill that allowed him and Lyra to perfectly fuse and temporarily grant Casper powers far above usual, even allowing him to use the blight affinity far more liberally than the few skills he was experimenting with.

Yet all this form had done was make him fall into a trap. The undead had hunted down the vampires in a prolonged war... Perhaps it was foolish to think they had not made up ways to fight it, including barriers and spells explicitly made to counter their magic.

"I'm sorry, Lyra... I didn't see this coming," Casper told her through their connection.

She was no longer able to respond, as she was weakened at an even faster pace than he. He innately felt that she couldn't hold on for much longer, and with her demise, he would most likely die. Perhaps he would have a faint chance of surviving... but that wasn't a life he would want to live.

Only a bit more time passed before Casper cursed loudly to himself, activated his Hunter Insignia, and left the Treasure Hunt. His only recompense was that at least the treasures he had acquired were brought back to Earth safely. He, along with most others, had given their treasures to someone else from their faction during the pre-battle grace period, as they all knew it was a risk to stay.

He had just never expected to be forced to leave like this.

———

An arcane explosion consumed the terrain as the Monarch was pushed back. He summoned orbs of blood to impede Jake, but he merely stepped down twice and appeared off to the side with the first—and right behind the Monarch with the second.

His entire body burned with stamina. He pushed himself even harder than before, his eyes filled with anger and annoyance. The vampire reacted to Jake's attack by summoning a barrier, but Jake's scimitar descended surrounded by dark and arcane mana, and he stabbed through it and into the Monarch.

That was when he felt the Mark of the Avaricious Arcane Hunter he had left on Casper disappear. Momentarily, Jake was afraid that his old office pal had died, but he quickly noticed that wasn't it. Instead, he had just teleported out... which in itself was also enough to piss him off.

The Monarch had managed to get some distance when the damn Abomination and blood clones had impeded him in his efforts to help Casper, allowing the vampire to cast his magic. Jake had only just reached the Monarch again when Casper was encapsulated by the sphere, and the moment he was, the entire sphere disappeared—teleported back to where he had fucking teleported away with Carmen last time. In other words, it was too far a distance, and one that Jake had no way of reaching.

If he did so, Sylphie, the Sword Saint, and the recently returned Caleb would be screwed. The entire situation was so fucking frustrating, as Jake felt like the Monarch actively tried to avoid fighting him in favor of picking off the others.

"Just fucking fight me," Jake growled as he pushed his blade into the chest of the vampire.

The Monarch looked up at him and smiled. **"That wouldn't be in my best interest. I have a mission, same as you."**

An explosion of blood meant to send Jake flying back came out of the Monarch. Jake, however, was done. Scales of the Malefic Viper covered his body as the blood energy washed over him, and instead of blowing him off, he just leaned in closer.

"It wasn't a request," Jake said, infusing even more mana into his presence as mana bolts condensed all around him and the Monarch.

"Truly the Chosen of the Malefic One," the Monarch answered with an impressed tone. **"I admit, I legitimately have no confidence in defeating you. But—"**

The vampire suddenly ripped himself free, allowing Jake's

scimitar to rip through his flesh. Quickly, Jake released his stable arcane bolts. They flew forward, penetrating the body of the Monarch. The vampire took the blows, and his body began glowing red as he sped away far more swiftly than Jake expected.

"—you cannot contain me either."

Jake cursed under his breath, chasing after the vampire who had changed his target yet again—this time going for Caleb, who was helping the others deal with the Abomination. After the Monarch had given the monster new instructions, it no longer bothered only fighting Eron and Sylphie, but had forced the Sword Saint to join in and fight it, with Caleb also coming. He seemed to have done so primarily due to how well Jake was dealing with him.

Caleb, to his credit, noticed he was the next target and reacted instantly.

"Ascension of Tenlucis."

For a moment, the red sky darkened as lightning stuck down, and an all-encompassing pressure covered the area—perhaps the entirety of Yalsten—for a brief moment before all returned to normal.

The only target of the lightning strike was Caleb himself, his form emerged shrouded in it. Yet instead of engaging the Monarch directly, he flew back towards the Mistless Plains. Jake followed close behind while the others stayed to finish off the Abomination.

I fucking hate team battles.

CHAPTER 56

TREASURE HUNT: HOLY BLADE

J acob opened his eyes and exited his brief meditation. He felt the currents of fate, and he knew that the Monarch of Blood was coming towards the plains. Of course, detecting anything was hard with all of the people present in the Treasure Hunt, but he at least could read something that simple.

He used a skill to swiftly contact Bertram and his team, telling them to retreat from fighting the Vampiric Blood Elementals while also tossing a quick message to the undead through tokens they had exchanged. The parties out fighting had a rotation of sorts in place for people to retreat and regenerate, and with Sven and the people from Valhal recently rejoining the battle, Bertram and the others had more space.

It didn't take long for Bertram to make it back, joined by the healer of his party. The swordsman, Maria the Archer, and their caster had stayed behind to finish off some more elementals before returning themselves. But that was fine, for Jacob only really needed Bertram.

"They are returning?" Bertram asked, some concern in his voice.

"Yes, they are. It is time to use the Holy Sword," Jacob stated. His guardian gravely nodded, as he knew what it meant.

They went over to the ritual grounds, where Jacob saw the people who stood around the ritual circle.

"My friends, our time has come," the Augur said as he went into the middle of the ritual and, out of his spatial storage, drew a weapon.

It was a gilded sword that seemed to be made of pure gold. He didn't hesitate to stab it into the ground at the center of the circle as holy energy breathed to life. He hurried out of the circle, then motioned for the ritualists to begin the infusion.

There were fourteen people in total. All of them had barely reached D-grade and, under normal circumstances, would have little reason to remain when they were given a chance to leave the Hunt. They were individuals who had only just reached D-grade through a final push of resources, and many of them would likely never even reach mid-tier of D-grade.

So... this was for the best.

The ritual began with them kneeling. Jacob closed his eyes, summoned his lantern, and held it out.

"Thank you."

One by one, the fourteen ritualists collapsed as the holy energy in the ritual circle intensified. Bertram stood solemnly beside him, Jacob knowing the man disapproved. However, Jacob stayed determined that this was for the best.

Wisps of light came from each of the bodies as they entered his lantern—at least their souls were saved, bound for the Holy Realm where their lives would continue in some form. It was the least they could do for those who sacrificed their lives for the Holy Church.

When the final ritualist lay dead on the ground, the ritual circle collapsed in upon itself. The sword was fully infused and ready. Jacob Identified it and sighed, glad that at least it was a significant success.

[Holy Sword (Ancient)] – A blade infused with intense holy energy, forged by a talented blacksmith with

unquestionable faith in the Holy Church. The sword has been elevated through a sacrifice of faithful believers to infuse the blade with further power and Records. Using the blade will grant the user incredible holy power for a limited time at the cost of their own life. Due to the intense holy energy in the blade, it can only be used once. Enchantments: Holy Ascension.

Requirements: Soulbound.

"I don't like this," Bertram said, vocalizing his distaste of what they were doing.

Jacob understood. It seemed unsightly from the moral perspective of the pre-system world. But... things had changed. Life had less value than before, and sometimes the best destiny was to at least die for the greater good of others.

"Do not speak ill words of those privileged to ascend before others," Noor, the priestess and healer of Bertram's party, said.

"It is fine," Jacob said, soothing her. "The choice was ultimately theirs, the same as the choice is yours if you want to wield the blade or not."

"Not much of a choice when I am the only one who can be resurrected," Bertram countered, but he walked forward nevertheless till he stood before the Holy Sword, ready to claim it.

Jacob conceded that one, as Bertram truly was the only one who could use it, outside of maybe the swordsman Lucian. However, Bertram would undoubtedly be the best, as his Toughness allowed him to wield the Holy Sword longer than anyone else.

Truly, for anyone else to wield it would be a waste, and potentially mean that all those sacrifices had been in vain.

Now, Jacob had considered many times if this was even worth it, much less required to defeat the Monarch of Blood.

To answer the question of whether it was required, the answer was likely no. Jake, the Sword Saint, and all of the others could likely defeat the vampire without the Holy Church even doing anything. However, ultimately, this didn't matter due to the answer to the second question.

Was it worth it? Most definitely.

There were few chances to so directly contribute to the community more than in an event like this in the multiverse. Jacob was fully aware that a single talented person being uplifted was worth more than ten ordinary people getting benefits. In this way, their deaths would directly contribute to Bertram gaining a higher level of contribution against the Monarch of Blood, netting him a better reward, and through that, making the Holy Church on Earth even stronger as a whole.

Reality was simply cruel like that. Jacob—or Bertram, for that matter—didn't have to like it, but they did have to adapt to it. A fact that at least Bertram accepted. It did help that the Holy Church had ways to still keep people alive in some form by allowing them to pass on to the Holy Realm.

His thought process was interrupted when he saw the dark sky in the distance and the approaching aura of the Judge, AKA Jake's brother. Swiftly, he took out a small token and sent a message to the undead faction, communicating for them to be ready.

He then tossed Bertram a look. "The time has arrived."

———

A high Perception stat was great. Jake loved being able to see far away usually, but sometimes it just led to more frustration.

He was flying and using One Step Mile while chasing Caleb and the Monarch, who were both flying at incredible speeds back towards the Mistless Plains. The Monarch was slightly faster and intermittently clashed with his brother, but luckily Caleb could handle himself in his current boosted form.

It also helped that whenever the Monarch did manage to touch Caleb, his claws just seemed to phase through the dark lightning mage, not truly injuring him. Jake was aware this situation was only momentary, and after only a few minutes, Caleb gradually slowed, showing his boosting skill was beginning to weaken.

This did allow Jake to get slightly closer and even fire off a quickly charged Arcane Powershot here and there. His eyes were also hurting from using Gaze of the Apex Hunter, every use of it allowing either one of his arrows to hit or for Caleb to smash the Monarch back a bit with his staff.

Luckily, they soon got close to the Mistless Plains. The Monarch did try to summon a clone or two and send them after Jake, but he just ignored them by flying past or using One Step Mile, showing that the Monarch wasn't the only one who could act like a little bi...

Anyway, when they got close, Jake saw the fighting in the distance between the humans and the Vampiric Blood Elementals. He saw far fewer on both sides, making it clear a lot of humans had either died or been forced to leave due to the prolonged battle.

He also noticed that some Ekilmares had joined in on the fun at some point, but had been swiftly slain. No doubt they had still contributed to the chaos of it all. Honestly, this entire final phase of the Treasure Hunt had just been a fucking mess, and Jake would have preferred to just fight the Monarch alone. But, sadly, things hadn't worked out like that.

Jake kept following and firing potshots, noting that Caleb had slightly changed his direction with a clear target in mind. Frowning, Jake wondered what the plan was... An answer came just a moment later.

A large figure of pure, ghastly light raised itself towards the sky right behind Caleb as he flew by, separating him and the vampire, surprising both Jake and the Monarch. Countless chains suddenly shot out of the hooded phantasmal figure, with the Monarch trying to turn to mist and get away, but at that moment, Jake felt like something had changed in the environment. His One Step Mile failed, and so did the vampire's escape as the chains connected to his body and pierced it.

They didn't appear to actually interact with his flesh, but simply phased through it and held him in place. The Monarch tried to release a blast of energy, but it failed. Before he could do anything more, a pillar of light shot up, this one of pure, holy light.

Jake felt a familiar aura from the light, and a moment later, it subsided and merged with a person who flew upwards. Glowing wings of holy light were on his back, his entire body covered in similarly golden heavy armor. In his hand was a shining blade that made Jake's danger sense react, revealing that the weapon wasn't simple at all.

Bertram was behind the armor, and he swung the blade in an opening attack. The Monarch reacted with clear concern at the approaching figure. Armor of red crystals covered him, and he also summoned a multi-layered barrier as quickly as he could.

However, it all quickly proved futile. The holy blade tore through the barriers and impacted the vampire's armor, sending large parts flying off together with blood and gore. The first slash broke the armor on his chest, the second cut off a blocking forearm, and the third one tore through the shoulder and down to just where the heart was supposed to be.

Every attack released shockwaves of light and burning holy power that ravaged the terrain around Bertram and the Monarch, and even the ground below looked scorched. Every attack was more powerful than Jake's fully charged Arcane Powershots. Jake didn't idle during this time, but instead split his attention. Trying to attack would prove meaningless, but that didn't mean he couldn't prepare. He held out his hand and began channeling Arrow of the Ambitious Hunter, never taking his eyes off the two fighting figures.

Not even five seconds had passed since Jake became aware of Bertram before he noticed something that didn't seem right. The armor on Bertram was already beginning to fade, and when it did so, Jake saw the glowing veins spreading all over his face as the skin around it was flayed.

He is overloading his body...

It was like when Jake had pushed Limit Break far further than ever intended during the fight with the King of the Forest, except with even more potent energy. The holy energy clearly came from the sword, and Jake was absolutely clear that whatever was happening couldn't be stopped. Whoever chose to use that weapon would die doing so.

Bertram didn't seem to let it bother him. He kept attacking, likely due to the bullshit powers of Jacob allowing him to resurrect him. A bullshit combo, actually. The Monarch was lined with golden cuts, his entire body filled with holy energy. For the first time, Jake saw the Monarch truly grow stressed and filled with anger. He bared his sharp teeth and appeared to almost hiss at the golden warrior.

Blood energy exploded out as his hair was raised, and his eyes began glowing an even deeper color than before. The forearm and hand that had been cut off regenerated, and then the vampire attacked back, tearing off a large part of Bertram's armor. Bertram countered by cutting a leg off the vampire, with the Monarch going for even more. The Monarch released a massive beam of energy that cut Bertram apart at the stomach. His legs fell to the ground below, not even able to hit it before the holy energy turned them to nothing.

The man seemed entirely careless as he raised the holy sword above his head. The Monarch attacked again and stabbed a large spear through Bertram's chest just before the already-dying man released the final attack.

"Judgement's Fall."

For but a moment, it felt like the entire Treasure Hunt was enveloped in light. The faint mirage of a six-winged angel appeared behind Bertram. The blade extended as it grew, and the man cut down. Jake didn't see exactly what happened next—

everything flashed, and an explosion of holy light pushed him and everyone else back.

It was like a new sun had appeared, and without his high Perception, Jake would have been blinded. The aura of Bertram disappeared with the arrival of the explosion, his body unable to handle the power he had just deployed.

But...

Light subsided as the sky returned to normal, and in the air, the spectral chains from the undead—as well as all traces of Bertram—were gone. All that remained was a tattered robe with what looked like wriggling flesh within.

For a moment, Jake wondered if the Holy Church had actually managed to do it, but his senses told him otherwise. His intuition once more proved correct when the vampire's form was revealed beneath the robe. He lived, but was far from fine.

A long, golden scar now went from the top of his head and down to his one thigh, crossing over the already-present mark left by Carmen's fist. His entire body was a mess, and he was even weaker than before. Both legs were gone, one arm remaining but dangling uselessly. It was the perfect time to strike.

"Thunderfall of Tenlucis."

At that very moment, a figure dropped from far above. The Monarch barely had time to look up as Caleb descended and passed right through him like a living thunderbolt. A shockwave of dark electricity was released, and Jake once more found himself slightly pushed back.

However, he didn't miss the opportunity to raise his bow and channel Arcane Powershot while flying back. Then, before the blast from Caleb's blow had even subsided, he released his own attack: Arrow of the Ambitious Hunter.

It flew true. The Monarch once more failed to respond, and the arrow sank into his body, sending him tumbling back. Jake had nearly expected a notification from that... but the vampire still lived. He quickly followed up by activating his Mark of the

Avaricious Arcane Hunter charge, making the vampire flash up one more time.

No mercy was shown by anyone else as attacks began arriving from all over the plains. Sultan fired from his ship, and arrows, bolts, beams, and all manners of ranged attacks bombarded the already-battered form of the Monarch. Although individually, most of these were too weak to truly do anything, combined, they still had to add up. Under usual circumstances, the Monarch would have dodged them easily, but he was in no condition to do so currently.

Jake nocked an arrow to keep attacking, then stopped at the final moment. On the tip of his arrow, he saw a reflection of the moon above. He looked up in shock and saw the moon looked different.

An eye stared down upon Yalsten from above.

The eye of the Monarch.

Jake stared back as the red glow of the eye intensified, and the voice of the Monarch of Blood echoed all around him.

"Color of Night."

And the world turned the palette of blood:

Sanguine.

CHAPTER 57

TREASURE HUNT: A FINAL FIGHT

"Iskar, I pass the responsibility on to you," the leader of Yalsten said as the vampire handed him the necklace in his cupped hands. "Know that even if Yalsten is to fall, the Legacy cannot enter the hands of the Church or the undead. No matter what."

Iskar nodded and accepted it. He stared at the beautiful item with the Legacy Blood of the True Ancestor within. An item more valuable than his entire world and the lives of all of them combined. Iskar closed his eyes in reverence, storing the Legacy as he prepared to send it somewhere safe. Even back then, he'd felt its influence on him, but he'd accepted it. No, he'd welcomed it.

The leader never returned after that, slain by the Holy Church in battle. All of the other kings fell one by one, too, leaving only Iskar left to desperately try to save his world. They starved. The Bloodless Night left them all starving, forced to feed to survive. He tried to fix it... but the ritual failed. In the end, he was forced to seal off his own world and kill his own kin to keep them hidden.

All to protect the necklace.

He was brought back to the present, the memories flashing through his mind. Reminding him of why he was there.

Iskar, the Monarch of Blood, stood in what had once been Yalsten, a massive world filled with billions of proud and powerful vampires, now crumbling to nothingness all around him. He stared up at the bloody moon. He felt his own weak body breaking like the world around him. Iskar wasn't sure if there was much sense in struggling... but he had a task. A final mission entrusted to him by the True Ancestor. Or was it simply the system that made him think so?

He didn't know, and it didn't matter. The Monarch smiled as pain ravaged his body, and he spoke without a single trace of regret in his mind.

"Color of Night."

———

Jake had felt it before. For a brief moment, an aura dominated the entire Treasure Hunt—one so powerful none of them could resist. Below, the Earthlings fell to their knees against their will, the pressure not allowing them to fight back in any way.

He saw Jacob, all of the members of the Noboru clan, and the surviving fighters all fall down. Only two humans stood against the pressure: the Thayne brothers. Jake felt the aura was similar because he had felt it many times before.

It was the aura of a god.

Yet as soon as it appeared, it was gone again. But the echoes of what had been remained. Also, while the aura had disappeared... the true effect of the skill had not. A dark red color hung over everything, bathing the landscape in the sanguine light of the moon.

Then Jake felt something was off. His scales absorbed mana, despite him not feeling like anything attacked him. He wondered what was happening until he heard screams from below. Looking down, he saw several of the weaker people in the larger camps fall to the ground with blood seeping out of their skin.

Within a few seconds, it multiplied. The humans began bleeding from every orifice and even out of their skin, sending tens of thousands of tiny droplets flowing upwards. Even the undead began letting out black blood.

It wasn't only the humans and Risen who were affected. The remaining Vampiric Blood Elementals also began dissolving as they floated upwards, some of them heading towards the moon and some towards the Monarch of Blood.

Like hundreds of rivers, the blood funneled into him and the moon. Humans below began making barriers, and the Holy Church activated some magic to try and defend themselves, but it was far from enough.

In less than a minute, hundreds of D-grade humans died or fled the Treasure Hunt—more than eighty percent of those who remained. Jake looked down and saw Neil and his party together with Sultan, and he hurried over to them as he saw Silas struggle.

He had a strong feeling attacking the Monarch or the moon would be completely useless right now, so he chose to help those from Haven instead. Jake touched down, spread out his hands, and infused a bit of mana into his presence as he erected an arcane barrier in the area. It was a bubble more than ten meters across, and in not that long, it filled entirely with people who took refuge under it—courtesy of Neil teleporting them in to save them.

Caleb had flown down to the rest of the Court and protected them, but soon enough, Neil also teleported them over. Reika, too, activated a powerful barrier to defend herself and others. People everywhere around the Mistless Plains did what they could to survive, but the death toll was still high.

Jake sent a message to Sylphie and got confirmation that she and everyone else at the Abomination were fine. The Abomination had apparently gone into some berserker rage as the red light hit it, and she, the Sword Saint, and Eron were handling it.

Honestly, it was expected, as all of them were powerful enough to fight the magic currently deployed by the Blood Moon. Especially Sylphie and her overpowered Green Shield thing.

Seconds passed as the Treasure Hunters on Earth simply tried to survive. On the other hand, the Monarch began rapidly regenerating his broken body using the blood channeling into him. If Jake's guess was correct, the moon absorbed the blood to keep the spell going, and with the supply cut off, it would soon be forced to end.

The only problem with this was the many blood elementals still being absorbed even after all the affected humans were either protected, dead, or teleported out. A few humans here and there still failed to keep up their defenses and found themselves exposed, but it was few and far between, and they often just teleported out right away using the Hunter Insignia.

Jake just looked on while maintaining the barrier. He didn't need it himself, but he was fine keeping others safe. Could he have perhaps interrupted the regeneration or something like that? Potentially... but he didn't want to. He wanted to see what this final skill or ritual or whatever it was called was all about.

Finally, after the entire thing had been going on for over five minutes, the Blood Moon began dimming slightly, and the constant funnel of blood from the elemental finished, as there was nothing more to feast on. The forces of Earth were in shambles, and just when Jake thought it was over, the eye on the Blood Moon opened as wide as it could, and the iris became a narrow slit.

A new kind of pressure appeared, pressing down on everyone within Yalsten. A mix of magic and the same god-like presence as before.

Jake dispelled his arcane barrier, and those around him looked sluggish and barely able to move, many even falling to their knees once again. He exchanged a glance with Caleb, who stood beside him. His brother breathed heavily, as his boosting skill had long expired.

"I'm spent," he said with a smile.

Nodding, Jake stepped forward and summoned his wings. The pressure didn't affect him, and even if it could, his scales would have kept it out. He felt the blood magic inherent in the pressure and how it was almost physical. It was almost as if people's own blood made everyone heavier, making only a handful of humans able to move. Even Jacob was completely downed.

Jake jumped and flew upwards. He stopped in the air not far from the Monarch. The vampire stared up at the Blood Moon, not even looking his way as he spoke to Jake.

"I made a lot of mistakes, you know?" he said, and for the first time, his voice was not infused with Willpower. Instead, he just spoke normally, and his voice sounded far less imposing than before. He finally turned to Jake, continuing, "Some parts of me think that the True Ancestor knew a day like this would come. Everything I have done, I did to fulfill the mission I had been given. It took far longer than anyone could expect back then... but I believe that today, I will finally complete that mission."

At the same time, Jake got the message that the Sword Saint was coming back towards the Mistless Plains together with Sylphie. The Abomination had collapsed along with Eron the moment the pressure appeared, with only Sylphie and the old man able to keep moving.

It was odd. Jake was completely unaffected, and below he saw Carmen sitting up, unbothered, with a sweat-covered Sven right beside her, unable to do anything. Reika also managed to stay upright, but everyone around her couldn't. It wasn't a scale of suppression... it was either-or. Jake felt absolutely nothing.

"What is this pressure?" Jake asked the Monarch, genuinely curious.

The Monarch smiled and gladly explained, "Judgment. Only those deemed worthy can stand and keep participating."

Jake looked up at the moon. "A test of some sort related to the Legacy of Sanguine?"

"Exactly," the vampire confirmed. The two of them stood there a bit longer, just staring up the moon, neither in a rush to begin what would no doubt be the final battle.

"All those unaffected are worthy, and I must say I am surprised there are so many. You being worthy is obviously no surprise, but for three more to be too? Truly a surprise. Ah, with two more coming, it seems."

Jake had obviously already felt them. The Sword Saint and Sylphie reached his side not long after, the Monarch not making any moves. He looked wholly healed, with not a single wound left from their fight... but Jake felt he was weaker. Everything had taken a toll. Jake and the Sword Saint weren't at full power, either, but they weren't that weakened, just a bit tired and potentially low on resources. However...

"Sylphie," Jake said to the bird.

She looked at him and understood. At this point, she was only posturing, and Jake knew she was barely running on fumes. Sure, she had a few good attacks left in her, but he would rather not risk it. Sylphie, a bit reluctantly, jumped off his shoulder and flew down to where Carmen was. Caleb had also joined her, as pretty much all the surviving humans had sought out the same area. None of them could fight, and even those who could stand knew they couldn't truly interfere.

Jake saw the Sword Saint throw a glance down to Reika. Jake agreed. While she was strong, this wasn't a fight she could join.

The Monarch approved of their decision, it seemed, as he summoned his blade and took a defensive position. "Come. Let us finish this."

Both humans took a step at that moment. One of them flew forward, his sword brandished and ready, with the other drawing a bow while teleporting backward and nocking an arrow. Jake took aim and fired, but the Monarch ready. Blood magic condensed in front of him to block it, and he also moved his blade.

The Sword Saint and vampire exchanged several blows,

seemingly even. Jake broke the balance as his arrows flew in, hitting the Monarch or forcing him to divert his attention and block. Black curse magic began revolving around the Monarch as he summoned the otherwise mostly unfused school of magic.

Black tendrils spread all around him, aiming to infect both Jake and the Sword Saint. The old man spun his blade, summoning planes of water that functioned like shields. When the tendrils touched the water, they simply sank into it as though the thickness of the water was far more than it was.

Jake, on the other hand, just teleported away from them, and those he didn't view as worth dodging, he tanked with Scales of the Malefic Viper. He had feared for a moment the scales wouldn't block curses, but that didn't appear to be a problem with the legendary version.

Blood clones then appeared, followed by a lot of the other usual tricks. Some of them flew for Jake while some stayed at the Sword Saint. Shooting them down one by one, Jake also assisted the old man by bombarding the clones around him.

Their teamwork didn't rely on them knowing how to work together, but on trusting each other's strength. Jake felt like he understood the Sword Saint well enough despite them having interacted so little. Because even if the old man talked about responsibility and how he did everything for his clan... Jake knew.

The old man enjoyed it. Perhaps not as much as Jake, but the Sword Saint just loved fighting.

That gleam in his eye whenever he clashed with the Monarch, the faint smile that he failed to suppress when the vampire managed to block his blow and counterattack... It was unmistakable. He could swear up and down how everything was for others, but Jake would call bullshit on that any day of the week. The old geezer was a battle junkie, pure and simple.

Jake also grinned as the two clones made it to him, both wielding their weapons. Jake's danger sense activated just before one of the clones exploded, while the other one dove through the explosion to attack Jake. In the distance, another clone exploded too. This time it included a teleport. The Monarch appeared right in front of Jake, his blade gone and claws at the ready.

Back at the Sword Saint, the old man had been ready and, unlike last time, managed to cover his body in a faint layer of water, taking the brunt of the impact. Another clone came for him, making him unable to keep up his assault on the true Monarch right away.

Not that Jake needed it. The claw of the Monarch tried to pierce Jake's chest, but he blocked it with his scimitar while quickly depositing his bow. With the other hand, the Monarch grasped Jake by the shoulder, with Jake also grasping the vampire in kind.

Leaning in, the Monarch tried to bite Jake, but he blocked by raising his arm, allowing the vampire to bite down on it. Jake, without thinking, also bit into the arm holding him. He felt pure vital energy draining out of him along with his blood, but he swiftly responded by channeling mana into Blood of the Malefic Viper.

At the same time, he pumped in venom with his own canines, courtesy of Fangs of the Malefic Viper. Jake had to admit, at that very moment, it would be hard to say who was the vampire and who was the human. However, one thing was clear... the Monarch was the first one to stop. Not because Jake was winning out, but because an old man with a sword tried to cut off his head from behind.

Jake tried to keep him still, even using Gaze of the Apex Hunter, but the Monarch managed to wrest himself free through a combination of pure physical power and blood magic. Jake was sent tumbling back as the Monarch barely managed to duck as a sword flew overhead, cutting a bit of his hair off.

Using the given space, Jake reequipped his bow and continued his ranged assault. The Sword Saint was now pushing the Monarch again as their melee brawl continued. Jake and the old man exchanged a quick glance, as it was clear they were both enjoying themselves, and amazingly enough, even the losing Monarch didn't seem the least bothered.

Below, everyone just stared on as the two most powerful people on Earth battled the Monarch with a clear advantage. Jake was tired, and so was the Sword Saint, but the Monarch was also far from healthy. The humans had spent a long-ass time with boosting skills active, and the Monarch had taken enough blows to kill someone like Jake tens of times over.

In the end, the three monsters battled as Yalsten crumbled around them, all of them having the times of their lives.

Twenty minutes after the final phase began, deciding the winning side couldn't be more straightforward. Jake and the Sword Saint truly proved themselves the two most powerful humans on Earth.

CHAPTER 58

TREASURE HUNT: VANITY & PATIENCE

The Monarch stumbled back, four arrows in his chest and a newly made deep cut that nearly severed one of his arms. He reacted by pulling the arrows out and tossing his sword to the other hand as he barely managed to block a blow from the Sword Saint.

His movements were slower, and he didn't heal as fast anymore. Every action looked draining, and Jake felt how tired the vampire was. However, that didn't mean he stopped as he and the Sword Saint kept pushing the Monarch repeatedly, making the wounds accumulate.

Everything had been pulled out at this point, and the Monarch was clearly out of tricks. At least it seemed so. Jake and the Sword Saint also weren't at their full either, far from it, but they had already won several minutes ago. All three of them knew it.

An understanding had been reached, and the Monarch got the final fight he had wanted.

A final clash sent them flying away from each other, and the Monarch stopped in mid-air. His stance made his exhaustion evident, and anyone could see he was on his last legs. Yet, a smile remained on his lips as he chuckled.

"I genuinely thank you... I never thought I would ever get a chance to experience something like this ever again when I entered slumber," the vampire said as he made a slight bow towards Jake and the Sword Saint.

His body began flaking as his skin peeled off, revealing glowing red energy beneath. At first, Jake thought it was his body had run out of energy to sustain itself, but that was over-turned as he felt the Monarch's aura spike.

"Now, if you will allow me a final moment of vanity."

Before Jake or the old man could react, the vampire turned into a blood-red mist and appeared down below in the midst of all of the remaining humans. Jake had a very bad feeling and was about to use Gaze as suddenly the Monarch teleported again – taking every single remaining member of the Holy Church with him, including Jacob and the party members of Bertram. In the final moment, before he disappeared, Jake had placed a Mark on Jacob.

Jake felt his Mark reappear several hundred kilometers away, only to disappear a second later. Jacob's disappeared just a moment before that as he no-doubt left the Hunt. As for the Monarch's Mark, it disappeared not because the Monarch had dispelled it... but because he died.

You have slain [Monarch of Blood– lvl 170] – Bonus experience earned for killing an enemy above your level

* 'DING!' Class: [Avaricious Arcane Hunter] has reached level 141 - Stat points allocated, +10 Free Points *

* 'DING!' Race: [Human (D)] has reached level 136 - Stat points allocated, +15 Free Points *

* 'DING!' Class: [Avaricious Arcane Hunter] has reached level 142 - Stat points allocated, +10 Free Points
*

> ***'DING!' Class: [Avaricious Arcane Hunter] has reached
> level 143 - Stat points allocated, +10 Free Points ***

> ***'DING!' Race: [Human (D)] has reached level 137 - Stat
> points allocated, +15 Free Points ***

The levels came in as confusion struck him for a brief moment. At least that is until he saw the red light in the distance.

An earthquake hit the entire Treasure Hunt as space shattered, and a massive shockwave of pure energy washed over him and everyone else present. It was by far the most powerful display of power Jake had ever seen by anything since back during the-

At that moment, it felt like so many things happened at once. The notifications from the kill, the shockwave of power, the realization of what the Monarch had done in his final moments, and the feeling he suddenly got from within himself... or perhaps more accurately, what was connected to his inner-self through the mask on his face.

The first thing he addressed was the thing on his face. Jake ripped his mask off as he stared down at it. The only lucky thing was that no one was looking with the Monarch's final moment of vanity taking away all of the attention. He stared down at the mask as he got heard a faint murmur in his mind. A familiar voice he had heard many times before whenever he was too deep in meditation or distracted as he remembered the most hectic fight he had ever been in.

"Patience."

It was a single word, but enough for Jake to go on full alert. Eron had dropped not-so-subtle hints. The description described the King slumbering... but now it was confirmed. The King of the Forest still lived, at least in some form. He identified the mask and instantly spotted the change.

[Mask of the Fallen King (Legendary)] - A mask born from the Records of the one once known as the King of the Forest; a mighty Unique Lifeform that died just as its path began. The mask is made of a wood-like material unique to the lifeform it comes from and does not obstruct vision when worn and regenerates itself from any damage taken. The Fallen King remains within. Enchantments: Living Wood. Passively absorbs mana in the atmosphere, increasing mana recovery rate by a large amount. Increases maximum mana by 25%.

Requirements: Soulbound

"The Fallen King remains within."

That was all the changes to it, and when Jake probed it further, he felt nothing different compared to before. If not for the changed description, he would have been inclined to think that voice earlier was simply his imagination... but something had changed for sure.

Jake wondered why something had happened now, but as he looked back at his level-ups, he understood. The King of the Forest had been level 136. Now, Jake had finally surpassed the level of the first D-grade he had ever killed. He believed that was it, and his intuition was rarely incorrect about such things. His intuition and danger sense didn't give him any negative responses towards the mask either... so he decided to just do what the Unique Lifeform dwelling within his headwear suggested.

He would have patience. Also, there were just too many different things to deal with for now. Hence he just tossed on the mask again and decided to deal with it later after the Hunt. For now, he turned his attention to more urgent matters at hand.

In his final moments, the Monarch had struck back at his hated enemy. With every last shred of his power, he had teleported them away, leaving everyone else unharmed, and detonated himself. It was only a few dozen people, but it was all their elites.

He didn't even bother flying over there as he knew that they had either teleported out or died. That is until he saw a single figure in the distance speed towards the plains surrounded by flames. Jake recognized her as the archer that had been with Bertram, and she flew like a meteor as she crashed down onto the ground. He was impressed she had survived and gotten out and looked down where she had landed. There, he saw her body... which was barely a head and a bit of the upper body. Her entire body was also still on fire.

Just as he considered if he should go help, he noticed that the flames on her didn't seem to injure her. Quite the opposite. They spread as flesh visibly healed, and Jake recognized that she wasn't in need of any help. She had no doubt deployed some very powerful life-saving skill to get her out because even Jake wasn't confident in coming out of that final suicide explosion from the Monarch without heavy injuries. It would likely even trigger his Moment of the Primal Hunter.

Also... for some reason, Jake couldn't help but chuckle a bit under his breath as he thought about the antics of the Monarch.

"Do share?" the Sword Saint asked with an amused tone.

"Just pretty funny the Holy Church did so much bullshit to get good rewards only to get shafted in the end by a miffed old vampire," Jake said with a shrug.

"I guess fate wasn't on their side," the old man answered in a playful tone.

Clearly, the Sword Saint wasn't a huge fan of the Holy Church in principle either. Additionally, the old man had clearly also gotten quite a few levels, so it made sense he was in a good mood. Now, Jake just wondered what would happen next.

Just as the thought appeared, the world flashed again. Jake and the Sword Saint both looked up as they saw the Blood Moon still hang above. Within a few moments, it shrank to nothing but a small blip, and a beam fired down and stopped right in front of them as a system notification appeared.

Quest completed: Fallen Monarch

The Fallen Monarch, given back his true form as a Monarch of Blood, has been slain as the Treasure Hunters stand victorious. Not only was the ancient vampire defeated, but the Treasure Hunters even passed the test of the True Ancestor. His Legacy is now theirs to claim.

Rewards will be given upon leaving the Treasure Hunt.

Due to the destruction of the world, the Treasure Hunt will end in: 9:41:41

Both of them had skimmed the message as the item appeared before them. A simple-looking necklace with a single marble of blood attached. Yet as the two humans stood there, they both felt the pressure from it, making it obvious it was no simple item. Jake naturally Identified it.

[Sanguine's Blood Legacy (Divine)] – A Legacy item left behind by the first-ever vampire and the creator of the vampiric race, Sanguine.

And it told him nearly nothing.

"Does your Identification yield any useful information?" the Sword Saint asked.

"Just that it is a Legacy item left behind by that Sanguine guy," Jake answered truthfully.

"Same as mine then," the old man said.

The two of them stayed there for a while, just looking at it. An obvious question was before them... who should get it?

Below them, the tomb the Monarch had slept in was utterly

destroyed. There was nothing else to be gained from the Monarch, and with the Monarch's self-explosion, there wasn't even any loot from his body to claim. Not that Jake thought there would be anything to begin with. A divine item wasn't a bad reward by itself, was it?

Cutting it in half didn't seem possible either. It looked pretty durable.

"So..." Jake tried to break the ice.

"Quite the conundrum indeed," the old man agreed.

Neither of them made a move to just snatch it up. Jake trusted that the Sword Saint wouldn't do it, and the man extended him the same trust. The problem was... someone needed to. With how the Treasure Hunt worked, anyone could potentially steal it if they delayed.

"I do believe we had a duel planned?" the Sword Saint said as he turned to Jake with his eyebrows raised. "This looks like a good piece to wager."

"Deal," Jake instantly agreed. "Ah, but you can take it for now. Just to temporarily hold onto it."

The old man looked at him and nodded, and at the same time, also waved his hand as items appeared. To his surprise, Jake saw three ancient-rarity coffins and altars, as well as the three weapons from Counts, and even two legendary-rarity items. Clearly gained from Vaults.

"Then you can hold onto my bounty meanwhile. We shall simply reverse the exchange in the event of your victory," the Patriarch of the Noboru clan agreed.

Jake didn't look at all the items as he scooped them up, and at the same time, the old man put the necklace inside his Hunter Insignia. Or at least he tried to, but instead, the necklace reacted as it gave off a faint red light, and a figure appeared in front of it. A very familiar one.

"We meet again," the projected figure said.

"I thought we just killed you," Jake pointedly stated as he stared at the clear visage of the Monarch of Blood.

"Technically, I killed myself. But, I shall admit, I did not predict this even if I perhaps should have. It seems like I was only revived due to the Legacy and my existence is inherently tied to it," the Monarch explained. "The will of the True Ancestor remains even after his demise. By his will, I am to serve as a steward of this Legacy and as a guide for its uses, as well as a teacher for any vampires created from it. Ah, yes, one of the abilities of this Legacy is to allow individuals of the enlightened races to become vampires."

"Oh. Cool, I guess," Jake shrugged, not voicing his thoughts of how much a demotion it was to go from Monarch to steward. Ah, he should totally call him the Steward of Blood now. Also... vampire transformation? Jake had to admit, his interest level in that was nearly in the negative. He gave up becoming a half-dragon thing, so becoming a human with sharper canines didn't seem that attractive. He already had Fangs of the Malefic Viper anyway.

"What causes me to be unable to store the Legacy?" the Sword Saint asked, just taking it all in strides.

"My acceptance. I believe it to be a better outcome if the Chosen of the Malefic One obtains it," the newly named Steward of Blood said.

"Nah, we agreed on betting it on a duel," Jake just explained. "I'll get it if I win."

"I did hear your conversation; I merely disagree with such an approach. The Legacy of the True Ancestor isn't something to be wagered so carelessly and is worth more than-

"As I said, we already made a bet. Besides, would it be that bad if the Legacy goes to someone who beat a Chosen?" Jake cut him off.

"No, but if he chooses to renege on the-"

"He won't," Jake just stated.

"I also find the insinuation insulting," the Sword Saint chimed in.

"See, all in agreement."

With a sigh, the Monarch disappeared, not even bothering to argue with the two unreasonable humans. When the Sword Saint tried to deposit the Legacy this time, it went into his Insignia smoothly.

"We got over nine and a half hours until the Hunt ends," Jake said. "I don't know about you, but I would prefer to not fight while tired as fuck."

Having had Limit Break active at 20% for long over an hour was quite draining. Amazingly enough, he didn't really feel that strained, though. Probably because his body had just gotten a lot stronger, and in general, the strain from Limit Break after reading D-grade was just far less.

"I concur. Let us take this time to recuperate and fight at our best," the old man agreed.

With that in mind, Jake and the Sword flew down to the ground with all of the others waiting. Caleb, Sylphie, Reika, and Carmen were all sitting on the ground, with the rest also sitting down on the bare soil that had once been covered by the blue grass.

All of them looked at the two of them, and Caleb gave him an approving nod. Jake nodded back and scooped Sylphie as she flew over to him. He placed her on his shoulder, and she didn't hesitate for even a moment to rub her head against his cheek.

Jake scratched her little head as he sat down on the ground too. There were only a few hundred people left in the entire Hunt, with most having left earlier during the "Color of Night" spell. Surprisingly enough, many of those had now gotten up and made their intentions clear. They said they would try and go explore a bit more of Yalsten before it totally collapsed.

He himself had no interest as he closed his eyes and began his recuperation process, already looking forward to a nice duel with the old man. Nothing better than celebrating a good fight with another fight.

CHAPTER 59

TREASURE HUNT: LIMIT SHATTER

No set time for the duel had been decided, so for now, they all just sat and relaxed as they healed. Jake shared his potions liberally, and no one tried to start anything. Silas and two other healers even joined in to help set up a ritual to boost everyone's regeneration.

Maria, as Jake learned she was named, also came over after her body was done being healed by her flames. That was also when Jake became fully aware she was the maker of his current bow. She seemed very interested in how he had quote-unquote "fucked it up" with his transmutation.

All in all, it was all a very good time, with many of the strongest people on Earth just sitting together and chilling. Jake learned that everyone was pretty cool, and it helped a lot that he had his brother sitting beside him to make him feel more comfortable with the entire situation.

He had always been a good brother when it came to social situations with Jake. The kind of guy who would deflect topics Jake didn't want to talk about, and would keep a conversation going so it didn't get awkward. Heck, Jake had a long-standing theory that his brother had become so good at dealing with people—and a teacher—from learning to deal with having Jake as a brother.

The humans talked about a wide variety of topics, most prominently the battle with the Monarch and the general state of Earth. It was a bit odd with the Holy Church not present, but perhaps it was for the best. Because a lot of them had some doubts about the large religion's intentions.

The undead were also all gone, aside from two random Risen who hung around for a bit before leaving to try and find a few more treasures. Even Priscilla had left at some point without Jake even noticing. The same was true for the guy called Sven and all of those people. Honestly, for many factions, this final phase of the Treasure Hunt had just been a complete disaster, and they likely praised themselves for at least getting all their treasures out beforehand.

They also began sharing some things the nominal leaders would perhaps not be happy to see shared during this time. Well, some were just sharing stuff without a care—like Eron, who was excitedly talking with Silas and two other healers about how to better heal people and how everyone should focus more on pure healing and less on all that supportive-magic stuff.

Jake didn't have much to share himself besides some tips on alchemy, but it wasn't something that could really be taught effectively with their limited time. The Sword Saint didn't have much, either, besides a few words of wisdom. Again, one couldn't really teach others swordsmanship in a few hours. At least, not without sparring, and sparring would make the entire restoration process wasted. All of them were dealing with backlash from boosting skills, after all. Well, *they* were. Jake, right now, was just focusing on restoring his resources.

Speaking of boosting skills... Carmen, who had been blessed by the presence of Sylphie in her lap, turned to Jake, as she was allowed to scratch the small hawk.

"You got Limit Break, right? What rarity?" she asked curtly.

She, Jake, and the Sword Saint had ended up being left alone as other people spread out and went away from them. Some had left to get more treasure themselves or were just sitting a good distance away.

Jake looked at her, wondering what she was getting at. He had a feeling she already had a good idea as he answered truthfully, "It is, and it's at rare rarity."

"I figured," Carmen said with a smile. "Honestly, that a skill like Limit Break even has a rare rarity is a damn tragedy. It's basic as fuck. When'd you get it?"

"During the tutorial, so quite a while ago," Jake once more answered truthfully.

Carmen turned her attention to the Sword Saint. "Hey, your boosting skill is an upgraded version of Limit Break, right? It seems quite a lot better and far more controlled. Really playing into that entire water theme you got going on."

The Sword Saint simply nodded in acknowledgment.

"What I am trying to say is that you should seriously consider getting that shit upgraded," Carmen said, turning back to Jake. "I am sure you've noticed by now how you can easily handle it even at the 'unsafe' level. That unsafe level is where your body is not taking any damage, but with a high enough Toughness, you can push it even beyond the twenty percent. Of course, it would be better to improve and not use stamina so crudely."

Jake looked at her for a bit, having not expected the unsolicited advice... but he appreciated it anyway.

"What would you recommend I do? I honestly haven't experimented as much with stamina as I should." In truth, it did feel a bit embarrassing to be called out like that.

"Well, first of all, do you have any other boosting skills interacting within the same archetype?"

Yeah, he didn't really get exactly what she meant by that but made a guess. "No, my only real boosting skill is Limit Break. Outside of weapon skills, of course."

He considered if he should mention his Big Game Arcane

Hunter, but decided not to, as he didn't think it was the same as Limit Break in any way. Sure, both gave stats, but he still found them very different. Primarily because the Big Game skill didn't use stamina—or any resources, for that matter.

"Then you really need it upgraded," Carmen said with a nod. "Boosting skills like Limit Break are the most fundamental kind there is, which means you can't get something to fit in the same place. Like... you can't have two skills that summon wings at the same time, or at least, you need some special stuff to make that happen, and stuff like Limit Break is the same. So, yeah, if you don't upgrade it yourself, you need to either waste a skill selection on it to get it upgraded or be stuck with shit."

Jake nodded along. He got that part. Getting two skills that did the same thing rarely worked. It was like wearing two hats at once or, as Carmen said, trying to summon two wings out of the same place on the body. It just didn't work, and the system wouldn't offer a skill to do that by default.

He brought up his current version of the skill and read it over.

[Limit Break (Rare)] - Sometimes, one needs to go above and beyond. Break your limits, temporarily increasing the effect of all stats at the cost of increased stamina consumption. Increase by up to 10% for double stamina consumption. Increase by up to 20% for quadruple stamina consumption, with the Hunter afterward entering a state of weakness based on Limit Break duration and magnitude. Increasing by more than 20% will lead to severe consequences.

Jake hadn't thought much about the skill, as it was still good. A 20% boost in all stats was just awesome, and it naturally scaled with him. It had been super tiring to use when he first got it, and he sometimes took a bit of damage from overstraining himself. That strain was completely gone by the end of E-grade, and after D-grade, he could use it at both 10% and 20% without any issues. Even the period of weakness was often a short one. This time he had used it for well over an hour, and now, less than an hour later, all the weakness had left his body.

"Tips for upgrading it, or just general tips for stamina usage overall?" Jake asked her. He had seen her fight, and she was clearly quite good at it.

"I am interested too. Also, young lady, if I may ask, you do not possess any mana anymore, do you?" the Sword Saint asked.

"No, I don't. I made it all into stamina after I reached D-grade," she shared openly. "Does have some drawbacks, but it also makes all of my stamina more potent and gives me a way bigger pool in return, so totally worth it. I didn't really do anything with my mana anyway."

Jake nodded along. That actually made sense in retrospect. He hadn't detected any mana from her, but he guessed that could just be because she didn't really use it during combat. That she didn't have the resource at all hadn't crossed his mind. He did wonder if it didn't lead to a lot of problems, but he assumed there were ways around everything. Maybe her stamina worked a bit like mana now when infusing it into items to bind them? Or did she transform it into mana? He knew one could do that.

"Anyway, for stamina use," Carmen began, regarding Jake and the Sword Saint, "have you two done any proper martial arts before the system? Well, you have, old man, but how about you?"

"I did archery," Jake answered.

"Alright, then those Powershots of yours make way more sense. You know how to properly use your upper-body muscles for shooting a bow, but you are utterly clueless about how to use your entire body. Limit Break just circulates stamina at a faster pace where it is already going anyway. So it is just brute-forcing a boost, and it is damn ineffective and wasteful."

Jake once more felt attacked but didn't really disagree with anything. The way he controlled his stamina during both Infused Powershot and Arcane Powershot was far more effective and controlled than during Limit Break. Limit Break was just him speeding it up and having it go real fast without giving it a second thought. It was a switch he flipped.

"On the other hand, the old man has infused clear intent into his stamina," Carmen kept explaining. "It is more gentle, probably with some form of water affinity merged into it, or at least something mimicking the effects, making it not cause the same toll as it passes and making it flow faster and more naturally. Been told about such an approach before, and it's a real good one.

"Your body is stronger than his, so I would advise you to first refine the basics. Optimize the flow, direct it more, compress it, avoid unnecessary flow, and maybe speed it up a bit; you can then work on more complicated improvements. Find a balance where you maybe lose a bit of health and be fine with it. Just push it to the limits of what you can handle for now. Should get you the Limit Shatter skill, which is just a better version."

Nodding along, Jake took her words in. The Sword Saint also seemed to be in agreement with what she said as he added, "Recall how your body moves as you battle. The places where the stamina passes are the most important parts and should be focused on. Control the ebb and flow as you master your inner self."

Mentally taking notes, Jake took it all in. He tried to focus a bit on his internal energy and moved it around his body. He hadn't really done it much himself outside of using Limit Break, as he quite frankly had some bad memories from it. The first time he tried to freestyle it, he'd ended up blowing off an arm, after all, and full-body stamina control seemed like a good way to make himself pop like a blood balloon. Perhaps that fear was unneeded and had mattered more back when his body was far more fragile.

A few hours had passed since the Monarch had "died," and

Jake was more or less fine now besides his still-low resources. Hence, he was fine doing a bit of experimenting. He activated Limit Break, and the energy began moving. He entered a half-meditative state as Carmen spoke,

"Now focus less on speed and more on control. Make it denser and lead it where you need it most. Focusing on where your muscles and bones are located tends to be the most effective. It may take a while, and moving around while doing it tend to be—

Skill Upgraded: [Limit Break (Rare)] --> [Limit Shatter (Epic)]

Jake's entire body exploded with stamina as the dust around him parted. It felt like his body was faintly tingling, and he noticed how he lost a health point after a few seconds, proving he had struck a balance of sorts.

The people around him just looked at him. Carmen looked weird, the Sword Saint began chuckling, and Sylphie looked like it was the most natural thing in the world.

"That was easier than expected," Jake commented as he got used to the feeling.

It really had been easy. He just activated Limit Break, directed it himself a while, and then pushed it over 20%. It quickly climbed to 25%, and then around 30% before his danger sense tossed him the slightest warnings, making him instantly stop the increase and search for a new equilibrium. He compressed it a tad here and there and took some inspiration from Powershot, and then it just clicked in place. Then again, reaching an equilibrium was something he had gotten quite good at, considering his entire arcane affinity was created by combining destruction and stability and balancing that.

With that done, he had gotten the notification, and he quickly checked it and saw the expected.

[Limit Shatter (Epic)] – Go above and beyond as you shatter your limits. Elevate yourself, temporarily increasing the effect of all stats at the cost of increased stamina consumption and straining your body. Increase by up to 15% for triple stamina consumption. Increase by up to 30% for six times the stamina consumption, with the Hunter beginning to take damage that worsens with prolonged use and makes them enter a state of weakness based on Limit Shatter duration and magnitude afterward. Increasing by more than 30% will lead to severe consequences.

Carmen kept looking at him for a moment. "Honestly? Fuck you."

"What?" Jake asked, confused.

"Just..." Carmen looked more grumpy than usual. "It normally takes just a tiny bit longer, but fine, I guess it's to be expected of the oh-my-god-he-is-so-cool Chosen one."

"Sorry?" Jake awkwardly apologized.

"No need to apologize; the vice of others is no fault of yours," the Sword Saint said, getting a glare from Carmen. "I do not doubt your body had already acclimated to the state of Limit Break long ago, making you prime for an upgrade. Often merely bringing attention to a blind spot is all it takes to get the final push when one is already at the precipice of enlightenment— only a slight nudge, all that is needed for a major breakthrough. It is like this everywhere."

That last one saved it a bit. Carmen nodded and agreed, "Yeah, I guess you were pretty much on the crux of the upgrade anyway."

"Still, I owe you one," Jake promised.

"I may just hold you to that. I do have a certain something I could use a hunter for." She wasn't willing to share more there and then.

They kept talking, sharing things that could potentially help the others. Jake gave a few pieces of advice on things like mana control and even the application of Willpower through most of one's actions. Sadly, he really didn't have much to teach about his combat-related skills, as that area was just a bit too unique and suited to him specifically. It was all so heavily rooted in his Bloodline, and it was hard to tell someone that the best way to dodge an incoming weapon was to just not think about dodging it and let your body react instinctively.

Carmen especially wanted some tips, as while she was happy tanking blows from most opponents, cases like fighting against the Monarch required dodging. Jake just said that it wasn't something he could really share, as it was an ability he couldn't teach anyone. Both she and the Sword Saint took his word for it.

As they got talking, the Sword Saint asked Jake about his weapon that had broken during the fight. Jake took out the remaining pieces of the Nanoblade, the handle and most of it still intact, but the blade itself broken. It sucked for sure, and he hoped Arnold could help him fix it. He really liked it.

"Do you not need a second weapon?" the Sword Saint asked. "You could simply use one of the Count weapons, could you not?"

"I guess I could," Jake agreed. It didn't feel as good as the Nanoblade, and it wasn't like Jake *needed* to dual-wield, as having a hand free for magic and other uses was quite handy, but he did also like two weapons.

He took out the Count weapon he had fused from three of the rare weapons to get a feeling for it in his hand. The Sword Saint and Carmen both looked at it before Carmen commented,

"Why haven't you fused all nine of them yet?"

Jake was about to answer that he could always do that later... until he Identified it out of habit and saw that last clause.

[Count's Vampiric Transforming Blade (Epic)] – A weapon created by fusing three weapons wielded by Counts of Blood, all of which have been soaked in the

blood of countless enemies throughout the ages. Crafted using a special type of steel, the blade can absorb the life-force of Vitality-based lifeforms to repair itself. The combined Records of the three weapons have allowed the blade to evolve and transform even further, allowing it to steal a portion of the lifeforce of anyone injured as well as change form between a sword, a dagger, and a rapier. This blade was originally crafted in a set of nine using the unique environment of the hidden world, and can absorb the weapons of other Counts of Blood to enhance itself. Three have now been fused, and six remain. Note: This functionality is only available within the Treasure Hunt area and will disappear once the event concludes. Enchantments: Hemoabsorbant Self-Repair. Vampiric Weapon. Transformation.

Requirements: Lvl 130+ in any humanoid race.

It could only be done within the Treasure Hunt area.

Jake looked at the Sword Saint and saw the old man look away, showing the faintest level of embarrassment.

"Well, because we wanted to fuse it after regenerating a bit, and—"

"You forgot?" she asked, looking between Jake and the old man, who still stayed silent.

"Yeah..."

She just blinked at him.

Anyway, weapon fusion time!

CHAPTER 60

TREASURE HUNT - THE DUEL BEGINS

In Jake's defense, he had a lot of other stuff to deal with rather than upgrading a weapon he didn't really plan on using anyway. It wasn't like he'd had all nine weapons before a few hours ago. Besides, the divine-rarity necklace kind of took away all other attention.

Now, while he was sitting around and waiting anyway, it was a great time to merge them. With the Sword Saint and Carmen observing, he took out the Count weapons one by one. He had a total of seven, as he had merged three into one already.

First, he tried to merge the other six into the upgraded one but got no response.

It can't be.

He then merged three of the weapons, creating an epic-rarity version. He repeated this and now had three epic-rarity weapons.

For real?

Putting together the three epic-rarity weapons, they all reacted by melting into black metal.

"A bit cliché, isn't it?" Carmen commented after the three weapons had all turned completely into liquid metal and blended with each other to form something new, its aura also growing.

"Totally," Jake agreed. Nine turns to three, and three turns to one weapon. It was like another damn video game. Well, perhaps that was only to be expected, coming from vampire Counts with terrible boss dialogue.

The merging process was smooth, and soon the process stopped, the metal assuming a more stable state. The weapon now gave off a powerful aura, and Jake had to admit it was likely the most powerful weapon he had ever seen. However, it didn't resemble a blade anymore; it looked more like a black metal stick. Not a staff, either, but a twenty-centimeter-long stick. It wasn't even thick.

Jake used Identify on it together with the two others.

[Vampiric Chimera Weapon (Ancient)] – A weapon created by recombining the full Chimera weapons once wielded by Counts of Blood, all of which have been soaked in the blood of countless enemies throughout the ages. Now that it is whole once more, it still hungers and seeks to grow. Crafted using a special type of steel, the weapon can absorb the lifeforce of Vitality-based lifeforms to repair itself. Allows this weapon to steal a portion of the lifeforce of anyone injured by its attacks. Can change form between various weapons. Enchantments: Hemoabsorbant Self-Repair. Vampiric Weapon. Chimeric Transformation.

Requirements: Lvl 150+ in any humanoid race.

Oh, so it's like the Omnitool, but a weapon? Jake thought as he read it over. It looked all nice and dandy until he got to the last part about the requirements. He needed to be level 150 to use it.

"Looks cool, I guess," Carmen commented again.

"Indeed a peculiar tool," the Sword Saint agreed.

"Yep," Jake said, putting it back into the Hunter Insignia. It looked like he would be stuck with only the scimitar against the Sword Saint in their duel anyway.

"Can't use it?" Carmen asked as she saw him put it away.

"Not 150 yet," he answered truthfully.

"Oh."

She looked at him up and down again. "I kind of assumed you would be around there. Wait, am I higher level than you?"

He quickly identified her.

[Human – lvl 136]

Jake shook his head and hid his smile under his mask while answering, "Nah, you still got ways to go."

"How many?"

"Oh, plenty."

Sylphie looked at them in confusion, flapping her wings and making screeches and odd gestures as she formed constructs of mana. Jake quickly tried to tell her to not blow his cover, but it was too late, as Carmen had understood what Sylphie tried to communicate. On that note, who the hell had taught his bird to summon green mana constructs, much less the numerical system!?

"You're one fucking level above me, aren't you?" she said, glaring daggers at him.

Jake just looked at Sylphie, who was rapidly switching between being confused and meek as she flapped her wings to make all her mana in the air disappear. "Little traitor. I'm gonna tell your mom and dad when we get home."

"Hoh," the Sword Saint laughed, joining in with a jovial mood. "Since we are sharing, then I appear to be lowest among us at 135. Seems like I cannot keep up with you youngsters at all."

They kept chatting for a while, regenerating and exchanging pointers. As time passed, Reika and Caleb also joined them, with even Maria joining in later on. She was especially interested in asking Jake questions about Haven and his city.

"If I may ask," Caleb said as he turned to Maria, "why did you choose to join the Holy Church despite being associated with a god that isn't?"

"Because I met them first, and it made sense at the time," she answered, adding, "Finding a competent party was also difficult, and Sanctdomo had the best there was to offer—not just when it came to party members, but also in providing materials for my profession and facilities to work. There is very much an 'ask, and you shall receive' kind of culture if you are one of the stronger ones there."

"And what do they demand in return?" the Sword Saint asked pointedly.

"Protection, order, and, to some extent, obedience. I am in a way better position than pretty much anyone else, as I am associated with another powerful god and thus far harder to control. I haven't experienced any serious issues besides the atmosphere being a bit unsettling."

"In what way?" Jake asked curiously.

"People are almost too kind... It's hard to explain," she said, continuing to be open. "It feels like no one ever says no, and you are handed whatever you want, but the same is also expected of you. If anyone in charge comes and asks you to do anything, you are expected to do it without question or even an explanation for why you have to do what they tell you to. Again, I am more or less excluded from this, but that this mentality is so prevalent does make it hard to make any friends, even with my party members. In my eyes, we are just colleagues, and I doubt I will ever be able to view any of them as true friends. Much less that they will view me as one."

"Why not just go solo?" Carmen chimed in. "Way easier to just be your own boss and do whatever."

"Contrary to someone else," she said, nodding towards Jake, "we archers don't tend to do that well alone. Sure, while we can hunt alone, being with a party is just so much more effective. It's like how a guardian or a healer isn't meant to hunt alone, but put a guardian, an archer, and a healer together, and you have a powerful combo far more effective than the sum of their parts."

"I guess," Carmen recognized. "By the way, you keep mentioning being blessed by some other god?"

"Gwyndyr," Caleb answered, with Maria nodding in confirmation.

"That name sounds familiar," Jake said, trying to remember where he had heard it before.

"It damn well should," Maria said, glaring at him. "He invited you to his divine realm after your tutorial, and you rejected him."

"Oh, yeah, that was a thing," Jake recalled. "Should have tossed in a bottle of vodka if he wanted me to come that badly."

Everyone just stared at Jake, who elaborated with, "Oh, it was this inside joke between the Viper and me where he promised me a bottle of vodka, and apparently it was also an excuse to toss me into a vat of poison that helped get me some skill upgrades, even if it usually kills people, and—"

Caleb put a hand on Jake's shoulder and laughed. "Sounds like quite the time, eh?"

Getting the hint to shut the fuck up, Jake just agreed. "Yeah, sure was."

"Good for you, I guess," Maria said. "Gwyndyr did ask me to not antagonize you and instead treat you as an ally, considering your position as Chosen of a Primordial. So, yeah, I guess he wants me to suck up to you."

"Quite open about it," Jake commented.

"Sure—it isn't like the gods can peek into the Treasure Hunt, so may as well be frank. On that note, you have met the Viper in person... Isn't it kind of unsettling? From what I heard, he is a monster with no regard for mortal life, a complete psychopath who likes torturing and has an Order that—"

"No, I'm good," Jake answered, frowning. "And I don't have

a habit of shit-talking my friends behind their back either. I think a better question is why some god is trying to invite someone who already has a Patron god to his realm when he isn't even associated with the tutorial?"

Maria looked a bit taken aback at Jake's shifting attitude but quickly recovered. "Sorry? And I think he invited you specifically because of that. He was curious who could get a Primordial out of hiding and even get a blessing. Not to mention become his Chosen right off the bat."

"How did he even know about me?" Jake asked, still more than a little miffed.

"With so much attention on your tutorial from other Primordials and powerful gods, he also spared it some attention. He didn't take notice of you till he found out he *couldn't* take notice of you. He discovered that you had been hidden by the Viper, and that truly piqued his interest. There was nothing negative about it; he just thought that getting positive relations with the Viper's Chosen would be a good move. I also can't rule out that he wanted to get a feel for the Viper's power through you."

"I am not sure why any of this is relevant?" Caleb butted in.

"What I am trying to say is that I don't really care about the Holy Church, and I don't want my current status as working with them to mean I am against anyone else," she said, defending herself. "I am not some spy or anything either. My true allegiances lie somewhere else."

"Why stay?" the Sword Saint asked curtly. "Many other organizations exist, and from what I know, Reika is looking for worthwhile team members, are you not?"

Reika, who had just been sitting silently, quickly nodded. "I am indeed, Patriarch. Of course, we always need more powerful members, and naturally do not impose any restrictions upon them."

"Thanks for the offer, but I have an agreement in place for now," Maria said swiftly. "Not with the Church itself, but the

Augur and Bertram. And no, I can't share details. Once more, not because I am not allowed to, but out of respect for them. We can always revisit it when those obligations are fulfilled."

After that, their conversation went to other, less serious topics, with the occasional important subject brought up here and there. More than anything, this entire situation created a foundation for the future. The Noboru Clan, Court of Shadows, Valhal—at least, partly—and Haven cemented their diplomatic relationships.

Carmen didn't really speak for Valhal, the same way Jake didn't really speak for Haven. She didn't have Sven, and he didn't have Miranda, so while they could make promises, it wasn't like they would enact anything. That meant that they really didn't want to swear up and down and make formal pacts and all that.

Hours passed by, and soon others began returning towards the center. Throughout this time, they also found that leaving the Hunt didn't actually spawn an Insignia, indicating that one would keep their loot. To be honest, that did make a lot of sense to Jake, considering the Treasure Hunt was more or less over, and all of this was just bonus time.

Also, the reason everyone was returning was apparent. From the center of the Mistless Plains, Jake could see the world collapse far off in the distance, and it was closing in. Yalsten didn't have much time left, and they all knew it.

Jake brought up the window with the timer and saw the countdown had passed to under one and a half hours.

Treasure Hunt will end in: 1:24:57

He looked at the Sword Saint, and the man made a big smile and nodded. He understood. The two of them stood up at the same time, drawing all attention to the two men. One a young, masked hunter, and the other an old man in a deep blue robe.

Caleb threw Jake a glance, and Sylphie made a loud shriek of encouragement. At the same time, Reika and those remaining from the Noboru clan gave the Sword Saint an encouraging bow or salute. Carmen, Eron, and many others were neutral, but that didn't mean they didn't pay close attention. They all knew this would be a battle to once and for all decide who was the strongest human on Earth.

The two of them entered the center of the Mistless Plains, not far from where the Monarch had been buried. The ground was bare, and destruction from the long battle was present everywhere, but neither was bothered as they looked at each other.

"A year ago, I was bedridden, my one leg having given out due to my age," the Sword Saint said. "I was deemed too old for a hip replacement, and I understood. Even when my grandson insisted to the doctor, I asked him to stop. I was ready for death, for I had lived long enough. I would never have thought a second chance like this would come. A second chance to stand tall and lead my clan towards greatness."

"Don't you mean a second chance to wield a blade and challenge yourself?" Jake asked teasingly.

"That is merely secondary. The method in which I uplift my clan. My own power is the power of my clan. If I was not there today, the Holy Church would not respect us, and would the name of my clan even be known to you?" He said this counter with a light smile, not offended at all.

"I don't disagree," Jake said as he rolled his shoulders and summoned his scimitar. "But don't delude yourself into thinking you're standing where you are right now for your clan."

"You're saying a proof of strength and growth from a duel such as this will not help my clan?" the old man chuckled. "I believe we are merely talking in circles at this point."

He also drew his blade as he shifted his stance.

"Still not what I'm saying," Jake said. "I am saying you're here right now because *you* want to be. Not for your clan or whatever. You want to fight—nothing more, nothing less."

"You sound like the Monarch and his insistence that the

pursuit of power and power alone is the only true way forward," the Sword Saint said, shaking his head.

"No, because I don't believe that myself either. Maybe he was right, and that is a good path, but I don't think everything is so black and white. Power is all fine and good, but you need to use it for something, or it is just there. For a long time, I also thought I just wanted power for power's sake... but I really don't." Jake flashed a smile. "I like power because it allows me to see more of the world and gives me the freedom to do whatever the hell I want. And what I want is to experience all there is to experience. Fight everything there is to fight. I am just a selfish asshole who likes fighting way too much."

He got into position as energy revolved around him. Jake pointed his blade at the Sword Saint, smiling as he charged the old man.

"And so are you."

CHAPTER 61

TREASURE HUNT: PASSION

J ake didn't give the man any time to object as he charged
forward. He only had a single scimitar, and chose to use it
here in the opening clash. Both of them had fully restored
resources and had ensured there were no potion cooldowns
or unavailable skills. Besides Jake not having his second weapon,
both of them were at peak condition, and him not having it
frankly didn't matter much.

His first attack was a simple swipe, and the old man easily
blocked him... or, more accurately, made him miss. He hit the
side of the katana wielded by the Sword Saint and charged past
with a deflected scimitar, still making sure to not give the man
time to counterattack.

Turning around, he attacked again, this time swinging from
a direction where the swordsman couldn't simply redirect it. Or
so Jake thought. His own sword ended up tearing up the ground
as he was once more thwarted, and he had to quickly dodge back
to avoid getting himself slashed.

"Enjoyment of battle does not give one an excuse to shirk
responsibilities," the Sword Saint said as he took the offensive.

Droplets of water began condensing around Jake, and he
responded by creating a blast of mana around his body to

quickly dispel them while also swaying to avoid the sword trying to cut him in two. More water began condensing, and Jake finally began to realize why the vampire had constantly kept his aura active... To deal with the old man's water magic. However, the water magic was so weak that Jake easily made it useless just with a bit of mana here and there.

Jake jumped back as the old man cut upwards, sending forth a screen of water that tore up the space between the two of them. Sadly for the Saint, Jake had already seen the movements of mana and easily dodged to the side to avoid it.

Screens of water began appearing all around Jake as the old man sent out crescent waves with his sword, but not directly towards him. They entered the screens and, to Jake's surprise, were reflected and redirected. He dodged the first few and saw them begin bouncing between the water screens. The old man was trying to set up a killing trap or something.

"Neat trick," Jake recognized.

Ultimately, not very effective, though. He reckoned that combination was more a relic of past skills, as it really didn't work well against foes with his mobility. Jake simply ran forward and dove under a sword wave before jumping over another one to get free of the trap.

Running straight for the old man, he attacked again with a swing. The swordsman blocked and redirected his blows again and again. It was at this point that one thing became utterly clear...

Jake was completely and utterly outmatched in skill. He was stronger and faster, yet he felt like a child swinging a stick in front of a swordmaster... because, in many ways, he was.

Yet, at the same time, he wouldn't lose. Because while Jake was unable to even get close to landing a wound, the same was true for the old man. Jake sucked at using a sword compared to the Sword Saint, but he sure as hell didn't suck at not getting hit by one.

He knew when dangerous blows approached, and he reacted

to those while blocking weaker blows to not leave an opening. He could do this since he was ultimately still superior in stats and likely also overall skill rarity and methods. Superior in every way but pure skill. Not that any of them had really shown anything else yet.

"You have not wielded cold weapons for long, have you?" the Sword Saint asked.

"Not since the system came, unless you count kitchen knives during cooking. And even then, I was a shitty chef," Jake answered, snickering.

With a deadpan expression, the old man said, "It shows."

Ouch, Jake thought as he struck back, this time going a bit harder. Arcane energy revolved around his blade as he upped the power of his blows. This forced the Sword Saint to be even more defensive, and when Jake didn't let up but kept pressuring him, he was finally forced to go a bit harder in turn.

Jake felt the spike of power from his opponent as his boosting skill was used. Probably at a low volume... but it was used. A faint teal mist came out of the old man's skin, and he pressed forward, suddenly placing Jake on the backfoot.

He dodged a few blows as the Sword Saint let loose, his blade now faster and stronger. He pushed Jake away and pointed the tip of his blade towards him.

"Thousand Droplets."

His danger sense exploded as he felt like hundreds of needles prickled his body. For the first time, Jake was forced to use One Step Mile, as the area he had just occupied was suddenly cut through by what he could only guess was a thousand tiny stabs.

Okay, that is dangerous, Jake recognized. He would, at a minimum, have to use Scales of the Malefic Viper to handle that one, as while each blow was far from a normal stab... well, there was value in quantity.

Jake decided that if the old man got serious... he would also kick it up a notch. Arcane mana began condensing around him as several bolts appeared, and in his hand, concentrated arcane energy gathered while he dodged another sword blow with One Step Mile.

Yet just before he could release his arcane bolts, the old man summoned a plane of water in front of himself, reflecting Jake and his bolts. For a moment, Jake felt like his bolts existed in two places at once, and just as he felt that, the old man cut across the water plane. Jake's arcane bolts and the mana structures fell apart at that same moment, leaving only the arcane energy he had gathered in his hand.

"That is a cool skill," Jake said as he dodged yet another blow, his One Step Mile taking him closer.

"Quite the durable mana constructs," the old man recognized in an impressed voice as he blocked Jake's scimitar.

"Yep."

Jake spun and pointed his palm at the old man, releasing a massive blast of arcane energy that sent both of them flying back. In a swift reaction, the Sword Saint had managed to summon a protective layer of water, but Jake still felt like he came out on top.

They charged each other again and exchanged blow after blow, sending rock and soil flying everywhere as they tore up the area even more. None of them landed any blows worth mentioning on the other as the minutes passed by, yet one thing was clear... This stalemate wouldn't continue.

Because while the old man pulled out more and more cards, Jake only had to use half as many. A new tipping point came when Jake decided to give his new Limit Shatter a test drive.

Energy revolved inside his body, condensing and speeding up. He felt full of power as it spiked to 15%, and instantly the situation changed. Jake summoned more mana bolts and bombarded the old man, who couldn't cut them down fast enough—not even with the water plane. Instead of summoning five simultaneously, Jake quickly made them appear one by one with his hand and more or less threw them in between his sword blows.

In response, the old man began also using more of his own magic. Large orbs of water that fired out pressurized blasts tried to block Jake's blows, and several planes of water appeared to somewhat successfully block Jake's magic. He even used reflecting planes to make his pressurized water beams come from different directions. That was just one of his many types of water magic, with large water explosions, more needle-like droplet attacks, and whatnot also mixed in.

However, none of it worked much. Sure, the water beam could cut well, but compared to the sword, it was nothing. Jake ended up still summoning his Scales to take a few blasts of water, allowing him to close in and push the old man back, finally landing a good blow for the first time in the fight.

Seeing the writing on the wall, the Sword Saint got some distance between them and said, "I must admit... seeing you fight and facing you is very different. It is like being hounded by a beast that turns into a specter just when you think it has overextended."

"Thanks for the compliment," Jake answered. "Meanwhile, you feel like facing a master swordsman who also decided to try and become a water mage at some point. Honestly, you got way more tricks than I expected."

The old man frowned. "Swordsmanship can only take one so far, and it would be foolish to abandon other types of magic when other means can be used to enhance oneself."

"I wasn't insulting you," Jake said, shaking his head. "But between facing your sword and your water magic... they aren't the same. The latter feels hollow."

"It is no lie—I am not truly a mage and have not invested as much in my mental stats as I perhaps should," the Sword Saint acknowledged. "We all have places to improve, like your swordsmanship and my magic."

"No... no, that ain't it." Jake shook his head again. "It just feels forced and boring. There is nothing in it. As I said... it's just hollow. Completely without passion."

The old man frowned again. "As said, I am not a mage. Magic is merely secondary and a requirement to—"

"Those shitty water balloons are doing nothing for you," Jake said, sighing. "It feels like someone with a gun deciding to toss bullets for some goddamn reason. If you don't actually care for using water magic like this... just stop and don't insult me by using it pretending to be serious. Stick to what you actually care about."

Jake didn't give him time to respond as he moved to attack again. The old man seemed to have taken his word to heart, though, as he didn't use any of his water magic but instead only blocked with his sword. Sure, there were still some water-affinity things... but he wasn't acting like a low-tier mage. Jake was fine with using things you were still practicing on... but that wasn't what the old man did.

He had just made some simple magic spells and gone with those. It was all low-tier stuff, not tied to what the Sword Saint was all about: his swordsmanship. Jake didn't feel the slightest tinge of danger from those water orbs, but he didn't care to take a single blow from the sword.

Now, magic that supported his swordsmanship was another thing. The reflection of spells to dispel them with a sword cut, or him making his sword waves jump between planes of water? That shit was cool and inventive, and overall supplemented the swordsmanship.

The Sword Saint wasn't like Jake—that much he was sure about. It felt like he only used that water magic out of obligation, not desire. Was it wrong to learn how to use spells like that? No... not really, but if you didn't really care about magic spells, why waste your time on it? Okay, maybe if it was to practice some concept and was a middle step, but then you shouldn't use it in combat. Same as how Jake didn't try to summon weapons out of arcane mana. Maybe he would do it one day... but not yet. Also... ultimately... if it wasn't fun to use magic while fighting for the old man, why bother? If there is no passion, why have it be part of your path and style?

Jake pressed his attack, showing that contrary to the Sword Saint, he actually cared about his magic. Arcane bolts supported him, arcane explosions made space where possible, and the arcane energy revolved around his blade as they clashed.

The old man got a bit faster when he pushed his boosting skill higher, allowing him to keep up and go even. However... Jake felt that his opponent couldn't go much higher. That didn't mean it was easy for Jake, but it did mean that it would be very difficult for the Saint to get anywhere.

Because while Jake forced the other party to show his cards one by one... Jake had yet to.

"You may be right," the old man said, appearing far calmer than Jake expected.

His blade sped up and pushed Jake away as the Sword Saint changed his stance. He gripped the sword's handle with both hands and pointed it straight at Jake, and the atmosphere shifted.

"But do not think for a moment my blade and the power of the rain are not connected. This skill was the first legendary one I got... Please share your insights," the Saint said as he breathed out and spoke in a low voice,

"Rainblade."

Jake moved just before the tip of a blade appeared where his chest had just been. The old man had moved even faster than ever before, making Jake remember his movement skill. *He was still holding back.*

Somehow, the Sword Saint's feet slid across the ground like he was a water strider on a lake. It was not teleportation, but swift movement in mostly straight lines. Contrary to Jake's One Step Mile, the old man could use it to build up momentum as he struck—at the cost of some speed and the risk of taking damage, as he still physically moved compared to straight-up tele-portation.

But that wasn't what Jake had to truly look out for... for if the sword was dangerous before, now it was on an entirely new level.

Visually, not much had changed besides a faint layer of water now covering the blade of the katana. It looked to be in constant movement as it streamed up and down the edge, but Jake knew there were some serious concepts at work... for with his Sense of the Malefic Viper, he felt a massive amount of mana from the weapon. Way more than he could pack into an Arrow of the Ambitious Hunter by a large margin. More surprisingly... it didn't look like it required much upkeep, as it was a stable flow.

As for what this Rainblade did...

Jake dodged and summoned a bolt of arcane mana, but instantly found it cut in two. He teleported back, and the Sword Saint swung in his direction, sending a few tiny droplets after him. Without hesitating, he teleported again. The droplets hit a small hill in the distance and penetrated it, each as powerful as the stab of a sword.

To make it worse, when the old man stabbed for real, Jake found himself forced to roll on the ground as the blade extended over ten meters. The extended part was made of only a faint outline of water, yet he knew it wasn't something he should try to tank.

I knew he had something more. Now, this is some proper fucking water magic.

The water level had been shit. Maybe rainwater was just superior to ocean water?

A moment of inattentiveness made Jake not teleport away fast enough, and the old man managed to get within striking distance. Jake dodged the first four swipes but was forced to block the last one. He raised his scimitar and clashed with the Sword Saint, feeling like he had just blocked another normal sword blow... yet when he did, it was like a part of the blade just kept cutting, ignoring that the physical part of it had stopped.

Using One Step Mile, Jake appeared off to the side, a wet cut across his chest with the scales torn open and blood seeping out, mixing with the rainwater.

It was his first time taking an injury... and it wasn't a light one.

Jake made a toothy grin as he yelled at the old man, "I guess it's only fair I also do what I'm best at."

With that, he waved his hand and summoned his bow, dodging again as he nocked an arrow.

The second part of the duel between the swordmaster and the hunter had begun.

CHAPTER 62

TREASURE HUNT: MISCONCEPTION

The Sword Saint was proud. He always had been, and perhaps the years had only made it worse. It was indeed interesting what the thought of imminent death did to a man. When he'd lain there dying, many thoughts had gone through his head. Regrets. Unfulfilled wishes. But oddly enough, also a substantial amount of pride. Pride for the things he had accomplished throughout his life. Pride for the clan he had built. It had always been powerful, but the Noboru clan had skyrocketed to entirely new heights under his leadership.

For fifty years, barely anyone had dared criticize him. Since the system arrived, none had. In any crowd of humans, he had been the strongest. This meant everyone respected him to an almost unhealthy level, and Miyamoto would lie to himself if he said he didn't enjoy it somewhat.

However, that didn't mean the Sword Saint believed he deserved respect. In his view, respect was earned, not merely given. He had seen where pride and arrogance could take you and had even observed his own family fall into the pitfall of thinking themselves superior to all others simply due to their heritage. They began to view respect as a given, not something that was earned, and if anyone dared disagree with this sentiment, they somehow viewed this as being disrespected.

It becomes their new worldview. A toxic mentality that would corrode any organization from within. Miyamoto had seen it seep in and grow worse since after the system. Power-hungry members of the clan working under the radar, gaining power through favors, seeming like good and respectful people until the moment they actually grasped influence, turning them into tyrants.

For close to a century, it had been his job to guide his clan to do the right thing. Even when he should have been retired, he kept working. Even when he had to use a cane, he refused to back down. Only when his body fully gave up had he stopped—the day Willpower lost out to the merciless march of time.

So, he'd had a responsibility to lead them when the system came, and he'd gotten a second chance. He had to be the figurehead. He had to be the most powerful, the wisest, the most respected. Gods surrounded his planet and his land, seeking to claim it as their own. Many welcomed this, but Miyamoto was not one of them... for he had yet to see why they deserved his respect.

For them, respect was not a question of being viewed as a person but being viewed as an absolute authority. Either you complied or were a blasphemer that believers would gladly put to death as a heretic. Miyamoto was intimately familiar with this... for he had experienced it himself.

Back during the tutorial, he'd been blessed by a god, like so many others. In the beginning, he had agreed simply to gain the blessing and the power given by it. The god in question had even been open and welcoming, not demanding anything, and treated him with respect—or, in better terms, like a person. Perhaps not an equal, but good enough.

That had all changed when he did exceptionally well in the tutorial. The god had spoken to him more, encouraged him. Miyamoto hadn't needed it, but had appreciated it as he moved forward and established his clan. All was well, until one fateful day when the god did something he had done not before. He told Miyamoto what to do. It was not a request, but an order.

The order? To go seek out the Holy Church, swear allegiance to them, and make him and his clan subordinate to the Church. It was a matter-of-fact order, leaving no room for negotiation. At least, that became clear when Miyamoto gave a stern no in response.

To truly see what a person is like, you need to have a conflict with them. A disagreement. Miyamoto and the god had been on the same page all this time, but the moment the slightest divide emerged, all hell broke loose.

What had struck him more was the obvious confusion the god displayed over Miyamoto even *daring* to say no. The god had clearly made plans and deals behind the scenes, seeing Miyamoto as a great way to connect with the Church. To him, the entire Noboru clan had just been another chess piece for him to further his own goals without any care or regard for them as living beings, viewing them as merely objects. Entities unworthy of respect.

In the end, Miyamoto had renounced his blessing and not accepted any invitations from other gods since then. In some ways, he had been greatly offended at the god... yet in other ways, he understood how a being consistently treated as above everyone else for so long could begin feeling like it truly was so. He did not reject that gods were powerful and deserved some respect for that... but that did not give them the right to treat him as less than a person. His pride did not allow it.

Miyamoto wanted to avoid falling into the same trap as that god and the many people who'd let power get to their heads in his own clan. But it was hard, as he saw this happened everywhere.

He had few people he respected on Earth, most of whom he had spent most of the day with. They did not treat him as an authority, but as a person, and hence he treated them the same.

It was refreshing... yet something gnawed at him. A feeling he hadn't felt for a long time.

Focusing on the battle between himself and the Hunter of Haven, he used his most powerful boosting skill and pushed his Revolution of the Northern Stream as hard as he could, increasing all his physical stats by over 50% with his Rainblade active. All other tools were also out of the kit... yet he still failed. He was still weaker.

Lord Thayne—no, Jake—teleported as he fired his bow, every arrow a harbinger of death, every single move seeming to be calculated, yet spontaneous and erratic. Unpredictable. Miyamoto even had his movements restricted, as he felt like he stood before a beast outside of his understanding, leading to injuries he would have otherwise dodged or blocked. However, what he truly felt was not fear or reverence...

Envy.

Yes, that was it. That was the feeling Miyamoto hadn't felt for so long... Genuine envy. Not because of Jake's power or methods. He didn't desire his magic or his equipment or even his relationship to a powerful god. Instead, he desired that genuine smile on his face and his unburdened attitude. The fact that he seemed to burn with passion at every moment during their fight.

He wanted the freedom his opponent had. The carelessness with which he carried himself and his utter disregard for anything but himself. He was completely selfish. Miyamoto did not think that as an insult, just his honest observation. Sure, Jake clearly cared for people like his family, but it didn't detract from his freedom.

Without any regard for his own life, he would seek out powerful opponents and challenge himself. Meanwhile, Miyamoto could not do that. The implications of his own death were things he couldn't bear. If he died, the clan would be severely weakened, if not outright collapse. Without the power to stand up to the more powerful factions, they would be in deep trouble.

Yet, he wanted that freedom. He yearned for it, more than he would ever admit to himself. He had been on the cusp of death. He had accepted it. Miyamoto was fine with dying, just not the consequences his death would now bring.

This was why Jake's words struck so profoundly. The young man didn't care and simply spoke his mind. He smiled and enjoyed himself to his life's content. Every battle was an event to enjoy. A challenge to overcome with a smirk.

To put it bluntly... Jake Thayne just had fun with life, damned be the consequences.

And for one day, the Sword Saint decided he would do the same. A genuine smile appeared on his lips, and he pushed his boosting skill further than ever before as he attacked with all he had. For just one day, he would be free and enjoy himself.

Perhaps this wasn't a fight he could win, but it was one he could genuinely enjoy.

No clan. No consequences.

Just two humans fighting.

———

Jake bombarded the old man sliding across the ground, sending droplets in return. Jake dodged away, returning fire as the two of them danced in circles around each other, the Sword Saint slowly closing in.

Once more, the old man had sped up after a power spike. The teal energy seemed to flow far faster both within and around him, giving him more and more power.

The Sword Saint closed in and cut across the terrain, sending dust and soil flying into massive pillars as the ground exploded, creating a fissure between them. Jake fled back, summoning a barrier of arcane mana to buy him time to nock another arrow.

He fired it through the dust, and just before it arrived, he made it split into six arrows. The old man was ready and dodged in between them—a decision he quickly tried to correct, as he noticed something was wrong, but it was too late.

BOOM!

All of them exploded as the Sword Saint was sent tumbling back, his robes torn in many places and quite a few wounds on both his arms from the blast. Jake nocked yet another arrow, and this time the old man slid to the side, always staying in motion. That was when Jake noticed something annoying... He had begun finding ways around Jake's Gaze.

As he slid across the ground constantly, Jake tried to freeze him but found that his opponent could still control his speed somewhat without physically moving his body. Because while Gaze impacted physical movement, it did nothing for movements of mana or even stamina, allowing the Sword Saint to pour in some more energy to slide faster or less to go slower, throwing Jake's aim off.

No worries, there are workarounds, Jake thought as he used One Step Mile to avoid a few more droplets, getting even more distance. He spun in the air, aimed his bow, and nocked the arrow as arcane mana whirled around him.

The Sword Saint saw what he was doing and charged straight for Jake at full speed. Jake channeled as long as he could before he released the Arcane Powershot, aimed straight for the Sword Saint's chest. He tried to use Gaze but suddenly lost vision of the old man as his form shimmered for a second— enough to allow the Saint to counter the arrow.

Sword and arrow clashed, and another explosion rocked the area. Jake's eyes opened wide as he summoned an arcane barrier in front of him just in time to get hit by a thin blade of water. It stabbed through his shoulder and out the other side, then ripped downwards, tearing through flesh and bone. Jake backed away to dislodge the weapon.

He got out, but not before getting a wound that ripped all the way through his body from his right shoulder to just above his navel, the blade having torn through everything in between. He would be dead if this had been pre-system, but now it was just a severe wound.

Yet Jake wasn't discouraged. The dust cleared and he saw the Sword Saint, who stood with his two feet steadfastly planted on the ground, his right arm extended with the katana pointed forward. His left arm hung limply at his side, as his entire shoulder was disfigured, and a large wound extended from it and towards his neck and chest.

The two of them stared at each other for a moment, then just snickered and moved again. The old man ignored his wounds and drank a potion while dodging another arrow—a potion Jake himself had made—and bought some time as his body healed.

Jake didn't need to regenerate himself yet, so he pressed his advantage. If he couldn't hit the Sword Saint, he would at least make him spend a lot of stamina and mana to avoid his blows. With the potion cooldown now in effect, there was no way to regenerate those easily, after all.

Their fight continued. Soon the old man was healed enough to use his left arm again, and thus he began attacking more, trying to corner Jake and get close enough to strike him. Jake wanted to avoid melee at this point, as he didn't see himself able to land a single blow on the old man without his bow, while the Saint wanted to be close to avoid Jake's arrows and, of course, land his own attacks.

Yet... some gaps were not meant to be overcome, and some distances were too vast to be easily crossed. Jake's advantage only grew as time passed. They clashed many times, Jake taking wounds repeatedly, but for every cut that Jake received, the Sword Saint was damaged even more.

For the fourth time during their fight, Jake blasted the Sword Saint back with an Arcane Powershot, sending him tumbling through the air, a large hole in his thigh. The old man could still stand, but his stance was weaker, and the final nail came when the old man's blade stopped giving off the same power as before.

He was unable to keep Rainblade active.

The Sword Saint still stood in a combat-ready stance when Jake stopped ten or so meters away. The old man looked down at his own body and sighed.

His robes were torn, revealing his bare upper body. Jake saw more muscles than he thought such an old man could possibly have, all of them lean and powerful. This was especially impressive, seeing as his entire body was covered in wounds from Jake's constant arcane explosions and arrows.

"I lost..." the Sword Saint said, sighing again. He took a more relaxed stance, stabbed his sword into the ground, and leaned on it as he looked towards the sky.

"Seems like it," Jake agreed with a nod. He didn't feel any particular happiness from the win, but he had thoroughly enjoyed the duel.

"Tell me... what am I lacking?" the Sword Saint said as he looked at Jake. It was a genuine question, not one veiled with sarcasm or ill intent. Just a genuine desire to improve.

"Eh... it's more that you have too much?" Jake tried to answer, attempting to articulate his thoughts. "The first part of the fight felt like I was fighting a weird mix between a second-grade mage and a damn good swordsman, while the second half was far more consistent. I don't get why you are so insistent in using magic like that... or at all."

The old man shook his head. "Magic seems like a necessity for progress... if not now, then later on my path. I cannot be an old man swinging a sword forever, stuck in the past as I dream of my younger years and memories of my prime. The world has changed, and so should I."

Looking confused, Jake asked, "... Why do you think that?"

"Pardon?" the Sword Saint asked, equally confused as he shifted his injured leg. Likely from the pain.

"What's wrong with just swinging your sword? Not gonna lie, you swinging your sword is pretty damn fucking scary already."

"For now, maybe. But I did not walk into this changing world blind. I sought advice from those more familiar with systems from our old world similar to this new reality. The path of magic is always the most powerful, and if I want to keep up, I need to also learn to wield it. Do you not liberally wield magic yourself?"

"I do... but it isn't like *you* need to? I am pretty sure you can do just fine only with a sword. Maybe keep the whole 'water affinity and the concept of rain' thing going? Those seem to be working well for you in just making you better at swinging your sword, but why try to be a mage? Why not just seek the absolute pinnacle of swordsmanship?" Now he was genuinely even more confused. Had the old man been told about old videogames or whatnot where magic was overpowered?

"If I can just add," Carmen yelled over from the sidelines, having heard their conversation, "you don't need to get good at everything. I just want to get good at punching things, and I am doing okay. Also... Valdemar, the leader of Valhal, became one of the twelve Primordials and is one of the most powerful gods in existence. And according to his wife, he is a meathead who only knows how to swing an axe..."

The Sword Saint said, "I am certain he has gone through severe magical—"

"He doesn't have any mana because he couldn't figure out how it worked. Ever," Carmen interrupted. "So he just got rid of it to get more stamina to swing his axe more."

"But a limit must be—"

"If there is a limit to just swinging a weapon, he hasn't reached it yet. Gudrun told me that when once asked if he thought one could become powerful enough to shatter an entire universe, he claimed that if he just swung hard enough, then why not?"

"Yeah, what Carmen said," Jake agreed. "There aren't some set rules on how to be strong, from what I know. Just do whatever the hell you want. Shit, there is a god who became like that just by being a mega fanboy and another who just always did alchemy and never bothered with anything else."

The old man frowned as he looked at the two of them.

"I guess what I'm saying is that you shouldn't conform to the system to gain power," Jake continued. "Instead, do what you want to, and make the system conform to your own will and reward that path. Simplicity does not make some worse... just simpler. It's all about forging your own path, defining your own limits, and setting your own rules while refusing to stop moving forward."

Jake had enjoyed their duel, and he actually liked the old man quite a bit. He felt they were very similar, but the Sword Saint was limited by outside factors, as far as he could see. Perhaps it was bad information, an assumption gained by seeing so many explore magic to get stronger, or maybe even some powerful entity being full of shit.

Either way, it didn't matter. Jake was just doing as he always did, speaking about his interpretation like it was fact... because it may as well be in his head. Hey, his entire interpretation was about just being stubborn enough to make the system go, "Fair enough, I guess that works," so why wouldn't he think the system worked exactly as he thought it did?

The Sword Saint stared up towards the sky, looking to be deep in thought. A few seconds passed before he glanced down at Jake, a new look in his eyes. "Tell me... what is your fondest memory?"

CHAPTER 63

SPRINGTIME ADVENT

"My fondest memory?" Jake asked, confused at the sudden question. He didn't know why the Sword Saint had asked him that, much less why he had such a sincere look in his eyes. Like the answer to his question genuinely mattered.

Thus, Jake considered it seriously. When he thought about fond memories, he was surprised to notice something... None of them were from before the system. He tried to remember some positive memories from before and did find plenty. That time they'd gone to the theme park, where Jake had just gotten tall enough to ride all the "wild" attractions. Or when he'd won his first big archery competition.

But... comparing them to the post-system ones, they seemed so much less. The first time he got a notification from a kill, the times he defeated any of the Beast Lords... his victory over the King of the Forest... the D-grade Storm Elemental he'd bombarded from long range... the damn blue mushroom... Altmar Golem... So many memories appeared over those traditionally happy childhood memories.

Yet, one memory emerged before any of the others. One that

had been the beginning of Jake's true journey into this new world.

"It was the first day of the tutorial... I was with my colleagues, and we made a camp to wait out the night. I was on watch alone. Ah, I need to add that we didn't do jack-shit for the first many hours, but just walked around and sometimes fought weak foes. Everything except killing a big boar was a waste of time. During this night, we were ambushed... Three men came for me. All of them were several levels above me, stronger and faster.

"By all accounts, I should have been fucked, but instead, I felt like I awakened after sleeping for a long time. Suddenly the world was more vivid than ever before, and I fought the three ambushers. No, I didn't just fight them. I dominated and killed all three of them while barely taking a scratch. That was my first true fight to the death, and the first time I ever killed another human. The euphoria I felt when I stared out into the night as I stood victorious... is something I will never forget." It truly was his most precious memory. It was the day he'd stopped being Jake the office worker and become Jake the Primal Hunter.

Across from him, the Sword Saint nodded along to his words. He smiled as he looked at Jake. "In some ways, we truly are similar. My fondest memory is not one I have ever shared... One I have been embarrassed to regard as my fondest."

He leaned on his sword as he sat down, making it clear this would not be a short story.

"When I lay dying, expecting my life to end at any moment, I recalled so many memories of my life. My marriage, the birth of my children, grandchildren, and even great-grandchildren. The day my wife passed, and the day I buried my firstborn son. I remembered all of it oh so vividly, happy and sad times both."

His body was covered in wounds. They both knew a winner was clear, and Jake merely stood there and listened. "Yet out of everything... I remembered one thing. One event that shaped me more than anything else. My fondest memory and my fondest moment, as I looked back upon my life."

The Sword Saint's eyes lit up, remembering ages past. Jake chose to simply listen as the man spoke with genuine passion and emotion. Even more so than anything before.

"It was during a war... a terrible time. Young men and women died, believing there was honor in such an honorless time. Oh, were we foolish. We thought ourselves heroes, and we wanted to stand out and bring praise upon our names and families." The Sword Saint stared up towards the sky, reminiscing over what had happened so long ago. Yet, there was a small spark of something else in the air Jake couldn't quite recognize.

"We achieved nothing but proving our own foolhardiness as we unwisely tried and go above and beyond our call of duty. You see, we were not the defenders at this time, but the attackers. In a foreign land, unknown to us besides a sparse few hours around a table and a small booklet that only one of us had read. This is all the knowledge we wandered in with. We had no personal animosity towards the enemy, but solely went to war due to our national pride demanding it and our honor not allowing us to say no.

"There, we fought and battled faceless enemies as we got further and further from home. Deeper and deeper into the unknown, we fared, but all we found on our way was desolation and desertion, the villages ransacked and destroyed as our foes retreated." His look turned sour, yet that spark remained.

"My squad and I tried to be clever—to get ahead and make ourselves stand out—so we went where we were not supposed to. A single vehicle and not enough rations were all we had. How could we have known our journey would end as it did? Perhaps we should have... but we were young and dumb.

"Our only means of transportation broke down in the middle of nowhere, and as we tried to fix it... it came," he said, his voice cracking slightly and his hand still holding the sword shaking.

Jake stood there, silently listening. He felt that the old man truly looked and sounded like he was back in the past... that whatever had happened back then was so thoroughly etched in his mind that he didn't need any Wisdom or magical stats to remember every detail perfectly, even if it had happened nearly a century ago.

"The snow fell. The biting wind from the north descended on us like a merciless beast as winter arrived. Ill-equipped and lost, we tried to return home, but we were too far away from anyone else. We had to seek refuge in a small, abandoned village, with only a few drafty houses left standing.

"From there... the longest winter in my life began. A squad of four, we tried to keep ourselves warm and our spirits high. They were my brothers and felt as close to me as my family at the time. I trusted every one of them with my life, and they trusted me with theirs. Which is why what came next was so hard." Tears fell from his eyes, and he gripped the sword handle hard enough to make blood fall to the ground below from his wounds.

"Our rations were... limited. We all knew it from the first day. The small book told of the brutal winters of the land. A winter we would never survive... so the hard choice was made. The hardest choice... made. We knew not all could survive... so we chose.

"The rations would last enough for only one of us. Haruto was the first... He simply asked for the one who remained to tell his family he'd died with honor, and to take care of his wife and child before he ended himself. Ibuki followed him soon after, leaving only his brother and sister in the care of the survivor. The final two were Aoto and me."

The old man spoke with so much agony it was almost tangible. Jake felt the intense pain in every word.

"I had a clan... and so did Aoto. We were both the only heirs remaining and had no children. We were the last of our Bloodlines, so if we died, our lines would end. There was no good choice... so... we flipped a coin. I won, and with tears in his eyes, he nodded in recognition and brought the gun to his head."

Jake felt the words almost echo as he saw the tears flow down the Sword Saint's cheeks, his head angled skyward. Jake felt like he saw clouds far above but couldn't quite make them out. He looked back at the old man and saw that glint in his eyes had never disappeared, and Jake now recognized it.... *Enlightenment.*

Something was changing; he felt like the atmospheric mana was affected somehow. Not just the mana... Everything seemed to be influenced.

"That winter was so long... so lonely. Every day was a struggle to simply stay alive, every second torture. Cold, alone, forgotten and abandoned. After the first month, my family would have no doubt received news of my death. After the second, they would have come to believe it. The third and fourth? My funeral had been long held by then.

"I cannot even begin to explain how it felt. I have experienced torture more than once in my life, but those months... were more than torture. There was not a day I didn't consider joining my fallen comrades... but I had made a promise to them. One I would keep. I was also simply not willing to accept death. Not a single fiber of my being believed that winter was supposed to be my end before seeing at least one more spring."

As Miyamoto spoke, Jake noticed something more. It was faint... but he felt like he saw tiny snowflakes falling. He saw them even in his sphere... and he couldn't detect any mana or energy... *They're real.* Not constructs, but real snow. He looked over at the onlookers, and they saw it too. Slowly, a faint white blanket of pristine snow fell upon Yalsten.

"But the body can only last so long; Willpower only take one so far. We had underestimated the relentlessness and merciless-ness of winter. It was rougher than even those that came before it, more adamant than anything my squadmates could have expected.

"Yet I lived. Day after day, I weakened, but I remained. Until finally, one day... I heard a tap."

The old man suddenly livened up, seemingly unbothered by his wounded body. He smiled and stood.

"One tap, and then another. I had been half-asleep, dehydrated, and starved. Yet, I recognized it right away. I managed to lift myself off the ground and pushed myself to the door. I will never forget opening it that day and seeing the rainfall upon the snow as it melted.

"It was... magic. For the first time in months, I felt hope; I felt a desire to truly live and believed that I would make it. I laughed out loud and yelled far louder than I thought a man in my state should ever be capable of. Then, however... a moment of pure relief and happiness swiftly changed as I heard another sound, barely audible over the rain."

The Sword Saint turned far more serious as he continued his narration. Jake wasn't even sure the old man knew if anyone was still listening.

"As mentioned, the winter had been long... far longer than usual. It had disrupted not just me, but the natural balance. Spring had come later, and the animals suffered for it... especially those who usually hibernated through it. For before me stood a bear, far larger than I had ever seen, thin and starved as it stared at my willow form.

"We met each other's eyes... and at that moment, we both knew. One of us would become the sustenance to allow the survival of the other. Or... perhaps only I thought that, for clearly, the bear did not view my small and weak form as a threat. Which, under usual circumstances, it really shouldn't have been."

He slowly raised his sword, holding it towards the sky as if to show it off.

"I had no guns or bullets left; all of them used to try and hunt for food during this time. I had no way to fight except for one thing. When I left home, I had taken with me an heirloom.

Something many families and clans did back then. I had chosen the sword that had been passed down to me. This very sword I hold in my hand.

"The bear stared me down as I felt its intent... and I drew. My body hurt. My bones protruded from my skin, as I had not eaten for weeks and barely had some melted snow to keep me alive for the past few weeks. Yet, as I stood there, sword in hand, the rain falling upon me, I felt none of this. All I felt was the rain upon my skin, and hope for survival."

His eyes lit up as he showed his teeth. Jake felt the mirages of snow around him turn to water, the atmosphere shifting. He was not the only one who closely observed the odd happenings. Caleb, Carmen, and many others looked with a mix of confusion and astonishment, silently watching and listening to the story.

"As two starved beasts, we clashed, sword against claw. Needless to say, I was no match in strength, barely a match in agility, and utterly outmatched in durability. It was a battle I was not meant to win, but one I, at the same time, couldn't afford to lose. Couldn't see myself losing.

"Time after time, we clashed, blood was spilled, and my blade—dulled by the weather and lack of maintenance—was barely able to penetrate the skin of the beast. The beast seemed unaffected and kept pushing me back. My body was fraught with pain. Yet at the same time, I felt my body overflowing with more power than ever."

Jake looked on silently and sensed the subtle gathering of energy, the Sword Saint at the center. It felt like the world itself was feeding him power as he stood there, seemingly unaware of all that was happening.

"The battle was long and painful, the physical difference larger than I could have imagined. Neither of us was willing to die or surrender, and neither willing to give up. At one moment, I slipped on the wet snow below my feet, which made me unable to dodge as the bear hit me in the side. I felt my arm break, my ribs bent, and the air was knocked out of my lungs. I rolled and fell to the ground, my body bloody and broken. Yet I stood once more, my left arm useless, my blade still in the other.

"A final time, the beast came. It charged me, seeing my weak form. I stood there, staring at the beast with my blade raised as the rain hit the tip of the blade. I saw it slide down the edge, and at that very moment, a miracle happened. The rain-filled clouds above parted. Faint rays of sunlight fell upon my blade, reflecting the rainwater and blinding the bear.

"I did not think. I simply felt at that very moment that the world had chosen to assist me. I was one with it, as I was one with my sword, and I merely swung a single time. My blade moved through the air, parting the raindrops, and when it met the neck of the bear, it did not stop. An impossible strike cut the head off without any resistance. I never even felt the impact in my arm as I stood there victorious, the beast dead beneath me. All I felt was warmth despite standing in tattered clothes in the melting snow, a single ray of sunlight bathing me."

The old man finally looked at Jake, the glint in his eye more evident than ever. More energy than before gathered towards the Sword Saint as Jake stared back into his eyes.

Deep within, he felt an emotion he hadn't felt for a long time...

"After that, I used the bear's body to provide food, clothing, and other necessities till I was rescued by happenstance nearly a month later when all the snow was gone. I returned to my home, became the leader of my clan, paid my dues, and never spoke of those months ever again. Yet that day in the rain never left me. The feeling of shame that came from the thought that the deaths of my comrades and those months of torture had all been worth it—for that one fight—never left me. My desire to experience such a thing once more... never left me. I merely forgot it."

Jake felt the world change at that moment, sunlight penetrating a sunless sky and rain falling upon Yalsten, visible for all to see.

"I believed that my second chance was another opportunity to help my clan. I believed my job was to bring upon a season of growth and push my clan into an eternal summer... at the cost of confining myself to my own personal winter as I abandoned selfishness for the good of others. Now I realize... my second chance was not for that...

"So as the snow melts and I usher the season of change..."

Jake suddenly knew what that feeling was. It was the same feeling he'd felt the first night he stood before the three humans.

"As winter ends and the rain falls..."

A feeling of competitiveness that could not be born from fighting beasts and monsters of the multiverse.

No, it was one that could only be realized through fighting those of his own species to stand at the apex. Jake did not comprehend what was happening and quite frankly didn't care to know. He just wanted to see the result.

"So let it come."

Jake grinned as rays of sunlight bathed Yalsten and the rain fell upon his skin. He felt the atmospheric mana of the entire area skyrocket to entirely new levels, as if the system itself fed more into Yalsten out of nowhere. He felt an aura wash upon him that made him aware that whatever monster stood before him was on another level than anything he had ever faced before.

"My..."

He felt his own heartbeat and Bloodline revel as he drew his scimitar and pushed Limit Shatter to 30% without any hesitation.

"Springtime Advent."

CHAPTER 64

PEAK OF HUMANITY

J ake stood with his eyes open wide in shock, blinded for a moment. Not only were his eyes blind, but so was his sphere. He saw nothing but pure energy as it washed over him, but only for a moment. Then a figure appeared before him.

Long black hair flowed through the air from the power exhibited from the man's body, a bare chest of muscles with not a single wrinkle or sign of weakness in sight. If not for the all-too-familiar wounds Jake knew he had caused himself, he wouldn't recognize the person before him.

For who now stood there was a man no older than himself, pointing his sword skyward. He looked up towards the sky, which was now filled with clouds that had occasional holes to let sunlight through.

The Sword Saint looked down, and what met Jake were not the same sunken eyes he had stared into so many times before, but two deep blue eyes that were in no way natural. Jake narrowed his gaze and bent his knees, ready for what was to come.

"I have been blind for too long," the Sword Saint said as he smiled at Jake. "Thank you. Now... this is presumptuous of me to ask... but—"

"Come."

Jake didn't need to say more. The swordsman grinned with a childlike smile that fit his younger appearance far more. Then, just as Jake thought it was kind of funny, his danger sense suddenly exploded. He raised his blade on instinct and blocked.

Just in time, too, as he felt an impact upon his blade stronger than even the blows from the Monarch of Blood. He purpose-fully lifted himself off the ground and allowed himself to be blasted back, giving him a chance to stabilize. He felt a faint pulse of mana behind him as the figure of the Saint appeared.

Teleportation?

Jake could see no other way to move that fast. He himself spun in the air and landed while facing the Sword Saint, instead teleporting himself backward the moment his feet touched the ground. The swordsman didn't teleport again, but merely stepped on the ground as the soil was ripped up. He flew towards Jake and slashed upward.

Stronger. Faster. What did he do?

He naturally didn't get an answer, as he was forced to dodge the swing of the sword. Jake barely managed to slip by it, but it turned in the air at an impossible angle. Once more, he avoided it by a hair's breadth only due to his near-precognitive intuition and danger sense.

How and why the man had transformed, Jake didn't fully comprehend. Had he suddenly gained a skill upgrade that allowed him to change? He had already ruled out the Saint awak-ening a Bloodline, as he didn't feel anything... so what else was there?

Jake blocked with his scimitar and was blasted back again. Without even being sure how it had happened, he got a slash on his arm, and he gritted his teeth as he landed, kicking up the soil.

It doesn't matter now...

He wouldn't figure it out just by asking himself. Instead, he would just have to ask the old man after their duel. The Sword Saint had changed, but the situation hadn't... They were still just two humans fighting, one of them suddenly getting an unexpected powerup.

Mana condensed all around Jake, and he stopped holding anything back. Pride of the Malefic Viper activated, taking dominion of the area around him, and his wings appeared and began pumping out poison mist. He also didn't hesitate to begin using poison on his weapons.

Surprisingly enough, the Sword Saint stopped when he saw Jake apply his poison, patiently waiting for him to be done. They exchanged looks, and Jake saw the absolute confidence in the face of the man. Jake felt his own heart beat faster as his excitement grew.

He pointed towards the Sword Saint and summoned his arcane bolts, and the formerly old man reacted by disappearing. Jake felt the movement of mana on his right, causing him to fire his bolts that way—just in time to hit the appearing form of the swordsman. However, he failed to do anything, as the bolts were all simply cut in two and failed to explode.

Jake used Gaze of the Apex Hunter to avoid getting hit while teleporting back, drawing his bow and firing off a Splitting Arrow. Once more, the sword simply swept to the side, and as all the arrows exploded, not a single trace of the explosion managed to reach his opponent.

Not that Jake was in any way discouraged. He teleported again, just in time to avoid the Sword Saint appearing. Twisting in the air, he drew the bowstring and felt time slow down as arcane energy revolved around him.

He released Arcane Powershot, but didn't wait to see it hit before he nocked another arrow and prepared to repeat the attack. He saw the Sword Saint appear, and, to Jake's surprise, he didn't even try to dodge the arrow. Instead, he simply pointed his blade forward and, in a move that left Jake completely dumbstruck, met it directly with the tip of his blade. The Sword Saint

THE PRIMAL HUNTER 5

barely made the two weapons touch, and with a slight movement of the wrist, he redirected the arrow and made it whistle straight past him to hit a hill far in the background.

Once more, they made eye contact as Jake fired a second Arcane Powershot while also giving a look of pure respect. Blocking his arrow that way wasn't something he had seen coming at all, and it quite frankly looked cool as fuck. Of course, Jake would have to make sure the Saint couldn't repeat the same trick for the next one.

The Arcane Powershot tore through the terrain, and Jake used Gaze without any hesitation or restraint, refusing to break eye contact. The old man froze completely as the arrow approached. Yet at that very moment, the world responded. Rain condensed to revolve around his outstretched blade, making it move even if the man's body couldn't.

It was another neat, unexpected trick... but Jake's Arcane Powershot was not weak either. The Sword Saint only partly blocked it. The arrow exploded upon impact with his blade, sending the swordsman flying back from the blast.

He elegantly floated through the air and landed on the ground, clear marks present on his arms and chest from the explosion, a bit of poison also mixed into the wounds.

Stronger... faster... but not that much more durable, Jake concluded.

Jake also began theorizing the Sword Saint's skills were somehow limited, as he had yet to see many used so far besides the teleportation and a few tricks with his sword. No shitty water magic like before, that was for sure.

Both of them moved again, Jake teleporting to avoid another swipe of the blade as the Sword Saint appeared right in front of him. He sensed his own body filled with power from Limit Shatter, and he was stronger than before for sure... about as strong as he'd been versus the Monarch of Blood, perhaps. The difference was that Jake didn't get any benefits from Big Game Arcane Hunter at all—and, of course, one other tiny detail.

The current Sword Saint was stronger than the vampire. The
only aspects he wasn't superior in were durability and means of
attack. Jake only had to repeatedly dodge the blade of his opponent and look for openings, as he believed that the Sword Saint
couldn't use all his ski—

"Thousand Droplets."

Jake's eyes opened wide. He quickly summoned a barrier of
arcane energy and readied himself with his scales while dodging
backward, unable to teleport since the attack had already arrived.
He barely managed to raise an arm to cover his face. Hundreds
of tiny stabs hit him and sent him flying back, leaving dozens of
trails of blood in his wake.

He had miscalculated... perhaps been baited in, Jake considered as he recognized his fuck-up. His entire body hurt, but now
was no time to wallow. He made a platform of mana below his
feet to teleport away, just in time to avoid the Sword Saint
appearing behind him.

Another teleport later, and he had gotten some distance. He
condensed bolts of mana along with orbs that he sent flying all
around him to make them explode. He didn't expect to hit, just
buy enough time to consume a health potion that began
repairing his damaged body. Coupled with the damage he'd
taken before the Saint transformed, it was needed.

It was also only now that he noticed he was actually losing a
bit of health from Limit Shatter. It was subtle and not much,
but it was there. Compared to the Sword Saint, his boosting skill
was clearly far worse. The formerly old man hadn't used any
boosting skills, as far as Jake could tell... or, well, he probably
had; Jake just couldn't detect it because the man was overflowing
with power. Or was the transformation a boosting skill? If it was,
that would be wild.

Stopping his wastage of mana from trying to hit the teleporting Sword Saint, Jake began firing arrows again, alternating
between explosive and stable ones, while also tossing in the occasional Splitting Arrow to try and hit his foe.

Jake decided to try and mix things up by using his Pride of the Malefic Viper to exploit a weakness. He tried to attack the man's feeling of responsibility towards his family, and how he was gambling a divine item on their duel in an attempt to get an opening. It was a trick that would likely have worked before, but now...

The moment he attacked with Pride, an illusory sword flashed in his mind. He felt backlash and was forced to stop right away, still feeling a slight headache. He was lucky that he didn't dodge attacks based on conscious thought, because if he did need to think, his failed attempt would have cost him an arm.

Continuing to dodge back, Jake felt himself pressured, finding fewer and fewer chances to counter. He tried different things, but the only real method he had to make openings was Gaze, preferably coupled with large explosions. His poison mist even proved ineffective as the goddamn rain suppressed it.

Yet, despite it all, Jake felt a rush he hadn't felt since that first night. It spoke to a particular part of him to battle a human on his own "level" in ways battling a beast or monster simply couldn't. He reveled in that feeling, and he felt the heartbeat that only came when he—and thus his Bloodline—was truly excited.

He pushed himself with everything he had as they exchanged blows, but no matter his excitement, one thing was clear: the Sword Saint was coming out on top. Their positions had reversed completely, with Jake now trying to adapt and find a way to fight back.

"Control the flow," the Sword Saint abruptly said as he made a casual swipe to send Jake away. "You still underutilize your abilities. You already know your path of magic; make it so your body does too."

Jake frowned when the Sword Saint didn't attack again, but looked back with scrutiny.

"If you do not overcome your limits, then this round is mine," the Sword Saint empathized.

Lose?

The sentiment was not one he would even dare entertain. Jake felt his heartbeat speed up, accelerating his energy in tandem, and he didn't wait for it to work. He just attacked, feeling every movement of his body.

With his scimitar, he engaged the Sword Saint in melee, the other party only parrying. "You also need to work on your swordsmanship," the Saint cheekily said as he purposefully deflected Jake's blade and kicked him in the stomach to send him back.

Jake got up right away and charged again. Arcane energy began revolving around him, making it momentarily look like he was casting Arcane Powershot. It wasn't entirely wrong, as the sentiment and mechanics were very much the same.

He felt his entire body as the energy ran through it. *Stability within destruction.* He needed destructive power while at the same time keeping it stable enough to not damage him. The energy began flowing faster and more directed, yet at the same time it seemed almost chaotic. Jake began taking damage from his body failing to endure his own energy, even more so than before. That was when a faint purple spark entered his inner energy.

The Sword Saint smiled at Jake. "Now embrace it."

Like a spark had been lit, his invisible expulsion of stamina suddenly changed color. An explosion of pure arcane energy pushed back the Sword Saint, and Jake felt his entire body enter a new equilibrium. He stopped taking damage as the arcane energy revolved within, boosting him up while keeping him entirely stable.

Skill Upgraded: [Limit Shatter (Epic)] --> [Arcane Limit Shatter (Ancient)]

Jake felt himself grow stronger in every way. He rushed forward with his scimitar, arcane energy and dark mana revolving around it as he used Descending Dark Arcane Fang with his full power, making space vibrate in his surroundings. The weapon shot down like a—

Cling!

A casual swipe of his opponent's sword sent all of the momentum of his attack barreling into the ground, poking a hole dozens of meters deep into the soil while not even touching a hair on the Sword Saint's body.

"Good!" the Sword Saint yelled as he swiped his blade up, making Jake scramble to block, only to be sent tumbling back with a long gash up his arm.

He spun around in the air and rapidly fired two arrows at the Sword Saint. The first was blocked, but the second one exploded.

A barrier of water summoned by his blade blocked it, but it gave Jake time to land and channel arcane energy as it condensed even faster than before. With arcane energy infused into his Limit Shatter, his connection to the affinity had grown even more. The magic was now both stronger and faster to summon.

More than a dozen orbs of arcane energy appeared all around him as he took a single step forward—bringing all of them with him. The Sword Saint now found himself surrounded by the bombs. For a brief moment, their eyes met as an explosion rocked the area. Jake was already soaring into the air, firing exploding arrows down one by one.

The onlookers were pushed back as arcane explosions stretched for hundreds of meters in all directions, Jake still feeling the Sword Saint in the middle of it. As a final attack, he aimed the bow down and began charging Arcane Powershot. All of the arcane mana in the bow was pulled out and formed an arrow. He took aim and fired it straight down, preparing to Scorch the Plains in pure arcane energy.

With great speed, it descended and smashed into the ground.

———

Neil was looking at the fight, completely immersed and dumbstruck. Two humans who had both been introduced to the system for as long as he had were battling it out like two absolute monsters. Their exchanges were faster than he could see, and he and his party members became utterly aware of how far they had to go. All five of them wouldn't even last a dozen seconds against either of them. What they were witnessing was the peak of humanity—Earth's humanity, at least.

He saw Lord Thayne use space magic and teleport forward, bringing the bombs tied to him along, as the entire area exploded. Neil was forced to summon barriers, assisted by Silas and others around him.

The more powerful people summoned their own shields or found ways to block it, but they were not gathered all together like before. Neil believed they could handle the fallout from Lord Thayne's attack until, suddenly, another arrow fell with incredible speed. He heard it explode, and suddenly a wave of pure destruction headed towards him and everyone else.

With wide eyes, Neil listened to the sound of people teleporting out in panic with their Hunter Insignias. Neil naively thought for a moment he could block it, but that thought was dispelled instantly when the blast got closer, and he activated his own Insignia to leave the Hunt.

Yet just before he disappeared, he heard a single word echo out from the epicenter of the explosion.

"Rainblade."

CHAPTER 65

SUMMER RAIN

E ven at a kilometer up in the air, Jake felt the arcane energy from the explosion wash over him as it completely destroyed the Mistless Plains below. It had to have done a lot of damage, and Jake was already preparing a follow-up when he heard the voice of the Sword Saint.

"Rainblade."

A feeling of dread spread up his back as he suddenly felt the arcane energy move. It began spinning around itself, gathering contrary to Jake's will. His eye opened wide and finally saw the Sword Saint stand there, his body covered in even more wounds. But he had the same stable and confident stance as before while he spun his blade in his hand, making the arcane energy spin along with it. Millions of raindrops guided and controlled it.

He pointed the spinning blade up towards Jake, who saw all of the arcane energy gather in the middle of what looked like a whirlpool of water. He stared into the eye of the storm that was his own destructive energy, and his danger sense reacted.

BOOM!

A massive blast of arcane energy and rainwater was blasted

up towards Jake as if fired from a canon. Jake reacted by teleporting away, narrowly dodging the projectile of pure energy fired after him. Then, with shock, he watched it fly into the air and blow up several kilometers above him, sending down a wave of force that momentarily destabilized him in the air.

Turning his head, he looked down at the confidently smiling Sword Saint and understood.

He didn't need to do that... he just wanted to see if he could.

Smiling, Jake nearly failed to hold back a laugh as he dove straight into continuing his attack. He shot down a Splitting Arrow, and the Sword Saint responded by swinging his blade. Jake believed he was doing it to block Jake's arrows... but he was wrong.

A crescent wave of water was fired up towards him, and contrary to what he would expect, it only grew in power as it flew through the air and absorbed any and all rainwater it encountered. By the time it reached Jake, it was more than fifty meters in length while still as thin as a string of hair.

Jake avoided it, but felt like he was being subtly pulled towards the attack as the rainwater impacted his body and softly pushed him. That was when Jake noticed something else. His Scales of the Malefic Viper had been active from the start, but now, after the Sword Saint had used Rainblade, he felt his scales slowly begin to absorb mana.

What did this mean? It meant that even the damn rain had become a passive effect that slowly began dealing damage or some other adverse effect. It was ridiculous, but far less ridiculous than what the Sword Saint did next.

The old man pointed his sword upwards, aiming at him. Jake expected him to maybe extend it or something like that, but his danger sense activated from all around him. In a swift move, Jake spread out his arms and formed an arcane barrier around himself, pouring in as much power as he could before the attack arrived.

"Torrential Droplets."

Every single raindrop within dozens of kilometers reacted, all beginning to glow with mana and move according to the swordsman's will. Millions of drops headed towards Jake faster than the speed of sound, and he knew his current defenses would in no way be enough.

Jake screamed as he fueled his mana and will into Pride of the Malefic Viper, pouring more mana into it than ever before. A purple glow emanated from his body and established a domain. Barrier after barrier appeared around him, creating a ball of nearly pure arcane energy more than twenty meters across by the time the raindrops arrived.

A battle between the rain and his arcane energy began. Jake was attacked from all sides, his arcane energy slowly being whittled away from the millions of small attacks. The sphere of arcane energy slowly shrank from twenty to fifteen to ten meters. It was shrinking by a meter every second. Jake held on until it was only a mere four meters across, still obscuring his body.

Then, suddenly, the attack stopped. Jake momentarily felt relief before his danger sense reacted again, making him twist his body. A blade of rainwater cut through his sphere and swept upwards, leaving Jake groaning in pain as his thigh was stabbed into and cut through.

It hurt, but it wasn't serious enough to impact him. The only bad thing was his mana expenditure, which was not insignificant. But at the same time, he had a feeling that the Sword Saint wouldn't be able to keep up his current power forever.

Because when he stared down at the Sword Saint below him, he noted the man's body was more damaged than before, but he also noticed something else. A few faint signs of wrinkles had appeared on his face, and a couple of strands of gray hair had appeared. It was subtle, but it looked like he had aged at least a few years since their battle began. That meant he was on a timer, and whatever he had done was temporary. Then again, they were kind of both on a timer.

Treasure Hunt will end in: 31:01

Around them, space was slowly compressing and breaking apart more and more, and soon it would encroach upon the Mistless Plains. Their battlefield would slowly shrink as time went by, but at least for now, they still had plenty of space to fight.

Jake stared down at the Sword Saint and, failing to hold back his curiosity, yelled, "What exactly did you do?"

The Sword Saint simply smirked and answered, "I do not believe the answer to that question is pertinent right now. What is more important is how long it will last. Spring is but one of four seasons, and as summer approaches, so must fall before we enter winter once more. It is a cycle that forever repeats... so please, as springtime remains, let us fight till the end of summer to our heart's content."

Jake shook his head at the non-answer. *Good enough, I guess?*

When he moved, the Sword Saint reacted by teleporting once more. Jake had finally figured out how the teleportation worked, and it was honestly bullshit. The Sword Saint didn't just randomly teleport somewhere. Instead, he switched places... with a fucking raindrop.

And when there was a goddamn rainstorm, it made no practical difference if it was just pure teleportation or not. The only real difference was perhaps the forewarning as the Sword Saint infused the drop with mana and then changed places. It was brief, but enough for Jake's keen senses to detect it and react every time.

Jake dodged the sword while flying backward, flapping his wings as the Sword Saint chased him through the rain. He wanted to avoid melee more than anything, as he was at a huge disadvantage in every aspect but avoidability.

It wasn't merely a question of power either. Every exchange they had didn't result in Jake being injured because he was significantly slower or weaker. No, it was that every single sword swing moved in virtually unpredictable ways, and he felt like his scimitar was magnetically pulled to his opponent's sword whenever he tried to counter, or that it was somehow pushed away whenever he tried to block.

Jake fled back and tried to kite the Sword Saint, but every once in a while, the man still found an opening and landed a blow, further bloodying Jake's body. However, Jake did begin to find ways of fighting back.

Dodging back, Jake summoned four small bottles and condensed arcane mana around them, breaking and destroying the glass entirely, leaving only the liquid within. It was an expensive way to fight, but necessary. Jake manipulated the four bolts manually while also firing his bow, looking for an opening. More bolts soon joined the original four, these ones without any bottles within. His head hurt from controlling them while also fighting semi-normally, but the domain from Pride allowed him to keep up the control.

The Sword Saint cut his bolts down, but Jake kept firing his arrows while trying to avoid taking damage himself. The occasional explosion made some space as Jake consumed his resources at high speed. His opponent seemed to not be in a rush, either, firing the occasional raindrop from his weapon or extending the blade to land a cut.

Jake smiled under his mask when he found an opening. He had bought time to channel an Arcane Powershot as Gaze activated, and the bolts closed in on the Sword Saint. Naturally, the Sword Saint focused on the Powershot. He swiftly moved his blade and released an omnidirectional cut from his body, making all of the bolts break.

Preparing to block the Arcane Powershot, he noticed the liquid coming out of some of the bolts too late. For the first time since his transformation, Jake saw the man open his eyes and display a hint of fear. Then his body was splashed with four bottles' worth of uncommon Necrotic Poison.

He reacted fast, channeling his abilities to get the liquid off. Rainwater gathered and revolved around his body to wash it off while also blocking the Powershot. Jake pressed his advantage, firing more exploding arcane arrows.

As a final thing, he activated something he had been waiting to use. Throughout their entire fight, arcane energy had been building up within his Mark of the Avaricious Arcane Hunter. Even before his transformation, it had been building up—and the transformation hadn't made the charge disappear either.

Jake activated it. The area flashed with arcane energy for a brief moment, further amplified by his Arcane Powershot exploding, and Jake felt himself be pushed back. He felt the damage done to his opponent and prepared to keep attacking... until a crescent wave made him abandon the idea.

A circular explosion of water pushed away all of the arcane energy, revealing the Sword Saint's form. His chest and shoulders were covered with signs of necrosis and wounds leaking blood, with faint arcane energy covering every inch of his skin. He was breathing heavily as he stood there, his blade raised. The only part nearly untouched was his face, which still had the same confident look.

Signs of aging were also far more evident now, as he looked almost middle-aged. The black hair had clear signs of graying, and many wrinkles covered his body and face. Jake felt like he was beginning to get an advantage, but the moment that thought appeared, it was crushed.

"As spring comes to an end, we enter the longest days. May we embrace the blessing of the sun, but never shun the gifts of the sky as we welcome the great treasure..."

Jake felt the temperature faintly increase around him, then the mana intensity. The rays of sunlight turned brighter as the clouds changed color and became darker than before, increasing the rainfall.

"Summer Rain."

Warm droplets fell upon Jake, and the mana density around him only grew. He did not fully understand what the Sword Saint had just done, but he looked up and saw the now middle-aged man simply stare at the sky as sunlight and rain hit him. That was when Jake noticed something... The rain was rejuvenating him.

Meanwhile, Jake noticed his body begin to feel worn down and heavier as the rain continued to fall on him. It felt tiring to stand there in the warm rain, even if it was also soothing.

Shaking his head, Jake nearly smacked himself while exiting his stupor. No, now was not the time to relax as the Sword Saint was slowly healed. He pushed the arcane energy within his body further to make himself properly wake up, then drew his bow again.

Every moment, he felt slightly slower than before, and even his mana and stamina didn't move as fast as earlier. Gritting his teeth, he still fired an explosive Splitting Arrow towards the Sword Saint, finally forcing the man to no longer just bask in the sunlight and rain.

The swordsman teleported and appeared to Jake's side just like before. Jake tried to also react like before, but his body just didn't move as he wanted it to. He was off by a few centimeters, earning him a cut in his side, and when he tried to block, he was also slightly too slow, receiving another cut on the arm.

This is...

Jake used One Step Mile to try and get away but found himself only traveling roughly half the distance he had wanted to. It didn't take long for the swordsman to catch up and force Jake even further back in a desperate struggle to not have his limbs cut off.

...like being underwater.

Drenched in the rain, he got flashbacks to being submerged deep underwater in the Vault. Arcane mana whirled around him as Arcane Limit Shatter was pushed as far as he could take it. He

ZOGARTH

managed to shrug off a bit of the suppression from the rain but still found himself pushed back by the Sword Saint, who relentlessly attacked.

I just need to buy time, he told himself as he narrowly dodged the blade, only to see himself caught by a follow-up attack. Each wound was small and barely did any damage, but they accumulated as he lost more and more ground.

He tried to summon some more arcane magic but found it far more difficult, as the rain seemed to corrode the arcane energy. One massive difference between the Vault and here was that in the Vault, the water had just been there. It was a natural part of the environment and was entirely neutral. But the rainwater? The rainwater was so full of intent and will that Jake found it suffocating.

With him being slowed down, Jake failed again and again to get enough distance between them. He used more magic, threw bottles, and did whatever else he could quickly think of, but every move was thwarted.

Jake was slowly absolutely clear on one thing... *I'm losing*.

Losing to someone two levels below himself.

Losing to someone who should at most be his equal.

Losing to another human.

THUMP!

Jake was cut again as the blade managed to swipe down his arm and through his thigh, leaving a long gash.

THUMP!

He was stabbed in the shoulder and upper arm, and his eyes slowly began shining more than before. Jake failed to hold back a massive grin beneath his mask. He refused to lose.

The Sword Saint tried to follow up, sensing the huge

opening purposefully made, allowing Jake to lean in and head-butt the Sword Saint in the chest.

More power.

Jake closed in, forfeiting his blade and instead punching the Sword Saint with his arcane-infused gloves, making the man block with his own hand. Not letting up, Jake kicked him and bent his body in an impossible shape to avoid a counter, moving with bestial intent.

More.

Arcane energy began whirling around Jake as he pushed all of his energy even further. Pink-purple fissures slowly formed on his skin and scales, and the remnant arcane energy flowed out of him. He had pushed Arcane Limit Break to above what it should be capable of, and was now overflowing with power at the cost of his own health.

More!

Jake felt his own body inside and out as he superimposed Pride of the Malefic Viper to contain and control the energy. He refused to see his own arcane energy run rampant when it was *his* damn energy. If it was going to destroy him, it would damn well be with his own consent.

MORE!

A faint layer of pure arcane energy covered the dark green scales and whatever skin was visible, pushing away the rain's effect. Jake's entire body exploded with energy and sent the Sword Saint flying back, blocking with his blade in surprise. The Sword Saint had barely stabilized himself in the air when an arrow hit him in the shoulder, sending him spinning through the air.

Jake looked down, his entire body burning. The bow and arrow he was nocking glowed with arcane energy as remnants of it left his body and fused with his weapon. The fissures of arcane energy emanated arcane-infused stamina, as it was contained close to his skin instead of simply flowing away. The rain hit the shield and slid down it without having the slightest effect.

Because while the Sword Saint could transform and reveal far more power and tricks than expected... Jake also had a Bloodline with a pertinacity to refuse to lose and push him beyond what should be possible.

Both men stared down at each other as the third round began, Jake barely taking notice of the notification.

Skill Upgraded: [Arcane Limit Shatter (Ancient)] —> [Arcane Awakening (Legendary)]

CHAPTER 66

A (POTENTIALLY) MOMENTOUS DUEL

Caleb stared up into the air, feeling the pressure upon him from the rain as well as the auras of the two men fighting. He still stood tall, more for show than anything else. While he really wanted to just sit down and take a breather, he had to keep up appearances as the Judge of the Court of Shadows.

Carmen was sitting on the ground, unbothered. There weren't that many more around, as pretty much everyone else had left, leaving only himself, Carmen, Sylphie, Eron, Reika, Maria, and one or two more who had managed to resist the wave of arcane energy earlier. Even people like Sultan had played it safe and left.

Up there, far above, flashes pulsed through the air every time their attacks clashed, a glowing figure of pink-purple energy flying and teleporting around at incredible speeds. On his trail, following him closely, was a swordsman only really visible due to the huge shockwaves of power every swing of his sword sent out. If this duel truly had any meaning besides a bet, Caleb truly didn't know. Perhaps it would be a momentous battle that defined Earth's destiny to come, or maybe it was just two people having a blast, with no real meaning besides their own personal ones.

As he stood there, Caleb had a theory about what the old man had done but no way to confirm it. If his theory proved correct or not didn't really matter in the grand scheme of things, because today had made one thing absolutely clear to every single faction of Earth who knew anything about the multiverse outside of their own isolated planet.

These weren't just the two strongest people on Earth. Caleb had access to information spanning much of the multiverse. He knew the standards of geniuses, and he did not have a shadow of doubt in his mind that both his brother and the Sword Saint were monstrous geniuses on a multiversal scale.

He looked at Eron, who stood and paid attention to the fight in odd ways, as though he saw things no one else could see. Caleb shook his head.

First two ridiculous Bloodlines... and now we may even have a Transcendent.

———

Jake spun in the air and blocked the blow of the Sword Saint with his scimitar, launching himself back as he rapidly swapped to his bow and fired an arrow.

Still spinning, his foot touched down on a constructed platform. He teleported away and fired a near-instantly channeled Arcane Powershot towards the Sword Saint. The swordsman reacted as expected by deflecting the first arrow and dodging the second, still chasing Jake closely.

Clashing once more, Jake shot his palms towards the Sword Saint. Both exploded with arcane energy, and as the two men flew away from each other, Jake raised his hand and rapidly constructed a long, spear-like mana bolt, which he naturally threw.

Sadly, it did nothing. It was cut in two, both sides flying around the Sword Saint, and even when they exploded, they only hit the constructed barriers of rainwater already covering the Saint's sides.

Jake took the opportunity to swiftly check his notifications as curiosity got the better of him.

***Skill Upgraded*:* *[Arcane Limit Shatter (Ancient)] -->* *[Arcane Awakening (Legendary)]*

[Arcane Awakening (Legendary)] – Arcane energy runs through your veins and body as you embrace the duality of stability and destruction. Revolve, empower, and infuse your stamina with your arcane affinity, making it far more potent while significantly increasing stamina expenditure. Arcane Awakening has four forms. Balanced Form increases all stats by 30% and inflicts no damage or period of weakness afterward. Destruction Form increases Strength, Agility, Intelligence, Perception, and Willpower by 50%. Stable Form increases Vitality, Toughness, Endurance, Perception, and Willpower by 50%. During a stable Arcane Awakening, your body is covered by a faint barrier of arcane energy at all times, while all your attacks are infused with a slight amount of arcane energy while embracing destruction. Fully awaken your arcane energy to enter Arcane Awakening Form for a boost of 60% in all stats at the cost of severe loss of health every second and a period of weakness after use. During this time, you benefit from both the traits of embracing destruction and stability.

That entire description made a lot of sense to Jake, as that was precisely how he felt it work. Needless to say, he was currently in what it called Arcane Awakening Mode. The fissures on his body were leaking pure arcane energy and dealing damage to him, and every single blow he made was infused with even more arcane energy.

His stamina was draining fast along with his health, but even so... it was stable. He did not lose more health as time passed, and the health loss was within an acceptable range. Jake had to admit he had surprised himself with the sudden upgrade, but he also knew why he had gotten it.

From the beginning, his arcane affinity had always been linked closely to his Bloodline and his instinctive control of mana. So to impose his affinity upon stamina was only a logical next step, and when he found himself pressed by another human, his Bloodline truly got unruly due to Jake's excitement and competitiveness growing to new levels.

Not a single part of him wanted to lose. Not because he would lose out on an item or prestige or anything else stupid like that. He just wanted to win because he was a selfish and arrogant asshole who really didn't like the thought of losing to another human around his own level.

"Got any more tricks?" Jake asked, not even a second having passed since their last clash.

"Perhaps, perhaps not," the Sword Saint said with a smile. "And I do believe it would be more reasonable for me to ask that question."

"I guess we'll just have to find out!"

Jake nocked an arrow and stepped down at the same time, dodging the expected slash just as the Sword Saint teleported up to him. Turning in the air, Jake prepared to fire the arrow—then saw the Sword Saint point his sword straight at him, having predicted Jake's move one step ahead.

What he couldn't expect was Jake's method of blocking.

He raised his foot toward the extending blade. It slammed into the sole of his boot, sending him flying back and grimacing in pain—yet not a single drop of blood was spilled. Not even the Sword Saint could cut the mighty boots. It still hurt like hell, and Jake was pretty sure he now had internal bleeding in his foot, which wasn't that big of an issue, as that was where blood was supposed to be anyway... right?

Getting more space between them, Jake fired another Arcane Powershot at the surprised Sword Saint. It was understandable; comprehending the comfy boots was not a simple matter after all. Not that the Saint failed to respond, as he did the redirection block again. By now, the Sword Saint could easily tell the difference between explosive and stable arrows, making it harder for Jake to bait him into blocking over dodging.

Jake kept shooting as they flew around a while longer. The shield from his Arcane Awakening suppressed the Summer Rain effect, allowing Jake to be slightly faster than his opponent, but it was a close race, and firing arrows while moving naturally slowed him down.

Yet Jake still thought he had a great advantage, as he managed to land the occasional glancing arrow and leave minor cuts. Minor cuts that became not that minor when factoring in the poison. Even though Jake had to admit his poison did not prove as effective as he'd hoped—the constant current of water running across the Sword Saint's body washed it away instantly, slowly healing him as they fought—the man was still slowly and surely losing health, but not as fast as Jake would have liked.

Ah, but Jake had his own healing too. He activated his oft-forgotten leg enchantment as he dodged another crescent wave of water, feeling the warm glow pulse through him, granting him a good portion of vital energy. It wasn't that much, but it helped to keep him going and offset the health-draining effects of Arcane Awakening.

They engaged each other again. The game of cat and mouse continued, Jake happily kiting and avoiding the swordsman, while his opponent did all he could to try and lock Jake down and land duel-winning blows.

Dodging a blow, Jake tried to follow up with a potshot, but the old man used another skill that shifted the rain around them.

"Thousand Droplets."

Knowing what was coming, Jake swiftly teleported to the side and appeared to see the Sword Saint had teleported to the exact same place, having read Jake flawlessly once more. His scimitar appeared and blocked two blows, but Jake was taken by surprise when the third came. The Sword Saint's blade moved in a circular motion, and Jake felt like his wrist was nearly twisted off. At the same time, the Saint moved in and jabbed his wrist. The scimitar shot out of Jake's hand and down towards the ground.

Without a weapon, perhaps the Sword Saint had expected Jake to be distraught. What he probably hadn't expected was Jake gripping his sword-bearing wrist and placing his palm on the Sword Saint's chest.

Touch of the Malefic Viper

A pulse of pure toxic energy was emitted as Jake activated what was perhaps his most potent offensive skill. The passive current of water covering the Sword Saint's body offered no resistance, failing to stop the energy rushing into his opponent.

The swordsman reacted fast, using his free hand to grab Jake's clothes and moving his feet. Jake suddenly found himself upside down with a foot smashing into his stomach, sending him flying downwards. *That was some jiu-jitsu shit right there.* Jake grinned as he stabilized, teleporting away to dodge a follow-up attack from the Sword Saint, who now had a dark green glowing handprint on his chest.

Jake came out of that one on top. He began infusing his gloves with mana while drawing his bow once more. A few Splitting Arrows and plenty of explosions later, Jake found a new issue creeping up on him.

Faint pulses of space mana reached them, as the arena was shrinking. The destruction of Yalsten had encroached upon the Mistless Plains as if they were within a shrinking sphere. It grew smaller and smaller every second, and faint cracks of space reached them while up in the air. The collapse became truly evident when a large crack suddenly appeared between them before quickly mending itself again.

Both of them stopped, no doubt both checking the countdown.

Treasure Hunt will end in: 10:47

None of them had expected their duel to take this long, and neither had any intentions of stopping even if the world was literally falling apart around them. Instead, they merely acknowledged it as another battle factor and moved on. Their clash continued, space shrinking evermore around them.

It did mean that Jake had less and less space to dodge with. Unfortunately, this meant it didn't take long before he once more found himself in melee. The Sword Saint cut towards him, forcing him to sway and weave until, finally, he met one he couldn't simply dodge.

Jake moved his hand, chopping towards the edge of the blade with pure arcane energy glowing around it. An arcane explosion shot them apart. Jake's hand bled faintly, as a bone or two had broken in it, but the glove was still intact, courtesy of the enchantment that made it incredibly durable when infused with arcane energy.

He chose to go against expectations once more, teleporting and appearing right in front of the swordsman, who now truly was beginning to look like the same old man. Jake punched forwards, making the man block with his blade, then kicked him in the side.

Chasing him down, the old man countered by swiping his blade forward. Jake met it face-first—literally—as he blocked with his mask, setting himself spinning. He used the momentum to kick the Sword Saint on the chin, which sent him flying upwards and Jake downwards.

Jake accelerated his descent and pushed blood out of his now broken nose as he reached the ground. Then a string of arcane mana manifested and pulled the scimitar embedded in the ground towards him.

A crescent wave of rainwater severed the string before the weapon reached him, trapping it mid-air as the Sword Saint's form barreled down towards him. Jake quickly recalled a similar situation, then grinned and summoned the Pillar of Encumbrance.

With full power, he increased the weight, infused it with arcane mana, and swung it straight at the charging man in a strike that would no doubt leave him with more broken bones than not. It was like when Jake had descended towards the Altmar Census Golem, but reversed, with him now in the striking position.

His entire body moved as he swung the long, tons-heavy pillar-staff against the blade.

Jake expected to feel a heavy impact when the two met, but instead, he felt like he hadn't hit anything. With his eyes, he saw the sword hit the Pillar, but somehow the old man merely moved his blade and brought the Pillar along with it, making it fly straight past him. Jake's swing continued, sending him completely off balance.

What?

To make it worse, the old man was still headed towards him with full speed. Jake tried to teleport in that final moment, but found himself completely restricted. Suddenly the rainfall intensified more than ever more, pressing down on him even through the Arcane Awakening shield.

He saw the deep blue eyes of the Sword Saint as the blade was swung again, headed straight towards his chest.

Halfway through the swing, it suddenly slowed down. The raindrops around him seemed to almost stop in mid-air as they descended, with even the movements of mana and space appearing to cease as Jake claimed the moment as his own.

Moment of the Primal Hunter

It was the first activation in a long time, and Jake planned on taking full advantage. The scimitar in mid-air was pulled faster towards him than before as he moved to attack. Yet at that moment, he felt faint movements of mana. The Sword Saint's teleportation seemed to be automatically triggered.

Oh, no, you fucking don't!

Jake caught the blade and swept it towards the body of the old man, the edge burning with pure arcane energy. It was as if the world itself then reacted. The slow rainwater between his blade and the body of the Saint became filled with mana, impeding his swing. It was undoubtedly a defensive skill like Jake's own Moment, but it was clear that the skill forcefully upgraded by his Bloodline came out on top. The Sword Saint did everything possible to stop Jake's attack, which landed just as he was whisked away by his magic.

The old man appeared a few hundred meters away as time resumed, then fell to his knees, grasping his side and heaving in painful breaths of air—quite a bit lighter than before the teleportation.

Back at where Jake was, he stood with a bloody scimitar as a severed arm hit the ground with a thunk.

The Sword Saint's entire left arm had been severed, and the scimitar had gone halfway through his chest, nearly bisecting him entirely before his own defensive skill had activated to save him with the teleport. A part of Jake was happy that the old man had shown him the respect of activating his Moment of the Primal Hunter, which was proof that he was taking the battle seriously and not holding back. Hence why he'd retaliated in kind, not holding back from performing potentially lethal blows. Also... Eron would probably help heal them if they really got close to dying. Probably.

They met each other's eyes, acknowledging the fight was

entering the absolutely final phase as space continued to collapse all around them.

Treasure Hunt will end in: 4:47

The Sword Saint stood up and lifted his blade, and Jake summoned and nocked an arrow as the duel moved onto its final phase.

CHAPTER 67

TO THE END

The rain fell upon Yalsten, not even affected by the fact that the clouds were no longer visible due to space having broken apart. As long as the effects of the Sword Saint's Springtime Advent remained, so would the rain continue to fall. Their existence contradicted all logic and rules, but such was only to be expected based on what had been used to summon them.

Down on the wet soil, two figures clashed again and again, sending explosions and soil flying everywhere. More blood than should have belonged to merely two people soaked the ground, mixing with the rain as neither party gave up.

Caleb stared at the rain and felt space close in on him from behind. Carmen and Sylphie now both stood up and also stared, concerned at the collapsing world behind them.

"I believe we should leave," Caleb said. He really wanted to stay and observe, but he also knew he could not get closer to avoid the collapsing space. All of them wanted to see how this duel would end, but sadly reality did not make that possible.

Even Eron agreed, as the man who was said to be immortal clearly didn't want to wrestle with what lay beyond the broken world of Yalsten. Understandable, as such a place was the domain of the gods and not somewhere a mortal should ever find themselves.

With resignation, their figures disappeared one by one, with Sylphie and Carmen being the third and second-to-last to leave, respectively, leaving only Caleb remaining.

Good luck, Jake, he thought as he disappeared, unsure of who would win.

———

Treasure Hunt will end in: 4:00

Jake and the Sword Saint sent each other flying away as the water and arcane energy mixed, their blades both soaked in their respective energies. The old man had lost an arm, but his movements were still sharp and powerful. Still, it allowed Jake to keep up in melee a bit more easily.

Both of them were low on resources, and time was running out in every sense of the word. The only place they were decently okay was in health points, and the reason for that? The potion cooldown. The Sword Saint had used one after he lost his arm, and Jake had also used it at the same time, as he'd had the opportunity and a strong feeling he would need it. The potion did not allow the Saint to regrow his arm or anything like that, and neither did it even come close to healing the more than a hundred cuts and stabs on Jake's body. What it did allow them to do was keep fighting.

The old man was now truly old, all his hair gray and wrinkles everywhere on his body and face. For every second that passed, he got closer and closer to his original appearance, and Jake felt like he had weakened, but far less than Jake would have expected. But even if he had weakened, it wasn't like Jake himself was in top form.

Jake felt the toll on his body, primarily caused by Arcane Awakening, as more and more of his skin flayed and broke. He'd already deactivated Scales of the Malefic Viper to save on mana, as they didn't help much anymore.

The Sword Saint didn't use his skills anymore, except for the occasional crescent wave, raindrop attack, and barrier of rain, but even those had stopped now. Jake was also certain the old man would not be able to keep going without the effects of the Summer Rain constantly rejuvenating him. Without it, the poison should have left him incapacitated by now.

A crack of space suddenly separated them once more, not only creating space but also making Jake's arrow disappear into nothing. For every moment passing, those cracks appeared more and more frequently, forcing the two of them to wrestle with them while battling.

The intensity of Jake's Arcane Awakening was slowly lessening, as the rainfall wasn't as heavy anymore. The Sword Saint barely manipulated it as they fought, likely out of resources to do so. Jake tried to take advantage, as the old man didn't want to teleport anymore, by firing a Splitting Arrow with the sparse resources he had remaining.

At the same time, he tried to use Gaze, but felt it only activate for an incredibly brief moment before his head hurt. Both of his eyes began dripping blood from overuse. However, it was worth it. The Sword Saint was struck by two arrows, one in his arm and another in his stomach, making him groan in pain. The only negative thing was that the Saint had still managed to deflect the arrow with poison on it.

Jake tried to use the opening but found the Sword Saint already attacking him, forcing him to draw his own scimitar to block. Jake stepped down and used One Step Mile, but the moment he did, his danger sense flared. Jake only teleported five or so meters before a tear of space claimed the area between where he had just disappeared from and where he was, forcing him to jump back to avoid it.

One Step Mile is out of the question, Jake told himself as both he and the Sword Saint saw the tear in space, the old man clearly also deciding to stay far away from anything even close to teleportation for good.

During the fight with the Monarch and the first part of this fight, the less stable space had been more helpful than anything to Jake. It made using One Step Mile easier, as if he had less to fight against to teleport, but now it was like he simply tore a hole whenever he used the skill, creating a dangerous situation. The brief thought of using it offensively appeared, but he seriously doubted he could make it work and was fully aware that he had just gotten lucky to not get caught in it himself. Additionally... he couldn't really afford spending the stamina on it.

Hunt will end in: 3:00

Jake struck first by firing an arrow, forcing the Sword Saint to deflect it. Another one swiftly followed, which exploded and slightly pushed back the old man. Arcane Arrow was simply the most cost-effective skill he had, which was why he kept using it, with the exploding ones costing a good deal more than the stable version.

Needless to say, Jake wanted to avoid running out of stamina. Arcane Awakening ending before the duel ended would be what in the fighting business was called a very bad time.

They kept up the exchange of arrows and blocking as the Saint slowly came closer, one step at a time. Jake could no longer retreat due to the world shrinking and was forced to seek downwards. Soon they found themselves on the solid ground of the Mistless Plains, Jake instantly dispelling his wings to avoid the upkeep.

If Yalsten was a sphere, then the center of the Mistless Plains at ground level was the absolute middle, making that the last place to collapse and forcing them closer and closer to it. Jake kept shooting arrows as long as he could before space finally shrank to only a few hundred meters across. With the Sword

Saint getting closer, he didn't have time to nock and release another arrow.

He switched to his scimitar just in time as their blades met, both of them weaker and slower than before. Three arrows stuck out of the Saint's body, reduced from four when the old man had ripped the one poisoned arrow out.

Jake exchanged several blows with the Sword Saint, losing out since he was simply outmatched in skill. He had it going for him that he managed to dodge most counters, but it was simply impossible to dodge them all.

Will end in: 2:00

Taking advantage of having more than one hand, Jake used the other one to try and grab the Sword Saint, infusing a bit of mana into his gloves. Probably afraid of Touch of the Malefic Viper, the old man avoided his hand and kept Jake at a distance favorable to him.

Gritting his teeth, Jake kept pressing the issue, as he felt himself now overpower the Sword Saint in strength. He wasn't sure if it was because of his Arcane Awakening or the old man getting weaker, and he didn't have time to think about it either.

Dozens of blows were exchanged as the blade of rain met the arcane-infused blade, sending droplets and arcane energy flying. Jake finally spotted an opening and prepared to attack, but thought twice when he identified it as a feint. Instead, he just did a more straightforward blow, ignoring the opening to take the Saint by surprise. He swung down and slashed the old man in the left shoulder, momentarily celebrating when he cleaved into flesh.

A celebration that soon turned to shock as he noticed he hadn't been feinted... He had been double-feinted. The old man smiled and allowed Jake's blade to sink in deeper, sweeping his own blade down and upwards in a fluid moment.

Jake tried to avoid it—and succeeded partially, as he only felt pain in one of his legs. However, he suddenly felt himself lose his footing, as there was no foot to step down with. Jake tumbled back and tore his scimitar from the Saint's body, desperately trying to roll as he blocked another swing from the Saint.

His wrist hurt from blocking two impacts. He failed to stop the first one, which left a long cut down his chest mid-roll, making the damage even worse. Using a bit of his last mana, Jake fired a blast of arcane energy out of his hand, sending the old man back and forcing him to block. He fell over, his footing lost, when another crack of space appeared where he was retreating to.

This gave Jake the opportunity to stand up again and even deposit his severed lower leg into his inventory, primarily to make sure he didn't lose the boot. He stood there with his blade drawn on only one leg as the Sword Saint got to his feet again and attacked. Jake, refusing to give up, dove forward and blocked another blow, making him lose his balance—or, at least, making the Sword Saint think he did.

In his one hand, the Pillar appeared once more. Jake used it as leverage to stop his fall and raise his entire body as he smashed his leg into the Sword Saint's side, sending him stumbling back. Then Jake made the Pillar lighter and swung it, still mid-air. To get full power and be able to lift the Pillar, he used both hands and let his own scimitar fall to the ground. This time he got the intended effect. The Sword Saint tried to block by instinct, not using the redirection skill in time.

The sword was knocked directly out of his hand, as the Saint chose between getting a broken wrist or weapon. Yet at that moment, he also had the awareness to wave his hand. A small collection of raindrops sent Jake's dropped scimitar flying away, making them both disarmed.

Well, Jake had the Pillar, but he didn't get the chance to use it much as the old man closed in on him. Before Jake had the chance to swing the massive weapon, he was forced to deposit it, as a staff really wasn't good in such close combat.

End in: 1:00

The old man struck forward. Jake avoided his one arm by swaying as he moved to counter, but found his balance too bad and was kicked in the stomach. Before he could recover, he received an uppercut, but just as the Sword Saint tried to elbow him in the chest, Jake grasped his arm and smirked.

Jake punched the Sword Saint in his face with the other, following up with a headbutt just as he received a low kick himself, making him fall over. Jake still had hold of the old man's arm and dragged him down to the ground with him, then got on top and began punching him repeatedly.

He managed to land a dozen hits before he was jabbed in the throat. A leg swept up and pulled Jake backward, smashing him into the ground, with the Saint rolling away to get standing again. Jake couldn't stand up properly for good reasons, but he still pulled himself to a better position as their brawl continued.

They exchanged punches and kicks, soiling the ground with blood, neither willing to back down. Both their armors were utterly broken at this point, Jake more or less only wearing a single boot and his mask along with some tattered pants, with the Sword Saint only clothed on his lower body.

00:30

Jake tried to use Fangs of the Malefic Viper but found himself missing. Instead, he was high-kneed in the face, still sending him back in pain despite the mask. Several bones in his face were broken. Evidently, trying to bite made the mask phase-through—not just for himself to bite, but also to receive attacks.

For a few moments, Jake was on the back foot. His vision was blurry, but with his sphere, he managed to dodge a blow and counter.

He yelled as he landed a right hook on the old man's face, sending two teeth flying out. Then he was chopped right in one of his deep sword wounds, making him wince in pain as the wound widened. Jake growled and palmed one of the arrows in the Sword Saint's body, making it penetrate even deeper. The old man stumbled back and painfully wheezed.

They separated, breathing heavily before engaging again.

00:15

A few more tired blows were exchanged before Jake's danger sense reacted. Space suddenly tore open just before they hit each other, blasting them both back in opposite directions, rolling on the ground.

00:10

Jake pushed himself up and noticed his bow in his sphere, only seven or eight meters away. He ran on three legs over to it as quickly as he could. At the same time, he noted that the Saint had been blasted in the direction of his own sword. The old man was rushing to pick it up.

00:07

Managing to pick up the bow, Jake knew he only had one real opportunity left. The Sword Saint had also picked up his sword and gotten to his feet, having the clear advantage in movement with two legs and all.

00:05

Jake stood on one leg as he summoned an arrow and willed as much energy to appear as he could, his Arcane Awakening almost flickering from the strain. Yet he tugged out just enough as he pulled the string fully back.

00:03

Arcane Powershot channeled as the Sword Saint charged towards him, his blade burning with far more power than Jake thought he should possibly be able to summon at this stage.

00:02

The two made eye contact, and Jake saw that the old man was fully back to his old appearance from before his transformation. Both of them were on their last legs and had pulled out all they had for the final clash.

00:01

Jake and the Sword Saint yelled simultaneously. Jake released the string just as the blade ascended with space collapsing upon them, the Treasure Hunt coming to an end.

00:00

CHAPTER 68

AFTER THE HUNT

Jake stood on the edge of the pond at this cabin, staring out onto the water. His body was fully healed, but the same couldn't be said about his equipment, as it was still in tatters, and he stood with only a single boot on his feet.

He heard sounds behind him as Miranda entered the valley. He was too lost in thought to even react.

"I came here as soon as possible. What happened towards the end? I heard some from Neil, but—"

She stopped when she spotted something lying to his side. Jake followed her gaze to the two pieces of wood lying next to him, only a loose string connecting them—severed by a clean cut.

Jake raised his hand and touched his neck, where a small scar was still visible. The feeling of the blade digging into it was also still there.

"... I think I lost?"

————

The courtyard of the Noboru clan's Patriarch was silent as Reika rushed towards it hurriedly, ignoring all the clamoring from the other clan members on the way. Given her worry, she didn't even knock before entering it swiftly.

Inside, she saw a single chair in front of a few paintings. The Patriarch was sitting there, his back turned. He didn't acknowledge her right away as she took in his weak form. His skin was bare, and he looked weaker than usual.

"Great-grandfather?" she asked, more worried than before, only calmed down a little when he finally spoke.

"Could you help me stand?" he said weakly, turning his head and smiling.

Reika was confused as she hurried over to him, lending him her arm to stand. Failing to hold back her curiosity, she asked, "What happened?"

Her great-grandfather smiled and touched a small scar on the side of his skull. "I wonder?"

She was only more confused, especially as she felt him lean on her, his steps unsteady. She frowned and asked, "Are... are you okay?"

He gave her a comforting smile as he looked up at the sky, a few sparse clouds hanging above. "After the growth of spring and the life of summer, fall follows where everything wanes before we settle into a restful winter. So to ask if I am okay... Right now, no, but eventually, I will be. With time."

"How long?" Reika asked, having understood somewhat.

The Patriarch shook his head. "You cannot hurry a season to pass like that. Once winter comes, I will return to normal and have to rebuild myself to prepare for spring once more."

"Rebuild?" she followed up.

He chuckled a bit, shaking his head again. "According to my level, I am only at 112, with a 135 in parenthesis... I believe I will have to regain those levels before I can call upon another Springtime Advent."

"That is... What did you do?" Reika asked, distraught. She knew he had powered up beyond what should be possible, but she hadn't expected the cost to be that high.

"That is something I am still uncertain of, even now... but the system calls it a transcendence."

He didn't elaborate, but simply asked for her to help him into his bedchamber, as he felt tired. For a D-grade, to truly feel tired was something Reika had very rarely seen, and it made her worried. She felt he was barely stronger than a regular old man before the system. Nevertheless, she helped him get into the bed, not even bothering to remove any of his tattered clothes.

The moment he lay down, he thanked her quietly, closed his eyes, and went to sleep. Reika stayed at his side till he woke up again, which wouldn't occur until more than twenty hours later.

———

Jake had taken a seat on one of his porch chairs, having asked Miranda to leave, as he needed a few moments to himself to gather his thoughts. He had even told Villy to wait, his godly pal understanding and waiting for him to reach out and talk. He sounded curious to know what had happened, but countless years of being alive had clearly honed his patience.

He looked at the broken bow he had placed on the table beside him, the wood cleanly cut through. He remembered the final moment where he'd released the string. The sword had come up a fraction of a moment faster than he had expected. The final thing he remembered was seeing his arrow hit the side of the Sword Saint's head as, simultaneously, the swordman's blade dug into his own neck.

I lost...

The thought dominated his mind as he sat there. It wasn't his first time losing a fight. He had lost to the damn blue mushroom more than once, technically lost to a bunch of random cloud elementals when he couldn't beat them alone, and some could also argue he'd lost to the King of the Forest.

But this was different. Jake hadn't lost to some powerful being tens of levels or a grade above him. He hadn't lost to someone it was expected of him to lose to. Instead, he had lost to another human who had been in the system as long as he had.

Okay, maybe one could argue it was a tie because even if Jake had died, so would the Sword Saint. The old man had still had poison flowing through his body at the end, and with his power-up ending, he would for sure have died—likely even without factoring in the poison. So both of them had been saved by the system event ending. There were no two ways about it.

There was also no doubt in his mind that they had both lost their heads towards the end, with him nearly losing it in a literal sense. It had truly become a fight to the death as they'd both refused to give up. But he didn't blame the Sword Saint at all, and he had a feeling the old man didn't blame him either. Both had willingly put their lives on the line.

He still wanted to figure out what the old man had done to get so powerful, but he would later ask Villy for some insight. For now, he chose to focus on something else entirely to make himself feel a little better:

Rewards.

Jake had seen the system messages right as he returned, and now finally opened them.

The Treasure Hunt has ended!

With the Treasure Hunt ending, the winners become clear as the truly talented Treasure Hunters are separated from the others. Due to your performance against the Cursed Monarch and subsequent triggering and victory over the Monarch of Blood, coupled with all treasures collected, you have proven yourself a Premier Treasure Hunter. Know that you stand at the apex, achieving the highest reward possible.

You have earned the title: [Premier Treasure Hunter]

Note: All treasures within the Hunter Insignia must be retrieved within the next 24 hours before the Insignia disappears. Any items not received will be dumped in your immediate surroundings.

It was short and sweet, in many ways. It didn't contain much superfluous information and more or less just told him that he was a good boy who had found a lot of treasures and beaten the Monarch of Blood. Maybe he had even gotten first place in the entire Treasure Hunt? It was possible, and it did help him feel better to know that he had at least maybe won that one over the Sword Saint, as it seemed to put a lot of emphasis on the Monarch of Blood fight.

Also, he did find it a bit funny how it mentioned just dumping everything if he didn't take it out. It would be funny to see someone walk in the street a day from now just to see the entire area filled with stuff.

Shaking his head, trying to cheer himself up with happy thoughts, he moved on. Next up, he naturally checked out the title, going in with pretty low expectations but finding himself pleasantly surprised.

[Premier Treasure Hunter] – You are at the apex of Treasure Hunters—not only a true talent when it comes to retrieving what was once lost, but also in defeating any who dare stand between you and your rightful bounty. +10% Perception, + 10% Agility, +5% Wisdom.

That is a lot more than expected, Jake thought. He had expected it to be more like the title from a dungeon or something like that, not a percentage amplifier. He also noted that it was in his three highest stats, making him assume that was no coincidence. That did help him feel a bit more vindicated with drinking a lot of Agility-enhancing elixirs, as he now had the percentage amplifier for that increase.

He quickly got to the thing the note mentioned by summoning items from his Hunter Insignia, which was still functional. Out of curiosity, he tried to redeposit something but found he couldn't. *So, only taking things out.*

Jake spent the next few minutes just taking all of the stuff out of the Insignia and placing it in his storage necklace. At least, he tried to, until he got to a few massive gates of black metal that just fell to the ground, making the earth shake with his failure to deposit those into his necklace.

Staring at them a bit, he asked himself why he was so adamant about getting those again, but was quick to move on with cleaning up the Insignia. To his surprise, he even found his own scimitar in there, the system having been nice enough to give it back after the collapsing world of Yalsten swallowed it up.

When all of that was done, he sat down once more, looking at the crater in the ground formed by the metal gates with a small snicker. He got an idea of what to do with them, but that could wait for later.

Jake stretched on the chair and opened his status menu to get a feel for his progress over the last ten days or so.

Status
Name: Jake Thayne
Race: [Human (D) – lvl 137]
Class: [Avaricious Arcane Hunter – lvl 143]
Profession: [Heretic-Chosen Alchemist of the Malefic Viper – lvl 131]
Health Points (HP): 30620/30620
Mana Points (MP): 48025/48025
Stamina: 27640/27640

Stats
Strength: 2243
Agility: 4202
Endurance: 2764

Vitality: 3062
Toughness: 2302
Wisdom: 3842
Intelligence: 3083
Perception: 8546
Willpower: 3012
Free Points: 0

Titles: [Forerunner of the New World], [Bloodline Patriarch], [Holder of a Primordial's True Blessing], [Dungeoneer VI], [Dungeon Pioneer VI], [Legendary Prodigy], [Prodigious Slayer of the Mighty], [Kingslayer], [Nobility: Earl], [Progenitor of the 93rd Universe], [Prodigious Arcanist], [Perfect Evolution (D-grade)], [Premier Treasure Hunter]

Class Skills: [Basic One-Handed Weapons (Inferior)], [Basic Twin-Fang Style (Uncommon)], [Basic Shadow Vault of Umbra (Uncommon)], [Hunter's Tracking (Uncommon)], [Expert Stealth (Uncommon)], [Archery of Vast Horizons (Rare)], [Enhanced Splitting Arrow (Rare)] [Arrow of the Ambitious Hunter (Epic)], [Arcane Powershot (Epic)], [Big Game Arcane Hunter (Epic)], [Arcane Hunter's Arrows (Epic)], [Descending Dark Arcane Fang (Epic)], [One Step Mile (Ancient)], [Mark of the Avaricious Arcane Hunter (Ancient)], [Moment of the Primal Hunter (Legendary)], [Gaze of the Apex Hunter (Legendary)], [Steady Focus of the Apex Hunter (Legendary)], [Arcane Awakening (Legendary)]

Profession Skills: [Path of the Heretic-Chosen (Unique)], [Herbology (Common)], [Brew Potion (Common)], [Alchemist's Purification (Common)], [Alchemical Flame (Uncommon)], [Craft Elixir

(Uncommon)], [Toxicology (Uncommon)], [Cultivate
Toxin (Uncommon)], [Concoct Poison (Uncommon)],
[Malefic Viper's Poison (Epic)], [Blood of the Malefic
Viper (Ancient)], [Sagacity of the Malefic Viper
(Ancient)], [Wings of the Malefic Viper (Ancient)],
[Fangs of the Malefic Viper (Ancient)], [Sense of the
Malefic Viper (Ancient)], [Touch of the Malefic Viper
(Ancient)], [Legacy Teachings of the Heretic-Chosen
Alchemist (Legendary)], [Palate of the Malefic Viper
(Legendary)], [Pride of the Malefic Viper (Legendary)],
[Scales of the Malefic Viper (Legendary)]

Blessing: [True Blessing of the Malefic Viper (Blessing -
True)]

Race Skills: [Endless Tongues of the Myriad Races
(Unique)], [Legacy of Man (Unique)], [Identify (Com-
mon)], [Thoughtful Meditation (Uncommon)],
[Shroud of the Primordial (Divine)]

Bloodline: [Bloodline of the Primal Hunter (Bloodline
Ability - Unique)]

Growth across the board, especially in Perception—Jake had
continued his path of putting all Free Points in it—but also good
growth in Agility and even Toughness, primarily due to his
Scales of the Malefic Viper upgrading to legendary during the
Hunt.

Speaking of skill upgrades, he had also gotten a few of those.
Naturally, there was Scales, but also Alchemical Flames in the
early day of the event, and during the last fight and the lead-up
to it, he'd gotten three whole rarity upgrades to his Limit Break,
making it into Arcane Awakening.

He had undoubtedly gained a lot from the Treasure
Hunt... but...

Jake sighed and stared up into the sky. He heard another noise behind him as someone entered the valley. He had told Miranda to leave him be for now, but there was someone who really sucked at heeding orders.

Sylphie flew over and landed on the table next to him. She stared at the broken bow and back to him as she screeched. Jake shook his head and nuzzled her, and she happily wriggled her head as he scratched her.

Smiling, he lifted her up. She didn't resist while he sat with her like she was a cat, just petting her and letting her enjoy every moment.

After a while, Jake finally spoke. "I'll win next time. And not in a way that will leave anything up to ambiguity."

To which Sylphie gave an encouraging screech in approval, clearly not having a single trace of doubt in her mind.

--

As the Treasure Hunt ended, humanity and the Risen were all returned to Earth once more, swiftly finding out that even if they had been gone for nearly ten days, not even ten hours had passed outside of the Hunt.

A few settlements had experienced minor attacks by beasts during this time, but most had made preparations to be gone longer, meaning none of the major settlements had any real issues. There were even signs that beasts had been less inclined to attack during the nearly half a day of absence of nearly all D-grade humans and Risen. This led to theories that perhaps they had their own event to participate in or opportunities, but nothing was provable.

An hour or so after everyone had returned, another message appeared before all of the recently returned people, reminding them and informing them of what was next to come.

System Announcement.

With the end of the Treasure Hunt, the Auction will begin a week from now. Further information will follow a day before the Auction begins. Note that any participant of the Treasure Hunt can also attend the Auction.

Many instantly began scrambling to prepare, while others took it more calmly. One such place was Haven, where nothing much happened for the first many hours after the Treasure Hunt ended. Miranda planned a meeting where they went over things; the city owner was suspiciously absent, yet none dared to go and check his valley without permission.

With so many items gathered from Yalsten, everyone knew the coming period would be even busier. The entirety of Earth and all of the factions had just received a big influx of valuable items to help them in the future, with the upcoming Auction a huge opportunity to get rid of items they did not need themselves and receive items useful to them.

But for now… for now, Jake just wanted to enjoy a few quiet hours with Sylphie and have a nice chat with Villy.

CHAPTER 69

REFLECTING ON A LOSS AND THE QUESTION OF WHAT THE HELL A TRANSCENDENCE IS

There were many things one could do after suffering a setback. One could wallow and feel sorry for themselves, blame someone else and act like it wasn't their fault, ignore it entirely and move on like nothing, or a slew of other things. Jake ended up going with a far more productive approach as he reflected on it all.

First of all, he had undoubtedly gained a lot from the fight. Skill upgrades and all that, but also some realizations that could only come with losing. Sure, one could argue if Jake truly lost, but in his mind, he had. Even if he had killed his opponent, too, he wouldn't exactly call it a win if he also had to die himself.

The first thing he realized was that he actually cared more about losing than the prospect of death. It was odd... His survival instincts were through the roof, and he naturally had no desire or intentions to die, and yet the thought of it didn't really bring up any innate fear. Just a feeling that death was a natural consequence if you fucked up too bad, and that was okay. Jake killed people, and he fully understood that death was always around the corner when fighting powerful foes.

It did take some mental gymnastics to be fine with death yet not fine with dying or getting killed. Or perhaps it was just a natural adaption he had made, potentially due to his Bloodline? If he walked around with fear, it would impede him and make failures far more likely. Or maybe Jake was just weird and had an odd mindset.

Either way, he moved on to continue reflecting on what had happened towards the end of the Treasure Hunt and the Hunt as a whole.

When you succeed, all you really learn is what works, even if the victory is achieved through struggle. It is often said that failure is far more valuable to long-term success, as you find out what doesn't work and what is lacking to succeed. Additionally, Jake hadn't magically forgotten his many years of formal education on business strategy and operations. There, failures were often viewed merely as learning experiences, and as long as the losses were not too significant, they could even be a good thing.

Hence, Jake tried to go with a logical approach as he analyzed the battle to figure out where he'd fucked up the most and how to improve. He knew he had fought a challenging opponent, and even if he'd made mistakes, it didn't take anything away from the Sword Saint. So he thought long and hard about both the fight with the Monarch of Blood and the Sword Saint, and a conclusion swiftly appeared.

"Do I kinda suck at fighting?" he asked himself half-rhetorically.

No, that isn't entirely right. In his own opinion, Jake wasn't bad with his bow, though he surely had room to improve. But melee combat? He had to admit... he didn't really know what he was doing.

The only reason Jake was managing was due to his instincts allowing him to dodge most blows and instinctively strike back. However, these counters weren't really thought about. Instead, he just reacted and attacked with straightforward slashes and stabs while coating his weapon in arcane energy and poison.

This was one of the reasons Jake preferred duel-wielding—his arms kind of just moved, and two weapons were just superior in his mind. At least, a part of him thought that. Jake had always been ambidextrous and good with both hands, and that had naturally only improved after the system arrived. He had a strong feeling everyone could be considered ambidextrous now, which raised the question: why did someone like the Sword Saint only use one sword?

Because one thing was absolutely clear, and had been from their first clash. The Sword Saint was far better at using his weapon than Jake, just as the Monarch had been. This was one of the reasons he could only dodge, while the Sword Saint had managed to not only block but also counter and land attacks despite his far lower stats than Jake during the boss fight.

Jake realized he had, in many ways, been ignorant and naïve, as he had begun to believe that he didn't really *need* to learn how to use a sword or melee fighting in general. If he could predict the other party's moves and instinctively counter, why would he need to learn how to actually fight like some martial artist?

Perhaps that would be partly right if the field of martial arts also clearly didn't develop. He had seen himself hit by blows he did not understand properly, seen the Sword Saint block blows far too powerful for his feeble blade and low stats to resist.

He shook his head and sighed. Sylphie had been silent throughout it all, just sitting on his lap and resting, not giving any input besides just cuddling up to him. Jake scratched her as he considered her and one of the reasons he had not really learned how to use weapons.

Why would knowing how to fight wielding a sword be effective versus a beast? Swordsmanship was inherently rooted in learning how to battle other human beings—blocks, techniques, attacks, methods, et cetera—all focused around beating your fellow man. Knowledge of lethal attacks also naturally all centered around hitting vitals in the human body.

Swords had, historically, primarily been used against other humans, and they were not seen as a hunting weapon. Jake could far more easily see how a bow and learning how to use that made better sense against beasts. Same for even things like spears or axes. Yet clearly, the Sword Saint did not struggle with non-humanoids.

He finally decided to stop only thinking about it himself. He opened up the line of communication to his Patron god and asked, "Hey, Villy... do I kinda suck at fighting?"

It took only a moment for the connection to fully form, and the Viper answered, *"Fighting? No. Knowing how to fight? Eh, a bit, I guess."*

Jake didn't need to ask the Viper to elaborate.

"A battle is very multifaceted, and there are many elements, some of which you excel in and others less so. I think you have a very disconnected style that certainly does need working on, but everyone has room to improve. Anyhow, what brought this on? Heard you muttering about losing earlier."

"Yeah..." Jake said, nodding after listening to the Viper more or less say what he already knew himself.

He began explaining what had happened during the final parts of the Treasure Hunt, having to backtrack a bit to tell him general stuff about the Treasure Hunt. It quickly became clear Jake had a lot of questions, but for now, they focused on the topic at hand.

After his explanation, the Viper was silent for a while and seemed almost a bit distant. A few moments later, he returned his attention to Jake. *"Well, I'll be damned. I didn't expect a random Transcendent to appear like that; you losing suddenly makes a lot more sense."*

Jake heard the genuine surprise in his voice, and he only had one question. "What the hell is a Transcendent?"

"Remember when I told you that only two kinds of things exist outside of the system and can break its rules? One of them is Blood-line holders, as you know, and the other is known as Transcen-dents. If someone with a Bloodline is a born cheater, then Transcendents are self-made cheaters."

638 Z<small>OGARTH</small>

"Still haven't told me what the hell it is," Jake commented impatiently.

"Getting to it. I think the easiest thing to compare it to is a mix between your arcane affinity and your Bloodline. A Transcendence is essentially a self-created skill that breaks some fundamental rules and does stuff otherwise not allowed within the system's current parameters and limitations. Transcendence is not something you can aim for, but something you just gain, and like Bloodlines, it is hard to say if Transcendence is even a good or a bad thing for the recipient, in many cases."

"Seemed like a pretty damn good thing for the Sword Saint. Also, how many of them are out there? Just on Earth?"

"First question first... Well, yeah, based on your description, his does seem beneficial, but with all things, there is cost. Breaking the basic rules of the system does not mean you break all the rules of reality. This power does not come for free, the same as any kind of boosting skill that makes you stronger temporarily. You still need to consume something to make things possible, and what he consumed was a resource he should otherwise not be able to use if my guess is correct. And I think I am, because I can already tell you now that his Transcendent skill has some serious drawbacks.

"As for the second question of how many there are... well, Transcendents are very rare. As in, you can find more gods than Transcendents by a good deal, and far from all gods have a Transcendent skill. And how I can know this? Well, same as how those with Bloodlines can feel others with Bloodlines, one Transcendent can recognize another. Also, while a Transcendent is essentially just someone with an extra skill made, it does have wider implications and does bring some benefits outside of the skill itself, courtesy of a title. And no, I will not share the details of what that is."

"Do you have a Transcendent skill?" Jake asked curiously. "If yes, how many?"

"I already told you they are rare, mate. I have one myself, and of the twelve Primordials, there is only one with more than one

Transcendent skill, and even some who don't have any at all. I need to make one thing clear—while having a Transcendent skill is good, it doesn't mean using it is or that having one is in any way required to be powerful. Again... they all have costs outside of merely using a bit of stamina, mana, or even rare catalysts. Costs anyone with one would prefer not to use.

"Some examples would probably help. Well, the most known Transcendent skill in the multiverse is the Holyland of the Holy Mother. It is a place anyone who is blessed by the Holy Mother goes after death, no exceptions. It directly messes with the Truesoul of those affected, transforming them into new beings known as Holy Spirits and making them reside in her realm. This entire skill is the basis of the Holy Church and why it is so damn popular, as it allows all members to live out the maximum lifespans of their souls in what some would argue is a paradise.

"The second example I will give you is the one possessed by our dear Eversmile. Eversmile's is a purely offensive one that allows him to completely annihilate someone through karma, severing all connections they have to the world and even erasing their Records, making them and all information related to them cease to exist. Their names erased from books, memories gone from relatives. This only works on people far weaker than himself, but he can also use it on the dead to remove them from the annals of history. There are some limitations, like the inability to make people at his own level forget, but it is a damn powerful skill.

"But as I said, both of these have costs. The Holyland is intrinsically linked to the Holy Mother's divine realm, and the cost is constant consumption of faith to keep it active. The activation cost was originally not pretty either. There is more, but I made a promise not to share such details a long time ago, and while I am a snake, I do keep my promises. Oh, but fuck Eversmile; the cost for him is that he has to sacrifice positive Records and memories himself every time he uses the skill. As someone who views himself as a researcher and scholar, to sacrifice knowledge is something he seriously despises. He really hates using it."

The Viper finished his explanation with Jake just slowly nodding. There was a lot in there, and he did feel like he had a far better understanding of what those skills were about. But one burning question was in his mind.

"Any advice on getting one?"

It was natural. Jake saw something great and wanted in on the action, as he'd seen what it had done for the Saint. To have something like that as a trump card...

"*Nope. Factions of the multiverse have tried to find a way or methods to get one—or at least increase the likelihood of getting one —since the very first era, and none have figured out anything worthwhile. If it happens, it happens; if it doesn't happen, it doesn't happen. But do know that having a Bloodline makes it harder, as the two seem to counteract one another. What this means is through whatever process you ever achieve a Transcendent skill, your Bloodline cannot have any impact, which is borderline impossible, as one is so interlinked with their Bloodlines. So, while it is not impossible for you to get one, it is just way, way harder. Also... you don't need one. You already got your Bloodline to be the little rule-breaker you are.*"

Jake slumped down a bit.

"*Ah, but this entire thing does bring up one interesting topic,*" the Malefic Viper continued. "*Transformation skills, especially ones that just make you straight-up more powerful—or, in this extreme case, a Transcendent transformation just making someone stronger—is the apex of temporary power boosts. Emphasis on temporary.*"

"You mean I should just buy time or run?" Jake asked, quickly catching on.

"*Tactically disengaging would be a better term. If someone is boosting themselves up significantly, they are also burning themselves out and will suffer the consequences for it—be it through a Transcendent skill or not. Sometimes the best thing is just to dodge or retreat as they tire themselves out. It's just the smart thing to do, and there is no harm in it. Fighting them is like running up and hugging someone who has set themselves on fire to try and hurt you."*

"Yeah, but if I use a boosting skill, too, we are both on a timer, right?" Jake countered.

While he did recognize that he could probably have just run away from the Saint if they fought outside of a collapsing world, he still wasn't sure if the Springtime Advent would outlast him. He had noticed how him damaging the Saint sped up his aging, so he really had no way to tell.

"Well, if they boost way more than you? Additionally, there is a classification of fighters you have not met, I believe... The truly suicidal ones. Those who burn up their entire being and souls as they practically kill themselves to try and take down their opponent without any hesitation. People who use a special item or participate in sacrificial rituals to summon far more powerful effects than otherwise possible. Rituals and items are far more normal, as often all you need is others to willingly sacrifice themselves, and naturally there aren't that many good skills making you into a suicide-soldier."

"I... I think I saw the Holy Church do stuff like that. Also, if there are many rituals and items, why not skills?"

"Yeah... that is part of the Holy Church's MO. Plays really well with the Holyland being a thing, making them far more willing to give their own lives for 'the greater good' or whatever bullshit they spew. As for why there are not that many powerful suicide skills... think a bit about it. Upgrading a suicide skill is quite hard, as one would imagine, as you can't exactly practice it, and with skill choices based on Records, it means that to get a good suicide skill at skill selection, you need to be truly suicidal and dedicated to killing yourself. And people really committed to stop living tend to not live that long, for some super weird reason. Besides, such people are weak cowards who take the easy way out if they can't handle things or are brainwashed morons. Either way, they tend to not be the most talented."

Feeling a bit dumb, Jake shook his head and directed the conversation away from the not-too-pleasant topic.

"Anyway, now I know what a Transcendent is, and that running away is fine if someone suddenly transforms and becomes way stronger out of nowhere. Now, where were we... Oh, yeah, something about me not knowing how to fight."

Jake heard the Viper chuckle and had a feeling their talk wasn't going to be a short one.

CHAPTER 70

COMBAT STYLES

The Viper was silent for a moment but quickly seemed to agree to the change of subject.

"I think I have made it clear in the past that I am not a big fan of giving direct advice on things to improve, as it often does more harm than good, in my experience, but fine. For once, I shall act like a proper Patron god and give some actual advice and direction.

"There are limitless ways to fight in the multiverse, and to call one method superior to others is fallacious and stupid. However, no matter the method, understanding yourself and the path you walk is essential. Someone such as a highly experienced warrior—a swordmaster, spearmaster, et cetera—is one such valid path. To them, their weapons become extensions of their bodies, and they live and breathe through their weapon, every part of them poured into it. A mere movement of their weapon can impose their will upon the world as they become one... but I must emphasize this is but one path.

"A mage mastering magic and comprehending all there is of their given element, a spirit that is one with their environment, or a snake mastering its toxins and embracing that part of itself all constitute a valid path. I myself have never learned to truly wield

a weapon, but I did learn to use my claws, tail, fangs, and generally just my body as a living weapon. And Jake, if I am honest... so should you. At least partly."

Jake frowned at the last part. "Are you telling me to stop using weapons?" he asked, a bit confused.

"I am not telling you to do anything, just giving my perspective. But no, that is not what I am saying. I am saying where to center yourself. So let me first ask you something very simple... Do you feel the edge of your blade as you hold your sword?"

Without waiting, Jake gently lifted Sylphie off him and placed her on the table with only a few minor protests from her. Then he walked down from his porch and took out his scimitar. He stood there with it in hand, not sure exactly what Villy was asking about.

"I'm not sure I get it?" Jake said.

"Do you feel the wind on your skin right now?"

"Well, yeah, of course?"

"Do you also feel it on the scimitar? No, not the slight nudging on it... Do you feel the wind slightly cool it down, the sensation as a small gust embraces and wraps around it, and yourself holding the handle not only in your hand, but like you are grasping your other arm or hand?"

Shaking his head, Jake just asked, "What the hell you on about?"

"That you never embraced any weapon—at least, not a melee weapon. You swing them like sticks, not extensions of yourself. You use them as tools, a sentiment any master would feel offended by. I would say you have decent skills when using weapons, but you do not have any knowledge of weapons, nor have I ever felt any desire from you to truly embrace and understand one."

"I thought that whole extension of your body thing was just some joke or over-exaggeration... but you're serious?"

"Dead serious. I am certain that the old swordsman you fought views his sword as fondly as you view your arm. Many weapon masters in the multiverse spend obscene resources on upgrading old *weapons or repairing them without sparing any expense when they could get better by buying new ones. I have seen one mourn his broken axe by annihilating an entire race of poisonous frog-like creatures, leading to their extinction after one corroded his axe into nothingness with their special toxin.*

"Getting a new weapon, for them, is like adopting a child. There is a long time where they are uncomfortable with their new weapon, and have to slowly adapt and get used to it before forming a bond. Meanwhile, you just pick up any new, shiny weapon you got and use it right away if it seems better than your old stuff."

Jake took the words in, and he couldn't really disagree. His Nanoblade had broken, and while he sure did like the weapon, he liked it for its usefulness, and he disliked it being broken mainly because he would have to find a replacement or spend time and money getting it repaired. Not because he felt like an old friend had died or something like that.

He then looked over at the porch table with Sylphie and the broken bow on it. Sylphie was having fun inspecting the ruined weapon, but Jake didn't really feel anything special there either. Again, he liked the bow, but it was, in the end, just a tool in his mind.

"How do I learn to really embrace a weapon, then?" Jake asked.

"I think your takeaway is wrong here. No one says that is the only option. I think an example of how it isn't needed is that girl from Valhal who only uses her fists. Her entire body is her weapon, and she has embraced that."

"So, we back to me not using weapons?" Jake once more asked.

"Not necessarily. There are other options, but I would consider going away from tools not fitting you as much. Your body moves like a weapon as you fight, and you have embraced it far more than I see with many seasoned warriors. Your instincts for self-preservation and avoiding blows are simply too powerful, and in many ways, I can see a large tool getting in the way of that. So,

maybe consider going smaller? Something where your weapon is only a small extension of your own body, and then if you need a longer weapon, you can use a method you have embraced: your arcane magic."

Jake furrowed his brows and considered that. "Daggers or knives?"

"Fangs in hands," Villy joked back, Jake imagining him snickering.

"I do have the Twin-Fang Style skill," Jake remembered. It was a skill he didn't really use much, but he did recall what it did. It was an actual martial art of sorts, all focused on stabbing and leaving narrow cuts with small weapons.

"Yeah, I know," Villy said, launching into a brief history lesson. *"It was a style developed all the way back in the First Era by someone following a powerful mammal-like creature with highly venomous teeth. The man managed to acquire two of its fangs with some of its venom still on them after the beast had battled a powerful foe, and he began using them as weapons and developing a style with them. The guy kept hunting down venomous creatures and getting their fangs as he honed his style, in the end becoming far more skilled at using fangs than the creatures they originally came from. After his death, others picked up his style from the Legacy he had left behind. They honed it to entirely new levels, and it just spread from there. Now it's a very well-known fighting method for those using poisoned weapons."*

Jake snickered and made a guess. "I am sure the guy would have loved some Malefic Viper fangs... I guess he bit off more than he could chew?"

"No, it was actually mainly me biting him," Villy answered, Jake certain both of them had silly smiles on their faces.

"Anyway, back on topic," Jake said after the brief intermission. "I guess daggers do work well. I did like using them, but the range was just limiting."

"That is where magic comes in. Extending the blade with mana is something you already do. Plenty of methods to get

around it, and honestly, even just scratching the skin is enough to deliver a good dose of poison most of the time. But again, it's all up to you. Just something to consider for the future. Daggers or short weapons are far closer to your body and are, in many ways, closer to using claws than actual weapons."

"Certainly food for thought," Jake said, nodding as he moved to one thing nagging him. "But... where does the bow come in?"

It was something he had been holding off on asking about, as he had a bad feeling about what the Viper would say.

"We were talking about melee combat here," Villy answered. *"Jake, you are already a jack of all trades, using magic, archery, and melee fighting during bouts, which is far more than most bother with at your grade. I would say that the type of combat you are best at is honestly magic, due to your level of energy control and skill in manipulating it and imposing your will upon the external world. Plus, your arcane affinity is potent when used to both attack and defend.*

"As for the bow... Well, now we're back to me telling you to do whatever you want. You certainly have more skill with your bow than your melee weapons, but I wouldn't classify you as some archery genius. You're decent enough, but my honest take is that giving up on the bow and focusing more on magic would be beneficial to you and also work more synergistically with your profession."

Jake nodded with a serious expression before answering, "Well, that is dutifully noted and promptly ignored. Besides, it isn't a waste; archery is a damn good way to deliver my poisons, and—"

"You can deliver it more effectively by just coating magic attacks or creating new spells integrating it directly," the Viper swiftly countered.

"Now, considering I have stacked points in Perception, it would be a waste not to—"

"Perception is a primary stat of magic users too, and you can easily specialize your magic to make better use of the stat. Besides,

you are still only barely mid-tier D-grade; you got plenty of room to adjust."

"You miss that many of the class skills currently require a bow to use, so abandoning it would be—"

"A choice that can still easily be made, as you have only been in the system for less than a year, and we are back to you having plenty of time to adjust," the Viper said, continuing to shut him down.

"But if I merge archery and magic, I will be able to make use of the best of both worlds—"

"I didn't know you had infinite skill choices, levels, mental energy, and time," Villy said teasingly.

"I like archery," Jake finally just said.

"And there we have it—the first thing you should have said. If you like it, do it. Your path will take you further than the engineered path of perfection created by someone else. Perhaps not in the short term, but most certainly in the long run. Bla bla, the path to godhood is a marathon and all that, and remember it is your marathon. Not mine. So while I will gladly share my opinion, do know that what you feel is best will likely be a better choice for you. Even if no one else sees it."

"Good, we agree archery is great," Jake said, promptly declaring his victory. "But really, magic? I am not that good at it, in my opinion. I just make big explosions and piercing bolts and the occasional barrier here and there, with a platform sprinkled in to step on for good measure."

"All of which are powerful in their own right, and I can see the potential for growth. Also, your magic is linked with your archery, and I will advise you to continue pursuing those methods. Make the bow a harbinger of your power, a way to focus your magic like one would use a staff. You already kind of do that right now, but I think that could be interesting and allow you to make better use of all your talents."

"Sounds fine... I just think I'll keep doing what I already do when it comes to archery while maybe focusing a bit more on improving my basics. But I definitely need to learn some more about melee combat and find a proper method for that. Anyway... Villy, while I do have more questions, I feel like those can wait. Thanks as always; we can chat later. Unless you got something on your mind?"

"Hm, not much besides the question of why you are wearing a living Unique Lifeform on your face without commenting on it or mentioning it as something important quite yet," Villy shot back, slightly teasing but with plenty of genuine confusion mixed in.

"Oh. Yeah. That."

Jake had totally not forgotten it with everything else going on. Definitely not.

He took off his mask and stared down at it. "Hey... so... got time now?"

Honestly, he was not sure where to start. First of all, how was the King still alive? Second of all, why was he in the mask? And third of all, what should Jake do about having him in his mask? The entire situation was also just super awkward, as Jake had naturally been the one to put him there. So, starting the conversation was just weird.

He looked down at the mask and waited. Seconds ticked by with nothing happening. Jake even went as far as to poke the mask with his finger and knock on it a bit to no avail. He used Identify on it and found the description hadn't changed.

Is he ignoring me?

That was certainly one possibility.

"I am not getting any response," Jake said with a shrug to Villy. "Odd, he did talk earlier—at least, I am ninety-nine percent sure he did. Either way... how is this even possible? I killed the King of the Forest and got the experience and all that. How the hell did he survive?"

"Oh, he didn't; the King of the Forest is dead," Villy just answered nonchalantly. *"But the death of the King of the Forest seems to have given birth to a new Unique Lifeform that now dwells within the mask. It probably still shares all of the memories*

and is the same individual, but it won't be entirely the same. As for how? No fucking idea, man. Unique Lifeforms are weird. It could be some survival skill, some way of binding a part of his Truesoul to later regenerate, or a slew of other possibilities. It is rare one gets experience for such kills, but it does happen. I know of a few creatures with the ability to self-resurrect even after true death, and their methods are never simple or straightforward."

"So, I shouldn't expect to be absorbed into my bow and magically resurrected if I die?" Jake joked back.

"I get the joke, but I think you are kind of misunderstanding something. The mask isn't some equipment off the King of the Forest; it was his true body."

"Wait... are you telling me I have been wearing a corpse on my face for months now?" Jake asked, staring down weirdly at the mask.

"Of course, we could also reframe it as you only wearing the severed head of a slain foe on your face for months, as it is only the most important part. Again, Unique Lifeform physiology is weird."

"In the end, all roads lead to me wearing a corpse." Jake shook his head and smiled. "Though that is pretty normal, right? Heck, leather and fur are made of pieces of dead things too."

"Don't forget how even a lot of rare metals and natural resources are, in fact, just old, decaying corpses of elementals, and a lot of rare plants are children of sentient plants, but still only infants yet to awaken."

"Slightly disturbing, though very informative," Jake laughed.

They kept chatting, during which time he tried to get the mask to react a bit more but still got nothing. Maybe the King was sleeping again or just being a little shy.

"What are your plans now?" Villy asked when Jake finally gave up on the mask and just put it on like before.

"For now, go meet Miranda and figure out if I have anything to do, as well as get the general directions to the city that houses the Court of Shadows," Jake answered, having already considered it. "The auction begins in a week, and during this time, it should be possible to travel there and spend some time."

"Hm... Oh, yeah, your relatives are here. I guess you can spare a week to visit them, just don't make it an excuse to do nothing for too long," the Viper warned.

"Relax, man, I don't plan on entering early retirement, just visiting family for a bit. Anyway, as always, been good chatting with ya, and cya around," Jake said, issuing a goodbye for real.

Then, with a smile, he waved towards Sylphie, who happily flew over and landed on his head. A bit wasted, as Jake went over to take the pieces of his bow anyway.

"Sure, and we may just meet sooner than you expect," Villy said, making it sound like a veiled threat. Totally on purpose, for sure.

Chucking to himself, Jake exited the valley and headed onwards.

He had lost one battle, and while he certainly didn't like it, he wasn't going to let it stop him. What he would do was take a brief intermission to recharge before it was back to the grind.

CHAPTER 71

TRAVEL PREPARATIONS

Miranda sorted through some lists Sultan had handed to her, as well as the formal contract he had written up mere moments after their return from the Treasure Hunt. She skimmed the contract over, already aware of what it was about, primarily looking for any word traps or phrasing she didn't quite agree with.

The contract was for him to act as a broker and sell items for Haven and Jake during the Auction a week later. The lists he had handed her included items he already possessed as well as people he had already made agreements with during the Hunt.

Reading over the contract, it became clear the man was giving extremely favorable terms to them, seeking to only take a flat fee for high-value items and a small percentage on lower-priced goods, though he did emphasize his belief that nothing below epic-rarity would be sold at the Auction simply due to the volume of items gained from the Treasure Hunt.

As for why Sultan was so interested in a deal—well, besides him being a businessman, that is—apparently, the Auction held some special implications and opportunities for merchants. If the World Congress was the arena of the politically minded and social classes, the Treasure Hunt the arena of the fighters, then the Auction was the event with the most opportunities for merchants.

Sultan had received a quest that was more or less just about selling a lot of things, and he would be competing against others. Miranda did not believe they could beat out the larger factions simply due to the sheer quantity of items a city like Sanctdomo had to sell, but if Jake agreed to use Sultan for some of his higher-rarity items, she did believe Sultan could do well. Of course, she would have to get some more benefits from the man if they helped him succeed in a quest, but Miranda suspected he already knew that.

"Lillian, is the report in from those who wish to sell through Haven?" Miranda asked the other woman in the room.

While it was clear primarily items from the Treasure Hunt would be sold, some held valuables not from there. Even from some who did not participate in the Hunt at all, such as Phillip.

"Most of them," Lillian answered as she brought over another stack of papers. "Neil and his party will sell through Haven, and a lot of the unaffiliated D-grades have also chosen to do so. Additionally, we have received thirteen requests to gain permanent residence from participants in the Hunt... which is all of those who returned but two."

"Hm, thoughts?"

"I do not believe there are many downsides to additional D-grades within the city, and if we wish to increase the average power level of Haven, it would be highly beneficial. The more we have, the more will also come by, as there will be more skilled crafters, more opportunities to find hunting parties, and more ways to sell and procure materials for everyone."

"You're right," Miranda agreed. "Just have some basic tests done; maybe ask Silas to help."

Miranda didn't really have much more to do right away, as she had spent the last few days before the Hunt hectically planning for her own absence. They'd been told the Treasure Hunt would last ten days, and while many had suspected there would be some kind of time dilation going on due to the length of it and the constant threat of beasts, no one had known. Hence, she had been on the safe side.

"Additionally, the sculp—"

Lillian was interrupted by a knock on the door. Miranda was surprised—mainly because they hadn't planned on anyone coming, but also because they'd heard it at all due to the enchantments meant to obscure sound.

She sighed and waved her hand. The door opened to reveal Jake standing there—the only one she would suspect of, for some reason, sneaking into the main office of Haven. Well, that or an assassin, but it would be an odd strategy to knock first if it was an assassin.

"Hey, Miranda, Lillian, anything interesting happen that I need to be aware of, or can I leave for a while?" he promptly asked.

"Only some minor things related to the Auction," Miranda answered just as promptly, knowing not to mince words or ask unnecessary questions.

She gave him a quick rundown, and Jake agreed without much hesitation to allow Sultan to sell some stuff for him. He didn't specify what, but Miranda was sure she would find out in due time. There were also a few additional minor points, and she asked him his opinion on giving what was effectively citizenship to the D-grades who had applied.

"Sure, why not?" he said with a shrug. "Just kick them out if they get annoying."

"Duly noted," Miranda said with a smile. "Where are you heading off to anyway?"

"Where the Court of Shadows is located. Sky-something. Ah, for that, I wanted to ask if you had any idea where it is, and also... would you happen to have a spare bow lying around?"

"I think asking Neil about directions would be a good idea, as he has been working on the long-range teleportation circles, and as for a bow, maybe check in with Sultan, as he no doubt possesses some." Inwardly, Miranda wondered why he would need a new bow.

"Thanks. If there is nothing else, I'll be off. I reckon we'll meet next in the Auction."

"Are you going to Skyggen to visit family?" Miranda asked, failing to hold her curiosity back.

"Yeah, Caleb more or less ordered me to go, and it is about time to visit, so it makes no sense delaying," Jake confirmed, moving to leave.

"Alright, have a nice trip. I still have the communication skill to contact you if anything comes up, so I will make sure to keep you updated on major events."

That got a nod of approval from him. They said their goodbyes as Jake left the room, his presence disappearing as soon as he left the office.

"Didn't you say he seemed down when you visited him just a few hours ago?" Lillian asked, confused.

"He was, and he still is," Miranda said, shaking her head. It was just what her gut told her, and she felt like she had interacted enough with Jake to detect it. But he was better now than before for sure.

"Either way, can you fetch Hank about the plans for expansion?" Miranda asked Lillian.

"I believe he is busy with that young man who visited the temple with Lord Thayne a while back," Lillian answered. "They seem to be working on some kind of odd monument, and I am truthfully not certain what it is about... but according to the young man named Chris, it should be related to the Malefic One, Lord Thayne's Patron god."

Miranda nodded, already feeling a slight headache come on from whatever they were doing. She seriously doubted it could be anything that wouldn't give her massive annoyances and the cause of many issues...

Jake had quickly located Sultan, courtesy of the large, floating ship that also acted as his store. The merchant had quickly sold him a rare bow for level 120 and above, which was far worse than his old bow, but it was made solely with resilience in mind without any fancy effects. He did also have an epic bow for level 100 and above, but Jake preferred the rare one. It wasn't the best, but it was all he had for now.

He did ask him if he had any idea on fixing his broken bow, but Sultan said that anyone else but the original craftswoman would find it difficult, if not impossible after his own transmutation of it. He wasn't even sure that the woman named Maria— who had made it—could fix the bow. Sultan instead recommended Jake dismantle it and reuse some of the materials, such as the two gems. It was a bit disappointing, but Jake took his words to heart and saved the broken pieces for later use. Now, he would just hope that a good bow would be sold at the Auction.

Before he had gone to meet Miranda, Jake had also had a good chat with Sylphie. To his surprise, she had wanted to split up to go hunt and grow stronger. He felt a strong sense of inferiority from her, and she had seemed a bit sad at how little she had been able to help against the Monarch of Blood. There really wasn't any need for her to feel like that, as she was already up there with the strongest on Earth, but she clearly still wasn't satisfied.

Needless to say, Jake wasn't going to get in her way. Her parents were also not in Haven—likely out hunting too—so that probably only added to her sense of competitiveness. So, before Jake had even made it to Miranda's office, she had taken off towards the forest like the zooming little hawk she was.

He would lie if he said he hadn't hoped to take her with him, but he wasn't going to tell her what to do. Well, at least he could now look forward to hearing about her progress during the Auction. Ah, who was he kidding? They still had their connection that allowed some communication, and he had barely managed to exit Miranda's office before she gave him the absolutely essential update on a funny-looking tree she had found and couldn't break with her whooshy wind.

Next up, he headed for the Fort where Neil was. The guy was still working on teleportation gates and had gone far enough to have one connect Haven and the Fort, which meant it only took a few seconds on a teleportation circle and some mana to travel the distance. Not that it would have taken him long without, but there was still like a hundred and fifty kilometers or something.

Finding Neil in the Fort wasn't hard either, as he was working on an even larger circle in his own house of sorts, which was more like a large warehouse or gymnasium. Jake had to respect his grit; the space mage had only been out of the Treasure Hunt for a few hours and was already straight back to work. In fact, he seemed even more filled with fervor than before when Jake saw him in his sphere.

Jake knocked on the door, and a second person in the house opened it. Jake hadn't seen a young lad before, and the guy seemed terrified, almost paralyzed, upon seeing Jake stand there. He stood there for a solid second before collecting himself, inviting Jake inside, and directing him towards Neil. Probably an assistant or something.

Walking into his practice room, Jake saw a lot of half-made magic circles and small devices he didn't recognize.

Neil looked up as he detected Jake and promptly greeted him. "Ah, hey there!"

"Hi," Jake said, giving a half-hearted wave while inspecting the room.

"I have to know, who won?" Neil asked as he stopped doing whatever he was doing.

"Not me," Jake answered. Even if the Sword Saint couldn't be said to have won either, Jake had sure as hell not come out victorious.

"Oh," Neil said, turning the situation far more awkward.

"Anyway," Jake said, changing the topic. "Looking for some

way to know the direction of Skyggen, as I am going there, and Miranda said you might have something."

"Ah, sure!" Neil exclaimed, happily changing the topic. He waved his hand and took out a small metal disc that looked like a compass. "This is a copy of the Spatial Compass tied to the receiver circle I gave to Skyggen during the World Congress. Just infuse a bit of mana, and it will display an arrow." Neil then took out a small metal cube. "Also, if you are going, can you bring this with you? It is a small storage cube containing some research and improved coordinates and directions to syncing our teleportation circles. With hope, we can soon have a permanent teleportation circle connecting our two settlements."

"Why not?" Jake agreed as he got both of the items. He instantly used the compass and saw it did indeed display an arrow, just like a regular compass.

"One more thing," Neil said. "Want a boost on the way? I can send you a few thousand kilometers the right way without any problems. Ah, but it will be a bit random, and I can't tell for sure where you will appear."

Jake shrugged. "Sure thing. Would be nice getting there faster."

"Great!" Neil said, smiling and muttering as he led Jake into another room with a circle already prepared. "I have been hoping to test the cost and challenges associated with teleporting someone substantially more powerful than myself..."

Less than a minute later, Jake found himself standing on a magic circle as Neil made some small alterations to get the direction right. He placed a number of items to act as catalysts, and Jake made a mental note to compensate him. When everything was ready, Jake gave the go-ahead. Neil activated it, and Jake felt space around him distort. He could easily resist the effect if he wanted, but he allowed it to take effect as he disappeared.

Jake felt himself travel through space for a second or two, his sphere acting up a bit, but nothing he couldn't reign in. Finally, when he regained vision, he found himself standing on a large, flat stone surrounded by small mountains and hills.

He barely had time to take in his surroundings before he detected movement. The rocks around him began moving on their own, and Jake turned his gaze and saw an almost humanoid-looking stack of stone assemble.

[Summoned Stone Elemental – lvl 102]

Jake raised his eyebrows as he looked a bit further and saw the head of a small figure atop a hill not far away. Soon, many more elementals appeared. Jake detected more than fifty figures surrounding the small vale he found himself in. Squinting, he finally got a good look at one of the small figures above as it peeked up to look at him.

[Mountain Goat Rockshaper – lvl 114]

A fucking army of goats?

Shaking his head, Jake just raised his hand and coiled arcane mana around it, and a dozen or so arcane bolts appeared. With a flick of his wrist, all of them fired out and hit the stone elementals, making them explode into dust instantly.

Only half had been blown up, while the rest just crumbled, and when he looked up again, he saw all of the goats gone. Jumping, Jake took flight and stared at the many goats fleeing in all directions beneath him. Jake couldn't help but chuckle at the cowardly beasts, and he naturally didn't bother pursuing them.

Killing such low-level beasts didn't give him any experience, and he didn't really blame the goats for attacking him either. He had kind of just appeared in the middle of what he assumed was their territory, giving off an aura he had been told several times wasn't the most friendly. So them running away upon seeing he wasn't someone they could deal with was just smart.

Goodbye, little goats, Jake thought as they all went into

hiding, and he looked out over the vast landscape in front of him with rolling hills, mountains, vales, and valleys. When he closed his eyes, he even felt the auras of some beasts that would perhaps be worth challenging hidden within their own territories ahead of him.

Jake found himself around three thousand kilometers away from Haven, which was quite impressive work from Neil. It was a nice head start for sure.

Smiling to himself, Jake looked forward to finally meeting his family again. It had been a while since he had seen them, and he had been putting off visiting for far too long. He wondered what his mom and dad had been up to and how the system might have changed them, and he would be lying if he said he wasn't nervous.

Not putting off going any longer, he took out the compass and, without further ado, began his trip across the land. He was perhaps only missing a single important detail before taking off towards Skyggen:

How far it was.

———

The story continues in The Primal Hunter 6

Thank you for reading The Primal Hunter 5!

We hope you enjoyed it as much as we enjoyed bringing it to you. We just wanted to take a moment to encourage you to review the book. Follow this link: The Primal Hunter 5 to be directed to the book's Amazon product page to leave your review.

Every review helps further the author's reach and, ultimately, helps them continue writing fantastic books for us all to enjoy.

———

ALSO IN SERIES:
The Primal Hunter 1
The Primal Hunter 2
The Primal Hunter 3
The Primal Hunter 4
The Primal Hunter 5
The Primal Hunter 6

———

Want to discuss our books with other readers and even the authors like Seth Ring, J.F. Brink (TheFirstDefier), Shirtaloon, Zogarth, Cale Plamann, Noret Flood (Puddles4263) and so many more?

Join our Discord server today and be a part of the Aethon community.

Facebook | Instagram | Twitter | Website

You can also join our non-spam mailing list by visiting www.subscribepage.com/AethonReadersGroup and never miss out on future releases. You'll also receive three full books completely Free as our thanks to you.

———

Looking for more great books?

———

Kullen is the Emperor's assassin. The sharp hand of justice. The Black Talon. *Gifted a soul-forged bond with his dragon, Umbris, Kullen is tasked with hunting any and all who oppose the Empire. But when the secretive Crimson Fang murders two noblemen before his very eyes, Kullen must discover the truth of who they are and what they want. What he uncovers is a web of lies and deceit spiraling into the depths of Dimvein. Natisse, a high-ranking member of the rebellion known as the Crimson Fang, has no greater goal than to rid Dimvein of power-hungry nobles. Haunted by her past, fire, flames, and the death of her parents, she sets out to destroy the dragons and those who wield them as unstoppable weapons of destruction. Until she, too, finds herself buried beneath the weight of the revelations her investigations reveal... The Empire is under siege from within, and one man, dressed in black like the night, stands at the epicenter of it all.*

Get Black Talon Now!

One bad roll catapults a group of friends into a new world... *Five friends gather for their usual game night like they have hundreds of time before. But when they use a strange new die, they are instantly transported to a fantasy world where all gaming ideas can come true. Together, the party must join forces to deal with the vile Necrolord whose plans will not only threaten this world, but Earth as well. Should be easy for a team of lifelong gamers. However, when gaming and real life collide, there are situations which can't be anticipated. Will Samo use science to solve all her problems? Will Wyatt always resort to violence? Will Bourbon discover lost treasure? Will Falcon restore his kingdom. Will Melf, the bard, find his pants?*

Get One Bad Roll Now!

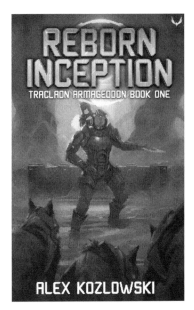

Eric Peters has been reborn. Sent back in time to change humanity's fate. *After experiencing a future where all of humanity's planets and colonies had been purged, Eric refused to fall. And so, the Entity chose him to be humanity's last hope—to be Reborn... The Reborn are galactic boogiemen. Myths and legends used to terrify children and curb the aggression of advanced alien civilizations. They are usually granted boons and abilities able to grow powerful enough to destroy star systems, making them the number one target of every alien race out there. But in Eric's case, the Entity had screwed humans. Instead of being given powers that could make him like a god, they are barely classed as special. With only his memories and a couple of minor boons, Eric needs to survive evil elements within humanity, the circling alien races that would do anything to eliminate him, and change history sufficiently so that when the Traclaon Empire declares war, his species can fight back. In his first life, Eric was inconsequential. In this life, he will be anything but....*

Get Reborn Inception Now!

For all our LitRPG books, visit our website.

Made in the USA
Middletown, DE
26 August 2024

59775573R00399